JOHN COWPER POWYS

Weymouth Sands

A NOVEL

WITH AN INTRODUCTION BY

ANGUS WILSON

Chief works of John Cowper Powys
with dates of first publication

WOLF SOLENT 1929
A GLASTONBURY ROMANCE 1932
WEYMOUTH SANDS 1934
AUTOBIOGRAPHY 1934
MAIDEN CASTLE 1936
OWEN GLENDOWER 1940
PORIUS 1951

Writers and Readers

Writers and Readers Publishing Cooperative 9–19 Rupert Street,
London W1V 7FS, England

First published in the United States of America 1934
Published in Great Britain as *Jobber Skald* 1935
Published by Macdonald & Co. 1963
Published by Rivers Press, Cambridge 1973

This edition published by Writers and Readers in 1979

Printed by Redwood Press, Trowbridge, Wiltshire and bound by
Burlington Press, Cambridge

INTRODUCTION

JOHN COWPER POWYS died in 1963 at the age of ninety-one. Longevity among artists of genius is not so very rare. To take a few outstanding examples – Bernard Shaw died at the age of ninety-three odd, Guiseppe Verdi at eighty-eight, and Titian, traditionally but doubtfully said to have lived to the age of ninety-nine, was certainly some years over ninety. Powys produced work that was strange and fresh almost until the year of his death; yet, if we think of the 'impressionism' of Titian's last years such capacity for new vision in extreme old age cannot surprise us. Powys produced what many of his admirers, I among them, consider his most original novel of genius *Porius* at the age of seventy-nine; but Verdi had already gone before him by giving the world *Falstaff* at the age of eighty. It hardly serves much purpose, indeed, to compare Powys's as yet largely unrecognized genius with the work of great and revered masters like Titian and Verdi. I have introduced this novel with these remarks on genius and longevity not so much for the comparison as for the difference between the career of Powys and those of other long-living artists, because in that difference lies an important clue on how to read and place his novels, a central clue to the nature of *Weymouth Sands*. John Cowper Powys not only lived and wrote into very old age, but he began novel writing very late; he wrote his juvenilia in maturity, his two conventional masterpieces – as near conventional as can come from so strange a writer – as he neared sixty, then with the remarkable bridge work *Weymouth Sands*, he entered a whole new world of fiction uniquely his own in his seventies, and finally, as an octogenarian, produced a number of eccentric fictions which I do not believe we have any likelihood of appreciating until the great works of his two previous productive periods – *Wolf Solent*, *A Glastonbury Romance*, *Weymouth Sands*, *Owen Glendower*, and *Porius* – have been very much more satisfactorily digested by critics and very much more widely read than at present.

It is more instructive to compare this career with that of the most widely read and appreciated English novelist of genius of our centufy – D. H. Lawrence. His, too, is an astonishing story. One sees with him as

with Powys the easy mastery and yet the impatience with traditional forms
– with narration, plot, character drawing and so on; one sees also with both
(at any rate, in their novels) a complete lack of concern for the experimental
techniques with which others of their contemporaries – Joyce, Virginia
Woolf, Dorothy Richardson – were seeking to escape from the conventions.
Yet it is clear from the beginning that for all their use of tradition, both
Lawrence and Powys are going to burst through it, not to start a new
tradition, but to force the novel into the strange, idiosyncratic shapes or
distortions demanded by their urgent and peculiar visions of life's meaning.
In their outset, despite all the differences of the two men, the forms of
their novels seem similar: a short novitiate, a contemptuous mastery of the
two main conventions – the novel of self-exploration and the novel of
society – the emergence from them into an entirely personal form of novel.
Lawrence's novel of self-education *Sons and Lovers* and his novel of society
The Rainbow share with Powys's *Wolf Solent* and *Glastonbury Romance*
that extraordinary quality of transcendence of their forms which makes it
possible for the conventional critic to say with conviction that they are bad
novels and for the critic of insight to see at once that they are novels of
genius to be judged by none of the ordinary canons of novel criticism. But
Lawrence's contribution, however quirky, to our traditional novel had
been made by the time he was thirty. *Women in Love*, his greatest, most
urgently personal (as opposed to autobiographical) novel was published in
1920 when he was thirty-five. Powys's two great hammer blows at the
conventional form were published in his fifty-seventh and sixtieth year.
It was not until his seventies that he was to produce his idiosyncratic
masterpieces. After *Women in Love*, Lawrence continued to pour out fine
novels, yet they all seemed to be alternate blasts, less striking, upon the
same judgement trumpet that he had already sounded through Birkin's
mouth. It is as though the incredible, awestriking rush of his career and his
output, also no doubt the increasing warnings of his physical health
however little he cared to listen to them, had kept his powers alive but
halted his will to explore further; there was so little time to speak that he
could only shout the same cry more loudly.

Quite otherwise and more lucky was John Cowper Powys's novel-writing
life. Starting twenty or so years later than Lawrence, he still had decades of
life before him; and the worst of his physical pains were behind him after
an operation of gastroenterostomy successfully performed in 1917, ten
years before the publication of his first important novel. With *Wolf Solent*
and *Glastonbury Romance* achieved, with as much of the conventional novel
conquered as he desired, he could make the journey to his own fictional
world slowly and expansively. *Weymouth Sands* is the first extraordinary
step in that journey. It is, perhaps, worth closing this comparison of two

geniuses – the hare and the tortoise – by noting another contrast in their lives. Lawrence was increasingly to seek his solution to life by travelling across the world and yet he never, perhaps, for all his wonderful empathy with the creature world, found the way out of his own self. Powys, on the other hand, announced his intention of seeking his own realm by returning to his native Britain from the United States where he had been a nomadic showman-lecturer for more than twenty years. Here, first in his boyhood Dorset and then in his ancestral Wales, he found in their geography, their zoology, their history, and their folklore the inspiration that released his ambiguous mixture of reverence and mockery, of occult agnosticism, of continuous single-purposed concern for multiplicity. Here he acquired that cunning innocence which allowed him to maintain his tough ego, and yet, unlike Lawrence, constantly to transcend it.

Weymouth Sands is the last novel he wrote in the United States, in a curiously named upstate New York weather boarded house Phudd Bottom – the house to which he had retired after his long years of lecturing up and down all but two of the forty-eight states, the house from which he had already produced *Glastonbury Romance* and where he was to write his extraordinary, very frank, very covert *Autobiography*. It is typical that all his books written in America from *Wolf Solent* (scribbled on scraps of paper in Pullman cars and hotel rooms while still on lecture tours) to *Weymouth Sands* should have been laid exactly in the England he had known in his youth. He needed distance to convey actuality. Indeed with *Weymouth Sands*, the sea, the quarries, the sands are dissolving the human characters and their concerns. The setting, though recognizably Weymouth and Portland, is much more than that, it is a claim for a pantheistic (yet never declaredly transcendental) universe in which men, their acts and the memories of those acts survive only through the timeless, so called inanimate world they live in.

With the Dorset of *Wolf Solent* and the Glastonbury of *Glastonbury Romance* there had been a concern for the sharp edges of remembered geographical reality which could only be written at the distance of the Atlantic Ocean. Now that place was to mean more but exactitude less, paradoxically John Cowper Powys's imagination could allow him to return to the land whose myths he was going to portray. For the reader of Powys's novels, *Weymouth Sands* with its qualities of disjunction, of fading in and out from one group of characters to another, of mild acceptance of good and bad, and mild expectancy of happiness and unhappiness may seem strange after the epic battles of good and evil that have marked his preceding great novels. Here there is no evil save that of the vivisection of Doctor Brush's laboratory, and that, so strangely when we know how the pain of animals in the service of medical science was to Powys the greatest of all modern abominations, is an evil more stated than felt. In any case, it is an evil half defeated (but the 'half' here is typical of the author's ironic acceptance of life) by the time the novel ends.

However for those who look more closely at the three great novels of his middle years the progression becomes clear. Wolf Solent, with his typical anti-hero's plagues of two loves (one lost and the other not gained) and the heritage of his father's sins, nevertheless works out or, rather, fails to work out his fate in a living community but above all in a countryside whose insects and flowers, whose ponds and fields brood over hero and community alike. In *Glastonbury Romance* all heroes are swallowed up in the interplay of the multi-fated inhabitants of the town, yet this human pageant, too, like the pageant within the novel, is overshadowed by the Tor and the Abbey, the caves and the Grail. In *Weymouth Sands* this changing balance is complete – the heroes are many, their fates various and compassionately but aloofly surveyed; the community glitters and shines as the sun strikes a group here or a group there, then it seems lost in darkness as a cloud passes overhead, or is dissolved in the sea mist; for a moment it seems that this or that human story has claim over the others but then some characters only dimly seen or even the nameless chorus of trippers on the beach fill the screen, crowding out the characters we have come to know; some stories are brought to an end happily, some are left in the air; place has taken over. Here, if ever, John Cowper Powys in his apparently clumsy, teasingly 'old-fashioned' language and techniques is making his contribution to the impressionism his contemporary Virginia Woolf was exploring. The seaside of *Weymouth Sands* is a Boudin painted by Monet. His concern is not so much like Mrs Woolf's with men and Time, as with sea, sky and Timelessness. And once this dissolution of men and their stories had been made in this novel, Powys, whose personal religion was far from anti-humanistic, was ready once again for men but in a richly imagined myth filled world, going back first to the fifteenth century in *Owen Glendower* and then to the fifth in *Porius*.

Certain aspects of *Weymouth Sands*, perhaps, remain to be commented on for the benefit of those readers who are coming to his work for the first time. What is the connection of the author with the seaside, and, above all, with Weymouth, that the scene plays upon his imagination so powerfully? John Cowper Powys was born in Shirley in Derbyshire, where his father was vicar. His father's mother lived at Weymouth. Here they came for visits which the boy remembered always with delight. But when John Cowper was still a small boy, Weymouth became a nearer paradise. His father received the living at Montacute, whose village and great house form a shadowy origin for the setting of *Wolf Solent*. From here his grandmother's home was a much nearer holiday resort. And when soon he was to go to Sherbourne and like it as little and as much as most sensitive boys have liked their boarding public schools, grandmother and Weymouth became for him and his beloved younger brothers a special delicious refuge. Something of his grandmother, no doubt, is in Miss Le Fleau; and Magnus's memories of his father as conchologist are certainly Powys's memories of his much loved botanizing father the vicar of Montacute. Already in *Wolf Solent* Weymouth had loomed increasingly large off-scene, now this idyllic seaside world of his boyhood took central place, but with a cruel irony attached. His previous novel *Glastonbury Romance* had been located exactly, because of the Glastonbury legends. It was not a town well known to him and he had to come specially from America to England for a visit to give his picture exactitude. Too much so, for the profits were soon eaten up by settling out of court with a prominent Glastonburian who claimed to recognize himself in Philip Crow, the ruthless business man in the novel. If such disaster could overtake by sheer chance a novel portraying a community entirely unknown, an indigent novelist only just beginning to get public notice could not afford to take risks with a town he had once known well. His new novel appeared in America in 1934, but the English edition of the next year came out shorn of all topical references, with all place names disguised, and entitled *Jobber Skald*. The true text and title did not appear in England until 1963. This sad but necessary tampering cannot have helped the book; especially, I think, the change of title which by emphasizing the Jobber's role removes the basic clue to the novel's central concern, as a novel not of heroes or even of men, but of men beside Nature.

But the sea goes further than Weymouth sands in the novel. The sea had haunted one of his previous books, *Rodmoor*, his second novel. But there the scene had been East Anglia, the only one of his novels not laid in the West Country or in Wales, although East Anglia was the scene of the opening of *A Glastonbury Romance*. East Anglia was the country of John Cowper Powys's mother, who, from all accounts, was of a melancholic, withdrawn nature. In the book, reflecting this perhaps, the East Anglian sea is a cold and cruel force; but the sea at Weymouth, the country connected with his father, a warm if magisterial and shy figure, is life-renewing.

Nevertheless if the sea and the rocks are paramount, the sands of the title have also an important *human* significance, on them swarms that happy ever-changing crowd of trippers and of Weymouth citizens on their day off or after work. Here, too, the loneliness and failure to communicate of so many of the men in the book – Magnus, Jobber, Sylvanus Cobbold – are made more cruel by the evanescent community feeling around them. Yet if Sylvanus preaches under censure or to deaf ears, it is also here that the girls listen to him – those nymphs who are half his childlike companions, half the objects of the chaste lust that saves him from total isolation. Here, I think, it is necessary to recall another part of John Cowper Powys's life central in his *Autobiography* and beautifully described there. After he left Cambridge, he began his strange adult life in Brighton, as teacher in a girls' school. It was here that he first felt that powerful voyeur pleasure in 'the hundreds and hundreds of beautiful girls I stared at as they bathed in the sea or as they lay prone for my delight upon the beach.' A chaste, happy, yet intensely lustful voyeurism was to battle all his life, and through all his novels, with a sadism which he feared, but which I suspect he never truly felt violently or, at most, left behind with his adolescence. Nevertheless in most of his novels the conflict gives the most strange sexual underweb to the epic battle of the forces of good and evil. As I have said evil is less fiercely felt in *Weymouth Sands* than in many of the others, for Lucinda Cobbold's malice is never fully unleashed, Cattistock's energy seems to ask forgiveness for his love of power, Sippy Ballard is left in pathetic defeat, the real evil of the vivisection 'labs' is perhaps lost by the restraint Powys had early placed upon himself of never portraying sadism too knowingly for fear it might touch and corrupt readers. But of the tender voyeurism, or, at most, 'immature' unfulfilled physical embraces that are at the other pole, we have some of his finest examples: Perdita's lying with young Larry Zed, Marret the Punch and Judy girl lying with Sylvanus, the momentary overwhelming happiness of Magnus when Curly Wix embraces him. All are frustrated and finally sad, but while they last they break the terrible human isolation that seems to make nonsense of our lives, if they were not given sense by the tides and seasons. The final reunion of Perdita and the Jobber seems likely to be of the same 'immature' kind but lasting.

How little sentimental Powys is, however, we are reminded by the Punch and Judy which delights the seaside crowds, for it is the show's proprietor, father of Curly, who out of the world's false sense of sexual rectitude puts Sylvanus in the asylum. The great clown Jerry Cobbold, too, lives sunk in sceptical indifference. There is no naive belief, such as Dickens had, in the saving grace of the circus.

Finally, I think, for a modern generation of readers, it is necessary to say something about the social texture of *Weymouth Sands* even though the novel shows the dissolution of social and personal values by an overriding nature. To many the characters of Sylvanus Cobbold, Magnus Muir, teacher of Latin, or even Jobber Skald himself may seem strange – what are these men, who appear somehow to have opted out of society, and yet live by little jobs and bits of inheritance in lodgings where they have the status of masters and gentlemen. In our own day the man who prefers to live poorly but as he wishes, who accepts shabbiness, even privation to pursue his 'philosophy of life' or his 'religion of life' or his art is likely to be a marked social rebel; if he does not accompany his protest with political anarchism, he will at least seek to live in a community or in a city group of other drop-outs. His family he will probably leave behind him. In the first part of this century this was often not so. There were many men and some women who contrived by a combination of small jobs – especially, for the highly educated, dead-end teaching or tutoring jobs – and small rents or inheritances to go their own way, yet did not cut themselves off (externally, at any rate) from their families, from society as it was accepted, or even from their class. Such gentlemen were seen rather as 'misfits' or 'cranks', or, if they fell very far, almost 'tramps' like the late Victorian Gissing or Thomson of *The City of Dreadful Night*. Such, to some extent, all his life, and certainly in early manhood was John Cowper Powys. Such are Magnus Muir, Wolf Solent, John Crow of *Glastonbury Romance*. Their search for love, for tenderness, for sexual assuagement is classless, but their status, for all their poverty, is that of 'gentleman'. Because such men are rare today, it seems desirable to explain their role, for they are at once social wanderers and men deeply rooted in the world from which they come. Of course, social roots have little importance ultimately in Powys's scale of values, but their existence, I believe, does explain why he came home to Britain to find the real world beneath its appearances that is revealed to us in the later novels; and it gives greater solidity to the social surface of even his most mythic novels than is often allowed to him by his modern critics. *Weymouth Sands* may be seen as the shore on which he set foot in exploration of this personal mythic land.

ANGUS WILSON

LEADING CHARACTERS

ADAM SKALD, the Jobber.

MAGNUS MUIR, a teacher of Latin.

DOGBERRY ("DOG") CATTISTOCK, a wealthy brewer.

SIPPY BALLARD, his nephew, an official.

SYLVANUS COBBOLD, a mystic.

JERRY COBBOLD, his brother, a famous clown.

RICHARD GAUL, a philosopher.

CAPTAIN POXWELL, father of Mrs. Jerry Cobbold and of Mrs. Hortensia Lily.

JAMES LODER, a lawyer.

RODNEY LODER, his son.

DR. DANIEL BRUSH, brother-in-law of Cattistock.

LARRY ZED, a mad boy.

MARRET JONES, a Punch-and-Judy girl.

DR. GIRODEL, an abortionist.

LUCINDA COBBOLD, Jerry Cobbold's wife, and a daughter of Captain Poxwell.

PERDITA WANE, companion to Mrs. Jerry Cobbold.

HORTENSIA LILY, a widow, sister of Lucinda Cobbold.

DAISY LILY, Captain Poxwell's grand-daughter.

PEG FRAMPTON, her friend.

GIPSY MAY.

TISSTY AND TOSSTY, dancers at the Regent Theatre.

CURLY WIX.

CONTENTS

NOTE BY AUTHOR

All the events and characters in this book are pure invention, except in the case of Magnus Muir and of Sylvanus Cobbold, where certain characteristics and peculiarities have been taken from the nature of the author himself. There is, to the author's knowledge, no such Institution as "Hell's Museum" anywhere in Dorset, certainly not near Weymouth, and if the author has used any well-known Wessex names for his imaginary persons, it was purely in order to enhance the verisimilitude of his tale.

1

MAGNUS MUIR

THE Sea lost nothing of the swallowing identity of its great outer mass of waters in the emphatic, individual character of each particular wave. Each wave, as it rolled in upon the high-pebbled beach, was an epitome of the whole body of the sea, and carried with it all the vast mysterious quality of the earth's ancient antagonist.

Such at any rate was the impression that Magnus Muir—tutor in Latin to backward boys—received from the waves on Weymouth Beach as in the early twilight of a dark January afternoon, having dismissed his last pupil for the day and hurriedly crossed the road and the esplanade, he stood on the wet pebbles and surveyed the turbulent expanse of water.

Lean, bony and rugged, with hollow cheeks and high cheekbones, the consciousness that looked out from his grey eyes assumed an expression that would have been very difficult for the cleverest onlooker to analyse or define. It was certainly to no easy, relaxed enjoyment of those darkening waves that Magnus was now yielding himself in his release from his day's labour. His face was wrought up rather than relaxed, strained rather than casual, grim rather than complacent; and if he had been a priest, occupied with the rendering of some complicated fragment of ancient liturgy, he could not have appeared more gravely concentrated.

It was with quite a different expression upon his bony face, whose broad nose, anxiously-twitching mouth and deeply-furrowed forehead carried with them a permanent air of physical discomfort, that this middle-aged man in his old but carefully-mended overcoat turned from his broodings by the sea's edge, placed the cap, which he had taken off, resolutely upon his head, pulling it low down over his eyes and regaining the esplanade by a couple of stone steps, began to walk in a westerly direction, moving with an absent-minded speed that was somewhat disconcerting to the people he met or passed in his rapid march.

His face was relaxed now; and yet it was animated by a mental intention which seemed to be moving, like an out-runner, about a hundred yards in front of his hurrying steps. An expression of disturbed surprise appeared in his relaxed features after he had passed the Jubilee Clock, that familiar landmark that always made him think of his father, so decently and self-respectingly did it mark the place where the esplanade curved a little, opposite the road to the station, for he now beheld beneath him on the beach a belated Punch-and-Judy performance going on in contempt of the cold and the gathering dusk under the foot of the stone wall.

A tall thin child with a red plush bag at the end of a pole was collecting money from the few bystanders, mostly children, who were crowding against the rails. The sound of Punch's high-pitched, strident voice crying out "Toby . . . Toby . . . Toby . . . Toby . . . Toby!" brought Magnus to a stop.

He moved to the edge of the esplanade and looked down. There were two sets of children's heads below him now, the upper group clinging to the rails beside him and the lower group standing on the beach. An especially violent Punch kept tapping the front of the little stage with his head, and at each blow upon his painted skull he cried "Toby! Toby! Toby!" The tone in which he uttered these words was like nothing else in the world. It was an indecent, insane, brutal tone and yet, Heaven knows, in some indisputable way not devoid of a curious poignance.

"Curly told me it went on in the winter," he thought. "I told her I was sure it stopped. But now I know I've *often* heard it—all through the winter! She said she'd talked to this little girl who's carrying the bag; and here *is* the child! I never noticed her before."

As if reading his thoughts the younger daughter of the Punch-and-Judy man moved her long stick deliberately towards him; and a moment later, while Magnus was searching his pockets for a three-

penny bit, she came right in front of him on the beach below and
looked up into his face.

"Make it a Bob, Mister," she said coaxingly, holding her bare
head, covered with a thick mop of hair, a little on one side. "Make
it a Tanner anyway, Mister, if you can't spare a Bob."

An elder sister of the child who had accosted him now appeared on
the scene, she, too, holding a bag on the end of a pole—for it was
evidently one of those desolate epochs in the lives of show-people
when methods of collecting are more in evidence than pockets to
collect from—and Magnus was struck by the wistful intensity with
which this elder girl, while she perfunctorily imitated the gestures of
the younger, kept straining her eyes, first to the eastward of the
esplanade and then to the westward, as if looking for someone who did
not come.

The esplanade was wet with recent rain and swept by a gusty wind,
and the few people who passed seemed more surprised than interested
to see the little group of children staring at so unseasonable a performance.

He himself beheld the whole episode in that special light with which
we look at something that reaches us through a glamour quite extra-
neous to the nature of the experience itself; for between these shrill-
voiced puppets and his search for pennies, as both the girls held their
forlorn poles towards him, hovered the enigmatic presence of Curly
Wix herself, not so much her actual figure as an emanation of poignant
sweetness upon the air.

He had just thrown threepence into the smaller child's bag and
twopence halfpenny into the elder one's, when he was aware of a
little group of persons advancing along the esplanade from the harbour-
end. The group was composed of that heterogeneous mixture of
novelty-seekers and nondescript adherents that one is wont to see
gathered around a Salvation Army drum; but the man who led them
was of totally different type from any conceivable Salvation Army
preacher. He was a tall lean man, the pallor of whose cadaverous
face and dark, wild-gleaming eyes were emphasized by his hatless
condition, by the loose untidiness of a thin black overcoat, whose
tails flapped in the wind, and by a long, almost Tartar-like moustache
whose ends drooped below his chin.

"Sylvanus Cobbold!" said Magnus to himself; and he drew closer to the rails with that instinctive gesture with which we nervously withdraw when someone we know is attracting unseemly attention.

But the elder of the two girls dropped her pole in wild haste and began running desperately to the nearest flight of stone steps. He soon heard the man's voice behind him.

"He's a born prophet," he thought as he stole a hurried glance round at the scene. There was the Punch-and-Judy girl, standing close to Sylvanus now, and gazing at him with shameless adoration!

When he realized how little aware this singular prophet was of any living person near him Magnus did not turn away as he had done before. It seemed to him that the girl was staring at the man in the rapturous trance of one who was as completely caught out of herself as he was. The man himself—taking advantage of the little group at the rails to turn his discourse in their direction—now fixed an excited, unseeing, inhuman eye upon Magnus and the children and hurled his wild cries towards the sea.

But for some reason, as often happens in a moment of unusual excitement, Magnus' own mind began teasing itself over a totally insignificant and trivial question. Why had not Curly told him that there were *two* Punch-and-Judy girls? Which of the two was her friend, the religious one, or the little flirtatious one? In spite of his desire to give himself up recklessly and happily to the thrilling sweetness of Curly's identity, he began to fret himself as to what exactly was her relation with these show-people.

But as the Punch performance moved to its lurid dénouement it came over him that there was something pitifully ghastly about the way Sylvanus was going on pouring out spiritual revelations, of which no one understood a word. Magnus began watching him more closely. The man held his hat in his hand as he spoke, and his grizzled hair was cropped so close that his skull had the tight, compact look of a nut neatly removed from its kernel. It made Magnus think of the sort of head that must have emerged from his fantastic helmet when Don Quixote lay unhorsed. Out of his hollow eye-sockets the man's eyes gleamed portentously in the dusk. He looked like a person who should have worn armour and carried an axe.

It was after the Punch-and-Judy show had ended, and while a

pallid and spasmodic individual, with a face like a hungry rat, was calling angrily to his elder daughter to come down and help them, that a policeman showed signs of interfering with the prophet.

Magnus felt torn between a desire to escape and a lively curiosity to know what the upshot would be. What interested him now was the curious name by which the white-cheeked girl was summoned so indignantly by her father.

"Marret! Marret! Marret!" he called up to her from the beach; and he kept retreating backwards, as he called, so as to try to get a glimpse of the girl where she clung to the preacher's side; but the esplanade was too high for this. The voices of the two men easily reached each other from where they stood; but Sylvanus was as one talking to angels and nothing could disturb him.

"Marret! Marret! Marret!" the Punch-man kept repeating and after each cry of "Marret" he would stumble yet further down the beach, turn round, and stretch out his neck, straining his frail body upwards in the hope of seeing her, for he suspected that she was doing exactly as she was, forgetting everything in the world while her whole soul hung upon the mysterious lips of the prophet. While he thus struggled to catch a glimpse of her he found presently that he had reached the sea's edge; and there he had to stop.

Meanwhile the policeman had begun addressing the preacher in very angry cockney.

"If I've told yer once, I've told yer a 'undred times! The beach is the proper plice for these 'ere hexortations. Get out of this! Do you 'ear me? It's all right, lady, I ain't going to 'it 'im, but the beach is the plice. No horficer will interfere with 'im if 'e will go down below . . . . Get out of this!"

"Do you know who I am?" said the prophet.

But the policeman did not budge.

"I knows yer well, Mister. We all knows yer! And what's more, *there be some what knows yer* 'as 'ave about enough of this; this hob-structing of 'is Majesty's Hesplanade!"

The preacher, his wild eyes flashing in fury at the policeman, lifted a little cane he was carrying, an old-fashioned soldier's cane, and was on the point—at least so it seemed to Magnus—of using it upon the astonished officer when the girl Marret whose complexion had changed from white to red, as the altercation went on, and then from red to white suddenly cried out some inarticulate words and collapsed in a heap on the ground.

This occurrence changed the whole situation. The Cockney officer showed himself a completely different person as he knelt by the girl's side; and the wrath of the preacher changed to violent remorse as he accused himself of being the cause of this misadventure.

Magnus was now resolved to escape; but before doing so he had the grace to lean over the rails and call out to the Showman to let him know what had happened. This done, he moved away; for he felt extremely disinclined that this man whose identity he knew well should recognize him. They had met more than once in those desolate rooms at the top of High House, where Jerry Cobbold, Sylvanus' famous brother lived, but the last thing he wanted was to renew their acquaintance at this particular juncture.

He felt a little ashamed of his pusillanimity as he quickened his pace along the dark, wet, chilly asphalt of the deserted parade; but the sight of a big steamer with many of its lights already lit—for the twilight was deepening—just outside the harbour, reminded him of the purpose of his walk to the pier's entrance.

He had had tea yesterday with Sylvanus's sister-in-law, Lucinda Cobbold, and she had told him that a young girl from Guernsey who had, in spite of what everyone had predicted, answered her advertisement for a companion, was due tonight on the steamer from Cherbourg and the Channel Isles.

"Is Jerry going to meet her?" Magnus had enquired, picturing to himself the embarrassment of the young woman when confronted by the world-famous clown.

But the eccentric Mrs. Cobbold, who rarely left her upper-floor in High House, had taken advantage of their long acquaintance at that point to beg the Latin teacher to go himself and meet the girl at the dock and in a sudden mood of altruism he had consented to do this.

He paused in his advance now and surveyed the incoming steamer. He set himself to imagine what the feelings would be—pretty miserable ones he supposed!—of the unfortunate companion, whose name Mrs. Cobbold had told him was Miss Wane, as she drew near her unknown destination.

"She'll never stand it!" he said to himself. "Lucinda works upon people so. She wears them out. Jerry ought never have let it go as far as this! Of course there *are* exceptional women who might—But, oh, no! Jerry ought not to have let this happen."

He pulled up the collar of his overcoat and sat down upon an empty bench facing the sea. He knew that as long as the steamer had not passed the little Weymouth breakwater there would be ample time for him to reach the pier before the gangway was down and the people were landing.

He put the unknown Miss Wane out of his mind and gave himself up to long, delicious thoughts about Curly. Some of the passers-by had their umbrellas up, though it was not actually raining, and it struck him as rather a queer thing that the sight of a few open umbrellas should bring back with such a rush the extraordinary delight with which he had held her on his knee that night in the cottage. Five times he had been out to see her at that Upwey Wishing-Well since he first made friends with her.

"Well!" he thought, "I am forty-six; and I have not had my share of love-affairs yet."

Shivering a little he cast a glance on the steamer. No! she was still in that same place by the breakwater.

"I'd marry her tomorrow if she'd agree," he thought. "I can't exactly say she's in love with me. But even if she never is *exactly that*, I believe I could make her happy."

The bench where he now sat, with his coat-collar up, his hands deep in his pockets and his legs stretched out, faced a particular spot where the road crossed the esplanade and descended by a natural slope to a flat expanse of dry sand, an expanse that was rarely, save in terrific storms, invaded by the sea, and where in the summer season the donkeys and goat-carriages were wont to await their patrons. How well he knew this spot! It was one of those geographical points on the surface of the planet that would surely rush into his mind when he came to die, as a concentrated essence of all that life meant! It was on this bench that he had sat five years ago when his father died.

No! The Cherbourg steamer was still in the same place. He could go on thinking of Curly! He now came to the conclusion, and by no means for the first time, that it was the unusual closeness of his link with this unique parent, for he had lost his mother in infancy and never had brother or sister, that had hitherto kept his occasional love-affairs from developing into anything serious.

"But after all," he thought, "I never felt like this for any of those others. Besides, with all my nerves and manias and so on, I don't believe I could ever get on with a girl of my own class."

And he began with a kind of excited, voluptuous ferocity to exaggerate to himself the characteristics in him that made him prefer a girl of the people.

"It's in tune with my whole nature," he said to himself. "What I want out of life is its poetry; and I'm like my father in that. Aye! how he used to cut down on the artificiality of things! He thought of nothing but mathematics and the weather and walking to Redcliff Bay and coming home through the rain to a candle-lit room and a good tea and a good fire. How he used to laugh at the conventionalities that our class makes such a stir about! I'm sure I don't know what he would have thought of my marrying Curly; but I know he considered that the social fussiness of our middle-class women destroyed all the enjoyment and all the dignity of life."

As he said this to himself the idea of his father rose up before him in a peculiar and special way. He felt ashamed of his shivering as he sat on and on there, waiting for the steamer to move. He felt as if the blowing of the wind and the breaking of the waves, nay! the very darkness itself, as it descended now upon land and sea, contained in it the spirit of his father, massive, primeval, and conceding nothing to human weakness and frivolity.

"Miss Wane! Miss Wane!" he muttered aloud. "I'm getting very cold for your sake, Miss Wane!" His impression of the luckless companion, so ignorant of what she was in for, was that of a middle-aged weary-looking spinster of French extraction.

Amid the gusts of wind that made him press his hands deeper into his pockets and drag his coat, as he hugged himself together, yet more closely across his knees, there now came one that lifted up an especially high wave and broke it into a towering mass of spray.

Any stranger who could have caught the look with which Magnus observed this phenomenon would have been surprised by its grimness, by its austere and almost savage delight. The man's bony figure and irregularly-shaped skull lent themselves to this grimness of expression, but it was quite different from his habitual look. In the normal cast of his countenance there was something formless and chaotic; something not exactly amiable, but certainly not stark or austere. It was as if in order to respond to the tension of the elements he had to gather up a power in his nature that came from his father's character and passed beyond his ordinary habit of feeling.

But the sea subsided a little after the breaking of this particular wave; and Magnus, noting that the ship, which he kept his eye upon, still lingered outside the harbour, let his thoughts fall back once more upon his recent encounter.

"I suppose I ought to have spoken to Sylvanus," he said to himself. "But it would have been awkward if he hadn't known me; and it wasn't the moment to make a mad prophet worry his brain with the names of people. I hope that girl came to herself and is all right now. It was the policeman put me off. Father would have gone right up to him and taken control of the whole affair. Curse it! It's my old cowardice again; my fear of any kind of row. I can't think how I ever had the courage to go so far with Curly. I wonder if that *was* the girl she told me about? I must ask her tomorrow when I go over there. But, oh dear! I wish I *had* stood up to that policeman. I wonder if they'll make Sylvanus stop preaching on the esplanade? What will happen if he defies them and goes on doing it? Will they arrest him? He's the very type to get into serious trouble with them. Curse it! I might just as well have gone up to them and said *something*. It wasn't very nice just sneaking away like that."

The vessel he was keeping his eye upon blew a prolonged whistle at this moment. Magnus could never hear that particular sound without a certain gathering together of his mind to meet a crisis, as if some angel of Judgment were blowing a trumpet.

On this occasion that sudden whistle of the Cherbourg steamer produced a very queer impression on his mind. It was an impression as if the whole of Weymouth had suddenly become an insubstantial vapour suspended in space. All the particular aspects of the place known to him so well, the spire of St. John's Church, the rounded stucco-façade of Number One Brunswick Terrace and of Number One St. Mary's Street, the Jubilee Clock, the Nothe, the statue of

George the Third, seemed to emerge gigantically from a mass of vapourous unreality. This hallucination, or whatever it was, lasted a very short time. A second blowing of the vessel's whistle dissipated it completely; but not before it had been borne in upon him that if he really was such a coward he would have to sink back upon some philosophy that included and completely allowed for such grotesque treacheries.

"A coward," he thought, "has a right to his own philosophy as well as everybody else; and I must get into the habit of accepting the fact that I am an undistinguished and unworthy person. It's possible to accept your cowardice and even to yield willingly to it, as long as you don't give up your—your pleasure in—your delight in—"

His thoughts stopped at this point; and he began—as he had often done before—to fumble in his mind for the right word to express a certain mental attitude which had become a matter of conscience with him, and to which he resorted as to an automatic, ritualistic gesture. But what he really felt now was a sensation as if St. John's Spire, the statue of George the Third, the rounded ends of Brunswick Terrace and St. Mary's Street, that great stone house on the Preston Road, called High House, where this unfortunate "Companion" was to go tonight, had become a cloudy ridge upon whose peaks the chilly bench on which he was resting was lifted up, and from which he could not descend, until he had found the exact word for this particular mental trick which he practised but could not define! Damn! He must give it up. He could not find the word!

With an impatient hopeless movement he jerked up his knees; and pulling his hands from his pockets, seized the handle of his stick which had been propped against the bench at his side. This stick had been his father's. It was of some hard, heavy foreign wood, of a dusky colour, and possessed a smooth curved handle upon which Magnus loved to lean his full weight till he felt he was leaning upon the undying strength of the formidable old man.

His hands were bare, and his fingers felt cold and stiff as he clutched this support, planted now firmly between his legs.

Still that steamer remained motionless between the pierhead and the Weymouth breakwater! What was the matter with it? It was surely long past the time when Mrs. Cobbold told him it would dock.

It didn't need a tug, did it? These Channel Isle steamers always came in on their own steam. He had seen them come in in that way all his life. Well, he must be stirring. He must find some shelter where he could wait, if the ship stayed out there.

The convulsed face of Sylvanus came into his mind again, with the white-cheeked Marret staring at it like a ghost. That man was heroic. There could be no two opinions about that. But he was stark mad. Only a madman would risk arrest by insisting on preaching on Weymouth Esplanade at the end of January.

"I ought not to have sneaked off. I ought not to have sneaked off. I ought not to have sneaked off."

He let go his father's stick for a second, but only in order to pull his cap low down over his eyes.

"But what I've got to do if I'm to keep any self-respect at all," he thought, rising stiffly from the bench, while his teeth chattered, "is to accept my cowardice, take it all for granted, and think of myself as a nervous insignificant book-worm, who can't do anything but teach Latin and be petted by Miss Le Fleau!"

He sighed deeply as he reached this conclusion; but in a flash he recognized that his grand interior moral gesture, this gathering up of his spirit for which he could find no name, *must* be made applicable to an organism, devoid of all courage. Mentally he saw again the Church-spire, the King's statue, the Jubilee Clock, the enormous stone house; and though that feeling of being lifted off the earth by these objects had completely passed, he still seemed to hear these inanimate identities—identities that had gathered to themselves all his memories of all his days—calling out to him to accept himself on the lowest terms and still hold on.

He now became aware that he was violently shivering with cold and he started walking rapidly towards the pier, thrusting as he did so not only his chilly hands into his pockets but also, into one of them, into his right-hand pocket, the handle of his stick; so that the stick itself protruded upwards from his side as he walked, making an acute angle with his body.

When he reached the landing-stage at the head of the pier he found quite a number of persons awaiting the arrival of the boat from the Channel Isles. These persons had already assumed that unique look which is always faintly uncomfortable to any newcomer; the peculiar look of human beings whose protracted waiting has given them a malicious uniformity. Any casual group of people who meet in common subjection to the waywardness of chance come to assume certain characteristics which humanity displays at no other time. At first they are totally unaware of one another, even more indifferent than if they passed on the street. But very quickly they become definitely *inter-conscious* and at first this takes the form of a vague, almost indecent awareness of one another. It is *after* this, when they have begun to get used to wondering critically about one another, that it is so especially awkward to be the last newcomer who joins their malignant vigil.

This was the precise rôle that Magnus was now destined to fill; and he very quickly found the situation so intolerable that, having ascertained from a luggage-porter that the boat's delay at the harbour's entrance had something to do with the tide and would probably be protracted for some while yet, he paid his sixpence and entered the enclosed portion of the pleasure-pier, from the end of which he knew that he would be almost able to shout to anyone on the steamer's deck.

"I mustn't start shouting at Miss Wane," he thought. "But, good Lord! she little knows what she's in for, going up to the top of High House, to be a companion to Lucinda Cobbold!"

He advanced along the harbour-side of the pier, passing the desolate closed doors of the summer Theatre, till he reached the end, where, like the wet deck of a ship, under a solitary light the jetty projected itself over the tossing melancholy waters.

The steamer was further off than he had anticipated, lying now with no motion of her screw, but with a long, wind-blown wisp of black smoke just perceptible in the gathering darkness trailing from one of her funnels, under the lee of the little breakwater.

Magnus found that he was still shivering.

"I need my gloves and my scarf," he said to himself. "Curse it all! I'll probably catch a deadly chill now and get pneumonia! What on earth did I want to fuss myself for about Miss Wane? No doubt she's used to looking after herself. But, good God! anyone who knows Mrs. Cobbold would pity a—"

His thoughts were interrupted by the shock of seeing a man's head, appearing quite close to him above the edge of the rail. The head was followed by a pair of broad, jersey-covered shoulders, and a tall seafaring individual swung himself lightly over the top, and jumped down on the pier.

"Why, Jobber—" Magnus cried in astonished recognition; but the man merely muttered something unintelligible and leaning over the rail began giving hurried directions to someone below.

Magnus himself peered down at the foam flecked darkness where the waves were breaking with heavy ominous sounds against the wooden piles. Close below the pier, pushed in against these piles, was a small, loudly-ticking motor-boat, obviously built for business rather than pleasure, and looking as if it had endured in its time heavier seas than this. Standing in the boat was a round-faced man in rougher garb than the person on the pier. This man was hanging on with some difficulty to a long boat-hook which he had jammed into one of the posts.

"Can 'ee hold her, Bum? Steady, Bum!" cried the tall man by Magnus' side. " Careful now, for the Lord's sake, be careful, man!"

"She be fast, all right, Jobber. Don't 'ee worry."

"Hold on to her then! I won't keep 'ee a minute. 'Tis only to tell Mr. Wool he needn't say anything, now we're back ourselves. See you again, Mr. Muir!"

The speaker now went off without further parley, running with long, easy, rapid strides, and disappeared behind the gloomy bulk of the closed Theatre.

"How be, Mr. Muir? I do mind 'ee well, though thee don't mind I," murmured the man who had been left behind, breathing hard as he tugged at the boat-hook.

"A bit unsteady, eh? Rather a ticklish business, eh? I hope Mr. Skald won't keep you waiting too long. It's not a nice night for—"

As he said this, leaning over the pier's edge, Magnus felt his teeth chattering again.

"Damn Miss Wane," he thought to himself. "I really shall be getting pneumonia if I don't clear off soon. What a fool I was to come!"

And then the excuse struck him that Miss Wane might think it was an impertinence, his arriving at the dock to meet her, a complete stranger! Oh, but *that*, of course, was absurd! How could *she* tell that he wasn't a much closer friend of the Cobbolds' than he was? In fact she might have never heard of the great Jerry. She came probably of quite simple people; and Guernsey was very much out of the world.

"I didn't catch your name," he shouted down to the man below.

"'Trot, sir!" shouted back the man, while the wind whistled through the planks of the pier, and the waves splashed and gurgled. " And they do call I Bum for short. Missus and me do keep house for Jobber Skald."

"Wouldn't it be better if you . . . threw up to me . . . a rope . . . or something?"

"No, no, Mr. Muir, thanking 'ee kind, all the same. Her's fixed tidy now. 'Tis only me asthmy that makes me breath so short."

"When's that ship going to dock, do you suppose?" Magnus asked him.

Mr. Trot glanced over his shoulder at the lights of the steamer, whose outlines—hull, mast, funnel, bridge—were clearly visible against the grey breakwater.

"'Tis the new pilot," shouted Mr. Trot in reply to this. "He be nervous of the tide. Jobber and me would have had she in an hour ago. There! That be her signal. She's off now, I reckon."

When the tall man came back Magnus felt so miserably cold that he resolved to take him into his confidence. Perhaps *he* would meet this girl from Guernsey! He had always felt rather drawn to this eccentric Weymouth character, nicknamed " the Jobber," who earned his living by running his motor-boat between the neighbouring coast-towns and who as a privileged personality was often to be seen at the Cobbolds'.

Adam Skald listened to him with courteous attention. Having got through his business more quickly than he expected he was in good spirits, his taciturnity relaxed, his air jocular.

Magnus was struck by the majestic proportions of the man's figure, and of his physiognomy, too, as he stood there listening to him under the pier light. His big hooked nose, massive chin, and corrugated brow had something about them that resembled those accidental features that people in a mountainous country come to detect in the lineaments of some jagged eminence. Magnus himself now struggled with a new access of self-accusation with regard to this second dodging of social responsibility; and his very feeling of self-humiliation enhanced his respect for this free-and-easy personage with such, emphatic features.

The Jobber agreed without any hesitation at all to undertake the obligation of seeing the new companion safely to High House.

"What shall I tell her?" the big man enquired. "Shall I simply tell her *I was told to meet her?*"

"Oh, she'll have full confidence in *you* directly she sees you!" said Magnus warmly. "My doubt is—poor, little, unknown woman!—how she'll ever manage to endure it with our friend Lucinda."

The Jobber stared at him.

"No, you're right there, Mr. Muir. I wouldn't like to be a young girl from Guernsey with the duty of entertaining Mrs. Jerry." The teacher noticed that this man spoke of Miss Wane as a young girl. Had he any authority for this, he wondered.

The voice of Bum Trot reached them now, informing them that the steamer was moving.

"Hang on a bit longer, Bum!" cried his master. "We'll let her get a good start of us before we run in."

He leaned over the edge of the pier and then turned quickly round.

"I must bid you good-night, Mr. Muir," he said. "It's Bum's asthma and this curst boat—"

He broke off at that point, all his own breath being required for the effort of clambering into the boat.

Magnus looked down at him as he took the boat-hook from Mr. Trot and made him sit down to rest himself.

"Don't worry! I'll deal with Perdita," the Jobber shouted as the boat rocked beneath him; and then he said something that, in the noise of the waves, Magnus couldn't catch.

Perdita? Yes, that was what Lucinda had called her; Perdita Wane. "What's that? I couldn't hear you."

The Jobber repeated his remark; but again Magnus couldn't catch it. It was apparently something satirical or sardonic; and it seemed to have to do with someone they both knew. Was it an expression

of humorous condemnation applied to Mrs. Cobbold? The big man
holding the boat-hook gave him quite an angry look when actually, for
the third time, he couldn't catch his words.

Mr. Trot intervened.

"Jobber be saying," he shouted, "that he'd like to have Mr.
Cattistock along wi' he, in this here lively sea; and maybe he'd gie' 'en
a clip with this here spike, along side of's ear-hole!"

Magnus heard this interpretation with perfect clearness. Nor had
he any difficulty in catching its grim significance. All the town knew
of the bitter feud between Adam Skald, and Mr. Dogberry Cattistock,
known as "Dog Cattistock", a feud which had gone to such lengths,
that they said in the Weymouth public-houses that Mr. Cattistock
went in fear of his life, as "the Jobber have sworn he'll do for he."

So the shivering teacher opened his mouth in the teeth of the wind
and wagged his head, and made a gesture with his hand, in the manner
in which aged men on the stage indicate by vigorous signs that they
are fully en rapport with what is going on among younger folk.

But afterwards, as he made his way home to Kimmeridge House,
Brunswick Terrace, walking as rapidly as he could to get back his
frozen circulation, he could not help associating this rough joke about
Cattistock with his own unworthy running away from two arduous
situations that night. He had left the Punch-and-Judy girl to the care
of that policeman and he was now leaving the Guernsey girl to the
care of the Jobber.

No! he was no honourable and dependable man of the world. He
was a hypochondriacal tutor of backward little boys! It came over
him, as he struggled against the buffets of the wind, longing for the
warmth of his room and the reassurance of his book-shelves, that he
would have been a much nobler figure of manhood, and one much
more likely for Curly to fall in love with, if he could have had the sort
of a quarrel with Dog Cattistock that the Jobber had.

"There's something contemptible," he thought with exaggerated
solemnity as he passed the Jubilee Clock whose hands pointed at five
minutes to six, "about the love-affairs of a timid person. In the very
marrow of human bones lies the instinct that, if we are to be lucky in
love, and to hold our own in love, we must have physical courage."

He set himself now to think of his father as he walked along,

glancing sometimes at the foam in the dark sea and sometimes at St.
John's spire. The same fear of his father, he thought, that made his
love-affairs come to nothing while the old man lived, was still latent
in his mind. *He* hadn't been a coward, though he had been a nervous
and not at all an adventurous man. But his nature was so massive,
his temperament so four-square, that danger itself seemed to growl
like a dog and draw back when he advanced.

It was in this shame-faced mood that Magnus permitted his thoughts
about his father to seize him by his shoulders as if he had been a
prisoner of war, and march him past the Burdon Hotel towards
Brunswick Terrace. It was at Penn House, at the end of Brunswick
Terrace, the last house but one of the row, that he had lived with his
father all those years.

The elder Muir had been a mathematical master of Weymouth
College, and had always hoped that his son would ultimately get a
job in the same institution. But Magnus had no gift for dealing with
high-spirited boys, and he followed the line of least resistance by taking
backward pupils in his father's house; not however in mathematics.
He selected Latin for this undertaking, although his personal predilec-
tion was all for Greek. But it was characteristic of him to take a
furtive pride in not allowing the drudgery of teaching to spoil his
private pleasure in the subtler and more primitive language, that
language which had come to form a sort of invisible barrier for him
between his interior world and the world of outer reality.

The elder Muir had been, it is true, not much more adapted to the
rough and tumble of life than his sedentary son; but he was one of
those men, born—for all their proud and shy withdrawings—with the
power of authority, and though never a popular master in the school,
he had always been respected by both his colleagues and his students;
and thus had grown old in his profession without losing heart.

But Penn House had passed at the schoolmaster's death into the
hands of strangers; and Magnus, retaining nothing but his books,
had moved into Kimmeridge House, where for years he had been the
one and only privileged border in the care of an elderly maiden lady
and her still older servant.

Miss Le Fleau was an old friend of the elder Muir and she treated
Magnus more like a relation than a lodger, though he always insisted

on having his meals brought up to his room on the second floor, and contented himself with brief periodic visits to the Le Fleau drawing-room. It was to this room that he now made his way, as soon as he entered the house; and he found the spinster sitting upright and peaceful at her book under her green lamp, waiting, in her neat black dress trimmed with purple, the moment when Martha would call her to her evening meal.

"Would it be giving her too much trouble, Miss Le Fleau," he began, "if I asked Martha for a hot glass of whiskey when she brings up my supper? I feel rather chilly tonight."

"Oh, I hope you've not gone and caught one of your bad colds. I'm so *glad* you asked me! I'll go down and see to it at once. About an equal portion of the spirit will you have, of the whiskey I mean, with the water?"

"Thank you so much, Miss Le Fleau, but let me go down and ask for it! There's no need for you to bother."

"Oh, *that's* nothing! I hope you'll *always* ask me when you need anything. That's what we idle women are *for*. Wait here, please, will you? And I'll bring it up to you myself. It'll do you no good unless you drink it on an empty stomach. And if I bring it myself I shall be sure that it's hot and I shall see that you don't forget it till it's cold, like you did that night when you got so wet, after walking to Upwey."

The long wrinkled face of the old lady contracted into such a sweet and tender smile as she went out that it seemed to Magnus to express a much deeper pity for him than the accident of feeling chilly quite warranted. He felt a faint tremor of alarm, as he bent down to warm his hands over the blazing fire. Had some friend of hers seen him at the Wishing Well with Gurly?

"She *can't* have heard anything. No, no! it's impossible. And if anyone she knows *had* seen me standing at the mother's door, they'd have only thought I wanted a cup of tea or a glass of ginger-beer."

He raised himself up and stood with his back to the fire surveying Miss Le Fleau's drawing-room.

"It *is* a brown room, this room," he thought. And he remembered how he had told its owner on one occasion that it was like "a brown study", and with what a wry face she had received that remark. But the effect of it *was*, in some odd way, brown; though except for the round mahogany table, and that was polished till it looked like deep water, there was not an actual brown thing in it. The wallpaper was a pale "Dutch pink", bordering on yellow. The cushions and carpet were a dull, rather muddy plum-colour. The pictures were all old, coloured prints, most of them of that smooth, mellow, *greasy* effect that is so peculiarly soothing—as if a misty, oily film, stolen from many natural twilights, had been spread over sketches in crayon; while the books in the three solid rosewood bookcases were almost all green and gold, their bindings carrying all those quaint curlecues and flourishes so popular in the middle of the nineteenth century.

How well Magnus remembered when as a boy his father brought him to call on Miss Le Fleau, how he had been wont to stare in long, quiet reveries at these bindings, absorbed in those queer interior fancies with which children transform almost any pattern into "worlds not realized" when there is no outlet for their restlessness, but from which they hurriedly turn away when such an outlet is found. Drawn back into his father's domination as he always was in this room, where several of the most characteristic pieces of furniture had been bought by Miss Le Fleau at the Penn House sale, Magnus became conscious that the whole Curly episode, when he lay back like this in pious quiescence upon his secure past, had something about it, like a glimpse of a surgeon's bag of instruments, or the sight of an accident on the street, or a sudden encounter with a hand-cuffed prisoner, that belonged to a region of existence where all manner of agitations took place that were completely outside, and even very shattering to, his enjoyment of Miss Le Fleau's drawing-room.

Was it a fatal mistake he was making, he a man of forty-six, with all the traditions of the professional class in his blood and bones, to contemplate marriage with a girl like Curly, not even a peasant-girl, as he saw only too clearly, but—for all her employment at the Upwey Wishing Well—a true Weymouth shop-girl? It was Miss Le Fleau's fire at his back; it was Miss Le Fleau's rosewood bookcases in front of him; it was this insidious Lethean brownness exhaled from the whole atmosphere of the room, that pushed Curly away; and as the circulation returned to his veins and he comfortably awaited his drink with an anticipatory glow of well-being, he found it impossible to help regarding the whole Curly incident as something frightening, disturbing, and out of control.

Miss Le Fleau brought his drink, as she had promised, boiling-hot and with a slice of lemon floating on it; and while he sipped it and stirred it with a tinkling spoon she herself sat down in a little purple armchair and picked up her knitting from beside her book under the green lamp.

"Do you know, Miss Le Fleau," he said, "I think there are two men in Weymouth who are heading for tragic disaster if something or someone doesn't intervene?"

The tall narrow forehead, wrinkled and yet so soft and white, and the proud aquiline nose above the pinched lips—her blue eyes needed no spectacles—remained bent low over her knitting.

Magnus knew well what this silence signified. It signified profound disapproval of the whole topic. Had he told Miss Le Fleau about seagulls or cormorants or a shoal of mackerel she would have greeted his remark with a lifted head and animated sympathy. But there were rumours about Sylvanus, about his immoral life that always made Miss Le Fleau uneasy. She knew it was of Sylvanus he was thinking and from her shining knitting needles to her smoothly-parted white hair she was clearly resolved to have no part or lot in such a discussion.

But the glow produced in his veins by the fire and the whiskey, and the spiritual relaxation produced by the brown room drove Magnus on.

"I saw Sylvanus just now on the esplanade having one of his rows with the police. That man's heading for serious trouble. I could see that the policeman—it was that cockney who stands in summer near the motor-buses and who's generally pretty polite—was at the end of his patience with him. He told him he could do what he liked on the beach. But of course the beach is empty in winter; though, it's true, there was today a Punch-and-Judy—but as a rule it's empty. Wouldn't you say so, Miss Le Fleau?"

Miss Le Fleau's head sank lower and lower over her knitting. There was a certain tone of unnatural emphasis about her guest's voice that made her suspect that her carefully prepared drink had not only warmed his veins but disturbed his discretion.

But Magnus went on talking louder and louder and more and more emphatically.

"The other disaster I see in the wind will be over this Cattistock business. I sympathize entirely with Skald. Don't you, Miss Le Fleau? My father always used to say that Cattistock would come to a bad end by his absolute unscrupulousness. Father couldn't endure him. But I wouldn't care to be in Skald's shoes all the same. I never meet him but he's cursing Cattistock and I can't see Cattistock putting up with it indefinitely. Did you know that at one of those public meetings at the Town Hall Skald went at him so furiously that he had to leave the platform. Something that he's done—and he's always doing dirty tricks—has driven the Jobber, as they call him, to desperation. And I can't see how it's going to end without some serious reckoning. Can *you*, Miss Le Fleau?"

He finished the whiskey as he spoke and advancing to the table, where the lamp stood, laid down his glass and began running one of his fingers round and round its rim. As he did this it was suddenly borne in upon him, like the rolling up of a great theatre-curtain, that a person like his father who had lived to eighty without really encountering the underlying chaos and violence and shame that exist in life was incredibly lucky.

He felt, as he thought of Sylvanus and the Jobber, as though anyone who could go on indefinitely from year to year in this "brown" room was separated from the real chaos of life by some muffled and muted screen. Very slowly, as he paused by that lamp-lit table, Miss Le Fleau stuck her needles into her ball of wool, and raised her eyes from her lap till they rested on his face.

He could not help feeling a vague uneasiness. Had she divined that something was on his mind beyond what he had been telling her of Sylvanus and the Jobber? What would she think if she knew how far he had gone in his mania for Curly? Her eyes met his now: and a long, troubled, inexplicable look was exchanged between them. As he looked away there came a pattering of rain on the window that made him turn round quickly and brought to his mind a renewed sense of the agitating dangers—emotional wrecks as well as physical wrecks—that occurred outside the snug bow-windows of Brunswick Terrace.

"I feel sorry for this woman who's coming from the Channel Islands tonight," he said, making a movement as if to seat himself in a chair near the one occupied by Miss Le Fleau. But the lady herself got up with reproachful abruptness.

"I think we've had enough talk of our neighbours for one night," she said. And then, seeing that he really looked surprised and hurt— "You can call at High House tomorrow, Magnus," she added, "and satisfy your—" she gave him quite a merry young girl's smile as she spoke, "your curiosity. None of us have been as kind as we might to Lucinda," she went on, grown grave again. "Perhaps this person will be very happy with her. Anyway we needn't expect the worst till we know."

Late that night, long after old Martha had removed his supper-tray, Magnus stood staring out of his open window into the darkness. His wide-margined Iliad—"Edidit Guilielmus Dindorf, editio quinta correctior quam curavit, Lipsiae—" was now buried under a heap of youthful exercises in Latin; and the teacher's three candles, for he detested lamps, and never lit the gas, were burning low down in their sockets.

He wondered whether Sylvanus had forgotten the policeman; whether that Punch-and-Judy girl had forgotten Sylvanus; whether the Jobber had forgotten Dog Cattistock; he wondered whether, in those gloomy rooms at the top of High House, Mrs. Cobbold's companion had forgotten the shock of meeting Mrs. Cobbold—all of these people deep-drowned in the ineffable release of sleep!

But for some reason, try as he might, he couldn't visualize Curly's small head, in its cloud of dusky hair, motionless on its pillow. She remained to him in his mind as he had first held her that reckless evening a couple of weeks ago in her mother's parlour; yielding and mischievous, tender and teasing, inscrutable to him as the cat that kept rubbing on that occasion against his legs. His father had once announced to him, in the grave tones of a Pontifex Maximus: "We can see their smiles, my boy"—he was speaking of women—"and we can see their tears, but we cannot see their hearts", and it was with this troubling doubt in his head that he closed the window at the bottom, opened it at the top, and pulled the red curtains a little way across that familiar oblong space of darkness and wet.

He then slowly undressed himself in front of the few crimson
coals that remained of his fire, while his candles spluttered themselves
into extinction. And as he undressed himself the familiar smell of
dead seaweed kept entering his room; and a strange phantasmal
Weymouth, a mystical town made of a solemn sadness, gathered itself
about him, a town built out of the smell of dead seaweed, a town
whose very walls and roofs were composed of flying spindrift and tossing
rain. Lying in bed in the faint glimmer from the grate he could hear
the waves on the beach, and a great flood of sadness swept over him.
Human hearts seemed all so pitifully frustrated! The prophetic frenzy
of Sylvanus; the passionate intensity of the white-cheeked Marret;
the feelings of the Jobber, tossed forth so automatically, as his boat
rocked under those dark pier-posts; that woman whose face he had
never seen, crying herself to sleep at the top of the desolate stone
house; they all belonged to something fatal in the world that turns
to sorrow and grief as inevitably as the compass-needle turns to the
north!

For a while he floated helplessly on the tide of this feeling, watching his big red curtains slowly inflate themselves and bulge forward,
only to be sucked back, with the retreat of the wind, into hollow
answering concavities. Then something in him gathered itself together, as it always did, to resist this hopelessness. And as he felt so
preternaturally self-conscious tonight he began once more trying to
analyse the precise nature of this power in him upon which at a pinch
he seemed always able to call.

But he could no more catch its real nature or even decide whether
it was a good or an evil motion of the mind than he had been able to
do when he was sitting on that bench in the wind. Whatever it was
it was clearly something that he had inherited from his father. It
had something to do with seizing upon some dominant or poetical
aspect of the physical present, such as this sea-wind now blowing into
his room, such as these dying coals, such as that bulge of the red
curtains, and drawing from it a fresh, a simple, a childish enchantment—the mystery of life reduced to the most primitive terms—that
was able to push back as it were by several mysterious degrees all the
emotional and mental troubles of life.

"With father," he thought as he turned his face to the wall, "it was just pure, massive, heathen childishness; and I am the same; only I have to be always fighting off other things."

Then while he settled down under the bed-clothes, there came before his eyes once more the spire, the clock, the statue of the king, the outline of the Nothe, as he had felt them when he sat in the cold opposite the deserted donkey-stand. And the impression gathered upon him that these simple things had a significance beyond all explanation; that they were in truth the outward "accidents" of some interior "substance", that belonged—by a strange law of transubstantiation— to some life of his that was independent of the humiliations of his ordinary experience; independent, for instance, of whether when he went to see Curly tomorrow she made him feel silly and old.

His last waking thought turned these things into a sort of magical abracadabra, devoid of all intelligible meaning, but offering, like some invocation in an unknown tongue, an escape from all his anxieties and shames! They were indeed, these things, in a very definite sense a lasting link with his dead parent; not a link with that parent's opinions or prejudices, but a link with the underlying continuity of his life—a life that had, after all, been so pathetically inarticulate.

He felt that as long as he could feel the presence of these things *in a certain way*—as a child goes to sleep clutching tightly some fragment of wood or cardboard or twisted tin—it would matter less whether he had or had not the courage to lift the Punch-and-Judy girl from the ground or to meet at the dock the companion of Mrs. Cobbold!

2

PERDITA WANE

PERDITA WANE, when her steamer from the Channel Isles did at
last move slowly into the harbour, was as relieved by the end of the
delay as Magnus himself would have been had he had the endurance
to prolong his chilly vigil.

The girl stood by the ship's rail watching the gradual approach of
the blurred shapes of houses, wharves and darkened office-buildings,
as the vessel steamed to her moorings beside the entrance to the pier.
Staring sadly at the water, which rose and fell amid the flickering
lights, she noted with a cold, unhappy meticulousness how each
separate wave that touched the ship's side differed from all the
others.

A vague hypnosis proceeding from these dark-flowing waters did
soothe her a little; for there is almost always, for the troubled human
mind, a degree of comfort in the presence of the inanimate, even when
it is attended by the sort of shivering forlornness that the look of a
dark tide at night-fall necessarily brings. Pure chance dictated the
particular forms that the white wisps of floating foam assumed; but
there did arise for the girl's desolate heart certain faint motions of
distraction as she watched from the deck this random hand-writing
of the elements.

What seemed to interest her fellow-passengers the most, in spite
of the fact that in that January season they were travelling for necessity rather than pleasure, was the long unobstructed curve of the
esplanade's lights; but the girl only lifted her eyes from the moving
tide with its red and green reflections to fix them upon an obscure mass
of swaying masts and dark bulkheads and bowsprits, beyond which,

41

further up the harbour, she could detect the dim shape of a massive stone bridge stretched across the water from quay to quay.

Mingling confusedly with all this shipping, as her mood thus showed its preference for the old and darkened over the new and illuminated, were the narrowest and most ancient of the Melcombe Regis streets; and just as the hulls and masts and rigging of all these little crafts were confused in the darkness, so the walls and roofs and gables and lofts of the dock-warehouses behind them flowed into each other and were lost in each other, till they became a conglomerate mass of antique masonry and woodwork broken by hollow spaces of velvety blackness and by flickering spots of light both of which seemed as arbitrary in their alternations as were the reflections in the troubled water.

The narrow little harbour, thus carrying the chilling airs and salt smells of the open sea into the heart of so much human intimacy, accentuated, for the girl who watched it all, the difference between the warm safety of the Guernsey home from which she came and the unknown encounters that lay before her. With her gloved hands upon the ship's rail she gazed at these things with melancholy intentness, trying, as we all do at such a pinch, to palliate the grimness of the future by concentrating on the immediate scene.

Perdita was neither a plain girl, nor a pretty girl. She was one of those young people whose physical appearance seems to admit of startlingly different verdicts, according to the degree of interest in their personality felt by the onlooker. Her face now, for anyone who saw it under the vessel's lights, was pitiably sad. Her forehead was contracted into a pucker between her arched eyebrows, which very soon —had she to endure many such experiences as this plunge into the great world—would become a permanent frown. The corners of her mouth, one of those mouths that find it so difficult to remain patiently closed, but must always be expressing some sort of intense feeling by their tremblings, were now drawn down in a woe-begone droop. Her chin was undoubtedly the weakest feature in her face; and in the light of that ship's lantern she allowed it to assume a helplessness and a hopelessness that would have disappeared in a moment had anyone addressed her. Then would have become more emphatic, as she raised her head, a certain proud curve in her nose, not to speak of a thoughtful dignity in her clear-cut brow, above which, beneath the rim of her hat, her brown waves, "that this is a winter sea and not a summer sea?"

Again and again as she followed abstractedly with her eyes the melancholy progress of some particular fragment of sea-foam, as it rose and fell on the rocking waves and entered the reflection of a red light or a green light, or got caught by some floating bit of wood or seaweed from which it extricated itself with difficulty, she found herself associating this wisp of whiteness in the dark water with her own fate! She felt pleased when it reached some particularly bright red reflection or green reflection and she could not bear it and had to turn her face away, when it showed signs of being sucked down under some cruel keel.

The keel that did finally suck down the latest of these simulacra of Perdita's life belonged to a motor-boat manned by two men and bearing the name "Cormorant"; but she had no means of knowing that the keen glances with which the taller of these two men swept the vessel's side were directed in search of herself. The little motor-boat, flying a local flag that the custom-officers recognized, ran along the portside of the incoming steamer, crossed her bows, and steering in under the slippery wall of the stone wharf came to rest between two flights of half-submerged stone-steps.

When her own vessel moved alongside the landing-stage, the girl, who was evidently in no haste to set foot on shore, hurried over to the other side of the ship.

"Would anyone know," she pondered idly, as she watched new circles and oblongs and pentagons of sea-scum carried up and down on the waves, "that this is a winter sea and not a summer sea?"

Her gaze wandered in the same weary, proscrastinating manner to a picturesque row of old-fashioned houses on the western side of the little harbour. Some of these time-mellowed habitations had lights in their rooms; and the rays from their windows fell upon stone steps leading down into the rushing tide, and upon quite a fleet of small rowing-boats that rocked up and down in the darkness. Above the roofs of these houses rose the grassy promontory known locally as the Nothe; but there was no one to explain to the newcomer that just as everything on this Nothe side of the harbour lay in the ancient borough of Weymouth, so everything in the lively resort now behind her back, belonged, in strict historic continuity, to the ancient sister borough of Melcombe Regis.

Drawing away her eyes with a sigh from the warm lamp-lit squares of human comfort presented by these small houses, every one of which she felt to be a world of homely drama from which in her loneliness she was excluded, the girl stared down again upon the blurs and blotches of floating spray which showed like streaked marble now in their wayward outlines as the waves beneath them grew darker and darker. How *would* anyone know that these waves were winter waves? Was there something in their colour, in their smell, in the look of their foam, that marked the season? Did the crew of the "Great Western"—those men she had avoided much less than she had avoided her fellow-passengers—feel a keener pleasure in reaching home, on these cold January nights, than they did on a sultry August eve?

It was one of these same sailors who now broke into her musings with the information that the gangway was down and she could land whenever she pleased. The steamer had slipped so swiftly into her accustomed harbourage that if it had not been for the cessation of the engines' vibrations, and the fact that the houses on the shore were now stationary instead of being in slow movement, the young passenger would scarcely have believed the man's words; but she followed him across the deck with reluctant steps to a particular spot on the starboard side where she had deposited her bag, a large paper parcel and her umbrella.

Here she found there was still another opportunity for delay, as there was a good-sized crowd waiting to disembark; and so to the accompaniment of the harsh grinding and rattling of the pulleys that swung the luggage to land she tried to forget where she was by pretending that the sea-washed stones of the jetty against which the ship was rocking belonged to a French pier instead of an English one.

"Would that have been better or worse?" she thought.

Slowly she picked up her bag and her paper parcel from the deck and moved towards the gangway.

"She said in her letter she could not meet me, but I was to take a taxi to High House, Greenhill, Preston Road. But I'd much sooner get a man to carry my bag, and walk, if it's not too far."

Perdita looked a very fragile and lonely figure now in her black neat clothes, as she stood clinging to her poor belongings on that red-funnelled steamer's deck, waiting her turn to hand over her ticket. She was the last to cross the plank; and as she gave up her ticket she enquired of the man who received it how long it would take her to walk to High House, Greenhill.

At mention of the name "High House" the official glanced quickly at his companion; and across both men's countenances there flitted that particular look which people assume when a complete stranger refers to some familiar spot, full of lively local associations.

"Pardon the question, Miss," he said, "but which floor in High House are you bound for? There are four or five of them storeys in that big house and different parties have different sets on 'em."

The stranger murmured the syllables "Cobbold".

"Cobbold of the Regent is it?" said the officer. "She's . . . going —to—Cobbold's," he repeated with interested emphasis looking at his companion. "'Tis nigh the end of the esplanade if you knows what I mean," he went on, again addressing the young woman. "Mr. and Mrs. Cobbold have the top with all the attics. 'Tis a fine view from the top . . . clear acrost the bay."

The other official broke in confidentially at this point.

"He've 'a lived there 'isself, you know, Miss; so if any can speak, *he* can speak. I've a only seed Jerry on the stage myself; but *he* have seed 'im in 'is 'ouse. Be you a relative of Jerry's, Miss, if I might be so bold?"

And to the girl's consternation the first speaker—while he still idly flapped her steamer ticket between his finger and thumb pre-paratory to placing it with the rest—began making signs to the two men who had just left the "Cormorant" and who were now standing at the end of the gangway looking at her as if they were waiting for her. Impatient at all this publicity the girl seized her bag in one hand, her umbrella and paper parcel in the other, and hurried across the plank without looking round.

"Good evening, Miss Wane!" said the taller of the two men. "I've been sent to see you safe up to Mrs. Cobbold's! This is my friend, Mr. Trot. Give me your things. Would you like to walk?"

It was unusual for Perdita to look so fixedly at anyone with her nervous hare-like eyes as she looked now, under that electric light, into the face of the skipper of the "Cormorant".

"*Can* I rely upon you?" her look questioned. "*Can* I trust you?"

She must have been reassured at once; for her critical soul slipped back almost instantaneously into its proud sheath. Letting the Jobber take her bag, her parcel and even her umbrella, she walked forward with a free step between the two strangers.

"I know Jerry Cobbold very well," said the tall man presently, as they passed the Jubilee Clock. This serviceable monument, so familiar and so full of memories for Magnus Muir, received a most cursory glance from Mrs. Cobbold's companion. Pivot for sightseers, Rendezvous for lovers, Resting-place for beggars, imperishable Association, like that of the lectern in their childhood's churches, to all dwellers in Weymouth who remember Victoria, the clock was just a clock to the girl from Guernsey. Even the ornamental adornments of this grandiose erection, adornments so entirely expressive of the era when it was put up, that like the blessing of a well-constituted, elderly relative they soothe with pompous benevolence the fretted modern mind, did not, though clearly visible, seduce this girl to a second look.

"Yes, I know Cobbold as well, I daresay, as anyone in town. He's not humorous in ordinary life. And yet he's very original. You feel it, you know; though it's hard to say *how* you feel it."

"What's Mrs. Cobbold like?" enquired Perdita. And then she could have bitten her tongue for asking such a question.

"Mrs. Cobbold, do you say? God! but *that's* a stumper! How would *you* describe Mrs. Cobbold to the young lady, Mate?"

But the short man, and to Perdita he looked much shorter than he really was, owing to the Herculean proportions of his companion, was not slow with his reply.

"Her be a snug two-masted's figure-head, lady, that's what her be, what none knows whether it be carved and painted new, or whether

it be old as Shamble's Light-ship! None knows and none'll ever
know! Mrs. Cobbold, lady, be what yer might call a drinking man's
'ooman. Her do walk in, dumb and 'andsome; and her do walk out
dumb and 'andsome. 'Ee knows 'ee's cuddled she and 'ee knows her's
cuddled 'ee; but what *she* do know passes all comprehension."

The Jobber chuckled shamelessly. "You see what you're in for!"
he said turning to the girl; and Perdita, wondering to herself why
she did not feel annoyed at the familiarity of these two men, laughed
aloud.

"I'm to be her companion," she remarked, feeling under the
Jobber's scrutiny a mysterious release from her accustomed reticence,
"so I shall soon find out."

The lights of the esplanade, as they moved on, kept giving her
new opportunities for taking in her companions' faces under their sea-
faring caps. Bum Trot had a most whimsically round face, ruddy and
wrinkled, out of which a pair of grey eyes glittered from beneath
shrewd eyelids. It was the enormous emphasis of the Jobber's lineaments that struck her most. The man's face seemed larger than
human in those glimpses of Rembrandtesque chiaroscuro. What
colour his eyes were she could not distinguish, for whenever their
glances met his pupils became so dilated that it was as if two spots of
animated blackness had been turned upon her.

After those words of hers, "I shall soon find out" had hung about
all three of them for several seconds the tall man touched her elbow
with the edge of the paper parcel he was carrying.

"Lonely, eh, young lady?" he said. "But it's only for a time. A
time and a time and half a time." He raised his voice to a mocking
chant as he uttered these words and the other man gave vent to a
guttural whistling, as a kind of accompaniment. "We three must
meet again, young lady," he went on. "That's the ticket, that's the
time of day, ain't it, Mate, and mum about the rest!"

The equivocal jocularity of this speech puzzled Perdita a good
deal; and she was still more surprised when a moment later he stooped
down, and tucking both parcel and umbrella under the arm that held
the bag, picked up something from the stone edge of the esplanade.
The girl glanced to see what he had found; and he promptly held out
to her a fragment of slippery seaweed, whose roots clung tenaciously

with their whitish tendrils to a small round pebble. She took the
seaweed into her hand while the man still retained the stone.

"What—" she began. But he jerked it out of her fingers without
a word and making a circular sweep with his long arm he flung this
pair of inseparable sea-dwellers over the dim bank of shingle into the
gloom beyond. They all three stopped and began listening to the
noise of the sea. It was impossible to tell in the obscurity whether
this composite waif, half-animate and half-inanimate, reached the
water. All that they could hear was a long wave breaking, down there
in the darkness, whose sound, harsh and distinct where they stood,
grew fainter as it died away in both directions.

"Oh why—" stammered the girl.

But "Come on, come on!" was all he said.

She was soon to receive a yet more serious shock from this man's
eccentric behaviour, for when they were passing the wide portion of
the roadway near the Burdon Hotel, where the rounded façade of the
corner-house of Brunswick Terrace gives to vehicles travelling eastward their first chance of a choice between turning to the left or turning to the right, the Jobber stopped and abruptly remarked:

"I'm anxious to get back to my room early tonight; so if you
don't mind, Miss Wane, I'll bid you good-bye here, and let Mr. Trot
carry your things up to Jerry's. Mr. Trot's feelings will be hurt of
course, if you offer him any money. Good-night to you! We're
bound to meet soon. Everyone meets here. It's a sort of Limbo.
Take care of her, Mate!"

Overpowered by the authority of his personality as he handed over
her things to the obedient Mr. Trot, Perdita felt too confused to
respond to his departure by anything but a stiff inclination of her
head.

There are moments in almost everyone's life when events occur
in a special and curious manner that seems to separate that fragment
of time from all other fragments.

One peculiarity of such moments is the vividness with which
some particular human gesture limns itself on the sensitive-plate of
our inmost consciousness, along with certain inanimate objects. It is
not with *every* object in the vicinity that it thus surrounds itself, but
with a selection of such objects, which, in place of being congruous

with the gesture they are accompanying, are often extremely incongruous. Another peculiarity of these moments is a sensation as if
there were a spiritual screen, made of a material far more impenetrable
than adamant, between our existing world of forms and impressions
and *some other world*, and as if this screen had suddenly grown extremely thin, thin as a dark, semi-transparent glass, through which
certain faintly adumbrated motions, of a pregnantly symbolic character,
are dimly visible.

Such a gesture—to the inner consciousness of this proud girl—
was the upraised arm of the man called the Jobber as he flung that
seaweed and pebble over the shelving bank into the darkened water;
and it was her complete absorption in this occurrence that held her
feet for a moment, after he had gone, as if rooted to the spot, though
she did not turn her head to watch him go as Bum Trot turned *his*,
but kept.it hanging down, as if in the humility of a sudden perception
of a movement of destiny.

They had not moved on many paces when Mr. Trot enquired,
with a screwing up of his eyes that distorted his whole physiognomy,
whether she would prefer to follow Preston Road, "back of Brunswick", or go on by the sea and "turn up Greenhill". This enquiry
broke the trance into which the departure of the Jobber had thrown
her. Perdita gazed round with bewildered hesitation.

"I like the look of Brunswick Terrace," she murmured, "so let's
go *that* way."

Obedient to her whim, the worthy Mr. Trot, whose Christian
name had been reduced to the single syllable "Bum", led her across
the road; and they walked rapidly along the narrow pavement in front
of the bow-windows of a row of comfortable little lodging-houses.
Some of these had lights in the windows and some not; but they all
stood back behind neat little area-gardens whose tiny patches of earth
were carefully dug up, and in many cases heaped with manure.

They had gone about half-way along the terrace when they passed
a house whose bow-window was brilliantly lit up, revealing the head
of a young man writing busily at a circular table. Perdita had just
had time to read "Trigonia House", inscribed beside the door-bell
of this snug retreat, when Bum Trot amiably prodded her arm with
the handle of the umbrella he was carrying.

"That be young Sippy Ballard," he explained proudly when they had passed on. His tone was like the tone of a Londoner pointing to the Mansion House.

"That fair boy at the table?" the girl murmured, glancing back over her shoulder. "He looked very busy."

"He be the new Officer," Mr. Trot eagerly explained. "Dog Cattistock put him in. He's his nephy or summat. Some do say he's his wone flesh and blood; but I don't gie' a horse-drop for such babblement."

Perdita was not interested enough in the young man at the window even to enquire who this "Dog Cattistock" might be.

There was nothing to arrest their attention about Kimmeridge House, where at that moment Magnus was drinking whiskey in Miss Le Fleau's drawing-room; and they soon passed Penn House with the same indifference. They were now following a path along a rough stone wall built at the foot of some quite considerable gardens lying along the slope of a steepish incline, from the summit of which rose several stately, solidly-built mansions. Perdita stood up on tiptoe and tried to look over this wall, but it was too high. They came presently, however, upon an iron gate in the austere fortification, and the girl stopped and peered through, clinging to the bars.

"Them be the lights of High House, Miss," said Bum Trot at her shoulder. "They yeller windies, up at top, be where Jerry lives."

The girl shivered. All her former dismay, temporarily dispersed by her encounter with the Jobber now came rushing back as her forehead pressed against those cold bars.

Her companion was not oblivious to her change of mood.

"'Tis lonesome-like, Missy, when us comes to places unbeknown," he muttered kindly as they walked on together, "but as the Jobber always do say: 'Time and a Time and half a Time, and all will be well!' "

The girl controlled herself by an effort, rubbing her cheeks with the back of one of her gloved hands.

The long-drawn descent of an extra big wave receded huskily into the darkness of the sea, scraping the steep pebble-shoal, as if it had been a hoarse musical instrument.

A couple of young sailors from a battle-ship in Portland Harbour drifted by at this point, their arms affectionately thrown round each others' necks and their steps lingering and reluctant.

There was something about these boys as they lurched by, with barely a glance at Perdita that made the girl's sadness feel almost unbearable. Her secret heart, troubled and disconsolate on her own account, melted within her to think of these two young neophytes of life carrying off their feeling for each other and all the dark pressure of their unknown future with this callous air.

"Boys are braver than girls," she thought to herself. And then she thought: "But what nonsense! They're only less aware of things." But as the two sailors pursued their way along Brunswick Terrace, the indescribable pathos of all human life struck her as something almost intolerable.

"Here's the lane, Miss! We'll soon be round at front-door."

The man breathed so heavily as they ascended the little asphalt path that Perdita begged him to let her help him with the bag.

"Nonsense, Lady," he gasped. "'Tis a touch of me asthmy; that be all. What I were born with, I reckon. 'Tis wondrous how a little bit of up-grade do bring it on. I can pull an oar, Miss, in the choppiest sea, for best half-a-day; but a bit of climbin' makes I pant like a wold hoss."

Arrived at the top of Greenhill Lane they turned to the left, and retracing their steps westward for about a hundred yards, stopped in front of a vast stone building that loomed above them with an impressiveness that was startling without being inspiring, and portentous without being sinister. The place looked indeed like an indestructible monument to that imposing epoch in English History when both Gladstone and Disraeli were young, and when Tennyson was writing "In Memoriam".

"Will 'ee ring the bell, Miss?" panted Bum Trot.

Perdita, who was shivering again, pulled out the great metal bell-handle and let it go clattering back. A remote tinkling sound within the huge edifice indicated that her effort had been successful. The door was soon opened by a pale-faced, elderly man who evidently played the role of a concierge.

"Top-floor. Cobbold's," murmured Perdita's guide in husky authoritative tones. To the girl's dismay, for she had come to feel a certain protection in the society of her asthmatical friend, Bum Trot handed her over with all her belongings to this attendant. Mindful of the words of the Jobber and unable to think of anything else to do, Perdita held out her hand to her guide.

"Good-night, Mr. Trot," she said, "and thank you, very *very* much!"

The staircase was such a stately and spacious one and so softly carpeted that the ascent to Mr. Cobbold's apartments was much easier than might have been excepted. The door leading to the top-floor, when they arrived there at last, was opened by an aged man-servant and once more Perdita's bag and parcel changed hands. The concierge disappeared, and the girl had hardly time to look about her before Mrs. Cobbold herself advanced to give her welcome.

"I must apologise," said the lady, "for my husband's not meeting your boat. The truth is he has to be at the theatre tonight. My husband is—I don't know whether you realized that, Miss Wane—a professional on the stage. He has his reputation over here . . . but I can't suppose it has got as far as the Channel Isles! This is your room, Miss Wane. No, *this* way—now to your right, and up three steps! Oh, that's right, Fogg; I see you've got Miss Wane a good fire. No! better let Miss Wane unpack for herself. We'll have our little supper by the drawing-room fire tonight, Fogg. And I expect we'll be ready for it in about half-an-hour. Yes, warm yourself, child! Warm yourself, warm yourself, warm yourself!"

Mr. Fogg glanced round as he approached the door; noted the fact that his mistress intended to remain for a while, and closed the door behind him as he went out.

"*That* means a good hour," he said to himself. "If she hadn't stayed with 'er 'twould 'd meant three-quarters. I'll go easy wi' they fried soles; and I'll 'old back that apple-charlotte."

While Perdita knelt on the hearth-rug and drew off her gloves in the comfort of the warm blaze, Mrs. Cobbold sat down in a large lavender-covered armchair.

When the girl turned her head to reply to what the lady was now saying to her she became aware that the room they had given her was much more like an actor's dressing-room than like a bedroom. Pictures of every kind of theatrical personage adorned the walls; most of them, but not all, framed in thin black frames, but some simply fastened to the wallpaper. Thus the room even in that warm, dim light had an air that was unhomely, transitory, insecure, and a little disconcerting.

Perdita replied nervously, and in broken, abrupt sentences to her employer's questions; but her agitation seemed to have no disquieting effect upon her interlocutor. Indeed Mrs. Cobbold gave expression now and again to quiet sighs of satisfaction, as if her relief was great to find her new companion so free from self-assurance and self-possession.

What Perdita could not get out of her mind as at last, like a bird in a cage making trial of an unaccustomed roosting-place, she rose from her knees and sat down on a gilded embroidered stool, a stool that had something about it that suggested a tarnished theatrical accessory —as if it were part of a throne-set in a conventional court-scene— was the feeling of the vast bleakness and desolateness of the enormous stone edifice all about her, of which these singular Cobbold apartments were the crowning strangeness.

"Warm yourself, warm yourself, warm yourself," Mrs. Cobbold repeated like an incantation. "I shan't let you say a word till you're thawed out."

Perdita had pictured her employer many times, but the reality was more disturbing than her most lively prognostication. Mrs. Cobbold was dressed in green velvet, bound with black satin. She had a thin gold circlet round her head, under which her glossy, blue-black hair, smoothed down and cropped, displayed a lustre as polished and gleaming as a raven's wing. Her head was large for her body, which was sturdy and shapely, although below the middle height, but what gave her face its extraordinary character was the extreme pallor of her cheeks, upon which, when she cast down her eyes, her long, dark eyelashes seemed to rest, like the eyelashes of a doll upon a countenance of colourless wax.

What struck Perdita at once about her was her unapproachable dignity. It was much more than the natural dignity of the eccentric wife of a rich actor. It was a dignity that seemed to separate her from ordinary men and women. The more the girl saw of it the more startling seemed its implications.

Before that evening was over—her first in the top-floor of High House—Perdita got the impression that Mrs. Cobbold was what might have been vaguely called a "dedicated" figure; though dedicated exactly to *what*, remained obscure. In fact, during all that first night, the girl's mind was tantalized by this particular riddle. She seemed once or twice on the very verge of a solution; but just as she touched it—and her feeling was that it was very simple when once it was caught—it slipped away and evaded her. Mrs. Cobbold was clearly set apart from the ordinary run of mortals by some fatality, which, whether for good or evil, endowed her reserved identity with an arresting emphasis.

Perdita wondered if Mr. Fogg was their only servant; but when the man knocked at her door nearly half-an-hour after her hostess had left her, and waited outside till she came out, and discreetly and courteously led her to the drawing-room, she came to the conclusion that this grave personage was quite capable of doing the combined work of the customary number of servants.

Mrs. Cobbold's drawing-room was no less theatrical in its general impression than was the room which Perdita had been given as a bedroom. There was more gilt and more tinsel, however, in the dominant effect of this spacious chamber, whose three large windows looked out over the waters of the bay. Most of the chairs were gilded while every cushion, every curtain, every bit of upholstery looked as if it belonged to a rather dilapidated stage-set.

Well, here she was, actually in the midst of her first "place"! And it was not so frightening after all, now that it had come to the point, thus to sit so close to this blazing fire, on a low gilded settee, while Mrs. Cobbold sat on the opposite side of the hearth in an equally low armchair. It was not frightening even when the lady began talking about what French authors they would read together. It was indeed a mighty comfort to Perdita to know that she wouldn't have to *talk* French; and that she wouldn't have to cope with any of the more scholastic aspects of this classic tongue. Apparently all she would have to do was to read aloud from some volume of fiction while her employer held in her hands another copy of the same work. Mrs.

Cobbold's "dignity" stood the girl in good stead over this matter; for it ruled out as disturbing and unbecoming all those aspects of learning a language which suggested school and school-books.

Perdita's heart did begin to beat a little when, drowsy and warm on a fantastical sofa by her hostess' side, she heard the sound of the hall-door opening and caught the voice of Mr. Cobbold speaking to Fogg. But when the great man had divested himself of his overcoat and goloshes, and when Fogg had ceremoniously opened the drawing-room door, as he did every night of their life, with the words: "The master, Madam!", and when a slight, unobtrusive figure had approached his wife—who did not rise—and kissed her forehead, and had shaken hands warmly with the new companion—who stood up very straight, and haughty, and shy—she felt that the famous Jerry was going to be the reverse of alarming. As a matter of fact no one could possibly have guessed from the tone in which he chatted to her, that he was the greatest clown upon the music-hall stage; and that it was only because it was his wife's caprice to live in Weymouth that he had retired from "Cobbold's Colosseum" in London.

He had bought the well-appointed, old-fashioned Play-House, called the Regent, and there for three nights in the week, and for one matinée, he danced his dance and made his grimaces all the winter long, greatly to the benefit of the lodging-houses and hotels of the town, which had not entertained, or been entertained by, so famous a visitor since the days of George the Third.

Mr. Cobbold had scarcely been talking to them for five minutes before the door opened and Fogg appeared. This time he carried into the room the same little card-table and the same white table-cloth that had served for the earlier meal, and very soon the comedian was enjoying a substantial supper. With perfect naturalness, and in the airiest manner Mr. Cobbold talked to them while he ate his meal and drank two or three glasses of wine. He was voluble upon the nature of the audience to which he had played that evening, commenting in a mischievous manner upon the various local characters— for his wife was a native of the town—whose faces he had caught sight of in various parts of the house.

Perdita was conscious that his liveliness was addressed more to his lady than to herself; though every now and then she fancied she read a look in his eyes which seemed to say: "This is the sort of thing I want you to help me do. Keep her mind distracted. Amuse her, amuse her, for God's sake! As long as we can do that, together, now that you are here, all will be well."

There was something about the man's concern for Mrs. Cobbold and the nervous way he watched her while he made his very harmless jests, that at once puzzled and disturbed Perdita. The drowsy feeling of luxurious relief which had descended upon her as she talked with the lady about French novels was entirely dissipated. She began to be almost distressingly awake now; and with her wakefulness there came over her a new and less pleasing impression of these curious rooms at the top of this formidable stone house. She began to feel as if she had been spirited into an inaccessible fortress, where her duty was to distract some distinguished prisoner and keep her mind occupied by perpetual card-playing.

The famous comedian doled out his lively commentaries—his humour in private, the girl thought, was more like that of a whimsical Abbé than a popular Clown—just as if his words had been cards from a well-considered hand. It struck her now that there was something —it was hard to say just what—something curiously forlorn about all these faded gilt chairs and theatrical hangings. As she noted with a puzzled intensity the expression and manner of her host she felt more strongly every moment that she was in the presence of some kind of desperate game; a game that this man was playing against some unseen antagonist, whose nature and quality hung about these desolate draperies and this unnatural furniture like a ghostly presence.

"We mustn't keep Miss Wane up, Jerry," said Mrs. Cobbold, in the first real pause her husband reached in his flow of lively discourse. "She must be tired after her voyage and even—" the lady turned with a graceful and intimate little gesture towards her new companion—"even if she isn't ready for bed, it's always nice to have a little time to settle down in a strange room."

She hesitated a moment, raising one of her shapely hands to her golden circlet, as if to assure herself that he head was carrying that adornment becomingly.

"Jerry breakfasts at nine," she said, giving Perdita a straight and calmly authoritative look, "and I know he'd love to have your company then. I don't myself come down till later. Fogg will knock at your door, and leave your hot water outside, at eight; if that's agreeable to you."

They were all three standing now, though it would have been difficult for Perdita to isolate the moment when she herself and Jerry rose to their feet. Her whole attention must have been absorbed in watching Mrs. Cobbold. And as they stood there, while Perdita hesitated whether to offer them her hand or just to bow and move to the door, she felt that both she and the comedian were engaged in a joint struggle to keep Mrs. Cobbold's mask in its place, to prevent her from dropping her appointed rôle, to prompt her with the right cue for the repetition of her habitual part. It was one of those curious moments when the entrance of a new personality into a situation that has become automatic by custom produces a tension, a strain, a nervous expectancy, as of some possible catastrophe.

"I am sure . . . I shall be . . . very—" Perdita stammered, feeling as if she were called upon to say something; but her voice sounded unnatural in her own ears, while its faint syllables hung in the air of that theatrical room with the harsh sea-murmur coming up from below; and Mrs. Cobbold—her hands still raised to the gold band across her brow—betrayed under the lowered fringe of her dark eye-lashes a mocking awareness of the embarrassment that held the two of them and a malignant desire to prolong it.

Suddenly she dropped her arms and, lifting her eyelids, gave her husband a quick sidelong glance.

"She'll go to sleep," she burst out in a voice quite different from any she had hitherto used. "She'll go to sleep and forget everything! She's lucky; isn't she? Go . . . to bed . . . and . . . go . . . to sleep."

"Good-night, Miss Wane," said Jerry Cobbold hurriedly; and he stepped quickly to the door and opened it for her. "There's your room—you remember?—on the left, down that passage. We'll meet in the morning at breakfast."

Perdita turned, as she went out, meaning to nod or smile at her hostess; but Mrs. Cobbold had moved to the fire and was standing with her back to them both.

Once safe in her own bedroom, Perdita hurriedly undressed, and, putting on her old faded dressing-gown, a present, years ago, from her

father, pulled close to the hearth, where the flames were now mounting up brightly, that same low chair upon which Mrs. Cobbold had
sat for their first conversation, and hugging her knees with clasped
hands set herself to ponder on all her impressions of this evening.
She had pulled the window-curtains aside before crouching at the
fire; and from where she sat she could hear the sound of the sea much
clearer than in that theatrical room downstairs.

The feelings which that sound roused in her were curiously mixed.
It awed her a little. It chilled her consciousness with the ebb and
flow of vast non-human forces that cared nothing for human plots
and counter-plots. It brought something into that fantastical bed-
chamber that was free and uncaught, whose very desolation was a
kind of comfort, obliterating with the release of the indifferent elements the unhappy morbidities of her race.

Out of all the impressions that had crowded upon her in the last
few hours, since she stood on the deck in the harbour watching the
drifting foam, the deepest was the one that it was hardest for her to
analyse or define. It had to do with the personality of the man called
the Jobber. She had never felt about any man—or indeed about any
human being—this curious disturbance of her inmost reserve. It
was as if some hidden self, hardly known to her own consciousness,
had at last found its recognition, its defence, its security, its refuge.

And this feeling did not seem to depend upon her ever seeing the
Jobber again. It seemed to fuse itself—when she tried to call up any
definite image of the man—with the lights and scents and murmurs
and darknesses of her whole impression of her landing. The Jobber,
when she tried to visualize his identity, seemed to melt away from the
clasp of her imagination and to lose himself in the sound of breaking
waves, the smell of tossed-up sea-drift, the rocking reflections of ships'
lanterns.

So abstracted in her thoughts as to be hardly aware of what she
was doing, she got up now from her crouching position and going over
to the mirror began combing her hair. It was an instinctive movement
with her to comb her hair when some subtle and absorbing emotion
took possession of her. Once in bed and the gas-flame extinguished,
she kept seeing the formidable sweep of the tall man's arm as they
stopped on the esplanade and he flung that piece of seaweed into the

darkness. She kept imagining the way that seaweed was now being washed, to and fro and lifted up and down, as the stone to which it clung rolled over and over on the ribbed sand under the dark tide.

"I am like that seaweed," she thought, "only I have no stone to cling to."

She lifted up her hand to the pillow behind her head and threw back the dark braid of her hair so that the exposed nape of her small neck should feel neat and free, as she liked to feel it.

But now, pushing aside the tall form of the Jobber, the lineaments of Jerry Cobbold limned themselves on the black square of her open window between the fire-lit curtains. She saw his mobile face with its premeditated animation, his big forehead, straight nose, weak chin and white teeth, all set in play by the intention within his skull, like a puppet's features worked by wires.

"I wonder what he's like on the stage?" she thought. "His face actually collapsed when he exhausted his rigmarole. It was like a candle, inside an Image, being blown out. What a changeable face he must have! I'm not sure now whether his nose was so small, or his forehead so big, or his chin so weak! I'm not sure of anything about his face. I only know it gave me a weird feeling, as if he *invented* it afresh at every moment, and as if, in itself, it was made of some ghostly neutral substance."

She now sacrificed all her careful adjustments of her neat braid by violently turning over on the other side. She wanted to catch again that delicious mood of vague romantic feeling which the incident of the seaweed had produced. She did not at all want to go to sleep thinking of Jerry Cobbold.

If a stranger had seen her lying in that flickering firelight, with the theatrical pictures all about her, such a person would have been surprised, noting by her wavy brown hair that she was a girl, to see, though she was lying on her side, how slightly the counterpane was raised! A young boy's hips, in that particular position, could hardly have lifted the clothes less noticeably. She tried to stay motionless now till sleep came; and she did turn over only once more; but that false, lively face pulled by wires seemed to hover over her like a mocking sentinel and refuse to let the Jobber's massive form and swarthy countenance come near her bed.

With the approach of sleep, however, it was not to Weymouth or to any of its people that her thoughts gathered, like roosting-birds settling down on a familiar bough, but to her home in Guernsey. An orphan since her childhood, she had been brought up by her uncle and aunt; and while her uncle lived, although as purser on a big easterly-bound liner he was seldom at home, her life had been in all outward matters peaceful and uneventful.

But with her uncle's death everything had changed. Her aunt was of French extraction, as indeed her own mother had been, and had always treated the girl as her own child; but the woman was an invalid, looked after by an elderly step-sister, and most of her husband's pension went in doctor's bills. Thus when Perdita, who had grown restless and unhappy after her uncle's death, begged that she might go to England and try to earn her own living, the two old ladies gave their consent. Between themselves, for Perdita had already, without anything coming of it, attempted some small jobs at home, they were certain that she would come back in a few weeks; and this certainty, while it lessened their enthusiasm for the project, diminished their anxiety as to how she would get on.

"Let her see for herself what work means, sister," said the ancient relative; and Perdita's aunt had sighed and acquiesced.

Deprived by destiny of all superficial prettiness—though not devoid, in moments of animation, of a loveliness peculiar to herself—Perdita had reached her twenty-fifth year without anything approaching a love-affair. She was proud and nervous and shy; and although she always got on well with older men, and was appreciated by them, her prejudice against lads of her own age—whom she regarded as insufferably conceited—was quickly enough divined by the young men themselves; with the result that they punished her—or fancied they were punishing her—by sheering off and giving her a wide berth.

Nor had she been much luckier with her girl-friends. Conditions of life in the little Guernsey town did not lend themselves harmoniously and easily to girl-friend hips. Family life was tenacious and very exclusive. Young girls attended convent-schools, helped their mothers with house-work and married young. It was only the flirtatious ones with a reputation for fastness, who went about in couples amusing themselves.

Perdita's few friends were older people, friends of her uncle, simple folk who petted and encouraged and wondered at her, as an intellectual prodigy, but made no attempt to understand her, and indeed saw nothing of her real nature. Thus she had been very happy, as a child, but very unhappy and very lonely as a young woman, and this rash and reckless plunge into independence was the result of her desperation.

Her reversion to her Guernsey memories at this moment was not, therefore, though they came to her with all the nostalgia of the familiar and dear, fraught with any sense of peace or tranquillity.

"Oh, how sad life is!" she thought, as she turned once more on her pillow; and there came over her the old hopeless longing to be safe out of it all, and really at peace. These desolate thoughts made her curl herself up in her bed, as she listened to the sea, as if by the mere hugging of her knees between her arms she could return to that unconscious state in which twenty-six years ago she lay, an embryo-mite, before she was born into a world like this; a world in which for a woman not to be beautiful, not to be seductive and appealing, means after all a series of futile desperations, of shifts and make-shifts, of pitiful and sorrowful turnings to the wall.

3

THE JOBBER

LITTLE as Perdita realized it, in her fixed conviction that fate had made her so totally undesirable, the Jobber's thoughts, though he retreated abruptly from her side, clung to her shy and evasive personality with an obstinate persistence that surprised and troubled him.

"What was there about that girl?" he thought.

But he had hardly begun to follow up this question than his mind swung back again to what had become of late its habitual preoccupation. His hatred of the person he thought of as Dog Cattistock had indeed mounted up within him in the last few months to such a pitch that it came to be nothing less than murderous.

As he strode now along the esplanade he hitched up his thick woollen blue jersey from his hip and thrust his hand into his right pocket where his fingers closed over the smooth, hard surface of a large pebble-stone. A week ago he had visited his parents in Portland and learned from his father who had been an independent quarry-owner, till Cattistock's tricks, as a promotor of companies, had reduced him to poverty, that this remorseless man of affairs was now going to close down the largest quarry in the Island and turn away a score of old Portlanders who had worked there from boyhood. The Jobber that very evening had picked up from Chesil Beach this particular weapon and had kept it in his pocket ever since. As he went along now his fingers closed spasmodically, as they had repeatedly done during these last days, upon this heavy stone, the cold, hard impact of which against his side gave him such deadly satisfaction.

"If I did it," he thought, "it would be my end as well as his. I should hang; unless I got away in time to drown! And what would be the result? It would kill mother; but he'd be out of the world! There's not a labouring man in this place but would breathe free. He'd be out of it—the devil!"

Something cold—colder than the stone he clutched in his pocket —struck into his vitals.

"To die, to go none knows where; most likely into nothingness, into the absolute Dark. But to take him with me—aye! there's the rub—to take that devil with me. No Dog Cattistock any more! Look for him tomorrow. Not there! That dog's face of his grinning no more. Gone. Quite gone. Weymouth free of him and his brute-tricks for ever and a day! And Miss Guppy at the Weeping Woman pouring out drinks just the same. . . . 'Have they hanged the Jobber yet?' 'No, they're waiting for the Sheriff. They say 'tis on Monday they'll finish thik little job!' "

At this point in his imaginations, as often had happened with him of late, he found he could not go on doing what he called *thinking the thing through*. It was like walking into that ice-cold sea over there without a shred of clothing.

"I mustn't think about it," he said to himself. "I *must* stop thinking about it. If I do it, I do it—and there it is. He'll be in black emptiness for ever, and I shall be the same. Both of us as if we'd never been born at all."

He stopped and swung round. "Thinking is bad," he said to himself "Nothing is ever done by thinking. So much added to thinking, so much taken from doing."

He let his gaze drift back along the esplanade till it reached the beginning of Brunswick Terrace, where it wandered to St. John's spire and to an obscure blur under a street-lamp which he knew to be the newly erected statue to Queen Victoria.

"That girl—I must see that girl again!" His mind followed Bum Trot and Perdita in their approach to High House. "She doesn't know what she's in for," he thought, "with that woman".

He could not help imagining how thankful "that girl" would be when they at last let her go to bed. He had often been in those rooms of the Cobbolds' and he had no difficulty in visualizing her going to bed in what they called "the Spare Room".

"They *must* be giving her that room," he thought. "The little one, next Fogg's, would be *too* bare and miserable."

He still stood motionless, staring at the vague outline of the church-spire and at the still more obscure figure of Victoria. These two objects—the one of stone and the other of bronze—were both so nebulous in the street-lights that they assumed an almost ghostly appearance. The fantastic notion came into his head that these two erections might well exchange their thoughts as they stood there night after night. This fantasy of the Jobber's as he contemplated them, himself a solitary figure between the lighted houses and the dark sea, was not without its natural congruity. But these monuments were modern; and though the Spire was half-a-century older than the Statue, there was an historic link between them. Both represented the inmost platonic essence of the Victorian era; for what the Spire had gained in its long experience of the Queen's subjects, as people went Sunday by Sunday to worship the Queen's God, the Statue made up for by being the living image of the Queen Herself. Thus while the elderly Spire respected the brand-new Statue, the Statue looked up to the Spire with solemn confederacy.

"It will be long," they both seemed to say, "before Respectability and Piety lose their importance in Melcombe Regis."

The Jobber glanced at these grave objects under particular conditions; for he was ashamed of following Perdita with his thoughts and at the same time he was reluctant to turn away. He therefore used the Spire and the Statue as objects of his official attention while he let his mind wander. He saw them, in fact, without seeing them. This does not mean that they had no effect upon his mind; for it is a matter of common experience that impressions thus made sink the deepest of all. But it means that their effect upon him at this particular moment was unconscious rather than conscious.

Both these monumental objects receded as he gazed upon them into some remote psychic dimension, while in their places appeared— like a cloud in an air-mirror—not the concrete image of Perdita, but a symbolic projection, composed partly of his unaccountable attraction to her, which was represented by something velvety and alluring in the darkness, partly of the actual contour of one of her cheeks, as he had seen it under the lamp-post when she was holding the seaweed, with a wisp of her hair, damp from the sea-spray, falling obliquely across her brow.

Ashamed of his moment of weakness he now turned his back to Brunswick Terrace, took his hand from his pocket, and with rapid swinging strides, thinking to himself, " I'll look in at the Weeping Woman before I cross the ferry", made his way westward.

But a man's thoughts—especially when hovering round the figure of a girl—are not dispersed by a few minutes of rapid walking; and the Jobber, when he found himself close to the statue of George the Third, was compelled to come to a second abstracted pause. This older monument, which has stood so many years at the bifurcation of St. Mary's and St. Thomas's Streets, was now in its turn destined to be teleported from its pedestal, so that its location in space might be used, as he had used that of those later landmarks, as a material support for his psychic evocations. Gazing upon this grey object— no remarkable work of art—he soon brought it about, in spite of the fact that there was more light here than in front of St. John's, that the well-meaning monarch, that great patron of the town, should vanish like those other phenomena, into whatever curious Limbo it may be that receives such things when the magic of human abstraction exercises its despotism upon them.

The Jobber's own bodily form disappeared under the tyranny of his thought as completely as did the form of the old king; and in their stead a procession of mental images and intentions filled that hollow gulf in time and space. If the emotional content of his musings at that moment had been put into words, such words would have run roughly like this: "beer-froth bubbling up in pewter; forget her wet cheek; Miss Guppy drawing beer; lull myself to sleep with Middlemarch; finish off Dog Cattistock without thinking about it." And then, as his thoughts ran on Perdita again, he began cursing the disobedient heart, as Homer would say, "within his hairy breast".

"Is it possible," he said to himself, "that I've waited all these years, nipping in the bud every affair that offered itself, only to be hit at last by Mrs. Cobbold's companion?"

The hollow statue of the old King now became a sounding-board for the Jobber's memories of his gross erotic life; a life which he had not scrupled to keep on a very earthy and a very sensual plane. This heathen method of his with the perilous nerve found its epitome in an actual mania he had acquired for never allowing himself to utter the three fatal syllables, "I love you", in any feminine ear. It was indeed in the strength of what had now become an automatic gesture of self-protection that he had made his clumsy excuse, a few minutes ago, and left this disturbing girl to the unromantic care of Bum Trot.

"I'll just drop in at the Weeping Woman and have a glass of gin and bitters," was his final conclusion. "That will give Bum a chance to get home first; and Cassy will give him a hot supper."

For a good many years now the Jobber had lived in a small house, in "Weymouth Proper", on the other side of the Harbour. The house was his own and he had furnished it after his own fashion, the chief characteristic of which was a fancy for things that were both ample and ancient. For *small* bric-à-brac Adam Skald had a curious dislike. He always said that such delicate things "made the tips of his fingers tickle". Upholstery and curtains and cushions he held also in detestation; but he had crowded his little house with big wooden armchairs, wooden tables, grandfather clocks and enormous brass cauldrons and earthenware jugs, till it resembled a humble lodgement of the giant Gargantua.

Skald's native home was in the neighbouring promontory of Portland; but for years he had lived an independent bachelor life, served with unsparing devotion by Bum and Cassy Trot. It was the rather original occupation by which he earned his living that had procured him his nickname of the Jobber. What he really was was a sort of amphibious Carrier, conveying in his motor-boat, the Cormorant, and in a Ford Truck, that he named the Slug, every conceivable kind of load, from cattle-dung and fresh vegetables, to flour, oil, and salted fish.

The Jobber was a man of thirty-five; a secretive person, living entirely in his own eccentric thoughts, but possessed of a sympathetic magnetism that had brought it about that he had more acquaintances, on both sides of the harbour, than any other person in the community.

The perturbed man now crossed the road and leaving the old King's statue behind him plunged into the town. He strode so fast along the outside edge of the pavement of St. Mary's Street, passing the Parish Church and the Guildhall, and, to make quicker progress, stepping frequently into the road to avoid the crowd, that he had scarce time to beat down the image of Perdita before he came among the dark warehouses and narrow alleys and reached the Tap Entrance of the Weeping Woman.

He was warmly welcomed by Miss Guppy, the barmaid, who paused in her service of other clients to mix his gin and bitters; and he was soon ensconced in his favourite seat at the end of the counter, which indeed Miss Guppy had kept intact, against his arrival, by the simple method of piling up in it, on a large tray, all the dirty glasses. The plump lady herself now looked down maternally and possessively upon him from where she stood, drawing out of him by one shrewd question after another, every detail of the Cormorant's recent trip to Lulworth. It was easier for the Jobber to ward off Miss Guppy's curiosity by enlarging on the business that had taken him to Lulworth than it was to prevent his thoughts, below the surface of his replies, from running upon Mrs. Cobbold's companion.

"Will she keep her up till Jerry gets home?" he wondered. "I suppose they're having their dinner or whatever they call it now, with Fogg dodging about their elbows."

"Good-evening, Mr. Skald!"

It was Witchit, a fish-monger from a shop in a neighbouring side street, who thus addressed him; and Skald cast upon the effusive little man, whose face was polished with affability, a ferocious glare.

"Oh, I'm all right, Witchit. I generally am. How are things in *your* line of life?"

The sociable physiognomy of the fish-monger did not diminish in the least because of his interlocutor's scowl. From the end of his pointed nose to the tips of his big, flapping ears his countenance gleamed with gregarious rapture.

"Fayther be the 'appy one, fayther be," Mr. Witchit's wife was wont to acclaim; and there had been a time when young Jimmy, their son, would boast among the other boys as they watched Punch-and-Judy on the hot sands in August; "Me fayther can smile more broader than thik poor poppet!"

There was indeed something grotesque about the invincible brisk-ness of Simon Witchit; and yet, if the truth were told, Simon was in reality a profoundly cynical man. The bleeding fish he chopped up and disembowelled on his shining counter had no inkling of this. The lively canary he petted so much, and who used to peck so affectionately at his fishy fingers had no suspicion of such a thing. In direct defiance of the vulgar opinion that an organism's feelings correspond with the expression of its feelings, Simon Witchit had the power of grinning with ecstatic affection like a warm-blooded goblin at the very moment when a deep distaste for all the ways of all living things upon earth chilled his inmost soul.

"Your dear father," Simon went on now, literally bowing and scraping as he pressed himself against the edge of the Jobber's table, but in his heart hating the sight of the Jobber's gigantic physiognomy, his thick, heavy under-lip and sullen dark-lidded eyes, "your dear father, Mr. Skald, was in my shop yesterday, and he told me of all the trouble he's been having with Mr. Cattistock. He said Mr. Cattistock had bought up the last of the large quarries on the Island. It's a bad thing for us all when these big men begin—"

Witchit stopped abruptly. He did not stop because the Jobber scowled; but for the contrary reason. He stopped because the Jobber smiled! The mysterious and profound phenomenon of smiling is curiously emphasised when man, the only animal who smiles, smiles from malice and not from amusement. And Simon, who knew something—few knew more!—about what can be hid under a smile, felt a spasm of uneasiness when he caught this ogrish grimace. Some electric fluid of nervous awareness, below the surface of Mr. Witchit's affable mask, leaped forth at the signal.

"I know what you are feeling," this awareness said. "I know how you hate Dog Cattistock. But has it ever occurred to you that there are people *who hate you both?*"

But the Jobber rose to his feet and took his seaman's cap from beneath his jersey.

"Good-night, Miss," he said. "Good-night, Mr. Witchit. No; I am going straight home by the ferry. I never go by the bridge when I can help it!"

Leaving the Weeping Woman the Jobber now turned down a short dark alley between high warehouses. Several of these buildings possessed open loft-windows, from which iron chains and dangling ropes, used for lowering bundles of hay and sacks of flour, hung suspended above the narrow pavement. Others, rented by some of the smaller ships' chandlers, had windows in them of very thick glass, through which, where they were not yet shuttered for the night, all manner of varieties of rope and twine could be seen, piled up between bundles of sail-cloth and interspersed with old, disused, second-hand, nautical instruments.

As soon as he reached the harbour's edge the man turned to the left and followed the wharf in a seaward direction. He walked slowly and cautiously between the single lines of railway that brought travellers from the station to where the steamers docked. It was muddy and littered between these railway lines; and many of the wooden sleepers, upon which the metals were laid, protruded from the mud in such a manner as to offer stumbling-blocks to unwary pedestrians.

With his mariner's cap at the back of his head and his hands in his pockets the Jobber advanced with cautious strides. The wind blew against him wild and strong just here and the harbour-tide at his feet was running out in gurgling darkness. When he reached the stone coping of the ferry, and was free of the metal rails and the littered mud he pulled his great wrists out of his pockets and rubbed his hands together in a fit of emotional excitement. As he rubbed his hands his face assumed a peculiar expression. His upper lip protruded itself and quivered violently. His nostrils dilated. His corrugated forehead swelled and lumped itself into rounded curves. His shaggy eyebrows twitched. His heavily-lidded eyelids narrowed. His head lowered itself a little and stretched itself forward over his enormous chest. His massive shoulders bowed themselves, as he walked, in a curious rhythm with the rubbing together of his great palms.

What had started this exultation in the Jobber was the sight of the high narrow bows of Perdita's steamer and its tall red funnel. With an irresistible rush, that whirled away all his efforts at suppression, the image of the girl as he had first seen her standing on the deck, was swept into his heart. But his emotion was not due purely to Perdita. It was due to the fact that his first sight of Perdita had taken place on this particular spot.

To all natives of this district—Magnus, for instance, would have confessed to just the same—the sight of the wave-washed steps leading to this ferry, and the experience of being rowed across this strip of tossing water, had a peculiar sentiment of their own, a sentiment that reverted back to earliest childhood. How many elderly people, peacefully awaiting the end of their days in Weymouth parlours, looking out to sea, must have recalled these slippery steps and these rocking boats as their first and perhaps their deepest impression of the unfathomable romance of life.

Crouching over an iron brazier of red-hot coke, as the Jobber came to the first stone-steps, there was only one aged ferry-man left at his post and he was fast asleep. But he knew the owner of the Cormorant well and was not in the least ruffled at being brought back to that gusty night from God knows what miraculous mackerel-catches in halcyon seas. As the old man rowed him with some difficulty across the harbour—but the Jobber understood marine etiquette far too well to put a hand to an oar—his mind, for the tide and the wind prohibited conversation, reverted to what Simon Witchit had told him of his father's words in the fish-shop.

Yes, it was only the bare truth! His father had inherited from *his* father three or four small quarries of the precious Portland stone; but little by little the crafty financier had been getting them into his hands, until, by purchase, by mortgage, by a system of commissions, by bullying and bribing, by leasing what were left of the old Prison Works, by monopolising the stone-cutting saw-mills, practically all the old hereditary quarry-men of the Island had lost their inheritance and had become mere agents and employees of the Cattistock Company.

As the water dashed over the side of the boat drenching his thighs, the outrage done to the actual *stone* itself of his native promontory tore at his heart. The Dog was an enemy of everything sacred in life! That Portland stone, ever since the far-off Viking invasion that had landed the Skald family among these Celtic stone-slingers, had been something to be handled reverently, piously, and *in fear of the gods*. And now came this brute—

The dark swaying waves, the rocking boat, which shipped a nasty bucketful when he rose to search about in his pocket for a silver coin, the look of the interior of the boat under the lights of this Nothe shore, the coiled ropes, the scooper for bailing, the rushing channel of bilge-water following the boat's tilt as he got up, above all the smell of the slippery seaweed, as the waves heaved and sank on the stone steps—all these things became a chorus of his whole life calling on him to strike this blow.

"Good-night, Mate!" he said, handing the old man a double fare.

"Good-night, Mr. Skald, and thank 'ee kindly, sir!"

He stopped before one of the oldest and smallest of the time-mellowed houses, looking on the harbour. The name "Cove House" was written in flourishing characters over its narrow doorway. There was a light in the window—a big bow-window from which it was possible to see the entrance of the harbour—and the Jobber had no sooner begun mounting the brick steps that led to the door than a muslin curtain was dropped down by a bony hand that had been holding it aside.

The man smiled as he took his key from his pocket and inserted it in the keyhole.

"I wonder how late I'd have to be," he thought to himself, "for Cassy not to watch for me?"

A gaunt cadaverous woman of about fifty greeted him in the little hall-way.

"Hello, Cass!" he cried affectionately, "keeping guard as usual? Has Bum come in?"

"Half an hour agone, Mr. Skald," she said now in a tone of deep reproach. "And he be eating supper in kitchen. He've a-finished his meat and be nigh to finishing his pudding."

"*So* sorry, Cassy dear," pleaded the Jobber. "Bring *my* meat in at once, will you? I'll be down in a minute."

He rushed upstairs to wash his hands, while Cassy returned to the kitchen. Cassy Trot lived indeed entirely for her master and her husband, like a fish in an enclosed pond, and though malignant curiosity might be written on her face her heart held nothing but an almost tragic fidelity.

As the Jobber was pouring hot water from a tin can with a big spout, into an old blue-and-white basin, whose accompanying jug he had deposited on the floor, his mind veered away again from Dog Cattistock and rushed off to the top-floor of High House. Had that girl got over her fright by now? He himself was not afraid of Mrs. Cobbold, but he knew well that many were; for there had been the wildest rumours about her in the town, when as Lucinda Poxwell of Old Castle Road, she had married the celebrated clown. They said she had driven old Poxwell into his crazy custom of collecting cowry-shells out of the pools at the foot of Sandsfoot. They said it was because of Lucinda's deviltries that the Captain's younger child Hortensia, with her daughter Daisy, had come to live with him.

"Lucinda's madder than her father," the Jobber said to himself, as following a harmless but extravagant custom of his he went on turning his soap over and over in his hands till he evoked a cloud of lather, "but whether *that* will frighten that girl I can't say."

As he brushed his hair before a mirror framed in old dark mahogany, a mirror so erratic in its tilt that Cassy was always restoring it to the appropriate angle by bits of folded paper, which would fall out the moment the Jobber touched it, he let his eye wander over the walls of his bedroom. It also, like the room downstairs, had a bow-window from which could be seen the mouth of the harbour and a strip of open sea. It also, like the room below, had a couple of gigantic armchairs with leather covers. It also had on its walls endless old coloured prints of ships. Some of these were warships, some passenger ships, some merchant ships, and the seas in which they sailed were sometimes stormy and sometimes calm; but it was characteristic of a certain vein of obstinate optimism in Adam Skald that not one of these pictures represented a *wreck*.

"Mr. Skald! Mr. Skald! Supper be in!" came the voice of Cassy Trot from the bottom of the stairs.

He went down at once and took his place at an enormous oak table, black with age and polishing. On a second table under a pair of green curtains, that half concealed the big bow-window, was an open library-book with the address of a shop in St. Mary's Street on the cover. The book was George Eliot's "Middlemarch"; and before leaving him with his plate of meat already cut, and with two covered dishes of vegetables of the same blue-and-white pattern as the jug and basin upstairs, Cassy had brought "Middlemarch" from the table by the green curtain where it lay beside a swan's egg which the Jobber had stolen from a pond beyond Chickerel, and had carefully propped it up for him against a candle-stick. Had anyone watched her face as she pressed the cover of the book open and forced back its pages before she balanced it, there would have been caught upon it that particular look of indulgent gravity with which a mother manipulates a favourite toy for a spoilt child.

Dead silence reigned now in the front room of Cove House, for the kitchen at the back was separated from the sitting-room by such a long passage that it was impossible for the Jobber to hear the voices of Mr. and Mrs. Trot when the doors were shut.

He ate slowly, turning over the pages of "Middlemarch" with patient resolution—one page to about ten mouthfuls—for the satisfaction he got from reading while he ate was not so much in the reading itself—the Jobber could not be called a bookish man—as in the consciousness that he *was* reading. For he genuinely liked the idea of reading a nice solid library-book as he ate his supper in his bachelor parlour. Old Miss Burt, the librarian of that St. Mary's Street Shop, derived extreme pleasure from assisting "Mr. Adam", for she had known him all his life, in the development of his literary taste; and as her own taste ran, or she thought it ran, to works far removed from "this modern realism", the Jobber had lived to see great Liners fed by oil without having followed the course of his country's fiction further than the middle of the nineteenth century.

Like many another lonely and egoistical man he was much more original in his personal philosophy than in his aesthetic taste. His taste was, it must be confessed, anything but his own. It was indeed entirely dependent upon others. In literature it depended upon Miss Burt and in bric-à-brac upon Mr. Martin of the Dairy-Shop in Abbotsbury Road. In his drinks the Jobber bowed to no man, nor to any woman, either; for it was in vain that Miss Guppy explained to him night after night the aristocratic superiority of Whiskey over Gin; but in other refinements his humility was pathetic.

"George Eliot must have been rather like Miss Burt," he thought grimly as he finished his pudding and began to light his pipe; but at this point he was astonished to hear a sharp ring at the door-bell. He swung round and glanced at the small ship's clock which he kept fastened up over the fire-place. It was half-past eight. Who, in God's name, *could* it be, at this time of night? He began to rise; but sat down again, hearing Cassy come along the passage.

"Something she's ordered, maybe," he thought.

There was a momentary pause in the progress of events while Mrs. Trot pushed back the bolts. This bolting of the door, as soon as night fell, was a persistent rule of his own. Neither of the Trots approved of it. Few people in Weymouth would have liked it any better, with their frivolous habits of running in and out. Perhaps it was an austere Portland custom, going back to days when the Islanders suffered invasions that were less insidious than those of Dog Cattistock.

The Jobber, while this unbolting went on, mechanically closed "Middlemarch" and placed the mustard-pot on the top of it. He suddenly found that his heart was beating in an abnormal manner. This was due to a wild notion that this unexpected nightly visit was in some way connected with Mrs. Cobbold's companion. Through the bow-window, which was open at the top, and between the curtains which were only half-drawn, came the sound of the harbour waves, splashing against the row of fishing boats moored outside. This sound made him wonder how much could be heard of the sea from the windows of High House and whether Mrs. Cobbold's companion would keep open the window of her bedroom during the night.

But Cassy had got the front-door unbolted now, and he felt, without actually experiencing it, the breath of salt air that entered into the little passage. Aye! But what was this? He suddenly became aware of a high-pitched young-girl's voice mingling with the whistling of the wind. The front-door closed. Cassy was talking to the visitor within the passage now. He rose to his feet and laid his spoon and fork carefully side by side upon his empty pudding plate. He brushed away some crumbs of bread from the polished oak surface—the Jobber rejected table-cloths—and gave his own woollen jersey several lusty jerks to improve its appearance.

The door opened and Cassy ushered in a young girl of about seventeen.

"Why, Daisy Lily!" he cried hurrying round the table and shaking the visitor's hand with lively and astonished cordiality. "Who would ever have thought of *your* coming here? How's the Captain?"

"Oh, Mr. Skald, *please*—" the girl cried earnestly. "Mother says, will you come at once! Grandfather's at Sandsfoot Castle and won't come home! Mother and I've been twice over there. The second time Doctor Higginbottom went with us. But the doctor made

Grandfather worse. Mother thought of you at once. She said: 'If anyone could get him home quietly it would be Mr. Skald!' And then she said—'It would be no good getting D—' I mean Mr. Cattistock. She calls him D, you know. 'It would be no good getting D,' she said, 'would it, Daisy? Because Papa hates him so.' "

"What would your friend Cattistock say if he heard that?" grumbled the Jobber; and he began, with a shameless disregard of the young girl's presence, to remove his slippers and put on his boots.

"Grandfather says he'll run away," went on Daisy unblushingly. "He says the day that mother agrees to marry Mr. Cattistock he'll run away and never come back! He says Mr. Cattistock is a man-eater and ought to go and live with cannibals."

"Bravo, Captain!" chuckled the Jobber in a thick, husky voice, as with his head bent down he struggled with the oily, leathery bootlaces.

"Mother's got her car out there, by Trinity Church," remarked the girl. "She said she was sure you'd come at once."

"Is your mother set on marrying Cattistock?" muttered the Jobber, cursing his bootlaces, but deriving, all the same, a dim pleasure from the peculiar smell of the leather.

"Poor mother!" whispered the girl. "I oughtn't to talk about her; but you know it all anyway; so what's the difference?"

It was not, however, till the two of them were hurrying along the edge of the quay towards the bridge that Daisy Lily spoke with real freedom to her Grandfather's friend.

"Mother's in love with Mr. Cattistock," she said. "But he's been a long time making up his mind. I think he'd like to make love to mother without being married. But poor mother's tired of taking care of grandfather. She'll be glad to leave him to Mrs. Matzell and me."

They found Mrs. Lily wrapped up in a big cloth ulster and bowed down over her steering-wheel. She had fallen into a trance of absorbed thinking. From this she rose with a start; but impulsively gave the Jobber her hand, and smiled a tender, grateful smile.

"I knew you'd come," she said.

Settled down close to Mrs. Lily in her little car, with Daisy Lily

sitting on one of his knees, the Jobber gave himself up to a procession
of the queerest thoughts. It gave him a deliciously soothing and
sensual pleasure to hold Daisy like this; but out of the lap of this
sensuality his mind kept shooting off in more serious and more poignant
directions. To High House it flew, straight and fast, like the wind
that was now blowing in their faces; and the girl who balanced herself
on his knee had no idea how his contact with her young body was
mingling and fusing itself with his romantic feeling for Mrs. Cobbold's
companion. But the Jobber was not permitted by destiny to remain
long in peace, enjoying this contact with Daisy and these thoughts
about Perdita. A casual word from Mrs. Lily, as they drove through
Rodwell, referring to the number of new villas that had sprung up
in that district, though he replied to it in a friendly manner—and
indeed there had always been something piquant to his fancy about
having a flirtation with the Dog's fiancée—set him upon his murderous thoughts again. The weight of Daisy's body upon him accentuated the pressure of the hard cold stone from Chesil against his
thigh and he thought to himself:

"This silly Mrs. Lily will be the only person in the world who'll
be sorry when I *do for* the brute."

It must have been the unusual rôle of being driven through these
Weymouth suburbs by Dog Cattistock's woman that gave the Jobber
the power to envisage this killing of his enemy as if it were *a dark
red bruise* at the back of his consciousness which he could not avoid
accepting, but which he could temporarily forget, as he enjoyed
himself holding Daisy and thinking of Perdita.

He became aware, as they drove on, and as his mind ran forward
to his encounter with his distracted old friend, that Mrs. Cobbold—
"Aunt Lucinda" as he had heard Daisy speak of her just now—had
come to occupy, when he linked her with Perdita, a position in his
thoughts of the same order, though not the same intensity, as his
feeling for the Dog. Yes, he thoroughly distrusted Mrs. Cobbold.
She was a type he detested. He believed, in his passionate naïve way,
that she was the sort of woman who deliberately indulges vicious
and heartless selfishness under the disguise of hysteria.

"She's madder than the Captain," he said to himself, "but it's the
madness of wickedness. She's like one of those evil women of History.

I wish the Dog had got mixed up with *her* instead of this silly Mrs. Lily. What a pair they'd have made!"

But if the Jobber was thinking of Perdita as he held Daisy, Daisy's mother—who was only thirty-five—was thinking of Dog Cattistock.

From this state of things it was brought about that there drove through the hilly suburb of Rodwell towards Sandsfoot Castle, in addition to three visible occupants of a small dark car, two invisible ones, namely Perdita Wane, dressed as she was when she stood waiting on the deck of the steamer, and Dog Cattistock dressed as he was when, three months ago, he declared his love for Mrs. Lily. It was perhaps too fantastic a conjecture—and yet not altogether devoid of analogies in the physical world—to suppose that as these invisible and purely mental passengers rode thus together across that quiet quarter of the suburbs there came to establish itself between these complete strangers some sort of relationship, some link, some magnetic bond, which subsequent events might cause to be materialized. It may be regarded as part of this psychic approach—of which Dog Cattistock and Perdita themselves were so completely ignorant— that after a long silence, as they drove up Franchise Road, Hortensia Lily remarked to the Jobber:

"Have you heard in town, Mr. Skald, whether my sister's new companion *did* really arrive on the Guernsey steamer this afternoon? Everyone in Weymouth seems to know she was expected today; and I thought you might—"

But the Jobber muttered something about having only just returned from a business trip to Lulworth and not having spoken to a soul. An irresistible instinct made him cautious of breathing to the paramour of Dog Cattistock the least word about Perdita. He replied so coldly that Mrs. Lily, anxious to please him tonight at all costs, threw back her heavy coat from her throat, as she held the wheel, and turned quickly to him with a smile into which she threw so much intimacy and sweetness that it quite startled the man. With naïve, masculine simplicity the Jobber welcomed not exactly the thought, but the vibration of the thought; might not this desirable Being be cajoled away from Cattistock? Had the painter Correggio been driving by Mrs. Lily's side, instead of the Jobber, he would have been forever afterwards trying to catch the Ariel-like equivocation

of this ambiguous glance wherein all the wanton nymph in a light
woman's nature threw provocative arms round the neck of her lover's
foe. Her smile was given him as she turned her vehicle round the
corner of Franchise Road into Rodwell Road. Few places could
have been more difficult to transform into a Correggio picture than
this suburban retreat of quiet tradesmen, where the very pavements
were kept so neat and even the fluttering eddies of little hard, dead,
metallic-coloured privet-leaves were soon caught, scooped up, and
carried away; but Mrs. Lily was one of those fair women whose skin
is so exquisitely white that any gesture, revealing a fragment of throat,
or neck, or bosom, acquires a kind of involuntary seduction, independent of place or time.

Hortensia Lily's head was as small as her sister's was large, but
her forehead, like that of Mrs. Cobbold's, was unusually high although
it was concealed by a thick fringe of fair hair, trimmed like a child's
and making a clear-cut yellow line, an inch above the blue of her eyes.

It was at this moment that Daisy Lily, whose attention was less
distracted than her companions', suddenly cried out—

"You needn't go so slow, mother. The road's clear!"

The young girl's words were justified. All the way down the
declivity leading to the sea-shore they met neither pedestrian nor
vehicle.

"Can you not hear the sea?" said the girl again.

The lights of the car now revealed a road that became less and
less suburban in character. There were patches of Tamarisk-bushes
in the low, straggly, wind-blown hedges, and here and there rose a
stunted thorn-tree, that like a living creature desperately escaping
from the tumult of waters, stretched out its arms with frantic panic
towards the uninvaded fields. They could certainly hear the sea now.
Indeed the sound of its waves, breaking on the rocks far down beneath the uneven ledges and terraces of the cliff's edge, reduced them
to silence. The Jobber was surprised and a little shocked by Mrs.
Lily's sangfroid at this juncture. Daisy kept fidgeting on his knee
and straining her neck to catch the first glimpse of the ruined castle,
but the mother drove steadily on, going slower indeed, so it seemed
to him, than she really need have done, if the Captain was in any
actual danger, and letting him feel as she drove a light pressure of her

shoulder. Seduced by the warm bodies of both these women and actually courted—for that is how in his masculine vanity he interpreted this pressure—by the elder one, the Jobber gave himself up, as they went along, to an irresponsible feeling of well-being.

Arrived at the path leading to the ruin, they all three scrambled out, and leaving the car by the roadside hurried down the slope, Daisy a little way in advance. The Jobber and Mrs. Lily overtook her at the entrance to Sandsfoot Castle and they entered the building together. Here they were confronted by the rays from a lantern and by its light the seated figure of the man they sought became distinct. Seated under an old-fashioned ship's lantern on a steamer-rug that he had brought out there early in the afternoon, and with a big woollen shawl wrapped round his shoulders, Captain Poxwell was absorbed in the construction of certain small improvised shell-boxes. He had carried down to this spot that afternoon more than one of these little cardboard receptacles. These he had covered with that species of adhesive clay such as they give children to mould. He was now engaged in fixing into this clay a great number of small shells, which he had fished up with his hands, all through that stormy twilight, in the rock-pools at the Castle's foot.

The old man rose as Daisy ran towards him, crying in a tender quivering voice: "Oh, grand-daddy, you dear! you dear!"

Tightly fitted upon the Captain's closely-cropped, silvery head was a yachtman's cap. This he now took off, making a polite and ceremonious bow first to his grand-daughter and then to his daughter.

"Aye, Skald, my boy! Glad to see 'ee! Glad to see 'ee! You'll be able to bring reason to these crazy women. They think I can do my work just as well in the house as I can up here. They don't understand I *have* to be near the rocks to throw back into their proper pools the ones that have fish in 'em!" He paused and approaching the Jobber whispered in his ear: "I've been quite happy about *Her*—you know?—since you swore on your dying oath she never had a child. I can trust *you*, Skald, but not another living soul!" Apparently satisfied in his mind, he went on in quick hurried, loud tones, addressing them all. "How could I remember what pool they came from if I had 'em up there in my cabin? And as for letting you, you fussy child"—this was addressed to Mrs. Lily—"how could I trust you with 'em? You'd chuck 'em over the cliff—I know you! But listen, Skald! Do you know what Hortensia did today? Yes, I *will* tell him, girl. So it's no use your making faces. She brought that old lunatic, Higginbottom, down on me. Did you ever hear such a thing? I knew what he came for, the old spy! He'd heard about my collection of cowries. He supposed I'd got 'em hidden somewhere in the wall and wanted to find 'em. I led him a rare dance; didn't I, Daisy? I can climb up a wall, can't I, Daisy? as well as any one. I led him a rich dance, Skald! You'd have laughed yourself weak to see it. In the end I gave him a kick in the belly and he went off threatening to call the police. Didn't he, Daisy? As if he could set the police on me! It's a joke; isn't it, Daisy? Isn't it, Skald?"

All the time he was speaking the Captain avoided looking at his daughter; and the Jobber who *did* glance at her noticed that she had relapsed into her own thoughts, just as if her Father's ramblings were of no more significance to her than the moaning of the wind round the thick walls of the ruin. The rays of the ship's lantern fell upon her cold white face. She wore no hat; and her cloak, fallen back from her head, displayed the clear-cut line of her fair hair lying smoothly upon her brow, from beneath which her large blue eyes stared into vacancy.

Adam Skald, little of a psychologist as he was, found himself conscious of something uncanny in the feverish excitement of the Captain confronted by such contemptuous indifference. He was aware, however, that Daisy was listening to the distracted old man with an intense and troubled concentration. The young girl's figure was quite outside the lantern's rays—just a blurred, wavering, girlish outline—but it was revealed to the Jobber that from her whole being emanated a passionate and desperate interest in the Captain's wild utterances.

Captain Poxwell had a long, lean neck, the muscles of which resembled the flexible cords of some tough ivy-trunk clinging to an emaciated tree. His nose was long and pointed, his chin a knotty, narrow, and retreating one, his forehead, like the foreheads of both his daughters, was abnormally high, while his cropped hair, grizzled and stubbly, covered a skull that receded at the back, in a curiously obstinate manner, like the skull of a cranky and heretical fanatic. His chin was tufted by a very small patch of wiry hair, hair that had not turned grey, like the top of his head, but remained of a straw-like colour, indicating that it was from him that Hortensia inherited her blond tresses. A patch of similar hair scarcely large enough to be dignified by the name of moustache, bristled upon the Captain's upper lip; and when the light fell full on his excited face it revealed eyes of the most vivid blue; eyes that burned with that particular kind of restless energy which, whether in sane or insane men, is of all things the most objectionable to women; for it contains a double quantity of that species of human magnetism that is always rending and tearing at the normal processes of nature.

He was still talking eagerly to the Jobber, explaining, exhorting, appealing, when Skald suddenly saw Mrs. Lily shrug her beautiful shoulders with a gesture of infinite weariness. Her look at that moment made him think of the ship's figure-head to which Bum Trot had compared Mrs. Cobbold. One such image in particular came into his mind, which had belonged to a ramshackle craft, long since gone to the bottom; but her figure-head had always stuck in his memory; and her queer name too. She was called the Medusa.

"I'll walk with you to the house, Captain," said the Jobber, taking advantage of the first real silence into which the excited old man fell, "and then we can let the women-folk ride. I expect your old Mrs. Matzell has kept some supper for you."

Captain Poxwell relapsed now into complete docility. He proceeded to take his shawl carefully from his neck and wrap it very meticulously round the little boxes upon whose clay lids he had been sticking the shells.

The girl Daisy, satisfied that all was well with her grandfather, had turned her attention to the old Castle's walls and the high, deep windows through which the stars began now to be visible.

"The wind's dropping," she remarked. "It's going to be a fine night."

Taught by her grandfather the girl had come to know every cornice and balustrade and window-ledge and rampart and coign of vantage in the old building, and had acquired for the place that especial kind of passionate tenderness that youth acquires for any locality— picturesque or otherwise—that has come to be a background of its long, long thoughts. Daisy had lived in Half-Mile Cottage with her grandfather and her mother for five years now. She had come here when she was twelve; and not one of her vaguest, wildest and most romantic reveries but was associated with Sandsfoot Castle.

The child had a tall flexible figure, like her mother; but her fair hair was far less striking, her nose thicker, her mouth larger, her grey eyes much smaller than Mrs. Lily's. Indeed, it was the kindness and frankness of her expression, combined with the spring-like charm of her fresh young body, that made older people—especially old ladies, who doted upon her—speak of Daisy Lily as "such a sweet, well-mannered, innocent child". Her relations with her mother—if all were known—might have disturbed the lineaments of this ideal image; for there had been occasions, especially within the last six months, since the elder woman's association with Dogberry Cattistock, when Daisy had astonished Hortensia by her fierce outbreaks of re-bellious bitterness.

Something of this sort, although tuned to a key of wistful sadness rather than of wild emotion, was upon her now, as she watched a cluster of faint stars through one of the square sea-ward windows. The windows of this Ruin were indeed quite large in spite of the thickness of the walls; for after all Sandsfoot was not a mediaeval building, having been built, as a protection against France in a fit of that cautious nationalism which characterized the Tudors, by Henry the Eighth.

"Why *doesn't* Uncle John come home?" she thought. "If he'd only give up the sea for a year, he'd soon bring grandfather's mind back to itself. Mother torments him almost as much as Aunt Lucinda used to. Oh, how she does hate him! What would she feel if I began to hate *her* just as much as she hates grandfather?"

Such definite thoughts as these now completely failed to express Daisy's feelings. She gave herself up to listening to the faint sighing of the wind—for she had been right that the weather was moderating—as it went round the old Castle, like a ghostly shoal of perturbed flying-fish, uttering a barely audible, high-pitched susurration, that grew thinner and more falsetto as it gradually died away.

When they were all safe back in Half-Mile Cottage, the Jobber found that he was not mistaken when he said that Mrs. Matzell would have a hot supper ready for the old man. That there was no other servant at Half-Mile Cottage than this faithful woman was worse than a mere social grievance to Hortensia. It was a daily series of annoying discomforts. Mrs. Matzell was devoted to the Captain; and her opinion of the Captain's daughters, as she expressed it to her familiar gossips, was as vigorous as it was brief.

"There's not a nail's paring to choose between them. *Ladies* do they call themelves? I calls them 'Arpies!'"

Simple-minded men are always being deceived by the verbal outbursts of women; for women have the power of abandoning themselves to the most volcanic revelations of grim truth and then of going on living, in the ordinary illusions of commonplace reality, as if nothing has happened. Thus after all that he had heard and imagined of what went on in Half-Mile Cottage it was amazing to Adam Skald, as he sat opposite the Captain, while the old man ate his supper in what he called his "Cabin", to hear the voices of Mrs. Lily and Mrs. Matzell engaged in what sounded like the jesting of two life-long friends.

It was considerably after nine when the two men sat down to their snug meal—for the Jobber, though he had already had an excellent supper, scrupled not to propitiate the Captain by sharing his little repast—and both Mrs. Lily and Mrs. Matzell, now absorbed in cooking something that could not wait over night, took for granted that Daisy, who had curled herself up on the drawing-room sofa with her book, was fixed happily there for an indefinite time.

But Daisy was not fixed there for an indefinite time. In fact, for the last five minutes, she had not been there at all. With her woollen cap and mackintosh-coat on, and her ungloved hands thrust deep into her side pockets, she was hurrying along Rodwell Road into Wyke Road, and up Wyke Road, past Rodwell Railway Station, to Gipsy Lane. Arrived at Gipsy Lane—and the walk there, so eagerly did she hurry, only took her about seven minutes—she paused by the broken fragment of a loosely-cemented wall. The narrow lane was as dark and silent as if it had been in the heart of the bare Downs instead of a suburb of Weymouth; but in spite of the solitude and the silence the girl glanced nervously round and waited, drawing her breath in quick little pants and fumbling with the belt of her mackintosh. Then, standing on tip-toe close against the rough cement so that her knees brushed its surface, she lifted her arms to the top of the crumbling masonry and began feeling about with excited fingers. She soon lifted up a large flat stone from the coping of the wall and hoisted it out of the way. By doing this she exposed two smaller ones, lying side by side. One of these she also lifted up and with a little gasp of relief snatched from beneath it an unstamped, unaddressed letter. Clutching this tightly in her hand and breathing more easily, she replaced all the stones, under that faint starlight, exactly as they had been before; and moving back from the wall surveyed with intense satisfaction her unopened envelope. In the silence of that dark lane she passionately pressed this opaque blur of whiteness several times to her lips and then, slipping it into her dress, under the mackintosh, proceeded, with even more rapid steps than when she had come to make her way back to Old Castle Road. No one had locked her out. No one had even noticed her absence! When, in about half-an-hour, Mrs. Matzell came into the room to tell her she ought to be going to bed, the woman saw her close her book with such a well-feigned sigh of reluctance that the old lady began murmuring a long discourse upon the danger of too much reading.

"Good-night, mother!" she called out, leaning over the balustrade. Mrs. Lily pushed open the door at the end of the passage.

"Good-night, Day! Don't forget to clean your teeth!"

The door closed again; but not before the innocent-eyed maid had put out her tongue at the narrow glint of steamy kitchen light.

"Why need she always say that so loudly?" she thought. "Mr. Skald *must* have heard her. Oh, she is so annoying!"

On the first landing she paused to glance at the Cabin door, from behind which she could hear the murmur of men's voices.

"Why *doesn't* Uncle John come home?" she said to herself. "Grandfather's a different person when he's got a man to talk to."

She ran quickly up the last flight of stairs and entered her own room. Daisy's room opened on the front of the house which was on the inland side of the road; but by standing at the extreme left-hand corner of her window and pressing her cheek against its pane, she could detect, even when the window was shut, a narrow fragment of sea between the opposite houses. This strip of water—a glimpse of

Portland Roads—was framed between a segment of Sandsfoot Castle and a segment of Portland itself, and Daisy who knew every curve and contour of its restricted shape—knew it as well as she knew her own childish countenance in the big looking-glass that stood in front of it—was never weary of watching the infinite variety of its moods.

Two gas-jets were burning cheerfully in large cream-coloured globes in Daisy's room; and the sheets of her bed, covered with a white counterpane dotted with faint blue spots, had been carefully turned down.

In the order of Mrs. Matzell's devotion to the people of her life, if Captain Poxwell came by far the first, it was certainly Daisy who came second. Daisy's only rival for this place, was, not her mother, but the absent John Poxwell.

There was a considerable-sized book-case hanging on the wall above the bed, whose crowded shelves had that particular look, at once very faded and very gay, that clings about any collection of childish books, whether they belong to a girl or a boy. Above the mantelpiece was a large photograph of Captain Lily; and in the grate—its blaze pleasantly falling upon a brass fender and a crimson rug—burned a glowing fire, whose sticks had been lighted an hour ago by Mrs. Matzell.

The girl bolted her door and turned up the two gas-jets, making the room as light as it was warm. Then, thrusting her fingers into her dress, she brought out the white, square envelope; once more pressed it to her lips, and then stood it up on the mantelpiece beside the picture of the bearded Captain. Thinking to herself, "I won't open it till I'm undressed," she began hurriedly taking off her clothes. She undressed like a child rather than a woman, flinging her things down, hugger-mugger, in one big heap. The chill of her cold night-dress, for Mrs. Matzell had left this on her pillow tonight, instead of hanging it, as she sometimes did, over a chair by the fire, gave her a delicious shivering-fit, and she rubbed herself with her hands, standing with bare feet on the crimson rug.

She snatched at the letter then; but suddenly remembering that she had not brushed her hair, she put it back again on the mantelpiece, taking care to balance it at the precise angle that it had occupied before.

With fingers just as feverishly eager as when she undressed she tore out
her hair pins, tossed them down anyhow on the dressing table, and
shaking out her wavy hair, which was neither as silky in texture, nor
as beautiful in colour, as her mother's, she passed her comb through it
several times making faces and crying "Goodness!" when the tangles
hurt her, and finally catching at it tightly with one hand she brushed it
out hastily in firm, strong sweeps of her arm, and tossing down the
brush with a clatter on the table, she extracted a light-blue ribbon from
the drawer of the looking-glass and tied it up in a neat bow.

"I wish I were twenty-one, instead of seventeen," she thought to
herself as she came back to the fire-place. Once more she possessed
herself of the letter, and this time, seated on the rug close up to the
fender, she tore it open and read it with breathless attention.

It ran as follows:—

"Darling Day—Oh, I had such difficulty in fetching your last from
our box! And heaven knows when I shall be able to post this! *Father
suspects us*—there's no doubt of it. He *wouldn't* have, if he hadn't come
in that day when I was dressed up in my Page's costume. He *wouldn't*
have, if I hadn't talked to him last year, when we first met, so wildly
about you. Father is thicker than ever with Mr. Cattistock and this
makes our seeing each other more and more difficult. Oh dear!
Sometimes I feel as if we shall have just to bow to fate and give up our
friendship. Perhaps, after all, that *would* be better. What do you think,
my little Double Flower? It is Mr. Cattistock who really makes it so
impossible to go on. I can't explain quite why in a letter; but it *does*
and my Double Flower must just believe me. I'll be furious if you
say again what you said in your last letter about my being tired of you.
It's all Papa's friendship with Mr. Cattistock that makes it so difficult.
I'll explain when we meet. Let's plot and plan and tell each other our
conclusions. Perhaps we *could* meet in Gipsy Lane as you say. I'll
think it over. *Don't* write by post. Gipsy Lane is the thing for that.
It's so exciting hiding them there, and your letters are *so* sweet! Here's
a D kiss, and an A kiss, and a Y kiss! Think of me when you go to
sleep.

Peg.

P.S. Yes of course you're right. What a funny child you are!
What we read on all the Brewery Carts—'Cattistock and Frampton'

—*is* Papa and him. Do you mind your old Peg belonging to 'Cattistock and Frampton,' while your People are all in the Navy?"

Daisy allowed both letter and envelope to fall out of her hands for a minute while she stared fixedly at the fire. Very slowly big tears gathered in her eyes and her under-lip quivered and drew down. Tossing her head, however, she knelt in front of the bars and tore both letter and envelope into little tiny pieces, flinging them resolutely into the flames. While she did this she bit her lip and swallowed down her tears. She even tried to smile. Then with her hands clasped behind her back, and her head bowed, she shut her eyes tight and remained motionless for a long time in the attitude of prayer. Strange though it may sound, Daisy Lily *was* praying. It was a peculiarity of hers—due perhaps to her never having been to a boarding-school— to pour out all her troubles to her dead father. Till she was sixteen she always used to add for "Jesus' sake". But from that time on, when she had finished her supplications to Captain Lily, she added no religious conclusions. As so often happens with self-made invocations a heathen change had slipped in. She fell into the habit of praying to the dead Officer as if he had been the only supernatural Being who could possibly be reached. Whatever her conversation with her begetter may have been about, Daisy Lily rose to her feet deeply comforted.

"I'll never write to her again," she said to herself. "She's silly and she's funny. She's *horrid*. She only played with me to amuse herself; and she's found some other kid now and wants to get out of it. Navy indeed! When did I ever talk in that tone to her? Besides, she knows perfectly well that both Grandfather and Uncle John are in the Merchant Service. It was a nasty, affected, horrid letter. It's clear as a pike-staff she's got another kid; and I'm glad she has! That's the last time you fool *me*, Peg Frampton, and the last time I'll have anything to do with you."

Daisy cast a glance at the red coals where the flames had now died down. On the inner edge of the top-bar lingered a scrap of charred paper. The girl seized the poker and pushed this down into the heart of the grate. A look of resolute defiance had settled down over her young face. Her under-lip was indrawn. There were two wrinkles in her smooth forehead between the eyebrows.

A certain element in Peg Frampton, who was a little older than she was, had always jarred upon her, a certain cynicism, a certain wild, fierce bitterness, but in the excitement of their passionate friendship, the edge of which had been kept poignant, by secrecy, she had been seduced into disregarding these discords. In her simplicity she had even allowed herself to be proud of the sophisticated tone her friend loved to adopt. Sometimes, like the young Gretchen under the spell of Faust, she had listened in awe-struck wonder to Peg's daring blasphemies. But this letter hurt her to the quick. Its grown-up cajolery, its obscurity, its weariness, its lack of direct emotion, a certain tone in it that the writer evidently thought was the tone of a disillusioned woman, filled Daisy's soul with a puzzled disgust. She had never cared very much for her friend's fondness for playing upon her surname; and the expression "Double Flower" just now gave her a sickly taste in her mouth. There had been something of an ardent boyishness in her idealizing of Peg; and this letter—though she could hardly have explained how she read such subtleties into it—made her feel that her idol had all the time been despising her, treating her like a child. Something about the letter even reminded Daisy of her own mother! Her very innocence and simplicity made her anger—when she judged anyone as she now judged her friend—sternly implacable.

"I'll never bother any more with her and her tricky ways," she vowed to herself.

She extinguished the two burners and scrambling into bed pulled the clothes tight under her chin.

It was then that the pleasant coolness of the sheets, the relaxation to her whole body of this prone position, the association of this particular moment, when she first turned out the light, with an idealized concentration upon her friendship with Peg, threatened to betray her resolution. Her window had been opened a little at the top by Mrs. Matzell and she could hear the subsiding wind utter faint expostulating murmurs in many different tones as it went zig-zagging down Old Castle Road. Some of these wind-tones she mistook for the sound of the far-off waves; and this thought of the sea intensified her feeling for Peg. She kept seeing against the fire-lit wall—and it was worse still when she closed her eyes tight and pressed her knuckles against them, making the "spangly darkness boil up" in phosphorescent bubbles—that sentence out of Peg's letter about "bowing to fate" and letting their friendship end.

But what was this? Once, twice, three times, just as she was going to sleep she was caught away from her feeling about Peg Frampton and entangled in a teasing curiosity. Daisy's whole being detested and despised curiosity. Young girls often pick up from some man's chance words, or from some chance page of a book, some queer, irrational, superstitious, but very authoritative *principle of avoidance.* This principle of hers about despising curiosity she had imbibed from her father. Captain Lily's abhorrence of this vulgarity was carried to an absurd extreme. He asserted that the *great* men of Science—like Charles Darwin—were totally devoid of this contemptible vice. They pursued truth, not from any base curiosity about the nature of things, but from an aristocratic desire to stamp their own theories upon the plastic clay of the universe.

But three times, ere she slept, Daisy was teased by an intense longing to know how the fact of Mr. Frampton's partner being enamoured of *Mrs.* Lily made any difference to Peg Frampton's relations with *Miss* Lily. The vexation of this riddle was aggravated by a pressure on her nerves that resembled the invisible presence of Dogberry Cattistock himself in her warm fire-lit room! Daisy was not frightened by this phenomenon, which was indeed no more than an intensification of what a human consciousness frequently suffers when a person is alone at night, but it had the effect of exciting her curiosity to a pitch that was certainly aggravating. She knew there was nothing supernatural about the way a powerful personality, like that of Cattistock makes its presence felt, when you call it up from a distance. Daisy's curiosity would, as a matter of fact, very quickly have died down, if chance had not willed it, that, at this very moment of the night, Mr. Cattistock, closeted with Mr. Frampton in the latter's house in Newstead Road, near Radipole Lake, happened himself to be actually speaking and thinking of Daisy. By thinking of Daisy Mr. Frampton's partner threw a projection of his personality so strongly into Daisy's room that before she went to sleep both of her emotions—her attraction to Peg and her indignation with Peg—subsided without her having the least idea of the reason into the automatic, resistant numbness, by which she defended herself from thinking about Mr. Cattistock.

Long before the daughter of Captain Lily was fast asleep in the little room from which it was possible to catch a glimpse of the sea, another girlish figure had hurried furtively to that crumbling cement-wall in Gipsy Lane and deposited another unaddressed envelope under the two stones on the top of it. This transaction was an easier one for Peg Frampton than the obtaining of the first missive had been for her correspondent, for Peg was several inches taller than her friend.

Miss Frampton, however, wore no mackintosh; and the little thin cloth jacket which she did wear was a poor protection against the chilliness of the night. Perhaps this was the reason that led her, after she had crossed the Harbour Bridge, to drift into the brilliantly lighted Palladium Cinema before retracing her steps home along Newstead Road.

To the surprise of the drowsy young woman who sold the tickets— for it was now considerably after ten o'clock and the performance had not much longer to run—Peg Frampton paid her entrance fee and entered the moving-picture building. She passed a tall gilt mirror in the entrance-hall and pausing there for a second adjusted her dusky hair beneath her dark-blue cap. The face that looked into her own as she did this was certainly not a beautiful one. Every feature of it broke the most elemental laws of feminine desirability. Peg's forehead was very low, her small hazel eyes very deeply set, her mouth with its sensual passionate lips hung open, disordered, unhappy, twisted awry, while her hollow white cheeks seemed all the more haggard, for a girl of eighteen, by reason of her high cheek-bones that possessed an almost Mongolian look.

Motherless and friendless, save for a series of passionate and somewhat morbid friendships with younger boys and girls—for Peg could be equally interested in both sexes—the girl had found herself at sixteen mistress of an unattractive, desolate house, an overworked, slatternly servant, and a father completely absorbed in money-making.

Mr. Frampton took no interest in the amenities of life. In his secret heart he regarded his child as responsible for her mother's death, for the woman had only outlived her daughter's birth by a few months, and though not an unkind man, felt vaguely hostile to her, as if she had wilfully usurped her mother's place. He was a cold, cautious, crafty man of affairs, with so little imagination, even in his business, that it was not until his employer promoted him from the position of a trusted subordinate to that of official partner that his industry and thrift received anything like their merited recognition. Mr. Frampton ate whatever was placed before him and drank whatever was in his decanter. He used the same bed, the same carpets, the same curtains, the same chairs, the same cushions, that he had bought for his wife, of whom he was idolatrously fond, when he was an under-paid clerk in Cattistock's office. Peg had only once in her life seen her father really angry and that was when she had bought at a fancy-work bazaar a brilliant oriental-looking cover for their faded drawing-room sofa. Nor, even then, had his anger been shown in any way except by getting very red. But as he was always extremely sallow, this event was as startling to Peg as would have been the hoisting of a Russian flag by a battle-ship in Portland Harbour. Mr. Frampton removed the rug from the sofa, folded it up very carefully, and hung it over the bottom of the banisters.

After this event—though she used the offensive object as a counter-pane in her own large, bare, chilly bedroom—the young mistress of Swan Villa attempted no more domestic improvements.

The girl was old enough to remember the time, before the building of the new Westham Bridge, when Swan Villa had overlooked the tidal Backwater. Some of her happiest childish memories were connected with these muddy, brackish reaches, on the edge of which she used to play for hours, imbibing the sour tidal smells and watching the swans and the wild ducks. But the Backwater had been transformed into an ornamental basin, rendered independent of the sea-tides; and although its smooth expanse of harmless water, like a pond in a Public Park, still stretched away as far as Radipole Village, a couple of miles from the old Harbour Bridge, the charm of the salt mud-pools and the tidal débris remained in her mind as something she missed. Children's aesthetic sense is a deep half-animal feeling and when it is outraged it leaves a wound behind it that never quite heals up. Unsanitary as the old Backwater may have been, and pretty as the new ornamental water doubtless was, these improvements had taken away from the lonely girl in Swan Villa something that left an unsatisfied craving in her nature.

When she was unhappy in her early teens it was always to the Back-water she went for comfort. The old Backwater Bridge itself, un-satisfactory for modern traffic as it probably became, had grown to be associated in her mind with alluring images of romantic continental bridges; and for all the new cleanliness and convenience that had recently appeared she did not find herself seeking refuge any more at her window, when the nostalgia for far horizons and remote places took possession of her.

Swan Villa, Newstead Road, could not be said to have moved with the times as had the view from its windows; for though in actual years it was not an old house—probably it was built about the same time as St. John's spire—its yellowing stucco, its straggling privet-hedges, its cracked, unpainted doors, its wistful, neglected rock-garden resembled one of those old Victorian editions of standard authors, covered with decorative arabesques, but bleached and stained by exposure to the weather. At the same time, since it is harder for a woman than for a man to shake off the deadening and sapping influence of monotonous drabness, Peg could not get the same solace from the old-fashioned qualities of her forlorn home that she used to get from the muddy Backwater and the picturesque bridge.

Since the girl was so late tonight in entering the Palladium Cinema she was compelled to take her seat by the side of a boy of about sixteen who was eating sweets, of more than one variety, out of a striped paper-bag. Peg was in a more than usually reckless mood tonight and it was not long—in the obscurity of that darkened house—before she had established intimate relations with this unknown lad who struck her as an unusual and exceptionally clever boy. At the price of putting into her mouth two or three sticky sweets from his paper-bag, she was able to encourage him to take her hand and to hold it with growing warmth, sometimes pressing it against her lap and sometimes against his own. She took good care to leave the house before the very end; and was not in the least dismayed when the lad followed her out. Here, close beside the big gilt mirror, but in no alarmingly sumptuous foyer, they began whispering eagerly together.

"If 'ee could come on Saturday, the day after tomorrow," the boy said, "I could be here at nine for the opening. Could *you* be here at nine?"

Peg pondered the matter. It was very unlikely that there would be anyone who knew her at this particular Cinema; and on Saturday the crowd would be an especially popular one and not in a mood to notice anything.

"A little *before* nine?" she asked.

He nodded with a glowing face. His cheeks were flaming.

"I be Jimmy Witchit of St. Alban's Lane. What be *your* name?"

"Oh, never mind about *my* name!" she retorted. "You can call me Peggie if you like."

"Do 'ee live in Rodwell or over there by St. John's?"

"Never mind where I live. That's my business."

"You baint—on the game, be you? There now! What be laughing at? I weren't being funny. I've a-known some wonderful decent girls what's been on the game."

"You don't go with them, do you, Jimmy? That isn't safe for a kid like you."

He looked at her with dumb indignation. She had deeply hurt his amour propre.

"Lots of girls older than *you* be—you ain't more'n seventeen, be 'ee? —have said I were like a bloke of twenty. I do know all there *is*, I reckon! No girl in Weymouth on the game or *not* on the game, can tell Jim Witchit nothink."

A crowd of boys, heralding the general exit, rushed wildly past them, shouting and jostling.

Peg's hands went up to her hair again at the big mirror, "Goodbye, kid, till Saturday before nine!" she whispered. And then glancing sideways at him, "Run off now, for mercy's sake!"

Jimmy nodded a temporary forgiveness to her for hurting his feelings on the subject of prostitutes, and slipped obediently away.

As he ran off he said to himself, "She ain't a day older nor I be, and she believes all I do tell to she. Maybe she'll let a bloke take her to Uncle Cob's. She ain't a factory kid, either. Looks to *me* as if she worked at one of them smart photographers."

Peg's lonely life and her mental superiority to social distinctions had given her an air that would have puzzled a much cleverer young man than Jimmy Witchit. He went home therefore to his parent's flat, above the shop in St. Alban's Lane, in a state of glowing elation.

"Peggie", he kept repeating to himself as he undressed. "Peggie be me girl! Sue were all very well, but she were a school-kid. Tisha were all right, but she were a biter and a scratcher when she loved anyone. Peggie be a girl a person could go anywhere with, and she'd tell the tale to anyone, before they meddled with she."

The girl in question now moved away to the edge of the harbour and loitered for a moment on the Quay near the Harbour Bridge. Everything was quiet here and the few ship-lanterns reflected in the darkness showed that the tide, no longer blown into waves, was swiftly running out. The sight of that silent volume of dark water rolling seaward filled her with desolation.

"What a life!" she groaned in her heart. "What a life!"

Behind her back the tall sombre warehouses full of hay and coal and casks of wine and crates of beer-bottles gathered themselves *into* themselves, and grew at once larger and less utilitarian as they accepted the passivity of another night. From a few upper windows on the further side of the water, lights could be seen. One little window especially, in a tall old house near the Bridge's end, caught her attention.

"Perhaps there's a girl going to bed *there*," she thought, "more sick of life even than I am. Think of that boy taking me for a street-walker! Well—why not? Perhaps I *shall* end like that. Father wouldn't care if he never saw me again. Who have I got but my little Daisy? And she doesn't love *me*. She loves someone else in my shape. She no more understands me, that sweet, solemn little thing, than Jimmy Witchit does! Less than he does. For he took me for one of *them*. And that's of course what I am—but not from necessity!"

She mounted the steps to the Harbour Bridge and paused for a minute to lean over the broad stone parapet and gaze down at the water, swirling rapidly now under the stately arches.

"Unhappy girls at night," she mocked bitterly, "leaning over bridges! Why is it that certain situations repeat themselves again and again when you're a girl?"

She thought of certain melodramatic scenes in the fantastic Cinematograph she had just witnessed.

"Clever people laugh at such things," she thought, "and simple people cry at them. But they keep on repeating themselves. Everything repeats itself! Perhaps everything that's happening now, at this minute, in all these houses has happened, exactly the same, through all eternity. Undress; go to bed; sleep; wake up; kiss and get up; dress; kiss and pretend; do the same with the same; and go to bed again!"

She left the bridge, passed the front of Trinity Church, followed the North Quay to Sidney Hall, and then hurried along Newstead Road. She passed the turns into Granville Road, Ilchester Road, and Abbotsbury Road and soon after this crossing arrived at Swan Villa. There was Mr. Cattistock's neat motor-car, still at the door. She opened her purse, took out her latchkey, and, twisting it in the lock as quietly as possible, let herself in.

Yes; just as she supposed! The voices of her father and Mr. Cattistock were droning on in the dining-room exactly as they had been when, a couple of hours ago, she had slipped out.

Did her father think she was in bed? If he heard she'd been fished out of the harbour dead, what would he say?

"Yes," he'd say, "it's *her* all right. If it hadn't been for her, my wife would be alive today."

"Is it pathetic," she said to herself as she stole softly upstairs, "or is it simply comic, the way I live? Not a soul to care, except Double Flower . . . and what does she know about me *really*?"

Her big, poorly-furnished bedroom resembled a bedroom in a lodging house. She turned up the gas-flame and throwing her hat on the bed stared at herself in the looking-glass.

"Another day over," she thought. "That's one good thing. Took me for a street-walker." She turned away from her staring, troubled eyes in the glass. "I wonder what it feels like to let a man do it to you, in a bed like that?" and she recalled the way Mr. Cattistock had kissed her when he found her alone in the house on a recent evening. "Would I let *him* do it, if he wanted to?" she thought. "Oh, I don't care, I don't care, I don't care! I don't care *what* happens, as long as everything doesn't go on repeating itself!"

4

HELL'S MUSEUM

AT the top of the house in Brunswick Terrace, where Mr. Ballard lodged, lived at this time another and very different young man, who, as their mutual landlady Mrs. Monkton would express it, "answered to the name of Richard Gaul". If Mr. Ballard was a daring and dynamic youth, dedicated to grow rich, Mr. Gaul was a dodging and debouching youth, dedicated to remain poor. It was lucky for young Gaul, who was as much alone in the world as if he had been engendered by a Pine-tree upon a Palm-tree, that he had inherited one hundred and twenty-three pounds a year. If it had not been for this piece of good fortune it is really a question whether Mr. Gaul would have been still in the world; for it is impossible to imagine the kind of berth that he could have filled under existing social conditions.

But if it were his good fortune to have an income of a hundred and twenty-three pounds it was not less a lucky chance, five years before this time, when he was only twenty-five, that he noticed the engaging announcement in Mrs. Monkton's window: "Rooms to Let. Gentlemen Preferred." Nor had Mrs. Monkton so much as once regretted, during all these five years, the day when she allowed young Richard Gaul to take the little top bedroom situated above the bow-window of the front bedroom, that spacious chamber where "Sippy" Ballard slept.

Two days after the arrival of Perdita at the Cobbolds', Mr. Gaul was eating his breakfast at his usual hour. His usual hour was eleven o'clock. By a device, of a simplicity that would have escaped the wit of anyone but an authentic philosopher, he had reduced his daily meals to two, having breakfast very late and making his tea, which he enjoyed at six, serve for both tea and supper.

It was a great surprise to the youthful official when he observed Mrs. Monkton's niece, an undersized girl of fifteen, carrying up Mr. Gaul's breakfast at this unconscionable time. The truth was that in return for this courtesy Mr. Gaul—for it was one of the things that were within his extremely limited powers—helped the little Miss Monkton not only with her English Compositions but also with her English Recitations. He had indeed—as her Aunt who knew "what was what" in education, secretly recognized—given the child, in these five years of his stay in that house, a real start in literature.

Mr. S. P. Ballard, or Sippy, as his friends called him, had twice made an attempt—the first time when he was drunk, and the second time when he had been appointed an official of the Council—to get upon speaking terms with the young man in the top-room but neither attempt was crowned with success. Beyond a nervous nod when they met, and Mr. Gaul took good care they didn't meet often, Miss Monkton's tutor kept the enterprising official at an implacable distance.

Richard was finishing his breakfast which Betty Monkton had arranged on a large black tray, covered with a white cloth, and placed on a small three-legged table in front of his window. He swallowed with a mild and dreamy satisfaction the last mouthfuls of his daily portion of Dundee marmalade; and when these had vanished he poured himself out his last cup of tea and proceeded, pushing back the table a little, to light his first cigarette.

Between the muslin curtains, yellow, though not with dirt, for they had recently been washed, he could discern the grey level of the sea's horizon, broken by two small fishing-smacks. The sea was calm, this Saturday morning, but it lay under a low, sad, cloudy sky, neutral and grey as itself. Richard derived, as he alternately sipped his tea and inhaled his cigarette-smoke, a peaceful and soothing pleasure from the faint contrast between the greyness below the horizon-line and the greyness above it. Both these expanses were reduced to the lowest possible level of emphasis to which any material phenomenon *could* be reduced without actually becoming invisible; and sad though these two levels were, with that indescribable line of demarcation separating the horizontal perspective of the one from the perpendicular perspective of the other, their sadness, like two muted notes in a wistful bar of music, was of a kind that had more of peacefulness in it than of sorrow.

Whenever Richard glanced away from the sky and the sea and from those two sails that sometimes seemed to be suspended in the one and sometimes in the other, his eyes rested on his desk which also faced the window and upon which, retained in several separate piles under various sea-shells, which he used as paper-weights, lay quite a number of manuscript-sheets, written in small, rather thick, though singularly clear hand. These sheets, which were already enough to make a considerable book, represented the work of more than five years. It was not only an ambitious work. It was not only a long work. It was one of those works that in the industry and devotion of an intensely concentrated mind seem to win a sort of battle over necessity and death, merely on the strength of having come into being at all! In plain words what Mr. Gaul had been engaged upon for the last seven years was a system of philosophy. Yes! this young man whose desperate hobby it was to read every metaphysical book he could lay his hand upon, old or new, was actually occupied in composing a cosmological system of his own that should offer to those few specialists in such things who could read it—for philosophers write for philosophers—a simplification of the chaos of life. Young Gaul was totally free from any egoistic desire for fame. He wrote his book solely and entirely to satisfy himself. The pleasure he took in writing it was its own reward.

If Richard's system could be said to have any really valuable clue to the mystery of things this clue was to be found in his own word "representative". His idea was that all the exciting concepts of religion, mythology and metaphysics were true; but not *literally* true. He held they were true in a "representative" sense; that is to say, he held that behind every human creed and behind every mythological figure lay a quite definite human craving, a purely emotional and very often a quite irrational craving, a craving old as the hills and apparently springing from something ineradicable in human nature. And just as there could be discovered, if you analysed far enough a concrete and quite definite human exigency behind every religion and every cult, so you could discover, behind every single one of the great meta-physical systems, precisely the same body of concrete palpable yearnings that existed beneath the cults, only with the stress laid upon first one aspect of them and then another.

The first part of Gaul's labours upon what he called his "Philosophy of Representation" had to do with the primitive pagan religions, the second part with Christianity, Buddhism, Taoism, Mohammedanism, the third part with the famous individual metaphysical systems. What Richard was engaged upon now was the fourth portion of his book in which he applied his definite list of concrete, basic, irreducible human yearnings to the objective realities of life. His idea was that instead of being, as the scientists declared, empty of all value, these yearnings when reduced to their dominant motifs were actually "representative" of certain eternal, natural facts; facts that very frequently contradicted the mathematical and chemical hypothesis most prevalent in our age. Gaul had a trick of using, all through his argument, the expression "imaginative reason" by which he apparently meant some super-vision, wherein intuition, instinct, emotion, imagination were in some artful manner synchronized with reason.

Unlike most philosophers who are content to use their one grand, basic inspiration about life and then bolster it up with infinite logical and rationalistic devices, Mr. Gaul by a bold original method of his own kept his argument fluid, flexible and porous; subject in fact to the various *daily* inspirations that came to him as he lived in Brunswick Terrace. What he would argue was that the rigidly *monumental* method of exposition adopted by most philosophers was an unnatural method and was a method, moreover, that sacrificed a great deal of organic flexibility to the dead hand of logical abstraction.

"I must get some more paper-weights," he thought as he lit a second cigarette and struggled with the tip of his tongue to extract a tooth-brush bristle from between his teeth, for it was a peculiarity of Richard's to regard the use of a tooth-pick as a coarse, disgusting, and altogether loathsome habit. It now struck him that in the greyness of those two expanses of un-solid matter, visible from his window, a greyness so neutral and unassuming as to hover on the edge of nonen-tity, there dwelt the essential mystery of beauty. For what was beauty if not a manifestation in the midst of objective reality of something half-created and half-discovered by the craving of our human organism?

"If I don't feel a melting ecstasy at this moment," he said to himself, "from that horizon-line between sky and sea, it is only that this damned thing that's got stuck between my teeth is so bothering that I can't give myself up. I like this sort of day particularly. Why is it that the line between sea and sky—just a regular, *natural* line, not perfectly straight, nor curved, nor wavy, but with its own peculiar identity, the sea-line, the sky-line, the meeting-line—should give a human animal, an animated skeleton, such a curious thrill?"

He frowned gloomily, rose abruptly from his chair and went up to the window, as if by a closer observation of these phenomena he could catch solutions of their riddle.

"Yes, it certainly *is*," he thought, "very nearly my favourite kind of day!"

The shock of seeing so much of the sea at one view, the interest of observing that there were now three sails on that grey horizon, and finally the fact that the coming together of these two vast entities, the sky and the sea, was enhanced by the brownish ridge of pebbles, a ridge that vanished altogether at the other end of the town where King George's statue turned its back to St. Mary's Street, led Mr. Gaul to forget this worrying thing in his tooth; led him in fact to the verge of a transport of delight in this inimitable greyness; when Nature as though impishly consistent in turning a philosopher's pleasures into a victory of matter over mind, brought it about that the author of the "Philosophy of Representation" had to hurry off with incontinent haste to the lavatory upon the landing beneath him. This was one of Gaul's diurnal annoyances, this trip to the floor below his own, not because he felt towards his natural evacuations as he did towards the use of a tooth-pick, but because there was always a danger of encountering Mr. S. P. Ballard in the passage there and even of seeing him emerge from that discreet glazed door. This morning, however, he got back safe to his top-floor without misadventure, and was on the point of sitting down at his desk when he heard the door-bell of the house emit a reverberant ring.

"Someone to see Alcibiades!" he muttered to himself, and going close to the window he tried to peer down on the head of the ringer.

This was, as he ought to have known from experience, an impossible procedure, for the bow-windows of both Mr. Ballard's floors jutted out over the pavement. He had amused himself by calling his fellow-lodger "Alcibiades" ever since he learned from their landlady of the young man's promotion to municipal honours. Unable to settle down to work till he felt certain that this morning call had nothing to do with himself, he stood, in nervous indecision, with his hands on the back of his desk-chair and his eyes fixed on the three fishing-smacks. He was still in this position when he heard steps ascending the last flight of stairs. It *was* himself, then, that this stranger sought!

"Come in!" he called out hurriedly in reply to a knock at his door.

The door opened to admit Magnus Muir.

"Oh, it's you," murmured the young philosopher with something of disappointment in his tone. He had hoped—when the knock came—for he was young enough to long for the unexpected, that some exciting stranger, perhaps someone who had heard of his life's work, would appear on his threshold.

"Yes, it's me," said the Latin teacher; and as he took the chair offered him automatically by the young man, he wearily repeated his ungrammatical greeting. "Yes, it's me. And how is our Richard this grey day?"

Mr. Gaul offered him a cigarette in silence. Magnus glanced at the brand and replaced the packet on the table.

"I can't stay," he said and looked at the young man as if pondering in his mind whether, after all, it was worth while to put his problem before him.

"I had a letter this morning," he burst out now, speaking almost reproachfully, as if Mr. Gaul had been responsible for this annoyance.

"*I* don't often get letters," remarked that sage.

"A letter from Cattistock it was," Magnus went on, with the same faint reproach in his voice. "And he's coming to see me in a little while and take me to lunch. He wants me to tutor his boy."

"Cattistock—with a boy?" cried the other. "I didn't know that fellow was married."

"Oh, his wife's dead. Been dead for years. They say he's going to marry Hortensia Lily. He says his boy is an incurable fool. That's the word he uses in this letter—an incurable fool."

Mr. Gaul took off his spectacles, a gesture of his which always accompanied the reception of anything startling. But he only twisted them in his hands and replaced them carefully. Had the event been more personally arresting he would have cleaned them with his coat-sleeve. Confronted by a shipwreck he might even have rubbed them against his trousers.

"Will you do it, Muir?" he asked.

"I ... don't ... know," replied the agitated scholar. "I ... suppose ... I'll have to go and see him."

"If you see him, you'll take him," remarked the young man with decision, "like you did young Zed, when Gipsy May came to you."

Magnus smiled faintly.

"I didn't do *him* any good," he said. "He wouldn't sit still and he terrified Miss Le Fleau."

"He *is* incurable," said the other gravely.

They were both silent, calling up in their minds the red hair and green eyes of the young protégé of Gipsy May.

"You know Cattistock?" enquired Richard abruptly. "I've only spoken to him once. He terrifies me."

"My father never liked him," remarked Magnus with finality, as if the elder Muir's opinion put the person in question beyond the pale.

"Then you'll refuse?" murmured the other, lighting a cigarette and glancing round at his manuscripts.

Magnus shifted in his seat, resumed possession of his stick, and began buttoning his overcoat.

"He wants to get to work," he thought. "What I really came to ask you, Gaul," he blurted out, "was the gross and vulgar question—how much, if I *do* take this boy, I ought to ask. My ordinary pupils pay very little and can't pay more. But Cattistock is the richest man in Weymouth. Ought I to be glad to have his son, simply for the name? Or ought I to ask twice as much as the rest? I've only got six; and three are leaving this spring. It's a chance to save myself from worry for the next couple of years, if I ask enough!"

Magnus clasped his hands on his stick and sat up straight, staring anxiously at his interlocutor. Mr. Gaul raised one hand a little way towards his spectacles, and then dropped it. The problem of his friend's salary did not seem to necessitate an immaculate vision. He found himself guilty of an irresistible spasm of gratitude to providence for his own small but secure income.

"I'd be frank with him, Muir, if I were you," he said firmly. "Tell him that you depend on your tutoring for—for everything. Perhaps"—his hand moved a little again, and again sank on the table—"he'll offer you enough for you to give up all the rest."

Magnus' features cleared. What, as a matter of fact, had really prompted this visit to his young friend, had been the daring thought that, if encouraged a little, he might strike out for enough money from this heaven-sent rich man, to enable him to marry Curly!

"I shall have," he began excitedly, "to see the boy first, of course! Do you think by his using the words 'incurable fool' that the child's not all there? Do you think he's an idiot, Gaul?"

Magnus uttered the word "idiot" with such agitated emphasis that his hearer, whose thoughts, to confess the truth, had wandered away to a delicate point in the "Philosophy of Representation", drew back his head with a start, as if the other had threatened him.

"An idiot?" he stammered. "No, no; I'm sure we should have heard of it if Mr. Cattistock had an imbecile son. It's only the way he talks. It's probably his idea of being funny. These rich people— you know! I expect the child is afraid of his father. Everyone says that Alcibiades, I mean young Ballard down there,"—and Mr. Gaul made a gesture indicative of lower regions in general—"is his natural son. The chances are that he neglects this little boy."

Magnus leaned forward over his stick and fixed his eyes on a place in the carpet where the pattern revealed a small brown triangle, enclosing a conventionalized tulip upon which lay a fragment of bread. Sunlight fell upon this spot and close to the piece of bread a fly was cleaning her fore-legs. The teacher was thinking of the rendezvous which he had at the Wishing Well that afternoon. Would this expedition with Cattistock be over in time for him to get there? And if he was late would Curly wait for him? It was only in the summer that she or her mother had to be there all the while. During the winter they only went to the place to rake the leaves away and keep the fountain clean. But there was a shelter and a seat hard-by; and surely Curly would give him a little grace if he *were* late! It wouldn't do to hurry Mr. Cattistock in their negotiations. He now became aware that his companion had stretched out his arm and possessed himself of a sheet of his manuscript. Mr. Gaul had done this with a casual, accidental, haphazard air, like a dog who strolls through a kitchen, and gives a nonchalant lick, in passing, at the cat's saucer.

Magnus grasped his stick and hat and stood up.

"Well, I must be getting back," he said. "He might arrive before his time and be cross if I wasn't there. Sorry to have bothered you, Gaul!"

The distance between Trigonia House and Kimmeridge House was only a few steps; but it was long enough for a grim array of dark thoughts to march through his mind.

"Except Gaul I've got no one to go to," he said to himself, "and I've got *no one* to go to about Curly. Miss Le Fleau would nurse me if I got ill; but in everything else—"

And, as he tapped with his stick against the rails of the small patches of earth in front of these familiar Brunswick Terrace houses, the ignoble and cowardly wish flew like a black arrow across the sky of his consciousness that he had never met Curly. If it had not been for the hope of marrying this little shop-girl—"for that's what she is," he thought, "Wishing Well or no Wishing Well,"—he would have refused to teach Cattistock's son, simply on the strength of his father's dislike of the man.

"I'm going out of my harbour," he said to himself, "and I see reefs of danger ahead."

At each step he took, along that well-known pavement, life seemed to loom up before him in more portentous array. He felt it now as a menacing engine-house that he was entering—a place full of cogs and pistons and wheels and screws and prodding spikes—and full of people with bleeding limbs. A vague horror, like that of extreme physical pain, oppressed him. He felt as if all the hidden places where sensitive life was tortured had opened their back-doors to him, and the moans from within were groping at his vitals. Yes, something that he had always known was there all the while, there under Miss Le Fleau's brown room, there under the warm seclusion of his study, something raw, grating, jarring, despairing, twisted by pain, menacing him, like the spasms of a skeleton on a gibbet the moment the wind came from a certain quarter. He found himself actually growing cold

in the pit of his stomach as he went along; and he hurried into Miss
Le Fleau's little hall-way, smelling, as it always did, even in the
winter, of old, long-forgotten summers by the sea-side, as if he were
seeking refuge in the lap of his mother—that mother whose real
personality he could barely recall! The peculiar smell of the interior
of Kimmeridge House, even when he was ascending the stairs,
brought its own assuagement; for a multitude of long peaceful lives
at Weymouth seemed condensed there, like ancient flower-petals
in some old pot-pourri, lives whose re-vivified exits and entrances
were at once cleansed by salt-blowing winds and mellowed by glowing
fires and flickering candles.

When he reached his book-lined room and had closed the door, there
came over him such a sharp distaste for allowing this alarming
intruder to enter his precious fortress, that he decided he would be on
the spot downstairs in hat and coat so as to avoid the necessity—if thus
it *could* be escaped—of Cattistock's coming upstairs at all.

He looked at his watch. Yes, he might be here any minute; and it
should be at the door, or even on the pavement, that he would meet
him!

Neither Miss Le Fleau nor old Martha felt that it was advisable to
interfere with their guest's movements, though the one in her drawing
room and the other in her kitchen, found it impossible to do anything
but wait and listen in intense participation. He had shown Cattistock's
letter to both these women—for after all they were like near relatives—and there had been a certain vaingloriousness in the response
of the whole of Kimmeridge House to the great man's overture.

But it was a miserable business standing there outside the house, and
he had twice been on the point of retreating when the dark-blue car of
the financier came to a halt at his side. Hurriedly he removed his hat
and was on the point of addressing the car's driver when it presented
itself to his mind that Cattistock had merely sent his chauffeur to fetch
him. Full as he was of every kind of aesthetic touchiness, cars like
this, and their chauffeurs with them, were intensely distasteful to
Magnus. He did not quite share his father's attitude towards these
luxuries of the rich; but after his own fashion he was scarcely less
prejudiced. The elder Muir, on the strength of the weight of his
personality, had the power of making anyone he spoke to feel that to

possess a car at all was in some subtle way both a lapse from all good
taste and a deviation from all dignity of character; and as his son now
sank back and contemplated all the familiar landmarks flying past
him, till, crossing the big new bridge over what used to be the Backwater he asked the driver whether he had been long in his master's
service, it was with a feeling of condescending to a vulgar necessity
rather than of enjoying a genteel privilege, that he allowed himself to
be driven towards Chickerel.

As he was carried along in a north-westerly direction, following the
ridge of the bare uplands, he could see under the grey sky the broad
silvery horizon of the West Bay; and he told himself how, if he could
have followed that horizon like a migratory sea-bird, it would have
receded and receded before him, until, beyond Cornwall and the
Scilly Isles, it led him into the desolate wastes of the North Atlantic.

The driver of the car set him down at a gate in a low wall which
ran along the edge of the road on the outskirts of the village of
Chickerel. Above this wall was a neatly-cut box hedge indicating
by the height to which it had grown that Mr. Cattistock's dwelling
was at least a hundred years old. It was a solid, but quite small,
Georgian building, covered with a rather desolate frontage of cream-
coloured cement. In fact this cement was so weather-stained, and in
some places so much of it was peeling off, that it was an agreeable
shock to Magnus to find the head of the Cattistock and Frampton
Brewery and of the Cattistock Stone Company living in such a place.

A white-faced little old woman in a black dress and apron, but
wearing no cap, opened the door to him now; and the moment he was
in the passage, taking off his overcoat and laying down his hat and stick,
he knew that the inside of Cattistock's house possessed the same
curious appeal to his senses as the outside. In what did this appeal lie?
When he had been seated for a few minutes in the room that the owner
of the house called his study, and had talked for a while with the great
man, he came to a very singular conclusion. It was characteristic of
Magnus when confronted by a new human presence, especially when
surrounded by its own especial background and its own psychic
atmosphere, to give himself up, without any ulterior purpose, to a
purely disinterested analysis of the whole phenomenon. In the for-
mulation of his verdict now, upon the financier and his home, Magnus

decided that the quality which appealed to him so much was due to a very singular cause—or rather to conjunction of two causes—namely, that the astonishing fellow had the concentrated, sleepless obsession about money of an impassioned miser and that the only woman about the place was the old servant who had let him in.

"It is," Magnus thought, "the absence of a dominant imaginative passion that makes the aura of a house so intolerable; and mistresses are like lightning-conductors: they absorb the imaginative passions of men."

Cattistock was in one sense easier to get on with than he had anticipated, while in another sense he was more difficult. Magnus had expected to be treated in a brusque, offhand manner, made to feel in fact his social unimportance, compared with the richest man in Weymouth; but instead of this he found himself, after the first few minutes, being deferred to with a courteous and interested tact, as if his views on the matter of Benny's education were of so complicated a value that they had to be approached delicately, indirectly, tentatively, as a respectful outsider would approach the reserved experience of an acknowledged expert. This attitude was such a change from anything that Magnus had ever known in the tone of his pupils' parents that it very soon completely disarmed him and he found himself talking to the man not only more freely than he was wont to talk about his occupation but with more diffidences, hesitations, waverings, indecisions about the whole thing than he had ever before realized existed in his mind with regard to it.

But all the while this colloquy was proceeding, Magnus was secretly struggling to define more clearly to himself his surprising conclusion that what appealed to him so strongly about this house was due to the fact that it had no mistress, and that its master, for all his daring financial schemes, had something of that romantic intensity of a miser's psychology which like all great passions possesses its own especial dignity.

Answering Cattistock's questions as he sat opposite him by the fire of this shabby room whose bookcases contained as far as he could see little else but leather-bound magazines, directories, dictionaries, and encyclopedias, he had ample opportunity to take in every nuance of the man's personal appearance. And his impression of him became still more significant when, as the talk began to centre upon Benny's difficult disposition, Cattistock got up from his chair and began walking up and down the room. The man looked about forty; but his hair had grown prematurely thin and grey, though it was easy to see from its peculiar shade—he wore what was left of it parted carefully in the middle of his broad low forehead—that it had been in his youth of a light straw-colour. The whole weight of his character lay in his chin, which resembled the pictures of so many of our military leaders, being indicative of immense reserves of massive, stubborn power rather than of any excess of nervous recklessness. Cattistock's chin seemed always bristling with sharp thick light-coloured hairs. He shaved carefully; but nothing seemed able, after a few hours, to prevent this forward-jutting feature from growing rough and hirsute. His chin came near, indeed, to being a deformity: and on the right side of his lower jaw, where it projected a little beyond the upper, was a noticeable mole or birthmark upon which grew a tuft of hair still lighter and still more bristly than the rest. His ears were unusually neat, and grew close to his head; while his eyes which were small and steady had a way of remaining fixed, in a look that was at once a fighting look and a kindly look, upon the person or the object he was regarding. This stare of the man's seemed to conceal a queer abstracted reserve, as if what concerned him was not the character of his interlocutor, or the nature of the object, but some interior "substance" within them both, which he was calculating how to employ for purposes of his own.

As Magnus watched him walking up and down that unstudious study, with its faded carpet, its threadbare rug, its ancestral portraits, so dark and neglected as to be almost indistinguishable, he noticed how the man had a trick of clasping his hands behind his back and thrusting his chin forward as he walked; and he noticed, too, that he walked in jerks, as if consciously pushing his way through serried ranks of antagonists.

It was when, after a while, he rang the bell and ordered the old servant to bring some glasses and biscuits, that Magnus was confirmed in his impression about his having the temperament of a miser; for it was only after closing the door upon that old woman and standing with his chin thrust out and his eyes on the door till the sound of her retreating steps died away, that he produced a bunch of keys from his pocket and carefully selecting one of them went to a bureau-cupboard and cautiously opened it, kneeling down on the carpet the better to investigate its contents. To the nostrils of Magnus was wafted from this dark aperture over the shoulders of the kneeling man a mellow fragrance of ancient liquor; but it was clear that the master of Peninsular Lodge was weighing and calculating down there as to which of the half-empty bottles to bring out.

"The back of his head," thought Magnus, "is desperately acquisitive; but it isn't meanly acquisitive. He certainly carries his mania to a pathological extreme. But I like him much better than I ever thought I should. How excited Curly will be to hear about all this!"

The whiskey that was finally brought out to be shared between them was dispensed generously enough. In fact the half-empty bottle was nearly empty before it was returned to the cupboard. Into the cupboard it had gone, however, before there was the sound of the stopping of a car in the road outside followed by a great scrambling and confusion on the garden-path.

"Why, the Doctor's come here *with* him!" cried Cattistock moving to the door.

But the door was flung open before he reached it and into the room rushed a pale-faced, thin, excited boy clutching in his arms a small yellow dog. Behind the boy came a clean-shaven, unassuming, reserved man, about fifty years old, who produced on Magnus an impression that was very difficult for him to articulate to himself. There was something about the new-comer's eyes that gave him the feeling that the man was living in another world, but the Doctor's trick of preserving his dignity by a queer kind of furtive self-depreciation jarred on the teacher's nerves. The little boy broke off in the mid-rush of an excited speech to his father when he saw Magnus. With his hands still clutching the small dog in his arms he stared at his prospective tutor with wide-open mouth and round astonished eyes.

"This is Mr. Muir, Doctor," said Cattistock hurriedly, and then to Magnus he added, "and this is my brother-in-law, Dr. Brush, who has been taking Benny off my hands today."

Magnus and the Doctor exchanged polite bows from where they stood while the master of the house, peering into the passage with out-thrust chin, as though to be sure that poor Lizzie Chant, who had been his nurse in the old days and would have given her life for him was not loitering about for no good, shut the door with emphatic deliberation.

"That's how undertakers shut doors," thought Magnus. "At least that's how the one did, who came to Penn House to measure my father for his coffin."

Benny's flow of nervous explanation was now resumed while Dr. Brush sat down by the fire, a melancholy smile hovering about his thin lips. These weary smiles of this silent man were like those of some priestly autocrat whose executive burden has been increased by some secret mental strain.

It was when Cattistock approached his son and was—as far as Magnus could see—merely attempting to stroke the dog in the child's arms that a flash of blind fury convulsed the boy's face and he kicked the man sharply and malignantly on the shin. Magnus was astonished at his host's behaviour at this moment; for he had caught the thud of that vicious kick and knew it must have hurt him sharply. But Cattistock merely seized the child by the wrists and pulled him to the door which he flung open, calling "Lizzie! Lizzie!" The old woman, who could not have been far off, turned up at once; and there were screams and scoldings and barkings and every kind of hullabaloo as all three of them, the boy, the yellow dog, and Lizzie, struggled and clattered up the echoing staircase to the landing above.

"I expect you can see like a map how all this happened, Dogberry," began the Doctor, as soon as they were alone. "My man Murphy— Benny didn't like the look of him in his white apron—was carrying the dog to the kennels when it got away from him, and as chance would have it, ran right between the legs of our little Ben; when, as you can see how it *would* be, the fat was in the fire."

The Doctor turned back to the hearth; and Magnus sat down while Cattistock continued pacing the room. There was a moment's silence in the study of Peninsular Lodge, broken only by the tread of its owner as he strode up and down, his hands behind his back. The casual mention of the assistant "Murphy", in his "white apron", had started the imagination of the Latin teacher upon a very sinister train of thought.

"This man is a vivisector," he said to himself, while a sickening sensation of anger and disgust took possession of him. "It's all wrong," he thought. "They ought not to be allowed to touch dogs."

It would almost seem as if Cattistock had read the tutor's thoughts, for he presently paused in his perambulation of the room to suggest that when Magnus was driven home by and by he should drop Dr. Brush on his way.

"For the truth is," he went on, as he saw the look on the teacher's face, "we people in Weymouth don't realize what we've got here in our Brush Home."

It occurred to Magnus to wonder how it came about that a man as parsimonious as the owner of Peninsular Lodge clearly was had ever arrived at being a patron of modern pathological institutions. But it was evident that his relative's flattery was anything but pleasing to the man by the fire; for Magnus now caught upon Daniel Brush's face the only expression he had yet seen there that pleased him at all. The great Pathologist had suddenly begun to look as abashed and uncomfortable as a youth who is praised in public by his schoolmaster. But in spite of what he felt about this man's dislike of praise Magnus found it difficult to look at him without an obscure horror.

"It's all wrong," he kept thinking. "They ought not be to allowed to touch dogs."

"It was my brother-in-law," remarked Cattistock, "who first mentioned your name to me. He tells me you did quite a lot for a lad who has been in the Home, a boy called Larry Zed; but you've probably been told that before! Well, Mr. Muir, won't you come upstairs and see whether you think you can make anything of *my* little idiot? Don't run off, Dan! I do so want you to show Mr. Muir the Home. It will impress him, I know."

Magnus felt dazed and confused as he followed his host upstairs. He was accusing himself for not having the courage to speak out all that he felt on the subject of vivisection. He tried now to shake off this feeling as he looked about him. That fascinating inkling he had had when he first entered the house began to be more confirmed than ever. Yes; this man, against whom he had heard the Jobber muttering inarticulate threats out of his wave-tossed boat, *was* a passionate money-saver. And what a curious thing that the violent prejudice

against him which he'd accepted from his father and which applied
to the fellow as representing the Cattistock and Frampton Brewery
and the Cattistock Stone Company should be dissipated almost completely by the sight of this faded, dilapidated, neglected miser's house!

The carpets upon the stairs and upon the landing were what Miss
Le Fleau would have called "a sight", and as for the doors and the
woodwork and the window-sills, they had lost all trace of the paint
and varnish that supposedly must once have adhered to them. And
yet the house, although so lamentably faded, was spotlessly clean.

"Lizzie Chant must be perpetually brushing and scrubbing," he
thought, as he followed his host's acquisitive skull down a long passage.
"I've brought Mr. Muir to see you, who's going to do your lessons
with you, Ben," the man now asseverated, as he opened the door to his
son's play-room.

They found Benny standing close up to the shining fire-place—evidently the room had once been the boy's nursery—where, taking some
little biscuits from a plate on the mantelpiece, he was tossing them into
the air for the amusement and education of his new pet, who was trying
in vain, with little barks of excitement, to catch them as they descended.
The rug in front of the hearth was littered with broken biscuits, some
of which had been trodden into it by the boy's heels. The appearance
of the room struck Magnus as very singular; and well it might. What
the room contained were, in fact, all the elder Cattistock's school and
college possessions; objects retained all these years by this passionate
money-maker with a pathetic intensity of possessiveness, and only
lately brought down from the storeroom in the attic—probably under
the advice of Dr. Brush—to inspire the little boy with manly instincts
and sporting ambitions. Since Cattistock himself had been good at
nothing, except algebra and rifle-shooting, at either school or college,
there was something quaint, if not touching, to see the proud
satisfaction with which he had arranged these memorials of his own
youth against every wall of his child's room. There were ancient
fishing-rods and airguns; there were old cricket-bats and hockey-sticks.
An extravagantly tall rocking-horse—for it was clear that Mr.
Cattistock's parents had spent money freely on such toys—stood with
its tail against a broken bagatelle-board which was propped up against
the wall; and near it Magnus could see a big archery-target into which

had been stuck, in some whim of the little boy, an arrow with vermilion feathers. There was no sign of a bow; but leaning against the side of this target were a pair of rusty foils that looked different from the other things and had an air of holding them all in aristocratic contempt. Save for the blazing fire and the old-fashioned nursery fire-guard the chamber was poorly furnished. On the right of the fire-place, where one would have expected a comfortable chair, stood a brass studded chest with the lid propped open, inside of which Magnus caught a glimpse of what looked like an ancient tennis-net.

"Well, Benny!" said his father, fixing upon his son that formidable stare which was so characteristic of him, and which seemed to isolate the object of his contemplation from everything else in the vicinity, "I see you're teaching your pet to catch. You'll have to give him a name, you know. Every dog has a name."

"He *can't* catch," replied the child peevishly, without answering his father's look. "He misses every time."

The financier approached the fire-place and placing his hands on the gilt rail of the tall fire-guard glanced down sideways at the yellow dog. Save for the brightly-burning flames the only light in the room was a small lamp upon a distant desk; and Magnus, who had seated himself upon the arm of one of the few chairs in the place, became the witness now of a curious scene in that flickering glow, where the father tried to coax from the boy some sort of attention by sharing in this game of breaking biscuits at arm's length above the jumping and snapping animal, who certainly showed himself no adept at catching, and who only snuffed at the pieces he missed as they fell to the floor.

As Magnus watched them together in that warm fire-light there came over him a feeling that he had grown to be very familiar with: the feeling of the impenetrable obscurity of what human beings call "the future"; a feeling that grew so dark and dense that it was like an actual substance of pitch blackness. Somewhere within that blackness, into which an inexorable force was pushing them all forward, waited the groupings, the encounters, the issues and upshots, of what was transpiring now. There, in that thick darkness—not to be pierced, however sharply this little dog barked—waited the future, prosperous or tragic, of this man with the prominent chin and of this child with

that white nervous face. There, in that darkness, waiting to be revealed, was his own fate with Curly; that very afternoon's meeting
with her, if it really came about, and all their subsequent life. How
much would he dare to demand of Cattistock? The glimpse he had
had into the man's parsimonious habits was anything but promising.
But still—and he let his optimistic fantasy run riot now—if this
little boy got fond of him, and the child certainly was a much more
interesting type than he was accustomed to, who could tell? Why, he
might keep this job till Benny was old enough for the university. He
certainly didn't seem the kind of boy they could possibly send to a
Public School. What was in their minds now, as they fooled with
that dog in the flickering fire-light? But who could pierce the dense
black darkness that lay across their path and across his own?

"How monotonous," he thought, "my life has been until now!
Day after day with father, year after year—and now day after day at
Miss Le Fleau's. I suppose I could go on just the same all the rest of
my life—as long as I was seeing Curly. He's always with me, father
is! My hands, as I rub them now up and down my knees—they're
his hands; the knuckles the same, the wrinkles the same! What
would he think if he knew I was going to marry Curly? *Do you really
love the young woman, my boy?* That's what he'd say! And I'd tell
him the truth. I'd tell him that I can't imagine giving her up. I'd
tell him that she's at the back of my thoughts, wherever I go, whatever I do—always there—mixed up with everything. O
father, father, I wish you *were* here, for me to explain to you how
it is!"

His meditations were interrupted by a decisive move on the part of
his host. Cattistock suddenly straightened his back, patted his son on
the head, and went to the door.

"Come down in a minute, Muir, will you? I want you to give Dan
a lift. He won't keep you at that place. He's too busy. But you
ought to see the sort of thing it is." He paused with his hand on the
door-handle. "About the matter of hours, Muir? Could you come
out to lunch here every day and stay till five? I presume you could
crowd your other pupils into the morning—with a little adjustment?"

Magnus murmured an affirmative; but it confused him, being
rushed like this. But of course he *could* manage it, if he got up a bit

earlier. And the man said "till five"; so he'd be free about his usual time.

"And with regard to salary," went on Cattistock. This word made Magnus' heart beat fast. Would he offer him enough? And, if he didn't would he dare—"The fairest thing for both of us, as I see it," said Cattistock, "will be to leave this point undecided till the end of the first week—then we shall know better how you and Ben hit it off. See you downstairs in a minute, Mr. Muir!"

With this he was gone; and Magnus was left alone with the boy and the dog. The child's face assumed a completely different expression when the sound of his father's steps died away. He came hurriedly forward, pushing back the little dog impatiently when it went on jumping up. He laid his hand on the lappet of Magnus' coat and pulled it towards him in order to make its wearer lower his head.

"His name is going to be 'Yellow'," he whispered. "That's what I'm going to call him—*Yellow*—only I shan't tell father, for he'd think it a silly name. Now you've come I shan't have to go for drives with Uncle Dan any more, shall I? Wait a moment—Down, Yellow, *down*, I tell you!—I want to ask you something, Mr. Muir."

Thrusting away the dog irritably and violently, the child ran to the door, opened it a little, and peered out. While this went on Magnus experienced a strong revulsion against his whole predicament. As had happened to him earlier in the day a cold shrinking from all this activity shot like a shuttle of dark ice across the depths of his heart.

"What I'd really like," he thought, "would be to go on to the end of my days enjoying Homer and my walks by the sea, and going out to see Curly at Upwey. Of course I want to have her to myself by day and night, but—but—"

The shivering recoil in the depths of his being which accompanied his contemplation of Benny spying for eavesdroppers resembled the tearing of stiff paper in the centre of his stomach. And this sturdy paper, that caused him such a twinge while it was ripped up, *was his father.* Yes, it was the protection of his father, the security of his father, his daily walks with his father, the way his father used to sit so close to the fire-bars at Penn House, warming his old shins and rubbing his legs with his wrinkled fingers, the indescribable safety, like the feeling anyone has who hugs himself in bed on a freezing night, that the sight of his father sitting opposite him drinking his tea always gave him, it was all this that was now being torn in his inmost vitals, and letting in a draught of cold outer space! The child had come back to his side now and was actually whispering something in his ear.

"Don't, Yellow! Lie down when I tell you to! Don't *do* that! When I say lie down I mean lie down!"

"He doesn't understand," murmured Magnus, when Yellow received quite a severe cuff. "He thinks it's still a game."

"He'll soon learn it's *not* a game! Do you hear what I say, Yellow? Lie *down* when I tell you and *stay* lied down!"

But the boy's whispering was more exasperating to Magnus than anything Yellow could do.

"I can't hear you," he said. "I'm a little deaf. You *must* speak right out."

Unabashed by this rebuke—for he seemed to know by an infallible instinct where he was safe with this stranger—the child began a long hurried, proud, shy, nervous recital about some picture of two girls that he had got hidden away somewhere. Magnus had sunk down by this time into the only arm-chair in the room. This had been the accustomed refuge, by his study-hearth, of Dog Cattistock's father, a silent man from the banks of the Stour, when his family became too much for him, and a certain musty air of a whimsical and scholarly escape from the brawling voices of the world emanated still from its ancient and fragrant leather.

"Hidden, eh? Well, we all have to keep *some* hiding-places and treasure-boxes, Benny! I've got a picture of a girl, too, hidden away in my room. Perhaps I'll show it to you one of these days when your father lets you come and see where I live."

Benny came forward very close and leaning against Magnus' knees pressed a cold little hand over the teacher's eyes.

"Keep them shut," he cried, "while I get it . . . *tight* shut, mind . . . on your word and honour!"

The pressure of the eager hand was then removed; and Magnus was left from his contact with the child's clothes with a faint fragrance as of pine-needles. He could hear no sound; and he obediently kept his eyes closed; but he was intensely conscious, as he sat there waiting, of his physical longing for Curly, which embodied itself now in a particular sweetness unlike anything else. He had come to know this vague, delicious feeling well; and whenever it surrounded him he became braver and more adventurous.

"The Brush Home," he thought, "is *somewhere* on the Downs. I've seen it often though I can't recall exactly where. I won't stop today. I'll tell him I'll come another time. I pray she'll wait for me at the Wishing Well."

He was roused from his trance by the renewed pressure of the child's form against him; and that same sense of pine-needles. The touch of the child blended with his craving for the girl and he began to feel that he had exaggerated the dangers of the plunge he was taking into the unknown.

"It's from the Melcombe Circular I cut them out," Benny was explaining to him now, while he unfolded a scrap of paper. "Aren't they nice, Mr. Muir? You see what it says? They're acting in the Regent with Jerry Cobbold. They're dancers; that's why they're showing their legs. They're my greatest secret. So you mustn't tell anyone I've got them. Aren't they nice? They're sisters—Tissty and Tossty! *That's* Tissty and *that's* Tossty. Do you think they'd mind if they knew I had them? No one's ever seen them but you. They're—"

His quick ears had caught his father's step outside the door and he was off in a flash. Magnus got up from his chair and when Cattistock entered he must have been surprised to see teacher and pupil standing on their feet with the width of the floor between them. But he made no comment.

"My brother-in-law's ready for you, Mr. Muir," he remarked, without advancing into the room. "Put your jacket on again, Ben," he added addressing his son. "We'll take your new pet for a stroll presently. If you keep him out of doors enough Lizzie won't mind him."

It was a quarter to one by the mahogany clock in the hall of Peninsular Lodge as Magnus went out with the founder of the Brush Home. He had arranged to meet Curly at half-past twelve at the Well, have a light lunch at the Inn, where they were both well known and accepted as a respectable couple, and then spend the afternoon, if it turned out fine, walking round the prehistoric, grass-covered earth-works called Maiden Castle, whose turfy ramparts rose up on the north of Upwey and were skirted by the Dorchester Road. Since it was Saturday, both he and Curly—who helped in the winter in one of the small village shops—had the whole day at their disposal; and the idea of taking her to Maiden Castle, where, since his childhood, his father had taken *him*, gave him a peculiar satisfaction.

Neither he nor Daniel Brush said very much to each other as they drove along the uplands to the remote place in the heart of The Downs where predecessors of the doctor had erected their sanitarium. The whole expanse of the West Bay could be seen in glimpses between the rounded hills and Magnus noted a change in the weather since he left Brunswick Terrace; for the sun was visible now through the mist, but so softened and blurred that he could gaze at its lemon-coloured orb without any hurt to his eyes. His companion seemed so meek and quiet and courteous, and his own head was so full of optimistic hopes as to what would come of this Cattistock business, that he began to experience, as they drove along, a sensation that he knew well. This was a queer feeling that he had suddenly grown to be of enormous stature, like a giant being borne along that portentous coast-line, with the yellow wintry sun above the Atlantic riding parallel with him. He felt as if he had only to stretch out his hand and clutch this great lemon-coloured orb. He began to rise completely above all those timidities that had so fettered his spirit. He felt strong to cope with his fate, to marry or not marry *as he chose*, and to treat his Father's majestic ghost as an equal, not as a cringing dependent. When, however, they arrived at the group of buildings over which his companion ruled this expansion of his nature was quickly pricked like one of those coloured balloons they sold on the sands at Weymouth.

What was now the Brush Home was hidden away in so out of the world a spot, that very few among what Homer calls "articulately-speaking men" who lived in Weymouth had ever been near it, though most people had heard of it. As its massive structures raised them-raised themselves now before his eyes Magnus could not resist his sick aversion and distaste. Merely to imagine that those red-brick buildings contained animals in the process of being vivisected, and contained also hopelessly insane people whose death would be a comfort and relief to everyone concerned, was something that gave the spot an atmosphere of such horror that he fidgeted in his seat and felt sick in his stomach as if he were going to see an execution.

"But what a thing it is," he thought, "that these Downs should shelter a place so appalling that a normal grown-up person should shiver to approach it!"

"You are looking at my flower-beds?" said Daniel Brush quietly. "Yes, I had ten pounds' worth of bulbs planted on this place this autumn. I'll have in time one of the best gardens for Daffodils east of the Scilly Islands. I have specialized in Daffodils, Mr. Muir, ever since I first had a garden of my own."

But all the gentlemanliness in Magnus deserted him now. He could only sit in that car stupified, confounded, mum. He began to feel like an animal; and he felt that he understood now that shuddering panic-terror which makes the eye of an animal shrink away from the eye of a man. It does not shrink away from that eye's commanding nobility. It shrinks from that eye's cold-blooded rational cruelty.

If Science had chosen a remote valley in the Chalk Downs wherein to build her sanitarium she had chosen one of the most featureless and expressionless of all the valleys in those hills. The place had been so vigorously restored—for the doctor, although he looked much older, was really a younger man than Magnus—that all about it there was a smell of cement and mortar and fresh-cut boardings upon the air. The more solid portions of these additions were of a pale red brick; but what struck the attention of any stranger was the amount of ironwork and glass work that had been used. It was doubtless the presence of all this iron and glass, combined with so much whitewash, that gave to the Institution an air of such sanitary immaculateness that it made the very motes in the afternoon sun seem like disorderly intruders; and the very droppings of the starlings on the galvanized roofs seem like an insurrection of Nature.

When the car stopped at the door of Dr. Brush's private house, which was a neat, trim, sham-Gothic villa surrounded by all the marks of a carefully laid-out garden, it seemed as if the man had actually read Magnus' thoughts, for he showed not the slightest sign of asking him into the house. All he did was to shake him warmly by the hand and say in a friendly voice, "I hope we'll meet again at Peninsular Lodge, Mr. Muir; and I hope I'll have to give you the prize for being a better psychiatrist than I've been with young Benny."

Unwilling that Cattistock's servant—honest and sympathetic though he seemed—should be the witness of his meeting with Curly, Magnus waited till the doctor was well out of sight and then told the man that he did not want to be driven back to Brunswick Terrace.

"Where do 'ee want for to go, Sir? Master told me to drive 'ee home. But may-be, since we're so far on the way, you'd like to go to Dorchester? Dorchester be a lively place on Saturday night."

"No, no," said Magnus. "I'll tell you where I want to go. I want you to leave me at the Old Church in Upwey. I've got . . . to see someone there . . . and if you'll just take me . . . to the gate . . ."

Do what he could, he couldn't say this simple thing in a natural way; and this very inability caused an unpleasant sensation to rush to his cheek-bones.

"Upwey Church? Surely, Mister! I'll have 'ee along o' there in less than an hour; if me old car doesn't turn nasty on me."

They were scarcely out of sight of these modernized buildings, when Magnus, who had taken his seat by the chauffeur's side after the doctor's back was turned, enquired of the man what he himself thought of the Brush Sanitarium.

"Would *you* sooner be sent there," he asked him, "rather than to the ordinary County Asylum?"

The man's brown eyes gleamed at him in a look full of subtle intelligence.

"Round about here," he said, "amongst such as be simple folk— only ye mustn't let on as I told 'ee so—they calls Doctor's place 'Hell's Museum'. 'Tis their ignorance. But 'tis because of things they hears tell of; and because of catching sight of they lunatics."

Magnus was silent. One of those icy, dark, wedge-like panic-terrors, that seem to visit sedentary people so much more frequently than active people, struck suddenly down into his very vitals. He had seen himself as a patient of Dr. Brush!

"Suppose it *were* my destiny," he thought, "to spend the last twenty years of my life in that place? *Hell's Museum!* Trust our Dorset cottagers to hit the nail on the head! That is the worst of this sort of Science. It feeds a diabolical curiosity. Its passion for pathology is not a passion for healing, but a passion for experiment."

And in his mind, as the car followed the windings of a white Chalk lane through the heart of the Downs, he began to feel how easily he, like poor Sylvanus Cobbold, might develop some anti-social mania that would bring him into trouble with the authorities. He stretched out his body as tight and taut as he could in his cramped quarters, as if by this physical movement to shake away the thought of Hell's Museum, but this irrational dread of being handed over to the Murphys of the Brush Home began to mingle with his nervousness about marrying Curly and presented itself to him as just the very sort of unexpected disaster that he might have predicted would occur, now that by going to Cattistock's he had deliberately broken up his peaceful routine at Miss Le Fleau's.

It had proved to be a rather complicated cross-country route that young Chant had to follow to reach Upwey Church. The valleys in this quarter of the Downs were narrow and winding, and the grassy slopes between them quite inaccessible to motors. It turned out, therefore, that it was a long time after the time Magnus had fixed to meet Curly at the Well, that he finally approached, alone and on his own feet, this legended spot. As he followed the little lane that led to the famous fountain—one of the most popular Wishing Wells in the West of England—his heart began to beat faster. He could see Curly's head vividly in his mind's eye now, with the wavy, flaxen hair crossing her brow, and rippling down by her soft neck, making the delicacy of her skin seem so miraculously transparent. He could see her deep violet-blue eyes with their long dark eyelashes so strangely contrasting with the white shell-like fragility of her cheeks. He began to feel that wave of intoxicating sweetness, as if a cloud of smoke from a bonfire of fragrant leaves had assumed a girl's shape, which always overpowered him when her image excited his senses in a particular way. Magnus concealed somewhere within him an intense and satyrish obsession for Curly's body, an obsession he had never felt before for any feminine form; and with this obsession, that resembled the tantalized craving of the starved senses of a monk, the girl wantonly and deliberately played. Not that Curly Wix was a designing or a cruel young woman; for she was both simple-minded and tender-hearted, but her own senses were left calm and unruffled by Magnus' caresses and it apparently seemed to her the proper, suitable, and traditional method of treating her admirer that she should be always leading him on and never allowing him any sustained satisfaction. It is likely enough that it was this intense vein of satyrishness in him, never aroused by any girl before, that made him feel he *must* marry Curly. He had been full of dreads and fears and alarms from the first hour he had dared to speak to her; but this craving for the way her limbs were moulded and the way her head drooped from her neck, and the way she would sometimes let him, and sometimes refuse to let him, take her on his knee, had been always strong enough to sweep aside these fears. Would she be there still? he thought. Would he find her sitting in that little shelter, as he had seen he do so often, long before he'd had the courage to speak to her?

He didn't even glance at the Well as he came up. For once in their mythical history these waters were totally and utterly ignored by a human consciousness approaching them! The Well was no longer there. Through a space peopled by no Well, but by the rough lintel of a classic arbour and by a laughing Curly, as she jumped up to meet him, he moved hurriedly round the front of the erection— only to find the spot quite deserted! He stood taking breath and looking round with weary hopelessness. Then his eye caught sight of a fragment of white paper pinned to the rustic table where so often last summer—before he dared do anything more than watch her as he sat on the edge of the Well—he had seen her absorbed, or apparently absorbed in her book. He hurriedly unpinned this little missive. It contained the words:

"Tired of waiting! I don't like to go to Public House alone, I shall get some buns at Aunt Phem's and wait for you at Beech-Clump, top-bank, nearest Maiden."

For one beat of a half-second of time, as he crumpled up this paper, the Wishing Well re-filled its place in space; but only for the purpose of reflecting in its sacred waters the image of Curly eating Aunt Phem's buns under those leafless beeches. Not all the wild, desperate, humorous, cynical, furtive, fantastic, scandalous wishes that had been

whispered in the ears of those waters could at that second of time
endow them, for the only consciousness that gave them just then
their human reality, with any other existence than to be the mirror
of Curly, eating buns on "top-bank, nearest Maiden."

He hurried off now, pressing the end of his stick into the soft-
sun-thawed mud at the side of the lane and walking with steps that
had grown almost fierce in their impatience, as he made for the long,
upward-sloping cattle-drove that led, by a couple of miles' winding
detour, to the base of the prehistoric Camp. As soon as he was about
half a mile from his objective, he began an eager attempt to distinguish
his girl's shape against that far-off clump of trees. She would be
wearing, he knew, a certain long grey jacket which she had often
explained to him had been purchased not in Weymouth but at a sale
in Dorchester; and he found it strange that she apparently chose to
remain concealed among those trees rather than to wave to him from
the open hill-side. He knew well that his own approaching form
must have been visible to her for the last ten minutes. Why, then,
did not she stand where he could see her and wave to him? How well
he knew that field-path, up there, leading to the base of Maiden
Castle! How often he had climbed that hill with his father! Yes,
he knew that ridge, that turf-battlemented ridge, now looming up
behind those beech-trees, at every season of the year. Most of all
did he people it with Marble Whites and Skippers, those local coast-
line butterflies, that always seemed to gather about their wings in the
hot summer afternoons, as he caught sight of them fluttering through
the aromatic fragrance of the crushed thyme that would rise from
his steps, the very breath and spaciousness of the blue sky and the
distant sea! But as he stared up impatiently at that ridge now, panting
as he climbed, and praying that Curly would stop concealing herself,
he could not help, even in his eagerness over the girl, recalling a
sensation he always had as he ascended Maiden Castle, a sensation as
if he were voyaging through the immense ether upon a fragment of
Matter that was not shaped as the ordinary heavenly bodies are, but
was just a ribbed and buttressed mass of turf-grown chalk, journeying
through space, under the guidance of a super-mundane pilot, with a
mysterious end in view.

And all this while, like an evil blood-clot upon his brain, the thought kept coming back to him of the vivisection he felt sure went on in one of those buildings of iron and glass and pale brick, where Dr. Brush studied pathology among the inmates of Hell's Museum, and he suddenly began telling himself a story about the spirits of the old tribes who had raised this huge earth-fortress, and now the captive souls from the Brush Home might at least in the liberation of sleep come flocking out through the night to Maiden Castle and be there protected and safe, along with a great ghostly pack of crouching, whimpering, fawning, cringing, torture-released dogs, all crowding close behind these phantom-warriors, as wave after wave of their enemies poured up the slope, trying in vain to repossess themselves of them.

He was never destined to catch a single glimpse of Curly after all his long climb, till he had made his way between the tall trunks of the beeches, among whose smooth pillars the vaporous yellow sunlight wavered from across the Western Bay; and when he finally did get to her, and when at last he held her in his arms, he discovered to his surprise that her cold cheeks were wet with tears.

"What is it, Curly? What is it, my treasure?" and he began pouring out to her a broken and incoherent account of his adventures that day. "Don't 'ee mind, my Sweet!" he kept repeating, as he took breath in the rush of his jumbled story, "don't 'ee mind too much! You know why it was that I snatched at this chance. You *do* know, don't you? It'll mean we shall have enough—not much, but enough —for us to get married."

She was submissive to the ardent embrace in which he held her, and she let him, as they leant against one of those tall tree-trunks, kiss away the tears from her cheeks; but though it was a resigned form that lay against his beating heart, her girl's breasts were cold and lifeless, her girls limbs limp and unresponsive, and her large, darkfringed eyes, in that wintry light, never once looked directly into his. Over the wide landscape her gaze wandered, over the roofs of Upwey, over the valley of Abbotsbury, over that abrupt cleft in the hills, where to the south-east it was just possible to catch a sight of a fragment of the sea reaching away to St. Alban's Head. All her accustomed wantonness and mischief, all her teasing provocations seemed to have been driven out of her by those implacable and decisive words, "not much; but enough for us to get married."

As she had made the long ascent from the village to this spot the girl had set herself to think as she had never thought before in her life. And all the while she was waiting for him she went on thinking. Sitting there under those trees in her grey jacket and grey scarf, hugging her knees with one hand and nibbling her penny bun from the other, her soft shell-like face, with a tremulous shadow thrown across it by her tight-fitting velvet hat, bore an expression of intense, puzzled, troubled, unhappy thinking. Now and then as she watched his dark figure from a mile away, looking like a fly on a thin knife-blade as he followed that chalky cattle-path, she changed her position so as the better to be concealed. At such times she would stand up, and turning her back to the misty yellow sun as it slanted towards her across the West Bay she threw an intensely watchful eye upon a certain strip of the Dorchester Road which at that point was clearly visible. There was a little round pond by the road-hedge just there; and the watery sunlight fell upon this pond, giving it a faint, sad lustre, like the memory of some felicitous occurrence so long since departed as to be almost forgotten.

"I told him it was a piece of silliness," she said in her heart, as she snatched these furtive glimpses of the Dorchester Road. "I told him Mr. Muir and me were as good as married; even if we *have* plighted no troth as yet! O Sip, O my dear, dear love, how could 'ee do such a thing? How could 'ee think to want to trouble my heart by spying on him and me on this day of all days?"

Then Curly would once more retreat to her hiding-place under one of the beeches and once more hug her knees, rumpling up her grey jacket, pressing her grey skirt against her shins, and taking another bite of her bun. And ever and always, like a black fly upon a blade directed towards her heart, this middle-aged stranger who considered himself already married to her, this book-worm with whom she had absolutely nothing in common, kept coming on and on and on!

Well did Curly know that Simon Pym Ballard, or Sippy Ballard, who had found her out and stolen her maidenhead long before Magnus had dared to breathe a word to her, would never, under any conceivable upshot, consent to marry her. To do him justice he made no bones about his reluctance in the matter. From the very start, when he had first swept her off her feet,. he had made it clear that she must expect absolutely nothing from him. Sippy Ballard had his own whimsical way of emphasizing this necessity; and some deep feminine impulse in her made her secretly derive—though she would never have admitted this to herself—a self-lacerating delight in feeling herself to be his slave, his plaything, his chattel, to be used for his pleasure without any return.

She had eaten half her bun now; but with nothing to wash it down, and with her heart so agitated—for it would be just what Sippy would be likely to do, out of pure wickedness, to drive out in that little touring-car, simply to spy upon this meeting; and than mock his rival with her when they were next alone—how could she swallow any more of this dry, sticky stuff? And she threw away the rest, with an impatient fling of her arm. "That's for the birds," she said aloud. But the phrase carried no mental or physical image with it, either of birds or of anything else. All that it carried with it was a passionate desire to tell Magnus right out that she could not possibly marry him. And when he asked her why, simply to say, "Because *my boy*, my clever, naughty, reckless, handsome boy, thinks you're too funny-looking, and too queer, and too fussy, for any girl to put up with!"

"Don't 'ee mind too much, my Treasure," Magnus kept murmuring. "I've never seen your face more beautiful than it looks at this moment. *Little* Curly! Oh, please don't turn your head away! Don't be sad any more! I swear I couldn't help it."

Under that long grey jacket, bought in Dorchester at the sale, and under the short grey skirt, put on especially for this walk, the soft pliant form remained passive and unresisting. But the girl had succeeded, by making a few surreptitious steps between his eager claspings, in regaining a position from which, by looking over his shoulder, she could see that strip of road below. The wintry sunlight had left the water of the little pond now, but the white surface of the road was just the same; empty, but heaving with expectation at each long breath she took while the mocking face of her young seducer swam before her gaze.

By reason of the fact that his words about their marriage and his news about Cattistock had set her whole nature in a turmoil, and by reason, too, that at any second she expected to see Sippy Ballard's car cross that strip of road and to hear his familiar horn, so different from other horns, Curly found herself yielding to the caresses of the teacher more submissively than she had ever done before.

Thrilled by this passivity, which on all previous occasions had been so quickly interrupted by some roguish gesture, and mistaking her silent docility for maidenly consent, Magnus let his embraces—though to say the truth, from the point of view of Mr. Ballard they would have been innocent enough—grow more and more confident. It seemed to him indeed, as his hands moved from one sweet pressure to another, and as his lips played over her cold cheek and warm neck, for she still kept her head turned away, that he had never, in his life before, known what it was to hold an unresisting girl in his arms. His feelings were like those of an escaped monk, who, in his flight from the cloister, finds a friendly country-maid, upon whom he lavishes the pent-up adoration of a life-time. That it should be himself, Magnus Muir, or rather that nameless hidden self, that was the self of all his secretest feelings, who was now actually holding this incredibly lovely being in his hands, seemed to him too exciting to be true. What a miracle! What a mystery! That these soft curves which he pressed under the grey jacket were in very truth a young girl's breasts, such as he was always reading about in his classical poets—Oh, it seemed a thing beyond expectation! That these limbs—what god had moulded them?—a real girl's limbs, warm, alive, and so maddeningly sweet, should be for him to enjoy, even at the double remove of the skirt bought in St. Mary's Street and the jacket bought in Dorchester, was a paradise beyond all belief. And if Curly's body was so ravishing to him, thus protected and thus pressed against him as he leaned against a beech-trunk, what would it be like when she lay in bed with him, lay between him and the wall?

Tirra-lirra! Tirra-lirra! What a queer sound was that coming up from the road? People were always starting new tricks with these noisy motors! Some Saturday folk, probably, going to the Dorchester market.

"Father, Father," his thoughts ran on, as, hugging her close to him still, his eyes wandered to the lowering ridge of Maiden Castle, "this new feeling shall never interfere with *you*, never come between *you* and me, never spoil those things that we have shared and shall always share together."

Tirra-lirra! Tirra-lirra!

"Don't 'ee mind any more, little Curly, my having kept you so long. I couldn't help it! It was only for our marriage-sake I did it."

But the girl's whole being was concentrated now on concealing from him her breathless agitation over her lover's presence down there. She knew perfectly well that it was quite impossible for Sippy to see their two figures up here any more than it had been possible for Mr. Muir to see her while he was climbing the hill. That little pond down there must be, she thought, at least a quarter of a mile away and these beech-trunks made a safe shelter. She could see Sippy only too clearly; but Sippy couldn't possibly see her, and he was waiting now and imagining no doubt, with lively and mischievous intensity, this scene between Magnus and herself! All this while she knew well enough that if she stopped letting the teacher make love to her he might become aware that that car, standing there on the road beside the pond, contained an interested spectator.

Tirra-lirra! Tirra-lirra!

How *could* he go on blowing that horn when he must know that sooner or later it would attract her companion's attention?

"It would be impossible for me," Magnus was thinking, "to feel a greater happiness than I feel now. Why do people make such a talk about consummation, when merely to hold her like this, even in such a thick jacket, is about as great an ecstasy as I could have?"

His eyes kept returning to her shell-transparent face, with its wavy cloud of flaxen hair escaping from beneath the brim of her velvet hat, and it was always with remorse for the long vigil he had given her, up here on this hill, that he caught the agitation in her expression. Holding her like this and attributing her agitation entirely to her anger at his delay, Magnus was suddenly conscious that by some re-shifting of the elements, as the vaporous sun descended into the West Bay, the fragment of that *other* bay, with its far-off glimpse of St. Alban's Head, had taken on a peculiarly enchanted glow.

"I hadn't thought," he said to himself, "that you could see so far from Maiden Castle; and I don't believe you used to be able to. I don't seem to remember Father's pointing it out, and he'd have

surely done that if you *could* see it. There must have been some
clump of trees cut down lately or some embankment levelled, that's
made *that* speck of sea-horizon visible."

Tirra-lirra! Tirra-lirra!

"Everything in my life is reaching a head," he thought, "and everything in my life has been mixed up with the Sea and with Father—
How quiet Curly is. She lets me go on holding her as if she were in a
trance! I expect that's what girls feel when—"

Tirra-lirra! Tirra-lirra!

"What's wrong with that car down there? Why doesn't it go
away? Everything I feel is connected with the Sea and with Father.
And now this ecstasy with this girl is mixed up with the Sea and with
him. Those cowrie shells he used to tell me were used as money
among savages, those shells—what *did* he call them, that were so
transparent and brittle and made of mother-of-pearl?—and those
pieces of *white* seaweed that he used to find in the rock-pools near
Redcliff Bay, and the white sea-horses that he always used to show me,
and say in his peculiar tone, 'It's blowing up for stormy weather
tonight, Magnus, my boy,' it is all these things that I'm feeling now
as I hold Curly like this, and her hair's exactly like that light on the
sea—if it really *is* the sea over there!"

Tirra-lirra! Tirra-lirra!

"Damn that motor-horn. But I know who's got one just like that,
and that's Sippy Ballard. But *he* wouldn't be making a fuss like this if
his car broke down. I wonder if that car *has* broken down and they are
making that noise for someone to come and help them?"

He let Curly go as this thought came into his head; but catching at
her hand now, he clasped it tight in his own, and stood for a while
motionless, staring at that strip of road, at that cold metallic-coloured
little pond, at that open car with one solitary figure in it. It happened
that the sun, although not yet sunk into the Atlantic, was low enough
now to be lost behind a rank of clouds which extended along the whole
western horizon. This sudden loss of the yellow sunlight, that had
been giving its chief element of interest to that neutral winter's day,
had the effect of making it very much more difficult for Magnus—
and even for Curly herself—to detect, at that distance, what was
going on down there, in connection with that blurred and indistinct

object beside that livid, steely-white pond. And something about the dying away of the sunlight, and the immediate chilliness that seemed to rise up from the dead beech-leaves at their feet, brought to Magnus' mind, as he held her hand, a sharp, horribly clear memory of Benny Cattistock's yellow dog and of those other dogs at the Brush Home who had no one to save them from the diabolical cruelty of scientific methods. What was happening to them now, those other dogs? *Was it over for the day*, this that they were daily subjected to, without even that remote chance of escape such as hares and foxes had, who are tormented by sportsmen?

"Science is far crueller than sport," thought Magnus. "I'd far sooner be a Mallard shot by young Ballard when he goes duck-shooting on Lodmoor, than be a dog in the hands of Dr. Brush."

Tirra-lirra! Tirra-lirra!

"Ought I to—ought we to—" he began, "go down the hill, Curly, and see what's wrong? I seem to have been hearing that noise for a long time. Look! There's someone passing. There! They didn't stop! So it *can't* be serious."

He was silent again, pressing the girl's fingers, while Curly prayed in her heart that Sippy would go away.

"If mother didn't get on my nerves to such an extent," she thought, "and if only I *could* go on as we are, I'd tell Mr. Muir"—she still thought of him in her mind as Mr. Muir—"I didn't like him enough to marry him. But, Oh, dear!—the comfort to be out of mother's hands; and so quickly, too! It isn't as if Mr. Muir wasn't nice. He's *very* nice. I do like him a lot . . and if I'm careful and not silly I can go on seeing Sip. In fact it'll be easier to see him when I'm married . . . for mother hates the sight of him. I wish to goodness she'd never found out about him. That's why she's driving me to marry Mr. Muir. She thinks at any moment Sip might get me into trouble. She doesn't know—" And Curly's mind, ashamed in this point, as she was otherwise shameless over her treatment of "Mr. Muir", recalled, with a shock of distaste the contraceptual devices so unblushingly forced upon her by her unscrupulous young lover.

"Because you were hurting me," she replied sharply, when Magnus asked her why she suddenly pulled her fingers away.

"I didn't mean—Curly, my Precious—I didn't know that I—I

was thinking of the days long ago when I used to come here with my father."

Tirra-lirra! Tirra-lirra!

It was then, as he tried to take her hand again, and she refused it to him, that he caught a look on her face which, for all his simplicity in dealing with women, it was hard to mistake—a look of intense nervous irritation.

"I'm sorry, Curly", he murmured. "I forgot we could be seen from the road. Come on! Let's go back now."

But as she followed him down the hill she wondered if she *would* be able to see as much of Sip when she was married to this solemn, fussy man. And Magnus said to himself, as they began their long walk home, that men who can be thrillingly happy with their girls for more than a couple of hours are men who don't worry about what these lovely beings have in their heads, or about what goes on in such places as the Brush Home.

Tirra-lirra! sounded triumphantly from the Dorchester Road.

"That car can go all right now, Curly," he remarked.

"They generally can," murmured Curly Wix with a sigh.

5

LODMOOR

THE important highway that stretched out of Weymouth to the east of Brunswick Terrace, and to the east of that great stone edifice known as High House, a highway that was called by the modest appellation of Preston Road—Preston being the first little hamlet it reached—began its long and stately approach to Winfrith and Wareham and Corfe Castle and Poole by skirting the edge of a wide expanse of salt marshes that had acquired the name of Lodmoor. All visitors to Weymouth remembered Lodmoor as a curious and arresting phenomenon amid their other impressions. Perhaps they did not give it much attention at the time; for the Preston Road is bounded on its southern flank by a picturesque, grey sea-wall and by the pebbly shore; but later it returned to their mind with what Thomas Hardy would call a taciturn congruity, and they then remembered how notably across its level expanse, if they debouched amid its peat-smelling cattle-paths, could be seen seaward, beyond the low roof of the Coast-Guard Station, the towering façade of the great cliff called the White Nose, and landward, above the grassy undulations of the Downs, the far-seen image of the White Horse.

Mid-way between the last houses of the town—of which High House was one—and the sharp turn to the northward that the road took where the Coast-Guard Station nestled between the cliff-path and the rocky shore, there rose on the edge of the highway and on the edge of Lodmoor a very singular little hovel. A hovel it was, a poor enough shelter from the sea-storms, but it presented to an eye accustomed to the West-Country that peculiar sense of the past which a turn-pike cottage, however forlorn and ramshackle, is wont to convey. The melancholy little erection, with its white-washed walls and its black-tarred roof, over-topped by tall bill-boards bearing weather-stained advertisements, was surrounded on the Lodmoor side by its own private enclosure. At this date this enclosure contained a small vegetable garden and a good-sized strip of grass; enough grass in fact to help considerably in the nourishment of a solitary brown-and-white cow, who even in the winter when the weather was not too stormy grazed peacefully there untroubled by either the screams of the gulls from the shore or the cries of the wildfowl from the marshes.

The inhabitants of Lodmoor Hut at this time were two in number, a woman of thirty who went by the name of Gipsy May, and a half-witted orphan-boy called Larry Zed whom the woman had befriended.

A few mornings after Magnus' visit to Maiden Castle, long before the sun rose, indeed while the marshes were still wrapt in a wet and ghostly mist, Larry Zed was standing in a tumble-down wood-shed that served as a receptacle for hay and was peering forth from this, through a crack in the time-worn boards, into a larger and better-preserved barn, where Blotchy the cow was staring back at him, alert in her clean straw-bed.

"Ye be always awake when I do come, Blotchy," murmured Larry Zed. "Don't 'ee *ever* lay head on straw and sleep dead-sweet, and let the Nothing-Girl take 'ee on lap and give 'ee her titties to suck? Don't 'ee *ever* let the Nothing-Girl love 'ee, like her do love I o' nights? No, no, Blotchy! I bain't talking of Gipsy May. Her be a kind one and a cuddly one, but her bain't all there be, Blotchy. There be a wondrous soft place between the Nothing-Girl's titties where she lets I lie; and maybe she'd let thee lie there too, an' a' didn't horn at her side."

The cow knew perfectly well that Larry was bound ere long to bring her the accustomed armful of hay; so she gave her head a few careless tosses and turning her rump to the crack in the wall set herself to observe the door.

"Voices," she thought, "may come from cracks. Hay comes from doors."

Her prediction was well founded; for presently young Zed pushed aside the great wooden fastener of the cow-shed and brought in the expected bundle. With his entrance a breath of the wet dawn came into the shed, together with a strange, almost mystical fragrance from the wide-stretching salt-marsh mud, as if in the night the silent daughters of the Old Man of the Sea had been sleeping upon it. It was not permitted by Nature that Blotchy should derive more than a very vague and very diffused aesthetic pleasure from the sight of that bare-headed human figure standing in the doorway. And yet with the cold, whitish light about him, with the curious dawn-smell entering with him, with the unique chilliness amid the vapours which suggested the slippery motions of great cold-bodied eels in the wet mud, with the sense in every direction of thousands of inert wintry marsh-plants invisible in the mist, Larry's figure had an almost mythical remoteness. Larry himself certainly derived a vivid sensual pleasure from entering the shed. He drew into his nostrils a delicious fragrance of trodden straw, mingled with a cow's sweet breath and a cow's wholesome dung; and mingled too with emanations of a more bitter savour that proceeded from a small heap of turnips piled up behind some rails and covered with a hurdle.

A few minutes later the boy's slender form might have been seen from the highroad—only the hour was so early that the road was empty—bending over the deep ditch that divided Gipsy May's little enclosure from the rest of the marshes. He was now muttering low curses to himself—chanting them indeed in the form of inverted prayers—so that it came to pass that the first human tones to reach that day's Dawn upon Lodmoor were a boy's imprecations.

"May Sippy Ballard be danged in 's belly-guts! May Sippy Ballard be hanged wi' a hemp rope! May Sippy Ballard bear Joby's girt boils! for being minded to turn me May out of her wone house!"

While thus cursing the new official, who was carrying the rights of Authority where no official had ever before thought of carrying them, Larry began pulling up one by one the eel-lines that he had dropped in that peat-dark water the previous evening. At the end of one of them alone was there any catch; and this turned out to be such a small eel that when he first jerked it out of the water he was tempted to throw it back. But Gipsy May having a customer in Belvedere Crescent, the most fashionable terrace in town, in the shape of a landlady named Mrs. Pengelly, who being at that time in the later months of her pregnancy was covetous of eels' flesh and prepared to pay highly for it, young Zed now took his knife from his pocket and opening it with his thumb-nail, cut off the eel's head. Kneeling on the black mud beside the ditch, while the eyes in the bleeding eel-head stared at the convoluted saraband danced by the eel-body, young Zed proceeded to take from off his hook the half-drowned lob-worm that had betrayed those unglazed fish-eyes; and hesitating a second before throwing it away, to ascertain if it still lived, threw it, *not* into the water but upon the mud at his side; where after a faint quiver it lay motionless, aware—in its obscure worm-consciousness— of an indescribable relief from the removal of that iron barb and for all young Zed could tell deriving only comfort from the white mist which wavered driftingly across that ditch-bank. Young Zed thrust his blood-stained fingers into the stalks of a little brackish plant that grew extensively round him and remained on his knees with his face towards the Coast-Guard Station and the far more distant White Nose. The twisting of that eel's body worried him; and the discovery that the worm which had caught the eel was still alive, after a night on the hook, worried him, too, but these were for him but slight emotions compared with a certain lodged hate and intense loathing to which he now gave full rein.

That particular flesh-covered skeleton in Trigonia House, "hanging out" as he would have called it, "at Mother Monkton's", was at that moment, as it lay with its head on a couple of snow-white pillows, the object of two antipodal currents of human emotion. For while young Zed knelt by the ditch, Curly Wix in Upwey with her bare arms behind her flaxen head and her dark-fringed eyes staring at the dawn through her cottage window, gave herself up to a protracted orgy of erotic yearning, in the course of which this somnolent official, at Mrs. Monkton's, became endowed with the beauty of the seducer of Helen of Troy.

Larry Zed on the contrary, as he knelt by those convulsed eel-coils, with the wet sea-fog in his red hair, projected towards the sleeping official such a deep and concentrated malediction, that it was enough, if wishes could kill, to have ended his career forever.

It must be admitted that the profile of S. P. Ballard as it lay so

peaceful, with the white sheet under its chin, in the front bedroom of
Trigonia House, possessed a certain youthful beauty of its own, with
the breath coming so softly and tenderly between the delicately-
moulded lips, curved, as the saying is, "like Cupid's bow"; for with
the closing of young Ballard's eyelids something treacherous, something foxy and shifty, vanished altogether, while a look of appealing
innocence appeared, resembling the innocence of one of those Floren-
tine angels that we see in the background of so many old Italian
pictures. As the waves came up below Brunswick Terrace that
morning, under the pressure of the high tide, mounting and receding
along the pebbles with hardly a trace of foam, only the faintest sound
of the sea penetrated Sippy Ballard's bedroom. But towards that
sleeping youth, through his half-open window, came these two intense
vibrations of emotion, the invocation of passionate hate from the boy
kneeling by that ditch, and the invocation of self-forgetful devotion
from the flaxen-haired girl in her Upwey bed.

Jumping to his feet Larry Zed now picked up the still twisting
body of the eel and thrust it with some difficulty into his pocket.
Throwing the head into the ditch and leaving the eel-line on the bank
he now set off with rapid steps across Gipsy May's forlorn patch of
withered cabbages, and going round to the back of the house crossed
the highway and scrambled over the sea-wall. Well did he know that
particular crunching and scattering under his feet as he climbed the
bank of pebbles and went down the other side; and it seemed always
to be his destiny to experience this awareness when his mind was
particularly disturbed. But he stopped today on the crest of the
pebbles and gave a deep groan of wonder; for the dawn-mists from the
marshes had broken into troops and squadrons of ghostly figures,
who, as they swept away over the sea, dissolved into thinner and
thinner vapour, until they melted into nothing at all; and it struck
Larry's mind as if he were contemplating a spiritual suicide, as if some
phantom Jesus, followed by all his disciples, had decided to perish in
the waves.

But scarcely had these vapour-ghosts vanished from before him than
a deep, narrow, crimson streak—as if it had been a bloody scar in an
ashen-grey forehead—appeared just above the horizon; and simultaneously with this blood-line which made him think of the decapitated

eel, the long saurian neck of St. Alban's Head, like some antediluvian sea-serpent, manifested itself on the horizon. And even as he looked at it, this red streak on the sea's rim, that was like a long thin trail of rusty blood that slowly incarnadined as the sun melted it from behind the world, changed its nature, and became crimson, and with it a galaxy of small feathery clouds that had been floating unnoticed in the eastern sky caught this glory and bloomed over the water like a towering cascade of gigantic rose-petals.

Impossible to detect the sliding second of time when the next change came! But as if the boy had been hypnotized into making a leap forward over some time-gulf, he suddenly realized, without catching Nature at her conjuring trick, that the whole eastern sky, and the whole horizon of the sea, too, had lost its crimson and become shining gold. And what was that blinding rondure, curved like a man's head, that now swept up from below the sea's surface, making it impossible for the boy to stare eastward any more; making him blink, and turn his eyes away? It swept up as if it were in pursuit of something, as if it would fain stare at something face to face and deluge it with glory; and Larry had the feeling that what it was glorying over was that same world-snake that it had slain from the other side of the world, drenching the universe in its blood. As he blinked at the sun now, it seemed to him as if it were not a stupendous globe at all, but, on the contrary, a small round hole, like a port-hole in a ship, through which he could see, if he were not driven to turn away his head, into the very furnace-heart of eternity. But Larry *was* driven to turn away his head! He had already stared at that burning orifice—and it had seemed to him of a dazzling levin-blue—a little too long, and as he stumbled down the pebbly slope towards Gipsy May's black-tarred fishing-boat, which he had himself drawn up there and bailed out carefully only yesterday, there seemed to dart forth from his eyes innumerable simulacra of that blue-white hole into heaven; and these blazes kept jumping about, like enormous sand-fleas, over the pebbles, and finally became stationary on the gunwale of the little boat. Pressing the palms of his hands against two of the sturdy wooden pegs that served as rowlocks he leant over and stared at the pebbles on the other side. In this position the livid sun-circles gradually faded away; and Larry was pleased to note that no rain had fallen in the night and the bottom of the small craft was as dry as he had left it.

"She don't need no tarpaulin today", he said to himself. " 'Tis going be one o' they 'pet' days. I best go home-along and tell she her were wrong and I were right; for her made sure 'twould rain afore dawn! No, she be baled out, dry as a life-craft. I bain't a-goin' to fret about she today."

Thus confuting, in one general refutation of feminine errors, both the woman and her boat, Larry gave one more hurried glance at the great luminary in whose rays he and the whole beach were now bathed, and turning his back upon both sun and sea made his way across the road and entered Lodmoor Hut by its front door which now stood wide open to greet the morning. The place had only two rooms downstairs, and only two rooms upstairs; while the staircase, opening out of the parlour, if such it could be called that was everything except scullery, reduced the space in that doll's-house sitting-room to smaller proportions than Blotchy's cow-shed.

"Oh, there 'ee be, Fisherman!" cried Gipsy May. And Larry knew by the use of this appellation, which had for both of them a vague, dim, mystical implication, that the gipsy was in an emotional frame of mind. "Do 'ee mind washing hands at yard-tap? I've a-got the sink pretty full-up looks-so, but all be ready; so don't 'ee linger out there, talking to Blotchy no more."

"I ain't been talking to Blotchy," replied young Zed in a reproachful voice as he went out. "And how can I look sharp when Rowena be fussing so? She smells eel-blood. That's what *she* smells!"

"Rowena, Rowena!" cried Gipsy May; and she made a particular tinkling sound with the metal milk-can that always brought the cat to her side. She was a sacred cat, this great sleek pet, for it had been handed over to May as a tiny little tabby kitten by the famous Romany Princess, Scarletta.

No sooner had the two denizens of Lodmoor Hut sat down at their breakfast-table, which was also their kitchen-table and stood near the shining dresser, than the roving eyes of the red-haired Larry noted that May's fortune-telling cards—both the ordinary cards and the Tarot cards—were lying, all carefully arranged, on a tall wooden chest which was always devoted to these daring shakings of the veil of Isis. Since she had settled down in Lodmoor Hut—roofless and windowless for years and a prey to all the elements—Gipsy May had forsaken her wandering life.

But it was not only to take care of the orphan Larry that she had patched up this ramshackle refuge and stored it with the treasures of her caravan. For though her care of young Zed was a deep impulse of piety, what really had forced her to break with her tribe was her infatuation for Sylvanus Cobbold whose discourses on the sands at Weymouth she had a passion for frequenting. Popular report, indeed, accused her of having carried her mania for Sylvanus so far as to have domiciled herself with him for a time, in his house on Portland, surrendering to him a good deal more than her instinct for roaming. This was before she saved young Zed from the work-house; a deed that was only done—so gossip hinted—when Sylvanus had begun to weary of her passion. Since then her chief concern had been to keep Larry out of the hands of Dr. Brush, who had found him a fascinating case, and indeed had carried him off for a week to Hell's Museum; but nothing short of bolts and bars could prevent the boy from wandering back to Lodmoor, and finally—after the signing of various official documents—the ex-gipsy became his lawful guardian.

The woman's Romany blood was clearly visible at this moment in the bright colours and shining utensils of this kitchen-parlour; and as the two sat opposite each other, eating their bread-and-treacle and drinking their tea, they might almost have been inside a caravan. Two supercilious china dogs, looking as if they had been stolen from the drive-gates of the Earl of Ilchester, and as if nothing short of an Earl, or at least a Baron, would cause them to drop a fraction of their contempt for the generality of mankind, stood at either end of the dresser's lowest shelf, just above the stove, and if two black noses could possibly be tilted in higher disdain, the conversation now going on between the outlaws whose shelf they honoured seemed to give them that extra tilt.

"Be she coming to ask 'ee to go back to he?" enquired Larry, with his mouth full of bread-and-treacle.

Gipsy May tossed her head almost as scornfully as the canine aristocrats above her.

"What do the like o' *she* know of what lies between him and me?

How can ye ask such dimsy questions? Me and Mr. Cobbold understand each other like as we were King and Queen of Spades. This
Marret girl, I be telling 'ee of, be the Punch-and-Judy girl who said
summat to we once, when us were on esplanade, last August. You
was minded to linger and diddle with she, but I dragged 'ee away from
the baggage! Don't 'ee mind thik summer night, Fisherman?"

"Ees, I do mind 'en," replied young Zed. "Her have black hair,
all in twisties and turnies, and her face be chalk-white, like a ghosty's
face. Mar't——that be her name! Oh, I've a-seed her many a time
when thik Cobbold be a-hollerin'; and her were looking at he out of
her chalk face. What have he sent her here for then?"

The woman drew in her breath and then a very curious explanation
burst from her—outlandish syllables, that perhaps reverted to the
camels'-hair tents of far Arabia.

"——izadek, Larry! *He* never sent her! When me and *he* feel like
saying something to each other we comes and sees each other! We
don't send little sand-girls along shore. What are ye starin' at me for,
Larry Zed?"

"I *weren't* starin' at 'ee, May; I were only looking; but your eyes
do glimmy so. And so Mar't bain't bringing naught from he?
Nothing ... nothing ... nothing! She be coming to buy an eel,
present, same as I got for Mrs. Pengelly? Or maybe she be coming to
play ducks-and-drakes with poor Lal? Or, 'perventure, she be coming
to ask 'ee to tell fortune by they girt Egyptian cards!"

Gipsy May's dark eyes opened to their widest extent at this last
word of his. She had often been visited of late by a secret suspicion
that young Zed was in reality "as clever as Sylvanus" and was only
supposed to be out of his wits when dunderheads like Dr. Brush and
Sippy Ballard mistook his cleverness for lunacy. That queer exclama-
tion with such far-drawn lineage broke from her lips again.

"——izadek!" she exclaimed, resting her chin upon the palms of
her hands and propping her elbows on the table, "——izadek! You
bain't a Romany, Larry, be 'ee, unbeknown to your own parents?
How did 'ee guess she were coming here for me to tell her the cards?"

"Be she coming this morning and bringing no word about he? But
if 'tis only for they cards she be coming, May, how is it, that your eyes
be shining so, and your bissom be going up and down?"

Gipsy May stared at him in mounting astonishment. Many women caught off-guard like this by a crazy boy, would have flown into a furious temper; but in the depths of her heart she had profound respect—indeed something like awe—for her youthful protégé; and that Larry should have penetrated, at one bold dive, into the bottomless ocean of her feminine ways, and should have divined—for so she supposed he *had* divined—that it was she herself, with the excuse of the fortune-telling, who had lured Marret into coming to see her, gave her a thrill of that delicious consternation that she used to experience when listening to the oracles of the princess, Scarletta.

"You mind thee wone business, Fisherman!" she answered shortly.

Something, all the same, seemed to have broken down what few barriers did exist between these quaint companions, as they busied themselves about their domestic tasks prior to the appearance of the exciting visitor; for May kept putting all manner of nervous questions to Larry, as to how many times he had seen Marret of late, and whether he thought she was pretty, and whether Sylvanus behaved natural with her, and whether she had a nice voice. No one listening to these snatches of talk, as the two went about their affairs would have thought that the red-haired boy was half-witted; or that the woman was so much older than he was. Once, as she was peeling potatoes, Larry found her fallen into a sort of trance out of the midst of which she begged him to swear by the dear heart of Jesus that he had never talked to Marret alone.

It was nearly eleven o'clock before the figure of the Punch-and-Judy girl was actually seen at the door; and when she *was* seen it was with as great a shock as if they had not been waiting for her all that morning.

"Come in, come in!" cried Gipsy May with nervous eagerness. "Where is Larry? Oh, here he is! You know our Larry, don't you, dearie? Our Larry knows *you* if you don't know him. He's been telling me how pretty you are, and you *are* pretty! Doesn't she look pretty in that nice black dress, Larry? How old are you, dearie, if a gipsy may ask? Ready to hear what the mystic cards have got to tell for a sweet, lovely maid?"

Young Zed's expression when he heard—almost for the first time— this wheedling, professional tone in his friend's voice was of a very

complicated character. He surveyed Marret from head to foot with
fascinated scrutiny; but his green eyes kept glancing sideways at Gipsy
May with nervous concern, as if he doubted what these caressing
words might be leading up to. But although the repetition of these
"dearies" was upsetting to the boy, they seemed to be taken perfectly
for granted by the visitor herself. She permitted herself to be led into
the caravan-like sitting-room and displayed no embarrassment at being
ensconced in the only respectable chair, and placed right under the
up-lifted black noses on the dresser; while the chest, with the two
packs of cards upon it, was pushed to her side.

"The police be worritting Mr. Cobbold again," was the first
sentence that Gipsy May's impulsive greetings permitted her to
finish. "They be after he for holding meeting on esplanade."

"Come in, Larry! Don't 'ee go away. The spirits of the cards
can't see no future doings while none but women-folk be around.
Now sit 'ee snug and cosy, dearie, on Scarletta's chair, while I
shuffles and deals. 'Twas Scarletta herself who always said: 'To make
the cards speak truth there must be a man's thing near 'em!' Sit 'ee
down, Larry! Sit 'ee down on table, if thee must. Hearken, dearie,
now! While I shuffles, dearie, I shuts me eyes tight, and while I
deals, the one we thinks on draws near. Don't 'ee stare at this pretty
girl, Larry, while I shuffles. 'Tis from a far place to the Romany's
tent she've 'a come; and 'tis the heart in her body what brings her the
message from they that know."

Larry did as he was bade and sat on the edge of the well-scoured
table, swinging his legs. Marret, looking terribly white, kept her gaze
fixed intently on her rival's face. Gipsy May closed her eyes; and
standing over the chest began shuffling the cards. There was a
profound silence in Lodmoor Hut while this went on. Retaining her
impassive expression, as if her thoughts were far away from the whole
transaction, Marret kept saying to herself: "It's because she be so
tricksy that he got so tired of she."

Young Zed, still swinging his legs, as he sat on the well-scoured
deal table, holding the edge of it tightly with both hands, watched the
rivals with absorbed interest, pondering on the difference between
them. For from these two feminine bodies, as they thus leaned
towards each other, there emanated a wordless hostility, below and

beyond their peaceable attitude and their quiet expectation. And the wayward spirit of the red-haired boy flung itself into the unknown consciousness of the absent Sylvanus, wondering which of them the preacher would be looking at if he were here. That shuffling of the Tarot cards—for the Gipsy had arrived now at the more portentous pack—seemed to him like one of those inanimate accompaniments that had so often been the background of his own emotional dilemmas. Yes, it was like the waving of the willow-branch that hung over his eel-catching pool. It was like the lifting and falling of the tarpaulin cover of their boat on the beach, when the wind blew under it. In his wanton fancy he wondered whether the grizzled head of Sylvanus had really rested upon both these bosoms; the elder woman's almost as girlish as the younger's and both stirring with each excited breath they took. He was not quite sure that he wanted to snuggle down upon either of these, himself, when darkness covered Lodmoor Hut; and yet he kept glancing at Marret and wondering.

"Me Nothing-Girl be best for I", he sighed.

It was not long before the Tarot cards began to cover the surface of that old chest with their upturned images of fantastic doom; and the sunlight streaming through the small-paned window fell on the copper pans, and on the bright-coloured mats, and on the supercilious dogs—who seemed to snuff at the whole business, as if they were saying to each other: "This must be the Heraldry of Rogues!"—and on the shining black of the Gipsy's towelled hair, as the cards trembled in her hands. Marret, her cheeks white as milk, and her pale grey eyes fixed, not on the cards but on the other woman's face, sat with her back to the window.

"She believes in it!" thought Larry in a mood of pitying wonder; for like so many other half-initiates in a famous mystery, his own attitude to fortune-telling had long been one of sceptical indifference.

There were only two cards left now in May's fingers; and it was with a gesture of unconscious ritual, handed down to her very likely from a date when the body of Agamemnon lay still unavenged in its golden tomb at Mycenae that she now opened her eyes wide, surveying that old sea-chest, strewn with ominous hieroglyphics, and the time-worn unrevealing backs of the two cards she held out at arms' length. The silence in that little room now became so intense, that young

Zed stopped swinging his legs. He began to feel that the very sun-motes in the thick golden light which streamed down over Marret's dark shoulders and fell upon those occult symbols were as they flickered there a sacrilegious interruption of that moment's indrawn breath! Rowena, trained in a caravan, surveyed from her seat in front of the stove her young mistress' outstretched arms and oracular gesture with the sleek and gnomic look of a centuries-old confederate in such matters; and if it had not been that Blotchy, tethered on a patch of wretched bent-grass at the back of the wood-shed, considered the silence within the hut to be propitious to her own purpose, there would have been a perfect psychic dénouement. But Blotchy's plaintive appeal that she might be moved to another spot broke the spell completely. And it did worse than break the spell. For those three persons, or four persons, if Rowena were included, thus aroused from their trance, acted as if the cow had been possessed by a demon. Gipsy May flung down one of her cards with a careless movement as if Blotchy's protest had taken the heart out of the whole transaction.

"Goodness!" she cried: "*The Man with Three Staves!*"

Larry jumped from the table and standing beside her threw his arm round her waist. While he did so he was aware that Marret, who had been sitting up very straight in Scarletta's arm-chair leaned forward over the table, causing a couple of the enigmatic Tarot cards to flutter to the floor. This accident, combined with the boy's touch, seemed to increase the gipsy's irritation. She flung the last card down so angrily that it, too, in place of falling on the chest, fell to the ground. It fell close to Marret's feet; who at once stooped down and began fumbling for it. But either the Punch-and-Judy girl was too short-sighted to find it, or the golden stream of sunshine was so localized that it dazzled and confused her, for there was quite a perceptible moment of delay before she lifted up her low-bent head and laid a card on the table.

Had Larry Zed been forced to tell upon his oath exactly what happened after that, he would have found it extremely hard. His first impression was that both the women, the moment they perceived *what the card was*, made a violent scattering of all the rest; so that the one in question, along with quite a few more, slid down beneath the table. His second impression, however, was that it was Marret who forcibly intervened to prevent Gipsy May—the moment that *she* saw what the card was—from mixing them all up and tossing them on the ground. At any rate the immediate issue was that Gipsy May, her dark eyes roving about the room as if the walls had been wind-tossed bushes of Tinkleton Heath, began fiercely accusing Marret of spoiling the whole event and of trying to cheat the Destinies.

"You saw what it was! You saw what it was!" she shouted; and Larry, who knew her so well, could see by a certain muscular contraction in her shoulders—like the quiver in a cat's body before it springs—that she was beside herself with anger. But it was characteristic of this singular woman, whose emotions never expressed themselves in the expected way, that she suddenly fell to abusing Sylvanus himself. "What does 'S. C.' mean," she cried—she habitually spoke of the man by his initials—" by aggravating the police? Why can't he go *his* way and let them go *theirs?* Don't talk about him; don't talk about him! He's just a fool, S. C. is. He's just a great fool!"

Larry could not help feeling a spasm of admiration for Marret, so calmly did she bear herself under the other's outburst. She did indeed draw back to one side of that queer-shaped chair, and her pale eyes seemed almost as dark as the gipsy's compared with the whiteness of her cheeks; but once fully at bay she folded her thin arms in their tight black sleeves, pressed them against her thin bosom, and holding her head high began her defiance.

"I *couldn't* see what it was! How can 'ee be so silly? I don't know one of they crazy cards from another. These bain't natural cards. These be devil's cards. If I *did* see a gallows on oon it weren't spyin', were it, for 'ee dropped 'em on floor? And there be other gallowses in world, beyon' they silly pictures."

Larry saw Gipsy May's right elbow give an ominous twitch.

"Don't 'ee, May, me precious darlin', don't 'ee," he gasped.

But at that point a new diversion offered itself in the movements of the big tabby-cat.

"Looksee!" cried Larry, "Looksee! Look at that girt cat!"

In truth, inspired by some occult contrariety, Rowena had actually jumped, at this agitating crisis, upon the lap of the Punch-and-Judy girl; and here she was curled up in her calmest and most inscrutable attitude, loudly purring. Larry Zed contemplated this scene, from behind his friend, in dumb amazement. The white-cheeked girl was bending over the cat now and stroking it; and it was borne in upon the mind of the boy how unaccountable both cats and women can be, in their ambiguous moves towards their desired ends. Suddenly the gipsy made a step forward towards the chair.

" 'Twas . . *the* . . *Hanged* . . *Man* . . that . . were . . thik . . last . . card," she gasped out, in a low, solemn voice, as if the mere mention of this formidable symbol were a sacrilege. "And you knowed it were! Didn't you hear her say, Larry, that there were other gallowses than what be in my cards? She were talking of thik wold Punch, and of his being hanged for Judy. Hanged for Judy!—when all the time it were *the Hanged Man* of me girt Egyptian cards what fell down . . . 'Tweren't no mommet in no doll's-house theayter what fell down . . . 'twas the . . . Hanged . . . Man!"

Larry was ashamed of his friend. Unbalanced as he was in his own poor wits, he felt that all this fuss about a card was silly and childish. He was relieved when the gipsy suddenly went over to the side of the room and still muttering something about S.C., began to turn the handle of a music-box. Rowena meanwhile remained on Marret's lap, in the dead Scarletta's chair, completely unmoved by the thin, faint, elfin notes that her mistress was grinding out. Larry noticed how quiet Marret herself was, too, just mechanically stroking the cat with one hand, while the other lay inert, as if there were no life in it. The music-box continued its wistful tinkling.

"How black her eyelashes are!" he thought. "Is she pretending to be asleep?"

Marret's eyelashes did, indeed, as they drooped against her ghastly cheeks, resemble those "earth-forgetting eyelids" that are beyond awakening; but this apparent phenomenon was a complete illusion. Her eyes were open all the time. She was looking down at Rowena and thinking hard.

"Aren't you going to say *anything?*" cried Gipsy May, putting an end to the music. But since Marret still remained mute, she now began restlessly pulling her hair-pins out of her hair. Zed was so used to these spasmodic outbursts of what could hardly be called vanity, that he only sighed when he saw her stand before their one little mirror and deliberately take down her dark tresses and then with equal deliberateness gather them up again and replace the hair-pins.

"Jerry Cobbold be joined with the world against him," were the words that finally fell from Marret's lips.

"It's that woman," murmured the gipsy. And suddenly to Larry's surprise she took her professional tone again. "I've gone to the Egyptian cards about she, dearie. Nor me, nor you, nor none other girl what loves he, need worrit ourselves about that woman. If ever a person were marked and sealed by the discerners of spirits, 'tis Lucinda Poxwell. How she ever got Jerry to marry she is past surmising. But Jerry'll live; and you mark the gipsy's words, dearie, to marry that little Tossty girl he be so crazy on."

"Yes, 'tis Tossty," replied Marret while Larry sank back against the table, yawning gratefully. "My dad declares all the theayter people say 'tis Tossty he do favour; though whenever I've a seed 'ee 'tis Tissty he were courtin'."

"Well, a man like Jerry, and his brother, too, I fancy," said Gipsy May, fixing a glance of triumphant malignity upon the white face below her, "as long as they have *some* girl to pass the time with don't worry much whether it be Tissty or Tossty. They wants a girl and that's all."

"My dad declares that Tossty forced herself on Jerry whether or no. The theayter people dad goes with say she won't *let* Jerry sleep alone. Dad says if he were him he'd roll her on floor! Dad says Jerry never could bide a dancing-girl till Tossty took up with him whether or no."

Moved by one of her unaccountable impulses Gipsy May opened a drawer of the dresser and, heedless of the supercilious dogs above her, extracted a crimson velvet band, which she now proceeded to tie round her head. There was a triumphant light in her dark eyes as she turned upon Marret now.

"Me and 'S. C.'," she brought out, "never tell no one what us'll do when the world turns against we and they police locks we up. No, us never talks of thik things; but if He were took I'd 'a know of it, and not by the cards neither; and if I were took He would know of it! He may amuse himself with all the little shore-girls he likes, but if he were took 'twould be his Gipsy May he'd send for, same as if I were took 'twould be He I'd send for—yes I would!—sooner nor even poor Larry here."

"Mr. Cobbold says Summat New be come into world," remarked Marret, slowly and solemnly, as if she were repeating a lesson, "and He do say this Summat be the Holy Ghost!"

Gipsy May's face had never looked more proud and scornful.

"Such sayings," she cried haughtily, "are what all and sundry do hear from He, when 'a be preaching on beach; and such sayings are what He do throw out to all they little shore-girls what run after He. But I'd scorn to tell a living soul—no! not even Larry here!—what His real secrets be. There be no Holy Ghost in 'em, Marret, me Dearie. But Him and I thinks best to tell to little gals what little gals can best understand!"

" 'Tisn't fitting nor right," Marret countered, without a tremor in her voice, "to play with they Devil-Cards about he. They cards can tell of Hangings and Buryings for them as hasn't talked and walked with God, but when—"

"I do mind what 'ee be thinking, milk-face!" the gipsy interrupted bitter and low, bending down above the figure in the chair. "Ye be thinking *The Hanged Man* was the last card. Ye be thinking"—here she lowered her voice to an intense whisper—"that 'tis of Him thik card did speak. But it isn't; it was for others it were meant."

Marret was silent, lowering her eyelids again and continued obstinately stroking the cat, while her left hand—more expressive perhaps of her feelings during the whole episode than anything else—lay inert, passive, helpless, dead, upon the edge of her lap.

"Why don't you say something, dearie?" the gipsy now asked her in that queer wheedling tone that sounded so unnatural to Larry's ears.

Marret's inert hand suddenly moved, and to the accompaniment of a pitiful mooing from Blotchy which had now become incessant in the rear of the hut the Punch-and-Judy girl looked straight at her rival and uttered, in a low, toneless, neutral voice, words that fell from her as if she, this time, were dealing portentous cards:

"He says he would like to see you again. He told me to tell you that. He said, 'Tell her I want to talk to her before I go to prison.' He meant—" she cleared her throat and lifting up the cat placed her deliberately and carefully on the floor—"that the police were going to take him if he went on speaking on the esplanade."

Gipsy May became, in a second, deadly calm.

"He .. sent ... *you*," she whispered hoarsely, "to call me to him? I wouldn't come to him because *you* asked me—no, not if he were going—" her voice quivered in a sort of muted chant—"going to be hanged by the neck ... like the man on my Egyptian card!"

Something in the tone of her mistress at this juncture led Rowena to approach the agitated woman and rub her warm sleek body against her legs; but even while the gipsy stooped, in half-conscious response to this appeal, the cat raised her head and turned towards the door of the hut. Yes! Someone had stopped outside. The engine of a car could be heard in the silence. Then it ceased; and as May and the boy looked at each other there came a sharp knocking.

While Larry and May had been excitedly awaiting the appearance of the Punch-and-Judy girl, the self-contained author of the "Philosophy of Representation" had been mounting the high, broad staircase leading to the upper rooms of High House. He mounted these steps with a firm, intent, and yet abstracted resolution.

Mr. Gaul rarely paid such a morning visit, even to his oldest Weymouth friends; but he had had an interview the night before with Magnus Muir which had considerably disturbed him. So disturbed, indeed, had he been by this conversation that he had found the usual serenity of his intelligence totally upset; and being quite unable to go on with his work he had decided to follow a hint of his landlady— whose curiosity was intense with regard to Mrs. Cobbold's companion—and make use of his ruined work-time in what might be called the interest of the gregarious appetite of Trigonia House. It is, however, a pity that the astute Mrs. Monkton, and indeed Mr. Ballard, too, could not have been witnesses of the encounter between the ambassador from Brunswick Terrace and the employer of the new companion; for *they* would have found many more interesting revelations in Lucinda's manner and words than a philosophical recluse had the wit to discover.

"It's all very well to be homesick and that sort of thing," he was now privileged to hear his hostess say, "but to turn away from me altogether, and to sit without a word at the writing-table, as if I were some kind of a criminal—it's what nobody could tolerate."

"Where is Jerry?" enquired the visitor.

"Out," she said laconically. "Always out, when there's trouble brewing! But as a matter of fact Jerry's got his own worries just now. They've sent for him to the Police Station about that brother of his. Jerry is really angry at last . . . done with that man for good, I hope! If he hadn't the patience of an angel and if *I* hadn't the patience of—I don't know what—we'd have let them shut him up long ago. Jerry says he's mad; but *I* don't believe it. *I* say he only does it to annoy Jerry and me, and make our life here difficult with everybody. I told Jerry I'd never forgive him if he 'went voucher' again or whatever they call it, for him. And I wouldn't, either! I've had enough of the man and all this fuss about him. The sooner he's put away the better. How can we be responsible for him I should like to know, when he delights, yes, positively delights, in making us a laughing-stock to the whole town? I told Jerry to tell them plainly—and I think he will—that this is the end. The sooner they arrest him and put him in an institution the better. If Jerry doesn't like the idea of the County Asylum they could send him to Dr. Brush. The expense will come on us of course. But I'm used to that. If it isn't one thing, it's—"

She stopped abruptly, hearing some sound that altogether escaped the abstracted senses of Mr. Gaul. She stood with her eyebrows lifted a little, staring at the door; and Mr. Gaul, as he clutched his hat and stick, for it was against his principles to leave such important adjuncts of his personality in other people's halls, was obscurely reminded—for his scholarship was vague—of Clytemnestra waiting for some signal-fire on some promontory. She was dressed in dark green and looked younger, but at the same time more enigmatic, than when in evening attire, with the circlet round her head. It was perhaps the height of her forehead and the blue-black glossiness of her hair that led her visitor to think of Clytemnestra, but the real enigma, to a more psychological person than Richard, would have been how a person, so occupied as it seemed, with ignoble anxieties, could be wrestling all the while with some dark and terrible fatality.

Blundering now in a way no one else in Weymouth would have done, Mr. Gaul, who must have known better, but who was attracted, as less wise men have often been, by the proximity of the precipice, enquired point-blank how Captain Poxwell was. Two little spots of colour came into the woman's cheeks, as she answered, with a smile like that of a waxwork figure on a pedestal, that her father's health was better than usual.

"It is a pity," she added, "that he is so opposed to my sister's second marriage. Jerry and I both think it would be such a good thing; and so nice for Daisy to have the little Cattistock boy to play with."

Mr. Gaul gave these words a far too literal attention; for Lucinda, swallowed up as she was in her own secrets, was able to speak of Daisy as being the same age as Benny, because both children were totally unreal to her—just names for phantom forms, more negligible than figures painted on a theatrical proscenium when the curtain has lifted.

"I believe," the indiscreet sage found himself blurting out, "I believe that Mr. Cattistock is thinking of finding a tutor for Benny."

Now Mr. Gaul knew perfectly well that he had no right to betray their friend Magnus; and yet he also knew that it was important to help this daughter to forget his unlucky mention of her father. Such were the convoluted responsibilities of human conversation. But he had done the harm; for while she waved him, hat and stick and all, to the nearest chair, she herself remained stationary, slowly rubbing, with the tip of one of her fingers, a large opal she wore on her bosom, and staring blankly into vacancy. And her mind, as if it were a vulture carrying of a reeking morsel of carrion to devour at leisure, pounced on a certain scene in her fatal past and dug sharp, spiritual talons into it, with a self-tormenting ferocity. She saw that detested vein-cord in the long neck of her father, that withered, energetic, super-masculine whip-cord vein, that she so particularly loathed! She saw his restless, electric eye, gleaming with that especial kind of fanatic concentration that always bit into her like a tooth; but she saw these things when she—not he—was the dominator. She saw them paralyzed, that neck-vein, that electric eye, under the corroding spell of what she did. As her fingers went on polishing that opal, and her great head drooped forward a little, she saw the red coals in that familiar room, that room Captain Poxwell called the Cabin, and she saw, Oh, so distinctly! the big lacquer tray he kept there, strewn with shells from the rock-pools below Sandsfoot Castle. She saw those curious little shells they call cowries, that he had such a mania for, and she saw a feeble blue-bottle fly hovering round these shells, longing to settle on them, but repelled by their bitter sea-smell. The red light

from those coals was the only light in that room. Strange that her
senses should have been so intensely acute—Oh, she was the daughter
of that brain-sick maleness! She was the daughter of that loathely
whip-cord neck!—to remember after all these years the look of that
fly. Yes, it went on buzzing and flying heavily—it was a feeble,
half-dead fly—all those long hours that dripped, like the rain dripped,
outside the window that night . . . plud-plop, plop-plud, plud-plop,
plop-plud . . . and it flew into the darkness and out of the darkness;
and that was what her thoughts were always doing. It was not only
because he had that whip-cord in his neck, not only because he had that
maleness, that brain-sick maleness in his eyes, that she had bled him,
humiliated him, taken his wits into her fingers and stretched them
taut; it was because the house, the road, the old castle, the rock-pools,
the rain, the waves, the light-ship, the break-water, had turned into a
great, mounting, moaning, pushing darkness that was thick, majestic,
irresistible! In and out of that darkness flew that blue-bottle fly
weak with the sea-smell of cowrie shells; and in and out of that
darkness flew her mind. Shells were curious things. Her sister—Mrs.
Cattistock to be—couldn't understand a man collecting shells and
sticking them on little boxes. But she could understand perfectly!
When you held cowrie shells in your hands you could go in and out
of that majestic darkness, that darkness that was like the sea standing
up straight, and not get weak, like that fly. He brought everything
on himself—everything! He ought to have bled that whip-cord vein
and not tormented her with an eye like the light-ship. What he
wanted to do to her and dare not, she did to him. But she was always
his victim. He could have stopped that light-ship's winking if he'd
wanted to. He knew perfectly well what he was doing when he let
her draw him out. He could get well tomorrow if he wanted to. He
thought it tortured her to know about his sticking cowrie shells on
little boxes. But between them the account was absolutely clear.
Everyone she talked to knew how clear it was! This fool of a Wane
girl was too selfish to listen. Everyone who really listened could see
her side; could see that he was much happier torturing her with his
little boxes, than she was, living with a man who wouldn't even sleep
with her, and who was known to be the slave of that bitch who called
herself Tossty.

"You'll tell Jerry that I was sorry to find him out," remarked the visitor at this point.

"Find him out?" she echoed. "Find him out? I beg your pardon, Find Jerry out? Oh, yes; oh, of course!"

She moved a step towards the table and began toying with the waxen petals of a bunch of gardenias that stood there in a green vase. Suddenly she swung round and faced him with a stupefying irrelevant question.

"Have you seen this new act at the Regent's, Dick? I hear it's quite a popular success; and I'd like to know from a man's point of view—a man less prejudiced than Jerry—what there really is in this Tossty's performance. I've only seen them play together, those two, and to tell you the truth I greatly preferred Tissty. Of course, they're neither of them—"

It seemed impossible for Mr. Gaul to take off his spectacles quickly enough. The blurred outlines of a confused vision presented themselves to him as his best escape from such an equivocal topic. But now when he looked at Lucinda standing by those gardenias, her smooth, white forehead, so eminently intellectual and spiritual, that forehead upon which when she was confirmed at Salisbury the great Bishop of South Wessex had laid so unusually a sympathetic hand, appeared to him one of the most shameless objects he had ever beheld!

"Tissty, anyway," went on Lucinda, still standing by the vase of gardenias, "is much the prettier of the two; and if either of them has a spark of talent she's the one who has it. *This* woman seems . . . don't you think so yourself, Dick . . . simply what the old Weymouth papers would have called 'a fetching piece'. She ogles the gallery. She flirts with the pit. But if you're going to talk of dancing or of acting— but of course, Jerry's head's turned, just as the crowd's. Jerry never did have any taste in his women."

"Not even when—" Mr. Gaul was chivalrous enough to respond with a quaint, stiff, little bow over the hat he held on his knees.

"Least of all then," laughed the lady, giving her shoulders a satirical shrug in a foreign manner. "But the unfortunate thing about Jerry is—"

She was interrupted by the appearance of Perdita who came into the room dressed to go out and began speaking at once, even while she was in the act of opening the door, in that particular tone of strained but calm desperation to which nervous people work themselves up as a result of a protracted mental struggle.

"You won't mind, Mrs. Cobbold, if I—" but catching sight of Richard, she stopped abruptly.

Lucinda transformed herself in a second from a personage who could be confused with Clytemnestra into a gracious and charming hostess introducing a young man to a young woman.

Mr. Gaul thought to himself, as he shook hands with Perdita—

"I must devote a special chapter, when I come to what with us today represents monasticism, to show how it came about that the old monks thought of women in connection with the devil. I believe there's a deep metaphysical secret here—only it needs working out. How Lucinda has changed from what she was when we were alone! And they're always changing like that. Little Miss Monkton does it, just the same as her mother. Daisy Lily does it, the same as *her* mother. I can see it's going to drive poor old Magnus out of his senses over his Miss Wix. It's *change* that they represent. Those writers are wrong who say they're the conservative force in life. Every woman is always creating Something out of Nothing. Parthenogenesis is their natural condition! We try to discover the laws of nature and then follow them; but women instinctively resist all law. They're what Goethe makes the devil say *he* is. They're the eternal daughters of Chaos."

While these thoughts flitted through the philosopher's skull, Lucinda had been introducing him to Perdita as warmly as if the girl were her own daughter; even carrying her cajolery so far as to touch Perdita's small wrist, in its tight black sleeve and lace cuff, with a caressing hand.

"But you're going out, my dear?" she remarked tentatively, as if she had nothing in the world to do but to humour the whims of pretty companions.

Perdita having allowed the young man to take her hand, and having given him a quick, searching glance, recovered herself sufficiently so as to be able to murmur, in a less tense manner, that she was anxious to find a chemist's shop.

"Why, what could be better?" declared Lucinda brightly. "Mr.

Gaul's just the person to help us. You'll do that for me, won't you, Dick? The one in the Dorchester Road is the one *I* always go to. But I daresay you'd like to show Miss Wane some of our other shops. She's seen positively *nothing* of the town. Take her as far as St. Mary's Street, if you're free this morning. Why not?"

It transpired, therefore—though Perdita displayed only the barest civility to the young man—that their forms might presently have been seen crossing the street between Queen Victoria's statue and St. John's church, directing their steps towards a chemist's window, in which stood—for it was a long-established pharmacist's—two of the biggest glass vessels, the one containing green liquid and the other purple, that the girl had ever seen. All these various objects as she took them in, became the mere stage-setting of her miserable mood, the heraldic "supporters", as it might be said, of her engrossing wretchedness. Her unhappiness took possession of the tall church spire, whose grey pretentiousness had become such a notable landmark and seamark for miles around; took possession of the embronzed imperial lady; took possession of those two jewel-like symbols of the wonders of chemistry; and made them carry her down a long diminishing perspective of frantic decisions.

"I won't stand it," she said to herself, "a day longer; and I won't go back to Guernsey either. I'll leave that place and get another job here. I wonder if this man—"

They were outside the shop now and she turned round towards him.

"Don't go away, please, Mr. Gaul! I've got something I want very much to ask you."

Mr. Gaul took off his spectacles and made a movement with them as if transcribing some sympathetic word on the air.

"I'll wait for you here," he said, and planted himself in front of the plate-glass window. While he waited he tried to make an orderly arrangement of his somewhat scattered thoughts. "She's unhappy," he concluded. "She's unhappy with Lucinda. I must give her some practical advice."

That he found it difficult to determine what precise form this sagacious assistance was to take was proved by a vague movement of the hand which still held his spectacles towards those brilliantly coloured objects that shone so purple and so green behind the glass.

Aware that he could now obscurely see the slender, dark figure within, standing alone at the counter, he hurriedly turned round to gaze at the back view of Brunswick Terrace.

"I can't talk to her in the town," he thought. "I must take her for a walk."

Mr. Gaul concealed in the secret depths of his guileless mind no small conceit of himself as a practical confessor to unhappy young ladies. He had often told himself a story about the competent manner in which he would act if he found a life-weary street-girl alone at night on an unfrequented part of the beach. Miss Wane was not a street-girl, but she was evidently very unhappy... Having purchased a small bottle of Eau-de-Cologne, for the more troubled she was in her mind the more extravagantly she always used this fragrance, Perdita paused for a moment before leaving the shop, to collect *her* thoughts, which were certainly a great deal more disturbed than Mr. Gaul's.

"It's not her being *mad* that's the worst," she pondered now, as she read, and yet read not, the chemical abbreviations on the glass jars on the shelves, "and it's not her forcing herself into my room, in that awful dressing-gown, and keeping me awake every night. I think she is a bit mad; but not in the sort of way . . . in the sort of way . . ." and Perdita, as she inhaled the health-giving odours of a cheerful row of various kinds of soap tried to define to herself in what sort of way Mrs. Cobbold's aberration might conceivably have appealed to her. "The truth is," her thoughts ran on, for she was deliberately prolonging her sanctuary among all these nepenthes and opiates and palliatives for human distress, "the truth is, there's something about the woman that's deeply and frighteningly *evil*; not merely evil in anything she's done, for I can't make out whether she *has* done anything; but in her attitude to herself all the way through. There's a *falseness* in her; not merely a theatrical pretending. For a thing like that would never have scared me so; but the falseness that the most frightening kind of criminal has: something different from humanity; and yet not in the least animal."

A little less humiliated by her failure at High House now that she had given her reaction a name and analysed her discomfort, she moved to the door of the shop.

"*So* sorry for keeping you, Mr. Gaul!" she murmured as she came out, "but there's something I did want to ask you . . . if I might . . .

could we find a seat somewhere for a moment . . . in that church perhaps?"

The idea of this foreigner suggesting St. John's church—whether it was locked up or not at the moment he could not tell—as a suitable place for secular conversation tickled Mr. Gaul's fancy; but it made him all the more resolute to take the girl for a proper walk; and it was then that the idea of Lodmoor—which was indeed, unless he took her across the harbour to the Nothe, the nearest place where they could be alone—became a definite decision. He looked at Perdita, while his round face was illuminated by this happy solution of their dilemma.

"I'll show you Lodmoor," he declared, with as much solemnity as if he had said, "I'll show you the grave of Caractacus."

"I'd like to see it," she said gratefully; while the sympathetic gravity of his countenance made her feel so much confidence in him that she did not even bother herself to wonder what sort of a natural phenomenon this "Lodmoor" might be.

"He's nice," she thought. "He's really nice. He may be able to help me."

Thus was it arranged by whatever invisible forces embody themselves in what we call chance, that before so many minutes had elapsed from their leaving the entrance of High House, Perdita Wane and Richard Gaul were once more overlooked by that imposing stone erection. But this time they continued on their way past it; and were soon upon the long level road stretching between Lodmoor and the sea-wall.

"You couldn't have known—no one *could* from a letter or two—what you'd find at the Cobbolds'."

It was when they were walking together by the edge of the low grey wall that he hazarded this bold remark.

"I think," said Perdita, after a moment's hesitation, "that she has got some frightful thing on her mind."

Mr. Gaul was flabbergasted. Had the girl begun already to listen to all the morbid legends that circulated in the town in regard to this lady? He cast about for some prelude to a less personal exchange of views; but all he could think of was the chapter in the "Philosophy of Representation" upon which he had been engaged when Magnus Muir had burst in upon him with his talk about getting married to a shop-girl. It was extraordinary how impossible it was to steer clear of unpleasant events, even if one didn't stir an inch from one's own quiet course.

"I am writing a book," he remarked emphatically.

Perdita glanced at him with some embarrassment.

"A book?" she murmured. "Is it"—and in an instantaneous revolution of her mind she tried to visualize Mr. Gaul as a writer of novels, but simply could not do so—"a book of essays?"

"Not exactly," he replied. "Well! To tell you the truth, it's a System of Philosophy."

Against the background of the dark desolation at her side, which he had told her was Lodmoor, and against the foreground of certain expressions on the face of Mrs. Cobbold, "a System of Philosophy" seemed one of the most reassuring things in this Weymouth scene that she had yet stumbled on.

"I suppose I shouldn't be able to understand," she said, "even if you told me, what the leading idea of it was?" And she thought in her heart: "He *is* nice. I believe I *will* ask him presently where I could get another job."

"Every system," replied Mr. Gaul, "can be *made* clear. There is a *clue-word* somewhere. Mine is Representation. When modern people deny the existence of God and of any survival after death and of free will, I answer that there is something in the deep places of life—though doubtless outside the material world—'representative' of such things. I don't say corresponding exactly, mind you; but sufficiently representative of them to satisfy all those cravings in our nature which half-discovered and half-invented these daring concepts."

He paused to take breath; but he did not lessen his speed, which for the girl at his side had become uncomfortably fast.

"Yes," she panted.

But she really did begin to feel a good bit happier; not through any practical advice given her by Mr. Gaul, for at the mere approach to what really was the matter he had shied off, but through the guileless charm of his disarming personality.

"And it can satisfy them not *less* fully," he went on, while the girl, struggling to keep up with him, wondered hopelessly to what "it" and "them" referred, "but more fully. For instance, take the concept

'God'. The truth of this concept has nothing in it of that gloomy fear, that solemn servility, that obsequious cringing, that moral cowardice, which human depravity has perpetuated in connection with it."

"I .. am .. sure .. you .. are .. right, Mr. Gaul."

"You see what I mean, don't you?" his voice went on. "The great thing is to put our basic human cravings into a rigorous mental crucible, until we extract their purest essence. This essence, when we actually get it sifted down, will turn out to be much more like the old feelings called up by such words as 'God', 'Immortality', 'Free Will', than it will resemble the sapless formulae of modern scientific catch-words. You see what I mean, don't you?"

"Yes, Mr. Gaul." And she thought in her heart: "By the time we have turned to come back he will have grown tired of my stupid answers; and *then* will be the moment for me to ask his advice about a job."

But even Mr. Gaul's power of abstracting himself from the pressure of immediate phenomena was now disturbed by the sudden stopping, with a good deal of noise, of a small open motor-car at their side. The occupant of this car blew his horn vigorously as he came to a pause, being apparently of the opinion that to arrest the attention of a peripatetic philosopher, discoursing to a girl-pupil, the *vox humana* alone was insufficient. Then from his seat at the wheel Sippy Ballard addressed the pair. It was the whim of a moment; for he was planning a descent upon Lodmoor Hut in his official rôle. But Richard's avoidance of him had excited his pertinacity and here was a chance to gratify his curiosity about the new companion.

"A fine morning, Mr. Gaul!"

The young man turned and surveyed this untimely interloper.

"I beg your pardon?"

"I said it was a fine morning for a walk."

Mr. Gaul took off his spectacles and looked vaguely round.

"Going as far as the Coast-Guards?"

Mr. Gaul advanced a little, so as to place himself well between Perdita and this young impertinent.

"The old Bay is looking its best this morning, eh?"

This remark was as much addressed to Mr. Gaul's companion as to himself; but Perdita, acting on the assumption that a casual encounter between two Weymouth men was no concern of hers, stepped lightly to the top of the low sea-wall at her side and pretended to be absorbed in the view. A little nonplussed by this manoeuvre Sippy Ballard also looked sea-ward.

"Wonderfully clear—the White Nore today," he said.

"The White *Nose*," corrected Richard Gaul drily.

"Well! Nose or Nore, I must be getting on," said the other briskly, "if I can't give you a lift?"

Mr. Gaul replaced his spectacles on *his* nose, and replied that cars were nice for getting about, but that he himself preferred his own feet.

"I'm going to pay a visit to that Gipsy-woman," remarked the intruder, starting his engine. "They keep me busy, our city-fathers!" And with that he drove off.

Gaul glanced at his companion, and seeing that the girl showed signs of preferring to walk along the wall, he obligingly humoured her, moving along by her side upon the narrow path at a slower pace.

"They might just as well have let that woman alone," he called up to her. "But new brooms sweep clean. He lives in my house," he added apologetically. "He is a pushing sort of person."

"So I imagine," laughed Perdita, who began to feel a childish pleasure in her present position. She even allowed herself, as her spirits rose, to recall the figure of the Jobber throwing back the seaweed. "Perhaps, after all," she thought, "I *might* give that woman another chance."

Mr. Ballard had been right about the beauty of the view that morning. In front of them now as they walked in silence—for Richard found it impossible to *shout* his philosophical ideas to a girl on a wall; and indeed he began to experience a mild sensual pleasure from the sight of those slender legs as they moved along above him—there could be discerned the whole expanse of that shining bay, buttressed, on the east, by the most remarkable stretch of cliffs, the most varied in geological formation, the most monumental in the grandeur of its curves, that can be found anywhere round the whole coast of England. This noble line of cliffs, beginning to mount up, as Perdita's eyes followed it now, behind the black-and-white building familiarly spoken of as "the Coast-Guards", stretched away in a south-easterly

direction, past the majestic promontory of the White Nose, till it
ended with St. Alban's Head.

As the girl moved along this low sea-wall she amused herself by
kicking down upon the beach below various isolated pebble-stones that
recent storms had deposited upon the grey surface of this rampart. In
many places, however, she had to cross, not only a quite heavy sprinkling of pebbles, but patches of loose sand and broken shells. Sometimes
her gaze would turn from the line of cliffs in front of her and veering
northward would wander over the wide expanse of salt-marshes by
which the road was bounded. One object alone, on this inland side
of the road, broke the dark monotony of these reedy flats and that was
the hovel now occupied by Gipsy May, and now invaded, as the girl
could see in the distance, for she had noted the stopping of the car
beside its dilapidated boardings and sheds, by the youthful official.
Save for this little erection the marshes stretched away in just that
kind of uninterrupted desolation that had the strongest appeal to
Perdita. Rushy bogs, where the brackish mud was hidden beneath
tall wavy grasses, alternated with beds of glaucous-leaved, crimson-
stalked marsh-plants, small as mosses, and then again there were dark
stretches of gloomy peat-sod, that bore little or no vegetation at all.
Patches of minute vegetable amphibiums, half-plant, half-seaweed,
with oozy, succulent, salty stems, grew along the edge of the broad
black ditch that separated Lodmoor from the highway, forming a
perceptible contrast to the taller and more astringent sand-shore
growths which in spite of their winter hibernation—especially in the
case of the bladder-campion and the sea-pink—still braved, with a
few withered petals and many unbowed stalks, "the extremity of the
skies".

"I haven't made it clear enough to her," thought Mr. Gaul, "how
in every human soul there is something that is beyond and outside the
astronomical world. It all depends on that point."

The agreeable glow that the sight of Perdita's legs gave him—what
a happy thought it was of hers to walk along the top of the wall!—did
not seem to disturb the current of his musings. The vague warmth of
diffused well-being that it cast over him seemed to reveal with a cul-
minating vividness that all material objects were unreal compared with
the mental activity in which they floated, like rocking driftwood on an

intangible tide. Being a philosopher, rather than a neophyte in sanctity, Mr. Gaul did not feel it at all incumbent upon him to refrain from contemplating Perdita's legs. And indeed the harmony with which his thoughts fell into perspective, as he did so, seemed to justify the indulgence.

"The mind is everything," said Mr. Gaul to himself, and he began to feel the actual flowing expansion of this mental mirror, wherein all these things, the narrow path by the road's edge, the grey pebble-strewn wall, the girl's black stockings, the far-away image, several miles off, of the famous White Horse, cut out of the Chalk Downs, hung suspended, with clear thought-spaces above them and beneath them, all rounded by the same unfathomable mystery.

If her companion's thoughts, save for the pleasure of looking at her legs, were thus idealized, Perdita's own thoughts, as she advanced along the top of that wall had grown to be completely resolved into the separate objects she looked at. She had often practised—even in her childhood—this natural nepenthe for human unhappiness, and she began now to be really successful in substituting the inanimate, as the burden of her mind, for the face of Mrs. Cobbold. Her thoughts became the pebbles; they became the sand; they became the waves; they became the crying of the gulls. Her thoughts became the sharp, bitter, overpowering smell of heaps of ancient seaweed. They became that peculiar dryness, a dryness that resembles a sound that sets your teeth on edge, of the shelving pebble-bank beneath her. They became those curious, indescribable waftures that floated over Lodmoor—as of thousands of years of dissolving vegetation, and, on the top of that, of thousands of years of the solidifying of such dissolution.

Such being the cogitations of this pair, it might almost be said that the two primordial symbols of man's mind and of woman's mind were advancing towards Sippy Ballard's empty car, with the sea on the one hand and Lodmoor on the other! Two aboriginal Silences they were, as they came along, a masculine silence and a feminine silence. And meanwhile this grey sea-wall of Portland stone, with the curved pebble-bank beneath and the recurrent breaking of the waves on the pebbles, went on with its non-human endurance. It was bearing the weight, those grey stones, that grey rampart of aged oolite, of more than a frail girl's slight form. It was bearing the weight, along with those pebbles and along with the flints in the road, taciturn, indrawn, unyielding, the weight of all the in-breathings and out-breathings of the orbic motion of the world, of the systole and diastole of space and time. Bearing the weight, they were, today as yesterday; as when the Jubilee Clock was built for Victoria; as when the great White Horse was cut for Victoria's Grandfather; as when John Keats, sailing for Italy, lay on his ship's deck and stared inland, riddled by sickness, racked by desire. Bearing the weight was that whitish-grey sea-wall, and those shelving pebbles; the weight whose expectancy never is satisfied, the weight of all the matter in the universe, and of all the out-breath and the in-breath of the universe. And the planetary expectancy, which that sea-wall bore, trembled and wavered in a reality that was only relative, hovered like a train of moving, motionless images reflected in an eternal mirage. And the thoughts of the one of this particular pair of human intruders who was a man continued to reduce these stones and pebbles and sea-waves to the insubstantiality of bodiless ideas; while the thoughts of the one who was a woman accepted each "minute particular" as a sort of absolute, *the way things were*, in this world, where a girl could be happy walking on a sea-wall and desperately miserable shut up in High House.

Mr. Gaul and Perdita were both walking quite slowly now—the one three or four feet higher than, and a little in advance of, the other, as if, in spite of an occasional car or truck driving in to Weymouth, they were so solitary there that the place had begun to take notice of them. This is a frequent experience with wayfarers. Leaving a town or a hamlet they chat to one another for a while, and are accosted by others; but let them walk long enough upon the same road; let them walk long enough along the same beach, and the time arrives when that inanimate pathway subdues them to itself, hypnotizes them into silence, into a curious passivity. It is then that under the spell of the simplest forms of matter, a mud-bank, a flint track, a stone wall, they are allowed to listen to a speech too deep for sound; and they become eavesdroppers of the ancient litany of aboriginal matter and grow confederate with the long piety of the cosmos, whose religion is to wait. The whitish-grey sea-wall under the girl's feet and at the man's side, had the air—as the sunlight fell upon it—of being something that had moved forward just the fraction of an inch towards their conscious souls. It had the air of posing a question to these self-absorbed intelligences. The shelving pebbles—whose surface was like a sound that might set a dinosaur's tooth on edge—seemed to join with the wall in asking them this question.

But the pair still moved on their way in silence, unconscious of an appeal that had been made to sentient organisms endowed with the power of movement for so many millions of years of planetary life. They had now arrived opposite Lodmoor Hut, where Ballard's empty car was still stationed. Mr. Gaul threw a nervous glance across the road and cried hurriedly to Perdita:

"Come down now, if you don't mind, and let's get on faster!"

The girl obeyed docilely enough and, taking his hand, jumped down. But they were too late. The door of the hut burst open and S. P. Ballard, followed by Gipsy May and young Zed, rushed out into the highway. Sippy Ballard's sharp eyes caught sight of them in a second, as Richard tried to hurry his companion off.

"Mr. Gaul!" he shouted, "Mr. Gaul!"

His voice was lost in the shrill vituperation that Larry Zed was uttering. He seemed calling down upon him some terrific Romany curse; and Richard, as he fidgeted and hesitated, found the occasion was too dramatic even for *his* power of dodging the agitations of humanity. Drawn, in spite of themselves, towards this group, and it seemed as if young Zed had laid his hand on Mr. Ballard to prevent him ascending into his car, the two pedestrians crossed the road. A volley of violent explanations was at once flung at them by the angry lad and they found themselves—much to Richard's annoyance and Perdita's bewilderment—the centre of a situation that, if the incident had occurred in the town in place of so lonely a spot, would speedily have become an excited crowd.

It was scarce noticed by anyone, Marret's retreat just then, as the shabby, dark figure of the Punch-and-Judy girl slipped quietly away; but Perdita—who, as a stranger, was more detached than the rest from what was going on—followed that figure with an interest she would have found hard to explain as she watched it scrambling over the wall which she herself had just quitted, and disappearing down the pebble-bank towards the sea!

Gipsy May herself had gone to her fowl-run; and here she could be seen bending over a black Minorca cock as if what was occurring at the moment was no concern of hers.

But Sippy Ballard, freeing himself from the indignant clutch of the boy, jumped incontinently now into his seat and, removing his cap with a whimsical bow to Perdita, set his engine in motion.

"You won't have a ride then?" were his parting words to Gaul, jerked out as his car spluttered off, "I've got another little job out Preston way!" and they could hear him sounding his impertinent horn, as gaily and viciously as some machine-bred Puck, as he overtook a lumbering lorry ahead of him loaded with Cattistock and Frampton beer-barrels. Meanwhile Gipsy May was approaching the hut with the bird in a paralyzed condition in her arms. "Something's bit it," she kept repeating intently to herself.

"Shall we . . . do you mind? . . . go in with them . . . for a moment?" murmured Mr. Gaul.

And Perdita, who was habitually anxious to be as inconspicuous as possible, heard her name mentioned by her companion, and found herself following the Gipsy, who went on repeating, "Something's bit it!" as if this mysterious disaster in the fowl-run were the only event of a serious nature that had taken place, across the threshold of the hut. On the table of the kitchen, among a number of scattered cards— some of them bearing pictures such as the Guernsey girl had never before set eyes on—lay an imposing legal document with the red seal of the local Town Council; and to this object, when the door had been shut behind them, the attention of Mr. Gaul was indignantly directed by young Zed.

"Take the young lady back of house and show her Blotchy, Larry, while I tend to this bird. Mr. Gaul can't put mind to thik lawyer's gibbery when ye be yallerin' at he!" And once more she muttered to herself, "Something's bit it!"

It thus became Perdita's destiny, still trying to be as docile and inconspicuous as she could, to follow this red-haired, green-eyed youngster, who looked anything but elated at the prospect of being her entertainer, into the enclosure at the rear. She found herself, however, decidedly impressed by the brown-and-white cow and she very soon, after looking at Larry gravely, as they stood in the shed, and meeting his furtive green eyes with her own steady brown ones, began to disarm his touchy aloofness. She had never been one to care much for boys, or indeed for young men of her own age, but the very thing in Larry—his unsettled wits and erratic movements—that made others shrink from him, stirred a deep reciprocity in her lonely heart.

As for young Zed himself, he had not been with her for five minutes before he began to forget his hatred of Sippy Ballard and his agitation over the Tarot cards.

"She's like 'me Nothing-Girl'," he said to himself, "who do cuddle I to sleep! If only she'd let poor Larry do it, how he'd hold she close!"

Never had young Zed made love to anyone in his life; and only with that presence at night, when his limbs were relaxed and the labours of the day released him, had he ever really known, even in his imagination, what a girl's body can do to drive away pain and suffering and anger and misery from the mind of mortal man.

"Come!" he suddenly said to her when she had been stroking Blotchy for several minutes. "I'll show 'ee me girt Hern!"

To Perdita's surprise he actually gave her his hand, as a child might have done, and stealing stealthily out of the little enclosure—too ramshackle to be called a barton—he led her softly along the edge of a ditch, where the expanse of the marshes was hidden from her vision by one of those little reed-shanties that sportsmen put up for the purposes of duck-shooting. On one side of this reed-shanty there was a high clump of dead bull-rushes, and on the other a half-prostrate but still living willow. He made her stand perfectly still for a few seconds when they reached this spot, and releasing her hand stole forward, like a limber-footed young savage, towards the tree.

Perdita as she stood there, her feet sinking in the black peat-mud and her nostrils inhaling the faint, sickly aroma of aeons of vegetable dissolution, had time to realize how much she was attracted to this queer lad. Compared with the romantic agitation in her empty heart which the formidable figure of the Jobber had aroused, this was nothing. It was just a gentle protective thrill of interest. But such as it was, it made her, as she watched his stealthy, wild-animal movements, feel that she could have caressed him as she had done Blotchy. She liked everything about him. She liked his green eyes. She liked his blood-red hair, with a matted elf-lock hanging loose over his forehead. She liked his white gleaming teeth. She liked his

long bare forearms, as free from hairs as were her own. She liked his
brown knees beneath his ragged knickerbockers. She liked his supple
waist and his thin slouching body.

Hurriedly and gravely she drew off her gloves and squeezed them
under her waist-band.

At last she saw him turn and beckon to her to advance. In silent
haste she obeyed him, moving almost as quietly as he had done himself,
and crouched down by his side behind the sloping willow-trunk. Here
again he possessed himself of her hand and she was aware, as he
clutched it tight and pressed it against his side, as they crouched together, that his heart was beating violently. Suddenly he became as
rigid, stiff and frozen, as a beast that catches sight of its prey. Then he
pulled the girl forward; and they leaned together across the tree-trunk
where they could see what was behind the reed-hut.

And Perdita was seized with such a spasm of awe-struck wonder at
what she saw there that it was she this time who pressed the lad's hand
against her side. For standing there with its back to them on a tussock
of grass, with one long leg curled beneath its wing, and its immense
beak suspended above a glittering pool of water, stood a great, motionless, grey heron. Breath after breath of incredible pleasure did Perdita
draw. She had never seen such a thing in all her days! It was not
merely the heron that created the spell that held her. It was the
melancholy waste of those dark brackish marshes behind it. It was the
pallid cheek and blood-red hair of the lad, across whose profile she
gazed at the huge bird, and whose fingers she was pressing against her
side. It would have puzzled her to put into words the emotion she
felt at that moment; but when the heron, catching the sound, one
might almost have thought, of the beating of those two young hearts,
spread its enormous wings and flapped away over the ditches, there
surged up within her, with a dark delicious trembling, a particular
feeling she sometimes had when she thought of death—its release, its
finality, its great escape.

"Where do 'ee live?" Larry asked her in a whisper as they walked
back to the hut.

Perdita was still holding the boy's hand, but the intense eagerness
with which he asked this question, in a tone more like that of a lover
than a child, made her feel a sudden sense of uneasiness. How could

she tell what might be the effect of exciting emotional feelings in this queer elemental Being? Of course if young Zed felt for her as she felt for the Jobber—so she said to herself as they crossed the paddock— just a vague, delicious quintessence of pure romance, careless of what came of it—all would be well. But who could discern what went on in the mind of a strange youth like this? Thus—in her feelings and impressions rather than in any definite words—Perdita pondered; nor was she mistaken in fancying that her appearance at Lodmoor Hut had roused an emotional tempest in the mind of Larry Zed.

"Don't let's go in yet!" he whispered now, when they reached the back of the hut. "Let me show 'ee me seaweed-book, will 'ee? 'Tis in hay-loft where I do sleep."

Perdita felt a little uneasy at the idea of this excitable lad coaxing her to his sleeping-place; but the inevitable reaction in a nature like hers had already begun; and as she contemplated the wooden steps leading to the hay-loft above Blotchy's shed, she suddenly felt a wave of such desolation of heart, such emptiness, such loneliness, such futility, that all sense of responsibility for her actions seemed to slide away.

"What does it matter?" she thought. "Do, don't do; draw back, go on; be brave, be cowardly; it all comes to the same thing in the end. It's just the purest fancy that that man gave me a thought! Why should I think of him? Up steps, down steps; in and out; back and forth! 'We know what we are; but we know not what we may be'."

With these flotsam thoughts in her heart, and the green eyes of young Zed shining like a cat's close behind her, she climbed the rickety stairway—"he can kick it down" she thought, "if he wants to, and keep me up there in the straw forever!"

The tiny loft was certainly bare, when she opened the door and entered; but there was a camp-bed at one side of it and although there *was* a heap of straw, it was all piled close to an orifice in the floor that opened upon the cow's manger. There was no straw immediately round the bed.

In her present mood the girl sat wearily down on the bed and stared out of the open door across Lodmoor.

"This boy only wants me because I'm a girl," she said to herself, "and that man didn't give me a second thought. I'll die if I go on with that woman, though. I must get out of *that*, anyway; even if I have to be a servant. I wonder where a person goes to get servants' jobs? But they always ask references; and that woman will be furious. I know one thing, though. I'll die sooner than go back to Guernsey!"

And all this while young Zed, pretending to hunt for his book of pressed seaweeds, was on his knees in the straw, moving it about with hands that positively shook.

"I've got a girl on me bed," he kept saying to himself, "and she be like all girls be. But she bain't scornful of poor Lal like them others. She did give hand to poor Lal to stroky and huggy. I've got a girl on me bed."

And then his shaking hands would encounter the old ledger-book he was looking for; but he would push it further under the straw the moment he touched it, afraid lest the figure on the bed would notice it and demand it. And he thought of all the times when he had walked up and down the lonely beach telling himself stories about some stray girl, some tramp-girl, some harlotry-girl even, that he might manage to coax to come up those loft steps—"I've got a girl on me bed"—and he thought of how he had waited hours and hours on the Esplanade— unknown to Gipsy May—in hope of exchanging a word with Marret when the Punch-and-Judy show stopped. But Marret never cared about him, whether he was there or not, whether he spoke to her or not, whether he helped her carry the whole Punch-Stage or not! Marret didn't care whether he was in the world or not—any more nor he'd been a dog-fish—"I've got a girl on me bed"—and as for his own precious May, she didn't seem like a proper, real girl, at all, save now and then, when she cried to him, same as she did when Marret knocked over "the Hanged Man". But now he'd got a real, proper girl—like what they all be—and there she were on his wone bed— "I've got a girl on me bed"—and all he'd got to do was just walk over to her and say:

" 'Tisn't time for seaweed-book yet, me Lovely!"—and put his hand on her knee.

Down on his own knees in the loose straw, he kept flinging little wisps of it through the oblong hole to where Blotchy's head generally was at night; but the cow was outside now, tethered by the edge of the ditch where Perdita had petted her before spying upon the heron, and he could see every stalk of straw that he dropped touch the smooth, soft-worn edge of the manger, where the sunlight fell in a heavy stream, coming through the half-open door and lying there, yellow and still.

"Why don't 'ee go over to she, then, Lal, me boy?"

Thus the quivering imp of desire whispered to his heart. But his heart could only repeat, with inane, monotonous repetition the same old burden; but something—he did not know what it was—just kept him there, dropping straws, fewer and fewer at a time, on that sun-warmed manger's edge. Presently he put a straw in his mouth; and fell to letting them drop by threes, by twos, and finally only one at a time. But, all the while, his thoughts ran a fantastic round of half-crazed poetical sensuality. He kept thinking of the maddening slenderness and softness of Perdita's body—such as, in a minute, he would be enjoying! Little peculiarities, which he had passionately noticed—and they could have been remarked in any slender girl who was not a skeleton!—swept over his senses now, till they made him tremble. The curves of her flanks, the veins in her neck, the way her hair was drawn back, the extreme littleness of her wrists—Oh, but these were the reasons why he kept drawing a straw through his teeth, and throwing 'em down a hole! She was too lovely for him to *dare* to touch. And yet *there* she was!—"I've got a girl on me bed"—and she was herself, all the time, he knew it, though he durstn't look straight at her, for fear of meeting her glance, staring out of the loft-door; staring with those sad, steady, mysterious brown eyes, like the eyes of the Virgin Mary!

And Perdita, all this while, was saying to herself:

"He never gave me a second thought. That business of the seaweed was some freak of his own and had nothing to do with me. When next I pass him on the esplanade—if I ever do—he won't recognize me. I'm not pretty; I'm not striking-looking. I look insignificant, pitiful, unappealing to all! The only man who could *possibly* ever be interested in me would be some queer, strange, non-human character like—like I *thought* the Jobber was . . . but I was a fool to think such a thing. He, no doubt, has scores of girls in Weymouth and Portland— yes, and in Lulworth, too! Why should the very first man I meet here be the one—queer, strange, unlike everybody else—that I can tell myself stories about? But I won't go home. No; anything but that! I'd stay at High House if that woman hadn't forced herself into my room. But Oh, dear! it doesn't matter what becomes of me. I'm nothing of any value. I'm like any one of the thousands and millions of people who might just as well be dead as be alive. I can see how my life will be—like a map! I shall leave this Cobbold woman; I shall find some appalling drudgery; I shall write to Aunt and tell her how happy I am; and I shall go on and on—getting novels out of the Public Library as a drug, to stop my thinking—and then, old before my time, with a passion for Persian Cats and the Works of Henry James, they'll come one day and find me stiff and stark—old Miss Wane of the Back-Attic!—and give me a pauper's funeral and chloroform my cats and sell my Henry Jameses—and that will be my story's end! There's that boy over there, who's probably never—just by unfair destiny—kissed anyone, except his Gipsy, all his life; and here am I, who've never had even a Gipsy to kiss. And the boy's desperately attracted to me and thinks I'm beautiful, and I *know* he's beautiful; and yet—"

And Perdita felt such a bitter contempt for her scruples, that she imagined herself jumping up off the bed, with the hot blood rushing to her cheeks, and running to the boy's side clapping her hands over his eyes and crying out:

"Let's *be* mad—"

Instead of doing this, however, which would certainly have so startled young Zed that it would have scared away every amorous feeling he had, she did—possibly inspired by great creative Nature— something that was much more to the point. She lay down on the boy's bed with her head on his pillow and shut her eyes. Young Zed knelt up in the straw and stared at her in a trance of adoration.

"I'll be cooming over to 'ee, present!" he said to himself. And then he thought, "She be whispering in her heart, 'Here I be, Lal! Here I be! When be 'ee cooming to I, Fisherman?' "

But Perdita's thoughts had flown far away from poor Larry. Lying prone like this, stretched out on the bed, vague emotional feelings that she had had since her earliest girlhood came floating through her nerves. She had always associated whatever romantic sensations she had with the presence of the sea. She had even, in her young-girl fancies, created a sort of vague, indistinct sea-lover, whose identity she would feel bending over her at night, when the wild Channel Island tides were riding high. It was indeed into this half-mythic image of masculine predominance visiting her maiden bed like an enamoured sea-god that in the excitement of her first landing the figure of the Jobber had transformed himself; so that during all these recent nights, when under the stress of her unhappiness at High House she had turned piteously, as soon as her head was on the pillow, to the sea-lover of her girlhood, it was—as happens in the old books of poetry—in the eidolon of the Jobber's form that her tutelary demi-god consoled her. In her weakness and her melancholy, careless of what happened to her, she let the nerves of her girl's body cry aloud to the nerves of this boy's body kneeling in the straw; but the feeling of her heart was all the while with the Jobber; for he, and he alone till the end of her days, would represent that vague sea-presence which had thrilled her childhood.

Young Zed had no idea when he imagined that her silence was calling to him how like his own innocence her's was. Here they were together, both of them waifs and derelicts; but though the boy might mutter "I've got a girl on me bed", and the girl might cry out, "Let's *be* mad!"— something, the natural shrinking of inexperience and the invisible chasm created by social custom kept them apart. But chance seemed resolute to give them yet another opportunity; for as a result of the dust that was wafted over to her from where he was disturbing the straw she suddenly sneezed—"Amor dextra sternuit approbationem!"—and this broke the spell.

With the quick spontaneous grace of a wild animal young Zed leapt to his feet and went over to her side. Very gently, just as if she had been made of some material more precious than flesh and blood, he stroked one of her bare hands which lay cold on her lap with the tips of his fingers. Perdita had closed her eyes; but in a moment she opened them again, for she felt by his quick breathing that he had fallen on his knees by her side and had tightened his fingers over the hand he had touched. For some minutes they stayed together in this position; and then something deep in the girl, which surprised herself by its sudden strength, stirred within her; and she knew that standing there behind the kneeling lad, in spite of her reckless mood, in spite of her sense of the futility of thinking about him, remained, for all she could do, the

great lowering figure of that tall man who threw the seaweed into the
sea! But she still went on gazing softly and tenderly into the face of
the kneeling boy; nor did she stir, nor did she make the least motion
to release her fingers, although, so strong was his feeling, she could
feel the burning pulse throbbing within his wrist. Larry's whole soul
gleamed in his green eyes as he hung over her. His brain felt dizzy;
but it seemed to him as though touching her so, and while she lay there
prone and still beneath him, that a veritable consummation of his
desire was already taking place. To his fervid imagination it was
enough that their eyes clung together and that she knew he was
ravishing her in his thought. Her bare hand, round which his fingers
burned, was to him then her whole body. For this was the first time
in his life that he had held a girl who knew what he felt and did not
stop him. His green eyes, as they clung to her soft brown ones, kept
saying to her: "I'm taking you! I'm taking you!" and it seemed
to him that she yielded more and more, as he bent forward, his body
pressed against the side of the couch; and it seemed to him that it
pleased her that he should be seeing her bare figure—as he *was* now
seeing it in his intense imagination—and that it pleased her to lie so
hushed and still, so that he could the more easily enjoy her; and it
seemed to him that this strange passivity, she knowing that he was
taking her, was the ultimate essence of her Being offered up to him;
and that her lying so still, with her bare hand in his, while he enjoyed
her, was the ultimate sign of what it meant to be a real, live, mysterious
girl; and that this was the secret of all girls, that they could not know
how exciting they were; and that this was their inmost nature that
they stayed so quiet while they were loved.

How could he know that it was only possible for Perdita to remain
so quiet, and to answer his impassioned gaze so calmly because her own
thoughts had once more grown pitifully sad. Weary and hopeless was
her whole spirit, as she lay on Larry's bed; and all, all seemed futile to
her. The fleeting quiver of response that the boy's beauty and passion
had roused in her had been stricken cold by that image of the Jobber
lowering above him. Perhaps it had been all the while her feeling for
the Jobber—for not a night had passed, since she saw him, but she had
gone to sleep thinking about him—that rendered her so sensitive to
this boy's infatuation.

It was indeed peculiarly characteristic of Perdita, that fate's best way of making appealing the near and the pressing was to incarnate in them something belonging to the remote and the evasive. Thus while to the ecstatic senses of young Zed there lay exposed before him, yielded willingly up to him, two of the whitest, softest, young girl's breasts that the world contained, behind those breasts the girl's heart had substituted a full-grown man, dark and formidable and full of the magic of the sea, for the boy's red hair and burning fingers. But since such ecstasies, whether spiritual, or physical, after dipping their possessed in Eternity, toss them back all too soon into Time the moment came when young Zed lowered his eyelids, removed his fingers, rose to his feet, and said in an abrupt jerky tone—

"Will 'ee bide quiet where 'a be, while I fetches me seaweeds to show 'ee?"

The girl smiled at him; and, rising from her recumbent position, shook out her dress, put her hands to her hair, picked up her hat from the end of the couch, glanced unconsciously round for some sort of looking-glass, and sat down again on the bed, giving vent to a half-suppressed yawn.

Had these two young people been really disporting themselves in equal rapture, they could not have looked more relaxed or more dragged back to dull reality. Larry crossed the room and wearily lugged out from under the straw an old, great Ledger Book, bound at the back and bearing the inscription in red ink— "Algae".

The lad placed this heavy volume on Perdita's lap and sat down by her side. The camp-bed creaked ominously; but they were both so thin that it did no worse than that, and he began showing her the seaweeds. The specimens were so arranged that only one lay upon each page, with a blank page opposite to it; and the result of this was that each of these blank pages bore a deeply indented imprint or natural tracing of this same sea-growth.

Perdita never afterwards forgot what she felt as she watched him turning, one by one, these thick brine-smelling leaves, and saw the beautiful shapes and colours of those sea-plants spread out before her. A strange, half-mystical detachment from all the poignances and confusions of life stole over her; and she thought:

"Oh, if existence could be reduced to this—just looking at seaweeds and letting the world go!"

And when the lad turned one particular page, and she saw before her what must have been a specimen of the very species which had been clinging to the pebble-stone that night on the Esplanade, she bent her head over it, as if enjoying its pungent sea-smell, but in reality to hide from young Zed the fact that her eyes had suddenly filled with tears.

6

RODNEY LODER

WHEN Lucinda told Mr. Gaul that Captain Poxwell was opposed to her sister's second marriage she spoke less than the truth. The Captain so cordially detested Dog Cattistock that Mrs. Lily had to take care they should never meet; not a very easy or pleasant task, unless she became the one to visit her admirer. But Mrs. Lily had taken a natural dislike to be a mere visitor in Peninsular Lodge, a place which was not only forlorn in itself, owing to the financier's miserliness, but was under the complete sway of Lizzie Chant, who viewed her presence there with ill-concealed hostility.

Thus it came about that most of their meetings, which as their marriage drew near occurred more and more frequently, were arranged for the afternoon, when, if not a hopelessly wet day, Captain Poxwell betook himself to his shells in Sandsfoot Castle. Here, since the wintry weather kept excursionists away, the Captain had come to make himself completely at home; and had even gone so far as to devise hiding-places in those ancient walls for the materials of his shell-boxes; the shells themselves being always procurable in the rock-pools at the sea's edge.

Mrs. Lily had at least been persuaded not, as will be seen, without certain secret reservations, to name the twelfth of February as their wedding-day, and so when the second week of that changeable month came round, Dog Cattistock's obtrusive chin and husky, grating voice were in evidence in Half-Way House nearly every afternoon. It was on the ninth of February, only three days before the day appointed for their wedding, that young Daisy Lily, instead of joining her grandfather in the ruins as she usually did while Cattistock was with

her mother, decided to walk over to a house called Spy Croft in Belle
Vue Road, where lived old Mr. James Loder, the famous Weymouth
lawyer, with his unmarried children, Rodney and Ruth.

James Loder had managed the affairs of Daisy's parents, just as he
had done those of her grandfather. In addition to this he was her
godfather; and feeling an imperative necessity to talk a little about
her mother's marriage to some sympathetic feminine ear, she chose,
from among all the people she knew, the one who was the quietest, the
least excitable and the most likely to keep things to herself. In making
this choice Daisy was actuated by a train of long, quiet, sagacious
reasons.

"Mother's hopeless," she said to herself. "She does nothing but
drift. If I don't look out I shall be living like that myself. She's a
warning to anyone; and I'm going to be as different from her as I
possibly can!"

In selecting Ruth Loder as her confidante, at this disturbing crisis in
her life, Daisy was certainly choosing the one person of all persons in
her circle most different from the future Mrs. Cattistock.

While the young girl made her way towards Belle Vue Road,
Rodney and Ruth Loder were standing at the window of Spy Croft
drawing-room waiting for their father to come down. Drawn up
outside the front door was the old gentleman's bath-chair in which
Ruth was presently going to take him for his usual afternoon's airing.
The girl had lately—though Daisy Lily had no idea of this change of
custom at Spy Croft—substituted herself for her brother as the old
man's escort; and today she had the idea, since the weather was mild
and windless, of pulling the bathchair down to a little cove called
Bincleaves, on the western side of the Nothe, where there was a strip
of beach. As she stood now at the window by her brother's side—
and it would have been clear to any observer that they were brother
and sister—Rodney turned his grave pale face and pallid hazel eyes
sympathetically upon her.

"Why must you go down the hill to Bincleaves?" he said. "It's such
a pull for you getting up again from that beach. When I agreed to
your taking him I never meant you to do anything like that. Does he
want so *very* much to go down there?"

She smiled and nodded.

"Well, why don't you let *me* take him today? We needn't be rigid in our new régime. Nothing's worth making drastic, unbroken rules about. Let me be the one to do it when he gets a mania for hearing the sea."

She looked Rodney full in the face with an imperceptible tilt of her clearly-marked eye-brows.

"You know what we decided," she said, "and why we decided it. You shall take him whenever I've got shopping to do or am feeling poorly."

A troubled expression, very complicated and indefinable, flitted over her brother's face.

"I can't understand his so disliking my pushing him," he said; and he set himself to stare out at the small lawn, where their black cat Mortmain, a special pet of the old man's, was prowling about, hoping that the sparrows twittering so noisily in the high laurel-hedge might come a little nearer. "Of course," he added, in a faintly querulous tone, "I understand his *preferring* you. Anyone naturally *would* like to be pushed by you rather than by me. But why he should work himself up like this, until——"

"Oh, my dear!" she interrupted, "don't 'ee go on like this! I beg, I beg you not to! We've gone over it all. We've decided what's best to do. And it's *so* upsetting to me to have to go through the whole thing over again. Be good, Rodney, there's a dear, and let what *has* to be, be!"

"Have Father and I *always* disliked each other?" he thought. "Has he despised me all the while for the way I submit to him? Has he been saying to himself, for the last ten years, 'If Rod had any spunk he'd clear out; but since he hasn't, what can you do with such a fool?'"

He turned to Ruth now with a particular smile on his face that, more than any peevish or unhappy words, always stabbed her to the heart.

"Mortmain hasn't caught anything for several days," he said.

The girl did not respond to this remark; but she looked long and long into his countenance.

"That was a shocking smile," her heart was thinking, "to be seen on a man's face."

Nor was Ruth wrong in her feeling; for the mental machinery that caused that smile to be engraved on his face was a gentle form of absolute despair.

Yes, Rodney and Ruth were so much alike that their resemblance, when their life became unbearably monotonous, amounted to something pathetic. Both had the same pale complexion, the same straight nose, the same thin melancholy lips, the same light-coloured chestnut hair, the same faded hazel eyes. Ruth's hair was pulled tight back from her marbly forehead where little blue veins could be seen in any strong light and where the skin itself fitted the skull so closely that wrinkles were impossible. It was a family peculiarity, inherited from James Loder, not to be able to frown; and no doubt this was the *fons et origo* of Rodney's ghastly smile. Rodney had a trick of damping his hair when he brushed it, thus keeping intact the clear white parting on the side of his head which had almost become an organic portion of his appearance. He brushed his hair so smoothly and so closely round his skull that you felt as if it were a thin piece of adhesive paper that could not be removed without drawing blood.

"It breaks my heart to see him smile like that," the girl said to herself; and it came over her that there was some subtle connection between this smile and the familiar furniture of that room, furniture that had been unchanged since their mother's death when he was five and she was three.

But Rodney had had that infinitely forlorn smile from his earliest childhood. Old Ammabel who had been their cook, and who now played the rôle of housekeeper at Spy Croft, always declared that the doctor who helped to bring the child into the world said he was born "triste". There was in reality no necessary connection between Rodney's ghastly unmirthful smile and the furniture around them now. That the chandelier had *that look* for Ruth, combined with the tinkling prismatic pendants that hung down inside their oval glass cases from a pair of gilded candlesticks on the chimney-piece; that the polished ornamental coal-scuttle had it; that the green curtains, with gilt braiding, had it; that the huge pink roses on the carpet and the convoluted pattern of the wall-paper had it, did not really imply that between the solemn unchangeableness of this room and the life-weariness of the son of the woman who designed it there was any link. Had Magnus Muir, for instance, been destined to spend his days, or at least his evenings, in Spy Croft drawing-room, the old-fashioned faded sumptuousness of these objects would have been the cause of a deep, almost sensual content. But when a man and a woman have suffered the same things from the same parent for twenty years even the most dignified furniture becomes an accomplice in the process!

The bedroom door opened now; and the old man began to descend the stairs. Both the young people, if they could be called young any longer, when Rodney was thirty and Ruth was twenty-eight, went out into the hall, so as to be ready to receive him, for such was their immemorial custom, when he got to the bottom.

Sippy Ballard who, in school-boy phrase, spent much energy in "sucking up to" the great Weymouth lawyer, always called him "General" when he came to visit him on business.

"Mr., *Mr.*, Sir!" the old gentleman invariably protested. "You mustn't make fun of an old man."

But in his handling of the innumerable cases that the young official would bring up for his consideration Mr. Loder showed no sign of any displeasure at this title. As he came down the big staircase with its soft matted carpet, identical with the drawing-room curtains, he certainly resembled what might easily have been the graceless Sippy's idea as to what—for he had not seen many—a General was like.

He was extremely thin and extremely tall, and a compact skull well covered with snow-white hair, combined with a clipped military moustache and a back-bone that seemed to grow straighter rather than crookeder, as if the passing of time were seasoning it like a good walking-stick, were all aspects of his appearance that justified S. P. Ballard's facetious flattery.

As he came down, now, one step after another, James Loder knew perfectly well that they were there waiting for him; but he did not hurry nor did he look at them. He looked sometimes at the banisters upon which he rested his hand and sometimes at the steps upon which he set his feet. This starting out, of a fine afternoon, for his bath-chair ride was an event of importance, perhaps the most important event in his day, and he preferred to savour every second of its only too fleeting joy rather than bother his head with conscious gratitude for punctilious pieties. It would have been a sharp shock to him all the same if in place of finding Ruth in the dark out-of-door coat, and her neat black hat with its blue feather, he had found Rodney in his grey felt hat and light-coloured overcoat. For it was human nature, and it was silly idealism to quarrel with human nature, for a person to like his daughter better than his son. Ruth never said things, or looked things, or thought things, that he couldn't understand and approve of and that did not feel comfortable in his deepest soul; whereas Rod was always thinking something—Oh, he knew *that* well enough!—even if he didn't put it into words, which was critical, unfriendly, and a little contemptuous. The truth was that Rod, poor lad, had never had the pluck to have his fling; and so had grown thoroughly degenerate. Think of having a degenerate son! But that was the truth. Rodney was like a Frenchman.

"Is it going to rain, do you think, Rod?" he asked his son as soon as he got to the bottom.

This was his inveterate habit, to address a remark about the weather to the one of his children who was *not* going to wheel the bath-chair; thus—for that was the way Rodney analysed it—involving them both in the success or failure of the excursion.

"Quite impossible, Father. Here's your hat, Father."

James Loder was not ignorant of the fact that his hat was there. Indeed it was a custom that went back to the young man's boyhood that at this particular moment he should brush, with a little velvet pad kept on the hall-table, the felt hat on week days and the silk hat on Sundays of his General-like progenitor.

Slowly the old man drew on his gloves, keeping his son waiting. It would be hard to analyse the precise impulse that led him to do this; but the truth was that at this moment he felt more affection for the slight figure with its neatly-parted hair than he had felt since this same occasion just twenty-four hours ago.

"Ready, Father, dear?" said Ruth.

She was herself removing with her gloved fingers a few of Mortmain's black hairs from the blue edging of her jacket; and as her brother watched her he suddenly had a mystical feeling that he had seen her make this precise gesture in some dimension of Time, where neither Spy Croft, nor even Weymouth itself, had any reality. The old man contemplated with satisfaction his daughter's face. Above that blue-trimmed black coat and under that blue feather Ruth's complexion had a charming softness and delicacy, and her pale hazel eyes met his with tender solicitude.

He thought: "I suppose when a man has ulcers of the stomach he's bound to get a *little* touchy. The truth is, even you, my dear, aren't really concerned about me in the way old Belle is!"

Rodney, with the old man's hat still in his hand, stepped forward and opened the door, revealing the bath-chair standing in the gravel-path.

"Thank 'ee, Rod," said James Loder, taking the hat and putting it on his head with a shaky hand.

"Oh, your stick, Father!" cried Ruth.

James Loder looked reproachfully at his son. Had the boy forgotten his fondness for having his stick with him in the bath-chair? No, we must face the truth; a woman's love lasted on even when a person became a feeble pantaloon, but a man's love got worn out. And he recalled his own egoistic dislike of ministering to the physical wants of *his* father in his long decline.

"We come back to the women-folk at the last," he said to himself, and as he received his stick from his son's hand and took his daughter's arm, he thanked the Lord for the blind devotion of his old servant.

Rodney helped her to place him in the chair and get it out into the road. Then, not waiting to see them start, he returned to the house and closed the door. Why was it that the happiest moments in his life, these days, were when he had Spy Croft entirely to himself?

"I hope Ammabel and Lettice *are* out," he thought, as he slowly ascended the stairs.

At the door of his room, which was a comfortable sitting-room as well as a bedroom, he paused for a second, listening. Yes! the house was absolutely quiet.

"This might be my own place in Paris," he said to himself, recalling a certain little painted dwelling, just big enough for a solitary recluse, that he had noted once near the Seine at St. Cloud. He sank down in his arm-chair by the fire and tried to obliterate from his mind that great odious table, occupying a third of the room, covered with law-papers. In vain! And the sight of those documents made him wonder whether he had been wise to accustom Mr.

Crouch, the partner, and old Mr. Titch, the head-clerk, to his habit
of only being at the office during the morning.

Gaffer Crouch—as this heavily-built, laborious personage had been
called since he was a boy at school—had recently slipped into a way
of saying to Mr. Titch, "Leave *those* things, Titch, for Mr. Loder
to take home."

Forget the Law, forget his father, forget his fears that his good-
looking sister would die unmarried—yes! forget the whole cart-load
of life's burdens, and give himself up to his "essences"! Rodney had
never told a living soul about his "essences", which were, after his
interest in his sister, by far the most important thing in his monotonous
life. They would not indeed have been very easy to explain to anyone;
being in reality nothing less than a certain trick he had of clinging,
consciously and intensely, to those floating, drifting, wayward, intangible memories, selected from the dusty pell-mell, which come to
us all sometimes and flood the most anxious human minds with a
mysterious happiness. These subtle and insubstantial feelings had
gradually become, for this sluggish and unambitious young man, a
sort of world within the world, or life within life, and he would rest
his chin on his hands as he sat at his desk in the office, or at his table
in this pleasant room, and fall into a deep day-dream, or vegetative
trance, in which all manner of insignificant little scenes, recalled
from his walks into the town, or up Wyke Hill, or by the shallow
backwater called the Fleet, or along the crest of Chesil Beach, seemed
to grow in importance, until they acquired for him a sort of mystical
value, as if they were the casual by-paths or hidden postern-gates,
leading into aerial landscapes of other and much happier incarnations.
Rodney now pulled up his arm-chair to the fire and stretched out
his hands to its blaze; not for physical warmth, for it was not a
particularly chilly day, but for spiritual comfort.

"It's nice," he thought, "when there's nobody in the house! I
wish I lived alone in Weymouth and walked over here to see Ruth.
This house, with Ammabel always the same, and father always the
same, and with Ruth and me so sorry for each other, is slowly eating
out my heart. Even my ' essences ' don't come as they used to! I
feel as if, unless something happens very soon, my power of going on
will come to an end. And what . . . will I . . . do . . . then?"

He lit a cigarette and blew several clouds of blue smoke up the chimney, still leaning forward. The conformation of his forehead—just as was the case with Ruth—made it difficult for him to frown; but there were beads of perspiration on his forehead, for he remembered when he was younger being taken to see his uncle—his father's brother—who was a patient of Dr. Brush, and how they found this man, he must have been then about sixty, in his bed in the middle of the afternoon, and how one of the attendants of the place told his father who took him, that it was a definite symptom of Uncle Edward's condition that he should refuse to get up save by compulsion.

"You ... don't ... think," Rodney Loder now found himself saying quite out loud, to a particular little blue flame that was running up and down along a charred log, "you ... don't ... think ... that I'll ever *take to my bed* ... like Uncle Edward?"

All the reply he got to this question was a small, soft sound of falling ashes, as one end of the log in front of him sank down into the bottom of the grate.

"Well, if there's anything in compensation," he thought, "I certainly deserve something to happen."

It then came over his mind with a funny sort of flap, just as if Ammabel had flicked at him with her duster, that by this "something to happen" he meant nothing less than the old man's death. Angrily he threw his cigarette at what was left of that charred log and it seemed to him as though that little burning end would sink through all those ashes and all that redness too, sink through the floor, sink through the *next* floor, sink through the foundations, and the rock-bottom and the fire within the rock-bottom; yes! sink through to the antipodal earth-crust on the other side—for that tossed-away cigarette-end was his wish *that something would happen to the old man!* He leant back in his chair and shut his eyes. What did Uncle Edward feel when he turned his face to the wall in that neat bed at Dr. Brush's; that bed that reminded him of the dormitory beds at school? Did he feel a blind hatred of this tall, healthy, elder brother, standing there and repeating: "How are ye, old chap, how are ye? I've brought young Rod to see ye!"

'But I certainly do deserve," he said to himself, opening his eyes again, "that *something* should change my life—change it, change it!

Ruth has no idea how unhappy I am; just as she has no idea how her own life is killing her chances of getting married."

It was very unusual for Rodney Loder to make any sort of emotional gesture; but something about the warm spring-like air that reached him now through the narrow space where his window was open gave him the kind of twinge which people get when happiness is tantalizing them without flowing through them; and giving a jerk to the gold chain he wore to guard his bunch of keys, he pulled it forth, and began swinging it backwards and forwards. Then with a groan he thrust this object back where it came from, and, rising from his chair, moved over to his law-table, and, snatching up a pencil, proceeded to write, in a big scrawling hand, across a sheet of empty paper: "Rodney Loder—at the end of his tether."

Having done this almost automatically, he set himself to pace up and down the room.

"What I'd like to find out," he thought, " is whether what *I* feel is an unusual feeling. Is Reality as prodding, as pinching, as hurting to every living person? And is it simply that I haven't got the gall to face it? God! I remember that day I went to see Magnus in Brunswick Terrace about young Zed's case. There was some angry parent down below, in Miss Le Fleau's room, waiting to see him; and I warned him the woman was there and gave him a chance to escape— but he wouldn't! I can see his ugly, distracted face now; and how he shook it into shape as if it were a face of clay that he'd been working at for years, and how he marched into that—"

His thoughts were interrupted by the clear, sharp tinkle of the front door bell. Instinctively he jumped to his feet and looked at himself in the glass. Then he thought:

"Why should I answer it? They'll suppose everyone's out."

But even while he formulated this conjecture he picked up his hairbrush, dipped it in his jug, and began, as his habit was, sleeking back his smooth hair from its straight, immaculate parting at the side of his head. There was a long silence then, during which, even while he kept saying to himself "I shan't go down", he was tightening his necktie and tugging at his shirtcuffs. At last the bell rang again, but with a feeble force, as if the ringer had thought:

"I may as well give it one more last pull, before I go away."

But it was the feebleness of this second appeal, as much as anything, that made him run down the stairs and open the front-door. There stood Daisy Lily! The young girl was wearing a purple jersey and a dark skirt, and on her head was a little round lavender cap of knitted wool.

"Why, Daisy—come in my dear, come in! I *am* glad to see you! Ruth's taken to taking Father out, since you were here last. He enjoys it much more with her than with me—and I don't blame him. Come upstairs to my fire, my dear! She'll be back for tea; and you'll stay for that, won't you?"

He ushered her upstairs so fast that Daisy, who was very slow at answering people and a very deliberate speaker herself, hadn't time to explain to him that she had to go and fetch Captain Poxwell from the Ruins and take him home. But she let him place her in his own chair by the fire; and when Rodney, conscious that the room was too warm for young blood after a brisk walk, offered to open the window wider, she shook her head resolutely. Daisy was so accustomed to living with people more egotistical than herself, and she was instinctively so docile, that it never entered her head to suppose that her own private preferences in the matter of heat and cold were things to be brought forward.

"I like fires," she said gravely, putting her stoutly-shod insteps side by side on the brass fender-bar. "Mrs. Matzell gives *me* a fire. Mother thinks it's wasteful; for she *has* to have one herself because of feeling the climate so damp, and grandfather has to have one in the Cabin; so there are three fires upstairs; and, of course, that *is*—"

While the young girl was speaking, Rodney watched her with a curious intensity. How quickly she'd grown up! He had once bought her a doll's house on one of her birthdays and he could hear now the intonation of her voice as she began wondering at once whether Quinquetta, who was a little china doll with a face like Marie Antoinette, would prefer to have her bedroom upstairs or downstairs.

"Cattistock at your place this afternoon?" he asked casually.

Daisy nodded, and then frowned a little, bending her head and picking with her fingers at the fold of her jersey. She had felt a longing that amounted to a necessity to have a talk with Ruth; and now she would have to return to her grandfather without it. She became aware, too, that she felt dizzy in this hot room and she remembered that things had been so much at sixes and sevens at the house that day that she had had no lunch. She was so little afraid of Rodney, however, though it was with Ruth she wanted to talk, that she asked him whether she might have a glass of water.

"Wouldn't you like milk better, and a bit of cake?"

She admitted she would, and gave him a slowly deepening and extremely grateful smile.

"One of Ammabel's own cakes?" she murmured.

"If there *are* any," he said, and hurried out of the room.

The second he was gone she got up quickly, so as to get away as far as possible from this hot fire, which she felt sure was the chief cause of her giddiness. Moving towards the window, and in all the fibres of her being longing to fling it wide open, she could not help noticing on his big law-table that sheet of paper with the words, "Rodney Loder—at the end of his tether". She stood looking at this with wide-open eyes; and her heart began to beat fast. Her first thought was a wild girlish notion, derived from Peg Frampton's pessimistic outbursts, that she may only have arrived just in time to prevent Rodney from shooting himself through the head. But seeing no sign of a revolver and no sign of any bottle labelled "Poison" she went up close to the window, and in place of opening it pressed her hot forehead against the cool pane. Here she remained, thinking over what she had seen and what it meant, until, hearing Rodney's steps returning, she hurriedly slipped back to her place. It was clear to her that he had remembered the scrawl on the table while he was down-stairs, for she was aware of his crossing the room behind her, directly he re-entered; and presently without a word he flung a handful of bits of paper straight into the fire, carrying off this action as if it were a customary and natural one with him. But the girl was deeply thankful that the business of drinking the milk and eating Ammabel's cakes gave her an opportunity of being the one talked to, rather than the one to talk; and in her slow-moving mind she pondered and pondered the meaning of those grim words. So sturdy was the soul of Captain Lily's daughter that never once since she was little had it occurred to her to pity herself or to regard her life as an unlucky one. It had been indeed the secret cause of a certain drawing back from her friend

Peg, the way Peg derived such a weird pleasure in abandoning herself to her "sea of troubles"; but this revelation about Rodney was a very different thing. She saw before her now, as she sipped her milk and felt her dizziness departing and the blood coming back to her cheeks, those words "at the end of his tether". She saw the three little dots, like three full-stops, that he had mechanically made after his final "r".

And as she cautiously, and even reluctantly, replied to his questions about Mrs. Lily and Cattistock—for it was not at all Daisy's wish to talk to Rodney about her mother—she stared gravely over the rim of her milk at his smoothly-parted hair, at his pale eyes, at his unruffled forehead; and as she stared at him little by little he was transformed before her to a totally different Rodney from the one that all her life she had been taking for granted. That neat parting of his hair, as he sat opposite her now, kept repeating "at the end"; and she vaguely felt that the word "tether" hung, like a touching and tattered escutcheon, about his neck, the trophy of something high, remote, unapproachable, tragic. There must have been something new to *him*, too, in the look of grave tenderness with which she enquired if he went any more, as he used to do, on those sea-trips with the Jobber.

"It's nice to go out in the Cormorant—don't you think so?" she said. "But I wish he wouldn't look as he does whenever anyone mentions Mr. Cattistock! The other day when he and grandfather were whispering together they stopped suddenly when I came in. He oughtn't to encourage grandfather like that, ought he?"

"Certainly not," said Rodney; and then he was aware that the grey eyes regarding him so steadily, as she held her cake to her rosy, unsmiling lips and nibbled at it absent-mindedly, seemed to be the eyes of a woman who knew what was the matter with him; and, from thinking this thought, he fell, even while they continued reminding each other of the different occasions when they had boarded the Cormorant, into a sort of waking trance, in which Daisy Lily's figure, so fully feminine, as it now showed itself to be under her tight-fitting jersey, flowed obscurely into some earlier image of her, as disembarking between himself and the Jobber on the sunlit beach at Lulworth she formed an intrinsic part of one of his most brooded-over "essences".

Perhaps it was the fact that as they sat talking in that over-heated room there came through the open chink of the window a sudden harsh crying of sea-gulls that that particular essence, caught and lost, lost and caught again, so many times since that summer day, came back to him now, connected so vividly with this girlish shape under the purple wool. But the sea-gulls of the actual moment he did not hear, so absorbed was he in this new feeling—this feeling that had suddenly swept in upon him from some open window-chink of pure chance—that a woman's heart had taken pity on him as none had ever done before. It *had* occurred to him, when he was getting her the milk, to fear lest she might have seen that paper on his working-table; but when he found her ensconced so exactly as he had left her and the paper so exactly as he had left it, he did not give *that* possibility a second thought.

"Ei-ar! Ar-ei! Ei-ar! Ar-ei!" came the shrill cry of the gulls through the window; but Rodney heard nothing of it. It was characteristic of the vein of unhappy sluggishness and inertness in him that only when impressions had subsided into the remote past could he be thrilled by them. The reality of the present seemed always weighted with something hurting.

Neither did Daisy—though at Sandsfoot Castle she would listen in rapture to this sound—give it more attention than he. Something within her that nothing had stirred before—certainly not Peg Frampton—was shaken in its obscure fortress as she looked at that smoothly-brushed head before her and saw in her mind those three full-stops after the last letter of "tether". The girl actually felt as if from depths within her that were boundless—depths that began at her breasts, but sank away into a solidity of such strong, calm, competent, pitying flesh and blood as would have needed the stature of some full-bosomed earth-titaness to supply—there rose arms, there rose hands, there rose a mounting up of irresistible protection, into which that forlorn forehead and pale unhappy eyelids might sink and be safe!

Thus while the seagulls, outside that over-heated room, kept on crying: "Ei-ar! Ar-ei! Ei-ar! Ar-ei!" those two pairs of human ears remained completely oblivious.

And the obliviousness of Rodney and Daisy to that crying of the gulls above Spy Croft added a new burden, a new weight, a new quota of insensibility to the age-old indifference of so many human souls of the two Boroughs to the objects and to the sounds that had become the tutelary background of the place. To a mind not grown quite callous to what Mr. Gaul would have called the "representative potentiality of inanimate identities" it might be easily conceived that between St. Alban's Head, the White Nose, the Nothe, Chesil Beach, the Breakwater, the Town Bridge, the White Horse, Hardy's Monument, King George's Statue, St. John's Spire, the Jubilee Clock, and this perpetual crying of sea-gulls and advancing and retreating of sea-tides, there might have arisen, in their long confederacy, a brooding patience, resembling that of an organic Being; a patience that approached, if it never could quite attain, the faint, dim embryonic half-consciousness that brooded in the sea-weeds, the sea-shells, the sea-anemones, the star-fish and jelly-fish, that lay submerged along those beaches and among those rock-pools.

But it was at the very moment when these two people were most indifferent to the sea-gulls, by reason of their new-born interest in each other that one of those devils who wait on all the encounters of the *Ying* and the *Yang* put it into the head of Rodney to utter, in that particular tone of a grown-up person addressing a child which is always so teasing, the apparently harmless words:

"How is Quinquetta?"

As a matter of fact it was a far-off glimmering memory from one of his most precious "essences" that put this remark into his head; but how was Daisy to know that? To Daisy it seemed as if, just when she was stretching out towards him the quivering antennae of a feeling she had never had for anyone else, he had got up and gone over to his washing-stand, and, snatching his jug from his basin, had poured the cold water over her beating heart! She had felt all this while with a certain discomfort the presence of this jug and basin; for she had often seen Captain Poxwell roll up his sleeves to wash his hands in *his* basin, and the sight of the rough hairs on the old man's forearms had always shocked her. It was thus an unfortunate chance at this juncture that when he said "How's Quinquetta?" Daisy should have been looking at his jug and basin; for these particular objects were indelibly lodged in her mind as the accompaniments of a certain hirsute grossness and a certain mature maleness; and now it seemed to her as if it were with a rough hairy masculine forearm that Rodney—for all his white, unruffled face—was pouring cold water on her deepest feelings.

"Oh, all right, thanks!" and she rose to her feet at once. "I'm sorry I can't stay to see Ruth," she said. "I wanted to . . . tell her . . . several things . . . and ask her . . . several things; but I must get back to grandfather before it begins to get dark. Mrs. Matzell was going to give us our tea alone in the Cabin if Mr. Cattistock was still there. Thanks so much for the cakes, Rodney. Do tell Ammabel how much I liked them."

"All right—if you must," murmured Rodney rather gloomily. Then he brightened up. "I'll walk with you to Sandsfoot, my dear! There'll be heaps of time. And it won't matter if father and Ruth *do* begin tea."

Daisy still felt strangely crushed and hurt by his question about Quinquetta. It wasn't so much the words as the tone that offended her. He would never have used that ordinary, uninteresting tone if he weren't *taking her for granted* as a little thing he'd known from infancy. But she was too well-bred and far too reserved to let Rodney have the remotest guess that she had suffered this reaction; and they set off together towards Sandsfoot, in apparent harmony.

It certainly was a peculiarly beautiful spring-like day for that early period of the year, but both the man in his light overcoat and the girl in her purple sweater continued to be absorbed in their personal feelings. The truth was that Daisy's response to the elements had throughout her girlhood been the response of an extremely sturdy and normal child. She was born to deal with people and things in the formidable protective manner of that long procession of pragmatic women who have kept the restless demons of the human soul from ruining human life. Mr. Gaul's thoughts about "the queer daughters of Chaos", though they may have applied to both Captain Poxwell's children, certainly did not apply to his grandchild. And Rodney, though it is likely enough that these windblown pools of dying sunlight, followed so soon by a drift of fiery cloud-petals from beyond Chesil, created for him some indescribable "essence" that he would feel months, or even years, later, was far too much stirred by his discovery that "little Daisy" had been transformed into a woman who had the power of seeing into the bottom of his grief, to look away for a minute from her rounded cheeks, her grave eyes, her full, sweetly-pouted lips. By the time they reached the ruined Tudor Castle, however, a heavy bank of warm dusky twilight, rolling up from over the West Bay, had quite swallowed every trace of the sunset; and a glaucous pallor that carried, all the same, a curious vitality in it, like the greenish spawn of shoals of ethereal fish, lay soft and transparent upon both land and water. Suddenly Daisy clutched the flap of his coat-pocket and stopped.

"Bother!" she whispered. "The Jobber's with him. There's the Slug!"

And sure enough, there by the gate leading from the road, stood the lumbering, antiquated little truck that Adam Skald used when he transformed himself from a sea-animal into a land-animal.

"Grandfather will have worked him up to a frenzy against Mr. Cattistock; now that he's there with mother in the house! Grandfather's just wicked when he does that. And he knows perfectly well that Mr. Cattistock has acted very well in letting me stay with him while they're together. Oh, there!" and Daisy gave vent to a funny little chuckling laugh, "I've let the cat out of the bag! But *that* was what I wanted to tell Ruth. Well, you must remember to tell her if you don't mind. It's only that mother and I would have argued— Ruth knows!—till Doomsday about it, if Mr. Cattistock hadn't spoken up quite strong and firm and said of course I must stay with grandfather. They're not going to have any honeymoon, Rodney." This remark was made in an awed whisper, while Rodney stared nervously into the Jobber's fish-smelling truck. "But she's going straight to Peninsular Lodge after the wedding; and the wedding's to be in Trinity Church."

Looking into her face, when her voice ceased, Rodney was caught for a second completely out of his self-pity; for he had the wit, even in that greyish-green twilight, to note that she would have given blood from her veins *not* to have said to him what she had just said. By so much as even referring to her mother, with anyone but Ruth, the girl seemed to outrage some peculiarly sensitive decency in her breast. And Rodney, being the person he was, knew in a second what she felt; for it was what he himself had so often felt when he spoke unsympathetically of his father; and it touched him deeply to see the way she bit her lips and the way the angry tears came into her eyes.

"You must forgive me, my dear," he said hurriedly, "if I led you on to talk of your family affairs! Don't say another word; and I'll act as if I'd been stone deaf! This fishy truck is enough to make anyone sick, not to speak of deaf."

Out of her swimming eyes Daisy gave him a look, that was the softest look—although Rodney didn't know it—that he'd had since he asked her how Quinquetta was; and side by side they approached the ruin. As Daisy had predicted they found Captain Poxwell, seated like a lanky demon of malignity upon a pile of fallen stones, on the top of which he had spread out his tartan shawl, contemplating with grim satisfaction the towering figure of Skald who was pacing to and fro in front of him. The Captain appeared to be in unusual possession of his wandering fancies, and though it was too dark within these walls to see that distended vein in his withered neck, or to catch that burning gleam in his restless eye that so roused the morbid love-hate of Mrs. Cobbold, it seemed clear to Rodney that of the two sea-faring cronies it was the owner of the Cormorant who was the more upset. So excited in fact was the Jobber that he had reached the point of being quite unable to greet Daisy with his usual aplomb, though he did extend his hand to her, while to Rodney he gave the sort of sulky little nod that a duellist, on the eve of a fatal affray, might bestow upon an undesired intruder.

"Mrs. Matzell will be waiting for us, grandfather," said the young girl, going straight up to the figure seated on the heap of stones. "Have you finished that box you brought?" And she cast her eyes to the place where the old cowrie-collector usually worked.

So strong a hold upon the Captain's established habits had the girl's affectionate appeal, that he made no attempt to resist her. Scrambling down from his pedestal he stretched himself like an old dog caught with a forbidden bone, shook his long lank body and stiffened limbs, and proceeded, without demur, to gather together his belongings.

The Jobber watched him glumly, his hands in his pockets, his chin sunk low on his chest, his shoulders hunched.

"How's my friend Trot?" enquired Rodney, while Daisy, with her arm in her grandfather's, remarked in his tone that same intonation—as of a grown-up person addressing a child—that had characterized his question about Quinquetta.

The Jobber took not the least notice of this enquiry. He appeared to be buried in some desperately absorbing thoughts of his own. He kept pressing his great wrists further and further down into his loose sailor trousers and hanging his heavy jowl still more broodingly against his chest.

"Has he gone?" asked Captain Poxwell, addressing his granddaughter.

During this whole interlude he had paid no more attention to Rodney than if he'd been a dog who had casually followed the girl into Sandsfoot Castle.

"I don't know, grandfather," said Daisy quietly. "Mother hadn't yet lit the candles when we passed the house. But they may—"

The Jobber raised his head with a jerk, took his hands from his pockets and strode over to young Loder who was feebly trying to light a match, while the wind, blowing through one of the big ruined windows, put it out every time he struck it.

"Want a ride home?" he said. "Those two can look after each other. Better leave 'em to 'emselves!" Then in a sullen whisper he added the words: "The Dog thinks he's going to be married on the twelfth . . . that's Thursday, me boy . . . and it's Monday today."

Rodney shifted his pale eyes uneasily under the tension of the man's towering personality. He looked at Daisy's sturdy yet soft figure supporting the demented Captain, whose wavering form in the gloom resembled a crazy Mephistopheles under the tutelage of some imperturbable angel.

"He's ruined my father," the Jobber's' hoarse whisper went on, "just as he's ruined my father's mates. And now he's closing up those quarries that have been open for a thousand years! Don't 'ee see, Mr. Rodney, he's grown to be more than the enemy of flesh and blood? Don't 'ee see he's grown to be an enemy of *the Stone?*"

Rodney Loder became increasingly disconcerted. A strong vein of conventional propriety in him, of sluggish bourgeois common sense, felt irritated against this big, glowering whisperer. Hadn't everyone in this world got their secret troubles? Why should Adam Skald, the Jobber, be alone permitted to raise the devil? Let him burn his own smoke! He felt inclined to say something to him as cold and crushing as his father the General would have said.

—"What is that to us? See thou to that!"—

And indeed this whole scene, in the greenish-coloured dusk of these crumbling walls, had begun to seem fantastic, unreal, absurd to him. Even if his own job had begun to bore him to the breaking-point he had no wish to exchange it for nocturnal colloquies in Sandsfoot Castle.

"Ruined," went on the Jobber, while Daisy, who had been waiting for this curious dialogue to end, began to lead the old man away, "ruined—that's what father and his mates 'ull be! And today's Monday; and he's going to enjoy that woman on Thursday. What do 'ee make of it, Loder, eh? eh? He'll be tumbling it at Chickerel, while some on the Isle have neither bread nor meat nor stone!"

The word "stone" exploded from the Jobber's lips like a heavy missile from a catapult. The chances are that those flirtatious overtures made towards him by Mrs. Lily when he was last on this spot, though they had been warded off by the memory of Perdita, had impressed the man's senses. At any rate as he thought of Cattistock enjoying this Houri of such a dazzling and satiny-white skin, he felt it was more than he could stand.

"It's Monday today, Loder, and she'll be bedded with the Dog, come Thursday!"

Rodney now began to fancy that he smelt whiskey on the Jobber's breath. The savage growls of homicidal emotion to which he had been listening were a totally new experience, and with the cautious timidity of his class he assumed at once that the man was drunk. He fixed his eyes on the Captain's departing back and noticed that the shawl the old man had been sitting on was again in its usual place round his lean neck. Then his gaze clung to Daisy's form as they crossed the threshold, and he found himself envying the Captain, with a palpable throb of irritable jealousy, the support he was getting from that soft, jersey-clad figure.

"Good-night, Captain!" shouted the Jobber. "Good-night, Missy! I'm giving Mr. Loder a lift; but I expect you'd sooner go ahead. The Slug's a bit fishy this afternoon."

There was a dead silence then, as the two figures receded; but something seemed to expand and contract like a flapping sail inside the pit of Rodney's stomach.

"Good-night, Daisy!" he shouted; and for a second it seemed to him as if she were on a ship's deck leaving the harbour and unless he heard her voice now he might never hear it again. He had only once or twice in his whole life wanted anything as much as he now wanted to hear Daisy's voice. Yes!—oh, thank the Lord!—she had turned round just as they got outside.

"Good-night all!" she cried in a clear, school-girl voice.

"She said 'all'," he thought, "because she didn't want to hurt the Jobber's feelings."

To such a pitch of excitement had this completely new Daisy Lily lifted Rodney's nerves that the owner of the Slug—and the fishy smell subsided when they were in motion—had no difficulty in persuading him to play truant from the Spy Croft tea-table, and come on with him to the harbour.

Not far from the western end of the Town Bridge where the ancient High Street of the Borough of Weymouth began, a district now devoted to warehouses and taverns, there was, at this time, a little cobbled alleyway. About equal distance between Trinity Church it was and the newly-built lecturing-place called Sidney Hall; and unpretentious though it appeared, it possessed no less than three public-houses. It was at the end of this alley, called Corder's Wharf, that a friend of the Jobber's had a large boat-repairing shed and it was here—in spite of a good deal of rattling and spluttering to get it in and get it out—that he kept his truck.

He had got it safely ensconced now and he was coming down the alley with Rodney at his side when they were accosted by a person who rushed out upon them from one of the above-mentioned public-houses. This was none other than Larry Zed, who had been waiting for them, and watching both their entrance and exit, from the bow-window of his retreat. The sight of the son and heir of the great Weymouth lawyer, for young Zed had twice been introduced to Rodney, in connection with the legalities of his adoption, reduced the lad now to a confused and angry silence.

But the Jobber caught him firmly by the hand, and holding his hand—in deliberate defiance of Corder's Wharf etiquette, which did not approve of public marks of affection between man and man—and walking between him and Rodney, he led them both across the front

of Trinity Church and along the edge of the water till they reached
the stone steps of Cove House. As usual, the curtain in the window
was hurriedly dropped, and Mrs. Trot opened the door the second they
were at the top of the steps. Both Rodney and young Zed had been
in the Jobber's house before—for the man's genius for de-classing
himself had made him a *persona nota* if not a *persona grata* with every
level of Weymouth society—but this was assuredly the first time they
had ever entered it together. They all sat down in the sitting-room—
the host's mania for leather arm-chairs being displayed to good
purpose—and if Rodney had suspected Adam Skald of being drunk in
Sandsfoot Castle he was soon put into a less carping mood by the
unusual quality of the Jobber's whiskey when enjoyed in person.

What with the admirable drink, of which Larry partook equally
with the others, and the visits that they all three made, in decent
succession, to the Jobber's bedroom, the hour from five to six passed
with incredible speed. It passed a good deal faster, it must be confessed,
for Rodney in the Jobber's sitting-room than for Daisy in her grandfather's Cabin.

It is perhaps hardly strange that human beings in their abysmal
craving for some over-consciousness that shall record and retain in
memory events and occurrences and words and deeds and groupings,
such as happen simultaneously in any spot on the earth's surface,
should have been tempted to attribute a consciousness like this to those
symbolic Inanimates in such a spot, that in our partial fancy we
conceive of as fumbling their way to some obscure, non-human level
of awareness. But it is very hard for the mind to endow a thing like a
church-spire or a plaster-statue or a harbour-bridge or an esplanade-
clock or a stone-breakwater, or even a far-stretching promontory,
with this sort of consciousness. Thus we are compelled—although
with the loss of a thousand dear and indelible affiliations—to have
recourse, if we are to satisfy this natural craving, to the unhomely
gulfs of spiritual invisibility. If any over-consciousness then, or any
sub-consciousness for such omnipresence need not imply superiority,
could have looked into the heart of Daisy Lily and of Rodney Loder
between the hours of five and six on the afternoon of February the
Ninth, it is difficult to suppose it could be a consciousness emanating
from the White Nose, from Hardy's Monument, from the White

Horse, from the Nothe, from the Breakwater, from the Clock on the Esplanade, from the stone arches of the old Harbour-Bridge; but it is easy to suppose that some invisible entity—such are the possibilities of life—contemplated these two, the man of thirty and the girl of seventeen, in their present attraction to each other.

Rodney's own attention kept wandering from his companions; and although he himself was the most conventional of the three, he was the one, during that whole hour, whose nature was most transported out of its normal course. But wander as his attention might—such is the harsh obduracy of material distance—he could not see what Daisy was doing in Half-Way House.

The girl as a matter of fact was standing on a chair in her bedroom —having barely tasted any tea and escaped as soon as she possibly could—reaching up to a high, wide, cluttered shelf, and struggling to drag down a small, wooden play-box. Clouds of dust descended with the box and got into her eyes and into her mouth, but she stoutly went on pulling at it and finally jumped down from the chair in triumph and, dusting the bottom of it with her pocket-handkerchief, laid it on her bed. Hurriedly she pushed back the lid of the box; and there lay the china doll Quinquetta! Quinquetta was about six inches tall when she stood up; but since Daisy had relinquished playing with her she seldom stood up; but on the contrary lay all day long, as well as all night long, with her blue eyes wide open, staring at the lid of the box with no less earnestness than she would have stared at the ceiling, or, if it had been possible, at the sky.

If we were permitted by the Holy Office of the Exact Sciences to dally with so-unprovable a fantasy it were a nice point to speculate as to exactly *when*, in the life of an object adored by a fetish-worshipper, this sacrosanct Inanimate becomes animate. At what point does the idol, the stone, the block of wood, the doll, gather to itself its living identity, and become—as its worshipper certainly feels it *does* become—something more than the inert substance which is all that reason sees in it?

Quinquetta, when Daisy had taken her carefully out of the box and propped her up against her own pillow, was certainly something more than an inanimate china form. This "something more" would have been instantaneously recognized by any savage who had entered

Daisy's room; but the scientific instrument to register it has yet to be invented. Round and about Quinquetta's palpable form there must have extended—like what the theosophists call an astral body—an impalpable emanation, which was a second, or more etherealized, Quinquetta. This second Quinquetta was created out of her young mistress' own warm life and glowing youthful vitality, and although invisible to the eye of reason it must have been very apparent to the clairvoyance of the human heart.

Daisy was far too practical a young woman to let her natural superstition run away with her; and she did *not*, at this juncture, cry out with tears in her eyes: "Forgive me, Quinquetta, for being angry with him for mentioning you!" but in her heart, as she carefully straightened the doll's clothes, she undoubtedly did apologize to the beautiful little image, or at any rate to that invisible eidolon of it which had usurped a living identity.

"You *shall* stay out, Quinquetta," she told the doll, as from its place upon the pillow it saw her clambering on the chair again to put the box away.

There are things, we may suppose, that a grown-up girl's doll does not need to have put into words; and so we may assume there was a perfect reconciliation between them before Daisy, who was too practical—and also too conscious of Mrs. Matzell's appearance presently—to leave her on the bed, balanced her very carefully, in an inconspicuous but comfortable seat, on one of her book-shelves.

Both Mr. and Mrs. Bum Trot were called upon to wait upon the three men—if young Zed could be called a man—while they ate their tea-supper beneath the Jobber's immensely tall candle-sticks. Rodney, as has been hinted, was nervous and very absent-minded, while the Jobber, who had never drunk so much whiskey at his own table as he did tonight, kept swinging from one extreme mood to another with disconcerting suddenness. At one moment nothing could exceed his exaggerated cordiality; at another he would fall into spasms of such arctic silence that they were like holes in the air, ice-cold air-pockets, to the devoted Mrs. Trot, as she went round the table changing the plates.

"I knew Larry was coming to see me tonight, Loder," their host remarked, when the things had been all cleared away and a bowl of fruit and nuts put before them, together with the whiskey. "That's why I wanted you to look in. Are you and Mr. Crouch so tied up with the Dog, that you wouldn't dare to defend these Lodmoor folk, if the Town really did try to evict them?"

" 'Tis that Sippy Ballard—gentlemen—he be the one," cried young Zed eagerly, "don't 'ee let there be no mistake. *He* be the one. Council be skeered of he, seeing that he be Cattistock's nephy or summat o' that. Me poor May do thinky and thinky how best to answer 'n and to answer thik girt King's Writ 'a plumbed down; but her can reason of naught but being drove back to they Gippoos, and of taking I along o' she, to bide in caravan."

When Larry had finished speaking the Jobber gave Rodney a triumphant and almost gloating look; as much as to say, "You see how right I am!" But his only words to young Zed were:

"You and your May ain't got the hang o' things correct, lad. Sippy's nothing. Sippy's a catch-paw. 'Tis the Dog, I tell ye! First and last, 'tis the Dog. But tell your May to wait a little. Tell her to wait quiet and do naught. Today's only Monday; and there are two days betwixt Monday and Thursday, when he be thinking to set his teeth in that white skin. Tell her to wait quiet. She shan't be turned out of Lodmoor Hut nor shall my dad's mates be turned out of Saxon Quarry. You note what I say, Loder, my gentleman; and you note what I say, Larry, my lad!"

"Be Captain Poxwell's darter such a white one, Jobber," threw in young Zed with gleaming eyes. "Be she's skin white as our Blotchy's milk? Be it white as yon Chesil foam, when wind blows west?" He suddenly gave a furtive glance at the door, as if afraid of eavesdroppers; and then brought out in a low, solemn, intensely grave whisper: "There were a girl come to Lal's bed. Her came with Mr. Gaul, that time when Sippy Ballard put King's Writ on we . . . and her were the beautifullest girl poor Lal ever seed! Her were a lady-girl, her were, but her were minded to lie in the straw with poor Lal. That were when her came to hay-loft, so snug and so warm. 'Twas shown to I who her were, too, later; and do 'ee know who her were, Mr. Loder? Do 'ee know who her were, Jobber? Her were thik girl from the Far Isles, what Mrs. Cobbold sent for, to keep she warm o' nights. And I do know she's name too."

Young Zed uttered this last sentence with an awed and yet formidable gravity. He evidently considered that, as in the case of magicians and their attendant demons, to know a girl's name gave you some special power over her.

The Jobber heaved up his head from an orange he was peeling and gave his red-haired visitor such a look across the table as would have flabbergasted Casanova; only Zed completely missed it, because one of the tall candle-flames was in the way.

" 'Tweren't from Mr. Gaul that she's name came to I," the lad blundered on, while the elf-lock across his forehead gleamed blood-red in the candle-light. " 'Twere May what larned it. May said the cards told she it begin with a P.; and when us took me eels to Belvedere, and when her asked Mrs. Pengelly, *so't did!* She's name begun with a P. same as May said. And do 'ee know what it were? It were Perd'ta Wane."

Young Zed breathed his heroine's appellation so reverently that to Rodney's ears its syllables were confused with the name of an unfortunate young gentlewoman who had recently committed suicide in the town of Poole; and he turned his hazel eyes, a little dizzied by the whiskey, with a good deal of bewilderment upon this singular fellow-guest.

"Perd'ta Wane be she's name," went on Larry, uttering the words as if he were a young priest at the altar. "And that's the reason why, when I goes to bed me Nothing-Girl don't come to I no more. They girls don't like to share a person betwixt 'un; so 'tis Perd'ta Wane what I thinks on, now me Nothing-Girl have stupped cuddling I. May do say that when the Man-with-Three-Staves be the last card it means that the man of the house will lie with a stranger; but I mind naught of what them conjuring-cards say when I cuddles me down in me bed and do thinky and thinky of Perd—"

But the Jobber was able to endure it no more.

"Here, drink, boy! Drink, I tell you! No, no, Loder; it won't hurt him, my whiskey, no more than it'll hurt you. Drink, you shining eyes! Drink, you blood-head! *That's* the ticket. *That's* my girl-stealer! Down with it. And here's another to follow."

As a matter of fact Rodney was amazed at the little effect the drink appeared to have on the boy. He himself began to feel so light in his head that he made up his mind not to stay much longer lest he might not be able to walk home. And in a few minutes, when they had been sitting there, so it seemed to him, for fully two hours, he got up unsteadily on his feet and began to explain, uttering each word with the unnatural precision of a man defending his sobriety that it was important that he get back to Spy Croft before his father's bed-time.

"I always mix his grog for him, Skald; and here I am, revelling with you and our young friend, while—And I've got that walk, too!"

"Listen, Rodney Loder," said the Jobber, sternly, as he helped him on with his overcoat, "I can't tell how much weight you have with Mr. Crouch, but I swear to you this—if Loder and Crouch don't take up the case on behalf of May and this boy, there'll be such a —— You can delay and hold everything up, anyway! I know enough of the law to know that. And today's Monday; and on Thursday the Dog thinks he's going to enjoy his woman! Those Cattistock and Frampton beer-barrels ought to have orange blossoms twisted round 'em— eh, Larry Zed?"

He moved round the table to get to the door, which he opened wide, calling loudly to Mrs. Trot to come and say good-bye; for his habit was—although she waited on him like a servant—to treat her on formal occasions as if she were the mistress of the house; but he now turned to Larry, while Rodney was looking for his hat and gloves.

"Did your May's conjuring-cards," he said in a cold, harsh, emphatic voice, "tell her anything about me and the Dog?"

Young Zed's Tom o' Bedlam wits seemed to grow more rational in proportion as the Jobber's manner became more savage and unrestrained. The Lad's mind rushed back, as the man asked him this direct question, to that scene in the hut when Marret and May quarrelled over the Tarot cards; and leaning forward in his chair, where he was cracking walnuts by pressing them together with his wrists, he remarked, in a low mumbling tone, as he spat out a bit of walnut shell, that he "were not one for taking stock in they fortune-tricks," when he could have a girl in his bed.

The Jobber had his fingers on the handle of the door when Larry used this expression, and he gazed at him in cold fury.

"So this boy and I will count on you, Mr. Loder," he finally remarked, while Mrs. Trot, having shaken hands stiffly with Rodney, began unbarring those absurd door-bolts, with which in his Portland manner, the Jobber loved to bar himself in.

Rodney hummed and hawed. Nothing was more objectionable to him than an eruption of his accurst profession into his ordinary private life.

"I'll mention to Mr. Crouch," he said, "that I have been making personal enquiries about the Lodmoor property; and that it *does* seem as if Ballard had been a little—impetuous. I will suggest to Mr Crouch that it might be well to ask for further instructions from the Council itself, before taking—"

He interrupted himself from half-way down the front steps—for it seemed as if he could not get away fast enough, now that the Law had been dragged in—to speak of his gratitude "for this splendid evening"; but the splashing of the waves swallowed up his voice, and Mrs. Trot closed the door on him without ceremony. If there was one thing more than another upon which Bum and his wife were in complete agreement it was their hatred and suspicion of all lawyers.

"Well, lad," said the Jobber as he returned to his supper-table, only to find the nut-loving Larry still cracking walnuts between his wrists, "I'm afraid your friend May will be coming to look for you if I don't pack you off home-along. I *think*—mind you I can't vouch for't, but I think—Loder and Crouch'll stop their turning you out; at any rate stop the Dog from *rushing* you out, as he'd like to do."

"Here! Put some o' they nuts in thy pocket, lad," cried Mrs. Trot, who had entered the room with her master; and as Larry, who had slouched obediently into the passage, was struggling with his weather-worn overcoat, smelling of eels and cow-dung, the woman began filling his pockets with both nuts and oranges.

"It's his red hair and his sweet tongue," thought the Jobber, as he opened the front-door and gave the boy threepence for the ferry. "I've never known a woman who didn't want to cosset him. You can see it in their eyes."

He waited till young Zed was at the bottom of the steps.

"Go by the Esplanade, lad," he called after him. "Don't hang about the Town."

It was no surprise to Mrs. Trot, a quarter of an hour later, to hear from her kitchen the Jobber himself leaving the house.

"Who could bide quiet," she said to Bum, "after eating and drinking with a lawyer?"

"Hush, woman! 'Tis no lawyer, and 'tis no idiot neither, what drives he forth," retorted Bum. "Us do know what drives he forth; and us do know what be in's mind! Haven't us heerd 'un yallerin' in's sleep, ever since the Dog shut down thik wold quarry?"

Such, however, were the unpredictable moods of the Jobber that his faithful adherents would have been thunderstruck had they known—as he walked towards the bridge harbour—that it was not upon his enemy at all, but upon Mrs. Cobbold's companion, that his mind was running! It can be well believed what an effort it had cost him to restrain himself and to hold his peace, while Larry was rambling on, after his fashion, about Perdita's visiting his bed.

"No ... no ... no," he thought, "she *couldn't* have done that!" And then he rounded savagely on himself. "*Why not?* Every woman he meets falls in love with that boy! Besides, what do *I* know of her? That she comes from Guernsey! Who gave me the right to quarrel with her if she's found a lad that suits her foreign taste? Young Zed isn't an ordinary boy. I've never taken him for an idiot; and if he's had the wit to attract that girl—"

Such were the Jobber's thoughts as he stopped presently by the edge of the harbour-wall and stared into the dark water. The tide was riding high at that hour, and towards the lantern-lit arches of the ancient Town Bridge joining the two boroughs the whole sea seemed moving with one vast up-gathered volume of dark, strange, far-drawn invasion. As he stared at that rushing water, the Jobber gave full rein to the impassioned craving for this girl which had been mounting up in him all these days. Instead of his murderous intention killing this violent desire, it seemed rather to have accentuated it. Love and hate as they seethed together in his nerves, seemed to double each other's power of obsession. But this boasting speech of Larry's and all the wild, exciting images called up by his rambling talk, made the Jobber realize, as he stared at that rushing tide, that you could walk with a strange girl for no more than a quarter of an hour along the sea's edge, only to discover that nothing else henceforth to the end of your days, no person, no thing, no cause, no idea, can ever be, in your inmost, secretest feelings, as important as this brief experience. It was not that he believed with his reason that young Zed had really embraced Perdita. Indeed he was clairvoyant enough to have got a pretty clear notion of what actually had occurred. It was as if his feeling for the girl had flown back over the intervening days like a greedy cormorant, and had devoured all Larry's feelings for her; so that as he stared into that rushing tide his desire for her was far more intense, far more tyrannous, than it had been when he woke up that morning. The Jobber's amorous experiences hitherto had been entirely sensual and transitory, hardly touching his deeper nature; so that from the moment he set eyes on Perdita there rushed to the intensifying of his feeling for her a whole suppressed world of passionate romance.

Mrs. Trot had often said to her husband: "If ever the master do love a 'ooman he'll go ramping wild like a mad elaphint!"

To this the faithful Bum had replied: "*He'll* never go mad about *they*. Of that thee may be sure. The only 'ooman *my* skipper'll ever love be the salt sea."

But the Jobber had drunk a lot more whiskey than usual this night, and all his senses were on fire. At this moment as he stood in a mental tumult, with both hands deep in his pockets, his fingers clutching his Chesil Beach pebble, it *was* of a woman he thought.

"I said to myself," he thought, "that I wouldn't see her till I'd done it; but I can no more go another twelve hours without seeing her than I can pray to Jesus."

The swirling of that night-tide below him, which he knew nigh as well as the beat of his own pulses, seemed to him now like the very rush of time itself bearing him on.

"I must see her first," he thought, "and *then* I'll do it."

And the swirling tide before him seemed to rise up towards him, for he had been drinking steadily glass after glass, as he listened to Larry's talk and his heavy nature was disturbed within him at its deepest roots. And as the black tide rose up before him he could see Perdita quite distinctly through its swirling mass, and she was looking steadily at him with those same soft brown eyes that had clung to his own underneath the esplanade lamp. And while she looked at him she smiled wantonly, provocatively; and, while she smiled, her fingers went to the clasp of her belt to undo it, and then to the hooks at the side of her skirt, to undo them also. Yes, he could see her funny, twisted mouth, drawn down a little at the corners. He could see her thin, tilted nose, and a brown wisp of hair fallen sideways against her sea-wet cheek. And he had only to go straight through that black tide to take her—there as she was—for she was waiting for him; but for some reason the stone in his pocket was growing heavier and heavier and bigger and bigger! He could hardly hold it with his fingers, it was growing so big; and it was weighing him down too . . . With a jerk of his shoulders and a hoarse chuckle he drew back now from the wharf's edge.

"What a thing a night-tide is!" he thought, and he began imagining the way it must carry up the harbour all manner of big fish, fish that never came up at all save when the night-tide was high, and all manner of fresh bits of seaweed, crimson seaweed, red as these ships' lights that danced on the black ripples, blood-red, like Larry's elf-lock, which had been the candle to light her to bed; blood-red, like the Dog's skull, when he'd cracked it with his great stone! What big fish there must be now, floating so easily, so calmly with great languid nocturnal fins and twitching tails under that black blood-stained water! How they danced and danced on the water now those blood-red ripples! The night-tide—aye! how many a wet evening had he watched it! Swirling, rolling, mounting, brimming up, against the slippery, green slime of this wharf-wall, it had always stirred him to the depths. Those foam-patterns that floated there—so livid-white in the lantern-flecked blackness—he always imagined them far out to sea, drifting across the bows of derelict wrecks, tossed against the flanks of "sea-shouldering" whales, bubbling up from the gasping of drowning men, blown aside from the sinking of inestimable treasure! Yes, the night-tide, the night-tide, was the thing! Day-tides were greedy, monotonous, miserly. They went up and down; they went down and up; and they didn't like it when the least bit of weed, or the least bobbing piece of cork got clear away, out to the open sea! *Back* they would have them come. Oh, there was something abominable about those day-tide motions and reversions . . . And then he remembered how the Town Council had cleared out the ancient Weymouth Breakwater across whose wide-stretching muddy flat the tides used to flow, and had built a great dam over there.

"So this swirling deep-sea water," he thought, "has *nowhere to go*. All it can do is to go back and forth, forth and back, till Doomsday."

He gave vent to a heaving sight that shook his whole frame; and then very slowly, and with feet that seemed to drag under his weight he moved on towards the Town Bridge.

"I'll go to High House early tomorrow," he said to himself. "I *must* see her once—just once—before I do it. Damn! It's no good my going to bed, no good, no good. I'll go to the Weeping Woman and make a night of it."

7

SARK HOUSE

AT nine o'clock on the morning of the following day, two days before his sister-in-law's marriage to Mr. Cattistock, Jerry Cobbold was slowly finishing his breakfast in his gaudy, tarnished, stage-set dining-room, at the top of High House.

Perd'ta Wane, as young Zed called her, sat opposite the great clown, looking comparatively calm, for it was these tête-à-tête breakfasts with Lucinda's husband that would have persuaded her to stay on here, if anything could have done so. Mr. Cobbold lit a cigarette and offered one, and his match-flame with it, to his young vis-à-vis.

"You are thinking of leaving us, Miss Wane," he said quietly, in the same flat, neutral, colourless voice with which he always addressed her; and indeed, as far as she could make out, always addressed Mrs. Cobbold, too.

She thanked him for the cigarette, began smoking it awkwardly, flicked the tip of its illuminated end against the rim of her saucer, and with her left hand folded up her napkin, avoiding his eyes.

"Don't think, Mr. Cobbold," she began gravely, still without looking at him, "that I am ungrateful for all the kindness you've shown me. And your wife, too, has been more than kind. It isn't that I'm not comfortable here or at ease with you, for I am very much so; it's only that *I can't keep it up!* I mean I can't go on being your wife's confidante. It's too upsetting. I'm not strong; I'm not a spirited person; I've got my . . . my own difficulties and I tell you—" as she spoke she drew in a deep breath of her cigarette smoke and exhaled it slowly, letting it rise up like a cloud between them. "The truth is," she concluded, "what your wife wants is a very cheerful person, someone whose own nerves are very calm. I'm far too weak a character to be any help. It only troubles me, the way she is . . . I just listen and feel perfectly helpless."

The comedian looked at her with his head a little on one side and a faint smile on his lips.

"I think," he said, "if you'll allow me to say so, you're being quite unfair to yourself! Mrs. Cobbold has been . . . of course . . . *you* can't know this . . . but I'm telling you now . . . better . . . than she's been for several months . . . since you've been here . . . and I'm sure . . . between us . . . we could——"

He spoke in a low, hesitating voice—a voice she had never heard him use before, though she had heard a good many different intonations from him—and he gave her the impression of pretending to be afraid of her; when really he would have liked to box her ears for a silly little weakling. She had seen enough of Jerry by this time to have come to the conclusion that whatever his real life might be, not a flicker of it appeared on the surface at High House. What she felt was that he was acting all the while, acting *sans cesse*, a different rôle, of course, from his comic one on the stage, and not always the same rôle here, but always wearing *some* kind of mask.

"I'm afraid, Mr. Cobbold," she said as resolutely as she could and with as little feeling, "I really cannot stay. But I don't want to leave you in the lurch and I don't want to be unpleasant. If you have anyone you could call in for a few weeks, while you advertise again, it would be——"

To the girl's consternation the clown stretched his arm across the table and touched her knuckles with the tips of his fingers.

"Don't run away today or tomorrow," he whispered, with the air of a conspirator. "See me through this Cattistock business. Stay till the end of the week; and then you shall go—if you must."

He removed his arm with an easy gesture; but it was clear to her that the automatic start she had given had impressed him; for his next words were more direct and more deprecatory.

"Stay till the end of the week, Miss Wane—if you can bear it somehow—and then, I swear I'll let you go. And I'll come back from the theatre earlier tonight, and the next night, and . . . yes! listen Miss Wane. I'll tell Mrs. Cobbold you must have a whole day off——

a bit of a holiday—and I'll take your place on deck, while you're off duty. Come now! Be a kindhearted girl and do this for me—if not for her."

Perdita sat up straight and bit her lips. Her cheeks got white with the effort of struggling against him. Some sort of pathetic appeal she had expected; but not quite this. He put her in the position of a nurse, who proposed to leave her patient at a crisis. Oh, how indignant, oh, how furious she felt with him! For by some indefinable instinct she felt certain that Mrs. Cobbold *could* get on perfectly well without any companion.

"She's wicked," she thought. "She's a false, tricky, selfish, neurotic woman; and what *he* wants is just to escape the burden. He knows, as well as I do, that I'm not necessary to her. I'm *a vice* to her. That's what I am."

"I am . . . afraid . . . I can't stay," said Perdita firmly but faintly, disregarding his reference to Mrs. Lily.

Jerry Cobbold pushed back his chair with a jerk.

"Oh, well then! Oh, all right then!" he flung out, in a tone like that of a phlegmatic school-boy, who resigns himself to not having the half-holiday he had been promised. "Want me to play you something?"

Perdita could not help smiling at this. The man's transparent cajolery of her was really too childish! But she suppressed a hopeless little sigh, flicked away some cigarette ashes and, looking straight into his eyes, said that she would be thrilled to hear.

"You know you said yesterday that you always heard me play after breakfast down all that long passage from your room? You thought it was queer. But it wasn't so very queer, considering that I invariably opened the door! I wanted you to hear me, Perdita."

His use of her Christian name discomposed her far more than his touching of her hand had done. Neither gesture was anything in itself. She knew that. But she had come to feel disconcerted, puzzled, embarrassed, *defeated* by Mr. Cobbold. She did not dislike him. In truth she rather liked him. But she never for a moment felt that she could predict what he was going to say or do next, nor did she ever have the least idea what he was thinking in his own mind.

However, she got up from the table; and as he sat down at the little grand piano, where she knew it was his wont to play, in this soft, quiet manner, every morning, she sank into an arm-chair by the fire and set herself to smoke quietly and to listen to him, a thing she had never done before. She soon found herself throwing her cigarette into the flames and drinking in this music with unexpected interest. How softly the man played! How rapt and absorbed he was! Perdita had a passion for the piano, and a fairly comprehensive one, though her knowledge was small and her training nil. But now, as she listened, she forgot everything except these muted, muffled, tenderly evoked sounds. She had not the remotest idea what composer it was. It had the technique—so she thought—of the older masters; and yet there was something about it that stirred her pulses and lifted her out of herself as few of the older composers ever did.

"Is it," she thought, "some modern musician imitating the old style? No, no! This is no imitation. This is life itself, life filling out the patterns and rules that it has made, *as if they were sails,* to carry it beyond itself, over unknown seas!"

She had never listened to such playing.

"Why," she thought, "he is making a lot of mistakes! He is playing from memory and blundering and stopping. Is he extemporizing? No! it is *old* music; it is in the old style! He has forgotten it, and is leaving out and putting in! There—I'm sure *that* was wrong!"

She turned in her chair and tried to catch a glimpse of his face; but there was a big vase of Mrs. Cobbold's favourite waxen flowers on the piano; and she could not see him. How could he stand those things there, in front of his nose? She was still puzzled by what he was playing; but it was very soft and low, and became more and more beautiful as it went on. Her critical, pessimistic intelligence began its usual trick now of trying to spoil her pleasure.

"He is amusing himself by cajoling 'the companion'. He is talking to me through this music and trying to seduce me to stay. He *is* clever, though. He knows just what I like. He's a famous man, a great man, and I'm a poor, ugly, little companion; but here we sit at the top of this tall house and he's concentrating himself on breaking down what he thinks is my silly obstinacy. I suppose there are thousands of women in London who'd sell their souls to be begged and beseeched

in this way by Jerry Cobbold. An insignificant, funny-looking, sulky
governess, alone with the great Jerry!"

She could almost feel the caress of the man's fingers as this soft
insinuating music rippled, quivered, trembled, rose and sank about her
as she sat there. Slowly her bitter thoughts began to yield to the spell.
No! she could not resist these ripples of lovely sound. She set herself
to listen, while first one figure in her present life, and then another,
came and went. The figure of the Jobber was the last to come; but
it faded away like the rest.

"He doesn't play like a musician," she thought. "I know he is
making mistakes."

But she had hardly thought, "He is making mistakes. He is
playing badly," than she felt compelled to shut her eyes. An immense
flood of happiness lifted her up and carried her away. Her irritation
with this man of many masks dropped from her and sank as if into
deep water. Her revulsion against Lucinda fell away, too, sinking
down like a pebble-stone. Her loneliness, her anxiety, her pessimism,
all were submerged. She was herself, and yet not herself! She became
a disembodied spirit that floated in, and over, this quivering flood.
Across these waves she skimmed, light as a seamew; and, as the man
went on playing, it was as if every moment in her past life, when she
had been happy, darted up from its hiding-place, an arrowy jet of
gleaming luminosity, and diffused itself through the whole air on
which she floated; till she felt as if she were drifting through the
liquid ether of a substance that resembled mother-of-pearl. But when
all that had ever thrilled her, whether of taste, or touch, or sight, or
smell, was transformed into a super-ether, this ether itself melted into
that sound-sea, that rolled and rippled and towered and toppled and
carried her along. Everything became sound. Thought had no reality.
Things had no substance. Memory had no meaning, hope no shape.
Sound was life. Sound was death. Sound was fate. Sound was the
pouring forth, out of the abyss, of something beyond all reason and all
knowledge! She herself, the Perdita she lived with, became a sound
among other sounds, a sound that was nothing but the rising and
falling of darkness and light. Past and future were lost in each other.
Nor did any present that could be called a present take their place.
This conscious sound, that *had* been Perdita's soul, was a thing that

had neither inward nor outward, neither subject nor object. It was an Absolute, self-existent, self-generated, self-complete. Only it kept breaking up into innumerable waves of darkness and light, that fell and rose, rose and fell, till they were an eternal oneness in their manifold, and an eternal manifold in their oneness . . .

Then the man, without bringing what he played to its natural conclusion, let his fingers drop from the key-board. He seemed totally unaware of Perdita's presence. Rising from the music-stool he walked over to the great bow-window, built like the rest of High House of solid stone, and stood with his back to the girl, looking out.

For some minutes Perdita was in a condition of complete numbness. When her mind began to return to itself she found herself thinking— just as she had done when he began playing—

"He makes a lot of mistakes. You can see he is no musician."

Then once again that curious numbness returned, as if her soul had left its body and refused to come back. When it did come back its coming must have had a disturbing physical effect, like the return of circulation; for without the least emotional or spiritual awareness, and from some purely physical cause, so it seemed, she suddenly found herself crying—crying silently, automatically, stupidly—and with no feeling behind her tears, save that of an indescribable bodily relief. Whether Cobbold realized the effect his playing had produced she never knew. Her silent tears dried up. Her normal intelligence resumed its function. Her pessimistic attitude returned. She felt as if she had disembarked from a voyage to the Isles of the Blest, only to find everything in this old, bitter, unredeemed world, just the same.

Stiffly she stood up. The man had his hands in his pockets now, and he was actually whistling, in a careless, lazy manner, an air from the piece he had been playing. She thought to herself:

"If I slip away without saying anything, he'll know what I felt." It needed a terrible effort to speak to him; but her pride was in command again. "What *was* that piece you played, Mr. Cobbold?" she brought out.

Her voice sounded identical with the hard, cold, unfeeling voice with which, only last night, she had been driven to get Lucinda out of her bedroom.

He swung round with his most courteous and uncommitted manner.

"I thought you would—" he began, when heavy steps and men's voices in the hall took the words from his mouth.

He looked at her and she looked at him; and one of those quick, subtle complicities, of people who have been tossed by a wanton chance into an unforeseen familiarity, passed between them, between an anonymous masculine soul and an anonymous feminine soul, driven into a forced and accidental reciprocity.

Then the door of the dining-room opened and the man-servant, ushering into the apartment the tall figure of the Jobber, announced, in a low but very emphatic voice:

"Mr. Skald to see you, sir!"

She had never dreamed that it would flow over her with a *double* over-poweringness, when she saw him again, her weakness, her helplessness, her enslavement.

"I love you, I love you!" was what every atom of her body was calling out now as she let him take her hand.

Jerry contemplated with some surprise and amusement this encounter between them. A vague notion flitted through his brain that the pair were old friends and had been friends in early youth. Perhaps her people had gone to Guernsey from Portland!

Perdita simply could not look the Jobber in the face. She hung her head and looked sideways at a gilded stool. This stool might have been the very one that Hamlet sat on, during the play-scene, when he cried out: "For if the king like not the comedy, why then, belike he likes it not, perdy!" but what Perdita noticed about it now was that the gilding had been knocked off from one of its edges, revealing a fragment of pallid, flaky substance, resembling cement rather than wood.

But the voice of the man holding her hand went on growling and muttering like low summer thunder above her head. Of course there was no earthly reason against the Jobber's holding her hand so long and talking to her so possessively in Mr. Cobbold's presence. They were breaking no law of society! He was a bachelor, she a spinster. He was of an ambiguous social position; and so most undoubtedly was she.

"Pardon me, Jerry Cobbold, I was so pleased to find Miss Wane here that I forgot my manners. We haven't met, Miss Wane and me, for a long time. No, not since that first day, is it, Miss?"

"Sit down, sit down, Jobber," broke in Jerry now; and he pushed the owner of the Cormorant into the chair recently vacated by Perdita. "Will you have one of mine?" he said to him when he had got him settled, "or do you, like the rest of us, prefer your own?"

But the Jobber's great brown hand had already closed mechanically on the little object; and he was—from the cloud of smoke that now encircled his head and the length of the fiery ash-end that soon burned between his fingers—prepared to despatch Jerry's cigarettes at the rate of one a minute.

"I hadn't realized that you two were such old friends, Miss Wane," murmured the clown. "Here—sit here—for I must go and see if my wife doesn't want to share this pleasure. She's as much in love with our friend here, as her—" He was going to say "as her sister", but he stopped himself in time.

The Jobber's threats of physical violence to Cattistock were common talk in all circles of the town.

"Won't you, for five minutes, Mr. Cobbold, before I go to see your wife—for I know at this hour she'd sooner see me—just play us a little of what you were playing before Mr. Skald came in?"

Jerry smiled quickly at her; and once more there passed between them that curious wave of intimacy or familiarity which had brought them together when the Jobber's steps had been heard in the passage.

"Certainly I'll play for you again," he said. "But only on one condition!"

Perdita was astonished at the ease, the freedom, the naturalness, the lack of all diffidence and all shyness which she now felt with the great man. And she looked straight into his eyes with an animation and a soft radiance that enchanted him.

Jerry's perceptions, when it came to the relations between men and women, were subtler than a woman's; and not the simplest woman but would have discovered the surge of mutual excitement that was rocking these two queer ones in their singular encounter.

"You ... two ... *are* ... a pair ... of sly ones," said Cobbold very slowly, evidently gathering his cue, as he went on, from Perdita's

illuminated face. "Who would have guessed you . . . were . . . such . . .
old friends?"

The Jobber's arm shot out now and his fingers closed on the lappet
of the girl's plain, tailor-made jacket. This he held fast—apparently
with the same unconsciousness with which he had a minute ago been
puffing at the cigarettes offered him by Cobbold and throwing them
into the fire—while Perdita's hand, raised as if to loosen his fingers
from her coat, remained, to the delight of the wily clown, in obvious
contact with the hand she would have removed.

"Well, if you'll sit on the arm of our friend's chair," he began, while
his glance never wandered for one second from the girl's brown eyes,
which struck him as revealing a startled and infinitely touching
happiness, "I'll willingly play a bit of it again; only I can't
promise, you know, to catch the . . . what to you call it . . . a second
time."

He turned from them slowly, with a characteristic shrug of his
shoulders that had become famous. But this particular gesture—
familiar to his audiences in half Europe—was entirely wasted upon the
Jobber and Perdita; nor when the music filled the room again did it
recapture one-twentieth part of its former magic. In fact what little
attention Perdita was able to give to it was quite distracted this time
by her awareness of the player's blundering technique.

"He isn't a real musician," she said to herself. "What I felt before
must have been some kind of—"

She was standing motionless now with shining eyes, just where Jerry
had left her, and her cheeks were almost as white and her body almost
as rigid as Lucinda's gardenias.

The Jobber, however, was evidently thankful for the music. He
seemed like a man in a trance who responds to a word or to a touch, in
a state of rapturous abstraction. He still retained his hold of the edge
of the girl's coat and presently she felt herself drawn gently towards
him. Unable, without destroying the solemnity of that moment, to
free herself from him, she did, in a state of mind as somnambulistic as
his own, precisely what the comedian had suggested. She slipped down
upon the arm of his chair. With a delicacy and restraint which affected
her far more than any audacity could have done, he relinquished, the
moment she was seated so close to him, his grasp upon her jacket, and

kept his heavy-jowled massive lineaments turned away from her face and directed steadily towards the figure at the piano.

Sitting on the arm of his chair, but free from his touch, she couldn't help letting her eyes take in every aspect of this man she had loved— so literally at first sight! He wore his usual sailor's garb, a rough dark blue jersey and navy-blue baggy trousers.

"What has he got in his trouser-pocket?" she thought, observing the protrusion of the hidden Chesil Beach pebble.

She was spared that usual melancholy gulf between the ideal features of a mental image and the reality; for what she now snatched furtive glimpses of, the Jobber's profile, as he stared at the piano, seemed like an incarnation of all the impossible images that had hovered about all her girlhood's broodings and trances and yearnings.

But both Perdita's drifting thoughts and Jerry's swaying fingers were interrupted by the re-appearance of the servant.

"Mistress is asking for Miss Wane, sir," the man announced.

Cobbold drew a fantastic flourish down the keys, as if signing his name, and closed the piano.

"Thank you, Fogg," he said, "I'll come myself. Miss Wane's busy just now."

But Perdita was already on her feet.

"No, no," she cried, "I'm coming of course. Tell the mistress I'll be with her in a second."

"Yes, miss. I'll say so, miss;" and the man closed the door.

"Good-bye, Mr. Skald," she said, holding out her hand to the bewildered Jobber, who had scrambled out of his chair.

"But why ... but can't we ... but wouldn't you ..." he stammered, his face getting very hot under his swarthy skin.

"What nonsense is this?" broke in their host, stepping between them. "There's not the slightest necessity for your going, Perdita."

She opened her eyes at being called "Perdita" by him for the second time; and the thought flashed through her mind:

"Does being in love lay a person bare to all sorts of liberties?"

But she let her hand rest, unresisting, in the hand of the Jobber, although in his agitation he was squeezing it with cruel violence.

"Of course I'm going," she repeated, smiling at Jerry, but avoiding her lover's passionate stare.

"Listen ... Listen, *Perdita* ..." stammered the Jobber in a hoarse whisper.

She suddenly was seized with a calm, steady, luminous insight into every aspect—so it seemed to her—of the whole situation, as they all three stood there between the table and the door.

"Why," she thought, as she stared at the fantastic piece of drapery which covered the square back which the little piano presented to the world. "It's Persian! I never realized *that* before!"

And in the strength of her new insight into men and things, in the strength of this inrush of infinite capacity and infinite competecy which she felt, she said boldly to her lover, smiling into his eyes:

"Are you busy all day tomorrow, Mr. Skald?" And then she hurriedly added, seeing so much pleasure, pursued by so much suffering, race across his countenance that it hurt her to behold it: "Tomorrow's Wednesday, you know."

While the poor Jobber, and it was for the first time that morning that the thing had returned, was confronted by the tragic brevity of the hours he had yet left to be happy in—Wednesday, Wednesday, Wednesday!—unless the Dog was to flesh his teeth undisturbed in that woman's whiteness, and while he faced these terrible Norse days, Woden's day, Thor's day, and saw them far more livid with disaster than ever the Three Staves or the Hanged Man were, in the Lodmoor Hut repertoire, his expression began to reveal what a crashing, cracking, groaning, rending, there was going on within his breast. ·

"Because," Perdita went on, "Mrs. Cobbold's arranged to go out to see Dr. Brush tomorrow, and the Doctor's asked her to both lunch and dinner. So tomorrow I shall be free all day; if *you* have any time."

His face was like some old battle-book—some Malory or Holinshed—in which tourney after tourney, mêlée after mêlée, is followed by solemn Masses under candle-lit gothic arches. He remained rapt, caught-up, absorbed in his indecision, while he still went on squeezing her hand and staring, without seeing anything, at the grey belt of her grey cloth suit. Of their host—who stood patiently in attendance upon this queer scene—he seemed entirely oblivious. At last he said slowly and very gravely—though with no lifting of the gloom upon the brow, with no relaxing of the tenseness between mouth and nostrils and between eyes and mouth:

"Will you meet me then, by the Clock, at about this time, about ten, tomorrow?"

He seemed relieved to have got the words said, and to have shifted the burden of his indecision upon the sequences of destiny, and his face did clear up a little now.

But Perdita, looking rather puzzled, repeated his expression, "at the Clock", with an interrogatory inflection of her voice.

"He means the Jubilee Clock," explained Jerry Cobbold, before the Jobber—who seemed quite taken aback by having a girl who did not know what "by the Clock" meant—had collected his wits to reply, "That Clock you pass on the esplanade, near the turn to the station."

Perdita gave him a grateful smile but the Jobber scowled at him. It hurt his pride that their first rendezvous should need an explanation by an outsider. He dropped the girl's hand; but Perdita, quick to catch his mood, snatched at it again.

"By the Clock at ten!" she whispered radiantly. "I'll be there—if I don't die in my sleep, good-bye!" and she plunged her brown eyes into his grey ones, like a headlong diver seeking fabulous treasure at the bottom of the sea. It was a look that he never forgot; for it was her way of giving herself wholly to him, there on the spot, there on their second encounter, there without a word of love having passed between them!

When she was gone and the door was shut Jerry Cobbold asked the Jobber whether it was too early to offer him a whiskey and soda. But the man stared at him, as he spoke, as if the clown had been talking to the large Mid-Victorian print of Prospero dismissing Ariel which hung on the wall, rather than to him. As he stared in front of him in this way his face, without being actually distorted by the trouble of his indecision, twitched and contracted as if he were confronting a shining row of musket-barrels.

"Don't do that," he jerked out, when he saw Jerry hurrying to ring the bell. "I must go. I've got endless things to do. I've got to go over to Dorchester with some fish for Witchit and I've got to get my car"— in his agitation he forgot to call her the Slug—"attended to. She's been wanting tinkering up for some time. A man's pretty helpless, moving about these days and attending to his business, when his car's out of commission." He looked meaningly at Jerry and winked. "We need our cars for our girls," he said, and then as if conscious that Cobbold might have thought this remark an unnatural one, he added, with an obvious darkening of his cheeks: "Anyone would be surprised, Cobbold, at the number of people I've given lifts to, in my time, between Weymouth and Dorchester. I tell 'em they ought to get me a bus-licence."

Jerry did his best not to look as if he realized the man was making a fool of himself.

"How few of us," he thought, "can carry off being caught 'on the hop' as I caught him with the funny little thing!"

It had become a private whimsy of his thus to belittle his wife's companion.

"The funny little thing," he said to himself, "is much too proud not to carry it off with the grandest air. I've never seen a woman carry off such a 'give-away' situation in a more natural style."

With the departure of Adam Skald, and this took place less than five minutes after Perdita had withdrawn from the scene, Jerry Cobbold hurriedly prepared to take himself off, too. He had promised his dancer, Tossty, that he would call for her this morning at the house of a mutual friend of theirs, a certain Doctor Lucius Girodel, a notorious quack, empiric, and abortion-procurer, whose house was a famous resort of a certain group of unconventional philosophers and their fair friends.

Among these cronies, who, by some obscure and furtive under-standing that had casually and inconsequentially grown up between them paid liberally for their entertainment, Doctor Girodel was known as "Lucky" and his large dingy mansion, was always referred to as "Lucky's". Jerry Cobbold had long been one of Doctor Girodel's most liberal patrons. He had indeed a peculiar fondness for this shameless quack, among whose various rôles the one which he played to the greatest perfection was undoubtedly that of bawd. But Jerry Cobbold was authentically attached to Lucky, and seemed able to be more entirely himself in the Doctor's company than in any other, whether it were that of man, woman, or child. Something about the complete freedom from ordinary human decency, dignity, propriety, seemliness, pride, honour and self-respect displayed by Lucius Girodel, tickled the comedian's humour down to its roots; and it may be believed how Lucky's prestige was enhanced in the town by the general knowledge that as long as the world-famous clown had a crust in the world he would share it with him.

It was not therefore of "the funny little thing" nor of her formidable admirer that the clown was thinking as he hurried on his way. Nor was he thinking of Tossty.

His face partook of the gusto of his feelings which were those of sweet satisfaction in the dirtiness and littered condition of the piece of road he traversed. The faintest and most pallid tinge of sunlight had just now broken through the clouds and its watery lemon-coloured light fell upon all the horse-droppings and all the broken boxes and all the puddles and all the mud. There were some high hoardings, too, in this ramshackle quarter at the back of the station, upon one of which the clown noted an advertisement of a well-known aperient, held aloft on the pinnacles of a Gothic Cathedral. But the old withered horse-droppings, together with certain wisps of dirty straw, were what seemed to please both this watery sunshine and the senses of Jerry most of all. A bit of blue paper, torn from the hoarding, flapped like a discontented flag in his path; but the comedian's grave eye, as it gloated with a sort of mystical ecstasy on all these manifestations of matter, seemed to rebuke the discontent of this piece of paper. He was soon traversing the yet poorer district of Ranelagh Road, a region that always fascinated him. Ranelagh Road at that time was a sort of poor people's replica of the grand esplanade; and it was above everything a parade-ground and rendezvous for the loves of the children of the poor. Here when the lights were lit at night the natural shyness of the large groups of boys and girls who met there concealed itself under loud guffaws, crude gestures, incredibly gross jests, and hysterical idiotic giggling. All this Jerry Cobbold sucked up with far more relish than he did the plaudits of any audience. Jerry had indeed something in him that went beyond Rabelaisianism, in that he not only could get an ecstasy of curious satisfaction from the most drab, ordinary, homely, realistic aspects of what might be called the excremental under-tides of existence but he could slough off his loathing for humanity in this contemplation and grow gay, child-like, guileless.

All his life Jerry was destined to remain to every person who knew him an insoluble riddle. Like Augustus Caesar—who also was a comedian in his time—he kept even his intimates at a great distance. They might call him "Jerry"; but "Jerry" when applied to him became a title of aristocratic remoteness. They might utter the syllables "Jerry" when they addressed him; but the meaning of these syllables instantly became "your Excellency", or even "your Royal Highness".

Jerry's "funny little thing" was not the only penetrating girl who saw the man as a sort of fragile Atlas, perpetually holding up the weight of other people's destinies and aiming above all, as he did with Lucinda, at keeping people from going mad, by an everlasting process of distraction! His elder brother Sylvanus said once of him that Jerry wasn't the child of human parents at all; but that his father was the Ghost of Swift and his mother a Lemur, a remark which, when it was reported to Jerry, received a *tu quoque* so profane as to be totally unprintable.

When he came in sight of Lucky's, which was an old, unrestored Queen Anne dwelling, carrying the name Sark House by the side of its rusty bell, Jerry Cobbold thought of that fragment of Russian music which he had played, after his amateur fashion, for "the funny little thing"; and he paused for a moment, while some noisy children quarrelled and jostled on the dirty, littered steps of Sark House, to give himself up to those ideal cadences. The comedian's passion for music was his one grand secret escape. Here lay—if anywhere—the solution of the mystery of his character; for Jerry's loathing for humanity was even deeper than that of Mr. Witchit, the fishmonger of St. Alban's Street, and the only pleasure he got from his fellows was a monstrous Rabelaisian gusto for their grossest animalities, excesses, lapses, shames! These things it was, the beast-necessity in human life, that he exploited in the humours of his stage-fooling; and because he loathed his fellow-men he was able to throw into his treatment of their slavery to material filth an irresistible hilarity as well as a convincing realism, a combination that always enchanted the crowd.

Another peculiarity of this enigmatic person, and one that helps to explain the weary meticulousness with which he upheld the social fabric of life, was the fact that normal sex-appeals had not the least effect upon him. What had drawn him to Lucinda—if the truth must be told—was a queer pathological attraction; and the same was true, allowing for the difference in her age and type, of his interest in Tossty.

With Girodel alone the comedian removed that mask which Perdita had so acutely divined. To the quack doctor he showed his real face, a face which was so sick of life that the sight of it would have disconcerted anyone less heartless than the cynical tenant of Sark House. Doctor Girodel, however, who picked up his living from the seamy side of existence, took his patron's life-hating mood as much for granted as if it had been the despair of a girl with an unwanted child. Indeed he had long ago discovered that of all emotions that release the clasp of a purse to a greedy hand disgust of life is the most potent!

"Oh, it's you, at last, is it?" was Tossty's scornful greeting, when across the great, faded, forlorn reception-room of Lucky's he moved to the girl's side. Under this chilly reception the clown fell into a very queer train of thought. "Do I know," he said to himself, "a single woman who could really love a person like me?" And then without any apparent reason the image of his wife's sister as she would look if Cattistock ill-used her, came into his head. "*She* might," he thought, "and I'd respond to it, too, if she were outraged and abject. I've caught her eye sometimes, and I almost—"

The flames in the big marble-manteled fire-place seemed to him the only objects just then in that melancholy chamber which he could contemplate with satisfaction. Great black-and-white, Mid-Victorian prints of public ceremonies—the Queen being crowned, the Queen being married, the Queen meeting her Cabinet, the Queen celebrating her Jubilee—hung round the walls, showing, against the stained and darkened wall-paper, which itself was the colour of Cattistock and Frampton's cheapest beer, like royal visitors in an asylum ward.

"Yes .. *she* might," he mused. And he visualized with a queer tenderness an ill-used Hortensia. But the little abortionist went skipping about like an evil bird from one guest to another. They had all evidently been drinking, though it was half-an-hour short of noon; for the battered and discoloured mahogany table was strewn with glasses, soda-syphons and bottles.

"It's not his money," the clown pondered, still thinking of Mrs. Lily. "I wish I knew——"

Lucky was a clean-shaved, restless personage. He had a sharp nose, a pointed chin, and long, straight, fair hair, which he wore thick in front, and was always running his fingers through and smoothing down, as if he were in a high wind; and with that mysterious instinct with which human beings often select some particular garment to suit their inmost identity, however incongruous with the rest of their array, he had caused to be made for himself certain striped trousers that were extremely narrow in the leg and which gave to his whole figure a sort of lively formality, mincingly important and preposterously obsequious, as he moved about, while neither the people he cajoled nor the people he twitted, for he was chattering *sans cesse*, felt him to be a person with whom you could exchange a single serious thought.

"Yes, I am alive again, Toss," Jerry cried suddenly, in a tone as if he had been under the power of some drug. "What is it? Tuesday, the tenth of February! A very good date. An excellent date. *Today's* date! Yes, Toss, you lovely one——" and here in spite of her angry, averted profile he gave her a fantastical kiss that seemed to go ricocheting round all the historic prints on the walls——"This tenth of February is not yesterday nor tomorrow. It's today. It's *today's* date, you beautiful one! Doesn't that seem odd to you when you think of——" Here he was interrupted by the lively host, who pirouetted up to him to whisper something, gliding upon his thin, striped legs as if they were external to his organic volition, as a pair of roller-skates would be——

"Hullo, Lucky! How are you? Champagne did you say? Has the beautiful one been referring to her favourite drink? Surely! Let's have a bottle—two bottles—three—enough for everyone here! But what was I saying?"

Tossty, who was neither listening to him nor apparently—since his kiss—aware that he existed, called out now across the whole length of the room to her sister Tissty, who was talking earnestly to Dog Cattistock.

"Have you asked Mr. Cattistock, Tiss, what you said you were going to?"

Cattistock looked up quickly, lifting his great chin from across the girl's figure, for she was leaning against him on a horse-hair sofa, a sofa that had become so disfigured by ill usage that its colour had changed from black to a curious black-grey that always suggested to Jerry's secret imagination the appearance of a hearse. But Cattistock, as he lifted his bristly chin and blinked with his eyes, was not one to let these two sisters chatter to each other as if they were alone.

"What *was* she to ask me, Toss? Hullo, Jerry! How are you this morning? Why didn't you say you were going to order that champagne? Tiss said she'd go over to Portland with me presently; but *now*—It would be cruel to carry her off! Can't you put it off till tomorrow?"

There was a very curious eye-encounter then, across the big room, between these two men, who were, in the eyes of the world, the most important persons in Weymouth at that time, and who always met each other at Lucky's with that half-embarrassed air with which two wellknown statesmen might meet at their accustomed brothel.

While his answer to Cattistock's request hung in the balance, Tossty began eagerly whispering to the clown, a red flush animating her swarthy cheeks, and more emotion and more interest suffusing her whole being than she had shown him since his entrance. It was characteristic of him that he dropped the matter of the champagne instantaneously, without even bothering to put his assent into words, thus lightly removing from in front of Cattistock's massive assault the sole prize of the financier's artillery.

But Cattistock was thinking: "I must take Tissty to the Sea-Serpent's Head up there. If those quarrymen grow nasty I'll have to leave her up there, till I've dealt with them. It'll spoil my night on Thursday completely if I haven't had Tiss first! I'd be pretending 'Tensia *was* Tiss, and I'm not clever enough for such tricks. Sippy's the fifth person already today who's warned me about Skald's threats. The man *is*, I believe, really going to try something. Well! I'll invade his terrain today, when he's in Dorchester selling fish; and then tomorrow, and that'll be in ample time, I'll deal with *him*."

So far he thought in the same quick, harsh, clear-cut sentences as he was wont to speak. But there came a minute later—and all his thoughts passed far more quickly than half-a-dozen of the smooth-drawn breaths that the fair-skinned Tissty was breathing so near to his rough cheek—when his thoughts ceased to be so definite, but still went on, and indeed grew in intensity. These thoughts were images; and the first of them was of the sea, of the sea carrying on its surface—a summer, not a winter, surface—one, two, three, red-funnelled Channel Island steamers, purchased by him from the railway. How fast over Cattistock's mental sea did these steamers move! And then the image came to him of Adam Skald, commonly called the Jobber, standing in the dock at Dorchester, answering to the charge of making murderous threats against his life. The unfortunate Jobber, in the dock at Dorchester, was not far removed from the smooth summer-sea over which the red-funnelled steamers followed one another so fast. In fact the dock, in this mental picture, became interchangeable with Portland Bill, until both of these vanishing, their place was taken by a bedroom at the Sea-Serpent's Head. This rapid survey of future events was now brought to an end by a repetition of his protest to the comedian at the other end of the room.

"Can't you put it off till tomorrow? Everyone who's here now could be here tomorrow, couldn't they?" He disentangled himself from the satiny pressure of his companion's lithe form and straightening his back looked round the room. "You could all come tomorrow, couldn't you?" he said, in that peculiar grating voice that he used when he asserted his authority in the Guildhall.

Doctor Girodel, who had already got to the door in eager obedience to Jerry's words, was clearly much put out. He would have liked to sneak off, pretending he hadn't heard Cattistock's remark, but it was too late. His one hope was—for he was not a believer in tomorrow—that his patron Jerry would indignantly reject this delay.

"Yes," he thought, "you can stick out your chin all you like, you ugly brute! If Jerry thinks Toss wants the drink, he'll make me get the drink and you can go to hell!"

Tossty herself was the one who now indicated, in a whisper to Jerry Cobbold, that it would be better to have the champagne tomorrow when they could all enjoy it.

"We'll have it tomorrow, Tiss," she indicated to her sister across the room in one of those mute signals which between ladies are clear and decisive.

They were alike in figure, these two dancers, being a pair of the supplest, the most sinuous, the most provocatively slender girls who had ever graced the well-worn boards of the Regent; but whereas Tissty the one now flirting with Cattistock, was startlingly fair, Tossty the tyrant of the great clown was extremely dark. Their real names were Gloria and Pansy Clive; but everyone knew them as Tissty and Tossty. They were in fact Tissty and Tossty to each other; and even—one must suppose—to themselves. Born in the little village of Radipole at the end of the old Weymouth Backwater, now Radipole Lake, the sisters could not even now catch the scent of any spring flowers without recalling those cowslip-balls that they used to toss from hand to hand as they danced on the green in front of the inn on Club day. They had grown up to be very successful on the music-hall stage; but throughout their varied and adventurous career they never separated from each other, and they never consented to be long absent from their first love, the sea. This latter peculiarity of theirs— their mania for getting jobs at sea-coast towns—they were in the habit of attributing to their health. Pansy Tissty, the fair one, would always say: "Tossty *has* to be at the sea for her asthma;" while Gloria, the dark one, would say: "Tissty has to be at the sea for that neuritis of hers!"

Lucky gave vent to a palpable sigh, dropped the handle of the smoke-darkened door into the passage, pushed back the lank, limp hair from his forehead, and pirouetted, with a mincing and yet a gliding motion, clear across the room, to where, seated on a faded settee not far from the fire, little Peg Frampton, the neglected daughter of Cattistock's partner, was being rallied for her solitary condition by Cattistock's nephew, who, ensconced in the only comfortable arm-chair in that large room, held on his knees the diaphanous and love-dazed form of Curly Wix. When the gliding Girodel had slipped down by Peg Frampton's side and had crossed his thin legs in their tight striped trousers, Ballard, with the tone of a petted favourite talking to an infatuated Sultan, enquired of his uncle, who was now on his feet helping the fair Tissty into her silk-lined coat, whether he could meet him here a little before the others came as he had something rather important to ask him.

Peg Frampton's hollow, dissipated young eyes contemplated with a sullen envy the serpentine sinuosity of the dancer's slippery form as it wavered half-in, half-out of its silken sheath, as Cattistock turned his chin in his nephew's direction.

"What is it, Sippy?" he said. "We're in Liberty-Hall here. What is it, boy?" As he spoke he gazed, not at his nephew but at Curly. "That girl is growing extraordinarily beautiful," he thought.

Ballard's handsome face flushed.

"You don't want me to drag in that ass, Skald"—he pronounced it "arse"—"do you, sir? You really ought to hear some of the pretty tales I've been picking up about what he's going to do to you. He says—" There was a sudden hush at this point throughout the whole room, broken only by an audible whisper of Jerry's to Tossty to the effect that the Jobber was the bravest man in Weymouth; but S. P. Ballard went on boldly: "He says you'll never consummate your marriage on Thursday. He says—"

But Cattistock interrupted him.

"That'll do, boy! That'll do! If all you've got to tell me is gossip of *that* sort you can keep it to yourself. Can't he, Tiss?"

But Tossty, leaving Cobbold with a hurried "Nonsense! You ought to be ashamed of yourself," ran across the room to her sister's side and began whispering earnestly to her, while Cattistock, with a contemptuous hardening of his face, flung his arm round Tissty and led her to the door.

"I'll tell him . . . I'll tell him, my dear!" they heard the fair girl reply, as she was forced out of the room.

With this departure a babble of tongues was loosed. Everybody began talking at once.

Curly, looking even whiter and more transparent than usual, moved a little on Ballard's knee to fix her great violet eyes with an almost horrified stare upon Doctor Girodel, who was making advances, of a kind that seemed on a par with his fantastic trousers, to Peg Frampton, whose own attention was absorbed in watching Cobbold, a personage she had never before seen at such close range. The Wishing Well guardian was saying to herself, "Jerry Cobbold doesn't agree with any of them about this nonsense. He doesn't like Mr. Cattistock. Nor do I! I wish Magnus hadn't gone and tied himself up with him. It was just like his foolishness to take that idiot child."

Having come to the totally erroneous conclusion about Peg that she was too nervous, in so many people's presence, to respond to his advances, the restless little quack doctor turned his malignant attention upon Sippy and Curly; for it was his custom to treat with repulsive familiarity any couple to whom in the past he had been useful in his ambiguous profession.

"Well, and how's Mr. Muir?" he enquired with a sneer, leaving Peg's side and standing with his back to the fire, while he jerked his hair from his forehead and grinned down at Curly like a drunken conjurer at a white rabbit.

Jerry was now helping Tossty into *her* cloak, which, being lined with white fur, enhanced the Spanish duskiness of her hair and eyes, and when it was on they, too, moved up to the fire.

"We're talking about Miss Wix's fiancé," grinned the doctor as they approached. "Do *you* know Mr. Muir, Tossty?"

"Do I, Jerry?" the beautiful girl asked languidly.

"*I* do, anyway," broke in the comedian. "Magnus is one of my oldest friends in the place. Don't you be nasty about him, doctor!"

"When's the marriage coming off, Curly?" enquired the doctor, with a leer. "I'm not being nasty, Jerry," he added. "I'm asking the young lady for information."

Curly got up from her lover's knee and moved off, without answering him, to one of the great melancholy gilt mirrors that hung about the room. Here, without bothering to touch her dress or her hair, she stared into her own troubled eyes.

"I'll die," she thought, "before I'll let Doctor Girodel meddle with me again." Then she turned to her lover. "Let's go, Sippy" she said. "I'm hungry."

"When you *are* married to Magnus," said Jerry Cobbold to her, in a clear, friendly voice across the room, "I'll ask you both to dine with Lucinda . . . and I won't ask *you*, you rascal, you may be sure," he added, smiling at Sippy.

Thrilled at being actually addressed by the great man, Curly recovered her spirits in a moment, and moved towards him, her eyes large and liquid with excitement.

"Why, you've never even been introduced to her," said Sippy.

The comedian ceremoniously caught up the girl's hand and kissed it.

"I've seen her many a time at the Well," he murmured. "We all envy you, you rogue, and Magnus, too! You're a wise child, my dear, to have two strings to your bow. May you never get them entangled!"

He said this with such a tender and grave air that Curly was enchanted.

Meanwhile the lecherous little doctor was doing his best to establish some sort of ambiguous rapport with the forlorn intruder from Swan Villa. His knowledge that Peg had been brought here for the first time by Cattistock that morning, and might never come again if everybody neglected her, was enough to draw him to her side. In his fantastic vision of Sark House as a rendezvous for all erotic eccentrics, and of himself as an unexclusive Cicerone to a universal Cyprian Alsatia, he could not endure to lose even such a woebegone waif as this. Besides, after all, she *was* the daughter of Cattistock's partner.

The great financier himself, though he had brought her, had dropped her and completely ignored her when it transpired that the lovely and capricious Tissty, whose skin was of a whiteness rivalling that of his bride, and to whom he had long been attracted, happened today—probably out of pure feminine pique over his approaching marriage—to be in a receptive mood towards him.

The only person who noticed the overtures Lucky was now making, on that sorry-looking settee, was his patron Jerry, who as he talked to the languid and preoccupied Tossty, near the half-drawn window-curtains, kept his cold non-human eye—the eye of a philosophical harlequin—fixed steadily upon the couple.

"What's the rogue up to," he thought, "with that pitiful little piece? Has he taken upon himself to besiege her maidenhood on general professional principles? Is he trying to seduce her on the ground that the condition of virginity is an unhappy one for everybody concerned, except the fortunate person who takes it away?"

"I do so love," Girodel was even now whispering to Peg, "the way your under-lip droops; and you're silly, you know, to put anything on it, for anyone can see it's got a delicious redness of its own. But the way it droops—no! don't bite it now!—is positively ravishing."

Peg stopped biting her lip and stared at him wonderingly. It was such a completely new experience for her to be courted in this sort of way that she was both pleased and bewildered. Was the man making sport of her? No—she could not believe that when she saw his animated face.

"I knew an artist once who used to tease me about my lip," she said. "He used to call it the coral-reef."

Girodel was delighted at the impression he was making.

"Those old poets would say, Miss Frampton, that a bee had stung it newly."

But Peg's unmoved expression, as if this were an extremely doubtful compliment, indicated to him that she was even more ignorant of "those old poets" than he was himself; and he hurriedly proceeded along a different track.

"You know you completely puzzle me, Miss Frampton! You look so quiet and still; and yet no one would think you hadn't had a lot of experience. You've lost all your illusions I expect. Well, so had I at your age. I saw all through the world's humbug when I was younger than you are. Since then I've got down to the bed-rock of things where you soon find out that everyone's got to fight for his own hand . . . yes, and against his friends, too! I love the good Jerry over there for instance—don't look at him; for he's watching us!— but do you think I sacrifice myself for him? I should say not, Miss Frampton, I should say not! I was neglected and alone when I was a little boy—" here the crafty Lucky looked down at his striped trousers, as if the emotion of thinking of himself as a boy was so great that he could not bear to meet a sympathetic gaze while he indulged in it—"but since I've grown up I've thrown overboard all that. Life is a battle in the dark, little girl, and the game wouldn't be worth the candle if we didn't meet a lovely spirit sometimes who's had the brains to see through all the humbug, too—especially if this spirit has a drooping scarlet lip and delicious, slender little fingers!"

Here this Panurge-like figure in the striped trousers proceeded to take her hand; and as he crowded her against the end of the tattered settee pretended to peruse with solemn intensity the extremely broken and ill-fated lines in her hot, feverish, hollow palm.

"He's rather like a monkey," the girl thought.

But dropping her hand and lying back against the settee he began to talk to her more seriously; nor was he altogether hypocritical in this. There was a vein in Girodel of transparent simplicity and almost wistful childishness; but it very rarely appeared in his dealings with women. Jerry, who knew this vein well and responded to it, scarcely realized what a heartless rogue his friend Lucky was in his relations with women, or how completely this simple direct mood vanished away where they were concerned.

But Peg's cynicism combined with her extreme youth was something that the little abortionist had never come across before. Thus the tendency to rascality which he habitually displayed where women were concerned was qualified while he talked to Peg by a recognition that she was in some way different from the rest and had a clear and unsentimental intelligence to which he could appeal. It was not long, therefore, before he launched—speaking in a hurried, earnest whisper —into an eloquent discourse on the advantages of prostitution, if a woman kept her head and got out of it in time.

"How can a girl," he said, "be really disillusioned with all this nonsense of virginity hanging about her like a blinding cloud? A girl with a mind like yours"—and he gave her a fervent admiring glance— "doesn't want to pay the price of some stuffy commonplace marriage for her experience; and a girl with brains like yours wants to come down to the real thing, and not be bothered by silly romantic illusions. Intelligent women need variety and change, just as men do, and they need the experience of these things without all the fuss and fume of what is called love. Of course a girl needn't 'go on the street' as we say; and all she has to do, if she gets landed, is to come—well! come to *me*. No, no, my dear Miss Frampton, a woman is made for these experiences. And it doesn't mean that she kills her power of falling in love. Girls who have been with endless men can fall in love in the end, just as we can; and when they *do* love, it's real, I tell you; for all the silly nonsense that virginity creates, the parthenogenesis of illusion," (here Lucky chuckled over his own inspiration) "has been squeezed out of 'em. You *can't* be disillusioned and remain a virgin;

and yet what intelligent girl, until she's desperately in love, and not always even then, wants to tie herself to a husband and children. A conventional married woman grows inured to dullness and boredom; but she *cannot* be disillusioned, because she's not had the experience for that. And how silly and flirtatious these women are, my dear! Whereas a girl who has had her adventures—a prostitute if you like— can be a decent friend to a man without all this silliness!"

Peg listened to all this with absorbed interest, nodding her head now and then with the gravest approval and saying to herself in her heart:

"Now this would be the very man for me to experiment with and to satisfy my curiosity with."

And she grew happier and happier as Lucky talked more and more freely to her; for she thought to herself:

"I want to know *everything* about these things: and here's a man who's evidently attracted to me, from whom I *could* learn everything."

Presently he was trying to persuade her to let him show her the other rooms in the house.

"If you'll come upstairs—do, Miss Peg! please, *please* do!—I'll show you every room in the place."

And Peg thought to herself. "I'd far sooner be undressed by this man than by Mr. Cattistock. I wish I'd put on my best under-clothes though! How stupid of me. But that's always my luck. I'm always thinking of things and never doing things."

And then, as she found herself being helped up from the settee and led across the room, so that she might have the pleasure of being shown by Doctor Girodel "what the upstairs rooms were like", she thought to herself, while her heart began to beat fast:

"I might have gone on forever, going about with that Witchit kid and with all the other kids, and *never* have known all I want to know! But now I *shall* know. I know I shall by the way he was looking at me just now."

Thus she pondered in her beating heart, below the narrow, consumptive boy-like chest; and not only was the hand that Doctor Girodel held hotter, dryer, more feverish than any girl's hand he had ever held, but she herself was conscious of a sudden fit of what she

called "the shivers". To plunge into the unknown world of all she
wanted to know—that world that had just received its intellectual
justification from Lucky's discourse to her, that world of the "upstairs" of Sark House, which she vaguely fancied would have furniture
such as George the Third might have used—was an event of such
startling magnitude in her life that it was no use pretending that it
was nothing.

"I like him," she thought, "and he does really seem to have respect
for my mind. I do think he understands me and sees what I feel, and
wouldn't treat me roughly. But oh, dear! Perhaps I'll be sorry about
this tomorrow!"

Peg had been rather a pitiable figure from the first in that motley
assembly. To any woman of discernment it would have been clear
she was motherless. There was something about her clothes, something about the way her hair was done, something in the very look
of her shoes and stockings which testified to the peculiar desolation of
her dilapidated man-ruled home by the edge of that ornamental water.
Any woman who had once seen Peg's bedroom in Swan Villa or seen
the meals over which Peg presided or seen the figure of Mr. Frampton
leaving his house for his office would have scarcely been surprised that
her life's destiny should have reached the point, on this tenth of
February, of being led upstairs by Doctor Girodel.

Jerry Cobbold, however, who had at last persuaded Tossty to take
a seat by those great Victorian winter-curtains, half-drawn at this
moment, missed nothing of what was going on. His eye upon Peg
was now like the eye of a manager of marionettes who is a little
uncertain what wire to pull to prevent the Cinderella-Puppet from
leaving the stage with the Don Juan-Puppet. Although endowed
by providence with a detachment from ordinary passions that amounted
to a monstrous perversity, Jerry had the instinct of a born clown for
certain poignant human situations; especially for such as had a touch
of the grotesque, or of the pitiful, or of the tatterdemalion in them;
and as Peg—who, as we have seen, could certainly not be called
loath to go upstairs, and in any case was too spiritless and reckless
to make any sort of struggle against Girodel's eagerness, even if her
heart did beat and she did feel conscious of a fit of "the shivers"—
glanced sideways out of her hollow eye-sockets in such a way as to

give to the expression of her eyes, with the dark lines round them, a desperation that the girl would certainly have denied she felt, and which she probably did not feel, the great comedian, exactly as if he had been Hamlet, ironically and hysterically applauding the players, suddenly began clapping his hands together, extravagantly, violently, noisily.

Tossty got up from her seat by the curtain and looked indignantly round the room, as if calling upon public opinion to defend her from such a madman, but the subtle Lucky caught his patron's temper in a second, dropped the girl's hand, and as if jerked into reluctant propriety by some invisible wire, proceeded to occupy himself with a series of fantastic and bird-like movements in the service of his own disordered hair, alternately inclining and lifting his head; and finally pushing his hair carefully away from his forehead.

For a perceptible fragment of time Peg Frampton stood unsupported, awkward, embarrassed, in the middle of the room. Then very slowly, and walking like a child who has only just come out to play with the others and does not quite know which of them to approach, she moved over towards the left side of the fire-place.

Here Curly had rejoined Sippy, after having received upon the head—so to speak—of her adulterous life the comedian's impious blessing, and here the lovers were whispering eagerly together in some grave argument as to the best methods and ways of deceiving Mr. Muir.

Peg's fluctuating and hesitating approach—in her self-chosen and self-patched finery which made her look like a slum-girl out for a bank-holiday compared with Curly who looked *exactly what she was* and with Tossty who looked like a Russian Princess—drew her by nervous degrees, as if she were anxious to get a clearer view of the Coronation of Queen Victoria, towards the great black arm-chair where Sippy once more held Curly cuddled upon his lap. To the bishops and statesmen who thus looked forth at Peg from the choir-stalls of the Abbey she must have presented the appearance, as she advanced towards them in this wavering, hesitant *pas-de-seul*, of some little street-girl, who had put on her Sunday clothes to see the sight, and had—God knows how—got past the authorities.

And when those dark-lashed, violet eyes of the lovely Curly were aware that her dialogue with Sippy was menaced by Peg's approach, she acted very much as the bishops in the coronation would have done: she put away, out of her face, every consciousness that the form of Peg Frampton was anything but thin air.

Peg—though not very solid, for her hip-bones were sharp as a consumptive's and you could have balanced a penny on her collar-bones—had enough substantiality to know when her feelings were hurt and she now hurriedly changed the direction of her *pas-de-seul* and began to manifest a desire to look out of the window of that large room, a window which was behind the figures of Cobbold and Tossty, who also—since the hysterical clapping of the clown's hands—were engaged in some intimate discussion.

"What cheek!" Peg said to herself. "Even if she *is* on Mr. Ballard's lap, she must know I've been with people hundreds of times to see the Well, when *she* was nothing. And what is she now, I should like to know? *Mr. Ballard's bitch*—that's what *you* are, white face!"

But her anger, as she paused in the pursuit of her new objective (for she saw that Doctor Girodel had approached Jerry and Tossty and had interrupted their dialogue) faded away now, as she stretched out her thin arms to their full length over the grate and leaned against the marble edge of the mantelpiece. It faded very quickly, for Peg Frampton in her secret heart had no malice against anyone in the world, unless it were its maker and sustainer. Profoundly and bitterly as she pitied herself and cursed her lot she blamed no one—not even her father. Had Lucky taken her upstairs just then it is extremely unlikely that she would have come downstairs a virgin; but she bore against the wearer of those striped trousers not the faintest feeling of resentment. She felt no anger against Curly either now, just an amused awareness that in the usual scale of social values in Weymouth her own position was that of a lady while Curly's was anything but that. But what did it matter? What did all these things matter? Here she was, in this big room, a little black figure with outstretched arms above a fire-place, and there was not a single soul who gave a thought—save possibly her solemn little Double Flower—to what became of her. Well? Why should they? Why should *she* care what became of her?

"The best thing that could happen to *you*, my dear"—thus, with her arms stretched out like a diver, she apostrophized her soul in the red coals—"would be to *take to drink*."

And then she suddenly thought of her young admirer from the fish-shop in St. Alban's Street, and with a faint smile playing round her drooping under-lip, naturally red, and being perpetually made redder, she took her arms from the mantelpiece and stood back a little from the fire, brushing her skirt.

"Miss Frampton, isn't it?" said Jerry, moving up to her now, and holding out his hand. "I've been wondering, Miss Frampton," he went on, still retaining her thin fingers, "if you'd care to come round to our rehearsal on Monday. Our regular chorus is filled up; but I want—I mean I have a notion that a page's dress—"

Peg's clouded face lit up with the first gleam of spontaneous pleasure that it had known for many a day.

"Shall I have to ask father?" she murmured. "I'm afraid he wouldn't—"

"Here, Toss," he said, turning to the dark beauty in the fur cloak, "what bribe can we offer Mr. Frampton to lend us his little daughter for a week?"

The dancer stared scornfully at Peg and remained silent.

"Oh, well," said Jerry. "We'll be seeing Cattistock again tomorrow, and perhaps his influence with your father—"

"But, Jerry," broke in the dancer at this point, "do be practical for once! It's no good raising Miss Frampton's hopes when you know what always happens at rehearsals."

She narrowed her eyes as she exchanged a quick look with Peg, a look that told the would-be page that she had no more chance of being accepted, when it came to the point, than of having a collar of white fur.

"He's forgotten that he's promised two kids already," she breathed wearily. "I wouldn't bother your father about it if I were you. Come, Jerry! We'll give her a couple of tickets for the opening night, but you really mustn't—" and sliding her arm under the comedian's, and whispering something in his ear that clearly extinguished all the girl's hopes, she led him away.

Doctor Girodel attended them to the street-door; but when he came back he informed Sippy Ballard in an aggrieved voice that it was raining and the wind was getting up.

"Did you come in your car?" he enquired, glancing at the neat grey dress worn by Curly, "or shall I telephone for a taxi? Jerry had his usual luck. There was one just outside."

The lovers jumped to their feet at that and fixed a dismayed look upon each other. Curly murmured something about telephoning to her aunt's shop in Upwey, if they weren't going back.

"Do you want to come up with me then," said the Doctor. "It's in my room. We'll be down in a minute, child!"

But no sooner was Peg left alone than she slipped out into the hall and put on her jacket and her little cloth cap. Making a face at the great forlorn staircase, a face that seemed to dismiss Sark House forever as an escape from her desolation, the girl opened the heavy street-door and went out into the rain. The wind blew her skirt against her thin legs and drove the rain against her flat chest. Before she got to the railway-station she was wet to the skin; so that when she passed the back of the buildings, where Jerry had contemplated the horse-droppings, she thought:

"What's the good of sheltering in there now? I'm drenched through and through."

A miserable recklessness came over her and she hurried down King's Street, making blindly for the familiar esplanade, like a rabbit seeking its well-known covert, even though its hole has been stopped up. She passed in the middle of King's Street a confectioner's shop where, because of the sudden darkness brought on by these floods of rain, they had lit the lights. People kept pausing at this shop and jostling one another as they tried to close their streaming umbrellas before entering, and every time the door opened a warm, sweet smell of new-baked cakes emerged only to be instantaneously dissolved in the pouring rain. So often had Peg hurried, on warm summer days, down this particular street, longing impatiently for her first glimpse of the water, and anticipating with quickened pulses all the delights of the beach, the performers, the comic singers, the onlookers, the chaffing boys, the satyrish leers of the old men, that in her present mood of numb desperation she automatically pushed on through this blinding rain-water towards the kindlier salt-water. She had no fancy about being

welcomed in its depths by the friendly daughters of Nereus, girls
kinder than any Tissty or Tossty, and where there was no Lucky
with striped trousers; but all the same the sea was to this child of the
old Backwater, as it was to many another native of Weymouth,
something almost personal.

She crossed the wide road actually at a run, with its crowded buses
and rushing motors, and turned westward from the Jubilee Clock
which indicated that it was five minutes to two. Not a soul on the
esplanade, and how the rain positively danced up from the hard, black,
smooth asphalt in little watery tongues! These tongues were like
flames; only they were water-flames; not like those fire-flames across
which she had been leaning at Lucky's when she thought of taking
to drink. What else had she been thinking about as she leaned over
the fire after that pretty girl of Sippy's had snubbed her so?

Soaked through and through she was, and there was no bus going
her way at the statue now till the end of the afternoon. Soaked to the
skin she was; all the fault of her having gone to this Lucky's at all,
just because Cattistock offered to take her. And when he *had* got her
there, he scarcely noticed her and went away with Tissty! Well,
that was natural enough. Anyone *would* prefer a clever girl like that,
to a badly-dressed, ignorant kid. It always came back to the same
thing: God not having made her beautiful. It wasn't Tissty's fault, or
Cattistock's fault, or Lucky's fault. It wasn't even dad's fault. O,
if God could only once *hear* what she felt towards Him—even if He
struck her dead the second afterwards—what a heavenly relief it
would be! It would be like the bursting of a blood-clot that had
grown and grown in her brain till she couldn't stand it.

"The harbour would be the best place for a girl to drown herself
in," she thought.

She was opposite the place now where the donkeys stood in the hot
sand in the summer; and where that Punch-and-Judy man used to be,
whose daughter they said—and she knew the girl, too, by sight—went
about with the elder Mr. Cobbold, the crazy one, who was called
Sylvanus. The roadway on her right narrowed considerably now,
and the houses became smaller, older, more picturesque.

"Is the tide coming in, or going out, in the harbour now," she
wondered.

But what was this? She was leaving the esplanade now and crossing the road and the rain seemed to be abating; but goodness gracious! where *was* she going? She was entering one of those quaint, old-fashioned narrow streets, where they sell those little boxes covered with shells like what Daisy's grandfather makes in Sandsfoot Castle. How odd that she had so often been down this street and never thought— The rain was certainly stopping; but she felt horridly clammy and chilly and sticky, and there was an odious smell of soaked cloth and linen always reaching her. Yes; here it was, the little fish-shop that she had passed so often in former days, when as a child these curious shops, full of sailor's souvenirs, attracted her so, but which she had avoided since she had been going to the Palladium with that kid.

"I smell like a corpse," she thought, and still feeling as if she were under the eyes of those girls in Sark House, she entered the shop.

"Something sent me here," she said to herself, and she remembered how she had thought of young Witchit as she leant against that mantelpiece at Lucky's.

The fishmonger himself was behind the counter and he greeted her with his usual eager obsequiousness.

"Miss Frampton, isn't it?" he said. "Your dear father still at Swan Villa? You used to come for his cod-fish, you know. Oh, yes! I never forget a good customer. Cod-fish—that was what he always ordered! Your dear mother liked 'em. Yes, she liked a bit of good cod-fish in them days. Aye! how time does pass! Well, and what can I do for you today, Missy? There ain't no cod today; but I've got some nice haddock."

Peg stared at the man. And as she became conscious that below his smiling chatter she was no more to him than a piece of fish that he would give to his cat, an unutterable desolation swept over her.

"No, thank you," she murmured in a weak voice; and then with a shiver, "I think the . . . rain . . . has . . . stopped . . . now. I must be getting on."

She had already turned to go out; and it was that moment, with the inability of getting any bus for hours and her sense that she hadn't the spirit to walk all that way, or the money to take a taxi, combined with the look of a disembowelled fish on a side-slab near the door, that was the breaking-point. She paused with her head hanging down.

"Peg," she said to herself, stupidly and dully. "Peg is my name."

A voice from the back of the shop made her turn round. Mrs. Witchit, a short and extremely plump lady, who must have been seated in a low chair completely concealed by the counter, was now on her feet, indeed was already at Peg's side.

"Why, Miss Frampton, you're soaking wet! Why—Lordy bless the child!—you're shivering and shaking. Oh, my! Oh, my! how wet you are, Miss Frampton! My son have told me how kind you've been to him, taking an interest in him and all that. Excuse me boldness, Miss Frampton, but I can't let 'ee go, like you be, catching your dear death afore you gets whoäm. Come into kitchen and warm 'eeself, Miss Frampton! Oh, my! Oh, my! how wet 'ee be!"

It was now the destiny of Mr. Witchit to see his plump wife lead, nay! drag, this customer, to whom he had tried to sell his last piece of haddock, into her warm kitchen at the back of the shop. Slowly he went across to his pet canary, which at once began singing, and proceeded to apostrophize it:

"These be queer doings, Chirpy; these be uncommon queer doings. Your mistress be took, Chirpy. She be took, worse nor you and I have ever knowed her took!"

If Mr. Witchit's misanthropy was outraged by the manner in which his lady was "took" when she dragged Miss Frampton into her kitchen, it was no less than thunderstruck when from certain sounds in a room above it became clear that the woman was actually putting the girl to bed in their own chamber. Not many minutes passed indeed before the plump little person, carrying in her arms every stitch of the girl's clothing, put her head into the shop.

"Her don't go a step from here," he heard her say, "till I've a-dried these here things proper and finical!"

The man made no reply; but he and the now mute canary looked at each other in astonishment. They both knew that there was nothing to be said or to be done to stem the tide of the surprising events. Whenever Mrs. Witchit declared that something was to be rendered "proper and finical" destiny had to be left alone, to take "unbewailed" its way.

Meanwhile in the big bed upstairs Peg Frampton, with hot brandy
inside her and a hot bottle above her, lay with her face to the wall,
softly, weakly, helplessly crying, from pure physical comfort. What
with the brandy and the warmth of the bed and the relief of her tears—
for Peg hardly ever wept—the girl soon sank into blissful unconsciousness and slept for more than two hours. She was awakened by the
sound of loud voices in the shop below and the dragging and banging
about of boxes and crates. She heard the high-pitched tones of her
friend, the Witchit boy, begging his mother to let him go up and see
if his young lady was still asleep. Peg could not help smiling, even in
her present weak and somnolent state, to think how the lad must have
boasted to his parents of his friendship with "Miss Frampton", for
she had not been able to keep up her incognito with him. Then she
heard the deep tones of the Jobber, who had just come back from
Dorchester where he had been carrying round boxes of fish all day.
There seemed to be something especially malevolent in Mr. Witchit's
tone when presently she heard him ask the Jobber if he'd inherited a
legacy since he saw him last.

"You be in such an on'nat'rel jubilation, Jobber! Seems as if ye
weren't so elated when I last set eyes on 'ee."

Then Peg heard the Jobber's deep voice.

"What's that you're reading in the Gazette, Missus?" he asked,
completely ignoring the fishmonger's banter.

" 'Tis about that racing-man in London, what they've condemned
to be hanged," replied Mrs. Witchit. "He were with his sweetheart
when they took he up. They caught 'un wi' she down at Broadstairs,
or maybe Margate 'twere."

Peg's somnolence melted like a cloud. High-class murderers with
sweethearts at Margate were what she, too, loved to read about.
What made the Jobber's voice so serious, though, when he asked
them if they'd heard that Gipsy May of Lodmoor could read the
future by mummy-cards?

"Maybe she can; maybe she can't," Peg heard Mrs. Witchit say.
" 'Tis as how the upshot be."

"Do you suppose, Marm," said the Jobber, "that this racing-man
enjoyed himself with his sweetheart just afore he did the job, as well
as just after he did it?"

Mrs. Witchit held clear and strong opinions on this delicate point, which she was beginning to expound when Peg heard the shop-door open and shut, and a completely new voice make itself audible. The moment the girl heard this voice she sat up in the bed and listened intently.

She looked a quaint little figure, as she saw herself in the looking-glass, sitting up like this, arrayed in an ancient night-dress of Mrs. Witchit's, which fell away from her thin flat chest in voluminous folds. But she felt compelled to drink up every syllable of this new-comer's vibrant words. Never had she felt like this before, with regard to any human voice; and as she leaned forward, in the plump Mrs. Witchit's white night-dress, something in the tempo of this person's intonation ran through her veins like the quiver of electricity.

"Wet through? Of course I'm wet through, woman," Peg heard him say.

But the queer thing about his tone was that it did not sound like one ordinary person talking to another in a fishmonger's shop. It sounded as if the "I" of this individual who admitted being wet, had broken some barrier, some obstacle, some customary reticence that closed people in and was uttering these simple words as if they came from a level of life that was outside ordinary experience.

"But I've been into the pub next door," the voice continued, "and have had a drink."

Then again she heard the Jobber's deep tones; and though she could not catch the full purport of what he said, it must have been something about "drinking to forget"; for the thrilling voice went on:

"We're all half-alive and half-dead. To be really dead would be——"

It was clear he was interrupted at this point by the clatter that the Jobber and Mr. Witchit were making with the empty boxes and crates that had come back from Dorchester. But after a pause the voice began again, more clearly and more vibrantly than ever; but he was saying something now too obscure for her mind to follow. She could catch single words, but the sense escaped her.

And then she became aware of a noisy disturbance of some sort going on, on the pavement outside the little shop. She could hear boy's voices; and it was through her window that these voices reached her ears——

"He be inside fish-shop. I've a seed 'un! But Jobber Skald be wi' 'un; so do 'ee mind, Herb' Johnson, what 'ee be up to!"

Then she heard the shop-door open and the Jobber gruffly bidding the lads be off. Then once again the voice continued:

"*Want what?* That's the rub. That's the sticking-point."

But once more young Peg could make no meaning—for *her* intelligence—of the words that followed.

"No, no, not there, Jobber, not there, if you *please!*" It was Mrs. Witchit's voice that broke in at that point.

"That's where he keeps his cod, and he's got a fancy for holding on to that fish till prices do rise; whereas I tells him he ought to sell it at any price, and get a fresh lot in, and keep our stock on the move."

"What we need is air, air, air," continued the magnetic voice, growing louder and more commanding in its tone, as if it were competing with all the noises of ordinary life both within and without that little shop. "People don't yet know that if we'd only stop loving and hating and wanting, all would be changed! Then the—"

"Father! Father!" and the shrill voice of young Witchit drowned every other sound. "Look out, Father! *There!* Catch her! She stole it off the floor when I dropped it. There!"

And Peg could hear a terrific scrambling and presently there came the shock of something heavy being thrown.

"Kitty-Cat, don't 'ee mind! Don't 'ee mind, little Kitty-Cat!"

Peg could now catch the mother's voice.

"You've gone and scared Kitty-Cat into one of her fits, Witchit. She be panting like her heart were broke."

There was a long pause at this point while some large fish-crate was being dragged across the shop.

"Thank 'ee, sir," she heard Mr. Witchit say. "Thank 'ee kindly, sir!" so that Peg gathered that the owner of the voice had assisted them in their tidying-up process.

At this point she heard the Jobber's deep voice growl something in protest, something about "grand words baking no bread", and about human nature being enough without any gods. And then Mr. Witchit's voice became just audible explaining in an ingratiating and obsequious tone to the company at large how nice it was that they still had real gentlemen in the land "who had the time to tell us poor dogs about all these"—Then the boy's voice was lifted up again and Peg gathered that he was asking what he should do with the last piece of haddock.

But once more the magnetic speaker went on; only now he spoke in so low a tone that the girl couldn't catch the words. She strained her attention to the utmost. No! 'Twas no avail. With an angry sigh she sank down on her pillow. But that murmuring voice seemed to be coming up through the floor like a current of electricity. There! It had slid under her bed-clothes, under Mrs. Witchit's night-dress, and was clinging, and quivering and vibrating and twisting, like coils of seductive magnetism round her naked body. The next thing Peg knew was that she was out of bed, and out of the room, and gliding stealthily downstairs on her bare feet. Swiftly and softly she opened the door that led from the kitchen into the shop.

There was a little confusion at this moment; for the Jobber suddenly opened the street-door and could be heard packing off what, from the noise that ensued, sounded like a party of intrusive children. An immensely tall man in tweeds thanked him for this proceeding.

"They always follow me about now," he said. "I don't know why they do."

Yes! there he was, this man who had drawn her downstairs by the tone of his voice, and she knew him at once, for she had had him pointed out to her since she was a child, many a time on the esplanade. He was certainly a more remarkable-looking man than she had ever realized. Tall though the Jobber was, as he stood by his side, this man was perceptibly taller. But that was partly because he was so abnormally thin and lean. He had grizzled hair, a long cadaverous face with bony hollow cheeks, a face that was fantastically elongated; and while otherwise clean-shaved he wore a grey moustache of immense length and thickness, not a military moustache, like old James Loder's, but a Viking's moustache, or a moustache like those worn in these islands by the old Cymric tribes.

So it was Sylvanus Cobbold whose voice had called her down to him! Well! she understood now why it was that these women followed him everywhere and gave themselves to him, body and soul. She could have run straight up to him herself, just as she was, heedless of Mrs. Witchit's night-dress! It was Sylvanus himself who was the first to notice her as she stood there in the chink of the kitchen-door; but he only did so after he had bought that last piece of haddock, stuck it into the pocket of his rain-soaked tweed suit, for he had neither hat nor great-coat, and had half-opened the street-door.

"Crossing the bridge, Skald? You can give me a lift, for I'm done in. I've been on my feet all day."

The Jobber murmured his good-bye to the fishmonger without turning his head and went out. Sylvanus followed; but just before vanishing he looked straight at the white figure in the crack of the kitchen-door and called out to her:

"Don't catch cold, little sleeper, now you've come back from the Dead!"

Before the door had shut on him the three Witchits had swung round towards her.

"*What had he got in his hand?*"

This was the question she asked of them all now, as she threw the kitchen-door wide open, and lifted her loose-sleeved arms to her head. She awaited their reply with the utmost calm, gathering up her mop of dishevelled hair with her hands, as if *it*, and not her bare feet, or the woman's night-gown, had been the shameless exposure of that moment.

It was young Witchit who was eager to reply, though he did so with wide-open eyes and an awed voice.

" 'Twere his cane, Miss Framp—Peg, 'twere one o' they private soldiers' canes what he do allus carry round. They tell I that out there to Portland he have two hundred o' such canes and all broke in halves. They say he be a conjurer, Miss Framp—Peg, and that he breaks his canes like Moses and Aaron broke their rods, for to conjure over his enemies."

"He spoke to me alone," said Peg to herself; but aloud she said: "He pointed his cane straight at me. Does that mean good luck or bad luck?"

But the motherly Mrs. Witchit advanced resolutely towards her; and she fled upstairs, and the door was shut.

Then said the boy to his father: "Why were the Jobber acting so queer today and why were he talking so funny about that Margate man and his sweetheart?"

"Listen to me, son," said Mr. Witchit in a low ferocious whisper, and without the flicker of a smile. "What you've got to do is to study and study and study till you be larn'd enough to go to East Afriky. 'Tis in East Afriky that there be gold; not here, where us be all lying in Hell like—like me haddock!"

This last remark was made with such an alarming contortion of the man's features that the boy positively jumped back. But the street-door re-opened at that moment; and with the appearance of a customer, Mr. Witchit's face resumed that air of exaggerated humanity by which he got rid of older pieces of fish than any other fishmonger in Weymouth.

8

THE SEA-SERPENT

Wʜᴇɴ the Jobber, with Sylvanus Cobbold by his side, had crossed the bridge over the harbour and had stopped in front of Trinity Church, he began to wonder if the man would alight there and walk to Rodwell to get the train, or if he were assuming all this while that it would be a natural and easy thing to carry him on, all the way to where he lived between the village of Weston on Portland and Portland Bill.

There was a press of traffic at this point owing to the cessation of the rain, so that he had plenty of time to consider whether to run his truck into Corder's Wharf as he usually did or to go on up the hill towards Wyke Road. What decided him was the sudden thought that he'd better go to his parent's house on the Island and warn them that he thought of bringing out Perdita to see them tomorrow. So he muttered:

"You'd like me to take you on home, I expect?"

The drooping moustache moved slightly; and the Jobber understood that the man admitted that he would be glad if this were done.

But it was still impossible to move; for since the opening of the big new bridge across what used to be the Backwater, there was so little traffic at this point that it was unnecessary to keep a policeman standing here, and so, when a torrent of rain upset the movement of vehicles, the classical façade of Trinity Church was compelled to contemplate a good deal of confusion and not a little cursing. Good God! and the Jobber stood up incontinently in his seat and leaned forward over his steering-wheel, peering into the mêlée in front of him.

"An accident, man?" enquired Sylvanus, beginning to show some faint awareness of the press of traffic and the agitation of so many drivers.

But a green-grocer's hand-cart, far in front of them, having been pushed out of the way and having vanished down a little alley beside the church-steps, there was now a general movement forward, and the Jobber was forced to resume his seat at the wheel. He was kept so intent on the work of extricating the Slug from the confusion around her that he didn't even bother to answer his companion's remark.

When once they were well under way, however, and having left Rodwell behind were ascending the great mounting incline of Wyke Road, he had ample time to meditate on what he had seen. And what he had seen was the reverse of pleasant; for he had caught a glimpse of Dog Cattistock seated in an open touring-car, with a woman heavily wrapped up sitting pressed against him, evidently directing his way towards this very ascent. Mechanically the Jobber accelerated the speed of his truck but of course the Slug could never hope to overtake a car like that! Not a word did he say of what he had seen to Sylvanus whose elongated head was now uncomfortably nodding over his tightly-buttoned jacket; but he thought in his heart "He's going to that quarrymen's meeting. That's where he's going. But have they asked him? Do they know he's coming? Has he agreed to keep Saxon Quarry open?"

They had now reached the top of the hill by Wyke Church, where the churchyard is crowded thick with the bones of wrecked men— most of them anonymous and buried together under the name of the vessel that carried them down and with whose drowned ribs they had been tossed so long in the humming surf. Here Sylvanus roused himself, straightened his back, lifted his long, bony, narrow face and tugged at the ends of his grey moustache, which hung down below his chin.

As for the Jobber, his quivering nostrils dilated like a gigantic sea-horse, snuffing his native element. For there—spread out before them in the twilight, with the lights beginning to flicker from the houses on its Northern slope, and a vast threatening bank of clouds rolling up from across the West Bay, was the dark mass of the Island of Portland, with Chesil Beach transfixed in its side, as though some

Being, accepting the ancient derisive challenge of Omnipotence, *had* put his hook into the gill of Leviathan! Across the dim escarpment of pebbles heaped together before them, the rising wind, which had been increasing in volume ever since the rain ceased, beat against them with the flapping of terrific wings. It was as if a sudden host of armless demons, with vast invisible wings, were whirling over those two men and over the fish-smelling Slug, and over the bones of the drowned people in Wyke churchyard.

"See *that*, Jobber?" Sylvanus' voice sounded hollow and yet not metallic. It sounded as if it came through a trumpet-shell that had turned into stone.

"It's coming!" growled the Jobber with a ferocious chuckle and an inflection that was like the neigh of a horse.

Sylvanus caught the exultation in the man's tone and it communicated itself to his own nervous system. "God!" he laughed tugging at the ends of his moustache with his long bare fingers and feeling about with his heels for something to press his feet against, "You're one for going fast, Skald."

The Jobber's answer to this was only to drive more recklessly still. The Slug—completely refuting her name—rushed down to the point where what is called Fleet Bridge crosses that strange strip of backwater that separates Chesil Beach from the mainland, making the beach—the Hook in the gill of Leviathan—a sort of elongated island itself.

Both the men realized that it had suddenly begun to grow dark, the darkness seeming to emanate from that solid bank of pitch-black cloud that the West wind was now carrying before it, just as a giant might come running up, carrying a coffin upon his head. The Jobber turned his truck towards Portland as soon as they had crossed the Fleet, and as he did so he slackened its pace. His mind was in a turmoil; and the approach of this storm from the deep Atlantic acted upon his mood like the low, hoarse, sullen tapping of some enormous tuning-fork. It was so dark now that the lights from the houses, clinging to the precipice-walls of the high Portland terraces, that rose tier above tier upon the northern extremity of his Wessex Gibraltar, glittered in front of them almost as vividly as if it were already night.

The Jobber drove along parallel to the stupendous pebble-bank which now hid the sea from him; and a sensation passed through him that would be almost impossible to describe in definite words. What it amounted to was the leaping up, in his excitement, of all his first childish impressions of Chesil Beach; impressions which might be best suggested by comparing them with that confused infantile feeling of how big a person one's mother is and how formidable, and yet at the same time how safe and secure a refuge.

"Did you see that fishing-boat's lights to the westward, Skald, as we came down the hill?"

Now the Jobber *had* seen those lights, which were those, he fancied, of a small schooner but preferred not to speak of them. A fishing-smack driving before a storm like that was hardly a topic to be discussed with a man like this.

"You needn't take me clear home," went on Sylvanus. "Drop me at the Sea-Serpent, for that's where I always go to get my supper."

The Jobber was too agitated to answer. He was wondering whether this move of Cattistock's meant that he *would* re-open Saxon Quarry.

Then Sylvanus said. "You'd better take your supper with me, Skald. Mrs. Gadget fries fish very well. Or do your parents expect you?"

This did bring an answer from the dark-browed driver.

"No, no! *They* don't expect me. Do you happen to know, Cobbold, what time the quarry-men are holding their meeting tonight?"

The tall man gave his touchy companion a sharp, sidelong glance.

"At their usual curious time, Skald, I take it—about five. In fact I half thought of going myself. But I don't think I will. I'm tired of hearing you people quarrelling."

The Jobber mumbled something as a retort to this, but the wind carried his words away.

"Very well, Cobbold. I'm much obliged to you for your offer. Yes, sure," he said, raising his voice as they approached Portland Railway Station, "I'll sup with you at Gadgets' tonight. We can see the sea from there."

While the heavily-driven Slug, with a great deal of groaning and exploding, was slowly dragging these two up the steep ascent, past one massively-built little house after another, whose stone roofs seemed

like organic portions of the hillside, in the curious Inn known as The
Sea-Serpent's Head, or just briefly, The Head, on the seaward side
of the hamlet of Weston, John and Ellen Gadget were hard at work
preparing for much more exciting guests than Sylvanus or the Jobber.
These were none others than Mr. Cattistock and Miss Pansy Clive,
otherwise known as Tissty.

To the surprise of the quarrymen's leaders it was not with the cold-
blooded Mr. Frampton, but with the senior partner of the firm that
they had been forced to negotiate; and though the result of these
negotiations had been less hopeless than they had feared when they
first saw Cattistock's bristly chin, they had much ambiguous information to announce to their wives when they went home to supper. For
one thing the more rebellious element among them had made a scene.

The Head was composed of huge square blocks of Portland stone;
and although a very small edifice—of not more than half-a-dozen
rooms all told—it presented itself when seen from the bottom of the
cliffs that sank down beneath it, in the form of a massive fortress,
that might well have defended the Island in ancient times. Immediately round it were several small paddocks, enclosed by rough stone
walls; but within a stone's throw of its door were two quite large
quarries, and all the table-land round that portion of the Island was
strewn with blocks of oolite, limestone lying upon limestone, as
human bones might lie upon human bones.

John Gadget was a sturdy, dark, short man and Ellen Gadget was a
sturdy, dark, short woman. Time and isolation seemed to have made
these two persons literally into the scriptural "one flesh". They looked
much more like brother and sister than like married people. So close
indeed was their resemblance that it would not have been hard to
suppose that the old heathen aura of the Isle of Slingers had betrayed
these two into the extremest form of in-breeding. Ellen was now
standing erect and busy at her stove in the back when John and their
youngest daughter Sue came in and settled down to disturb her.

"Well, mother," said John, "Sue and me have been and got all
ship-shape upstairs! Fire be blazing chimney-high; table be laid;
bottles be on table; and me and Sue have worked thik wold warming-
pan up and down bed, till you'd think Mr. Cat'stock had had three
wenches in't already."

"How is it, mother," demanded Sue, a stolid child of fifteen and the living image of her parents, "that Mr. Cat'stock can enjoy 'isself with another lady when 'a be going to be married at Trinity Church, come Thursday?"

"Yes, mother," chimed in John Gadget, in a tone of innocent astonishment exactly parallel to that of his daughter: "How can he be so sure that no little bird'll tell Thursday's Missus how he've enjoyed 'isself tonight?"

"*And* mother," went on Sue, untying Ellen's apron-strings and tying them up again more neatly with little smoothings and pattings of her plump hand, "Daddy do say they *aren't* going to stay the night; only enjoy themselves, and drinky and cuddly, and then go away. Be that the truth, mother? Be Mr. Cat'stock and the young lady going to get out of bed in the middle of the night and drive through the storm over Fleet Bridge?"

Ellen Gadget turned round, saucepan in hand, and smiled at John. " 'Twould be a turble taking to our Sue to get out of *she's* bed on such a night as this be," the woman remarked, "even if her good man were as prickly as they sea-urchings."

"But, mother, what *would* happen if anyone what knowed about such doings told Mrs. Lily, afore she stood up to altar, where he were tonight?"

"Yes, mother," repeated Mr. Gadget, echoing his daughter's words, "where he were tonight?"

But instead of answering them, Ellen removed her hands from her pots and pans and brought them thoughtfully together, twisting her own wedding-ring round and round her finger. It was her habit to fall into deep fits of meditation like this; and in these ponderings she frequently came to conclusions that would have bewildered and astonished both John and Sue. They would even have astonished the two other members of her family who now appeared, first 'Melia the eldest child, and then Celia, the second child, drifting into the kitchen, each holding an open book and both of them hazy-dazy and brain-fuddled with long reading by darkening windows.

"The storm's getting awful, mother," said 'Melia.

"The storm's shaking the house, mother," said Celia.

"We don't believe, mother," said 'Melia and Celia, "that anybody will come tonight; and so we came to ask you if—since the storm is so bad—we *need* lay Mr. Cobbold's table in the dining-room?"

The quizzical contempt with which John Gadget and the practical Sue contemplated these two dazed book-worms, standing there in the kitchen-door, with the pages of their books hanging open and their heavy eyes blinking, was not shared by Mrs. Gadget.

But she was not one for curtailing her preparations even if the storm did shake the house. "Of course you must lay the table, girls," she said. "He may—"

She was interrupted by a loud ringing of the big brazen bell that was fastened to the bar-door; not *outside*, under the indecipherable signboard, which, with its pair of large cow-like eyes of a supernatural guilelessness contained all that was left of The Head, as it swung and rattled in the wind, but *inside*, opposite the dark, old, polished counter of the bar where there were shelves full of curious glass bottles of ancient and fantastical shapes and tints.

"Go, my dears, and see who 'tis," commanded Ellen, hastily smoothing down her dress over her rounded hips, and giving her apron-string a jerk to bring it into position.

Sue pushed past her sisters to rush to obey her mother, but the others, still holding their books, dawdled down the little passage in her wake, ashamed of showing any extravagant curiosity, but conscious that this wild night might realize their bookish imaginations beyond hope; for 'Melia was reading a thrilling History of Russia, while Celia was absorbed in Percy's "Reliques."

Thus the tall forms of Sylvanus and the Jobber, as they stood in that darkening room between the still vibrating bell and the gleaming bottles, presented themselves simultaneously to 'Melia, Celia, and Sue; while their three names, chanted in a sort of lyric sing-song by Sylvanus, rang through the house, as he made the silent Jobber shake hands with each one of them in turn.

"And now, my dears," said Sylvanus, "get Mr. Skald a drink quickly—whiskey, I expect, eh, Skald?—and give *me* a taste of Meliodka."

There was a burst of giggling when the man uttered this word; for 'Melia, who was the one reading the History of Russia, had been full, for the last fortnight, of Russian names, and had amused herself by filling one of those lovely, twisted-necked, old green bottles with a mixture of spirits that she had found described in some detail by her romancical historian. No one but Sylvanus, who seemed to have the digestion of a sea-lion, would have prepared for the most important meal of the day by even sipping such stuff; but Sylvanus disposed of no less than three whole liqueur-glasses of it, while the three girls stood in a row before him, watching him with a mixture of pride and consternation, and giggling delightedly when he ostentatiously pushed back his great Caractacus moustache and pretended to lick his lips like an epicure.

When the two men were seated comfortably by the fire in this small bar-room, each one with his glass of whiskey on the drink-stained chimney piece—for even the inventor of Meliodka considered that Sylvanus had had enough of that beverage—Ellen Gadget came in to say that their supper would be ready in ten minutes. It was now only ten minutes to six, so this was extreme punctuality; but the truth was the Gadgets had been consulting together and had resolved to satisfy these two tall men as quickly as they could, hoping that they might get rid of them before Cattistock appeared.

The girls were repeatedly summoned by their mother to help lay the meal; but only Sue could be persuaded to obey. 'Melia and Celia were dark and stodgy and short, just as Sue was, but unlike Sue these elder girls wore spectacles, and unlike Sue, whose square face had no blemish, 'Melia had a reddish birth-mark clear across her left cheek. As the two men sipped their drinks and stretched out their long legs on the floor and knocked the ashes from their pipes against the bars of the grate 'Melia and Celia stood hand in hand against the bar-counter watching them with intense absorption.

Every now and then an especially violent gust of wind would shake the whole house; and when Sue opened the front door to throw something out, for there was no hall-way at the Head, the sound of the sea—harsh and menacing, could clearly be heard from the rocks below their cliff. Twice Sue was commissioned by her mother to throw away some refuse; and the second time she remained outside for several minutes. This behaviour caused 'Melia to look significantly at Celia.

"Mother says," she remarked, addressing both the men but keeping her eyes—as Celia did too—fixed entranced upon Sylvanus, "that Sarpint's eyes be open tonight!"

"Why? Aren't its eyes always open?" said Sylvanus.

"Yes, they be open in a kind-o'-way," explained Celia, "but they bain't awake. But, when a girt sea be cooming, then they wakes up. 'Tis because of they drowned sailors them wakes up then. Sarpint do mind how sweet they bodies were in they wold times, afore light-ship were thought on."

There was a silence in the bar of the Head while the two men and the two girls stared at one another listening to the howling of the wind.

"Sue had mother's shawl on," remarked 'Melia at last.

"Sue be looking at Sarpint by light 'o thee's head-lights," said Celia to the Jobber.

"What?"

The man sprang to his feet and hurried to the window.

"Poor . . . old . . . Slug," he muttered. "I'd clean forgot 'ee," and he opened the door and went out.

He found the youngest of the Gadgets contemplating with absorbed interest the swaying sign-board, which was tossing in the wind and rain like the flag of a derelict ship. The girl was so muffled in her shawl that for a moment—his mind being all amort—he took her for a very old woman; and it flashed into his head: "Is there a grand-mother here, who never appears?" but the child addressed him by name.

"I can't see whether Sarpint's eyes be waked up, or whether they bain't, Jobber Skald," she cried out, plucking the shawl from her mouth, and challenging the hubbub with her shrill young voice.

"I can't afford to leave my lights any longer," he replied, proceeding to the body of the Slug, whose form, wearing an illuminated nimbus of streaming rain, the long shafts of which resembled a thick array of transparent spears, was an amalgam of darkness and light.

Sue Gadget rushed up to him with indignant protests, and tried to pull him back.

"I *almost* saw Sarpint's eyes and you're going to turn the light out; and it'll all be over!"

There was such a woeful strain in her voice that the Jobber paused, leaning against the body of the Slug, which now looked like a gigantic glow-worm.

"What'll you give me not to turn 'em off?" he said; and then without waiting for an answer, "Out of the way child!" he shouted, jumping into his seat.

He ran the truck close up against the front of the house and stopped it just beneath the tossing sign. Then, standing erect in it, he managed after several stumbles (for it was no joke to balance himself in that position) to catch the sign-board and hold it tight and still.

"Come on, girlie! Up you jump!" he cried.

Side by side, when he had her there, clinging to him with both her arms, they gazed into the obscurity of the Sea-Serpent's Head. The Slug's glow-worm lights did them very little good up there; but, for all that, the Jobber did seem to make out something curious about these darkly-discerned eyes. As for Sue, she was in a state of ecstasy. He could feel the throbbing of her belly, as it pressed against him, heaving like a bell-buoy in a high tide.

The girl knew the daylight stare of these weather-washed lineaments so well that her imagination was alert to anticipate any change caused by the storm.

"I can see it! I can see it!" she kept crying; and she clung to him tighter and tighter while he clutched the sign-board.

The Jobber could see in his truck's long search-lights several great heaps of square stones piled up near the mouth of the nearest quarry, and these stones, combined with the stone walls of the Inn, made him visualize the whole vast mass of that promontory of oolite stretching out into the sea. The unusualness of his position seemed to hypnotize him in some way, while from the warm body of the young girl under her flapping shawl, as the wind and rain whirled round them came a feminine magnetism that he diverted to his feeling for Perdita.

In her ecstasy as she clung to the Jobber Sue happened to turn her eyes away from the dimly-lit sign he held and to plunge them into the moaning, hissing, swimming darkness towards the cliff's edge. In the midst of this darkness she suddenly fancied she saw a light rise up; a light which wavered and fluctuated and then sank as quickly as it had come. With characteristic caution she said no word of what she had seen; but heaving round in his arms, she fixed her gaze—neglecting the Sea-Serpent altogether—upon the approximate place, in that humming and swimming darkness, where the light had appeared.

But the Jobber, noticing nothing of this move of hers, continued obstinately holding the sign-board for her supposed enjoyment— though to him it had become by this time no more than a square of obscurely painted wood—and letting his mind plunge freely into his own sea of troubles. He found that he shied away now from any reasonable attitude, or any *rational* attitude towards his resolution to kill Cattistock. There are those who would maintain that a deep, healthy instinct in the man had leapt up from the profound blood-pools of his being to save him from such a disaster; and that this instinct was using his love for Perdita to get him out of it. But such an explanation would find it hard to account for the exultant madness with which, as he hugged the shawled figure to him with his one free arm and abandoned himself to the feeling of its being a girl's, he gave himself up to the two great passions of human life. Those blocks of Portland stone, over there by the quarry, became an enlarged replica of the beach-pebble in his pocket, while the beating, stinging darkness became the eternal oblivion into which he was plunging both the Dog and himself.

"I'll kill myself," he thought. "I'll dodge the rope any way." And then he thought: "Ten o'clock by the Clock! And I'll bring her out here. I'll take her to dad's. I'll take her to the Bill. I'll take her to those light-house-keeper's graves. I'll take her to Saxon Quarry!" And in the hurly-burly of his mind the eyes of that painted Head to which he was clinging seemed to be like the eyes of all the stone of Portland and all the pebbles of Chesil. "I'll drag the Dog down with me," he thought. "*By the Clock tomorrow at ten!* And I'll have her for twelve hours; and perhaps all night—twelve hours more; and then I'll have you down, Dog. That will be a tit for a tat, and a pro for a quo! That will be hire and salary, and a brimming demi-john, Dog! And then when I've done it I'll drown myself. No one shall catch me. I'll see to that. And, by Dum, I'll have her again, *after I've done it* . . . like that man at Margate! By Dum! But they won't catch me with *her* as they caught him."

There. Sue saw that light again . . . not in the same place . . . much more to the north . . . and she knew what it was well enough . . .

this was not the first time . . . *a ship signalling for help* . . . they must have given up all hope of getting round the Bill . . . they must be drifting on Chesil . . .

"There's a wreck, Mr. Skald! I saw a rocket. She's driving on Chesil."

"*What's that?*" He couldn't hear her. He couldn't hear a word in the roaring of wind and sea. "What's that, Sue? *What* did you say?"

"A wreck, Mr. Skald! A wreck, Jobber Skald!"

Her shawl flapped against his face, as, letting the sign-board go, he lifted her down; first upon the body of the Slug, then upon the ground. He stretched his arm across the machine and turned off the lights. Now, for the first time since they had been immersed in that rain-pierced dazzlement, they could see the warm red glow of the bar. Sue, round whose shoulder the Jobber had mechanically thrown a protective arm as they moved to the door, thought that she had never seen a house more like a castle than their house was.

"I'll tell 'Melia," she thought, recalling some of their everlasting arguments, "that there's no need to read about Russian Castles. And I'll tell Celia that the Head *was* awake as mother said it would be. This is my fifth wreck . . . and who'd have thought I'd have shown it to Mr. Skald!"

There was no small stir inside the Inn when the two entered and told their news.

"The first thing *you'll do*, Sue," said her mother, "rockets or no rockets, is to change your clothes to the skin. Jobber Skald, you be as wet as she! You be as wet as if you'd carried she up cliff-path. Do 'ee want John to lend 'ee naught?"

"It doan't seem likely to I, mother," said Mr. Gadget, "that these here folk from—"

He broke off when he received a ferocious glare from his wife.

"No, no," said the Jobber. "What's the use of changing now? Come on, Missus, let me have a bite o'meat and a swallow o' drink and I'll be off to the Beach. Sue said she were running near Beach when she saw her. Didn't you, Sue?"

Sue's reply to his words came from the top of the stairs, where, apparently in the passage, so as to lose nothing of this exciting evening, she was hurriedly obeying her mother and stripping herself of every strip of clothing.

"Her were as near beach, mother—her were as near beach, father—as 'tis from here to Weston."

"I'll come down to the beach with you, Skald," said Sylvanus, whose figure, with one arm round 'Melia and the other round Celia, was looming in the back of the bar-room.

"Well, girls, help me to dish up quick," said Mrs. Gadget "and give them something to keep them warm afore they go."

So quickly did Ellen move upon this task that by the time the youngest girl had descended the stairs the two men, the one dry and glowing from the fireside and the other drenched to the skin, were half-through their hasty meal. Mrs. Gadget commanded her daughters not to tease the gentlemen, and the girls remained very quiet.

The whiskey he had drunk, the warmth of the bar-room fire, and now the well-cooked morsels which he swallowed, soon loosened the tongue of Sylvanus Cobbold and it was not long, in spite of the Jobber's taciturn preoccupation, before he was discoursing as if these short, dark, young women standing before him in a row were a large audience. His words were mingled with the howling of the wind in the stone chimney and the lashing of the rain against the window; and very soon, so magnetic was his voice, Mr. and Mrs. Gadget came out of the kitchen and stood at the open door of the dining-room.

"Those people in that ship," he was saying, "whose signals are going up as they drive on Chesil—don't they know more about life at this moment than any person safe and sound and snug under a Weymouth roof? What's at the bottom of the sea, 'Melia, Celia, and Sue? Most people don't think death's there at all, any more than the sea-serpent is. But it *is* there; and it's under this house, and under this cliff. Your sea-serpent wakes up in a storm like this but what we've got to do is to be awake all the time. That tragic half-life of the dead in Homer, that I heard Mr. Muir talk about once at High House, lies behind everything. Mr. Muir is right there, my dears. It lies behind everything."

The girls exchanged a certain glance that had the appearance of a mutual understanding about Sylvanus, not arrived at for the first time.

"If you," he went on, "take that half-life as if it were the bottom of the sea you give the sweet light of the sun its true meaning. Unhappiness comes from not realizing that life is two-sided. The other side of life is always death. The dead in Homer are tragic and pitiful, but they are not *nothing*. Their muted half-life is like the watery light at the bottom of the sea. It is like that faint stirring of the wind at the end of a summer's day that is so sad and yet sweet beyond description."

Mrs. Gadget, waiting in the doorway for the gentleman to reach a pause, began signalling now for Sue to come and carry some coal upstairs, a pantomime which ended in her dropping the shovel out of the scuttle.

Sylvanus turned his head slowly to the door and, stretching out his long arm, pulled 'Melia towards him by her voluminous skirt and went on.

"That Homeric death-life is tragically sad, but it has a beauty like the dying away of music when instead of becoming *nothing* music carries us in its ebb-flow down to this sea-bottom of the world—"

The clock in the bar-room which had the peculiarity of commencing its travail of striking with prolonged rattlings and heavings now began to deal with the hour of seven. As the last of its brazen strokes died away Sylvanus' voice could be heard again continuing his discourse.

"—where it's all echo and reflection, where it's all memory and mirrors of memory and brooding upon what is and is not. You girls are women," he went on, while Mr. Gadget, as if to make plain that at least he wasn't a woman, wandered off with a chuckle into the bar, "and for you the sea-serpent is always awake and the bottom of the sea laid bare."

He was interrupted by the discordant sound, carried into the house even above the roar of the storm, of the harsh honking of a motor-car. There was now a general confusion, the girls running to the window and Mrs. Gadget hurrying into the bar to confer with John. There was a quick exchange of whispers between them; and then as Mrs. Gadget came back into the dining-room, her husband came forward and announced in a loud voice:

"You'll have please to excuse me, gentlemen, but I must close this door."

A great gust of wind, shaking even that massively-built house, tearing off some slates from the roof which fell crashing down on the stone path, itself closed the door with a bang.

"What was that?" cried Mrs. Gadget in alarm at the terrible strength of the wind for she had always said to her husband even in the by-gone days when she resisted his passion, "Our place be too near the edge of cliff, John." In her nervousness she actually laid her hand on the Jobber's shoulder; but the soaked condition of the man's clothes changed her mood in a trice. "Off with your jersey, Mr. Skald, for Jesus' sake, and I'll lay 'un by fire, if it be only till Mr. Cattistock and the lady have come in out of storm and——" she caught her breath in dismay, realizing that after all it had been she and not John who had let the cat out of the bag! "Then you can put 'un on and slip off quiet and unbeknown, for I know how 'ee be, over he, and small blame to 'ee, *I* say."

And with that, so upset was she and so all-amort, she actually set herself to tug the wet and steaming jersey off the man's broad back. But the Jobber, stunned by this news of his enemy's expected arrival, awkwardly resisted; and there was something very childish in the way he looked round at her as he did so but she still went on pleading with him, and all the time pulling at his jersey, till Sue caught a glimpse of his grey flannel shirt and his red braces.

"It's girls like you," Sylvanus was now saying, and he was certainly justified in merging the three together, for in the excitement of the moment they had clutched so tightly at one another's hands that when he tugged at 'Melia's skirt, which was as voluminous as her Russian ladies', he caught, so to say, three fish with one hook, "yes, it's you, 'Melia, Celia, and Sue, who are nearer the common element, by which, you must understand, I mean what lies at the bottom of life and death, than any of the rest of us, because there's something in virginity—if you'll pardon my using that word—that is more passive to the ultimate forces. Virginity has something about it"—here, as his voice grew louder and his hold upon 'Melia's skirt tighter, the girl struggled angrily to release herself, and did release herself, but not till she had pulled his fingers apart with all her force—"that melts and dissolves into the 'common element' and is porous to the 'common element', and that's why when you remember, 'Melia, Celia and Sue, this night, later on in your lives, you'll see that it has done something to you that couldn't be done to any of us older people. It has sunk into ye, already, this storm; and, for all we know, it has dragged away some part of ye into itself, so that when these sailors, who are at the end of the vision of their past lives, perish, it will be into a storm, into a death, *into a life*, that has got something of 'Melia, Celia, and Sue in it, that their souls will pass!''

The Don Quixote-like gravity and earnestness with which this was uttered arrested the attention of Ellen and saved the Jobber from being stripped of his wet jersey.

Mrs. Gadget stared at Sylvanus' high cheek-bones and long-drawn-out cavernous face, as he sat there unconcernedly swallowing the supper she had prepared. He had released 'Melia's skirt at the end of his last peroration, and as Ellen watched his figure now, outlined against the heavy mahogany sideboard, and the old pewter flagons and pewter plates, and against the portraits of her parents above it, done—so it might seem from their dark and faded condition—by the same artist who did the Sea-Serpent's Head, she wondered, as she had often wondered before, whether this man in the frayed tweed suit really had a prophetic gift, or whether he was, in reality, just simply a madman.

Seated at the wheel of the machine whose horn had so disturbed those within—for the spirited girl had driven up here from the beach by herself—Tissty, or Pansy Clive, felt nervous of leaving the protection of the car to enter this lonely house by herself. She had been waiting outside there for quite a while, watching the dark shadows of unknown people cross and re-cross the glowing window-blinds. But though she had kept on mechanically sounding her horn, she had really been rather relieved at the opportunity to lie back in this comfortable equipage, while the rain beat on the closed windows, so that she might collect her thoughts.

She had flirted with Cattistock for months, proud of attaching to herself a personage of such wealth and prestige, but had not bothered her mind much about him till his imminent capture by Mrs. Lily had aroused her languid interest. Even then it was more out of pique, and because she saw the moments slipping away so fast that were leading him to Mrs. Lily, that she felt impelled to bestir herself. It was the sight, that afternoon, of Cattistock's encounter with the quarrymen; and his facing, immediately afterwards, the tragedy of the wreck, that had suddenly changed her mood of random mischief into something almost like a romantic hero-worship.

The place of the meeting with the quarrymen had been at a Working Men's Club in Chesilton, the oldest quarter of the straggling township that extends along the high terraces of Portland's western slopes.

Tissty had received one exciting emotional shock after another that evening. She noted how sardonically and humorously Cattistock had treated the whole incident; but a hundred little details returned to her mind now as she lay back on the cushioned seat, thoughtfully powdering her face and touching up her lips. He had intended to take her to the Head before the meeting and leave her there, but they had entered a private bar at the Railway Hotel and the time had slipped away so fast that it seemed tiresome to drive half across Portland and back when the place of the meeting was so near. He wanted her to remain in the Railway Hotel till he returned but this idea was so distasteful to her that in the end—though she knew he felt nervous about their being seen in public together so soon before his marriage and especially by these quarrymen—he yielded to her wilfulness and let her accompany him. Deeply had it impressed her, as from her sanctuary in the car she watched the hostile reception he got from the crowd outside the Club, the imperturbable way he had kept his head and his temper. She was near enough to the building to catch the sound of the voices inside; and it was soon evident to her that they were shouting him down. And when he came out and a lot of the younger ones followed him jeering and hooting and making sarcastic references to "Dummy Skald" she began to realize that this was no dull matter of business as she had supposed but a human situation full of dramatic and dangerous possibilities. What broke the meeting up was not only their refusal to listen to what he was suggesting—something about what they kept calling "Saxon Quarry"—it was the wildness of the storm and the news of the wreck; and what came to her now as she went on sounding her horn in front of this jerking sign-board and closed door was the way he had talked as he drove her to the beach.

"I'll just take a look at this wreck," he had said grimly as he got into the car. And when she had shown her anxiety and surprise about the evidences of ill-feeling she had just witnessed he had made an odd grimace. "Here today—and there tomorrow," he said. "It's just the same to be their hero as their devil. Disregard their moods and dominate them! Never mind their catch-penny driftings. Skald's the fellow for them today, but I could easily be in his place tomorrow. You'll see!"

She had reached this point in her thoughts when John Gadget, armed with an enormous carriage-rug that was a kind of heirloom at the Head, appeared at the window of the car, prepared to escort its occupants—two of them as he supposed—into the Inn. He was surprised to find the lady alone; but full of his wife's concern over the Jobber's presence, the absence of the girl's companion was a comfort to him.

The dancer hesitated for a second before letting him wrap her in the rug he was carrying, for the thing smelt like the very skin of Caliban; but when she had extinguished her lights and stepped out into the storm, she was glad enough to be enveloped in it and half-led, half-lifted across the threshold.

"There aren't any quarrymen here, are there?" were her first words when she was free of the evil-smelling rug.

"Nay, nay, Missy-Marm, there ain't no quarrymen, nor no smugglers neither. There be only Mr. Cobbold of the Beale and our Adam Skald, what be having a bite o' summat with me fam'ly."

"Isn't he the one they call Dummy Skald? Isn't he the man they call the Jobber?"

Mr. Gadget's mouth dropped, for he saw that his wife's admonition not to reveal their guest's presence was going to be justified. He nodded dumbly. Tissty snatched off her hat with a sweeping gesture and making for the dining-room door, flung it wide open.

The Jobber who was seated directly opposite the door was the first to take in this brilliant apparition and, having expected to see his enemy, met her angry stare with a ferocious scowl.

The eyes of 'Melia, Celia and Sue opened wide with an expression of thrilled wonder. This girl standing on the threshold of their familiar room, with her dazzling white complexion and scarlet lips, seemed to fulfil in a moment all that the Russian History and Percy's Reliques had ever conjured up.

Sylvanus, whose long neck and bony face were averted from the doorway, turned round rather wearily and, surveying the intruder without any visible emotion, continued mumbling under his breath some fleeting half-thought connected with what he had been just saying to the three girls when this interruption had occurred.

Had the intruder upon this quiet gathering not heard her sister so often tell of Jerry Cobbold's difficulties with his eccentric brother, the sight of this formidable gentleman in a tweed suit, with moustaches such as she had always imagined—probably from stage-memories of Macbeth—the early Kings of Scotland to have worn, would certainly have quickly subdued the impulse with which she had entered. But her newly aroused emotion for Cattistock, which this evening's events had inspired and then cut short from any natural expression, now made use of this chance encounter with his well-known adversary to clear a channel for its pent-up force. Thus there descended on the head of the Jobber, who obstinately remained in his chair, pretending —as soon as he realized that his enemy was absent—to be absorbed in his meal, and whose woollen jersey, wrinkled up above the straps of his braces, still allowed his flannel shirt to be seen as he bent gloomily over his plate, a torrent of feminine abuse.

"So you're the man, are you, who's threatening to kill Mr. Cattistock! I'm glad to have a chance to tell you to your face what I think of you. All the town knows, but that's what you wanted of course, what you've been threatening about Mr. Cattistock. Yes! You wanted all the town to know and everybody to know, so as to worry Mr. Cattistock without running any risk of danger. You're just like your friends, the quarrymen. Cowards all! I was there and I saw how they would have mobbed him if they dared, but they didn't dare. And where was Mr. Jobber Skald all this while? Not even at his friends' meeting! No . . . not even there . . . nor nowhere else where there's any danger. All that *you* can do, you great huckster, who dresses himself up like a sailor in order to win favour from the people he peddles to, is to go round town whining and whimpering and talking of killing Mr. Cattistock. Kill him, will you? Oh, yes, you'll kill him! You're one of these dangerous, strong, silent killers,

you are. You're not one to talk; you're not one to threaten; you're
one to strike and quickly, too! Oh, no, you'll tell no one your
intentions—only the whole town! Bah! you're nothing but a black-
mailer. You're nothing but a dirty fish-peddler who curries favour
with people."

Here Tissty glanced at Sylvanus' fingers that were nervously
tugging, first at one moustache-end and then at the other. As for the
Jobber, who kept cutting John's cheddar cheese into fanciful little
squares and thrusting great unnoticed hunks of home-made bread
into his mouth, he could do no better than repeat over and over again
under his breath:

"The Dog and his bitch! The Dog and his bitch!"

Then looking contemptuously at 'Melia, Celia and Sue, who were
standing against the wall, each one of them clasping one of her sisters
by some piece of clothing, as they listened open-mouthed to her
tirade, she renewed the attack.

"You're a humbug in everything! You wear that great sailor's
jersey just for show. You're no sailor; you're not even a quarryman.
You're not a working-man; and you're certainly not a gentleman.
You're nothing but a peddler; that's what you are, trying to blackmail
people. What are you doing here, I should like to know, when Mr.
Cattistock, and even your precious quarrymen, are all down at Chesil?
He sent me away because I was hysterical. I'm glad he did now;
because you've had a chance, Mr. Peddler, of hearing the truth for
once, in your sham sailor clothes! Eat, drink and be merry is the way,
isn't it? And let the other people die!"

She turned away, wrapping her cloak tightly round her, and went
back into the bar-room. Here she asked John to pour her out a
drink; and very soon both their voices were audible, in cheerful and
lively tones, discussing the qualities of various liqueurs.

When the Jobber, a few moments later, without a word or sign to
anyone, passed through the bar-room on his way out of the house she
did not even turn her head to watch his departure.

Ellen meanwhile stood listening to the Jobber outside trying to start
the Slug which was a process always attended by a series of such
explosive sounds as neither wind nor rain nor tempest could muffle.

Sue, who had drifted close to the front-door, suddenly snatched up a mackintosh of her father's which was hanging on a peg and, unseen by her mother, who was still in the other room, let herself out. The explosive noises made by the Slug now ceased altogether, and nothing could be heard around the Sea-Serpent's Head save the howling of the wind. It often happens, that in some human group, in some pause of the human drama, one consciousness alone, out of the rest, will catch the significance of what has been going on all the while among the inanimate elements. It was Ellen who thus detached herself on this occasion from the others, and it was the intensity of her abstraction from all these human beings just then, that prevented her from remarking that Sue had not come back, after running out in her father's mackintosh.

But Ellen standing at the dining-room window, while Tissty went off, ignoring Sylvanus and fraternizing with John, to select a drink from among those old-fashioned bottles behind the counter, gave herself to her wildest storm-fancies in which she always told herself a story about a real sea-serpent coming trumpeting out of the sea on a night like this. Tissty's references to the wreck had stirred this vein in this short, dark woman; for both Ellen's parents had been drowned off Chesil Beach; but it was the wind itself that seemed to catch her soul now, and strive to fill the place of her imaginary sea-monster. Yes, the wind seemed to set itself to force her to listen to it and to enter into its non-human passions. It forced her to follow its wild path over the whistling wave-crests and amid the flying surf. It forced her to follow it, as driving the scudding spray before it, it shrieked round those jagged rocks, while beneath it, below the sea-floor level, deep-gurgling rock-chasms drew the waves in and spewed them out. The wind made Ellen follow it when it left the turbulence of the rocks, and began whirling up the face of the cliff. Up the face of the cliff it twisted like the sea-serpent. It whirled up through dead tufts of bent-grass and through the wind-blighted elders and ashes and stunted gorse. It whirled up over patches of samphire, and over patches of grey rock-lichen, and over whistling stalks of sea-lavender and over chittering seed-pods of sea-thrift. And as it rose higher, it wheeled and eddied and coiled, and it became easy for Ellen to feel that it really was the original of that pictured Being whose eyes had been quickened that night, come up from depths unimaginable.

It was not till three whole minutes had passed by that she turned from the window and called to 'Melia and Celia who were standing at Sylvanus' side to ask where Sue was.

"She went out to see Mr. Skald off," said 'Melia.

"She was out there saying good-bye to Mr. Skald," said Celia.

"She *must* have come in! What are you girls talking about?" repeated Ellen, beginning to get frightened. "John!" she called out, unscrupulously interrupting Mr. Gadget's flirtation with his beautiful guest, "John! Sue hasn't come back and Mr. Skald has gone!"

It was Sylvanus' turn to rise to the occasion now; and he did it with an obvious effort and with a heave of his body which made his lean bones creak like the boards of a wagon.

"I'll go and bring her back," he said; and then he came straight over to Ellen and bent his long, pale Hidalgo face over her short, dark one; for Ellen Gadget had the very stamp and seal and unmistakable look of that ancient, mysterious, short-statured, dark population that the Celts dispossessed, ere they were dispossessed themselves by the invading Saxons; and a little crustily as if cross at having to leave such good listeners as 'Melia and Celia, he told her that he was sure Sue had gone off to see the wreck with the Jobber.

"I saw her eyes," he said in a low tone, "while that girl was tormenting our friend. The child fell in love with him, then and there—if she hadn't before! But I'll bring her back, if you'll only not work yourself up into a fever. I'll bring her back *within two hours from now*. I promise!"

Ellen felt a strong impulse to make Mr. Gadget leave his gallantries behind the counter and accompany Sylvanus on this errand, but no sooner had she crossed the bar-room, with this intention, than Sylvanus snatched up his little soldier's cane and, just as he was, slipped out, and set off on foot for Chesil.

He hurried along the grey and rain-swept way, going westward and while that "way" was too narrow to be called a road, and too wide to be called a path, its peculiarity was that it was designed for walking alone. No one could ride on it. No one could drive on it, and it was wondrous smooth to the tread. He had to go nearly a couple of miles before he came to the westward slope of the great promontory, and when he did so, though he could see flickering lights, and a great many of them, along the beach, and could clearly catch the white foam of the breakers under these flaring illuminations, he could see nothing of any wreck.

"It's all over," he thought. "She's gone; and the life-boat's come in. I doubt if they saved a single life."

It was only about half an hour since he had left the Head and it would take him now no more than ten minutes before he reached the beach, so there was no need to hurry. The ship had broken up. The dead had gone down. There were only the sight-seers and the talk, and the jealousies, and the heart-burnings, and the loves and hates.

"What spiritual eyes and yet what vicious, dissipated eyes that girl had! I must see her again. I must talk to her properly. She'd quickly give herself up to what I tell her."

A man's thoughts—and not only when he is descending a declivity as steep as this of the Isle of the Slingers—could be as easily interpreted in a wrong sense as in a right sense, even if it *were* possible to overhear his wordless words! No sympathy, no understanding, no devotion, no passion, no clairvoyance could, for instance, have indicated to Gipsy May or to the Punch-and-Judy girl, had either of these infatuated women overheard this thought, "I must see her again: I must talk to her properly," and the person whose image accompanied this thought, this wish, this intention, was *not* the beautiful Tissty, to whose eloquence he had just been listening, but on the contrary was that white, haggard-faced figure in the doorway of the fishmonger's, who had stared at him out of such dark-circled eye-sockets, as if she were extending her very soul towards him.

The bare hill, upon which he now paused, rose abruptly over the most populated portion of the Island. Under him gleamed the motionless window-lights of many solid stone houses whose roofs were crowded together against the steep incline, with that effect of dim, rich, intricate, *Gothic* confusion, which human dwellings acquire when mingled with the massive irregularities of ancient hills. Not a living soul had he encountered in his walk to this spot! Not a living soul could he see from where he stood. Nothing confronted him here except the unknown mysteries of the life behind those glowing windows and the unknown death-tragedy beneath those flickerings on the beach!

He stood perfectly still for a couple of minutes, letting the rain beat on his bare head and on his long, Quixotic countenance. His thoughts gathered up in haste the whole essence of his recent life, his life of the past five years, since he had come to live in that lonely Portland house between the hamlet of Weston and the wind-swept "Beale". Always a rebel, always dwelling in a mystical borderland of his own, Sylvanus was one of those beings who seem to draw from nature the power of escaping from the ways and customs and habits of his own race. The man himself had come to feel more and more as if his real home were not upon the earth at all but rather in some Cimmerian twilight belonging to the chemistry of a completely different star. His whole life now consisted in the self-pleasing enjoyment of a curious mystical contemplation; and he treated all actual occurrences, whether happy or unhappy, as if they were only half real. Certain words that have come down to us in the fluctuating borderland between religion and philosophy, words such as "absolute", "essence", "eternity", "immortality", conveyed when Sylvanus made use of them, a much more concrete and much more definite meaning than is usual with such expressions. By reducing the sensations of consciousness to the most primitive elements he had at last arrived at the point of establishing a certain rapport between himself and the cosmos which gave him a deeper sense of power and a deeper feeling of satisfaction than most people experience all their lives. It was, however, his relations with women that had come to be the most singular thing in his existence; and this element in his life had intensified itself of late. He was always trying to make clear to himself what he really was after in his dealings with women; but this seemed to be the evasive point in his days. He could not formulate it or define it. In fact he could not understand it. He only knew that he was driven more and more obstinately by some secret urge within him to do what, as he actually experienced it, he felt to be a sort of gathering up of women's most secret responses to life; as if some half-crazed Faust had found the magic oracles of those Beings he called "the Mothers" in the nerves and sensibilities of every ordinary young Gretchen he encountered. Well! not *quite* ordinary, for there had been, as can be seen in an obscure resemblance between Gipsy May and Marret, and between Marret and Peg Frampton, a certain indefinable quality that might perhaps be indicated as erotic virginity, a quality that had something in it of the classic abandonment of Bassarid and Maenad, and that it would not be inappropriate to name *unravished obsession*. What this quality really consisted of, in the women to whom, like a metaphysical ancient mariner he was compelled to reveal what Lucinda called his "wicked craziness", was a certain susceptibility to "religious prostitution", or in more ideal language, a latent passion to offer up their amorous life, as mystics offer up their souls, to some object of spiritual idolatry. What Sylvanus really was attempting to do, as he swept these prepared spirits into his mania for what he called the Immortal, the Eternal, the Absolute, it would be impossible to say. What he felt in his secret being was, that he had battered and bruised himself so long in his desperate struggle to reach the secret of life, that he had come now, in a kind of forlorn hope, to fumble and grope towards the world's mystery through the more receptive souls of women. One thing was certain. He never talked love-talk to them. He never made love to them. He never made promises to them: and when Gipsy May actually shared the same bed with him he scarcely touched her. Their passion was for him; but his passion was for the Eternal Being; only he had found his masculine reason so much of a hindrance in his struggle to attain what he called the Absolute that he was forever seeking to learn from the souls of women, attuned, as they were to strings and to chords which were hidden from him, some secret entrance to the Deathless and the Immortal which as a hermit and as a solitary he had been unable to reach for himself.

Sylvanus was older than Jerry by some five years; and their father, before he passed from the world under the care of Dr. Brush, had seen to it that this elder son, who from the time he left college, had shirked all human obligations, should enjoy an annuity, whose capital he could not touch. Even this paternal foresight had not, however, been sufficient; and when Sylvanus moved from Weymouth and established himself in a lonely house on the southern extremity of Portland, it soon became clear that his income, small as it was, would have to be doled out to him week by week if it was to last to the year's end; and this arrangement, by the aid of the firm of Loder and Crouch, was finally arrived at, not a little to the relief of Lucinda, for the man had contracted the habit, when his funds vanished and he felt hungry, of appearing uninvited at the High House dinner-table. But now, for the last few years, the High House pair had seen very little of him; and all seemed to be going well; until suddenly this new mania of his for expounding his ideas to anyone who would listen among the crowds on the Weymouth esplanade broke up the status quo and led to endless embarrassments.

It became one of the most popular topics of conversation in Weymouth society whether the elder Cobbold had "begun to go as his father did" but since apart from this mania for preaching, or rather for *expounding*—for Sylvanus' methods were more Pythagorean than Evangelical—he showed no sign of mental aberration, unless his fondness for the society of young women could be called by that name, not even Lucinda, who had always loathed him, had come to the point of suggesting having him confined, as they had done with his father, in the world-famous Home for pathological cases that the shepherds of the high downs called Hell's Museum. But with young Ballard's accession to municipal authority a new régime had commenced at the Guildhall, and within the last few weeks this expounder of the Absolute, grown so familiar a figure on the esplanade with his tweed suit and his uncovered head, had received repeated warnings that if he persisted in disturbing public order in this flagrant way he would find himself "in trouble". Sylvanus was not ignorant of what this "trouble" meant; for he knew that his brother's thoughts—egged on by Lucinda—would naturally turn to the famous establishment where their father had passed his last years.

But though he felt no attraction to Hell's Museum he had reached a point, in his meditations upon the Eternal, where the locality of his temporal domicile mattered little. He *had* vaguely wondered lately, as he lay in his bed, with the periodic revolutions of the great Portland light-house flashing across his face, whether they'd allow him to talk freely to the other inmates, in case he were "put away"; but in his heart of hearts, if the truth must be told, he had an instinct that something would happen to prevent his incarceration.

Had anyone less scientific than Dr. Brush, or less habituated to the evasive movements of animals under experimentation, peeped into the inside of that long Quixotic cranium at this moment, he would have found no evidence of insanity. He would, on the contrary, have found, if he could have read the man's thoughts, a very natural concern as to how he was going to keep his promise to Ellen Gadget and get Sue home, and an equally normal concern as to what would happen when, under these exceptional conditions, his friend the Jobber encountered Mr. Cattistock.

"Well, here goes!" he said to himself, feeling nothing but the most healthy-minded nervousness as to what he was plunging into, as he scrambled down the declivity to Chesil Beach.

He soon discovered little Sue. The girl was running from one to another of the men of her acquaintance trying to get all the information she could about what had happened before she came on the scene. She hurried to meet Sylvanus as he came clattering and crunching down the slope of the beach, where the life-boat—evidently of no more use—had been pulled out of the surf, and lay on her side, like a beautiful circus-performer whose "turn" was over.

"She were broke up afore we got here, Mr. Cobbold," the girl announced, gasping for breath, "and they life-boat men were wading in sea, and swimming in sea, tied by girt ropes. One o' they told Jobber, when us first came, that them had seed summat tossing in sea what weren't a plank, nor a mast, nor a yard-arm. I heard 'un tell how they tied ropes about 'un and swimmed out. It were two on 'em what swimmed out. But they got nothing. If it had been a corpsy, they told 'un, 'twould have been the same, the sea were that high. Them two what swimmed out were dragged in they woneselves like corpsies. So 'twas a *real* wreck! 'Melia and Celia ain't been at a real wreck, like I've been at, have 'un?"

The dark beach upon which Sylvanus stood, listening to the excited child, who had let him take her by the hand, was now crowded with agitated human figures. The news that a ship had been broken up on Chesil had reached Weymouth a couple of hours ago, just about the time people were finishing their evening meal, and quite a number of enterprising individuals had hastened to the spot.

Among these sensation-seekers was Sippy Ballard, in his belligerent little car, and Magnus Muir and Richard Gaul in a hired taxi. The primal cause of this last appearance at the scene of the wreck, which was astonishing to everyone who saw the two book-worms there, standing side by side facing the flying spray, was not the mutability of the ocean but the mutability of a woman.

Curly, with the rain as an excuse, had easily been persuaded by her lover and by the little doctor to content herself with what they could find in the larder of Sark House and to stay there all the afternoon. From this paradisiac interlude in the arms of Ballard, who, when he was not embracing her, was relating to her the drollest stories, it was more than even Curly could contemplate to go off and sit for two hours opposite the solemn countenance of Magnus; and so, though she had promised to have a high tea with him at the Regatta—an innocent, popular restaurant not far from the old king's statue—she had instead gone straight back to Upwey, little dreaming that both her men, the one filled to the brim with the after-taste of her sweetness and the other fretted to the breaking-point by the lack of it, would—in their opposite reactions—meet on Chesil Beach.

Sitting in front of her empty chair in his favourite windowseat at the Regatta, looking out across the esplanade, Magnus was persecuted by the proprietor of the place who, being an ex-yachtsman, had received special news from Portland of a wreck on Chesil. He not only recommended to Magnus—who would not touch a mouthful—to go and view this spectacle, but he expressed the opinion that "the young lady you are expecting, Mr. Muir, has heard of the launching of the new life-boat and has gone to see it". When Magnus fixed him with an eye which was as angry as it was bewildered, the man coolly added:

"I've never known a woman, Mr. Muir, who weren't crazy over life-boats."

Disturbed beyond what he himself would have believed possible Magnus had actually hired a taxi, driven straight to Trigonia House, and implored Mr. Gaul to accompany him on this wild-goose chase. Mr. Gaul, contemplating his friend's pitiable condition with unruffled detachment was, all the same, too good-natured to increase his agitation by refusing to ride through a storm. It was not, however, till they were nearly at Fleet Bridge that either of them uttered a word. Then Mr. Gaul remarked.

"That man at the Regatta makes models of life-boats. He brings them out to show you. They're not very good. They're too thick."

Magnus made no attempt to follow up his friend's knowledge of boat-building. He repeated mechanically the words "too thick" and fell once more to conjuring up in his mind a drenched and remorseful Curly who would rush up to greet him and throw her arms impulsively round his neck. He had even reached the point of vaguely considering where it would be best to deposit Mr. Gaul, when the taxi drew up.

"Do you want me to wait for you?" the driver called after them, as they moved off towards the beach. " 'Tis a wild night for all con-sarned," he said, as they came back, "and I'm sorry, gentlemen, but I have to arst you to pay my fare afore you goes. Such be me orders, after dark."

Mr. Gaul found it discreet at this juncture, in spite of the tearing wind and rain-wet darkness, to rub his spectacles on his coat-collar and even to glance casually and lightly at them, holding them in the air at a suitable distance from his face, as if he were sitting on a seat in Victoria Gardens listening to the band, instead of standing dazed and uncomfortable, within a stone's throw of drowning people.

"Shall I wait for ye?" reiterated the taximan, mollified by a good tip above his fare.

"Shall he?" said Magnus to Mr. Gaul; and it was then that the latter uttered the enigmatic words:

"Better leave it uncertain."

Grasping the truant Sue tightly by the hand, Sylvanus was indeed astonished when he found himself greeted by these two academic persons. He looked at them self-defensively and a little quizzically, for he had met them at High House under embarrassing conditions and Mr. Gaul had been present at at least one of his really nasty scenes with Lucinda.

"You're wondering," he said to Mr. Gaul, "whether I saved this girl from the wreck?"

Mr. Gaul looked completely nonplussed. The wind and spray lashing his face did not save him from the sensation of blushing. He had, as a matter of fact, been wondering exactly what Sylvanus said he had.

"I think I'll walk about a bit, Gaul," said Magnus. "We can't lose each other here."

He went off accordingly.

"After all," he thought, "it does sometimes happen in life that a fool like that Regatta man gives you the right tip. She may be here. It's not an absolutely mad idea."

"The storm's over," said Sylvanus, "and the sea's settling down. When I was up there on the hill and had a bird's eye view I could see, by those lights those men are carrying over there, the surf blowing across the top of the beach. We couldn't have stood where we're standing now *then*, could we, Sue?"

"What a lot of people there are here!" remarked Mr. Gaul. "What I can't understand is, where's the wreck they've all come out to see?"

There was a solemn intensity in the gaze the young man fixed upon the seething waters in front of him that was almost pathetic. Had his mother been alive to see that particular expression it would have reminded her of the look the small Richard used to assume when he stared for hours into the unknown, from above the rail of his cot.

Meanwhile, as he shuffled over the slippery pebbles, deafened by the roar of the breaking waves, Magnus hunted in vain for any sight of Curly. From group to group he went, and many a Portland fisherman told his wife, as he lay down by her side that night, that "there were a bloke on beach who must have knowed one o' they poor beggars. 'Twere a holy fright to see the feäce he had on him!"

It was no wonder that by the flaring lights thrown on that strange scene Magnus' expression was a shock to these men, used as they were to human perturbation in the presence of the elements. The extremity of what he felt was a surprise to his own heart. He had known too well how much he loved her, but the shock of this wild spectacle and the bitter vanity of the hope raised in him by that modeller of "thick" life-boats, stirred up in his very midriff a feeling that made the pit of his stomach flap, like his old wind-blown ulster. Manfully he struggled with his unreason.

"She was scared by the storm," he thought, "and her mother wouldn't let her go out. It's natural enough. She's probably in bed already. Oh my Lovely, my Lovely! your bed will be *my* bed before a fortnight's over!"

What he could not help himself from doing now, was thinking what his life would be if Curly had been on this vanished fishing-smack, if that shell-like, brittle little head were even now being bruised and broken in this black welter! Not a plank, not a barrel—the fishermen assured him—had been washed ashore.

" 'Tis like the wreck of the 'Festy'," they explained, "what had five men and a boy a'board. There be under-pulls in these here spring tides, what sucks 'un down and out-along. If 'tis fair weather, come the New Moon, we may see summat! But not a 'ooman who suckled 'em won't know the poor sons of bitches then."

Magnus wrestled with a terrible terror that something would happen to take Curly from him before he'd got her to himself. Her image became for him on that dark beach what he never thought any human image *could* become. Desperately he strove to gain the mastery over his wild fears. There *was* a vein in him, inherited from his father, of formidable exultation in such a furious mêlée as this. He tried grimly to get his old life-illusion back, whereby he thought of himself as a strong, primeval spirit, linked to a shrinking and cowardly set of nerves. He imagined himself as he moved up close to those towering, crashing waves, and let their foam drench his face, being called upon to rush into that seething blackness by the sight of human arms outstretched to him. An overpowering shame for all his habitual weaknesses shook his whole nature.

"Oh, my Lovely, my Lovely!" his spirit called out into that swirling chaos, "if fate will only give you to me, if fate will only let nothing happen, you shall find what I can be! You shall rest on me as on a rock!"

He stooped down once and picked up a fragment of tarry sacking. It was nothing. It had probably been floating out there in mid-ocean for months. But to touch with his fingers anything that had been in their roaring whirlpool gave him a queer feeling. He found at last that he had been scrambling along the edge of the waves till he was alone in the darkness. Turning round he could see the moving groups of people he had left, lit up weirdly and grotesquely, like a mask of demons, in the lights that some of them carried. What a place this Chesil was! As he turned again and tried to pierce the darkness where the great embankment stretched away westward, heavy with moanings and sobbings and inarticulate storm-wails of its own, he had a queer sensation as if he had walked along this pebbly ridge, on the verge of these ghastly down-sucking gulfs, many a time before! As a matter of fact this was the first time in this life he had been on the great beach in a night of storm. Was it then, he wondered, that he was *re-thinking the memories of his father?* Suddenly he became aware that he had not yet reached the bound and the limit of the other spectators of this madness of the waters.

The tall figure of a man was advancing towards him out of the westward-stretching darkness. Magnus recognized him before he spoke. It was Jobber Skald. In a flash he recalled the man's hoarse threats against his enemy from that tossing boat at the pier's end the night he transferred to him the task of meeting Mrs. Cobbold's companion. The sight of the man standing there, the sound of his voice, made him recall another thing, too, the fact, namely, that at the extreme eastern end of the crowd of excited watchers he had caught a glimpse, that night, of Cattistock himself, talking to his nephew. Magnus had undoubtedly for some odd reason lost his early prejudice against the man, when he found out that he was a miser. Thus the idea of this singular character now standing opposite him, with his heavy jowl and dusky, passionate features, going about threatening to kill him gave him only a feeling of distaste. Cattistock *the miser* was a very different sort of person from Cattistock the promoter of companies, and he was a person, too, towards whom it seemed simply absurd to cherish such murderous emotions.

If the place the hour, and the tragic vanishing—as if into fathoms of down-sucking chaos—of the lost fishing-smack, had revealed to Magnus the strength of his passion for Curly, they had certainly worked up the less balanced nature of the Jobber into a yet more grievous turmoil. There had been established a reciprocity—with a vengeance —between this man's soul and the elements about him.

"Did you see him over there?" were the Jobber's first words after the two men had shaken hands.

"See whom?"

"*Him*, the Dog."

"I saw Mr. Cattistock talking to Mr. Ballard; but I didn't speak to him. I don't know him very well."

"You're teaching his son now?"

"Why not, Mr. Skald?"

The words that they spoke to each other had to be shouted, to be heard at all, against the sea's uproar, and the mere fact that from these two figures standing so near each other, the one in his flapping cape and the other in his clinging, drenched clothes, there came these alternate shouts, reduced the interchange between them to something at once primitive and grotesque.

"He's an idiot, isn't he?"

"No, he's not! He's a very nice boy. You wouldn't say that if you'd ever talked to him."

"We all talk too much! There's too much talk, Mr. Muir."

"Too much *what*, did you say?"

"Talk, talk—too much talk!"

"Have you seen, by any chance, anything of Curly Wix down here?"

"There were a lot of women by the life-boat. She was probably with them. I didn't look."

"By the life-boat did you say, Skald?"

"The life-boat! The life-boat!"

"Are you sure you saw her?"

"By the life-boat! That's where they are!"

"*Who* is by the life-boat?"

"The women, the women, man! A score of 'em maybe, waiting for the bodies to come ashore."

"Was Curly Wix with them?"

"Oh, *that* girl. No, no! *she* wasn't with them. I'd have known *her*. I thought you were talking about Sue Gadget."

"You're *sure* you didn't see her with those others?"

"The Island's never had a worse enemy. Someone must finish it and soon, too. There's too much talk in this world, Mr. Muir! I'm a talker, am I, Mr. Muir? Is that what you think?"

It seemed to have sunk into the Jobber's head that this tutor of the Dog's son was hostile to him; and he now thrust his great face so close to Magnus' face and seized him so brutally by the arm that the Latin teacher was startled. But it was a peculiar thing in Magnus that while his reason was riddled and perforated with nervous terrors, there was something else in him—an inheritance perhaps from the elder Muir—that was liable at times to mount to his head. He shook off the Jobber's hold now.

"I don't know you well enough to say," he shouted, "but I do know this: that if you were doing to me what you're doing to Mr. Cattistock, going about through the pubs threatening to kill me, I wouldn't submit to it for a second!"

A responsive shock of anger quivered through the Jobber's frame and it rushed to the tip of his tongue to shout out to this touchy schoolmaster that he *was* "submitting", quietly enough already, while the pubs of the town mocked him as a wittold! It was on his tongue to tell him that at the Weeping Woman the other night he had heard some wag speak of him as "Mr. After-Sippy". But let him go! It was the Dog he was after, not this fool of a tutor. To the devil with him and his German cloak! He moved off and, shuffling down the dangerous slope of the sea-bank, stood staring into the swirling blackness, striking himself mechanical blows across the chest to warm his blood.

As for Magnus, he had no sooner expressed his anger than it died out of him completely; and when he saw the man warming himself like a frozen cab-driver, he experienced an unpleasant spasm of remorse. But he remained standing where he was, just above what would have been the water's "windrow" in any ordinary time, gazing into vacancy and letting his soul travel to his love. In that convulsed chaos of heaving ridges, slippery crests, tossing water-spouts, both men were now visualizing the faces of their women; but while the Jobber, whose case was the more desperate, took *his* girl's faithfulness for granted, Magnus, in whom caution and commonsense were once more entrenched, felt as if the shell-like face of Curly might dissolve at any moment, and be lost to him forever.

But even as they were standing in this position, the Jobber with his heels in the crunching slope of pebbles and Magnus with the cape of his ulster switching against the back of his head, and both of them half-deafened by the shrieking wind, there rose and broke in the welter before them a wave larger than the rest. They could see it towering up there, before it collapsed, in its precipitous and slippery bulk, and the resounding crash with which it fell, whirling its spray round the heads of both of them and covering the Jobber up to his knees, drove all thought away.

For the second time that night there came over Magnus a curious up-welling of something that was as one with these wild elements, and instead of retreating, when the fatal back-drawing of the wave's ebb began, he deliberately staggered, *with the wave*, down that dark pebble-slide and, digging his heels in, stretched out his arm to the Jobber. It was lucky he did this, for had the Jobber's foot-hold loosened, as it was on the verge of doing, the man would have been swept down, and once down there, in those churning waters, his chance would have been small; but the other's hand gave him just the necessary minimum of support and he quickly stumbled up the shelving bank.

They were no sooner side by side than the inherent weakness of Magnus' character—or what most people would call weakness—displayed itself in an invincible impulse to refer to the elder Muir. The elder Muir had been really remarkable in this one particular, namely that he had endowed each separate one of the material phenomena of the place of his earthly sojourn with a curious mythological identity for his son's mind. Thus every one of these objects, the White Horse, Hardy's Monument, the White Nose, the Nothe, the Breakwater, Sandsfoot Castle, and above all this great pebble-bank where he now stood, was seen by Magnus in a different way from the way others saw it. *It was a piece of his father's life.* Thus the moment they were out of danger he set himself to shout in the Jobber's confused and preoccupied ear:

"My Father, you know, Skald, was one of your old-fashioned sort, and he never could abide our friend Cattistock, but in those days people were more independent than they are today. But all the same, my good man, we simply can't,"—here Magnus raised his voice to a shriek, and as he raised it he was aware that another terrible wave was breaking—"can't avenge ourselves by force! 'Leave it to God', is what my Father always used to say. I've heard him say it often when people cheated him, just like you've been cheated by Cattistock; and my Father, Skald, was one who—"

But what looked like a water-spout from the jaws of Leviathan was now pouring in upon them and over them and past them, out of the shaken trough of that many-sounding blackness, and they had to stagger still further up the pebbly slope, till in a second the torrential back-swirl of another foamy retreat tugged at their legs. When once more he was able to take breath Magnus stubbornly finished his sentence about the elder Muir:

"—was one, Skald, who refused to be bullied!"

Aye! what comfort it gave Magnus to say—gasping for breath and dripping with salt water on this ridge of Chesil—that his father refused to be bullied.

"He refused to be bullied, Skald!" he repeated again, with a peculiar vibrancy in his voice; and he felt as if he heard those words blown on the wind, tossed on the waves, mounting up on the long spears of the rain. "He *refused* to be bullied, Skald!"

And as his voice sank, for the Jobber had fallen into his thoughts again, behaving towards these words about the elder Muir as if they were only another example of "too much talk", it came over Magnus that what he was disputing about with this man on the rim of the world was a blind, a screen, a joke, an organ-grinding jig, a pattern of marionettes, while all the while something much more important— something that had to do with the way his father used to stay so long bent down over the sea-anemones in the rock-pools below the Coast-Guards and the way he would say, "Magnus, my boy, I saw a little fish in this pool!"—was being transacted, behind and beyond all this unreal posturing. But he became aware now as he watched the Jobber's absorbed and frowning trance, that the salt which had gathered on his lips and in his nostrils tasted differently from usual. It had a dangerous taste, a fatal taste. What had set him thinking of such a thing? To find the taste of sea-salt in his mouth on Chesil Beach making him think of kissing Curly, when at last he had got her safe in his own bed, what kind of thought was this?

"A fair thought"—ha?—like Hamlet's about Ophelia's legs.

Suddenly, while his mind was thus obsessed with exciting images of passionate delight, he became aware that there was something important going on among the rest of the people on the beach. Looking back past the Jobber's abstracted figure, whose face was turned towards the west, his attention was arrested by a disorderly scattering of the glaring lights that the men near the life-boat had been carrying; and it seemed to him that there was a wild stir of some nature, amounting to something really serious, going on over there, away to the eastward, even nearer the Isle of Portland than the spot where he had spoken to Sylvanus.

"Something's happened; something's happening!" he shouted; and it was his turn now to tug roughly at the other's arm. "Come on, man!"

But the Jobber gave him the kind of stare that a person on a scaffold might give to a town-crier bawling out the news; and with the look of that contorted face, decomposed, wavering, torn by indecision, receding from his brain, as he went, Magnus hurried off so fast to ascertain what had occurred, that he didn't look round again to find out whether the Jobber was following him. He found the life-boat men busy with the struggle of launching their craft once more; but he did not wait to ask them any questions. On he went at a run; and it was still with the fantastic notion at the back of his mind that Curly might suddenly materialize, out of the sea, out of the wind, out of the midst of the crowd, that he joined a tense and wrought-up group of men, surrounded by a solemn and awe-struck crowd, who were watching them hold the end of a long rope while a solitary figure, rising and falling like a cork in the surf, was fighting his way towards a round, dark object that kept appearing and disappearing as the waves swept it shoreward. There were several lights at this point flickering on the men who held the rope—one of whom was S. P. Ballard—and on the man in the water, and the rather ghastly illumination flung, like a search-light, on the latter revealed—not a little to Magnus' astonishment—that this reckless swimmer was none other than Cattistock himself. The man was indeed forcing himself onward towards this dark object which bobbed up and down in the surf about ten yards in front of him while the life-boat, now safely launched, was making a circle in the illuminated water so as to reach with all possible accuracy the same surf-tossed objective.

Magnus soon learned from the excited remarks of Mr. Ballard, who was roundly reviling a couple of fishermen for letting his uncle do such a mad thing, that they'd seen what resembled a human form clinging to this barrel, but it certainly looked to the Latin teacher at this moment as if the barrel, bobbing up and down in the swirling spray, were empty and alone. But no! no! it wasn't *Something*—and it *was* a human form, only a very little one—was clinging tight to that round, gyrating cask. No! no! it *could not* be clinging to it. It would have been washed away from it an hundred times over as the thing leaped and danced and revolved, like a drowning Jack-in-the-Box. What he saw must be *tied* to it!

Cattistock's own thoughts, as he struggled forward, always being hurled over and rolled over, always being battered, pounded, half-choked, half-stunned, far from being confused or bewildered, remained sardonically cool.

"I'll show 'em, I'll show 'em, I'll show 'em!" he kept repeating.

He had come down to the beach without any definite purpose; simply from that obscure intuition of destiny that men of action so often have. His determination to deal with this serious animosity of the quarrymen was to a man of his kind such a compelling force that he couldn't just let it go and retreat to the Inn. His instinct was to follow up his enemies relying on some unexpected dénouement of circumstances to give him an unforeseen advantage. They had hooted him mercilessly at the quarrymen's meeting. Voices in the crowd had called out:

"Dummy Skald'll settle 'ee! Look 'ee out for Dummy Skald, master!"

At first he had not realized that "Dummy" was their pet name for the Jobber; but when Tissty explained it, for she "did not care now", as she told Tossty later, "whether he were the greatest skinflint in the county", he had seen the possibility of some spectacular gesture establishing his ascendancy in the Isle of the Slingers more effectively than argument or hard cash. The man was totally devoid of any poetical or emotional response to the storm himself, but he was shrewd enough to see that its effect upon the crowd lent itself to what he required. Never was a more strategic nor a more searching eye cast about for a move this way or that in the march of events than was turned that night upon the crowd and upon the waves and upon the life-boat and upon the beach and upon the sight-seers from the town, by the sharp-chinned president of "Cattistock and Frampton". He had seen this floating barrel when he was talking to Sippy, and what certainly did look like a person clinging to it, for several minutes before he told a living soul. Indeed he despatched Ballard to get a flask of brandy at the Portland Railway Station before he made any move at all. Then when Sippy was out of sight he joined a group of excited fishermen, among whom was the bareheaded Sylvanus still holding Sue Gadget fast by the hand.

"Someone ought to swim out," he remarked to this whole group, "and bring that thing in. It looks to me there's a man tied to it."

"Life-boat be being launched, sir," said one of the men. "They must have seed 'un, same as yourself. But I don't believe there be a man, 'ooman, or babe on 'un."

Cattistock glanced round. "By God!" he thought. "I'll have to hurry up. They *are* launching the damned life-boat." "If that's a person on that barrel," he remarked, "he'll be dead before the life-boat reaches him."

Sue Gadget stared up with big, wondering eyes at this courageous man. Could be actually be going to share with that girl the next room to her own that very night? Her heart began to beat fast at this thought, and she recalled the way a stream of light, when her own room was dark, came through a little narrow opening near the ceiling from this neighbouring room.

" 'Melia and Celia haven't seen the Head with Jobber Skald to hold 'un," she thought. " 'Melia and Celia haven't held hands all evening, at a real wreck, with Mr. Cobbold. They won't have a light shining into they's room, neither, from where Mr. Cattistock be stroking his beautiful lady."

Meanwhile Cattistock was watching the barrel—that sometimes looked as if there *was* something else there and sometimes not—with a measuring exactness.

"It's a chance," he thought. "It might—"

He picked up the end of a long rope and then, dropping it, began to take off his overcoat. Then he picked the rope up again and dropped it again. Then he bent down and with some difficulty, for the wind was very violent, unlaced and removed his boots.

Meanwhile the long white face of Sylvanus, as he watched the fishermen knotting the rope round Cattistock, began to show un-mistakable manifestations of a goblinish desire to laugh.

"There's nothing tied to it," he murmured a little later, letting his eyes rest first on the barrel in the surf and then on the back of the man who was already off his feet and swimming desperately in a deep sea-trough.

And to Sue's consternation—and after this she became one of the very few women who shared the view of Lucinda and the police that Sylvanus was really mad—the man in tweeds, suddenly aware of the humorous irrelevance of this absurd display in the bosom of the Absolute, burst into a fit of Gargantuan laughter. Little Sue tried ineffectually to pull her hand away; and even the fishermen, occupied though they were by the vibrating rope, looked at each other with disapproval.

Meanwhile Cattistock, dizzied and dazed by the first shock of his plunge into that swirling sea, did not lose his wits.

"If I get through the next *two* waves," he thought, as he spat out a great mouthful of brine, "I'll do it. But the life-boat'll pick me up anyway."

His conscious thought was swallowed up now in a great drumming and humming. Then he was aware of what seemed like a terrific trumpeting. Had Ellen Gadget been stunned by such a sound she would have thought the original of the "Head" had lifted itself out of the waste of waters to bark at the North Star. But Cattistock, as he beat the waves in his final struggle, had a fleeting but intense awareness that Tissty was waiting for him in the upper room at the Head.

"She'll love me tonight as no woman has ever—"

He lost consciousness, in fact, before he clutched the barrel; at least he had no memory of clutching it; nor did he recall how they pulled him in, nor did he notice whether, at the last moment, "anything" was washed away that had been tied to the barrel. . .

It was a bitterly tragic face, about a quarter of an hour later, that from above the tight-fitting jersey of Dummy Skald looked over the shoulders of the excited crowd that surrounded the half-drowned but sardonically well-satisfied Cattistock. The Jobber heard people talking about the heroic bravery of the man. He heard them say, too, that a body—probably the body of a child—had been washed away in spite of this gallantry. Meanwhile the lights which people were carrying flickered about so erratically that it was natural enough that, when one of them fell upon the Jobber's face, Dog Cattistock, his cheeks a bluish white, his forehead and great chin bleeding, the seawater trickling from his clothes and sinking down into the pebbles, should have fixed his gimlet-like eye upon the staring face of his enemy.

As for the Jobber, he could not have looked away from this extraordinary eye-encounter—no, not if the voice of Perdita had called him! Quietly, therefore, for Cattistock's head was in a very comfortable position upon Sippy's lap, the two men gazed at each other, and in the prostrate man's eyes was a cryptic expression that seemed to the Jobber like the words "check-mate"! Skald's whole frame began to tremble. His teeth chattered. For the first time that night he realized how soaked to the skin he was. He felt a monstrous desire to snatch the brandy-flask which Ballard was holding to the rescuer's lips and take a long pull at it himself. His hand plunged back into his trousers-pocket where the stone lay.

"I'll say good-bye to her tomorrow," he thought, "and then I'll do it. Damn him! Oh, damn him!" and then he turned and walked, dragging his feet heavily, up the beach and down to the road where he had left the Slug.

Magnus, who had rejoined his friend Gaul, observed the Jobber going off, and together they hastened after him.

"Can you find room for two, Skald?" he cried in his most genial tone, when they caught him up.

The Jobber growled something in reply that was scarcely articulate; but the wanderers from Brunswick Terrace were not in a mood to be nice about trifles. They had had enough of Chesil Beach. All the way into town, before they left their driver at the Harbour, they argued between themselves the important question, which many people were discussing that night, namely whether or not there had been a human body tied to the barrel that Mr. Cattistock had dragged in. Magnus assured Gaul that he had heard several fishermen declare that there had been a body fastened to that barrel when it was first observed.

"The life-boat wouldn't have put out again," he said. "Though of course a corpse—"

But Mr. Gaul corrected him for his use of the word "corpse".

"I have heard," he said gravely, "that people can be recovered from drowning after several hours' immersion. But it's true your friend

Cattistock would never have rushed into the sea like that *if he hadn't seen something*. He isn't a man to risk his life for a barrel."

Magnus, whose mind had reverted to Curly, had no comment to make on this.

"Perhaps, though," continued the philosopher of Representation in a tone of balanced cogitation, as one who gives every aspect of conflicting events its due proportion, "perhaps it was one of his own barrels."

9

MR. GAUL'S ADVICE

ALL the next morning, which was Wednesday, the eleventh of February, Magnus Muir, as he stoically went through his task of hearing three little Weymouth boys stumble through that stately Horatian poem that contains the famous admonition about remembering to keep an equal mind under the pinch of adversity, saw before him, as if they had been floating in the air, the pencilled lines scrawled on a post-card in Curly's neat unrevealing hand:

"Mother wants me to herself all day tomorrow; so you'd better not come then; but can you be at the Clock on Thursday about twenty to twelve? I *must* go to Trinity Church to see the Wedding! I'll wait for you till a quarter to twelve, but not a minute longer; or we'll miss seeing the bride go in.

Love.

Curly."

Now it was impossible for Magnus to detect in this letter anything but what was natural. Curly's mother was a doting and sentimental woman and he felt she had never liked him. He could not read the old woman's thoughts. He could not know that the avidity she displayed at this juncture for her daughter's presence was by no means just simple affection. Mrs. Wix was afraid of her daughter's spending too much time with Magnus until they were actually married for two sound maternal reasons. She feared that he might learn about Sippy; and she also feared that Curly might get so exasperated by having Magnus too much on her hands that she would break it all off in an uncontrollable fit of rebellion. Mrs. Wix had the wit to see that Magnus in his simplicity attributed her attitude to pure fondness, and she played up to this with instinctive cunning.

"You know, Mr. Muir," she would say, "how soon I shall have to face a life without my darling."

Magnus bit his lip with annoyance when he read that their next meeting was to be at Cattistock's wedding. Like a map he saw how it would be his destiny to sit for hours afterwards at the "Regatta" listening to Curly flirting with that accursed yachtsman, while the two of them discussed—treating him like an ignorant outsider—every detail of the ceremony at Trinity Church.

"*Aequam memento rebus in arduis—*"

With his three boys' heads, a round one, an oval one, a square one, and each of them cropped, for cleanliness he supposed, like little convicts, grouped round his desk, while they made faces and fidgeted and yawned and scribbled and erased, for he had told them to turn into Latin verse the lines: "I could not love thee, dear, so much, loved I not honour more," he was presently able to walk up and down the room. This was always a prodigious relief to him, especially when, after executing a crafty flanking-movement round the three cropped heads, he managed to snatch a surreptitious glance at the sea.

"*Aequam memento rebus in arduis—*"

No! he would not weep, he would not tap the ground with his head, he would not walk into the sea if he lost her. But the point was—supposing something *did* happen to her, supposing this very day, in her own Upwey village street she should be killed by a motor-cycle—would he be able to enjoy anything in life again? He'd probably go on talking to Miss Le Fleau, and being sent for to teach Benny, and coming back, and taking his walk before tea. But would there be any pleasure in any of these things?

"Is Muir in?" his friend from Trigonia House would ask at the door.

"He hasn't come back yet, Mr. Gaul," Miss Le Fleau would say. "He must have gone the Round."

Now "the Round" was a walk he especially relished, and only took when he was in the best of spirits. He went clean over Lodmoor, skirted the hedge of a little spinney, crossed a rough cattle-grazed hill where there was sometimes a bull to make him quicken his pace, and following a narrow lane at the foot of the Downs returned by the Dorchester road.

He incidentally decided that he would go the Round this afternoon when they brought him back from Chickerel! But if Curly caught a fever and died—as might happen to any beautiful girl—would he ever go the Round again? No, he'd go to the Coast-Guards and straight back, as the elder Muir used to do. But would he visit those rock-pools by the sea over there and look for sea-anemones? *That* would be the test! And he tried to imagine, as he watched a small one-funnelled steamer moving along the horizon and leaving a trail of smoke in the grey sky, what it would feel like to scoop up out of those rock-pools those precious cowrie-shells that old Poxwell had such a mania for, and bring them home in his pocket, and put them in a bowl, if Curly wasn't there to see them! It didn't matter whether she took any interest in such things. He smiled faintly to himself—after a hurried glance round at the three cropped heads—to think how little interest she *did* take in these matters. But the point wasn't her interest; the point was *for her to be there.* Yes; those sacred hieroglyphs of the place, the White Horse, Hardy's Monument, the Coast-Guards, St. John's Spire, the Nothe, the Old King's Statue, the Harbour Bridge, as he told her about seeing them, or *not* seeing them in his walks, were the mystical links between his true-love and his father.

He had to get rid of his pupils before eleven today; for the Poxwell sisters wanted him at the Loders' as a witness to their signing certain papers. Taking his coat and stick, therefore, as soon as the boys were gone, he looked in, as he often did before setting out on any important excursion, to have a chat about it with Miss Le Fleau.

The lady hurriedly rose from her chair, where she was as usual reading and sewing at the same time; but on this occasion it was the Melcombe Regis Circular which she held in her hand, that small daily paper devoted especially to social news.

"It's all just as you told me, Magnus!" she burst out eagerly, and then conscious that he caught the twinge in her face as she rose to her feet: "My rheumatism has been more troublesome this last winter. There! I must try and move about more. I get stiff in my chair."

But with one hand resting now on the edge of her table she read aloud to him what the paper said about Cattistock's heroic plunge into the sea.

"It is understood on the Island," she read, "that negotiations have been resumed between the quarrymen's leaders and the shareholders in the Saxon Quarry. These negotiations are, we gather, entrusted to the well-known firm of Cattistock and Frampton."

While he chatted with her Magnus kept peering out of the window and it was not long before Miss Le Fleau referred to this fidgety uneasiness of his.

"I know," he admitted, "I'm sorry. It's because when Chant comes for me today he's got to call for Mrs. Cobbold and Mrs. Lily. They're going to sign papers at Spy Croft and then go out to lunch at the Sanitarium."

"Not that poor little boy, too, Magnus?"

Magnus frowned.

"Yes, I'm afraid so, Miss Le Fleau. I feel about it just as you do. I asked Mr. Cattistock whether Benny and I couldn't lunch quietly at Peninsular Lodge instead of going to that place. The truth is, I think he wants Dr. Brush to see the improvement in the boy."

Miss Le Fleau gave her lodger a glance of proud affection.

"Well, you've done wonderfully with him, Magnus. I should think they're all grateful to you. Does the boy mind it *very* much, Hortensia's going out there to live?"

A curious expression of nervous reserve came into the tutor's eyes and hovered about the lines of his mouth.

"Oh, well, my dear," the lady hurried to say, "I don't want to be inquisitive. But I should have thought after living alone out there, with no one but that old Mrs. Chant, it might be—"

But Magnus had turned his eyes to the window, and with a murmured "forgive me" he now moved close up to it. Suddenly the lady saw him tap the pane with his knuckles and make signs to someone below.

"It's Gaul," he explained, returning to her side with the smiling look still on his face with which he had greeted his friend from Trigonia House. "Well! Good-bye, Miss Le Fleau!"

He hadn't *meant* to tell Gaul about Curly's post-card; at least he hadn't known that that was what he would do the very second they stood together on the pavement.

Mr. Gaul was in unusually good spirits. He had been for many weeks pondering on the problem of a metaphysical representation of Hell; and this morning he had been inspired with the thought that the status quo of Hell comes instantaneously and automatically into being, when, in a mood of cynical recklessness people let everything go and rejoice in the thought of universal disorder and destruction. When Magnus had tapped at the window Mr. Gaul was actually making little skipping motions with his feet as he went along, in the process of which he would rest the end of his cane on the pavement in front of him and then give it a lively kick. He was inspired to advance in this manner by reason of the fact that there entered into his brain at that time so many proofs of his interpretation of Hell that he was positively overwhelmed by them. The disturbing tantrums of his landlady's daughter for example, when she learned how independently a little girl called Sue had been behaving at the wreck, lent themselves with a mathematical exactness that was like Euclid to his solution of the problem. He had not yet mentioned her usefulness in this important branch of metaphysics to the little girl herself. She had destroyed the peace of Trigonia House till late at night. She had even brought S. P. Ballard out into the passage. But Mr. Gaul had long since found by experience that it is wiser to conceal than to reveal to the feminine mind its superb value as an illustration of philosophic truth.

It may well be imagined, however, that with his intellect all a-gog for living evidence of our human desire for universal disorder and destruction, he pounced joyously on Curly's unlucky post-card. Not lifting in his elation so much as the tip of a finger to his spectacles, he hurriedly advised Magnus, with a radiant countenance, to disregard Curly's commands and to go in spite of her to Upwey tonight.

"The thing to do with them when they're in this mood," he said emphatically; "for it's clear that to want to drag a thinking human being to a performance like a wedding is pure childish malice, is to disregard what they say completely. Keep your temper, my dear Muir, that's the great thing! Just smile, *whatever* she says. But go on yourself quietly doing what it is best and wisest, as if she didn't exist."

The young man's round face gleamed with such guileless satisfaction as he pointed his friend to the philosophic path, that Magnus, who had a mania for humouring everyone, lacked the heart to tell him that his wisdom was a little self-contradictory in one particular, since a person would hardly take the trouble to visit a girl against her will only to prove to her that she didn't exist. But Mr. Gaul's words, in spite of this small lapse in pure logic, sank deeply into his mind, for they revealed to him that he really *had* a grievance against Curly, and they indicated a direct way of getting even with her, a way, nevertheless, that did not carry with it the punishment to himself of not seeing her.

He was pondering on this point—for Magnus' secret thoughts, unknown to any of his friends, were very often on lines of drastic, vigorous blood-and-iron action—when Cattistock's big car drove up, and the warm, brown eyes of young Mr. Chant looked down at him from the driver's seat. Lucinda Cobbold, who was the only occupant of the car, began rallying them both for their absorption in each other's society.

"We have to pick up Hortensia," she said, "otherwise I'd offer you a chance of continuing that absorbing subject—whatever it was—"

"It was about you!" burst from the elated lips of Mr. Gaul, as he watched his friend stumble awkwardly into the seat by the lady's side and stretch out his long legs with a sigh of achievement.

But it was a more composed and less exuberant Mr. Gaul who now continued his way to St. Mary's Street, where he intended to purchase at a stationer's shop a copy of Faust in the original. It had occurred to him that in many isolated passages of that enigmatic work there were paragraphs that bore out his contention that the "ultimate repose" of Hell, as Milton calls it, is rather a psychological than a geographical revelation. But the truth was he had thrown so much suppressed wit into his bon-mot to Mrs. Cobbold that it was as if virtue had gone out of him. His inspiration drooped. His high spirits flagged. He felt no further inclination to kick his cane. And so dangerous had he proved it to be to exchange brilliant remarks with a society woman that all the way to the old King's statue, and all the way to the stationer's, he resolved that under no future temptation would he let himself be betrayed into such badinage.

"You can't serve philosophy and society," he said to himself, as he gazed into the royal countenance. "I wish I hadn't said those words. She looked astonished, though. They don't often get answered as quick as that, I expect."

Meanwhile Magnus, who felt no inclination to indulge in his friend's "esprit d'escalier", murmured something about hoping that Hortensia would have a happy life.

Mrs. Cobbold raised both her hands to her hat, which with its elegantly twisted green velvet band seemed to be a deliberate substitute for that classical fillet about the brow with which, in her home, she preserved that air of dedication that Perdita found so exasperating.

"It's a mystery to me," she said. "Of course, just like everybody else, I thought at first it was his money. Jerry *never* would believe that. Jerry has odd glimpses sometimes. And I've begun to come round." She leaned forward with such a gleam in her eyes that Magnus was filled with distaste. "She's infatuated with him, I tell you! I've found that out. And it's not an ordinary infatuation either. It's about as morbid and unhealthy as it can *well* be." She touched Magnus' knee with the tips of one of her gloved hands. "I know 'Tensia *so* well," she whispered. "She was always bored to death by her Captain. Your father used to say Cattistock was a Cro-Magnon. He meant just a plain brute. Well *that's* what 'Tensia likes! I give them twelve months—not a day longer, and it'll be over."

She drew back, and sank down into the capacious seat, settling the waxen flowers in her bosom and letting her eyes soften into a swimming haze of satisfied prediction.

Magnus sighed. "You mean he'll desert her?" he murmured uneasily.

But the lady laughed, and the sound of her laughter reminded Magnus of the popping corks of those tiny little homoeopathic bottles that old Dr. Higginbottom used to carry in a black bag and open one after another with such assurance.

"No, my dear," she said. "I don't think *that* will be the way it'll end."

It was only a small gathering of relatives into which Lucinda and

Magnus now plunged when they entered Spy Croft drawing-room. With its green curtains and green carpet, with its green valances round its green arm-chairs, with its green tassels round its vase-bearing brackets, this spacious chamber, designed to pleasure their dead mother before either of them were born, was like a mausoleum to Ruth and Rodney.

Magnus shook hands agreeably enough with the people he knew, and bowed politely to others as he was introduced to them by Ruth, but he soon sank down at one end of the great sofa—whose cushions and antimacassars seemed the only objects in the place *not* of this sepulchral green—and fell into solitary meditation. One of the windows was barely open at the top, but the heavy curtain stirred deliciously with the spring air that entered, even through so small an opening, and as Magnus felt this air floating in full of sea-scents from the near-by shore and looked at the people gathered in this room it occurred to him that there must be signs and tokens when spring touches the unharvested sea answering to those when it stirs the fields of the earth! Certainly *something* was affecting the people gathered here that was more than the fact that they had come to sign marriage documents. Those two Poxwell sisters—and how alike they were!— were dressed so much more strikingly than the other women that it was hard not to stare at them. What queer, high foreheads they both had! Hortensia concealed hers with her smooth-brushed, silky hair clipped straight across, and it struck Magnus that if he were Cattistock he would get pleasure from ruffling back that hair with his fingers, from that lovely white brow! It didn't take him very long to get the psychic import and mental implication of this group of people. It had long been a trick of his to treat occasions and gatherings like this as if they were some inanimate group of rocks and trees, with the light falling and the air stirring according to a spontaneous, natural art.

"This spring air," he thought, "is calling up these people's souls from fathoms of subconsciousness like a shoal of fish, and calling up their good and their evil, too, more unmistakably than generally happens. It's odd how uncomfortable it seems to make me to see Mrs. Cobbold talking to that lovely Mrs. Lily. Damn it all! I wouldn't be surprised if it didn't make a person uncomfortable to see Mrs. Cobbold talking to *any* sensitive and receptive person!"

His attention veered now to their host, "the general", who was evidently not to be driven from the room by the fact that he was suffering from his usual physical discomfort. James Loder looked happy enough, however, the moment his ulcers became quiescent. For one thing he was particularly fond of this room. He would no more have thought of changing anything in this drawing-room of his than he would have thought of shaving off his moustache. The happiest moments he had now, in his extreme old age, except the times when Ruth took him in his bath chair, were the moments on Sundays when, with the servants gone out, Ruth used herself to lay their tea on a little card-table in front of the drawing-room fire or, if it were summer, in front of one of the drawing-room windows. It was by the fire at this moment that the soldierly old man was standing, although every now and then he would cross over, in defiance of propriety, to the sofa where Magnus was, where he would stretch himself out, uttering audible groans. It was in fact one of James Loder's bad days. The chronic trouble which was the affliction of his old age was specially acute today. But Mr. Loder always enjoyed coming down from his bedroom to suffer in public, finding in the sympathy he excited and also in the distaste and disgust he excited, an important alleviation of his pangs. He really *did* suffer! The thing was no joke. But the very fact that it was a shock to people to see him twist about made it the greater relief. He derived an almost sensual pleasure from doing it. He experienced a satisfaction in bringing down the high spirits of others by flinging over them, so to speak, the mantle of his leprosy. There were doubtless subtler aspects still of this desire in James Loder to suffer in public; for Ruth and Rodney noticed that if ever they had anything resembling a party in the house on one of his bad days the old man was certain to insist on being present. On this particular occasion in the intervals of his visits to the sofa he chatted benevolently and with a certain old-world grace with the two sisters, rallying the beautiful Hortensia on Cattistock's heroism of last night, which he declared was in the best tradition of the West Country's historic chivalry. But after daring to hazard a repartee or two with the formidable Mrs. Cobbold, he thought to himself:

"How that son of mine does hate me! There's something sickening

in such hidden-up, sneaking hatred. Yet he owes everything to me ...
life ... career ... sister ... talent ... and I *am* his father, after all!
I wish the young parricide could feel for five minutes what this pain
of mine really is."

The telephone-bell resounding violently now in the passage
outside, caused everyone to glance at the door. To this insistent object
that seemed animated by so importunate a devil at that moment that
the whole apparatus shook as if it had been the body possessed by the
demon named Legion, Ruth anxiously ran, and put the silenced
instrument to her ear. It was Mrs. Matzell speaking from Half-Way
House and speaking with no little agitation, but Ruth soon learnt all
that was needed. Back again in the green chamber—and how stuffy it
seemed after the cooler air of the hall—how scented with the exotic
perfumes the Poxwell sisters always used!—she hurried at once, not
to Mrs. Lily, but to Daisy.

"Come out with me a minute, my dear!" she whispered.

They got out of the room without anyone, except "that
gloomy Mr. Muir, who always sits by himself at parties," noticing
anything.

"Mrs. Matzell telephones that Captain Poxwell's got into his head
that Mrs. Cobbold's here, and nothing could hold him. He's on his
way now!"

Daisy turned white and bit her under-lip as she stared at Ruth.
Then without a word she shut her eyes. She did this in order to think
clearly. Had she been a Field-Marshal she would always have shut
her eyes when the enemy's attack opened. Ruth stood waiting. She
had full confidence in Daisy's power to handle this crisis, and she was
unwilling to interrupt her cogitation. Finally Daisy said:

"There are only two ways by which he can come, Ruth: by Underbarn Path, and by Old Castle Road and Belle Vue Road so if *you* go
by the road, I'll go by the sea-path and then we're *bound* to meet him!
Quick! Oh, quick, *let's go!* Will you tell Rodney about it and tell him
to get mother and Aunt Lucinda off, if he—oh, *where's* my jacket,
Ruth?—if he *can* ... I ... don't ... think ... he'll ... be able ...
to"—Daisy was panting now with the effort of getting into her
things—"because ... Aunt Lucinda ... likes ... tormenting ...
There! I'll go now. Mind! I'll go by the sea and you go by the

road. You'll come quick, Ruth, won't you, when you've told
Rodney?"

"But . . . Daisy . . . what if the Captain insists on coming?"

"He won't, he won't, Ruth! I could easily have stopped him if I'd
been at home. He *never* does anything that hurts anyone! Mrs.
Matzell doesn't understand him, though she loves him so. It doesn't
do to let grandfather think you think he's not perfectly ordinary and
like other people. Good-bye, Ruth! You'll be quick, won't you?
And if he comes, *don't let Aunt Lucinda see him!*"

But the elder girl had more difficulty in getting a private word with
her brother than she could have believed possible. Thus it was fully
ten minutes after Daisy had set out, that Ruth found herself walking
up Belle Vue Road and thence into Old Castle Road. She had hardly
gone half-a-mile before she saw the Captain. He was walking very
fast in his heavy cloth suit, holding a plaid shawl wound tightly round
his lean neck. In fact he was bearing down upon her like one who
contended in a race with an invisible opponent. He walked with such
alacrity and his eye had such a bright, bird-like intensity, like the eye
of a demented sea gull, that it was difficult to get his attention.

"Captain!" Ruth cried, "Captain Poxwell!"

But he swept on past her as if she were a casual acquaintance in the
town whom he could legitimately pass with a nod and a lift of his hat.
Ruth flushed hotly. She felt embarrassed and nonplussed. She felt
angry with Daisy for assuring her that all would be such smooth
sailing. Here she was, entirely disregarded, and there was the man,
marching on with long strides like some terrible wound-up automaton
to which she had lost the mechanical key that stopped it! But she ran
after him and caught hold of his arm. Luckily at the point where she
stopped him there was a little field-path, going straight down past the
backs of some private gardens, to that shore-path, called Underbarn
Walk, which leads from the Nothe to Sandsfoot Castle.

"I must get to the sea. I *must* get to the sea, Captain," she coaxed
him now, in an unsteady voice that seemed singularly ineffectual to
her own ears.

Yes, Daisy was right. He hadn't realized who she was at first but
now he was at her mercy!

"I'm going to your house. You've got a party there. And my

eldest girl's at your party. Please don't make me take you down there! It's easy to go down there. You're grown-up."

"I must get to the sea," she repeated, "and I can't go alone. I can't, I mustn't, I dursn't go alone. So you *will* take me down to the sea, Captain Poxwell?"

He moved his stubbly head with its restless blue eyes backwards and forwards, like an unhappy doll that found itself in the hands of an alien mistress. He would first glance towards the path going down to Underbarn Walk and then twisting round, gaze yearningly towards Belle Vue Road. His sun-burnt neck, whose corded veins resembled strings of leafless ivy, had such a pathetic appearance as it craned round that Ruth felt sorry for him. There was something touching and pitiful about his helplessness under her light pressure when it would have been so easy to shake her off and go right on. There must have been a distressing struggle in the man's mind as he wavered there. To her dismay, as she clung to his arm, she noticed several big tears roll down his leathery cheeks and fall on the plaid shawl. This she could hardly bear, and she was almost tempted to go straight on with him to Spy Croft. Probably Daisy exaggerated the shock it would be to him to meet Mrs. Cobbold. But no! She recalled the look of that sturdy little figure in the hall with her eyes tight shut. She must keep faith with Daisy.

"Well . . . I shall have to . . . give it up . . ." he said in a low, unhappy voice. "If you *must* be taken to the sea, you *must!* I . . . expect . . . you're afraid of the nursery-maids down there looking for soldiers who never come. I'm sometimes afraid of them myself! They have such white cheeks and such red lips and such staring eyes. The real reason why I live in Sandsfoot Castle is not a thing to talk about with a little girl like you, but it has to do with those nursery-maids' eyes—always staring like that . . . always staring for the soldiers."

They had begun to descend the path now towards Underbarn Walk and he stopped her and looked down gingerly into her face.

"Those soldiers aren't dead," he whispered. "Did you think they were? Oh, no! They're not dead. But they won't come back. No, no, it will never, never be." He lowered his voice still further. "They've heard something about those girl's fathers. Mum's the

word! The word's mum . . . but all fathers aren't like Mr. James
Loder . . . such a good, kind, virtuous, thoughtful, righteous, God-
fearing father! A father who's got nothing on his mind, a father with
whom a girl like you can sit and talk and tell old tales and cuddle and
laugh and enjoy yourself! Take an unhappy wretch's word for it,
Ruth! To be able to kiss your father good-night, when there's not a
wind stirring and you can't hear a sound of the sea . . . it must be like
heaven. Nothing on the mind! And day following day so calm, so
snug, so safe. No, no, no, no! I don't wonder you dursn't go down
to the sea alone, for fear of nursery-maids. 'Tis terrible what stories
go round to keep those soldiers away, so that they'll never, never,
never come back!"

A sigh shook him from head to foot, that made the girl realize his
trouble better than any words could have done. Slowly supporting her,
or being supported by her, down the slope, and the girl caught sight
of a couple of sea-gulls' feathers, as they went down, reminding her
of some event in her infancy that she had completely forgotten, they
arrived at last at Underbarn Walk.

Here they sat down on a bench and Ruth let her eyes rest in peace
on the smooth oily expanse of water bounded by the two breakwaters
and extending away, without one ripple that glittered or danced, to the
base of Portland. How familiar to her was the outline of that great
promontory! Several war-ships lay at anchor in the Roads, and their
heavy, motionless forms intensified the pearly shimmer of that
unruffled expanse. The sun was veiled in a tenuous gossamery mist.
Not a breath of wind stirred; nor, since it was the hour of most folk's
mid-day meal, did any passers-by disturb the impenetrable quiet. Still
as a lake the great placid roadstead lay out-spread before her and the
huge bulk of Portland seemed to float upon some tremulous substance
more stable than water and more vaporous than glass. It was not
Ruth's nature to deal in introspection. Self-pity was unknown to her.
The young woman was by temperament an unquestioning accepter
of Fate. But for all that, there *did* stir faintly in her, as she sat by this
"child-changed" father, a vague sense that her dutiful service of old
James and young Rodney did not satisfy the whole of her life-craving.
Something slid into her being from that empearled surface that
stirred up the mute, dumb life of her deep-rooted nervous system.

She knew perfectly well—as indeed did all the town—that the old man's mania took the form of imagining that he had got his eldest daughter with child. But woman-like she was not in the least shocked at the idea of incest in itself. Much nearer nature than the old man by her side, she could not comprehend that mystical horror and shuddering guilt, that feeling of sacrosanct awfulness as of some Mysterium Tremendum that can so quickly be worked up in the masculine conscience. But, "all the same for that", as Homer would say, the best of women are sensitive to the erotic electricity of any masculine companion, positive or negative, and Captain Poxwell's agitation was not without its indirect effect upon her steady nerves.

But that unruffled, pearly expanse she now gazed upon, possessed something in its own inherent nature—for it was the eleventh of February—that bore a curious correspondency with the first dim stirrings of early spring. Whether Ruth could have detected any subtle spring-change in the crimson seaweeds, that were now swaying to and fro in that lazy tide in the rock-pools below, is doubtful, but what is not doubtful is that from the actual chemic substance of that undulant mass of oily, opalescent water there emanated something of that relaxing perilous-sweet mystery of the spring to which all human nerves are porous.

There were few women's natures in the two boroughs more inherently virginal than Ruth's. Magnus did not know it; but if he had wanted to find a fellow-denizen of the elder Muir's Ideal Weymouth, one whose attitude to the Nothe, the Harbour, the Bridge, the King's Statue, St. John's Spire, Sandsfoot Castle, Chesil Beach, was as mythological as his had been, Ruth Loder could have been that person. Just because of her chastity, and her almost morbid indifference to men, Ruth enjoyed with a passionate and proud exclusiveness every light and every shadow, every breath and every calm, that touched these familiar landmarks. By slow degrees, for she had come to note changes of the seasons in her sea-atmosphere that most subtly corresponded to the same changes in the land-atmosphere, Ruth began to find in these changes, and in the varying moods they threw her into, something that represented, as Mr. Gaul would have said, the fitful and perilous magic of Eros.

Captain Poxwell had by no means been talking to her incessantly all this while. As soon as the old man realized she was enjoying something especially precious to her, he left her to enjoy it in peace; displaying in this restraint a delicacy of which one would hardly have supposed his crazy egoism would be capable. At last he said to her:

"I was trying to persuade my son John to take a year from the sea and live with Daisy and me, now she's off to Chickerel, but he writes me he's already signed up on the Tonquin, Captain Fred Hutchings, sailing for the West Indies. So Daisy and I will have to make out as well as we can! There'll be some things we shan't miss, however, you may be sure, when she's gone!"

The old gentleman's face was wrinkled now with a most natural and normal desire to laugh over some interior vision. He took off his hat and wiping the perspiration from his forehead with the end of his brightly coloured shawl emitted a series of half-suppressed chuckles. The expression in his blue eyes as his eyelids screwed themselves up, must have been a very familiar one to his subordinates in his master-mariner days.

"The Old Man's all right," their looks must have told one-another when he came on deck like this.

"You women," he brought out, wagging his grizzled head roguishly at her, "think that all comes to an end when you leave us to ourselves. But we know better. We get on very pretty. Daisy and me will be deuced well-pleased to run things in our own fashion. We'll pack off Granny Matzell, too, if she ain't careful. Yes, by God, we shall get on like flying fish, Daisy and me!"

He ended with more chuckling, and the big veins in his thin, red neck stood out unpleasantly. They seemed to pulse with a humorous desire to make every woman in the world realize how well he could get on alone.

"I believe you; I believe you, Captain," murmured Ruth, but without any responsive smile.

This sort of genial sex-badinage, so popular with sailors, to whom women's ways are one long, delicious exasperation, was peculiarly distasteful to her. Her self-centred independence was mingled with the fastidious intelligence, serious and deep, of a girl of instinctive intellectual power; and much as she shrank from Captain Poxwell in his insane mood, this mood of jocular facetiousness was even less

agreeable. She was immensely relieved, therefore, when she suddenly
saw the sturdy figure of his grandchild coming swinging round the
corner from the direction of Sandsfoot; but that this relief was nothing
to the child's own feeling was proved by the happy shout and impulsive
scamper with which Daisy Lily flew towards them . . .

The only flaw in the harmony of the lunch-party at Hell's Museum,
to which Magnus presently escorted the two Poxwell sisters, was a
certain malignant impishness which Benny manifested more and more
boldly as the meal went on towards his father's bride. But to his
surprise it seemed to the teacher, when at last the two characteristic
Poxwell voices, a little husky but always so seductive, were brought
to silence by their host's getting up from the table, that the meal had
ended all too quickly. It was then that Dr. Brush carried off Mrs.
Cobbold, with a view to their professional interview, which was the
real purpose of her visit. The Doctor did this as easily and lightly as
if he were going to show her a collection of rare prints, while Magnus,
leaving Benny with the prospective mistress of Peninsular Lodge,
went off to find his friend, the young chauffeur.

Mrs. Lily retained the child at the tall large-paned window, looking
across all the gardens of the Institute, and set herself with a passionate
naïveté to overcome his malice. Magnus would have been shocked
had he seen the impish devilry with which the little boy—as if fully
conscious of the lady's pathetic longing to win him over—played with
her desire and without being in the least rude or brutal, pushed her
away, kept himself free of her, held her at arm's length.

When the tutor came back with Chant and his car and called the
boy to him for their return to Chickerel he was startled by the pitiful,
bewildered look in the new step-mother's face. With far more of the
emotionalism of girlhood in her mood than her young daughter often
displayed, Hortensia, in her exaggerated desire to win the boy, felt so
rebuffed by his malicious coldness that as she stood at their car door
there were tears in her eyes and her mouth was drawn down and
trembling. Not having been present at their solitary dialogue Magnus
was puzzled by her emotion, and being inclined to attribute it to her
dread of being left alone in the precincts of Hell's Museum he tapped
at the window, just as they were off, to make Chant stop. The bride's
gloveless white fingers were clinging to the side of the car as if she

would have tried by her own strength to hold it back, and she must actually have run a few paces with it before young Chant brought it to a pause. It was then that Magnus heard her ask the boy to say good-bye to her, "for you won't see me again, Benny, you know, till I come to live with you tomorrow night!"

But at this instant of time an event occurred that put the lady completely out of his mind; for he saw over her shoulder and across the boy's profile the door of one of the Laboratory buildings open, and a white-coated person issue from it.

"*Murphy!*" he cried in his heart. "It's Murphy, the Sworn Tormentor!"

No, no! he could not be mistaken. He had heard Benny describe this man with that excess of horror that makes a child's words irrefutable.

"Get out of the way, Benny!" he shouted at him, for he saw that Benny had not seen the man yet. "Let her come in! You'd *better* come in with us, Mrs. Lily; you really had! Your sister may be all the afternoon with the doctor; and this is a terrible place to wait about in."

But with that same passionate unreason that seemed to characterize everything she did at this epoch of her life, Mrs. Lily only drew back, peevish and wilful and uttered a little silly laugh.

"It's all right," she murmured, while Benny fumbled at the door-handle and resisted Magnus' attempts to pull him out of the way. Then Magnus could see her telling young Chant to drive on; and as the car started he heard her call out over Benny's thin wrists, "It's all right. It'll be my wedding vigil!"

All the way to Chickerel, while Benny continued chattering, just as if Dr. Brush's party were not yet over, the image of that man in the white coat, issuing from that building, nailed Magnus' imagination with a bodkin of torment.

"They're at it, in there!" he thought. "And these others are probably worse than Brush. What a coward I am! This vivisection is like the old gladiatorial shows. It won't be stopped till someone dies to stop it!" He lay back and closed his eyes, pretending to sleep, so as to keep the boy quiet, but under his darkened eye-balls his thoughts had never been so rending. "How can any one of us have a single moment of happiness," he thought, "when there's such a thing as vivisection in the world? And yet would I, to stop it once and for all, and to burn all their operating tables and all their straps and all their instruments, be prepared to sacrifice Curly?"

The coming together of these two electrified nerves in Magnus' nature, his erotic passion and his sickening twinge over vivisection, threw him, as the car wound its way along these narrow lanes, into a series of jumpy contortions. He kept experiencing a twitching in his long legs, and every now and then with a muscular contraction that corresponded to what he visioned was happening under Mr. Murphy's devotion to science he would draw up one of his heels along the floor of the car.

"I suppose,"he thought, "the only thing to do is to *assume* that life contains cruelties so unspeakable that if you think about them you go mad! That's what it is! To think about Murphy and Dr. Brush's dogs brings you into the care of Dr. Brush! I wonder how many of his patients lie awake at night thinking of the dogs?"

It was curious how powerful Magnus' imagination became at this moment as he contemplated young Chant's back and grew aware that Benny was now counting . . . one . . . two . . . three . . . four . . . the beats of his own pulse by his Ingersoll watch. His imagination made his passion for Curly take the form of holding in his hand a girl's belt with which he kept warding off the active fingers of Mr. Murphy from his dog's vitals. It was a peculiarity of Magnus' nerves— especially of these two major nerves of his, the erotic one and the one that identified itself with physical suffering—that when they obsessed him to any extreme tension they always induced in his brain *the image of dancing.* This scene, therefore, which his sympathetic demon now called up under his throbbing eyeballs, quickly became a dance, himself beating off the flickering wrists of Mr. Murphy with the girl's belt while the very air round them jigged and dazzled with the iniquity of these cruelties in the name of science.

One curious thing about what he felt at this moment was that the ground underneath his feet—for Cattistock's car seemed to fade into non-existence—was not the chalky mud over which he was really moving, but the smooth, wet sea-sand, ribbed, glittering, warm, and covered with tiny little pyramidal hills composed of minute models in sand of the sand-worms that threw them up. This sea-sand—as his

long legs kept giving these queer frog-like spasmodic jerks—was the
wet sand of the Weymouth Beach, down there beyond the *dry* sand,
where the donkeys and goat-carriages always stood. And as his
tormented brain made these desperate attempts to bring the intensity
of his passion for Curly into some mystical relationship with what
those dogs felt, he began to be aware that when he thought of the
"wet" sand—and it had to be the "wet" sand, not the dry—there
arose in his memory some saying, like the "logos" of an oracle, that
must have been uttered by his father when he was too young to
comprehend it. The "Logos" itself thus uttered by the elder Muir
when he may easily have been watching the little Magnus dig canals
for the inflowing waves, escaped the grown man now completely,
but a kind of aura of it hung in the air and came to him in his tension
like the clear light at the end of a tunnel.

His lesson with Benny went better than he had dared to hope, after
the way Dr. Brush's ego-orgy had stirred the malice in the child, but
he could not help remembering that pitiful look in Mrs. Lily's face as
she clung to the car when he left the boy at five o'clock with the little
yellow dog scrambling all over him.

"There was a new picture of your darlings, Tissty and Tossty in
yesterday's Circular," he remarked, as he stood up to go.

"Oh, Mr. Muir," cried Benny with gleaming eyes, "is that picture
. . . I mean does that picture . . ." the boy blushed and stopped.

"You mean," said Magnus with the full gravity that such a topic
required, "does it show their legs as well as yours does? Yes, old chap,
I swear I think it's still more exciting. Only listen, Benny: The
Eumenides will bring you bad luck if after enjoying Tissty and
Tossty you torment your dad's wife. Never mind how much the
devil drives you to do! You mark my words. You'll have no luck
with Tissty and Tossty if you're cruel to this poor lady. The great
thing, old chap, is to enjoy our Tisstys and Tosstys to the limit; but
to *pay it back to the gods* by being awfully decent to our step-mothers!"

"But I don't *like* her, Mr. Muir. I don't like the way she—" and
the boy screwed up his small face and person in a simulated shudder of
physical distaste.

"That doesn't matter;" said Magnus very gravely. "We've all got
to put up with that sort of thing. How do we know that people we're

awfully fond of, like Tissty and Tossty, wouldn't feel *us* getting on *their* nerves sometimes?"

"Why did you make that funny face, Mr. Muir, and frown like that? Does your girl, that you're going to marry in a fortnight, not like it when you kiss her?"

Magnus got very red.

"No one likes to be kissed *always*. That's just what I'm telling you. And that's why, in such a mix-up as this world is, we ought never to be horrid to people if we want good luck for ourselves."

"Do you mean, Mr. Muir—"

Magnus burst out at him:

"Don't be so silly, Benny, pretending to be stupider than you are! Because you don't torment a woman, that doesn't mean you've got to submit to her always. You know very well what I'm trying to say."

Magnus was rather astonished when just as he was leaving Peninsular Lodge old Eliza Chant appeared on the scene and asked him if he knew where the master was, and whether she had better hold back Benny's tea till he came in.

"I don't know, I'm sure, Mrs. Chant! No, if I were you I'd give Benny his tea. I think he must want it after our lesson today."

The man who had told Benny so dogmatically and so crossly that he "knew very well what he was trying to say", wished bitterly enough that he himself knew of a formula for these difficult subtleties, when having said good-night to young Chant, he made his way on foot through the village of Upwey. Had his friend Gaul been right in so strongly recommending him to disregard Curly's direct command?

The Wix cottage, a little thatched one of the kind that has been for centuries the dominant feature of English villages, lay at the end of a by-lane that led to some high ground bordering the railway-line; an eminence from which, as you passed it in the train from Dorchester it was possible to get a glimpse of the whole of Lodmoor and beyond Lodmoor of the towering precipice of the White Nose stretching out over the sea.

When he drew near enough to the cottage as to be able to catch the glow from its windows he could actually see through the gathering twilight a gleaming point of light, down there, which, though it must have been more than a couple of miles away, marked the position of

Gipsy May's hut. He now lessened his pace to a very slow walk, and presently stopped altogether.

"Damn young Gaul!" he thought. "It's easy enough to give advice when you're safe in Trigonia House. How would he like it to be invading the lonely habitation of two women who had emphatically told him not to come?"

And Magnus smiled grimly at the impossibility of imagining Mr. Gaul in his own present predicament. Then his mood changed.

"But he isn't a fool. He isn't an idiot. He's seen *something* of the world. He visits Mrs. Cobbold. I expect I'm frightening myself ridiculously. Curly doesn't know that I dislike weddings. How should she, when I'm always wanting our own to come so quick? She thinks it will be nice to go there together. And after all I *can* sympathize with her mother's wanting her these days. She won't have her for long. Oh, my love, my sweet love! shall I be able to make you happy?"

He looked about for some convenient place to sit down, so that he might collect his thoughts and light a cigarette.

"Perhaps they're in the middle of tea," he thought.

And then the unpleasant idea came to him that they might even have visitors . . . her aunt from the Upwey grocery, or some shop-girl friend from Weymouth. At last he found what he was looking for in an old disused pile of rough blocks of wood, of the kind known as sleepers, that are laid under the metals across railway tracks.

In the now deepening twilight he could detect far to the East two more lights in addition to the little faint glimmer that he assumed to be Lodmoor Hut. One of these was high up, and far distant, the other nearer, but more out to sea.

"The White Nose cottages," he said to himself, "and a ship off Redcliff somewhere!"

The idea of Redcliff made him think at once of the elder Muir. He couldn't help smiling a little, even in his perturbed state of mind, as he wondered what his father would say if he saw him sitting here, making every sort of excuse to put off intruding on the girl he hoped to marry in a fortnight! He began an imaginary explanation to the dead man of all the practical moves he had been making. He explained to him how he had made a sort of tentative arrangement at another lodging-house in Brunswick Terrace; and how he had been able to reach the penetrating conclusion, even without aid from Mr. Gaul, that Miss Le Fleau's was not the place for this daring venture. At this particular season, he reminded the elder Muir, there were so few visitors that it was possible to leave this important matter quite open. He even confided to the dead man how he found Curly evasive and a little non-committal when he introduced such domestic problems. He went so far as to confess to the elder Muir that he had thought of purchasing a special licence to avoid the publicity of having their banns published.

What he did *not* tell him was that it seemed rather odd that Curly should be so lack-lustre over all these arrangements and so ready to drift on with nothing decided! His own private notion on the subject, compounded of all manner of Mid-Victorian refinements, was that a modest and simple-natured girl was shy about these details, shy as she would be about the purchasing of a trousseau, a word that he always connected, perhaps because it was French, exclusively with under-clothes. He knew that the girl's mother had no illusions any more as to his power of purchasing trousseau, or anything else, but he suspected her of being the cause of all his difficulties with the daughter.

"She puts silly ideas into her head," was what he had decided from his first encounter with her.

Contemplating now these four lights, Curly's, the Lodmoor Hut, the White Nose, and the ship off Redcliff, the vibration of the thrilling excitement within him, when he thought of that shell-like head on a pillow at his side broke against the thought of that horrible emergence of the white-coated Murphy from the laboratory door.

"Had he left a dog strapped down there," he thought, "till Brush was finished with Lucinda?"

It came over him that he could easily imagine a sensitive person, who brooded night and day upon vivisection, going mad from the horror of it.

"It's queer," he said to himself, "that I should have come across Murphy at this moment of moments. What would Curly feel if I *did* throw everything to the winds and give up my life to fighting vivi-section?"

He buried the burning end of his cigarette in the damp earth by his side, and leaning forward as he squatted on the sleeper, hugged his shin-bones.

With a hoarse detonation, as it emerged from the long tunnel near Maiden Castle, a passenger train from Dorchester rolled by, throwing out as it did so jets of white steam in reverberating spasms. It did not stop at Upwey; and he could hear the low rumble of it dying off down the valley, as it ran along the edge of Radipole Lake. The shock of the train's passing helped Magnus to gather up his forces. He very soon knew, as his fingers clutched the edge of the damp sleeper beneath him, that this was a turning-point in his life.

"The struggle for happiness," he thought, "is no joke. Every living thing struggles for it, while anguish, like that which these devils inflict on dogs, writhes, tosses, screams, moans around its pursuit."

It was now nearly dark and the four spots of light had grown much larger and brighter. He hugged his knees and swayed from side to side. He began to feel as if in the process of staring at those four glimmering points he was slipping clean out of his bony carcass. As this feeling intensified itself it was accompanied by a curious half-consciousness *of what his body would look like to his soul* if he were completely outside of it.

"I shouldn't kill myself if I lost Curly," he thought. "I should just go on, taking my walks, teaching Latin, reading Greek, talking to Father's spirit. But would such a life have any happiness *if she weren't here?*"

On this question he concentrated, as he sat there in the darkness, the weight of his whole organic being; and it came over him that in all these years, whose passing had left him a middle-aged man, he had gradually—under the influence of the elder Muir—accepted a certain grim resolution to force himself to be happy, as his sole human religion. And it seemed to him that he saw the difference now between himself and his majestic begetter with a deadly clearness.

"Father," he thought, "was happy by nature. *My* soul takes my body as though by a leash, like an animal, and forces it to go through the motions of happiness."

Magnus had the peculiarity of being thoroughly "anti-narcissistic", that is to say it gave him a real twinge of unendurable discomfort to think of his physical appearance. It is the more remarkable, therefore, that at this moment as he imagined himself holding his body by a leash he did get an intensely vivid feeling of himself sitting there on a sleeper and looking at those lights! There wasn't a muscular excrescence, or a bony contour, or a fibrous hollow in his whole flesh-covered skeleton that he didn't *feel*, as he crouched there, hugging his knees and swaying a little from side to side. He felt the bone-points of his buttocks against the pressure of the sleeper. He felt the brittleness of his skull against the pressure of his cloth cap, and he got the sensation that he was travelling through immeasurable gulfs of empty, black air, he and those four lights, Curly's, Lodmoor's, the White Nose's and the vessel's off Redcliff, towards nothing and from nothing. Yes! and *with* nothing except an ultimate, defiant self-awareness, one skeleton's and four lights'; destructible and yet indestructible, travelling, travelling through eternity!

It was only by indulging himself to the limit in such thoughts, thoughts wherein he lost the rational proportions of things, that he got the courage at last to jump up from his seat and rush to the cottage-door.

The interior of Mrs. Wix's front-room was certainly the reverse of welcoming, when, as if to punish him for his disobedience, the old lady ushered him into this fireless and airless throne-room of propriety. There he had to wait, in company with a new-lit lamp, with which at this close acquaintance it would have irked him to compare his soul, for it smoked, stank, flared and spat, and acted towards him with a malignity that seemed inspired. Sitting miserable and chilly in this place, in constant fear lest that lamp-glass would burst, and aware that the stolid and unsympathetic faces of Curly's relations, all of whom seemed to be glowering at him out of extremely stiff wedding clothes, held nothing for him but icy disapproval, Magnus felt, for the first time since he had approached her cottage today, a faint but very definite anger against the girl.

There was not a sound to be heard in the whole house. Was Curly in bed? Were they playing some game with him and keeping silence on purpose? Oh, how stuffy this room was! It smelt as if from every thread of every tassel and from every bit of fluff on every mat, there emanated a purgatorial entelechy of joyless and pitiless propriety. At last there came the sound of the opening and shutting of the kitchen door. There were steps in the passage and Curly's mother came in, a little, wizened old woman, scrupulously neat, who had the peculiarity of picking up her crochet-work whenever she got on her feet, although when *not* on her feet no one ever saw her crocheting, and who now put down this humbugging fabric on the table as she took a seat; but immediately afterwards got up, went over to it, and replacing a loose end of it which she had left hanging over the table's edge, folded it into a form that might have been called a qualified rhomboid.

"My darling will be down to say good-evening, Mr. Muir. You must excuse us. We were struck all of a heap when your knock came."

"I hope nothing is the matter, Mrs. Wix?"

To this the old woman only gave a portentous sigh; and he went on:

"Perhaps . . . couldn't we . . . it would be rather nicer . . . I should feel much more at home . . . they are such friendly places I always think . . . much nicer if . . . in fact *won't* you let me come . . . won't you let us go—*into the kitchen*, Mrs. Wix?"

He rose as he spoke, to give emphasis to his words, and gazed fixedly at the door, as if he could find it in him to *project* Mrs. Wix like one of those conjurer's ladies, either intact, or in temporary halves, clean through this closed portal into warmth and welcome.

"My darling and me thought we'd do a little sewing for the wedding."

Still on his feet Magnus was compelled to pause in his spiritual teleportations.

"Oh, Mrs. Wix," he cried, inhaling this deadly hundred-years-old fluff, mixed with modern lamp-soot, with less hopeless exasperation, now that he learnt that Curly was taking advantage of their separation to work on her trousseau, "Oh, Mrs. Wix, that's sweet of you to help her! I knew it was a bother to her; but I know very well how she feels; and leaving you, too, so soon, and living in Weymouth besides, and having so much to think of in addition! How stupid I am! I never thought of how she must want her time for . . . for this necessary sewing."

The old lady regarded him with stony bewilderment.

"I told her," she thought, "I told her all along that he was not quite *all there*. They takes it in different ways, these tutors what teach dead

languages, but I always told her that tutors be neither plain people nor
plain gentry, neither quite sensible nor quite dotty. They be a tribe
by their wone selves, tutors be; and if this one doesn't beat all—"

And she explained, as if to an infant, or to someone not quite "all
there", that when people went to weddings of such gentlemen as
Mr. Cattistock, if it were only to be as you might say in the back
seats, people had to do a considerable deal of needlework first, "let
alone what such as have got men, who lays themselves out to be good
providers, may think it only right to buy in the best market!"

So it was for Cattistock's wedding, after all, not for her own at all,
that this precious evening had been filched away from him and flung
into the unrestoring past!

He left the door and moved over to the table, feeling quite nauseated
now by the stuffiness of the room. He began picking absent-mindedly
at that carefully-folded piece of masquerade crochet. A rush of hot
anger suddenly burst up from somewhere within him. His face
assumed that particular look of the elder Muir's, when the head-
master of the school tried to bully him.

"Mrs. Wix" he said, in a low vibrating voice looking down upon
the little woman from his full height. "Will you kindly go up at
once to Curly, and tell her that I want to speak to her before I go
home?"

"Sure-*lie*, sure-*lie*, Mr. Muir," murmured the old lady, as she
glanced quickly up at him and saw the ominous quivering of his long
shaven lip. She rose from her chair and gathered up the crochet-work.
Once in possession of this symbol of a life of blameless activity, her sly
composure re-asserted itself. "He's angry," she thought. "I must
send her down to him! I can't have her throwing away such a simple
party—though he *is* a tutor!"

Aloud she said: "Come into the kitchen, Mr. Muir, and I'll send
my darling down to 'ee, though she *be* all dimsy-dowsy with her
sewing—and with no dress on, neither!"

Left in the kitchen Magnus' habitual good-nature speedily returned.
The warmth emanating from the stove, the wholesome smell of some
savoury stew under a lid that kept heaving itself up and down, the
brightly polished utensils, a rose-coloured Primula in the window, all
combined, after his misery in that terrible front-room, to restore his

ruffled equanimity. The idea of clasping his sweet girl to his heart in
another second began to make his pulses beat deliciously.

"Perhaps she'll send the old woman to bed," he thought, as he
recalled one heavenly evening when this desirable consummation had
been brought about.

His face shone with expectant delight when he heard steps descending the airs; but it was only the mother again.

"She do say to tell 'ee," Mrs. Wix gasped, out of breath from her
hurried embassy, "that anyone what won't put 'isself to the trouble of
taking anyone to the season's best wedding, and hasn't even thought
to bring her a rose or two from flowershop, don't desarve to be said
goodnight to. But she do say that if 'ee promises to be there, by clock
tomorrow, with a bouquet of pretty roses, 'ee shall have a kiss, and
maybe two on 'em, afore 'a goes."

Magnus capitulated without a moment's hesitation.

"Tell her I'll be there," he said, "and I'll bring the roses. Only *do*
tell her to hurry up! She needn't—" It was on the tip of his tongue to
say "put on her dress" for an image of white soft loveliness with bare
shoulders hovered before him; but he closed his capitulation more
discreetly. "She needn't titivate herself," he added with a smile,
using a word characteristic of the elder Muir.

When the old woman had retired once more with this message of
warm surrender, the image of Mr. Gaul's philosophic countenance,
gazing accusingly at him through its spectacles, did penetrate his
glowing mood for a moment; but he said to himself:

"I'll tell him he was right and that we had a happy evening."

A more than "happy" quarter-of-an-hour the tutor certainly did
have, when Curly, but not with the bare shoulders he had presumed
to vision, came hurrying down. Seldom had he found her sweeter,
more yielding, more tender. This may have been in some degree due
to a sagacious hint from her mother; for the old woman had had time
to whisper,

"Don't 'ee afflict the poor soul too far, me pretty. I seed 'un just now
at the end of 's patience; and I tell 'ee he's a man like any other when
blood be up!" but it was also due to the excitement of the great
Cattistock ceremony, and to the fact that she had been spending such
an industrious, uneventful, cloistered day.

Although not "sent to bed" Mrs. Wix left them discreetly alone, and Curly did think to herself, as over her enraptured fiancé's shoulder while she yielded less coyly than usual to his ardent caresses, she stared wistfully into her own beautiful eyes in the little mirror among the plates on the dresser:

"It might have been much worse. He's a real gentleman in the way he touches a girl. I wouldn't wonder if I couldn't keep him from doing it for months after I sleep with him. Perhaps he'll *never* make me let him do it. That bar-maid at the Weeping Woman, that day I was waiting so long for Sip, said she knew a case when a girl never let a man have her, though they'd been married for years. Oh, deary I! I wish to the Lord a person could marry and sleep single!"

And then, while the warmth of the man's dalliance, as she tried to make herself soft and yielding, carried her thoughts back to her seducer's bolder usage, she couldn't restrain a sad little smile, as she gazed into her own eyes.

"I'm thankful," she said to herself, "he only does this . . . but oh, Sip, oh, Sip! if it were *you*, my sweet Love, my clothes would be off of me before I could say—"

And she made a protesting, endearing, girlish little click with her tongue, as if she had actually felt her frock slip to the ground.

10

SEA-HOLLY

Nᴇᴀʀʟʏ two hours before Magnus left Brunswick Terrace to join the Poxwell sisters, Perdita and the Jobber were enjoying their first rendezvous. They met at ten by the clock on the esplanade and were both in such a trance of delight at meeting that they stood talking for a quarter of an hour eagerly and passionately without moving from the spot. The Jobber was telling her about yesterday's storm, though he made no mention of Cattistock, and she was telling him how kind Jerry had been in helping her to get off early without having to see Mrs. Cobbold at all. At last the Jobber said:

"We've got the whole day haven't we? You don't have to be back for supper, even, do you?"

Perdita, smiling a smile of school-girl radiance which made her look extremely young and almost beautiful, shook her head.

"Well then," he went on, "the first thing we'll do is to go to Corder's Wharf where I keep the 'Slug'. You won't mind riding in *her*, will you, even if she is a bit fishy? Then we'll decide, as we're driving, what we'll do in Portland."

Perdita, "feeling nothing to the revairse", as Bum Trot would say, obeyed without a second's hesitation when he told her to take his arm, and they moved along the esplanade with faces so transformed by the blind delight of being together that several people who knew the Jobber well but could no more arrest his attention now than they could have stopped one of yesterday's waves on Chesil, turned round, when they had passed by, to stare wonderingly at them. But Perdita thought in her heart:

"What's the use of being silly about it? He has no ties that I know of. I am absolutely free. And, besides, I'm earning my living. There's no one in this whole town who has a right to say a word if we go about together!"

They went down St. Mary's Street, and he led her slowly along the pavement in front of the Guildhall, stopping to make her admire the Queen Anne carving above the entrance.

"That's where Sippy Ballard works," said the Jobber. "In just about an hour he'll be coming down those steps to go to lunch. He'd wonder how on earth an old dizzard like me got hold of such a beautiful girl!"

"Hush!" cried Perdita. "I *know* young Ballard. He'd want to stop and talk to us. Don't mention his name, for heaven's sake, for fear he'll come through that door now, before we've got past!"

He thought to himself:

"I wish we'd gone straight along the esplanade to the ferry! I'd like to have her in a boat more than anything. Well, we'll be nearer the 'Slug' by crossing the Bridge."

But, as luck would have it, by taking this particular way to the harbour they were compelled to walk close past the door of the Weeping Woman. As they passed this spot it came over the Jobber with the rush of an exigency too imperative to be disregarded, that it would be nice to take Perdita into this old haunt of his.

Perdita was in such a happy trance that she would have stepped straight into the "Cormorant" if he had led her to its side—and the Cormorant *was* moored within a stone's throw of the Weeping Woman—so that to enter a tavern that reminded her of a particular old wine-shop in Guernsey, where her uncle, the Purser, used often to take her, required no effort at all. She found it a little difficult to adjust herself to the situation, all the same, when she was inside. The bar-room was so thick with smoke and so murmurous with a low-muttered buzz of conversation, and the dim light, for the old house with its narrow Gothic windows was over-topped by tall ship-chandlers' stores, appeared so obscure and misty, compared with the glimmering atmosphere out-of-doors, that for a minute or two, although she felt not the slightest agitation, she did feel bewildered. He took her straight up to the bar-counter and introduced her to his friend Miss Guppy, who treated her—perhaps because of a certain air that her Channel-Island clothes gave her, but more likely out of feminine curiosity—with an exaggerated deference. He made her sit down opposite him at the little round table directly under the bar-counter which the bar-maid always kept for him by a thousand charming devices.

It was not, indeed, till he had disposed of two glasses of whiskey and had refilled Perdita's wine-glass, that he became aware that the striking figure of Sylvanus was seated at a table at the further end of the room between two young women. The Jobber recognized both these girls at once. He was surprised and rather amused to see them in such proximity and apparently in such singular harmony under the big man's dominance.

Helped by the whiskey, he succeeded in keeping intact a rigid mental barrier at the rear of his mind through which no thought of Cattistock, no thought of tomorrow, was allowed to break in upon his felicity. Luckily it was quite in accordance with the Jobber's character to be ready to live with absorbed passion in the emotion of the present, while he let the future take care of itself.

Little did Perdita know the full peril to their love of what he was suppressing; but she did divine, even while she gave herself up to this fate-given happiness, that there was something dangerous, disordered, desperate about his mood. But, after all, she had never had a lover before; and what did she know of the Jobber, beyond the town's gossip? Of this gossip she *had* heard a little, and she had resolved, when she got an opportunity, that she would challenge him about it, but she certainly could not have gone on quietly sipping her wine and staring into his eyes with a dazed and drugged beatitude, if she had known that it had become a maniacal imperative with him to prepare for killing his enemy before nightfall tomorrow.

Having nodded at Peg Frampton and smiled at the infatuated Marret, for Sylvanus was in one of his Seventh Heavens, the Jobber bothered his head no more about them, nor did he even take the trouble to explain to Perdita, whose back was towards them, with whom it was that he exchanged signals.

Perdita was too happy to think of anything save that the impossible had come true! Here she sat in this little old-fashioned place, knowing she was loved by the one man she had ever met who could give her the magic feeling "that redeems all sorrows". With an almost savage realism she found herself noting every smallest physical peculiarity in the man opposite her—how he had a small white scar over his left eyebrow, how his drinking had brought out a little drop of sweat, that was trickling down towards this white spot, how he had put on, for this special occasion, a new blue jersey that was of a rather lighter colour than the one he wore yesterday when he came to High House, how his eyes, though grey in the main, possessed several little marbly markings in them of a faint yellow and green and amber, how his lips, though full and finely turned, were rather babyish-looking than sensual; how often, when he got agitated and breathed heavily, which seemed to be a peculiarity of his under any slight stimulus, these lips of his remained apart, showing with startling clearness where one of his large white teeth had been broken off short, leaving a rather disconcerting irregularity.

The Weeping Woman was so close to the Harbour's edge that at one moment she thought she could hear the lapping of water, when Sylvanus' voice—and a vague notion that it *might* be Sylvanus crossed her mind—sank to silence. Yes, for a moment she fancied she could hear the gurglings and suckings of the tide round the wharf-piles and its motions against the slippery stones. She thought to herself, even while with her lips she was telling him certain simple details about her life at home in Guernsey:

"I never knew how love casts out fear! If he asks me to sleep with him tonight I'll do it. Why not? I don't care! He may easily turn against me when we know each other better; and I'm going to snatch at all of his love—all! all!—while I can get it. Yes! Uncle was very fond of me. We used to be together all the time when he came home from his trips." But her excited thoughts went recklessly on. "Better go as far as possible, while I've got the chance, so that when he gets tired of me I'll have something. I wonder what a child of ours would be like? It would be sure to be more like him than me; though it would be more mine than his!"

She felt angry with Sylvanus now—yes! it *must* be Sylvanus—for talking so loudly; and she felt suspicious of him too, and hostile to him, while all manner of scandalous stories about him floated through her

mind. She had indeed listened so often to Mrs. Cobbold's version of
the man's peculiarities that it would have been strange if some
sediment of evil had not clung to her vision of him.

"I suppose," she thought, when turning round for a moment she
glanced with an obscure distaste at the back of that grizzled elongated
head, protruding from the frayed tweed coat. "I suppose he captivates
these young girls with all this mystical rubbish—Oh, how I dislike
these emotional preaching voices!—and then, when he's spoilt their
innocence and got hold of them body and soul, he tires of them and
picks up new ones!"

It surprised her to note that none of the other guests in the bar of
the Weeping Woman shared her hostility to the rising and falling
inflection of this man's voice. They seemed rather pleased than
otherwise to continue their private exchange of furtive whispers—
they were mostly couples of opposite sexes—under cover, as it were,
of this metaphysical drum.

Perdita herself went on telling the Jobber all sorts of stories of her
early life and of the Guernsey coast. And as she talked it became
clearer and clearer to her that all her girlhood's imaginings about some
mysterious lover who was more like a merman than a human being,
had really and truly been fulfilled in this man.

By degrees a natural desire for a closer intimacy than was possible
in a place like this mounted up in the Jobber. But where could he take
her so that they should be alone? Till this moment the Jobber had
never suffered from the conventional obstacles to free intercourse
between the sexes which, as Magnus had discovered, blight the
furtivos amores of middle class persons in England. To take her to his
own house was impossible. He had once brought in the redoubtable
Miss Guppy and Mrs. Trot had been positively rude to her. To take
Perdita to his father's dwelling, which was between the village of
Easton and that "Last House" where Sylvanus lived, would have been
easy, but he would have had almost as much difficulty in being alone
with her *there* as under the tutelage of Mrs. Trot. What the devil
should they do? At last, even as he listened to her telling him about
the autumn fishing season at her home, the thought crossed his mind,
why not steal a leaf out of his enemy's book and take her to the
"Head"? The Gadget woman was a good friend of his. 'Melia,

Celia and Sue were romantic-minded girls, entirely free from spiteful-
ness and worldliness. Very few quarrymen frequented the place.
"By Dum, that's the ticket!" The blood seemed to leave the pit of his
stomach altogether and rush violently to his head. If the Dog could
take a room at the Gadgets' why couldn't he? He had come to feel
towards this eleventh of February as if it were a whole month. And
if the night was added to it—for what, after all, did Mrs. Cobbold
matter?—it would be more than a month. It would be a whole year;
and let come what *might* come on the morrow. He would have had
his day! He wouldn't tell her, by Dum! no, he wouldn't tell her,
about its being the end, the last of him, till 'twas near dawn and they
had to part. That Margate murderer, they found with his girl, must
have put much worse things than an unacted tomorrow out of his
mind!

"Yes, as soon as she's finished what she's telling me now I'll get up
and pay; then we'll go. By Dum! what moonshine that bloke *is*
jawing about! It beats me how Peggie Frampton can stand it or the
other one either."

What Sylvanus was "jawing about" in his queer manner just then,
and he made it sound like something midway between a magician's
invocation and a tipsy commentary upon Spinoza, was an impassioned
appeal to Peg and Marret to sink their souls fathom-deep—even as
they sat drinking in the Weeping Woman—into the everlasting
Absolute. As he kept murmuring and muttering about the "Absolute"
it was perfectly clear to both Peg and Marret that the feelings he
described were rather obscured than revealed by the words he used.
What annoyed the Jobber in the man's way of talking, what got on
Perdita's nerves in his prophetic voice, didn't touch Peg and Marret at
all. They loved him in the real "absolute" sense about which he was
talking, and what they got from him was made up of sidelong intima-
tions, droll by-issues, quaint betrayals of personal peculiarities and little
unconscious gestures. The "Absolute" which these two girls got
from him was indeed much more akin to the Chinese "Tao" than to
any Parmenidean equilibrium. It was an Absolute that saturated with
itself certain concrete objects more than others; and the girls began to
divine that they could find it in the smallest "minute particulars" of
their own lives. They loved him indeed with such disinterested

intensity that it was what he was feeling behind his words, and what he *was* behind his words that caught them. They used his masculine discriminations like a skiff, in which they could ride the rocking waves of their own slippery and evasive natures.

With the clairvoyance of love they noticed that Sylvanus would stop every now and then and stare, with the simple gravity of a reverential animal, at a window through which the harbour-noises seemed to be entering the bar-room. They had come to know him so well as to be able to catch him out, as it were, and to get the essence of his spirit, in a thousand quaint unconscious gestures; and it was from these odd little physical tricks of his that his everlasting Absolute came filtering into their souls. They had come to detect, for instance, what a mania he had for such mysterious inanimates as air, earth, water, fire, and how he seemed to worship, not poetically, but *really*, the sun, the sea, and the sky. They weren't in the least surprised, therefore, when he suddenly stopped his oracular mutterings, and gave a funny little ritualistic nod, which was clearly a religious obligation to him, as if he had caught sight of an altar, in the direction of the harbour. This, they knew, was his quite personal worship of the sea, his superstitious acknowledgment of the divinity of the sea, and they always got more of a shiver of real awe from it, when he made these awkward little nods, which he evidently thought no one observed than when he chanted his ponderous metaphysical runes.

To Sylvanus' own mind his peculiarities were a simple, direct categorical way of living upon the earth, that had no connection with affection or nonsense or silliness. In fact he regarded them as an evidence of shrewd common-sense.

Perdita had learnt from Mrs. Cobbold to consider him an arch-humbug, a man made up of evil subtlety and vicious hypocrisy; and this was precisely the sort of misunderstanding that, when Sylvanus encountered it, puzzled, bewildered, and disconcerted him; though it never made him change his ways. How could it do this when his ways were a fatality with him—much more integral than his Viking moustache—and born of a really *awful* simplicity in his temperament to which his intellect gave a shameless "carte blanche"?

What he thought at this very moment when Peg and Marret saw him—though no one else saw him—make this ridiculous bow to the sea through the smoke-begrimed window of the Weeping Woman, might be put into words like this:

"Sessa! Sessa! The beer in this bar has better froth than any John Gadget sells. What divine intelligence young girls have! I think they grasp the most difficult conceptions. These two are perfect. And they have no jealousy of each other. Aye! what celestial good fortune that I ever met these two! I understand them completely, and they understand me. Gipsy May is one too many for me. I'm too simple to follow her. But who *could* follow her? She's a scaramouch-woman! She beats me at my own game. I've had to think myself free of our race's nonsense, while she was born independent. She'll play me some shocking trick one of these days and only love me the more afterwards! I can't understand her. Life would be easy without her; but its salt, its bitter, smarting, tickling, rousing salt would be quite gone. I can't live with her. I've found *that* out. But to live without her—I can't imagine it! What goes on in her head no human being knows. She's completely inhuman, but that's her witchery, that's the essence of it. I hope she *does* come tonight and see me, but I feel a trifle uneasy when I think of it. If she *does*, what will she say to Marret? She could be heavenly to her if she *wanted* to, but *will* she—*will* she—"

It was at this point that he realized that without question he could hear the harbour-waves.

"O everlasting Sea!" he said to himself, talking to it quite quietly, just as if it were a person he had suddenly realized was present, "O divine, eternal, mysterious Sea, I never knew you were so near!" and it was at this point that he made his hurried, secretive, spontaneous little bow before he went on thinking about Gipsy May—

"Will she be nice to her? She won't be jealous in the ordinary sense. But you never know with May. She might hide her shoes or burn her clothes!"

Thus pondered Sylvanus as with Quixotic obstinacy he continued his oracular words. But his rhapsodical discourse was soon interrupted by an event that disturbed everything and everyone in the place. This was the sudden opening of the bar-room door and the spectacular entrance of none other than his brother Jerry accompanied by Tossty. It was not the clown's fault that his entrance with the haughty dancer created such a stir. Tossty had been seduced by the amenity of this spring-like day to wear a cloak of such a brilliant scarlet hue that towards this surprising adornment the whole heterogeneous company directed their fascinated gaze.

"Hullo!" cried Jerry. "Why, look who's here! And how are *you* enjoying this heavenly weather?" and he went straight up to his brother and kissed him in a somewhat un-English fashion. "Here," he went on, "I don't know whether you've met our great Regent star, Miss Clive—better known as Tossty? Toss, old girl, here's luck for you! She's been teasing me, Van, for the last month, to be introduced to you; only you never come to our little performances. Well! What do you think of him now you *have* met?"

Marret took the opportunity of this brotherly greeting to move up close to Peg, to whom she rather pitifully clung, as if from the other's superior social knowledge she would get support in this pressure of events.

Glancing down from where she stood, her hand resting indifferently in that of Sylvanus and a slight frown upon her face, as if angry with Jerry for what he had just said, the scarlet-cloaked dancer gave a start when she recognized Peg, and then, pleased to find an excuse to be contrarious, she snatched her hand away from the tweed-coated man and extended it to the girl.

"Why, Jerry," she cried. "Here's your little friend of Sark House!" And then, stooping gracefully over Peg, from whose side Marret now felt impelled to draw back, she murmured in a penetrating voice. "You must come round to the theatre one of these days."

Meanwhile Jerry, calling to the bar-maid to bring them "some of that old brandy of yours, dearie, that you gave us the other night", caught sight of Perdita and the Jobber and greeted them in his most affable manner. Perdita half rose in response to this, but aware of the black cloud that had descended on her lover's face contented herself with giving the clown a grateful and almost confiding smile.

"You see how happy we are," this smile said. "And it's all due to your indulgence!"

It was then, to poor Marret's consternation, that the exponent of the Absolute called the scarlet lady's attention to his other companion; and he twisted one of his great drooping moustache-ends with self-forgetting satisfaction when he saw the wilful beauty shake hands quite sweetly with the terrified Punch-and-Judy girl.

Miss Guppy, full of fluttered delight at having been called "dearie" by Jerry Cobbold, now came bustling up with shining eyes and panting bosom and cleared a table not far from the one where Sylvanus had been sitting. Here she placed the refreshment ordered by her new guests and gazed in fascinated approval at the scarlet cloak.

The presence of the great clown and his dazzling companion, brought into such close contact with them in this small place, evidently discountenanced one or two couples, for there was a movement to pay and clear off. But a few simple-looking sailors and their wenches remained, though even these, in place of continuing their whispers, stared in silence now at that silky, dark figure with its flaming background haughtily sipping neat brandy while Jerry talked to his brother, who had resumed his place between the two young girls.

"No, I didn't know you could hear it so clearly here," the clown was saying. "Listen, Toss! Do *you* hear it? It's nice, isn't it? It makes you feel as if you were in a ship. Do you remember, Van, old man, how they took us, when we were kids, to that old training-ship—the Boscawen, wasn't it?—and how we heard the water gurgling outside and how scared I was, but you said 'It's only the sea.' That quieted me. 'Wherever it flows,' you said, 'it's always the same sea!' And I've often thought of that since. Yes, you've said some good things in your time, brother! 'It's always the same sea'; I've often thought of that when life's got me by the hair. 'It's always the same life,' I've thought to myself; and known I had to stick it out somehow."

"I've been trying to make these girls," said Sylvanus, "recognize just what you say, Jerry; only it's so hard to get it into words. But it isn't *life*, brother; you're wrong there, if you'll excuse my saying so. It's no more life than this sound we hear in here is the harbour! This sound—you certainly *do* hear it today—is *in* the harbour but it isn't the harbour. Come, Miss Clive, can't you help me out? Tell these girls that Jerry's wrong when he says it's *life* that's 'always the same'. When you're dancing at your best—at your *very* best I mean!—and strike one of those wonderful balances that everyone tells me about, a pose that's like death itself, don't you feel as if you were floating on something beyond both life and death? Don't you feel so, Miss Clive?"

His voice was so solemn and his long El-Greco-like face, above his bottle-shaped, tweed-clad shoulders, wore such an unearthly look at that minute, that everyone waited for Tossty's answer, as if a ghost had been addressing her.

Never had this spoilt and petted native of Radipole such an opportunity to be provoking. She took it with the most teasing sang-froid.

"Do . . . I . . . feel . . . anything . . . Jerry," she drawled languidly, "at . . . all . . . like . . . what . . . he's . . . talking about?" She lifted her glass to her mouth and put it down untasted. "It's hot in here," she murmured hiding a yawn with her hand. "Jerry always tells me what I feel," she said, and she gave the impression, by some artful trick of tone and voice, of addressing herself exclusively to Miss Guppy. Then she threw back her head and extending her silk-sleeved arms in the air as if to stretch herself she yawned naughtily and rudely in the face of them all. "It's too hot in here Jerry," she repeated.

Sylvanus sighed; but his face brightened when Jerry spoke up, completely disregarding the girl's uncivil behaviour. But it did not remain bright, for Jerry's words, though tenderly affectionate to him, suddenly acquired a vibration that disturbed him and worried him, for in his fraternal concern he attributed it to the naughty ways of Tossty.

"You are the same old Cassius still," he said, "but it makes me angry to hear you deceiving these children. Behind . . . behind . . . behind—that's where you tricky mystics always put the secret, as if life had a rainbow-coloured rump like a pet baboon. It makes me sick to hear you, you old blackguard. Peace to all beings! Our only comfort is to rail, since we're not brave enough to die! Your baboon's arse may be an Aurora Borealis for all I care, since we shall never see it! The point is, pilgarlic darling, your jigging monkey-world is a Monsieur sans queue, an arse-less Monsieur! Like the Moon it has never turned round; and it *never will!* Dead shall we all be—"

The clown's voice gathered volume at this point; and Tossty, after one angry glance at him, wetted her finger and drew it round and round and round her glass with a frown even more gloomy than the

Jobber's who had begun to fidget as if he were suffering from what is sometimes called "pins and needles".

"Dead we shall all be, dead as those Dinosaur bones that that girl found at Ringstead Bay. And the only good thing about life is that it *does* end! Poudre de Perlinpimpin! If we sick lepers couldn't lie down and *know* it was the last, we'd *all* be candidates for Doctor Brush's Summer House. Come now, Miss Wane, *you* speak up and take my side, for I know well what *you* think about all this."

Tossty left making music with her wet finger and bent hurriedly towards him, letting her sinuous body make the same kind of engaging angle with the droop of her cloak over the chair that the spears of the plants known as Lords and Ladies make when they are fully disclosed. Her whisper brought Jerry back to his infinitely meticulous rôle of master of ceremonies.

"True, Toss," he said earnestly, and then to Perdita. "Miss Clive here says she's never been introduced to you. That comes of being a friend of our good Jobber. He knows everybody and everybody knows him; but you of course—"

Tossty made an inclination of the head, so prettily appropriate and yet so delicately exaggerated that Perdita felt very uncomfortable as she nodded to her in return and began murmuring some old-fashioned compliment.

Jerry was evidently suppressing an irritable disapproval of the way Tossty was behaving this morning, and her perfunctory and unsympathetic nod to Perdita, to whom he felt curiously protective, touched off the explosion. To the astonishment of everyone, except Sylvanus, who had anticipated exactly this very thing, Jerry suddenly cried out:

"Yes, I'll tell you what the other side of Life is, about which Van tells you his lies!"

With these words he leapt to his feet, bounded across to the bar-counter, vaulted lightly over it, and turning round, to face them all with one arm round Miss Guppy's shoulders and the other waving a beer-glass he'd picked up, he burst out into wild fooling:

"Piffer-rary! love your dearie! and I tell ye all for once and clearly... But *my* dearie here *knows* all," and he hugged Miss Guppy more tightly still—"that at the bottom of our hearts—O me! my heart, my rising heart! but down! cry to it, nuncle, as the cockney did to the eels when she put 'em in the paste alive; she knapped 'em o' the coxcombs with a stick and cried 'Down, wantons, down!' 'Twas her brother—*and that's you, brother*—'that, in pure kindness to his horse, buttered his hay.' Piffer-rary! love your dearie!—and I, *moi qui vous parle,* the dancing bear, have peeped behind that Curtain, when brother was playing his scrannel pipe and *there's nothing there!*"

The Jobber would have remained in his seat, right under the bar, scowling over his whiskey and grimly wondering what force was keeping him from flinging down what he owed and carrying Perdita off. But Perdita had become so interested in Jerry, and in a sense so fond of him, that she got up hurriedly now and moved to a table in the open, whither the Jobber had to follow her, to see what the man was doing.

And to their amazement Jerry was now, for he had dropped Miss Guppy, talking rapidly or pretending to talk on his fingers in dead silence, but with a hundred queer grimaces all addressed to Sylvanus as if he had been Panurge arguing with Thaumast. Something mute, violent, gross, inarticulate, in the Jobber's own nature now roused itself up to respond to the way the clown was letting himself go; and as he watched him, and he was unaware that Sylvanus had got up and was now standing close behind them, and as he saw him reverting to certain irresistible facial expressions that had gone—like inspired tunes—all over the world, he whispered hoarsely to Perdita:

"By Dum, the chap *is* a fellow!"

The only person who was not startled by these queer happenings seemed to be Marret. She apparently associated it all, in some natural and mysteriously intimate way, with the paternal performance with which she was so well acquainted.

But it was reserved to Miss Guppy, and to Miss Guppy alone, to have, so to speak, the best seat at this singular comedy; for except Jerry himself she was the only one who had the privilege of being able to see Sylvanus' face. Miss Guppy's conduct up to this point had been perfect. While being embraced by the clown she had worn upon her countenance that particular expression of good-natured protest, mingled with an irresistibly whimsical second-thought of "making hay while the sun shone" which certain charming elderly people always assume when their dignity is playfully rumpled. But it was

Miss Guppy's privilege on this eleventh day of February, and hers alone, to see Sylvanus' face as he set himself to exorcise this wild devil of Tartarean burlesque that had suddenly possessed his self-controlled brother.

Perdita felt very uneasy for the man; and as for the proud Tossty, she did a thing that the emotional Tissty herself might have done, save that Tissty generally got rid of such tensions by impulsive action; she put her hands to her head and thrust her fingers into her ears, thus repeating a gesture which had evidently come to be her last resort when her friend's pessimism touched the breaking-point.

Watching his brother with concern, Sylvanus thought to himself: "What a fool I was to let him begin this!" and remembering how when they were children he used to startle Jerry into quiescence by playing the ghost, he raised his arms high above his head and began waggling his long lean fingers, horizontally from his bent-over wrists.

But it was not at Sylvanus' lifted hands, nor at these queer fish-fin movements that his lean fingers made, as they sawed the air, that the petrified Miss Guppy stared. She stared at the long, white face of the man which had suddenly become like a narrow window-blind through which two holes had been pierced into a burning outer darkness.

In the presence of this formidable apparition the antics of the breathless clown abruptly ceased. His dominant desire, the moment he ceased, was, it seemed, simply and solely to reassure Miss Guppy, and sweeping an imaginary plumed hat from his head, he made her a bow like a cavalier and kissed her hand. Then with his brother's help he scrambled back across the counter and returned to Tossty's side.

"Well, Toss my dear, you've seen the original first act I ever put on. I call it 'Arsiversy' or 'Heads and Tails'. 'Tis an old comedy, Toss. Commedia Antiqua Veritatis! Or Devil cast out Devil. You saw the way he waggled his hands? They catch corncrakes so!"

Perdita was not the only girl in the smoky bar-room of the Weeping Woman whose inclination to "weep" that morning came from a tide of radiant happiness. Those words of Sylvanus that had seemed pure moonshine to the Jobber had been to Peg Frampton like the milk of Paradise! Brought up so drably and desolately, always so lonely, neglected, embittered, she had come to loathe the very name of religion. Her vice had been until now her one solitary refuge. For it was no glowing sensuality, but rather an acrid drug, a wretched intoxicant, distracting the sorry forlornness of her days. But this mysterious Absolute about which this man talked seemed to gather to itself everything lovely and sweet and satisfying that she had missed in life. There was nothing about it that suggested the conventional morality that stank in her nostrils, that was in fact actually mixed up in her mind with a certain musty-fusty smell that emanated from her father, whenever he gave her his formal and undemonstrative embrace. Peg had read little, but she had an inquisitive and receptive brain, and she had formed her own ideas as to the meaning of good and evil. Thus when her Don Quixote of metaphysics talked of this Tao-like presence that included and underlay everything, it at once occupied the place in her mind of all those vague desires, not vicious, but sweet and sensual and mysterious, which the drabness of her days had blighted.

To sit by his side and listen to him was all she wanted, and not the faintest jealousy of Marret entered her thoughts. Peg's susceptibility to her own sex had of late met with so many rebuffs from Daisy Lily, that to find in this new friend a tender if not a magnetic response was a surprise and pleasure. But the greatest moment of all came when Sylvanus went over to the bar to stop the clown's outburst. That elevating of his arms in the air and that queer movement with his hands was what gave her her greatest thrill of this whole morning. His hands seemed to her like fir-tree tops, like the indignant feathers of swans, like huge seaweeds from the bottom of the sea, like floating zenith-clouds, like windmill sails, like smoke from the great brewery in Dorchester, like storm-signals on the White Nose, like the weather-cock on the top of St. John's, like sea-gulls on Hardy's Monument, like the turning chimney-tops of Sark House before she had entered it, like the revolution of the Portland Bill searchlight that shone through the windows of Last House. She even went so far— and it was the reverse of blasphemy in her—to mix up the swaying of those horizontal fingers from the man's bent wrists with her childish ideas of the Holy Ghost. The grotesqueness of the action was what led her to do this. It seemed to contain a rebuke, a retort, a defiance, a challenge to Evil, from an armoury of the perverse, the weird, the monstrous, the half-mad; and this—with her loathing of conventional religion—was precisely her own private notion of how the Absolute *should* go to work, when it broke out.

Jerry Cobbold seemed extremely reluctant to separate from his brother. In his curious Atlas-like tendency to hold up the status-quo of the whole world he fancied he discerned in this singular rapprochement in the bar of the Weeping Woman a dedicated opportunity for persuading Sylvanus to stop discussing metaphysics on the esplanade.

So it came about that Peg induced the nothing-loth Marret to accompany her to the "Regatta", there to partake of the sort of lunch, consisting of lettuce salad, and a great deal of pastry, which young women, when left to their own devices, invariably select. Peg was compelled, before issuing this extravagant invitation, to un-click as surreptitiously as she could her tattered bead-purse. Thank the Lord! She had almost the whole of her weekly allowance left, an allowance that had been increased by Mr. Frampton on her last birthday from three and sixpence to four and nine-pence.

The day was such a lovely one, and began—as noonday arrived—to feel so warm that when they found themselves on the esplanade nearly opposite their destination Peg impulsively suggested that they should go down to the edge of the sea. Here, as they stood side by side on the shimmering sand watching the tiny ripples lose themselves at their feet, they saw that a boy and a girl, who were evidently visitors for the day to Weymouth, had taken off their shoes and stockings and were boldly paddling in this shining water.

This sight roused Peg's adventurous emulation and she persuaded Marret who would much sooner have gone on standing where she was with Peg's arm round her waist, to take off her stockings with her. It is a proof of the lonely and independent life Peg had led, and of how, her father being so immersed in business, she had succeeded in practically de-classing herself, that she didn't give a fig for what the world might say at seeing the daughter of Cattistock's partner paddling in the sea with the daughter of the Punch-and-Judy man. When the two young women did follow that boy and girl, and made their way into the shimmering water, they quickly became a most natural pair of very youthful companions, chuckling, giggling, shivering, exclaiming, as they felt the shock of those cold ripples. A great deal of their attention was taken up by the effort to keep their clothes from getting wet; and they behaved like children rather than like grown-up people in the way in which they kept hitching up their drawers and letting their skirts, which were constantly trailing down at the back, nearly touch the water; but as they stood side by side, and indeed turned their faces landward when they saw that the boy and girl were laughing at them, they did not lose the chance of exchanging a few remarks about Sylvanus.

"Do you live with him now, Marret, just as if you were married to him?"

"Not ... quite ... like that," said Marret, speaking slowly and choosing her words with the utmost nicety. "We sleep together, you know, and he presses me to him, *but*," and she finished her sentence with the natural frankness of a girl brought up among the donkeys and goat-carriages of the "dry-sand", "but *he never does anything*. He never seems to want to, and I don't think he ever will."

"Don't *you* want him to, Marret?"

Peg began to find a strange vicarious pleasure in all this. The fact that she herself was attracted to this girl seemed to make it all so much more natural and nice. She felt a tremulous excited curiosity as to what these two really did. She would have liked to have known everything, *everything*. She would have liked to have waited upon them as they lay side by side. She would have liked to have been their servant and carried up their tea to them on a tray, and put it on their bed, and sat on the edge of their bed. She felt herself in this position now as she pressed Marret with her questions, and her red lip—that lower lip which always hung down—had a tiny drop of saliva on its outer edge.

Marret was silent under the directness of this last interrogation.

"*Did* she want him to?" she wondered to herself, letting her eyes wander across "the wet sand" and across "the dry sand", to the white wall of the esplanade. There was a young man sitting on a bench on the esplanade, and Marret instinctively let her clothes drop down. "*Did* she want him to?"

"I don't know whether I do or not," she murmured at last, and there crossed her face, as Peg sympathetically watched it, a far-away, passive, infinitely mysterious look, that strange annunciation-look that the early Italian painters are such adepts in giving to their extraordinarily youthful madonnas. There was a long silence, while Marret kept turning her head with a slow abstracted thoughtfulness, as her eyes rested upon the old King's statue, upon the Jubilee Clock, upon St. John's Spire. Then feeling a sudden shiver of cold in those sunlit ripples, for the water still retained its wintry chill, she suggested to Peg that they should return to land.

Peg received this intimation with protective sympathy and at once began heading for the beach; though, if the truth must be told she regretted having to give up the delicious sense of erotic stimulus which sprang from her knowledge of being ardently watched from the esplanade by the young man on the bench and furtively watched from the deeper water by the young man who was paddling.

"His girl isn't much to look at," Peg said to herself. "No wonder he looks at Marret and me!"

In saying "Marret and me", she was obeying a deep inner imperative. Shamelessly immoral as Peg was, she was as austere as St. Augustine in regard to certain human weaknesses. When she was attracted to a younger girl, as she had been to Daisy Lily, and now was to Marret, it would have seemed to her a shocking disloyalty to allow a breath of comparison to enter her thoughts between her own physical desirability and that of her friend. But though it was with considerable regret that she approached land she was rewarded for her unselfishness by growing aware—and Peg was an expert in this kind of awareness—that the young man on the bench was spell-bound by the sight of her bare legs.

Marret—still with that Old Master's annunciation-look—mechanically shook out her skirt as they advanced. This the Punch-and-Judy girl did not only because of her natural modesty but because she was in love. The girl was in truth as deep in love with her prophet as Perdita was with the Jobber, but being less pessimistic and much less intellectual than Mrs. Cobbold's companion, her love took the form of a childish hero-worship that knew no bounds. At Peg's outrageous question as to whether she wanted to be possessed by Sylvanus she had answered with literal truth, "I don't know whether I do or not." Her feeling had indeed the very chastity of devotion in it. If Sylvanus had wanted to cut off her hair as well as to possess her, her heart would only have murmured: "Be it unto me as my lord wishes!"

But it was far from Peg Frampton's thoughts to drop her skirt over her shining legs. Tantalizingly they glittered in that spring sunshine. They seemed crying aloud for some wild dance of the Naiades on those sparkling wet sands.

The two friends did indeed make a subtly contrasting picture as they came up out of that pearl-soft sea. If Marret in her long black skirt resembled the little Virgin dressed up in an old robe of St. Anne's, Peg had all that air of brooding secretiveness which allured the sophisticated Botticelli to diffuse something cryptic through the wind-blown movements of his Sea-born. Peg's vicious excitement kept mounting higher and higher as she came nearer the young man seated on the bench. When at last she fancied she was near enough for him to know that she knew what his emotions were, a smile of the most equivocal abandonment flickered across her face. Almost immediately after smiling in this way she recognized who her admirer was. He was no other than that studious young man who lodged at Trigonia House.

Marret also recognised Mr. Gaul, and quite spontaneously—as she would have done had she been standing beside her father's puppets—she waved her hand to him and even shouted to him, a high-pitched little-girl greeting.

With some trepidation, and not without a nervous glance around him lest Miss Monkton, his landlady's daughter, should be returning from school, Mr. Gaul descended the stone steps leading to the dry sand and very soon had arrived at the spot, which was not hard to perceive, where the girls had left their shoes and stockings. He reached that spot indeed before they did themselves, and it came into his head that if some student at Jena or Heidelberg were to ask the famous expounder of the Philosophy of Representation what object or group of objects would most vividly "represent" the sea-coast of his native land, he might very well reply: "A couple of pairs of girls' stockings carefully kept in their place by pebble-stones, and sprinkled by drifting sand!"

As with most human events it was a consensus of fatalities that led to Mr. Gaul's presence at that particular juncture. That he was alone there, and that the esplanade had no loiterers to share his interest in this classical scene was due to the fact that it was the hour for lunch. But that he had sat down on that bench at all was brought about by the most exquisite balancing of second causes. He had set out in high elation to purchase a copy of Faust at that same book-shop where it had been the Jobber's destiny to procure "Middlemarch". But the encounter with Mrs. Cobbold and his facetious remark to her "taunted", as Curly's mother would have said, his mind. The book-shop used to possess, so the Jobber's friend assured him, quite a number of foreign books, "but people don't read as seriously as they did when you and I were young, Mr. Gaul." Whether this addition of at least thirty years to his age was, like his own remark to Lucinda, a "jeu d'esprit", evoked by the warm day, he was unable to decide, but as he ran his fingers up and down the shelves of the Lending Library— every volume of which, as he took them out at random, seemed to smell of sea-sand and of hot sunshine in bow-windows—he began to fall into unphilosophic thoughts. In plain words Mr. Gaul began to feel the influence of the spring. He thought of his bold advice to Magnus to visit his girl willy-nilly; and there slid into his disturbed senses a forlorn wish that he himself had a girl to visit. Presently, still keeping his back to the Jobber's friend, who was now occupied in a triumphant conversion of a reader of "these terrible modern books" to the lost culture of George Eliot, Mr. Gaul turned abstractedly the pages of a work of Rider Haggard and stumbled therein upon a little vignette, for it scarcely amounted to a real illustration, of two engaging young women arrayed, "or rather disarrayed", in antique attire. The book was nearly thumbed into obliteration. Every page looked as if it had been "kept", while its reader bathed in the sea, by having bits of sea-weed stuck across it. There arose from it an "aura" of half a century of summer holidays, spent between the dry sand and the wet sand.

And it came into his mind—as if from the long afternoon fantasies of the last reader of "Alan Quartermain"—that he ought to find some really enlightened interpretation of the theological notion of sinfulness as applied to erotic feelings. And as he replaced the book, and bowed to the Jobber's friend, whose correction of the taste of her young man had evidently left him confounded, it came into his head that it was impossible to philosophize adequately upon the mystery of lechery without yielding to it in *some* degree. These thoughts ripened rather than faded in the hazy sunshine, as he crossed the road at the back of the blameless King, and when he saw the visitor-boy and visitor-girl paddling in the glittering water and Peg and Marret watching him, he sank down upon that convenient bench and allowed the perilous spring weather to work its will upon him.

As the girls came drifting towards him, now stopping to enable Peg to pull down her under-clothes, and now stopping to pick up, and drop into the water again, some irresistible piece of seaweed, Mr. Gaul found that he *had* learnt one very serviceable piece of erotic knowledge —namely the important part played in the various stages of lechery by the element of the impersonal. The sight of Peg's polished limbs, gleaming so beautifully in that pearl-soft sunshine, when he had first contemplated them had been an intense amorous delight, full of poetry, full of a delicious tremulous satisfaction, that diffused itself over the whole surface of the shimmering water. But the moment he recognized that the girl knew he was looking at her *in that way,* and that she, too, was deriving pleasure from it, the thing came over him with such over-powering force as to be shaking, agitating, destructive of peace, creative of disturbing desire. A yet further stage was reached— so the philosopher in Mr. Gaul observed, commenting upon his human senses—when he shook hands with Peg and Marret and began talking to them and enjoying their company, and he came to the conclusion that in this social stage of the affair a woman got far more satisfaction than a man, so much satisfaction indeed that Mr. Gaul began to wonder whether all love-passages were not a sort of rape committed upon the essential gregariousness of women, like picking a rose from a rose-bush.

But the truth was—though he could scarcely have brought this into his analysis—that Mr. Gaul had it in him to be a charming companion to young girls. Little Miss Monkton had already found this out to her cost, for what her teacher attributed to the Devil in her moods and her tempers was really due to the poor child's first consciousness of the darts of Eros. With Peg and Marret, as they slowly ascended the stone steps to the esplanade, Mr. Gaul was well-nigh perfect as a companion.

Even Marret seemed to lose her shyness, for, as she said afterwards to Peg:

"You can't feel funny and think of things and all that, when you sees them shinin' round spectacles a-watchin' of 'ee, like the old gent from Regent's Park what used to sit all summer in front row at dad's show like he were gone on Judy!"

A delicate situation emerged, all the same, as the three of them crossed the road to the "Regatta"; for Mr. Gaul resembled Peg in that his purse was anything but inexhaustible. Neither he nor Peg had enough in their pocket to treat the other; and yet it was hopelessly contrary to Weymouth etiquette for each to pay for himself. But Mr. Gaul had a droll frankness when it came to such matters. He made the girls sit down with him on his bench, which was still unoccupied, and insisted that they should all three empty their purses into Peg's lap.

"But I want to treat Marret anyway!" protested Peg.

"Empty your purses!" repeated Mr. Gaul.

And then it turned out that in an ornamental leather case that looked as if she had picked it up at the feet of that visitor from Regent's Park, Marret possessed a golden sovereign.

"Put it away!" cried Peg. "She musn't change that, Mr. Gaul! No, no! Put it away."

But Mr. Gaul was rather tickled by the idea of the Punch-and-Judy girl being the one to pay the bill.

"I'll like to see the face of that life-boat modeller," he said to himself.

In the end the whole contents of Peg's purse was transferred to Mr. Gaul's, and they assured Marret that it was only because they knew they'd got her gold to fall back upon, that they dared enter the "Regatta" at all.

The Jobber had never felt that unique character of his native "Isle of the Slingers" as poignantly as he felt it today as with Perdita by his side he drove the "Slug" across Fleet Bridge and along the inland side of Chesil Beach. They had been, after all, the last of their group of acquaintances to leave the Weeping Woman, the delay being due to Perdita's shyness both at the idea of pushing unceremoniously past the others or of bidding them a formal adieu, and Miss Guppy not knowing whether to laugh or to cry at the thought of having been dragged into what she called "Mr. Cobbold's foolishness", insisted on providing them before they left with an "elegant fish-lunch", fresh that morning from the emporium of Mr. Witchit, and a couple of bottles of local beer, which she was careful to pour out before she set them on the table, lest the label Cattistock and Frampton should raise ill thoughts in the Jobber's mind.

Such ill thoughts were indeed obliterated just now as he drove slowly on, resting his eyes now and then, as he talked to the girl, on the great sea-bank towering above them. But Portland, as it lay before them, rising tier by tier over its terraces of old walls and grey roofs, seemed to be tugging at its tether in that luminous and liquid haze, seemed to be straining at this gigantic rope of transparent stones, agates and carnelians, which bound it to the mainland. The huge limestone rock seemed to have no roots, under this enchanted light, in any solid earth. It seemed to be riding, just as the battleships in the harbour seemed to be riding, upon a liquid abyss of opalescent water that sank down to the antipodes. And the Jobber got the impression that this stupendous mass of oolite was really afloat today in this translucent calm; not only afloat, but longing to drift off, to sail out and away, over the surface of that halcyon sea. All the way up the narrow steep ascent above Chesilton as the faithful Slug snorted and spluttered and groaned, the Jobber gave himself up to the paradisal happiness of explaining to Perdita the nature of all this limestone, its long history lost in prehistoric aeons of time, its different sections and layers and strata and qualities, and what it was that made one particular old quarry, like Saxon Quarry, superior in its stone-bearing power to all the rest. Perdita could not prevent the tears coming into her eyes as she saw how moved he was, and how his voice took on a tone so solemn and reverential when he talked of his native stone.

"It's extraordinary!" she thought. "I know I love Guernsey and its rocks; but *he* seems"—so far she gave her friend no human name, nor did she want to give him a name—"closer to this place than I've ever thought anyone *could* be to the place of their birth. I think it's this element in him, just as if he had a vein of oolite in his disposition, that makes him so far-off from everybody and yet so familiar with everybody."

Skald had to get out, when they were half way up the incline, to do
something to his spluttering engine, and the girl had a long opportunity
to meditate on his character. It was not at all Perdita's nature to
idealize where she loved. It was her nature on the contrary to be
critical to the limit; to analyse, to question, to sift out. Psychological
generalization was a passion with her and quite inseparable from the
working of her pessimistic mind.

"He's lacking in intellect," she said to herself now. "He's not a
thinker at all. He would have been happier, too, if he'd worked with
his hands as a quarryman than become—just what he has! This
jobbing business isn't what he was born for at all. It's the last thing
he was born for."

She stared happily, but with many wild fantastic thoughts, at the
man's great, dark profile as he bent over what he was doing.

"No," she thought, "he's not an intellectual person at all. He's a
bit stupid. In fact he's worse than stupid. He's pig-headed. But one
thing about him does please me so *very* much! He's neither ashamed
of his lack of culture nor affectedly proud of it. He just *is* what he is,
and lets it go."

Perdita's generalizations about the nature of the man to whom she
was prepared to give herself, body and soul, were really pretty shrewd.
Of course had she seen him with his book-shop friend and seen him
submitting so patiently to a prolonged study of "Middlemarch", she
might have got a new light on his desire to be cultivated, if not to be
intellectual, but it was a significant thing that during the very earliest
hours of these first twenty-four hours of their real acquaintance she
detected so clearly that it was to be her destiny to feel herself as much
cleverer than the man she loved as she was less clever than Mr. and
Mrs. Cobbold.

Having successfully dealt with the infirmity in the Slug's belly, the
Jobber clambered back by her side and they went lumbering on. At the
top of the hill he brought the truck to a deliberate stop and proudly
called upon his Guernsey friend to contemplate the vast sea-and-land
landscape spread out before them. He showed her the White Horse
and the White Nose. He showed her Hardy's Monument and
Maiden Castle. He showed her St. John's Spire and the outline of the
Nothe. He showed her the long line of Chesil Beach, curving away

in a vast, unending half-circle towards the low-hanging mists of the legendary West.

"By Dum," he cried, "I can't tell what it is about this view that stirs me up so! That old church-spire is nothing in itself. Those old Nothe forts covered with grass aren't anything. Sandsfoot isn't a real castle at all. And yet there's something about all these things, when you see 'em like this that just bowls you out—if you know what I mean!"

"I can see partly what you mean," said Perdita cautiously. "I can see that that Castle and that that Spire aren't as romantic as they *might* be, and I can see there's something striking rather than poetical about your White Horse on that hill. Do you suppose it's by looking at these things from earliest infancy that they've become what they've become to you?"

The Jobber stared at her blankly. His great hand rested on her thigh and his tobacco-scented breath hovered about her cheek and about the wisps of brown hair that began to slip—as they had done that night he first saw her, for it was a trick of her hair to fall loose like that—across the lobe of her ear.

"By . . . looking . . . at 'em so long, Perdita? No, no, sweetheart! They're what they are, these things—just look at Hardy's Monument now, with the sun on it!—independent of anything we do. No, it's something more than that. But *what* it is, by Dum, my precious, I can't tell 'ee!"

He squeezed her thigh yet more tightly as he leaned forward, staring over the wheel of the Slug at that familiar scene, and as he stared at his own land and at his own sea under that glimmering haze, they both became to him something unutterable, something written upon over and over and over with the hieroglyphs of the spirit, and he felt as if he were offering up to them at that moment the very flesh and blood of his love.

"Yes," he began again slowly, "I know the spire isn't anything particular . . . and it's not old either of course . . . and I know the old Nothe isn't anything . . . just a fort . . . a deserted fort . . . with turf over it . . . but . . . but when things have been in sight of each other for many years . . . you feel as if they were *connected* in some way . . . as if they were part of something . . . as if they were

... *making* something ... yes, by Dum! as if they were making
something."

He sank back as if exhausted by a mental effort that was beyond
his power.

Perdita snatched at the heavy hand that now lay inertly in her lap
and, bending her head, lifted it to her lips.

"I think I *do* understand what you mean about these things," she
said, "and if I stay much longer I shall understand a lot more. But I've
noticed already the way everyone talks about the Spire and the White
Horse and the Nothe and the Harbour-Bridge. I heard Mr. Muir
talking to Mr. Cobbold the other night about the shape of Portland
as he sees it from his window. It's quaint to think of *his* landscape
being your home and *your* landscape being his home."

The Jobber had his arm round her waist now, and as his fingers felt
the beating of her heart a great wave of tenderness for her went
vibrating through him.

"I have my left hand now," he thought, "on my Love's left
breast. Isn't there something about that in the Bible?"

But Perdita did not think of the Bible, or which of his arms was
round her, but she did think that she would have liked to tell him that
except for her uncle, for she had never learnt to dance, this was
actually the first time a man's arm had been round her waist.

"But I can't do it," she thought. "Yet it's funny that I can't! Am
I afraid he might think I was *odd*?"

Then as she looked at the outline of Weymouth, stretched before
them, with the Nothe at one extremity and St. John's at the other,
some vague, obscure, difficult thought began to revolve like a tortuous
serpent at the gateway of her brain. It was something that had to do
with the implication of what all these people said about their town's
landmarks and seamarks. It was a revelation to herself—but no! it had
escaped. She couldn't remember it. But she said to herself:

"I believe the way every strip of coast has come to look, after all the
tides and landscapes and earthquakes, is like a piece of ancient writing.
But that spire is a different thing, and the fort is a different thing. But
what came into my head just now included these as much as the shores
and bays! It had to do with the whole look of a place being in some
way—What ... was ... it?"

When they got within half-a-mile of the Head, which stood in the loneliest spot on the westerly coast of the island, the Jobber jumped out of the truck and told her in a very authoritative voice to remain where she was while he went on a little way to see someone and make some enquiries. Nothing suited Perdita better than to be left alone for a while, with the weight of all the accumulated mass of recent impressions fresh in her mind, and no sooner had his jersey-clad figure vanished behind a great pile of stones than she climbed out of the "Slug" herself and scrambled on to the top of the wall that bordered the road. Here she made herself as comfortable as she could.

"He has yet," she thought, "to become acquainted with my mania for climbing walls, trees, cliffs, fences, anything, in fact, where I can get a foothold!"

She had settled herself sideways along the top of the wall, with her back against a leafless elder-bush that had managed to get rooted in that stony place. Never had her mind been clearer than it was at this minute! She stared at a little patch of cold leaf'd, cold-stalk'd stone-crop that grew where her heels rested and she thought:

"I am as happy, at this moment, as I shall ever be in my life. He's gone to find out if we can stay the night at that Inn! He knows I'm ready for anything, and I am ready—for *anything?*"

She stared at the little greenish-yellow plant and at the grey stones out of which it grew.

"I must manage somehow to hold tight to this moment," she said to herself. "How tight that plant holds to that stone! But I feel in my bones that this affair of ours will not run smooth. He's not a man for quiet, established things. But it won't be our *love* that will end."

Her whole body grew taut, rigid, stiff, and her flexible face paled a little and took on a look—if there had been anyone there to note it—different from any she had ever worn. Perdita had a very small chin and a mouth that naturally fell open and drooped with a grievous droop at the corners. Her lower lip, red, and rather full, although a much dryer one than poor Peg Frampton's, drooped habitually also, and there were lines from her nostrils to her mouth of a very sorrowful kind, and other lines, too, beneath her eyelids, that answered to these in gloomy conspiracy, giving her whole face a curiously forlorn and abject expression.

But this eternal bond between them that they had now both come to recognize had brought out, since yesterday morning, when he came to High House, a change in the girl's face. Something about the bony structure of it, especially in brow and cheek-bones, dominated the rest, giving her a look that was stark and even a little bit stoical.

"Our love is no ordinary love," she thought. "We could quarrel fiercely, we could separate in blind anger, but nothing could ever really divide us, now we've once met."

Her thoughts sank deeper and deeper down into the nature of this eternalized moment, into the heart of the experience through which she was passing. The hardness of the wall, as with her body thus immobile she pressed the stones with her fingers, gave her the feeling that her soul was sinking into this vast promontory of oolite as into the shaft of a bottomless quarry.

"I'm glad I came straight to his home," she thought. "It's funny how I don't really admire him or respect him or even altogether *like* him!"

She gripped the stone with her fingers so hard that her knuckles went white. That bony structure of her face showed itself now in her death-stillness, as if it were her very skull seen through the transparency of her soft, weak, drooping fluctuating lineaments. Her intellect seemed clearer than it had ever been in her life before, and she derived a savage pleasure from tearing away every shred of sentiment, every tag of reverence from what she felt for this man.

"It's as if something of him were inside me and something of me were inside him. It's as if there were no need for him to take me, more than he has taken me already! It's as if when I hurt him I hurt myself and when he hurts me he hurts himself."

Her fixed gaze, with its new "skull-look" transforming her sorrowful features, seemed to penetrate the very roots of that stone-crop at her feet and plunge into the substratum of this stupendous sea-rock, into the foundation of it, into what lay fathoms-deep below the sea-surface.

"I'm sure I don't know whether people would call what we feel for each other 'being in love', or whether it's even passion. I think if he *does* take me tonight he'll do it clumsily, awkwardly, brutally, *and I shall be the same.* He doesn't seem to want to kiss me very much, and

I don't want to kiss him very much. It's as if we were both digging into each other's soul to find a self that was put there before we were born."

The Jobber came back highly elated from his visit to the Head with the news that they could have the very room that Cattistock and Tissty had had yesterday. Instead of annoying him, as might have been expected, it seemed, by some quirk of his queerly-constituted nature, to please him to think of this coincidence.

"I'm going to take you now to the Beale," he announced, "where the light-house is and where you can see the Race."

She had jumped down from the wall to meet him feeling very cramped and stiff.

"Couldn't you leave the truck somewhere," she asked, "and let's walk a bit?"

He agreed willingly to this, and having disposed of the Slug in the sawing-yard of one of the quarries near the Head, hand in hand they set out through that windless afternoon. He skirted the little town of Easton and showed her a dusty field-path which he told her led to his parents' house.

"I first thought I'd take you there," he muttered. "But I changed my mind. You don't mind, do you?"

And there was actually a gleam of suspicion in the dark glance he darted at her. She shook her head, and then she heard him repeating under his breath that mystical line from the Book of Daniel that he was so fond of:

"A time and times and half a time."

"What's the matter with him?" she thought. "Why can't he be open with me in these little things? I'd far sooner *not* meet his father and mother today. Why couldn't he have asked me what I felt?"

But it had already—in these brief few hours of their coming together—established itself as a peculiarity of these two that they could recover from a divergence without the least tendency to sulk.

"Here's Last House!" cried the Jobber when they had gone some distance along a straight dusty road, bordered by the same monotonous stone walls that gave the whole place its character, "Here's where Sylvanus lives! I doubt if he can be back yet, for he hasn't a car, but isn't it just what you'd expect of that bloke?"

Perdita surveyed a dingy discoloured stucco wall, with a couple of symmetrical stone windows and a pair of cracked chimneys above them, looking like the pricked-up ears of a startled ass. Between the house and the road were heavy, massive, iron railings, and five cement steps led up to the door. Upon the surface of these steps both green moss and yellow lichen, in variegated patches of contrasting colour, were growing very freely. There were two cement posts with iron rings in them at the bottom of these steps, between which hung a rusty chain, firmly padlocked in the centre. By the side of this padlock someone had once, long ago, tied a luggage-label which, turned yellow with age, served as a sort of weather-vane for the snails that explored that desolate spot. And this luggage-label, as it stirred in the faint airs of this halcyon day, flickered almost imperceptibly north-north-west.

"He doesn't use his front-door very often," remarked the Jobber.

"*Never*, I should say," agreed Perdita.

Slowly they moved on past those deep-set staring windows and those melancholy asinine chimney-ears.

"It only needs the moustache," thought Perdita, "to be exactly like that great humbug. Does he bring *both* those girls up here with him? That's the sort of thing I used to hear about at home, but I hadn't supposed it went on in Weymouth."

The whole personality of Sylvanus, his tall form, his frayed clothes that looked as if he slept in them, his long, peaked parsnip-shaped head, those odious moustache-ends, and all the unctuous religiosity that flowed from him, returned to Perdita now as one of the most repulsive impressions she had ever received. She pulled at her companion's arm to get him away from this odious house.

The Jobber yielded to her pressure but as a matter of fact he would have liked at that second to stand much longer there, just as he was doing, staring at a tuft of dead, thick-feathered grasses that grew at one end of the steps and stirred even less than the luggage-label in that windless air.

"I've always seen grasses like that," he had been thinking—"they're common as dirt, too, but you don't always notice them!—when something important's going to happen. By Dum! it's funny that I should see them now! They make me feel that today could last

forever. They make me feel I'd be able to send the Dog down
without having to go down with him. They make me feel that
something at the end might even let me off settling the Dog! They
make me feel I'd seen them on some great moor in Wales or Scotland
where I'd gone for hours and hours and was numb and stiff and
hungry, but enjoying myself like a curlew."

But he let Perdita drag him on without protesting and before long
they came to that smooth level end of the Island called the Bill, where
there are two great lighthouses, one disused and one in use, and where
the land itself, reduced to a tongue, or rather to a flat-stretching beak
of narrow rock-floor, juts out, as the slippery, naked prow-deck of a
ship might do, over the gurgling, churning, dark-green water, and
offers the wayfarer a circumference of double horizons, one infinite
and one finite, both conveying an impression of boundlessness, but the
boundlessness of the one being physical and the boundlessness of the
other metaphysical.

The Jobber and Perdita made their way out, till they reached the
very end of this sea-jutting platform of solid rock. Here they found
themselves standing side by side upon what resembled some dancing-
floor of the sea-nymphs, so smooth it was, or the level tombstone of
some ancient sea-god. It was a floor upon which a herd of seals might
have lain down to sleep, shepherded by Proteus! It was dark brown
in colour, spotted with some variety of yellowish sea-lichen, and in
particular places its surface was roughened by living shell-fish that
clung tenaciously to it and by minute fossils whose indwelling entities
had perished millions of years ago. Under it the dark-green water
swirled and foamed and gurgled, and beyond it, below the tossed-up
surf—for the waters of Portland Bill were disturbed by other agencies
than the day's weather—there were endless whirlpools and revolving
maelstroms of green water. It was one of those spots where Nature
arrives at an extremity of contrast that suggests a sublime intention,
for while there was gathered up in that rocky floor, which itself was
about twenty feet long and about half that distance wide, the very
absolute of immobility, there was flung abroad in those breaking
waters the corresponding absolute of never-ceasing movement.
Standing upon this platform a person felt himself held by gravitation
to the very bed-rock of our planet's substance, whereas in that rushing

whirl of waters he was aware of gaping holes out of which jets of the aboriginal chaos kept bubbling up. But this was not all. As though she had been roused by some human challenge into putting forth all her powers, Nature had decreed that clean across this great floor of stone there should be a slit of about a foot wide! By bending down, as the Jobber now proceeded to do, and staring into this chasm, you realized that there was a confluence of two water-courses wrestling here, namely the current that swept *in*, towards the inmost wall of this sea-level cave, and the opposing current that swept *out*, towards the whirlpools of foam.

"Look here!" cried the Jobber. "Look down here!"

Perdita knelt by his side on the brink of this slit in their platform. She could feel a cold breath coming up from down there, like the breathing of a monstrous sea-beast. Lightly he encircled her waist with his arm.

"Not much chance," he said, "for anyone who was pitched down there!"

There was something, even to her ears, a little ghastly about the tone in which he used the word *pitched*. It suggested—as indeed was the case—that the man's murderous obsession was still paramount in the deeper levels of his mind. She snatched off the flexible hat she wore and bent down a little, bent in fact, for his arm was tight round her, so low that her mouth touched the edge of the crevasse. Suddenly the arm that held her began to tremble, not just gently, but violently. Instead of frightening her this trembling gave Perdita a strangely reckless feeling. And it made her cry under her breath,

"I belong to you! I belong to you!"

But it was irresistibly borne in upon the Jobber, with one of those cold, shuddering certitudes that strike us as if a wedge of appalling reality of a different dimension altogether from any as yet known in our experience were being thrust into our warm human senses, that the thing to do, "when he had given the Dog his settler", was to come here and end it for himself by one leap into this firmamental crack. He thought of this quite calmly for all his shivering, for his mind had been able to turn the next twelve hours into something like twelve days, so that though his body trembled at the thought of ending it, his mind managed to blow *tomorrow* clean away, as if it were one of the airy foam-wisps that kept turning round and round as they danced on that platform before melting into nothing.

"That would finish us!" he whispered to her now. "And it would solve a great deal and spare us a world of fuss, if we tumbled into that froth! How long would our consciousness last? A minute? Two minutes? You couldn't swim a stroke! I'd just hold you tight and think to myself, 'I've got her. I've had my day'. Listen to that noise down there. Do you catch what it's like? *It's like flames!* Aye? *Isn't* it like flames?"

But he gave her no time to verify this startling assertion. With a sudden swing he lifted her up on to her feet again and, still holding her round the waist, made her look sea-ward, where, a league or two from where they stood, the surface of the sea seemed convulsed under some invisible tyranny. He now began a confused account, in terms far too nautical for her to follow, of the precise causes of these whirling foam-gulfs. She gathered that it was the meeting-place of two far-drawn sea-tides, one travelling eastward and one westward.

"In old days this was a terrible spot," he said, "but the light-house has changed everything."

They both stared at that churning expanse. The windless weather seemed to make little difference to its sea fury.

"Not much hope for the old Cormorant there," he said, "if she once got caught. She'd spin round like a top. There's a sea-hole under there, that goes down like a shaft. Think of those dark, slippery under-sea walls! Do'ee suppose our two skeletons would go on whirling round and round down there, when the fishes had picked 'em shell-white?"

They walked back along a high cliff-path on the western side of the promontory so that they did not pass Last House again, for which Perdita was heartily glad. After seeing that abode of Sylvanus' with its chained-up front-door, her prejudice against him had grown.

"I can't make out why Jerry is so nice to him," she thought. And aloud she said, "It's funny how much I dislike that brother of Mr. Cobbold's. I shouldn't mind if I never saw him again!"

The Jobber's great mahogany-coloured countenance became a little blank. He experienced that vague uneasiness with which men hear the strong opinions of women about other men. Finally the only answer he could discover to make to this arbitrary outburst of feminine criticism was to squeeze her slender figure tightly against him and murmur a mumbled question as to what was wrong with the fellow except his crazy notions of religion?

"Maybe you'll feel before long," he said, "the same shrinking from me! But come now. Tell me straight out what's wrong with him."

"I think he's the kind of person," she replied gravely, "who could commit a murder and go on without minding it *or being afraid of his victim.*"

"What would you do, Perdita, if I told you *I* had committed a murder?"

His voice sounded so vibrant that she turned quickly and looked at him.

"Don't talk nonsense!" she said. And then because she did not like the look on his face, "*There!* did you see that little brownish moth cross those stones? Isn't it too early for them up here? This place must be deadly cold at night."

"The Island's a great place for moths!" he boasted proudly. "You should see them in the summer. There are more moths than butterflies. I suppose it's the sea."

They went on in silence for nearly half a mile and then—

"By Dum!" he exclaimed, and stooping down he picked a small, glaucous-leaved plant at the edge of their path.

"What's that?" she asked.

"I'll tell you in a moment."

Again they walked in silence for another half mile, and while they walked Perdita looked about in vain for any other specimen of the thick stalk and strangely-shaped leaves which her companion was carrying so carefully. Every now and then, as they walked in silence, his arm round her waist, the Jobber would start humming, not very musically the words:

> "Awake, O Reinian, awake!
> Awake, O Reinian, ho!"

"Is that an old song?" she asked when the repetition of these monotonous syllables, mumbled so close to her ear, began to make her nervous. "It sounds," she went on, "as if it were a sign to some

smuggler friend waiting down there! You haven't got Mr. Trot
with the Cormorant waiting for us, have you?"

As she spoke she swerved at the edge of the cliff and peered over the
steep edge. But he pulled her back and again they went on and again
he began humming:

"Awake O Reinian, awake!"

"I mustn't let things like this get on my nerves," she thought.
"He's so inhuman that he hums and drums when anyone's with him,
as if he were by himself!"

At last they came to a place where half-a-century ago there had
been a land-slide. The result of this had been that about six feet below
the top of the cliff there was a broad, level ledge along the brink of
which grew several sturdy bushes forming a natural but quite effective
barrier against the precipice. But this was not all. There had been
brought down by this land-slide, which must have occurred in one
terrific subsidence a large and very curiously shaped stone composed
of the same oolite as the rest of the island but looking as if some early
race of men with prehistoric tools had at one time worked upon it.
Beyond the ledge where crouched this singular stone, Perdita as she
lifted her eyes, saw the whole level expanse of the West Bay, stretching
off towards Cornwall and the Atlantic.

The late afternoon sun, from a western sky that looked as if it were
made of one piece of unbroken gold-leaf, drew a motionless golden
path across the dark-blue water, producing a curious effect of elemental
opacity, and also, in the emphasis upon blue and gold an effect of some
ritualistic selection. Had the philosopher of Trigonia House been
with them at that moment he would doubtless have recalled to their
minds what Spengler says of the Magian Culture. Perdita felt that
this was exactly the kind of watery floor which the sea-god of her
girlhood would have crossed to reach her, and it was natural enough
for a mind like hers, engraved since infancy by fantastic images, to
imagine such a Being now—in reality an immensely enlarged Jobber
Skald—striding away towards that far-off horizon where the wide-
arching goldenness touched the dark-blue pavement. But the sun,
though it was low enough to create this Magian mystery was still a
long way from the sea's surface, and it threw a light, a glamour, a

transformation over the ledge and over the fallen stone. Such land-slide-ledges are often, above all other terraqueous spots, friendly and comforting to wayfarers. Warm are they beyond what one would expect, and for some reason both sea-ward winds and land-ward winds sweep over them without ruffling them, so that the grass-snakes and the adders, as well as the slow-worms and the lizards, appreciate their qualities even better than man.

"Come on down!" said the Jobber, after a pause, when he had given the girl time to take in the beauty of this ledge, poised per-pendicularly so high above the sea and yet illuminated by the horizontal sun.

He helped her to descend, and she soon discovered that the presence of that stone Idol, if such it were, and of those elder-bushes, entirely prevented any of the giddiness she might otherwise have felt from the height above the shore. Ensconced on this ledge they could hear clearly the monotone of the sea and the cries of the gulls seemed nearer to them there than on the top of the cliff.

"I chopped those out!" said the Jobber as Perdita laid her hand on some indentations resembling steps that marked the side of the stone. "Can you see what it is?" he asked her.

And then the girl did see that in the slow process of aeons of time this stone had been carved into a tremendous torso of love. Man's nakedness and woman's nakedness locked together in the primordial creation of life were suggested here by the straining together of god-like flanks and thighs. Neither of the two figures possessed arms, head or shoulders. Neither possessed legs below the knee. And yet the effect of this huge organic work of art was neither base, nor gross, nor bestial; but god-like, cosmogonic, life-creating.

The old Cornish ship's purser, Phileas Wane, who had married a Guernsey native, would have been puzzled to see the look of radiant happiness which illuminated his niece's face as she stood with this man looking at this shameless stone! Love-encounters the most absolute are those between characters who are devoid of the more supple, more whimsical, more civilized sense of proportion. The Jobber and Perdita were alike in this, that all the various gradations and fine shadings of our middle-class sense of decency and humour and common sense were lacking in them, and they were proud that they were lacking! In Mediæval times it is likely enough that both these quaint persons with their archaic attitudes would have been very happy. But exasperated by the clever cruelties of Modern Science and hunted by the hostility of people like Mrs. Cobbold and Sippy Ballard, they were both forced to take refuge in their own secret fancies, and it had been just as if Perdita had found a piece of her soul lodged in this "Brown Adam", and he had found a piece of *his* soul lodged in this Channel-Island waif, when they met that first evening on the sea-front. The phrase "children of nature" applies, as a matter of fact, very rarely to any civilized individuals. But Perdita and the Jobber, as they allowed their feeling for each other to steal new stimulus from this stone of the centuries, were as little under the domination of the society to which they belonged as a Neanderthal couple would have been in a community of Cro-Magnons.

"I chopped out those steps!" repeated the Jobber complacently. "You can climb up there now and join *those two*. It isn't anything to have done of course, and no one seems to have noticed it since I did it."

She ran her fingers over the indentations. The stone was about ten feet high. It was clear to her that contact with its mysterious antiquity had been a profound pleasure to him.

"When I was little," said the Jobber, "no one used to come to these cliffs except people after birds' eggs and a few moth-collectors. I didn't find this stone by myself. A gentleman from the White Nose who used to come over here in those days to see the light-house keeper's daughter told me about it, and then I took to coming here on Sundays. Father lived in Easton then and the path up there didn't exist. But after what that gentleman said I used to come here often. There's not a stone in the isle that's had more foolishness thought into it and chopped into it than this stone. I've worked here so long on summer afternoons that there was an old sea-gull who used to take me for an idiot and came so near I could see his eye. Puzzled he was at my goings on, and not quite satisfied! He had his eye on me all the time."

Perdita surveyed the rough love-torso above her head.

"I'd *like*," she said meditatively, "I'd *like* extraordinarily well to climb up there with you. There's a stone in Guernsey—Men and women used to sit on it, and it brought them luck. Uncle and I sat on it once and it brought *him* luck, for he died the next month."

"Is it luck to die?" asked the Jobber, while that lethalized and chloroformed *tomorrow* pressed its chin, a chin with a mole upon it, against the window-pane of his mind. Perdita laughed happily.

"Well," she said, "give me your hand and I'll risk death!" And she thought in her heart, "Who knows if it wouldn't be the luckiest thing that could happen to me if I *did* die after today!"

He helped her up and they balanced themselves as best they could, on those entwined limbs.

"Now," he said, taking the little plant into both his hands. "Let's try our luck with this!"

"What do we do?"

"Eat it," he replied laconically. "Eat it—*mouth and mouth about!* I *was* lucky to find a bit up here. There's lots of it down on Chesil, but it's rare on the Island."

Perdita, propping herself with some difficulty where she sat, looked at the little glaucous plant in her friend's brown fingers.

The Jobber himself seemed hard put to it to keep his balance. Twice, nearly dropping the plant, he clutched at the edge of their stone seat; nor did he dare to touch the girl for fear of bringing them both down.

Finally, their balance obtained, they turned to each other and exchanged a long clinging look. Perdita, woman-like, smiled as they stared at each other in their shaky position, but the Jobber, who was not one for smiling, remained as sombrely grave as he used to be on those old Sundays when the sea-gull took him for an idiot. It was one of those occasions when Chance having blindly prepared for a dramatic climax through aeons of time, seems itself to emerge like a palpable presence, out of the criss-cross accidents of its whirling possibilities and to survey its achievement. The queer-shaped block of oolite, the hint of "the gentleman from the White Nose", the ancient land-slide, the accident that this slim figure in her black cloth dress, and this bony figure in his jersey and loose trousers—a male skeleton and a feminine skeleton—should be there at all, with that particular plant clutched in his fingers, were all elements that had prepared for the haggard-rapturous stare with which these two now embraced. In this stare there was no voluptuousness: there was no gaiety. They shared the gravity of two animals drinking at a longed-for stream.

"Well," he said, breaking the spell, "shall we eat it?"

He stripped the plant of its three small leaves and flung the stalk violently away. Nor was this the first time that Perdita had noticed that when the Jobber threw anything away he always flung it as if with the words—"That's the end of you!" But she obediently put the little leaves into her mouth and proceeded to bite them up. This proceeding was by no means a pleasure either for touch or taste; but she chewed them gingerly while a certain amount of their astringent juice trickled down her throat. Then she smiled at him and asked him what this plant was.

"Why—don't 'ee know? Don't they have 'em in your Isles?"

He held his broad palm towards her and she took out the little chewed fragment from between her lips and placed it in his hand. With one of his curious solemn chuckles that were as totally devoid of any human humour as if a sea-lion were to display levity, the Jobber clapped his great hand to his face and swallowed the morsel at a gulp.

The next thing that occurred was not very surprising, although it was a shock to them both. The disturbance of exchanging the leaves upset their balance, and Perdita, finding herself slipping, clutched at his jersey, with the result that as she slid she pulled him down. Luckily the grass was soft at the stone's foot, so they got no hurt. They had rolled round, clinging tight to each other; so that finally, when they reached the earth the girl found herself in what the poet calls "the very lists of love". The Jobber however, did not forget that they could be clearly seen by anyone following the cliff's edge above them. He held her beneath him long enough, all the same to kiss her as she had never been kissed before. And lying there on that sun-scented grass Perdita responded to his embrace. She was a grown girl. She was no child. But this was her first experience of what it was to be pressed against a man's body. What he was feeling aroused responsive desire in her own senses. But the Jobber knew the danger of their position, so exposed from above, and scrambling to his feet he lifted her up by her wrists with a powerful swing of his arms.

"Well!" he panted, "that proves it's true!"

She gazed at him with a countenance flushed, ruffled, discomposed, but radiantly happy.

"What proves what?" she gasped.

The Jobber wagged his head and then nodded at her, still breathing hard.

"Why didn't 'ee *really* know what that plant was?" he returned. "It's Sea-Holly! 'Pilgrims of Love' and 'Brides of Quietness' used to come to Portland and Chesil Beach from all over England in old days. Old wives in Chesilton in *my* memory used to make a concoction out of this that brides would put into their tea. You're mine now altogether, Perdie, since we've swallowed Sea-Holly under the 'Clipping Stone'! 'Twas 'Clipping' *he* used to say, though its called 'Cuddling-Stone' on the Island."

Their sunset walk to "The Head" after this incident at the place so dear to "the gentleman from the White Nose", was so happy that for the third time that day the Jobber came near to forgetting the Chesil-Beach pebble which he still carried in his trousers-pocket. Though in her excitement at the moment the girl did not notice it, she found afterwards that she had received a bruise in her thigh as they fell, from that primitive weapon concealed by her lover. He had feared lest, with her superior social usages and more delicate refinements, she might be embarrassed by the fuss that the Gadgets would be sure to make over her, but it turned out quiet otherwise. Those moments when they lay at the foot of the Clipping Stone seemed to have inspired her with something of her lover's own easy indulgence and careless tolerance. It is true that for the Jobber, thinking of the morrow—for after all it was with a condemned man she was to be bedded that night—there were several occasions when he fell into miserable abstraction but whatever he might be feeling the girl noticed nothing of it.

And the Jobber was rendered proud as well as relieved by the attitude taken by the family at the Head. It was clear they were deeply impressed by Perdita's manners and ways, and it was also clear that they were honestly very happy for him that he should have the good luck of such a companion. They accepted the pretence that this was her bridal night just as sympathetically as if it really had been, but while John kept his grosser jokes to himself Ellen lavished her yearning for romance upon this quiet girl's head. 'Melia and Celia were so excited that they actually changed rôles, 'Melia turning the pages of "Percy's Reliques", and Celia wondering whether it wouldn't be nice to put a glass of "Meliodka" on the little table by Perdita's bed.

Long after Perdita was sound asleep the Jobber's mind went whirling on in the same blood-stained circle.

"It's God!" he said once to himself.

But what he called "God" was really his life-illusion, a sullen imperative that sucked up the whole fatal necessity of his nature. Half-awake, and yet not normally awake, he kept falling into a feverish delirium, in which the fact that he had possessed this girl at his side mingled their identities. It was not merely himself who kept striking the Dog with the stone he held, it was a double personality, made up of some incredible fusion of their bodies. It was something thickened, fortified, charged, with the spirit and the blood of both of them. And as he held the unconscious girl, who every now and then "made sweet moan" in her sleep, his delirious fantasy turned this new Being that was them both into the pressure of the fatal imperative that he kept calling "God". It never once occurred to him that his original motives, righteous indignation, his long-nourished hatred, his sense of the man being a Power of Evil, had been totally transformed since yesterday morning when he went to High House.

Once when Perdita in her sleep threw her arm confidingly across his body he felt such infinite tenderness well up within him that he had a moment of relative lucidity in which he deliberately tried to realize what his life would be *if he let Cattistock alone*. What yawned for him *then* was a chasm in his central self as wide as that slit in the Beale-rock, a chasm in that soul of his soul which made him what he was in his own eyes. *Not* to strike down this man seemed to him like jumping to safety from a sinking craft, a craft of which he was the master; saving his own skin by a denial of his living honour, more than of his honour, of his uttermost life-sensation, of the integrity of the very "I" in his central consciousness. It was as if, in the full public gaze, he were to let the Cormorant, with Bum Trot on board go down to perdition, while he swam off, to start, a new life—a wretched, meaningless dishonoured, coward's life!

As he tossed from side to side in that windless, starlit silence, with the sea-airs from the unruffled West Bay flowing in through their open window, there came moments when his hold on objective reality grew faint, and when a strange exultation seized him, made up of his love's lost maidenhead and his passionate possession of her, made up of the wild mixing of their blood; and in the tide of this exultation he felt as if blood and death and the blow with which he would rid the world of the Dog, were all part of some mystical transaction, beautiful, terrible, miraculous, that he had only to carry to its appointed end, to redeem all. It must have been about three o'clock when this final exultation came upon him. For a long time he had been answering to something in that feverish half-sleep, to something which held out a clue, a solution. Once he had disturbed the girl by a start and a jerk and a convulsed groan.

"Blood ... blood," he had heard her repeat; but she had sunk again into unconsciousness; and he took it for granted that she had no notion of what he was suffering in his mind.

But this "something" in his half-sleep which had been the clue to everything—what was it? It had seemed to him a complete solution, turning everything to peace, to satisfaction . . . but *what* was it? When he recalled it now, in this cold, clear, deadly lucidity into which he had roused himself, it seemed to him as though it had been the Clipping Stone! But how could the Clipping Stone be a clue to anything— least of all to what he was going to do to the Dog? The Jobber began to suffer. A cold, grey, not-to-be-pushed-off wedge of desolate misery seemed to come in now through that window opposite him. He felt as if in the act of possessing Perdita he had lost his main-spring. All was done, all was over. To sink down upon blood and ashes and let what must be be—that was all that remained. He now felt towards the killing of Cattistock as if it were a private "debt of honour" to the people of his home and their heritage of freedom. If it wasn't for this he might—for Perdita's love hung deadly sweet about him—have tried to live out the rest of his days as so many cowards do. He shifted his position, and sitting up a little, he squeezed his pillow into a shapeless ball and thrust it behind his neck, between his scalp and the woodwork of the bed. There was, somewhere in the sky, he knew, a shapeless moon at the beginning of her last quarter, but he could not see it in the little oblong space of sky which was all his window revealed. But a diffused whiteness which came from this dying moon threw a corpse-like pallor on Perdita's face, as he watched it now, turned so trustingly towards him; while her even and quiet breath, like the wistful air that had stirred in that lonely tuft of grass outside the barred door of Last House, seemed ready to carry the Jobber's mind, as he watched her, to some far-off Limbo, where such purposes as his melted away.

But he could not respond! Stark, grey, and cold, the lucid wedge of his self-imposed imperative brought him to the brink of despair. Here was his girl, her face turned towards him in confiding sleep, one thin arm, bare of the coverlet, lying exposed, a faint twitching movement, even as he watched her, still troubling her limbs. How could he tell her what he had laid upon himself to do: this penalty of losing the taste of food, of drink, of sleep, of the sea, of life itself, and *of her?* He must wake her. He must tell her, and he must do it now!

Her brown hair was trailing in a long, neat braid across her pillow, and her face, as she lay towards him, bore on its lineaments what struck him at that hour as being the enviable security of the faces of the dead. She wore nothing but her slip, but there was a knot of dark blue ribbon round the end of her braid, which had been all there was left for little Sue to provide, since it had been allotted to 'Melia to lend her her comb, and to Celia to lend her her bedroom slippers.

But the girl now woke with a start, and the first look of bewilderment that crossed her face at reassembling the events that had led to her lying in this strange room changed to a look of dismay at seeing his roused and watchful pose.

"It isn't morning? No, no. I can *see* it's still night. What's the matter? It isn't *nearly* morning!"

Her eyes had opened wide. There was moonlight enough to see she was not smiling. But neither did she look frightened. She just woke to consciousness to perform the natural, womanly act of beating back the movement of time.

"Haven't you been asleep?"

"No, my beautiful. I haven't slept a wink. You're perfectly right there. I've been——"

He stopped because it was not very nice to see the droop that came at the corners of her mouth or the wretched misery-lines that dragged at her tender sleep-relaxed cheeks.

"What is it?" she cried. "You're not going yet, are you? Is it all over? In stories it always says that men want to be off and away. They get up and put on their hunting clothes—and—'give their bridle-reins a shake!' "

She stopped. She could not help smiling at the word "bridle-reins".

But the Jobber gave her a look now as much as to say "I'll stop your damned feminine nonsense," and jumping out of bed he began impatiently fumbling about above the table where the matches and candle were. In this process he knocked down upon the floor the little glass of "Meliodka" which had been placed at their bed's head. Violently striking the floor this glass broke into a hundred bits, and a curiously pungent and very aromatic fragrance diffused itself through the room.

"There goes Celia's drink!" cried Perdita, lifting herself up a little in the bed.

She seemed to feel that even brides, at the third hour of their new day had to bestir themselves when things were broken and spilt.

But the Jobber, who had now laid his fingers on the matches, struck a light in a silence so portentous that it reduced Meliodka to its proper place in a world of blood and iron. But none of this grimness saved the man from receiving a sideways thrust when he noticed the way the grease had dripped down the edge of the candle. This had been caused by the fact that, teasing the girl, who wanted to blow out the light, he had pushed it away from her, while the air from the window kept blowing the flame sideways.

"Oh, Skald, whatever shall we tell her?"

This rather wistful voice from the bed as he squeezed the spilt candle grease away from the side of the candle only increased the Jobber's stubbornness. He replaced the spluttering candle upon the table with an intense solemnity. Then throwing upon her a look that was full of tragic reproach he went over to the door where he had hung his trousers the evening before. He had slept naked that night and that he had done this was not devoid of a curious appropriateness, because in Perdita's girlish fancies about a Being who was a kind of merman, and came to her out of the sea, the mysterious lover was always naked. Thus, as with the single candle between them, with its tiny heart of blue fire and its tremulous yellow pyramid that kept bending towards the wall as the night airs wafted it and ruffled it and spread it out like a flickering fan, the Jobber moved across to the door, Perdita could not help admiring his mould. His shoulders were so broad, his hips, flanks, and buttocks so thin, that his form did actually resemble a classic figure on an archaic frieze. As he unhooked his trousers he received yet another of these heart-sickening tragic stabs, for he could remember how his hand was so trembling with excitement as he hung these up, that he couldn't as he always did in his own house unbutton his braces from them and hang them separately. He didn't put them on even now, but he thrust his hand into one of the pockets and brought out that heavy grey-blue pebble, of the bruise from which, after sliding down with him from the Clipping Stone Perdita was already conscious.

"See that?"

He held it out to her across the side of the candle's flame. She looked at the stone; and then looking at his face she realized in an intuitive flash the connection between this object and all those dark rumours of his threats against his enemy that hitherto she had put out of her mind. Why hadn't she realized before? Women are sometimes much less subtle, much easier to deceive than men! Till this very second of time she had not the least suspicion that he was intending to leave her before dawn, not the least notion that all this long day, all the time since he met her by the Jubilee Clock, he had been brooding over this projected violence. The first shock of it—for her brain moved fast—when he held out that stone, was to fling her back, like a vessel striking ice beneath its keel, upon the cold substratum of her pride and her pessimism.

"What do you mean?" she asked.

"Feel its weight," he said, "for where I go you go, and what I do you do."

Her cheeks went white and she sat straight up in the bed.

"I shall do nothing of the sort!" she declared. "And what's more if you don't throw that thing away—"

She stopped, biting her lip, while a frown of intense concentration puckered her forehead and her unseeing gaze was fixed not on his face but on his navel.

"It doesn't matter much to either of us *now*," he said, "*what* you do. There would have been a time! But we're one now."

She leapt out of the bed and faced him.

"Throw that stone away!" she said in a low voice. "*No!*—don't you dare touch me!"

"Take care!" he cried in panic, conscious of the broken Meliodka glass.

And without a moment's hesitation he swung her off her feet and back on the bed. She gathered herself together, shaking from head to foot. She sat up and looked at him steadily, hugging her knees. Not only her body was trembling. Her teeth were chattering. Curious lines in her face appeared that he had never seen before, and her eyes grew larger and wilder every second.

"Take yourself off," she moaned. "I don't want to see your face. It's monstrous, this thing you're going to do."

She must have grown aware of something in his look that overcame her completely, something that was like a stricken animal, something helpless and pleading, something bewildered as well as hurt; for her anger melted out of her, and an intolerable tenderness for him surged through her, like a wave through a sea-sponge. She stretched out her hand towards him.

"Skald," she whispered hoarsely. "Skald, my dearest love, I'll go with you everywhere, always, through everything, if you throw that stone away, if you give this madness up!"

She suddenly realized that his eyes had grown small and that his cheeks had grown puffy from sleeplessness. He now opened and shut his mouth like a great dusky-armoured sturgeon.

"All Chesil Beach is behind that stone," he said.

"All the salt sea," she retorted, "is with me to bury it where it belongs! Give this up, give this up, you don't know what you're doing!"

Both her thin arms were stretched out to him now.

"Don't torment me, woman," he said. "I've got to do it. I'll go down too, you may be sure of that. They shan't catch me! Nor you nor mother nor dad'll have any disgrace. The Dog'll be gone, and the Jobber'll be gone. That'll be all!"

"But our love, Skald, our love—is *that* nothing? Listen, Skald! It may be little to you, but do you think I can go on, as I was, without you? Do you think I could bear it?"

But even while they were talking he was feverishly putting on his clothes and by the time she uttered the words "bear it", his trousers were on and the stone was in its old place.

"John and Ellen will see that you get safe back," he said, and now to her consternation she realized that he had his jersey on and was lacing up his boots.

Each new stage in his dressing was like the pause in a march to an execution. He was dressed completely now and was standing, terribly still, in the middle of their chamber.

"If you can't bear it," he said, in a voice that quavered and shook, "with me and the Dog gone, by Dum! do 'ee think *I* can bear it, to be a talker, a *talker*, and hear the Dog jeering, and all pubs in the town jeering. No, no, no, my girl. I was awake thinking about it all night, and I tell you when there's a man like the Dog to be brought down, the only way is to go down with him. Don't 'ee see, Perdie, my little Perdie, I should be a laughing stock forever, if after so much talk I let him go?"

There rushed through Perdita's whole being now a surging torrent of anger against this man, standing there before her, this man who actually was weighing the opinions of friends and enemies, pot-houses and Peninsular Lodges, in the balance with such a thing as their love, the life they could have together—the life that was to end tonight.

"How can you—" she began fiercely, but a speechless amazement took the place of her anger and the words died on her lips.

She felt, trickling down, drop by drop, upon her heart from their eternal cistern of futility, the old, cold deadly poison of her familiar hopelessness. They had had their happiness—for just twenty hours! And meanwhile totally unknown to this girl in the bed and to this man obstinately condemning both her and himself out of his wicked "Hubris" as Homer would say, the measureless starlit heavens above the silent stone roof of the Sea-Serpent's Head were slowly crossed, several hours before dawn, by a long procession of small white clouds.

And as if in occult confederacy with these clouds, by flying in the opposite direction, three large migratory birds, such as few Portland dwellers could have identified, passed swiftly, one behind another, with flapping soundless wings, over the Head's chimney. At all spots on the earth's surface, in these hours when the life-pulse is lowest, every slightest material movement is accentuated to an impressive degree, and rendered fatal and significant, like a solitary football in some vast empty universe.

Simultaneously with the passing of that procession of clouds and those unknown migratory birds across the spaces above the Head's stone roofs, the raised voices in the guest-room of the Gadgets seemed to disturb, though nothing articulate could be caught, for the walls were thick, but the psychic vibration of the talk, the quiet repose of 'Melia and Celia who shared the same bed. For both the girls, stirring in their sleep, murmured confused and troubled nonsense, but there was no one to listen to or try to interpret it. Ellen Gadget, however, in the room next the girls, rose on her elbow and whispered to John, who, like his daughters, had been talking in his sleep:

"Did 'ee hear summat, me precious marrow?"

But all the answer she got for bothering the landlord of the Head was a sulky growl:

"Get thee to thee's wone side, 'ooman; ye be shoving I over, ye fool, to bed's bloody edge!"

When in cold blood human beings recall the frantic agitations they make one another go through there is a curious tendency for the playing of strange tricks with Time. Human emotion seems as if it had the peculiarity of drawing Time in, or stretching Time out, like a telescope between the fingers of a child; so that an hour becomes five minutes or five minutes becomes an hour, independently of the glory or shame of clocks.

"I . . . will . . . not . . . let . . . you . . . go!"

How did the reverberation of this cry of Perdita's in her own ears get transformed into so many things? How did it get transformed into a cold, wet stickiness, under her feet, that, in the state she was in, seemed to her to be blood? How did it get transformed into the thud of her own head against the floor? How did it become the unbolting of the door downstairs and the starting up to a wild series of explosions of the Slug's machine? How did it become the bursting into her room of three white-faced, white-robed, white-footed young girls? How did it become the voice of John Gadget saying to Ellen Gadget:

"Better leave she to she's self, Ellen, and get fires lit and kettles on! She'll be all right present! 'Tis Jobber Skald's little way to curse and to threat Mr. Cat'stock. Us do know thik little way, and that 'un means naught, and never *have* meant aught; being only the man's way of relieving his feelings; but pore Missy Wane, being a stranger, though she *be* Jobber Skald's girl, be unaccustomed, as you might say, to thik wold zong what 'a hollers and zings about killing of the good gentleman. What made him drumble her head on floor, say ye? I knows well what made him act so! 'Twere because she thought his leaving of her afore dawn were a cruelty to a bedded sweetheart. I knowed 'a was leaving, and I knowed what 'a had to do, too! 'A had to take a fine load of fish for Mr. Witchit to Sherborne for one o' they School Festies. I do know what's what, Ellen; for 'a told I, his wone self. 'A mighty fine load of fish,' 'a says; 'and I've got to drop some wondrous mackerel,' 'a says, 'on me way, as I goes by Chickerel'!"

It was one of the things Perdita remembered afterwards that she had, at this juncture, enough heart left to be glad it was Sue, rather than either of the elder girls, who was left to scrape up the broken glass from the floor and to see that "her had a few sticks in she's grate zet a-vire".

She lay on her back, stretched out perfectly straight and still, with her sheets, attended to by Sue's silent care, tucked neatly in, and folded smoothly under her chin. She remained with her thoughts numb, inert, dazed, quiescent, in a species of half-sensual, half-mystical trance, recalling the passion of their love. Then—as sturdy little Sue, with tumbled hair and sleep-swollen face, kneeling before the grate, caused the sticks to crackle and send forth an exquisite-smelling smoke, which the dawn-wind, blowing up from the sea, carried to her pillow— the thought came to her with a certain surprise that it had not come to her before—

"But I can—always—die—too."

11

SYLVANUS COBBOLD

The morning of February the Twelfth, as it dawned upon Weymouth and Portland, was even warmer than the preceding one. It seemed as if nature were bent upon making up to the inhabitants of the two boroughs and their adjoining promontory for the violent mood in which she had disturbed the elements on the day of storm.

Curiously opposite were the local comments upon this second fine day, when it became manifest that the sun was intending to shine more and more warmly as the hours went by. Both in the trading districts and in the lodging-houses and the villas, both in the spacious Georgian apartments of Belvidere and in the small houses that adjoined the dingy mansion of Dr. Girodel, there was the same quaint divergence between the reaction of the men and the reaction of the women to this auspicious weather. The women, rich and poor, with complete unanimity, congratulated the Creator of all things on having realized, as *they* did, what a notable day this was, being the day of Mr. Cattistock's marriage; whereas the men with equal unanimity expressed satisfaction that the sky should be cloudless on the one day of the week when the shops and business-houses of the town closed their shutters in the early afternoon.

Awaking early—not, it may well be believed, on Mr. Cattistock's account, but on his own—Magnus let himself out of Miss Le Fleau's front door, without disturbing Martha, who was having her first cup of tea in the kitchen, and proceeded hurriedly down the terrace in the opposite direction from Trigonia House. When he reached "Fernlands", which was the elegant, if inappropriate name bestowed by Corporal Dawson upon his final retreat, he regarded this quiet abode with that tender attention, different from any other in the world, with which a lover contemplates what he hopes will be his first ménage. With a wise caution that explained the fact that Magnus was the only permanently successful private-tutor in the town, he had boldly asked Miss Le Fleau—whom he found still up when he returned from Upwey—whether in return for a comparatively small rent—nothing comparable to what he now paid—he could go on using his room, just as it was, for his daily lessons, until she should find some other use for it. Well did the crafty scholar know that for the pleasure of keeping up their daily affectionate talks in her drawing room his father's old friend would have let him use that room, free of all cost, forever; but he knew the elder Muir would wish him to pay *something*, and so it was settled that he should pay every week the sum of five shillings.

"Will she like it here? Will she? Will she?" was his one thought now, as he paced up and down in front of "Fernlands", observing every detail of its pleasing exterior and noting with satisfaction that it had far the best "garden"—if you could judge by cultivation—in the whole terrace.

The much-travelled Corporal, having watered flower-pots under the eyes of half the Orient, was not one to mind being seen scattering a little manure—bought at the stables of the Burdon Hotel—at the edge of a sunny Weymouth pavement. Corporal Dawson's appearance in this minute railed-in enclosure, wherein he had whitened with his own hands every pebble-stone that bordered the path to the door, coincided with Magnus' fifth approach during that early hour from the East or from the West of the terrace. To find that his prospective lodger had the peculiarity of a sentinel on patrol was by no means unpleasant to the Corporal. Instead of making him suspicious, it reassured him. He leaned in his shirt-sleeves upon the little gate and prepared to enter into a rambling discussion as to how far the Nothe Fort was still in use, and how, when it was most in use, it compared with other historic defences of the country.

"Missis be still in bed, Sir. My first wife, Sir, were one to sleep late, and so be my last. My second were always up afore day-break. But she died in the first year of our union, Mr. Muir. 'Twas in Singapore she left me."

The Corporal sighed; while Magnus, whose mind was all hazy-dazy with thoughts of Curly, concluded that the old soldier was accusing Providence of rewarding slug-a-beds with longevity, while early risers were cut down in their prime.

"I'm afraid," he remarked with a rather embarrassed smile, "that my young lady will be more like your present wife than like your second one, for she says she finds it very hard to wake up in the morning."

Saluting the Corporal warmly, if absent-mindedly, Magnus now crossed the road, stepped up upon the white-washed edge of the esplanade, where little, massive, squat posts with holes through the middle of them, indicated where ornamental iron chains used to hang in the days of George the Third, crossed the parade's shining asphalt surface and, jumping down on the crunching pebbles, descended to the sea's edge. The sun had not risen long and the teacher was met by a dazzling stream of unbroken rays reaching him directly as well as indirectly. Directly from the luminary itself these rays reached him, and they reached him indirectly from the dancing, glittering sea-path which was its reflection. And for one second Magnus forgot "Fern-lands", the benevolence of Miss Le Fleau, his spiritual distress about vivisection, yes! and even Curly herself!

That young woman had wakened early that morning, her head full of the Cattistock wedding, which after all *was* the greatest social event, second to the August Regatta, in the whole year; and at this moment, after her mother had with the greatest difficulty made her swallow a little breakfast, she was standing erect in the centre of her bedroom—which was also their sewing-room and their summer sitting-room—while with pins between her old teeth and her fingers fluttering under and above the edges of the precious fabric, Mrs. Wix fitted on her daughter's new dress. This dress was of a shimmery grey; and as the girl stood there under the eaves facing the small window—upon whose broad sun-warmed sill, in a chipped soap-dish, was a little bunch of snowdrops—her eyes seemed as lovely in their translunar remoteness as her slender figure was bewitching in its delicate charm. Curly's eyes, as she let her mother pull her about and lift up her arms, and pinch her waist, and smooth her shining hips, with a patience that knew no limit, had such a far-off look of mysterious beauty in them

that many an onlooker would have considered both Magnus and
S. P. Ballard totally unworthy of her.

The early morning light, for the room faced east, flooded the
deepest little window between the gables and caused to be thrown
upon the girl's pale brow and delicate cheeks a radiance that was
unearthly. Curly certainly was more than ordinarily beautiful that
morning. That faraway look in her eyes, those transparent cheeks
bathed in the freshness of the morning, that supple form in the dove-
grey dress, would have made any outsider feel that such loveliness
almost had a right to be supported by one man and loved by another.
A less faultless figure, a less far-off trance of luminous wistfulness, and
anyone might have condemned her as a designing whore. But the
idea of infidelity fled away abashed and the idea of cuckoldry hid its
head in the presence of such angelic grace.

"Oh, Mother, Mother," she presently sighed as she looked down
at the devoted little woman, whose hypocritical piece of crochet-work
lay untouched on the table, "I keep thinking that if I *were* still free—
and Mr. Cattistock's wedding and all coming on—Sippy *might* have
changed his mind when he saw me—you know?—in a nice dress and
might have thought I wouldn't be a shame to him. Of course I know
he has to meet real gentle-folk and so forth and go to their houses and
put on evening dress and talk about the Germans and the Chinese,
but though I'd have been scared at first by all that, I'd have done it all
right—*wouldn't* I have done it, Mother?—and made him feel proud
of me? That's to say if he'd only spent a *little* money on my clothes!"

Mrs. Wix smiled sadly, and standing back from her latest adjustment, took three pins from between her teeth.

"You'd be a perfect lady in a twelve-month, Love," she said.
"But don't 'ee mind too much. You'll be *a kind* of lady when you be
Mrs. Muir of Brunswick Terrace."

But Curly's thoughts at that moment were flying higher than
Brunswick Terrace. Strong if obscure feelings, just then were
moving in her heart, moving in that region of a girl's being where her
whole nature is stirred up but where emotion, desire, longing, are
only vaguely articulate. Her mind wandered back to her meeting with
Tissty and Tossty at Sark House; and, although not half as aware of
her own beauty as most girls are, she felt stirring within her a dim

sense that there *was* something unjust about her fate, thus torn between
an elderly fiancé and a selfish lover. Her passion for young Ballard
and her respect—for she had a genuine respect—for Magnus, kept
gathering up from the surface of her mental perplexity like wisps of
foam from a troubled tide. She *felt* rather than realized how unsatisfied was her claim upon life, her claim upon happiness, upon a
free escape from the imbroglio she was in, upon a richer, fuller,
sweeter, more exalted destiny! Not Curly's intelligence, but, as it
were, *her beauty itself*, beyond the margin of her reason, began to
make its demands out of the dumb sub-rational levels of its own
tender being. It was as if the soft petals of some ill-placed plant
should protest, while its root and stalk made no sign, against the sterile
spot in which fate had opened them to the air. Her incomparable form
and face—standing pensively there by that attic-window, while her
mother's swollen knuckles and bird-like fingers played once more over
the surface of her dress, seemed themselves to protest that they
deserved something better than to be the plaything of a Sippy, or the
petted idol of an elderly impecunious teacher! These dumb protests
from the transparency of Curly's skin, from the lovely wistfulness of
her far-off gaze, from the delicate curves of her slender body, were
uttered in voices much more poignant, much more tragic even—for
no self-pity can really touch the bottom of the pitifulness of such
waste—than the abrupt and rather contrary sounds emitted by her
young lips, as she murmured to her mother her hopes that she would
get a good view of the wedding, and her doubts whether Magnus
would select really "nice" roses.

Her mother's replies were brief, evasive, practical; but something in
the old woman did respond—for a deep and mysterious link exists
between a mother and the loveliness of the daughter under her
cherishing hands—to this wordless spring-stir in the indignant flesh-
and-blood she was adorning.

"You look pretty as a picture, my treasure," Mrs. Wix said at last;
but the girl only gave an impatient shrug, and thought to herself:

"What is the use? Oh, why, Oh, why is not this my marriage with
Sippy?" And then she did quite definitely formulate the thought: "I
am really as good-looking as either of those actresses though my skin
mayn't be quite as white as Mrs. Lily's!"

Even when Magnus was back on the Esplanade it was still only barely eight o'clock and he thought to himself:

"Martha never brings up the things till a quarter past. I'll walk a step towards Lodmoor."

Keeping to the esplanade, therefore, and turning his eyes away from Trigonia House lest he should be waved to by his friend Gaul, or even by that impertinent youth, Ballard, whose motor made such an unpleasant noise, Magnus had soon passed Penn House and arrived at that high wall and those various iron gates where the gardens of the Preston Road mansions descend to the sea. This was the place where, under the protection of the good Bum Trot, Mrs. Cobbold's companion had received her first impression of High House, and Magnus himself now looked up at High House, as he saw it towering above him, with no little interest. With a good deal more interest, however, he surveyed a striking mansion of yellowish cement that showed its superiority to all its neighbours by the possession of a tower. From the top of this tower, composed of what looked like stucco or painted brick-work, was suspended a flagstaff, and on the top of this flag-staff flew a small pennon.

This was the house of old Dr. Higginbottom, that choleric physician who when summoned to attend Captain Poxwell, the Captain being at that time most obstinately entrenched in Sandsfoot Castle, went off in a savage huff, uttering threats about summoning the police. Magnus had always cherished a certain romantic feeling for this stucco tower overlooking the bay. When he was a child it was Pearl Water, old Higginbottom's daughter, who occupied that tower-room. He remembered Pearl talking to him once at this very garden-gate and how she made such an overpowering impression on him that when she died her figure always haunted this spot. The girl had married an assistant of Dr. Brush and it was her death that had first drawn Magnus' attention to the appalling facts of vivisection, that secret horror behind all modern civilization.

Pearl had indeed quarrelled with her husband over Dr. Brush's experimental laboratory, but Dr. Water had died when influenza attacked the Institute, and Pearl came back with little Caddie to her old tower-room.

Rumour said that Higginbottom wouldn't have a thing changed in the turret-room after Pearl died, and that instead of getting a proper governess for Caddie he let her grow up in any sort of casual manner with all that tower-space to herself. He had indeed a good excuse for putting her physical health above her mental training, for Caddie Water was subject to epileptic fits. She was now eleven years old and not altogether, Magnus thought, as friendly to him as she used to be when she was five or six; but the Homer-loving teacher of Horace was still one of her best friends and Caddie Water's friends were very few indeed. She was an extremely plain child, heavy and awkward in figure, sullen and sulky in face; she would sit for hours in solemn lassitude staring across the sea. Caddie's best friend of her own sex was none other than Gipsy May, whom her grandfather had known from very early days. Among all the other local eccentrics, alternately patronized and bullied by the old gentleman none indeed was such a pet as the tenant of Lodmoor Hut. It was a wonder to see how well these two queer characters got on, and how the doctor humoured the gipsy and how the gipsy held her own with the doctor.

It was not, therefore, with any particular surprise in spite of the earliness of the hour that Magnus found a group of excited people, including old Higginbottom and little Caddie, standing at the garden-gate of "The Turret". He would have turned all the same the moment he came upon them there, for he sorely wanted his breakfast and felt anything but sociable, had not the doctor called to him by name.

"Muir! Muir! Come here a moment! Come here, please, Muir!"

Quite a disturbance it seemed to be that the teacher of Latin plunged into, when he arrived at the garden-gate of "The Turret". It had been May and Larry who were making the trouble in some private disagreements, but Caddie had seen them quarrelling in the road from her tower-window and had come hurrying down through house and garden to find out what was the matter; and she had very quickly—for the old man was an early riser—dragged her grandfather into it. Dr. Higginbottom was always plastic as clay where Caddie was concerned and he was much more occupied with her now than with the angry pair. But Gipsy May was terribly excited. There were red spots on both her hollow, consumptive cheeks and her great dark eyes were luminous and black as coal. After her fashion she approached the gist of the matter sideways, glancing at it, pecking at it, diving at it with a swoop before it reached the surface like a sea-gull snatching from a ship's deck what *might* be bread and *might* be a bit of paper!

"It's a beautiful day, Mr. Muir," she said, addressing him at once and fixing him with the fleeting eye of a swallow, who had been caught persecuting a gosling. "Don't you think it would be a nice day for me to go to Portland? Larry's afraid—no! no! give him your proper hand, Larry. You're not a child, are you? Your *right* hand, like a good boy, and don't look so sulky. I'll tell Mr. Muir what's all about, if you do—Larry's afraid I'll be making trouble at 'Last House' if I go over there, Mr. Muir. He's afraid I shall tell 'S. C.' what a little viper he's got there; but I never say nothing to anyone of what I knows from the cards."

"That's how she goes on, Mr. Muir," interjected Larry, his green eyes shining with the phosphorus of anger, "and she's got nothing against Marret at all 'ceptin' only that she bides with Mr. Cobbold. If she goes up to Last House like she is now, she *will* make trouble. Mr. Cobbold ain't one to be meddled with—and her be in a mood for meddling today—yes! meddling with Satan!"

The slow, hesitant voice of little Caddie now lifted itself up tremulous and hoarse, as if in her tower she had been copying the cries of sea-gulls and ignoring human speech.

"Does Marret," she began.

"Ugh! Hum!, Ugh! Ugh!, Hum! Hum!"

Such were the sounds, but far more charged with significance than the mere syllables suggest, with which the old doctor invariably saluted any company of people when little Caddie began to speak; and even as he now said "Ugh! Ugh!" he pulled her shawl more closely round her neck, and as he said "Hum! Hum!" he looked with doting idolatry into her white heavy face, poring anxiously over the quivering frown that now puckered up her forehead.

"Does . . . Marret . . . live . . . *with* Mr. Cobbold?"

Caddie articulated these words as if they were not her own language, as if they were a language she had learned with difficulty. This was the impression Caddie gave everybody, as if she had learnt the language and ways of men very carefully and thoroughly but was in constant danger of forgetting them, being in her heart, as far as the human race was concerned, as remote as if she had been a sick seamew.

"Ugh! Ugh . . . Hum! Hum!" repeated the doctor, looking at Magnus fiercely under his bushy brows as much as to say: "Careful now! Be careful in your thoughts, my friend! You can see who is speaking, can't you?"

But Caddie went on quietly, looking at no one in particular. She seemed to be asking her extremely touchy human question of the large tolerance of universal space.

"As his servant . . . or as . . . his . . . lady-love?"

"Missy! Missy!" cried young Zed, clutching with his eel-ditch finger-and-thumb the end of Caddie's shawl and giving it a beseeching tug. "Don't 'ee let May use common speech about Mar't! Mar't be woon of they gals what the stories tell of, what be beyond the sweet ways and the thorny ways, what be like Pelicans in Wilderness. Mar't have never once, no! not all the times I've seen she, said woon word against May, or about May and Mr. Cobbold, or how Mr. Cobbold could never bide May's mischief and how he never could bide thik girt music-box she carries with her, and how she let loose his pet sea-parrot that a sailor-boy gie'd he, and how it got into field and couldn't fly and a cat killed 'un. Mar't never once talked to I about woon thing o' such tales."

It was Gipsy May's turn now, and her retaliation took, as all her emotional moves did, an angle so totally unexpected and so remote from the whole issue, that at first Magnus supposed she was about to be reconciled with her protégé out of consideration for her friend Caddie.

"Larry here doesn't know," she said, addressing the little invalid, who was now leaning heavily upon her father's arm, "doesn't know what Tarot cards have been telling about S. C.'s being in danger from Minerals. Animals couldn't hurt the flick of a finger of him. Vegetables couldn't hurt the tick of a pulse of him. 'Tis minerals where his danger lies. 'Tis Minerals what'll be his undoing. And that's why I be taking to S. C. this very morning, and take it I will, what Larry have persecuted me for and teased me for, ever since us first lived as we be now."

As she spoke she let go her hold on Caddie Water's shawl and tapped the bones of her own hollow chest. She always kept her collar-bones exposed to the air, as if by that means to retain some lost link with the elements; although, below her collar-bones, her incredibly thin bosom was always covered up in a bright-coloured, beautifully clean wrap.

"It be *in here* I've got thik Magnet for he, Larry Zed; and if thee hadn't made such a fumigation about me going to 'un I'd have gived it to thee, thee own self! Never will thee set eyes on it no more. 'Twere Gran' Holt's Magnet. And now Gran' Holt's Magnet be going to Last House; there to bide; there to keep Hurt-from-Minerals away from S. C. So your pretty Mar't's—" and she impishly imitated the way Larry pronounced her rival's name—"Mar't's silver bodkin her told 'ee of, 'ull never prick S. C. in a bed May's ever made, but Gran' Holt's Magnet 'ull draw all they bobbikins after 'en, and her won't be able to keep a prick-point on her bussum so hard and so strong will Gran' Holt's Magnet pull!"

But Gipsy May had gone just a fraction of an inch too far in her tormenting of young Zed. She *nearly* achieved her purpose, which was to throw him, before them all, into a paroxysm of childish anger, while she herself slipped quietly away, but she missed the fact that since the scene in his hay-loft bedroom with Perdita, the lad had changed and matured in some subtle manner so that he was less easy to handle.

It was Caddie Water, who—with a child-invalid's psychic susceptibility—realized the stress of young Zed's feelings as he stood, stunned, taut, and trembling, his eyes full of angry tears. Thus he stood, staring and quivering, as if she had thrown a spell over him, while Gipsy May with that peculiarly vibrant glide characteristic of her, which combined bewildering furtiveness with unassailable dignity—hurried off along the pavement. She passed Penn House; she crossed the road; she mounted the esplanade, and very soon she was hidden behind bath-chairs, rain-shelters, boat-men, notice-boards, and those characteristic figures of early-risen athletes of both sexes, who, with season-defying towels and wet bathing-suits, seemed to be accusing all the rest of the world of effeminate and contemptible degeneracy. Among all these did Gipsy May vanish; but if it had not been for Caddie Water the chances are that young Zed when he got his wits together would have run after her and made a distressing scene. But Caddie Water snatched her hand from her father and seized the lad by one of his wrists.

"Come up to my tower, Larry," she cried, "I've got something to show you."

The Doctor gave Magnus a most complicated look then, in which a desire to make things unpleasant, and to make them unpleasant *at once*, for someone or other, struggled with a desire to please his grand-child at any price.

"May I take him up? May I take him up? May I take—"

The child's insistent voice brought back to Magnus Pearl's tones, as she stood and talked to him that day at this very gate.

"It was Pearl," he said to himself, "who first put vivisection into my head."

"Won't you go up with them, Muir?" said the Doctor.

Now Magnus knew perfectly well that this was a serious request, in making which the old man snatched at a chance to begin his breakfast with a free conscience. But in little physical exigencies of this sort Magnus was liable—as the elder Muir before him had been—to display adamantine selfishness.

"Not just now, thank you, Caddie," he said. "Martha must have taken up my breakfast long ago. I must hurry off!"

"How's Miss Le Fleau's rheumatism?" enquired the old man in reply to this, jeering at the teacher's restlessness out of one eye, while with the other he followed anxiously the little girl's figure as she went off with young Zed. "Oh, yes! and *did* you find a room at the Corporal's? Miss Le Fleau told me you were seeing him."

"I hope so . . . I think so . . . but it's too long a story to go into now," murmured Magnus. "Excuse me, Doctor, but I really *must* be off."

The old man returned slowly into the big house and went into his sunny dining-room where his silver coffee-pot already awaited him, in the window, close to a stand of red geraniums, and kept warm by the blue flame of a little spirit-lamp. He never smelt that peculiar methylated smell without thinking of Pearl. He could see her figure now as she poured out his coffee for him. How he always dreaded a certain curious look of unearthly detachment that used to come into her face. As he stood gazing at the geranium-pots behind the silver of his breakfast things, he suddenly set himself to listen. Could he hear any sounds from the tower? No; all was deathly silent through-out the house. Then there came the opening of a door and a hurried patter of feet.

"Damn!" the old gentleman thought, "It's Sarah."

It was indeed Mrs. Piddle who came cautiously in with the jerky movement of an anxious moor-hen exploring a suspicious weir.

"May I speak to 'ee a minute, sir?"

The Doctor countered her question with one of his own.

"I suppose young Larry Zed has had his breakfast long ago?"

Mrs. Piddle nodded. Then she said:

"I've 'a had a Card of Invite, Sir, from Eliza Chant out to Chickerel, and it says she's celebratin' Cat'stock's weddin' tonight at the Lodge with a few old friends and would *I* care to drop in. She says Mrs. Matzell from Half-Way House will be there and Mrs. Monkton from Trigonia House may be coming and Mrs. Wix from Upwey has promised to come. 'Twill be a nice little gatherin', Sir, such as I mayn't live to see the likes of again."

Old Higginbottom glowered at her.

"I suppose you're thinking of strolling up to Trinity Church this afternoon?"

Mrs. Piddle's face expressed dismay that he should even mention a matter so profoundly to be taken for granted.

" 'Tis the great event of the year, Sir," she murmured reproach-fully, "and I could scarce believe me ears when John said you wasn't going to the Church at all."

The Doctor flew into a half-real, half-pretended passion.

"Sarah Piddle!" he cried out, in the fashion of Oliver Cromwell, "Sarah Piddle! The Lord deliver me from Sarah Piddle!" Then looking at her more calmly. "If your Cattistock's a rogue," he said, "this Poxwell woman he's marrying is worse still!"

But the old lady had cocked her head on one side and was listening intently, very much as her master had listened a minute or two before.

"Is Caddie calling?" he said, his face anxious and concerned in a moment. "Yes, go up and see, Sarah! Go up, good Sarah, go up and see!"

When the housekeeper was gone he bent down and pinched with

his fingers one of the scented leaves of his favourite ivy-leaved geranium. And a terrible longing for his dead daughter swept over him. His moroseness, his savage anger, his moods of violence had all come after Pearl died. Secretly at the bottom of his heart he considered that Dr. Brush's Sanitarium had killed Pearl; and he never could endure a moment of the famous man's company. He used to say to John Piddle, whenever Sarah had hysterics:

"We'll send for that Sark House rogue, won't we, Johnny, and try an honest quack before we let her go to that fellow out there?"

While matters thus settled down to their usual unquiet quiet at the "Turret", Gipsy May was approaching the Jubilee Clock. The more disturbed, the more angry, the more upset Gipsy May was, the more tortuous and the more roundabout would grow her ways of mental procedure. These ways elaborated themselves until one would have thought it would be difficult even for herself to acknowledge the original cause of some puckish, impish, scandalous action which seemed to be the finest flower of pure motiveless mischief. If the seriousness of her anger could be measured by the convolutions of her track she was very angry now, for instead of going to the station to catch the train, instead of going to the King's Statue, to catch the bus, what must this circumambulatory woman do but visit the preparations for the wedding, outside Trinity Church and there wait quite aimlessly, it might seem, for a couple of hours. After this long delay she proceeded to the Pier and remained there, eating tangerine oranges, for no less than an hour more in order to catch the only morning boat there was, going to Portland!

A person clairvoyant of human thought would have found it an easy task to read and understand the thoughts of Sylvanus Cobbold; but he would have found it an impossible task to catch and explain the thoughts of Gipsy May. The truth perhaps was, as we might surmise of the thoughts of a raven or a magpie, that this singular woman jumped from one entirely concrete matter to another, pouncing upon it, snatching at it, picking it to bits, wrapping it up and hiding it and all the while thinking of it with a whimsical interest that was far removed from covetousness, an interest that was prepared to relinquish it at any moment with a complete gaiety of temper! Dr. Higginbottom used to say that Gipsy May was born under Saturn and was the true Saturnian type; but Pearl—those were in her happy days before she met Dr. Water—denied this and said there was nothing that happened in the world, unless it happened to a non-human animal, that May couldn't enjoy with a sideways relish of mischief.

Long before this mercurial Saturnian sucked her tangerines and collected the skins in little piles beside her, for she soon discovered that throwing them into the tide was a tantalization to the sea-gulls, out at Last House, which was the Gipsy's objective, Sylvanus Cobbold had been lying in his bed holding Marret between himself and the wall in his mystic-sensuous contemplations. The young girl had fallen fast asleep in the dark hour just before dawn; but as Sylvanus held her, pressed close against him, his own thoughts literally "wandered through eternity". He had long ago acquired that precious power, in which, they say, the Lamas of Thibet are such adepts, of reducing the intensity of his physical desire to a level that lent itself to the prolongation rather than to the culmination of the erotic ecstasy. And as he now held this slender young being in his arms, who, even in her sleep, made little natural movements of confiding contentment, he began using her young warmth, even as the aged King David did that of the youthful Abishag, to strengthen his colloquy with the mystery of the cosmos. Desperately in that chilly hour did Sylvanus wrestle with the dark angel of outer space. What tormented him now, at this very second, as the great search-light from the Beale Light-House swept, moment by moment across his window, throwing his own hollow-cheeked physiognomy and the ends of his great moustache that hung down over the collar of his faded, washed-out, light-blue pyjamas and the pathetically youthful profile of the Punch-and-Judy girl into an illuminated revelation, was the difficulty of explaining the atrocious suffering in the world under the hypothesis of the kind of Absolute he had hitherto imagined. Beads of perspiration stood out on his forehead and trickled down the slope of his high cheek-bones from his hollow eye-sockets; for not even the delicious sensuousness of holding Marret could make it easy to reconcile an Absolute that was good with the monstrous cruelties of the world as he knew it.

"How *can* you let these things be?"

These words Sylvanus uttered quite distinctly in his secret mind, though he did not let them pass, as Homer would say, "the barrier of his teeth", and then he fell to contrasting the pleasure which he was deriving from the satiny smoothness of this girl's body with the wretched suffering that even in Weymouth and Portland so many sentiencies were enduring. He shrank away, in all these thoughts of his, from every kind of physical self-consciousness. The subtlest of all differences between human beings has to do with their attitude to themselves when they are thinking about themselves. Some caress themselves when they are alone and consciously dote on themselves, whereas others hold themselves apart from themselves with a certain despotic contempt for themselves—and this, too, even in the midst of their liveliest sensations.

Of these last Sylvanus was an extreme example. Any idea of himself considered physically was nervously antipathetic to him. Sylvanus was more than shy of himself. A hot rush of blood causing him a curious discomfort, would mount up to his head at the merest approach to physical self-consciousness. He *had* to forget himself, or he couldn't go on! And yet he was a very sensuous man. Physical sensations he loved, cultivated, pursued, and fiercely sought; but physical self-consciousness shocked and outraged him. It seemed to give a twist, a tug, a squeeze, a jerk, a pull, a horrid twinge, to some invisible, *nervous navel-string* that was the devil's wire of his puppet-hood. Of all the men in Weymouth and Portland Sylvanus was probably the most egoistic and yet the least of a coxcomb. Such a shrinking had he from physical self-consciousness that it always worried him and gave him a nervous spasm even to set eyes upon his own shadow when he was going about! One of the most curious instances of this mania against physical self-consciousness actually arose at this very moment, while, satisfying his senses by holding the girl, he kept up an intense prolonged monologue addressed to the Absolute. For in talking to his God he never called himself "I" or "me" or "your servant" or even Sylvanus; he always called himself "Caput." But even this was not enough; for, since the Absolute was Everything, it was necessary to place the lowest function of his body side by side with the highest. Thus to the word Caput, in speaking of himself to God, what must this fantastical being do but add the word "Anus", which had the double advantage of indicating his spasmodic body-shame, and, incidentally, of rhyming with Sylvanus! As he lay there, in that incredibly hushed pre-dawn, thrilled through and through by a diffused sensuality, his mind gave up the struggle to reconcile his Absolute with the cruelty of things, for this began to seem beyond his power; and in place of it he wrestled with the Spirit in a frantic effort to make it include the Gross, the Repulsive, the Disgusting.

"Show yourself to Caput-anus! Oh, God, Oh, God, show yourself, show yourself, to Caput-anus!"

Thus did the cry of Sylvanus rise up from his bed in Last House, while constantly, like the repetition of some primeval creative act, like the index finger of the Absolute thrust into the gulfs of Nothingness, the revolving ray of the Portland Bill Light-house, that recurrent Pharos-Blaze, swept into the room and swept out of it.

Curious would it have been—but where was Peg Frampton to see such a sight?—to observe these two heads, the little doll-like head and the monstrous Quixotic head, with that minute-gun of blinding disclosure shot at them all the night! It was just as if the Eye of the Absolute itself had been turned in displeasure upon this unnatural assertion of mind over instinct, this side-steering, controlling, curtailing of the great erotic force that creates the world!

Nor was the grotesquerie of Sylvanus' thoughts at that time without its corresponding parallel in certain extraordinary movements he saw fit to make. He would, for instance, hitch himself up a little and crane his head forward, while his long neck, soft and malleable compared with the sinewy neck of old Captain Poxwell, would assume a striking resemblance to the head of a tortoise or a turtle. Straining himself in this way he seemed to have a remarkable power, which perhaps also was a trick known in Thibet, of being able to hold his neck extended, as it stretched upward and forward from his pillow, at an angle that might have given his bed-fellow an extremely uncomfortable feeling, if she had been willing to regard it. Gipsy May, of course, whose slumbers were lighter than those of a squirrel, had often been disconcerted by this peculiarity in her "S. C."; but it is doubtful if Marret, even if she had caught him at it, would have worried very much. Marret had watched so long those grotesque puppets of her father that she tended to consider such movements in a living man as the natural emotional expressions of the human frame.

But to Gipsy May, when she would wake up in that final watch of the night to find her companion in that queer position, and the salt air around Last House withdrawn into itself in a strange constriction, there was something upsetting to the nerves. The woman used to feel at such moments as if the very darkness itself, in the in-sucking sharpness of its suspense, were pulling in its cheeks along with its cold breath, in its passionate waiting for the dawn. And there was something about this turtle-like outstretched neck, with its super-independent moustache, that made her think of the twisted shape of the Hanged Man of the Tarot cards! There were few things, as Caddie's mother said, that could confound Gipsy May if they did not cause distress to beasts or birds or fishes, but always to wake up, just before dawn, and always be reminded of what those other, those non-human necks must have looked like, at this hour, hundreds of millions of years ago when that indrawn air shivered and yearned between the dawn's teeth for the red sun to touch the stalks of the pre-historic Mares'-tails, and to gouge great blood-pools out of the whitening swamp, was something towards which she at last had begun to feel rebellious.

Marret's more docile nature, a nature, too, that was "native and indued" to the spasmodic movements of immemorial dolls, gave itself up without question to everything that Sylvanus did. As to what he *said* she seldom understood a word of it; but it gave her a physical sensation of ineffable peace to hear him talking and to know that he was talking to her. Virtue came out of the sound, and the meaning of his words reached her through the aura of this virtue, like the cry of sea-birds through a sunlit mist reaching someone who lies motionless upon a deck.

It was curious how Sylvanus and his young bed-fellow slept and waked by turns; for when the light of day was actually penetrating their room and the revolving search-light had ceased its spasms of illumination it was the girl who was awake. She woke up this time with a sudden, startling feeling of what it would be like to be driven out of Last House by Gipsy May! Her feeling at this moment isolated itself and projected itself into that air-swept chamber. It became a living part of that chemistry of reality to which she had to adapt herself. She knew Sylvanus was expecting Gipsy May today;

and she said to herself now, just as if her leaving him could not be avoided when her older rival came:

"I shall go, if she stays; but they'll quarrel again, and I shall come back." Staring with wide-open eyes straight in front of her she said to herself, "He doesn't know how fond he is of her. He doesn't know that when she comes I must go. But when I go I mustn't be angry with him. When I go I must say to myself, 'They will quarrel again and I shall come back'. Whatever happens I must not get angry with him."

But though she said this to herself, and could not imagine any possible change in her docility, in reality, deep down in her feminine nature, deep down in her long thin body, the old eternal anger of a woman against "the other woman" *was* beginning to stir.

"I must stop thinking about her coming," she thought. "I must enjoy every moment while she isn't here, while she is still at Lodmoor!"

With her wavy brown hair tumbled loosely about the pillow her little oval face fell now upon a pathetic placidity that had an almost inanimate patience. She made no attempt, however wakeful she felt, to hoist herself up and survey her companion! She shrank from staring at him in his sleep, as if it would be something in the nature of a sacrilege. But the first rays of the sun roused up Sylvanus and he forthwith entered into a singular conversation with the motionless girl by his side.

"What's the first thing you can remember in your whole life, 'Mart'?"

He called her "Mart" because of the way she herself pronounced her name, which was almost exactly the way young Zed pronounced it.

Marret was thinking to herself:

"That's the sun on the end of the bed! That's the sun on the blanket over his raised-up knees! That's the sun on his forehead! I must remember exactly how *everything* looks, so I'll have something to think about when it's all over," but she replied to his question without hesitation. "The first thing I remember was Father hitting Mother with a water-jug. He held it by its handle till it broke. There was water in it and Mother's clothes got all wet. She minded that more than being hit. Mother was never one for water. She always said water were made for fishes, not persons."

"Did your father kill her?"

"No, no, no!" cried Marret while her little oval face—which, when she had been asleep, had looked exactly like a small china doll—puckered itself up into a number of anxious creases, "Ermentrude, the Salvation Army woman, who lived under us, came running in and she said to Mother, 'did he hit you, dearie?' and Mother said 'no, he didn't'; and she said to Mother, 'did he do anything to you, dearie?' and Mother said 'no, he didn't'; and she said to Mother, 'was yer a-quarrelling, dearie?' and Mother said 'no, they wasn't'; and she never said another word after that and when Ermentrude went to her she were gone and her feet were cold. I knew they were cold, because when Father camed in he said, 'Mart, thee may feel her feet just once, if thee likes, so as to say you've touched Death'."

"Did he say anything else before they put her in her coffin?" enquired Sylvanus gravely.

Marret looked at him with a radiant face while the newly-risen sun turned her dusty-brown hair into the metallic shimmer of a copper beech-tree. It was wonderful to her that she could interest him by her conversation.

"He only said, when the parish-woman came to lay her out, that he hoped they wouldn't wash her with water. 'My wife,' he said, for Father were one to talk high and mighty with strangers, 'never were a 'ooman for the water; so let 'un be; do 'ee hear? let 'un bide in peace!' "

It had been a daily astonishment to Sylvanus, since Marret had come to live with him, how quickly the girl would fall asleep after being intensely awake. He remained quiet now stretching out his neck in his swamp-turtle manner, and watching her puckered little doll face.

"She'll be asleep in a second," he thought, when he saw her eyes close. And in this conjecture he was completely justified.

Quietly he slipped out of bed, and even as he did so the girl turned her face to the wall and pulled the clothes tight as one who had no wish to awake. He went to the window and promptly addressed to the dazzling sun the same kind of formal little bow that he had directed towards the sea in the Weeping Woman. Having propitiated the great luminary by this brief gesture, he proceeded hurriedly to dress, paying, at present, as little regard to soap and water as Marret's mother seems to have done. Leaving the room very quietly he now descended the stairs and, going into the kitchen, proceeded to light the fire in the stove. When this was done, and thick fumes of acrid smoke had filled his nostrils, he transferred his attentions to the fire in the Last House parlour, which as a rule in spring weather he left unlit.

"May'll be here *sometime* today," he thought. "Since she sent that card, nothing'll stop her! I wouldn't be surprised to see her turn up before we've had breakfast."

He then went back into the kitchen and picked up the pail of refuse. Opening the front door by the handle—one of his quarrels with Gipsy May had been his custom of never bolting his doors—he carried the pail along a little path leading to a patch of desolate cabbage-stalks, where the barren ground had been disturbed many times. Here there was a fragment of a ruined fence and a few wooden posts. Against one of these posts leaned a fork which Sylvanus now took up and began to dig. As he dug he pretended to himself, in his peculiar whimsies, that he was digging a grave big enough to contain every living person who at that hour, all over the face of the earth, was giving up the ghost!

"Rise to life, Human Beings!" he repeated in a perfunctory and mechanical chant. "Rise to life, Animals!" And then, after a while, as he stamped down the earth on the buried refuse: "Rise to life all other Souls of the Dead!"

Replacing the fork against the post he now proceeded to a large woodshed with a high-raftered roof. Here he set himself to chop wood and sticks, cutting them into convenient lengths for tomorrow's fire-lighting. When his pile was complete he made that same formal little bow to the axe which he had just been using; and then following a fixed ritual which he had obeyed since he first came to Last House, he uttered a kind of Homeric Litany to all his tools, not forgetting the fork with which he had dug the hole for the refuse.

"The Pick," he repeated in a droning liturgical intonation. "The Pick, the Spade, the Fork, the Rake, the Hoe." And then he added, peering into a portion of the great barn where stood a substantial wheelbarrow—in a tone exactly as if this last object's dim identity exacted more propitiation than the rest—"and the *very good* wheel-barrow!"

The next thing he did was to gaze upwards where there was an old swallow's nest on one of the rafters. To this object Sylvanus began chanting afresh, raising his great parsnip-shaped head, till, with the moustache hanging from it in that dim light, it came to resemble an upturned gothic gargoyle with two wisps of trailing ivy.

"The swallow," he chanted, "has built him a nest, where he may hide his young; but the son of man hath nowhere to lay his head. Hold up the roof, beams! Hold up the roof, cross-beams!"

Finally as he went out of the shed carrying the wood very carefully under both his arms, hugged close against his ribs, he suddenly with a weary and a rasping sound, as if there were a croaking raven in his belly, uttered the words:

"Damp Straw! Damp Straw! Damp Straw!"

With this he left the shed, closing its large wooden gate behind him.

Once when Gipsy May—who was totally devoid of all reverence and all sentiment, save for cats and dogs "and such small deer"—spied upon Sylvanus as he went into his barn and from her hiding-place behind an old boat-sail which he had put up, so as to be able to make water when he had a mind, unseen from the windows of his house, listened first to the Homeric list of noble tools, then to the reference to the son of man, she was startled and shocked by this demon-croak in the man's belly, as if it were the groan of the ghastly Man with Three Staves, contradicting all the worth and dignity and meaning and value of the rest of his ritual.

"Damp Straw! Damp Straw! Damp Straw!"

At least an hour had passed since Sylvanus had left the house on these daily tasks and when he returned he found that the two kettles he had left on the kitchen-stove were boiling. He filled a small can from one of them and with this supply of hot water, making his way upstairs, knocked as discreetly and politely at Marret's door as if she had been the most virginal of visitors—as in a sense she was—and informed her that it was time to get up.

"Time, Girlie!" he shouted, without so much as touching the door-handle.

Then, retreating into the parlour, where he secretly in the depths of his crafty mind intended to entertain Gipsy May, he made up the fire, putting on several pieces of wood and some lumps of coal. He so greatly enjoyed the sensation of coming in from an extended walk and finding that Marret had already got breakfast, that, after putting some more wood on to the kitchen-stove, he sallied forth again, this time picking up, from a rack containing quite a lot of them, one of his soldier-canes.

Skirting the side of Last House he emerged into the public road, where he was met by an eddying cloud of dust, that seemed travelling at its own volition across Portland. Totally oblivious to the forlorn-ness of the front of his dwelling, Sylvanus now waved his cane towards their bedroom window feeling that if by chance Marret had already got up it would please her to be waved to; then he strode on, cheerfully brandishing his cane towards the great light-house. The wind blew fresh and cool from off the sea; and as the land narrowed to the Bill he felt as if the whole promontory were lifted up, up and out and away, from all the rest of the earth and was propelled by some unknown force to sail alone through empty space. This is a sensation that almost everyone experiences in the early morning on Portland, but it was an impression peculiarly transporting to Sylvanus, because it lent itself to his most characteristic way of thinking. It gave him a feeling as if Nature were returning to God, as if the Relative were returning to the Absolute, as if Life were returning to some mysterious Beyond-life. As he advanced now, almost due South, towards that tongue of rock which stretched out into the everlasting turbulence of the opposing tides, he became aware that beyond the Beale the risen sun, now blindingly in his eyes, had made a dazzling path over the water. Upon this sun-path, just as Magnus was doing at the same moment in front of Brunswick Terrace, he fixed his eyes.

"What have I done," he thought, "that I should be permitted to see a thing like this and live?"

In the extremity of his emotion he thought of those panegyrics to his strange Absolute which he still insisted on pouring out to all and sundry upon the Weymouth esplanade. Jerry Cobbold had used all the subtleties of his influence to persuade him to yield to the police in this point. Jerry had made the strongest personal plea, begging him, for the sake of their boyhood, for the sake of their father, for the sake of all the memories they shared, not to bring this thing to so final and fatal an issue.

"It'll be no use," Jerry said, "arguing with them. You're such an old offender that you've got their back up. They're just desperate. They'll finish you off, as *his* police-authorities finished off Socrates; and the whole thing will hurt me, my dear, more than you've any idea of! If you do this, Van, it'll be the cruellest thing you've ever done—and to what purpose?"

Thus had Jerry implored him only yesterday; and he had promised the clown that he would avoid the esplanade for a day or two while he plunged into his private equivalent of "fasting and prayer and the seeking of a sign from heaven". He could not help feeling as if this enchanted sunrise after his concentrated pre-dawn vigil, with his arms about his girl's polished limbs, were like an answer from his gods. He could not recall any morning by the sea, that he had ever seen, equal to this morning. He made a face of wicked buffoonery when he thought to himself:

"It's in honour of Cattistock's wedding!" and then, as he walked through the white dust, with the grey stones piled about his path, and in front of him that glittering, sparkling, dazzling trail across the motionless sea-floor, like the track of some immortal wanderer from an empyrean of sea-serpents, it seemed to him as if the Power that expressed Itself in this fire and air and water *must* be strong enough to give him the victory over Sippy Ballard and his Guildhall cronies!

It was an ironic thing—bitter with the grim tragedy of mortal contrast—that at the very moment when Sylvanus was thus exalted with happiness he should have proved the cause—and deliberately the cause, too!—of a poignant tantalization to another living soul. But of such events and of such coincidences is the very fabric of this world composed. What he did now was to suddenly swerve aside at a sharp angle, when he approached the tall light-house, for he caught sight of a woman's solitary figure standing at the very end of the Beale— standing, in fact, just where the Jobber on the previous day had shown Perdita that ghastly crack into eternity. The grand new light-house furnished with every modern device, knew nothing of the romantic legends that belonged to its vanished predecessors, knew nothing of this woman now standing on the edge of that rocky cleft. To the light-house she was merely an eccentric personage living in the little town of Easton!

How could this splendid modern erection, for all its searching scientific apparatus know that this eccentric individual from Easton was the enchantment, the magnet, the Hesperidean fruit, the Golden Fleece, that in former days attracted to this spot the Jobber's "Gentleman from the White Nose"? The latest phase of this woman's life had been a passionate devotion to Sylvanus. She had come to know his ways, his hours, his walks, and she had grown addicted to meeting him just about this time as he made his way to a certain favourite resort of his. These encounters were attended with almost as much emotional excitement for this woman as had been those former ones with "the Gentleman from the White Nose"; but today, his mind full of his long night with Marret and freshly aroused to the expected visit of Gipsy May, Sylvanus felt compelled to avoid her, a compulsion that caused bitter and cruel disappointment to the woman at the end of the Beale. Sardonic indeed would her comment have been upon masculine pharisaism could she have followed all her friend's superstitious mumblings when he reached his retreat.

Turning away from that watchful figure, and not refraining from a goblinish grimace that wrinkled up his whole countenance as he changed his course, Sylvanus now clambered down a sloping fragment of the eastern cliff's edge at an angle that actually faced the aforementioned White Nose as it stretched impressively into Weymouth Bay. Here he approached the entrance to a little ramshackle hut, which clung like an ancient fungus to a rabbit-burrow or a barnacle to a stranded keel, where the cliff sloped down. It was in reality the deserted tool-shed of some former light-house-keeper in the days before the new erection was built, but Sylvanus on the strength of being the tenant of Last House had boldly appropriated it to his own purposes. Here, for when the door was wide-open it made a pleasant three-sided shelter, he loved to sit, hugging his long shins, tugging at his long moustaches, and muttering crazy invocations to sun, sea and sky. It was his humour to keep up constant soliloquies in this little sentry-box with two inanimate objects, for each of which he cherished a fanatical fetish-worship.

The first was a rope which he kept twisted round one of the main beams of the shed and made use of sometimes as a help in climbing down the cliff to the rocks below. The other was a half-obliterated oil-painting. He had no sooner entered his retreat today than he fell to apostrophizing this rope, using a rhyming jingle that had come into his head of its own accord one day:

> "Rope, rope, hang Sylvanus!
> From caput to anus
> His doings profane us.
> Rope, rope, hang Sylvanus!"

Having delivered himself of this rigmarole he proceeded to twist about his turtle-like neck and to peer intently and anxiously into every portion of his sentry-box. It was clear he was searching for something and it was clear that what he searched for was very important to him.

Trivia, Trivia, Trivia!

There she was, the object of his concern, a small, palpitating, quivering, dancing sunbeam! This sunbeam, since it behaved always in the same excited manner, he had come to endow with a definite personality and he called her Trivia. He was so intense and so mystical a worshipper of young women that whenever he saw Trivia dancing on the wall he was ravished with pleasure. On this occasion, by resorting to the simple expedient of shaking with his hand a water-butt that stood outside his door he flung his little visitor into a frenzy. When quivering like the liberated spirit of an aspen-leaf she began this furious dance Sylvanus turned to the rope above him, which, as it dangled its frayed strands exactly over his head, had the air of accepting the use he had suggested for it as something that fell in very naturally with what it had observed during its life of the general tendency of earthly events.

"The rope I see up there," murmured Sylvanus, as if he were propitiating an extremely stupid and rather touchy judge, "is a very *strong* rope and a very *wise* rope!"

And once more he began gabbling his suckfist gibberish:

"From caput to anus Sylvanus profanes us!"

And then returning to Trivia he supplicated her to have pity on him in a voice so beseeching that if the woman standing by that crack into eternity had overheard him, she would certainly have thought there was a real girl in the shed.

"Trivia, Trivia, Trivia, Trivia, Trivia!" he repeated, as if pleading for remission of sins.

And Trivia, after a fluttering series of coy hesitations, would plunge once more, shivering and quivering, into a veritable maenad-madness. That old water-butt outside the tool-shed, which was always full of rain, fell into its rippling disturbance the very second the planks of the little building were disturbed by any movement. And the sun shone upon the water-butt. Such was the material cause of Trivia's saraband, but the effect upon Sylvanus was profound and quite immaterial. That shivering dance of reflected light from the heart of our planetary universe had a more mystical effect upon him than any other phenomenon between earth and sky. The only thing superior to it in its power to stir him was the dazzling glitter of the sun on the sea. Sunlight and water—whether the water were salt or fresh—always struck Sylvanus as being the nearest revelation of the Ultimate Being that man could attain.

But even while Trivia went on dancing Sylvanus betook himself to the most curious ritual of all. He had picked up on the rocks, somewhere below the old Portland Prison, a little, worthless, unframed oil-painting. There were other discarded objects in that particular neighbourhood; quite enough of them to indicate that someone had deliberately exposed this wretched derelict with the hope that the tide would wash it away. The tide *had* washed it away but had brought it back again with its colours not quite obliterated; and Sylvanus, after referring the matter to a solitary lad he found down there with as much nervous respect as Socrates would have used with Phaedrus, had saved this despised object thinking to himself:

"It will do for my shelter."

Here indeed he had fastened it up; and not a day passed but he saluted it in grandiloquent words, words of which both *the picture itself*—to such an insane length had Sylvanus' superstition gone—and the artist who painted it, were supposed to be aware to their occult satisfaction.

"*What* a masterpiece!" were his words at this moment, uttered in the tone of a person contemplating Rubens' "Judgment of Paris". "*What* an artist! What rosy tints in the sky! What livid whiteness in the lake! What tree-trunks with water between them! What blue distance! What an artist! What a masterpiece!"

As Sylvanus returned to Last House—and he made as long a détour as he could so as not to approach the woman from Easton—he felt exultantly happy. Indeed he felt so happy as the wind whistled in the blocks of oolite, twittered in the telegraph-wires, hummed in the stones of the walls and roofs, jigged in the wooden quarry-cranes, and made the whole stone promontory drum to a monstrous tune as if it were covered taut with the skin of the sea-serpent's belly, that he wondered if any living person had ever felt as happy as he did. He did stop again, even now, and hesitate once more, before he was out of sight of the woman on the Beale, but this hesitation, which might have excited hope in that patient watcher had nothing to do with her. He stopped in the effort of remembering and what he tried to recall was whether in his salutation of those old, immemorial Homeric tools in his wood-shed at Last House, which he always fancied gave his day a lucky beginning, he had forgotten to salute his axe!

The thought of this omission, on any other day, would have sent him home in such a mood that Marret would have at once asked what was the matter, but today he was so happy that he soon forgot his forgetting. His estrangement from Gipsy May had been full of distress for Sylvanus; not so much for himself—for as far as happiness went that Shameless Being within him which we all consult in our devilish moods would, in this case, have congratulated him most heartily if he had never, to the end of his days, seen Gipsy May again—as for her sake, and for his sake only as far as she was concerned, as being responsible for her jealousy, suffering and pique.

He found Marret ready for him and breakfast more than ready, for the girl had made the tea twenty minutes ago and poached the eggs a quarter of an hour ago; but since it was evident that the Punch-and-Judy man, however vicious and vindictive—for so rumour whispered him to be—in other directions was easy-going over his meals, Sylvanus was fain to imitate him. He therefore hummed the tune of one of the Regent songs that he was always hearing on the esplanade, insisted on having their meal in the kitchen, and sat down, drumming the table with his spoon and feeling like an amiable ogre.

"Then the other room will be all ready *for she!*"

This he said with a sardonic grimace that made his long white face wrinkle up like the Ghost in her father's repertoire.

Unknown to herself even—and certainly unknown to Sylvanus—there had been mounting up, all the while he was away, a volcanic outburst of jealousy over Gipsy May. If only it had been her friend Peg who was coming! Gipsy May was perhaps the only woman in the whole world that Marret whole-heartedly hated; and the pathetic thing was that Sylvanus imagined that the two were good friends. As she sat opposite him in the kitchen now sharing their belated meal and the extremely strong contents of the tea-pot, she did not conceal from herself that she was feeling perturbed about the appearance of this other "she", but she never suspected the strength of the emotion that was smouldering under her ribs. She had not forgotten her visit to Lodmoor nor all the agitation over the Tarot cards and the Hanged Man. Gipsy May's equivocal temper and round-about ways made her likely to be an extremely disconcerting enemy, and heartily did Marret wish that their paths had never crossed. Was it merely out of wanton curiosity, that this woman was coming now, or was she resolved to oust her and replace her? Marret began to long bitterly and sorrowfully for the support, at this juncture, of her friend Peg. She smiled to herself as she thought how cleverly Peg had flirted with Mr. Gaul at their lunch at the Regatta and yet had evaded making any appointment to meet him again.

"But Mr. Gaul would be a very nice one for Peg," she thought. "He's the nicest young man, *I* think, in the whole town."

Marret's thinness was so extreme and she was such a tall girl that there were times when she resembled a pathetic doll's head at the end of a broom-handle; but the wistful smile which crossed her face when she thought of Mr. Gaul was so sweet and quaint that Sylvanus smiled in sympathy.

And then an unlucky thing happened. With all his mystical attraction to that inarticulate life-worship in women and girls, which flows round and about and under their conscious realism, as a stream flows amid the stalks of its sub-aqueous plants, with all his subtle divination of the porousness in them to the washing of these magical life-tides, he had not yet learned the importance of what might be called the psychic atmosphere of speech. It is not *what* is said—few women give much attention to that—it is the air, the tone, the atmospheric weather, so to say, of what a man says, that is the essential thing. A man who wishes to propitiate a woman by his lies *must make the atmosphere lie,* and the same thing applies to the prosperity of his persuasions when he speaks the truth! Forgetting, or never having learned these things, what must Sylvanus do now, in his sudden rush of tender sympathy as he saw this touchingly grave smile on Marret's little doll-face, but blurt out:

"If she insists on staying the night—"

"Just as you please," the girl murmured briefly, and relapsed into a silence that lasted for several minutes.

"A penny for your thoughts, girlie?" he said at last.

She looked straight at him.

"Father told me on Monday," she said, "that he was coming up here to fetch me home."

"*What's* that?" cried Sylvanus.

"Yes," she went on, "and the neighbours said they'd heard him say he'd send the police after me and prosecute you for having me."

She was again silent, and it became clear that some new current of thought and emotion had begun to mitigate her disturbed mood.

"Father thinks Tiny can't collect the money like I do. But she *can.* She does it *just* as well and better too. It's only an idea of his, but men are funny when they get ideas."

"Do you really think," asked Sylvanus, "that he'd stir up the police about us?"

"He can't! It's all nonsense. People are allowed to live together without them great sillies interfering. Why! Father lives with a girl himself! We calls her Zinzin but that isn't her real name. She's foreign. She's nice to Tiny. She don't let Father hit Tiny. But she wants for me to come back for fear Father'll ask *her* to collect."

Sylvanus' face became grave. After all he had had a great many exquisite moments of happiness since he had lived in Last House, and he saw with a shrewd eye what would happen to him if they got any serious charge against him. He'd be among Dr. Brush's *compulsory* patients.

"Would you like Jerry to put me into a strait-waistcoat at old Brush's, Martie?" he said.

So he spoke; but when a tall thin girl who has lived all her days with hideously grotesque puppets shows signs of beginning to cry it is not an ordinary sight. It is an unhappy sight and a fantastic one, too. Marret wrinkled up her cheeks, opened her mouth, and turning her head away from him, presented to him so pathetically comical a profile that it hit him to the heart, till the big tears rolling down her face washed away every human expression, save the expression "of one," as Dante puts it, "who weeps".

"Don't 'ee mind, don't 'ee mind, Mart darling," he cried, rising and going round to her and taking her on his knee. "I'm ready. I expect they'll let me talk to the other inmates in the grounds; though I'm afraid they'd never let little Mart come and see me."

It is not an easy thing to hold a tall thin young woman on your knee and cajole her into relaxed peacefulness; and the Punch-and-Judy girl hardly ever broke down like this which made it worse. If the truth were known, this was the first time the girl had lost her self-control since the far-off day when her father forced her to begin "collecting". With a strained white face she now regained her feet and without looking at him began clearing away their breakfast things.

Sylvanus caught sight of a dancing shape on the floor. Had his wanton elf resolved to follow him everywhere?

"Trivia! Trivia! Trivia!"

He was so much alone, and his superstitious imperatives had got such a hold on him, that he could not resist uttering Trivia's name aloud. This brought down on his head the first outburst of real anger that he had ever seen in Marret. She came and stood by the edge of their kitchen-table and struck it several times with the sauce-pan with which she had poached their eggs. Sylvanus had never realized how big her eyes were till he met them now.

"That's it. That's the way," she cried. "Play, play, play, play, play! *You're just like your brother*! You've no real feeling. The whole of your life is a game, and now you whistle to sunbeams when they're coming to shut you up in Hell's Museum! Did you know they called it that, out there on Downs? Hell's Museum, or Once in, Never Out! We used to take our Punch-Box over there one time, but Tiny got so frightened when the people spoke to her that we gave it up. There's something else too"—Here the girl lowered her voice to an awed whisper. "They cut out the brains of live dogs up there. The mad people don't know it, nor their friends neither. But Father knows the man that sells dogs to them. Zinzin knows him, too. Zinzin's been out with him when he met a man called Murphy over there. This Murphy let Zinzin peep through a hole into where they were cutting out a dog's brains. She said it screamed like a human being. She said the way its eyes looked when they had their fingers in its brain made her so sick she came away from thik hole. The mad people don't know about this; but *I* know about it, through Father and Zinzin."

She stopped to take breath and then burst out again. "You're thinking of May—that's who *you're* thinking about; and what's more you've been thinking about her ever since you woke up this morning! It's her coming that's made 'ee so jubilating and so beyond thee's self. You don't think as I hàven't see how 'twer, all this while, ever since you got that letter from she? Very well! The best thing you can do is go into the other room and keep putting on wood till she do come! When she *be* come you'll not be thinking of fires nor nothing else. You'll be thinking—"

As she worked herself up in this way to greater and greater anger, she began, to his consternation, slipping off her apron. She had already put down the sauce-pan. When she came to the phrase "the best thing *you* can do," she ran into the small passage, snatched up her coat and hat, came back to put them on in front of a hand-mirror on the dresser, and concluded her defiance with the biting words:

"You'll be thinking you wished she were back here, with her 'Hanged Man' and her pussy-cat ways. Well! You can keep her here this very day if you want to, *for I shan't be here.* I'll be—somewheres else! You was hardly listening to me—was you?—when I were telling you about they screaming dogs. What's a dog's Hell to you, and what's a girl's feelings to you either, you great Booby, with your baby-bunting sunbeams? You think, with your crazy airs, you know everything there is. But I can tell you you don't know *me*! No! you don't know me or love me either, as well as, as well as, as well as, *little Toby does!*"

This final reference to the popular pet of her father's show made Marret's mouth go down at the corners, but she had no tears in her

eyes this time and her contorted white face on the top of her tall
body resembled the proud decapitated head of some woman-rebel of
the old days, carried on a sword's point.

That she should have appealed to the dog Toby's love of her
against his own did make an impression on Sylvanus, and he rushed
after her as she went to the door. Twice he followed her and was
rebuffed. Twice he caught her by the waist. Once—getting irritated
by what he regarded as mere childish hysteria—he tried to pull her
back into the house by sheer force. But it was all to no purpose.
Marret's anger with him this morning was almost as deep as her love,
and he had simply to submit to it and let it take its course.

It was with a heavy heart that he went out into the backyard when
she was gone, and round to the front of the house and into the road
between Easton and the Beale. There her figure was—what a tall
girl she was and what a quaint hat she was wearing!—and how far
she had already gone! Should he run after her even now and make one
more last desperate appeal to soften her? No, she was passing some
quarrymen. It wouldn't do! Besides, there *were* limits—If the kid
understood him as little as this what was the good of anything?
They'd be forever having rows. Better let her go. Besides if he *was*
going to decide to go on with his talks it was no use having two rows
with the police! If her father was the little devil she pictured, he
would probably have been soon blackmailing them! He watched her
till she was out of sight and then returned to the back of the house
with dragging, weary, absent-minded steps. He thought of what she
had been telling him.

"I'd like to meet that Zinzin!" he said to himself. "But I wonder if
it's true that Brush goes in for vivisection up there? It seemed a
weird thing to do, with all those patients. But, God! it *must* be true.
She couldn't invent all that. Oh, deary I! I don't like it, I don't like
it, I don't like it!"

As the malice-demon of the inanimate willed, when he got to his
parlour that accursed fire, which by his fussing over it, had done all
the damage, was completely out. He found now that he had no heart
to light it. He found, too, that he had no heart to go into the kitchen
to wash up their breakfast-things, and still less heart to go upstairs to
make their bed.

"God!" he said to himself. "You need have no great passion for a girl like that to feel miserably lost when she's gone!"

He sat down in his armchair by the empty grate. He glanced at the door which he had left ajar. He had no spirit to get up and close it. Her absence had taken all the livingness out of everything. The desolation of this familiar room of his was appalling. What had the child done to him? It was absurd to suppose he cared for her in any serious way. He cared for her only *after his fashion* and she had known it and accepted it. Why then had she gone off like that? Well! she was a woman. When they like you they loved you, and when they loved you, "Prenez garde à toi!" Suddenly he jumped to his feet. This miserable desolation was more than he could bear! What had she done to him, and what to his house, this broomstick body with the little white face?

"I'll go into the kitchen," he thought. "I must wash up before the other one comes."

He went out into the passage and walked to the kitchen-door. They had left it ajar when she tore herself from him and now he suddenly found—he, the worshipper of the Absolute—that he *couldn't* push it open and go in. He stood stock still, staring at it like a dunderheaded simpleton. He fell to pulling at his moustaches and twisting them, first one and then the other, round and round in his fingers.

"I *can't* go in there," he thought, "and see her cup and plate and her chair. I *can't* look at the frying-pan, that she always put water in —so careful!"

He turned on his heel and walking back to the front of the house found himself, without his ever having *thought* of their bedroom, ascending the stairs. Into their room he went. There was her new brush, which he had himself bought for her in St. Mary's Street, when he found she always shared Tiny's. There was her big white comb, kept so beautifully clean, that she had bought with her own Punch-and-Judy pocket-money last summer. There was her night-gown carefully folded up and laid upon her side of the bed. She never *had* had any sort of luggage, not even a handbag. She had come to Last House with her nightgown and her comb wrapped up in news-paper. Sylvanus stood in the entrance to their room gazing at everything in it. She had shaken their pillows and thrown back the bed-clothes. He wished he could have seen the dent made by her head in her pillow.

"It's more dangerous than I thought," he said to himself, "to have a girl to your bed and board. They leave a feeling behind them that's unbearable. It's like homesickness in some foreign place where there's no one you know!"

He could not bring himself to touch a thing in the room, and down he went again, and this time hurried with a rush into the kitchen. Oh, curse it all! She'd taken off her bracelet when she got the meal and there it was on the lower shelf of the dresser! How he had twisted that bracelet round and round her wrist, as he held her in his lap the first night she came! She'd come entirely of her own accord. But, of course, these curst police wouldn't believe *that!* He picked up the bracelet. It was a cheap childish thing and of no value. He put it down again, exactly in the same place.

"What *is* it in a woman's presence," he said to himself, "that a person misses so? It's nothing that they say, that's certain! What the devil is it? Mart! Mart! Mart! *Where are you now?*"

The extremely unpleasant idea came to him that she might have met Gipsy May on the road, or at the little Portland Railway Station. He took the kettle off the stove and began slowly and ponderingly washing up, leaving to the last, however, her cup and her plate. From this latter he picked up a fragment of toast-crust and put it in his mouth.

"It's not *love*," he thought. "I'm no more in love with her than I am with May, or with Peggie Frampton."

He stood now at the back-door, with her cup in one hand and her saucer in the other, shaking them vigorously in the air. This he did, not as a libation to any of his endless deities, but to make sure that nothing she had touched went down the sink!

When he came back and had put her cup and saucer away, where in a shockingly quick second of time they became like all the other cups and saucers, he was aware, probably because of his having left the back-door open, that Trivia had entered the kitchen and was engaged in one of her liveliest dances on the stone floor. This was too much for him. Cursing Trivia from the bottom of his heart, he rushed away to the foot of the stairs. Here he hesitated again. But he could not resist the feeling that the girl was definitely present now in the bedroom upstairs, where during the lowest pulse of Time's great Mill-Wheel he had pressed her to him so tight between the curved horns of his skeleton shape.

"It's not love . . . it's not love . . . it's not love!" he said to himself.

Then he rushed upstairs again and into their room. Here he went over to the chest-of-drawers and touched her brush and touched her comb as tenderly as if they had been the brittle eggs of hedge-sparrows.

"If she only knew May as well as I do," he said, "she would come back. Perhaps she *will* come back when May's gone."

He came down after that, so full of her presence that he forgot to close the door at the top of the stairs. He deliberately left the parlour-door wide-open now in his superstitious fashion, so that any flickering residue of her faded consciousness should be free to approach him there.

"Caputanus", he mumbled; and having thus in the numbness of his loss jumbled his two words together, he repeated this curious expression several times over with that deep craving to be comforted by symbolic gibberish that attracts children to certain ancient nursery rhymes.

"Caputanus . . . Caputanus", he repeated over and over again and while his voice died away something took the place of this gibberish within him which really did seem like a new clue to his Absolute and which henceforth he would always associate with this flight of his Punch-and-Judy girl.

Outstretched on this faded rug-covered sofa from which emanated the same kind of animal smell of solitary maleness as emanates from a mat habitually occupied by some large dog, with his eyes tight shut and the ends of his great grizzled moustaches pushed forward by the wrinkling up of his coat collar, Sylvanus went through one of those moments in which a man really tastes the bitter-sweet dregs of mortal life. He felt as if a false bottom had suddenly sunk away below him. He felt as if all the surroundings of his days, the sands of Weymouth, the stones of Portland, the pebbles of Chesil, and even the stained, discoloured wall-paper of this unappealing room, had changed into something more real, something more raw, something that included

tragedies of human relations thàt shocked him with their unexpectedness. It was a crushing blow to his life-illusion to find that he *could*
suffer a desolation like this desolation simply because a young girl
had quarrelled with him and gone off!

"Caputanus!"

Was it by some abysmal Pythagorean magic of sound that these
blind nonsense-syllables lapped up and soaked up the sharp-smelling
fishy life-sweat of the sea-serpent of truth? Sylvanus received a final
revelation then of what he had often suspected, namely that the
Absolute was to be found in the concrete and not in the abstract, in
thought dipped in the life-juice, and not in thought gasping in vacuo.
But it was in thought, none the less, *in thought first and last*.

She was with him completely, his Punch-and-Judy girl, *more* completely, now she was gone, than when she was here! She had left
behind an essence of her soul, and it was coming in through the open
door and it was hovering about the dead fire, that was more entirely her
very self than even the feel of her long thin body when he held her in
bed! But she had done something, or her going off like that had done
something, to the actual thought-reality of the whole world.

The great "S. C.", as his gipsy called him, had played the platonic
nympholept a bit too far! He began to feel now as if everything about
him were suddenly endowed with a raw, scraping, deadly reality, twice
as intense as anything he had known before. The old carriage-rug
beneath him, his rumpled coat-collar, creased up under his chin, the
stained and peeling wall-paper, a certain damp sepulchral odour, like
dead men's bones, that always breathed, for some reason, from the
parlour of Last House, the feeling of all the piles and heaps of naked
stones that covered the stark surface of Portland, all these things
seemed to emerge from a pleasant nebulosity into a biting clarity, in
order to scrape and harrow his consciousness.

Caputanus! There was only one loop-hole of escape for a man to
whom everything had become like vinegar spilt upon dust, and that
was the heavenly escape of sleep. This, luckily, or unluckily, his
whole nature craved, and it was as a natural result of all his recent
night-vigils with Marret that he presently fell into so heavy and
profound a sleep that he was able to forget the loss of her. Why
didn't one of his starlings, or one of his robins or at least one of his

sparrows, for whose sakes he had so steadily refused to keep a cat, enter the house now, where all was so open and so still, and rouse him to the danger he was in? Instead of anything of the kind, Sylvanus' very tamest robin, along with a pair of starlings and half-a-dozen sparrows, actually followed the stealthy invader, when she came, hopping in her footsteps, making flutterings as if to alight on her shoulders, and, as it were actually guiding her to these defenceless rooms.

Arrived at the door, all these treacherous feathered accomplices watched with alert interest the way the gipsy kicked off her shoes beside the scraper, and the clandestine manner, with steps light as a faint gust of wind, with which she entered the house. Except perhaps in certain tribes among the red-men, there were no human beings anywhere who could *act on the chance* as May could, and so often did. By "acting on the chance", I refer to a certain throwing yourself into the current of events, and then just floating there, until a nod, a sign, a touch from the adjacent water-flags gives you the hint of your opportunity. Her opportunity now, in having Last House entirely to herself while its tenant slept, she only realized step by step, but anyone who had noted the stealthy swiftness of her movements and her quiet assured air would have sworn she had known from the beginning that it would be like this. Why couldn't that blue-bottle fly, so stupid and heavy from its long wintry quiescence, instead of settling on Sylvanus' tweed coat-sleeve, settle on his face and stir him up with a blow-fly's bodkin?

The woman's black eyes as she stood in the doorway watching the way his moustaches hung down and the way his arms hung down and the way one leg hung loosely over the sofa's edge, were gleaming with so much mischief, so many convoluted fancies, so many airy alarums and excursions, that no one—not the subtlest psychologist who ever lived—could have followed her thoughts. Her thoughts couldn't be followed. To get at them you would have to hop and skip sideways and round and in front, until at last from some intelligible idea floating, drifting *among* her thoughts, you might discover the faintest, filmiest, most tenuous clue to a vague general direction.

Certainly S. C.'s moustaches had never looked more like those of an amiable walrus than they looked now as he lay there. Moreover all ordinary human expression—possibly this was the result of his metaphysical struggles before he slept—had left his face. Sylvanus' face had indeed ceased to be that of a man, but at the same time it had not become that of an angel or a devil. It had become like one of those forlorn, denuded Homeric dead, those *ameneena kareena*, who, while they can remember and forget, are completely deprived of all the creative energy of the power of thought.

No one who had watched her watching him would have thought for a single second that Gipsy May was in the least fond of Sylvanus, and as for thinking that she loved him, as a woman loves a man with whom she had fallen in love, anyone would have mocked and scoffed at such a notion. She might have been saying to herself in an airy, casual, chanting voice:

"Nonny, Nonny! *He's* asleep! Upstairs .. upstairs .. upstairs .. and we'll see if the little Hide-and-Seek is sleeping too!"

Upstairs accordingly she went, and since all the doors were open and she had taken off her shoes, it was the easiest thing in the world for her to enter their room up there without disturbing him. Something like the flicker of a beetle's flight over the silence of a burdock-leaf full of raindrops did cross the woman's face when she caught sight of Marret's night-dress on the bed. She went up to the chest-of-drawers, however, and while she fell there into what seemed like a brown-study, she began fumbling with the girl's brush and comb and also with a pair of scissors that lay beside them over against Sylvanus' shaving things. Then she proceeded to look at herself for quite a long while in the looking-glass, pondering gravely and intently upon every feature and even closing one of her black eyes and pressing her fingers against her eyelid, as if to see what appearance she would present if she had only one eye. All this time she did not relinquish the scissors and presently with a slow pensive, contemplative gesture she lifted them to her forehead and cut off quite a considerable tress of her own hair. Then she proceeded—and no one could possibly have told whether she did it in a fit of absent-mindedness or after full premeditation—to twist this tress of hers round and round, and in and through, one of those convenient turning-points or pivot-hinges whereby such simple looking-glasses as this hang upon their supports.

You could have looked at yourself here for some while without being aware of anything exceptional; then by slow degrees it would have dawned on you that some sort of human hair had been twisted in at the side of the glass.

Still holding the scissors in her right hand she now fixed a long last look at her own black eyes and, lifting her left hand to her cheek, she touched the feverish red spot which burnt there with the tips of two of her fingers. The faintest flicker of a smile crossed her face as she did this and as she removed her fingers from her burning cheeks she pensively touched with them the edges of her wet lips. Then with the scissors still dangling from her hand, she went downstairs, treading with unbelievable stealthiness, but as she went she panted in little, quick, hurried gasps, as if she were in the throes of a fit of asthma.

Sylvanus was lying in exactly the same pose, one arm and one foot hanging loosely over the sofa's edge.

Gipsy May, holding the scissors tightly, stepped up to his side and using her free hand to secure what she was stealing, she deliberately cut off, in that same quiet absent-minded manner with which she had clipped the lock from her own brow, *both the man's moustaches.* Without waking him—for her movements were deft as those of a flycatcher—she slipped off with her booty down the passage to the kitchen and flung these twisted grey coils that seemed to desire to cling to her fingers into the kitchen stove.

She had pushed open one of the round iron lids of the stove with a special poker kept for this purpose, and as she hovered like a tragic moth over this fiery aperture, she was shocked by two things: by the deadly speed with which the hair was licked up and by the smell that arose. It was this smell more than anything in the whole transaction that gave to her feelings something of that sick throb of ghastly sacrilege such as in former times must have attended the roasting of human flesh. She felt fascinated and a little triumphant, too, as she stood there, staring at the orifice, but her dominant sensation was as if she had sold her soul to the devil and therefore could afford to linger by the way and see what happened. Meanwhile, the unmistakable smell of sacrilege ascended the kitchen chimney. Into the sunlit atmosphere above the roof of Last House it went. Not as from the

ancient halls of Thyestes, whence rose a more ominously-charged
smoke into a bluer sky, it went up, for it carried the loss of a man's
pride, not the loss of a living soul, but it was full, none the less, of the
fatal mischief of arbitrary destruction, only it was the destruction of a
person's life-illusion it carried, not of his mortal flesh.

Gypsy May firmly and quietly closed up the stove-entrance and
with the air of a sorrowful executioner she moved to the back-door and
went out. Here, in the yard—to the extreme agitation of a row of
sparrows perched upon a clothes-line set up by Marret, she proceeded
to put on her shoes. Her soul must have been hovering then between a
sense of almost fairy-story guilt, as if she had singed the King of
Thule's beard, and a childish interest in finding herself again in
Last House backyard!

Her black eyes began roving about from side to side of the little
enclosure, and ere long it chanced that they fell upon a perfectly good
Brazil nut, that the Punch-and-Judy girl must have thrown by accident out of the kitchen door. Upon this nut Gipsy May pounced, and
cracking it with her heel against a flagstone she scraped up the broken
bits and began separating the edible morsels from the fragments of
crushed shell with the absorbed concentration of a squirrel. She held
the trampled nut—not unmixed with dust and dirt—in the palm of
one hand, while with the fingers of the other she picked out what she
wanted. As she was thus engaged she kept casting the hurried glances
of a thievish magpie at a little cinder-strewn path that led, through
some straggling currant bushes, to a gap into the main road.

Had a wayfaring philosopher—if such persons still exist—rambling
speculatively through Weymouth and Portland, and having just
beheld the dense crowds assembled for the Cattistock wedding filling
all the space in front of Trinity Church and even blocking up the
Harbour-Bridge, looked casually down that path through the bushes
and caught sight of this figure at the back-door, he might have said to
himself:

"What a peaceful time that girl in that red shawl *is* having! *She*
isn't thinking about any mortal thing but 'the pleasure which there is in
life itself'!"

Some such wanderer—at any rate a stranger to the Beale road—
did as a matter of fact come along just then, and paused to stare,

attracted by the brightness of her costume; and that was quite enough for this offerer of burnt-offerings to the Infernal Gods. Throwing the nut-shell away, she made a hurried indecent gesture with her fingers at this onlooker, and ran into the house.

Then it was that with a deliberate clattering and creaking of her shoes, which she made to sound as loud as if they'd been clogs thumping down the passage, she re-entered the parlour, crying out in a clear voice:

"Well, I never! Well, I never!"

Sylvanus opened his eyes with a start as she entered, struggled up awkwardly to his feet from the sofa and bending forward took her head affectionately between his hands and pressed it to his lips, kissing both her hair and her forehead many times over.

"But God! May," he cried in astonishment when he held her at last at arm's length from him and surveyed her brow from which she had cut that lock of hair.

His big hands completely hid her small snake's ears, but she knew well what he was saying!

"*What have* you done to yourself?"

"Feel . . . your . . . own—" was her quick reply uttered in a whisper as his hands dropped from her head.

And it was destined to Gipsy May to know then how revenge tasted. It was like discovering a new Tarot card. The truth was she experienced a diabolical rapture from that first expression his countenance assumed as his hands went to his face and he found those familiar adjuncts gone. And yet it was not a look of anger that he gave her. Nor was it one of bewilderment. It was a look of pure shame, and it was accompanied by an unnatural rush of red blood to his usually very pale face. This flush on Sylvanus' face was something that she had never seen before. In fact it was something that no one in Weymouth or Portland had ever seen. The last time it had appeared was when Bacon Major and Buckingham Minor tied his legs and tied his hands and left him at the gate of the Public Workhouse in the little town where he went to school. The tramp who untied him told his friends later.

"Thik young gent were as red as a bleedin' raddish. He'd have bust 'is innerds, seems so, if I ain't coomed by and let 'un loose."

But there was no tramp to "coom by" now through the open doors of Last House and put Sylvanus' moustaches on again!

For the passing of one second Gipsy May's black eyes drank up that extraordinary dusky red and that look as if he had been exposed to the mob, with a wild, wanton glee. She never expected to have a revenge quite as complete! She had fancied that Sylvanus would display a flash of anger and then laugh. Instead of which, out of that unnaturally red face, eyes were fixed upon her that contained the last bitter dregs of the cup of human shame. For a second of time Gipsy May tugged like a greedy child at the nipples of intoxicating sweetness.

"I'll larn him," her ecstasy might be translated, "I'll larn him to have girls' nightgowns in his bedroom!"

But the metheglin draught of sweet revenge resembles very closely the erotic obsession which exacts it, and there had no sooner appeared little, glittering drops in the man's eyes than the woman experienced a violent reaction.

"I'm sorry, S. C., I'm bitter sorry," she said. "Don't look like that, S. C. for your old Egyptian can't stand to see you looking like that."

"No, I won't! No, no, of course not; certainly I won't! In fact I don't!" he replied hurriedly, and his voice had the tone of a man who speaks to his nurse while he is performing some humiliating function of nature.

"I'll make it up to you, S. C." she cried hurriedly, "I will! I will!"

And she watched him imploringly while very slowly all that dusky red began to ebb from his countenance, leaving a terrible pallor.

"Don't 'ee put yourself out, my precious," he murmured quietly. " 'Tis a hard thing to take on yourself what another feels, but what I feel will—will be—all right in a minute!"

His mild philosophical tone brought with it a hurried, quite unconscious resorting to his old trick when anything disturbed him or when he desired to gain time. He raised his hand to his face, clearly with the instinct of getting hold of some philosophical idea through the familiar contact with his great moustaches. But there was nothing there! Only his upper lip had a small outgrowth, bristly and rough, thicker at the sides than in the middle, an outgrowth that gave him, when he touched it with his finger, the sensation of something weird having happened, not exactly as if he had a patch of sham hair on his lip, or as if a wandering thistle-head or a prickly burr had stuck to his skin, but as if his own hair had, in some terrifying manner, *changed its character!*

"What was that you were saying, May?"

And he sat down square and straight on the sofa and stretched out his arms to her. The woman gave her voluminous skirt a deft twist with her fingers and perched herself on the extreme end of his long knees; from which position she leaned toward him and took his chin between her finger and thumb. This immemorial gesture of humble supplication—the impact of which would certainly have made the harassed scholar at Kimmeridge House think of Thetis at the knees of Zeus—was less than nothing to Sylvanus.

"What . . . was that . . . you were saying . . . May?"

With that he thrust back her hands, and raising his own to his mouth licked the tips of them and rubbed them backwards and forwards over his denuded upper-lip, which to his sympathetic imagination began now to feel actually sore.

"Why don't you ask why I did it to you, S. C.?" she said, watching him intently, while she pressed her thin knuckles against the pit of her stomach and frowned a puzzled emphatic frown.

"Because you thought it attracted women towards me?"

She nodded vigorously.

"I did it first to myself," she said.

"Oh, *you* are different. *You'd* be attractive if you cut off every scrap of your hair!"

She jumped off his knees and stretched out her hand to him.

"Come on S. C.!" she cried, "I'm going to make it up to you! You've got your boots on. Do you want your hat? Never mind locking up. Come on. Let's go. Quick! Quick! Quick!"

It was quite clear to him that the idea of his sulking, the idea of his sending her away, the idea of his being tragically hurt by what she'd done, never for one second entered her head. She was so used herself to being a show, a spectacle, a laughing-stock, a cynosure, that it never struck her that what she had done to him was parallel to Larry Zed's dying his hair black.

"Poor May!" he said to himself. "She's terribly upset because she did this. Why, *there* are the scissors—on the floor! And they're

Mart's, too. I'll go with her, I don't know what she's going to do with me. But I'll go with her."

The woman now re-appeared with a sheaf of his soldier-canes in her hand.

"Go on; choose quick!" she cried.

"She likes doing the same old things," he thought, "that she used to do all those months."

And as the howling of those November storms came back to him, and the patter of those November rains, he submissively chose a cane at random and they went out together. . . .

"There's your girl, sitting with Peggie Frampton on Bridge!" his companion suddenly remarked, when, after vainly trying to make her say where they were going, he found himself hopelessly entangled in the excited crowd round Trinity Church. "I saw her push her way through to Missy Frampton, who were sitting where they both be now. 'Twere when I saw thik flock of people there that I decided to come out by boat."

Sylvanus could not but be thankful that, where he stood now by the gipsy's side it was difficult for those girls on the Bridge to see anything of them. And the crowd was packed so close that when once anyone was jammed into a particular vantage-ground it could only be by a violent struggle that freedom was obtained.

The gipsy soon gathered from their neighbours that all the important people, except the bridegroom were already in the Church. The bride had gone in, they learned, a few minutes before they appeared. In fact they could see from where they stood the helmets of the policemen who had cleared a path for her conveyance. Never, they learned, in all the history of the Two Boroughs had so many notables come together. Not another soul, they were told, could possible get into the church. Jerry Cobbold himself, they were assured, had the greatest difficulty in getting into the building. He had come late and alone, for Mrs. Cobbold was with her sister, the bride.

Again and again as in his familiar tweed suit Sylvanus towered above his bright-shawled companion, people nudged each other and whispered and giggled. There was no mistaking him! It was clear to them all who he was, and it was abundantly clear to them all, too, that he had lost his moustaches.

Just in front of the two friends, however, as they stood there, between them and a gentleman who was frantically struggling to open a lady's parasol to keep the sun from his head, a short man and a gaunt woman were engaged in such earnest whispers between themselves that they were totally oblivious of the presence of Sylvanus and the gipsy. These were none other than Mr. and Mrs. Trot.

"If only us *knew* he were wi' his father and mother last night," Bum Trot was saying, "us 'ud feel different. 'Tis them turble words Jobber were allus uttering what do taunt *me* mind, Missus, zay what 'ee 'ool. Jobber bain't woon vor yowling and growling without doing naught. I be afeared for 'un, 'ooman, and that's God's holy truth. I be afeared for 'un!"

"Mr. Cat'stock 'ull be here present, man," responded Mrs. Trot, consolingly, though her troubled face belied her words, "and then us 'ull know the master ain't done no unlawful deed. I be more acquainted wi' high-life ways and such, than thee be Bum, and 'tis the custom I tell 'ee for these here bridegrooms to keep their brides waiting. Them grand ladies don't think nought of a man what's at beck and call. Be 'ee sure Cormorant ain't gone? 'Tis like the master to go off by his wone self when all the world be sight-seeing."

"Cormorant be where she allus do be," replied Bum Trot gloomily. "I wish to sweet Jesus her weren't!"

The grossly loud words of a neighbour a little further off now drowned the murmers of the Trots. This person was commenting upon Sylvanus' appearance in language so emphatic that it could not but reach his ears.

"'A have had they circus-twisties pulled off, look so," he heard this critical spectator say. "I allus knowed they things weren't real. 'A must have surmised 'a'd look more genteel without 'un. But 'a don't, do 'en? 'A looks like Bart Looney, the Four-in-Hand man, what drowned 'isself for love of Molly Dingle the school-teacher. Thee remembers Mr. Looney, doesn't't? 'A were nephy, or summat o' that, to Herb' Dandin, the Radipole clerk. 'A had a monstrous long face, Mr. Looney had, and a sour, too, and 'twere no wonder neither, seeing 'a couldn't do it. Never *could* do it, try all 'a would and try all *she* would to help 'un. 'Twere *for that* and not for's sour face that 'a lost his Moll. He would try and she would try, and 'tweren't till they knowed 'twere no good that 'a drowned 'isself. Aren't I right, Elizabeth? And ain't thik wold Cobbold there, wi' his Roosian twisties gone, the living Superscription of Mr. Looney what never could do it all his days?"

No one will know what Gipsy May felt as she listened to this voluble wretch, who was an extremely shaky old man talking to a purblind old woman, nor what she felt as she saw Sylvanus' hand go up again and again to his face, and as often fall to his side. She suffered most when she saw him lick his fingers and rub his upper lip, as if it were sore or even bleeding. Nervously and furtively she glanced sideways at his mouth, half afraid that she really *might* have hurt it with the point of the scissors. But no! It was all right, though she had to admit that her S. C.'s mouth, without those moustaches, looked like the mouth of a gigantic rabbit.

"Oh, S. C., S. C., why did I, oh, why did I?" she moaned in her heart. " 'Twas that card that were the cause. 'Twas 'the Man with Three Staves' that were the cause!"

And what, meanwhile, was Sylvanus himself feeling and thinking? He also was occupied—if the truth must be told—by the problem of Causation. He was engaged in a dialogue with his Absolute.

"Are you the First Cause, or are you not?" he kept asking this evasive Entity.

And it seemed to him that the Absolute, like that Nothingness which must have confronted Mr. Looney before he drowned himself, replied that It was not the First Cause, or the Last Cause, or any other Cause! It simply was Everything, and there was no room in Everything for the idea of Cause. There was only All there was; and it was the inherent nature, throughout eternity, for All there was to change.

"Everything," the Absolute continued, as his clean-shaven devotee stared at the green parasol with which the elderly gentleman in front of him was trying to protect himself from the sun. "Everything has always changed, and always will. Outside Me, who am Everything, there is Nothing."

But the strain with which Sylvanus had forced himself to become for the nonce the Absolute arguing with the Absolute now broke down and humiliation swept over him. He felt that without his great moustaches, that secret belfry of wisdom at whose ropes he could always tug, he had become some one else, a different person.

"I must think it out," he said to himself, and still staring at the green parasol he resolutely faced his humiliation.

He analysed his whole character as he had never analysed it before.

"I depended on the idea of myself with those moustaches," he thought. "They were like my suit of clothes. They were like my cane. They were like my being Jerry's brother. When I talked to my girls, when I talked to strangers on the esplanade, when I drew Lucinda on to berate me, I was always *myself with my big moustaches!* When quite alone, in my shelter over there, with my strong and wise rope and my wonderful oil-painting, I was always myself with my moustaches. It was my moustaches more than this old suit and this cane," and he bent his cane between his fingers against his knee, for it was not long enough to touch the ground, "that were my leopard-spots. They were Me! Even when I was in my privy over there they were Me. When I held Marret in bed this morning, they were always Me. When I had cream to my porridge and that dark treacly sugar that I used to buy at that little shop in Easton, for I *can't* afford to feed Marret *and* have that treacly sugar, too, though I like the way it mixes with cream and I wish I were going to have some for lunch today, they were Me. When I hummed my old Caput and Anus song in the potato-garden which invented its own tune, Me, still Me, always they were Me! When boys ran after me in the street and tormented me and when people stared at me on the sands in summer when I paddled with women, that no one else wanted to go into the water with, it was always 'Me and my moustaches'. And as I thought to myself, 'I go with people that have no one else to go with! and as I thought to myself:—'boys wouldn't hunt me if I wasn't like a Lama with my moustaches' it was them—but what will I do now?"

He tried to force himself to accept himself as Mr. Sylvanus Cobbold, with a weak-minded mouth, like a prehistoric hare, going about help-lessly over the surface of the earth! And then he left that attempt and tried to think of his soul as a mathematical dot in Space and of his body as being a bundle of negligible Matter that his soul dragged about with it.

"I can enjoy my sensations," he thought, "even if my face *is* a laughing-stock. I can enjoy life even if I *am* the ugliest man. A dung-beetle can enjoy things as much as Tossty Clive. A lob-worm can enjoy things as much as Sippy Ballard. What I must aim at feeling myself to be now is one of those Freaks in Barnum's Circus, only going about freely instead of on Show! I'm lucky to *be* still free. I must think of that. If I go on talking on the esplanade they'll make Jerry give me over to Brush. At Brush's I'll be more in keeping as a mathematical dot, than if I had my moustaches. Yes, I'll take it as fate. I'll shave my lip tomorrow and henceforth I'll shave it till I die. Maybe they'll grow again, in my coffin. Well! They were the longest moustaches ever seen in Weymouth!"

He had stared so fixedly and so intently and so long at the green parasol opposite him before he reached his conclusion that he felt bewildered and confused when he came to himself. The crowd had grown excited now as it waited for this long-coming bridegroom. There began to be jeering cries, gross sallies, malignant facetiousnesses. One hoarse voice, speaking in the Portland accent, cried out suddenly:

"Where be Dummy Skald, then? Dummy Skald had zummat to zay to Master Cat'stock, us have heard tell, afore this little job can be car'd out!"

So dazed and abstracted was Sylvanus, and so separated from the jangle of the world, that Gipsy May had now to repeat a remark of hers twice before he caught it.

"Isn't that Mr. Muir over there, son of old Muir, the Schoolmaster, standing on top step, near Church door, with that fine lady holding them lovely roses. They be moss-roses, looks so, but maybe not!"

She paused, staring intently at the couple she mentioned, who were standing wedged in and helpless in the thickest part of the crowd.

"Why, 'tis Curly Wix, the Wishing Well girl, that's who it be, the one they say he's marrying, now he's the Cat'stock tutor. They be going to live at Corporal Dawson's, if Mrs. Pengelly ain't got it all mixed up."

Sylvanus succeeded in singling out the strikingly dressed Curly, who did indeed make it seem as if Magnus were standing there with some famous county beauty who by some blunder of the officials had not been yet escorted into her reserved seat.

"Did you begin to think, S. C., that I'd forget what I promised?"

He looked down at the bright-shawled figure at his side and smiled for the the first time since Marret had left his house.

"Don't 'ee fret yourself, May," he responded.

But the woman insisted:

"I couldn't sleep tonight," she said, "if I knew you was grieving for your sand girl. She's a poor preference, S. C., among so many, but when a person wants his choice 'tis his choice he wants. You stay where you be, S. C., and I'll run round and fetch them two. Don't 'ee let nothing move you, S. C., from where you be standing for I don't want to be left with neither of they kids."

If she hadn't darted off before her last words were out of her mouth he would have clutched her arm, so mad did it seem to think of forcing a path through such a crowd. But all he could do now was to obey her command to the letter. Do what he could to stop it the sudden thought of Marret's seeing him as he was now, with his grotesque rabbit-mouth left naked, caused a hot flush of burning shame to mount to his face.

Presently there was a tremendous upheaval of the crowd and great disturbing currents swept it backwards and forwards. It became increasingly difficult to obey the gipsy's mandate, for his neighbours were flung against him by *their* neighbours, and the whole space between Bridge and Church soon became a seething arena of anger, scurrility and indignant panic.

But the near approach of a light, open touring car that had caused all this confusion helped in a measure to allay it. The police constables on foot had now been reinforced by several more on horseback and it was by the aid of these that the machine drew up at the foot of the Church-steps, so close indeed to that beautiful girl in the grey dress holding the moss-roses, that she was seen to draw back as if in considerable trepidation. Simultaneously with its stopping, one of the policemen three open its door and a man holding a silk hat was observed descending. Cries arose of "Cattistock! Cattistock!" and one small boy—he was an office-boy in the brewery—piped up in a thin quavering voice: "Three cheers for Mr. ——" but young

Witchit who happened to be with this audacious youth but who was himself speedily learning the ways of the world, put his hand over his friend's mouth. When, however, the man with the silk hat paused before ascending the Church steps and began to converse with Mr. Muir and the lady with the roses, there ran through the crowd that angry murmur of disappointed expectation which is often the precursor of reckless, wild, and dangerous movements. The man with the silk hat, who had been talking earnestly and rapidly to the lady in grey, now swung round and stood up very straight and very slender and handsome.

"Sippy Ballard," cried one rude humorist in a loud voice, "Why don't 'ee take thee uncle's pleace, Sippy?"

But a much more official voice, although a much feebler voice, now made itself heard.

"Ladies and Gentlemen," it said, "we have something to announce."

It was then that Mr. S. P. Ballard rose splendidly to what everybody later admitted was a very awkward situation.

"Friends of the Two Boroughs," he said, "who have come to do honour to our distinguished—to *my* distinguished uncle"—he was felt at this point to indulge in a very artless and very charming hesitation—"you will all be very sorry to learn that Mr. Cattistock's wedding has—has been—indefinitely postponed—owing to—owing to—"

But by what subterfuge, by what diplomatic euphemism, this youthful Talleyrand explained the non-appearance of his master was totally swallowed up in the clamour and hullabaloo raised by the grosser elements of the crowd, and Sylvanus, drawing back from the violent struggles his elderly neighbour was making to close the green parasol, saw that the bright shawl of his gipsy friend had almost reached the parapet of the Bridge upon which Marret and Peg were sitting.

There must have been something in the interior mechanism of that green parasol which had a power of vivid reflection, for as Sylvanus' hand went up to his mouth for the hundredth time that afternoon, there fell upon the broad back of Bum Trot a dancing sun-beam. Such, however, was the noisy exchange of agitated exclamations all round him that neither of the devoted adherents of the absent Jobber caught the automatic response of "Trivia, Trivia, Trivia!" that broke from the shaven lips of the tall man in the tweed suit.

12

CURLY'S ROSES

THERE was not a single one of the elderly persons summoned by Eliza Chant to partake of refreshments that evening in the old-fashioned Servants' Hall at Peninsular Lodge, who did not say to herself when the news reached her of the postponement of the wedding:

"Well, thik party will be off, then! No taste of wine for we out to Chickerel, seeing as the Lord 'as decided contrary. But, all the same for that, I think I'll go round just for a minute, *by myself*, to see Eliza, if only to find out how thik poor woman be bearing up."

One by one, therefore, at any time between seven o'clock and nine o'clock that night, all her various invited guests rang the back-door bell of Mr. Cattistock's home and were admitted by Mrs. Chant.

Assuming that all her friends could not possibly have heard of the "Fee-asky", as she called it, at Trinity Church, and that, among those who *did* hear of it, would be some in whom curiosity would prove stronger than discretion, the wise Eliza had not failed to place on the big table in the Servants' Hall adjoining the kitchen, a cold but substantial supper. Here, accordingly, were assembled, volubly discussing every aspect of the day's occurrence, Mrs. Matzell from Half-Way House, Mrs. Monkton from Trigonia House, Sarah Piddle from "The Turret", old Ammabel from Spy Croft, and finally the two women who were her most especial cronies, though in no way connected with domestic service, Mrs. Wix of Railroad Cottage, Upwey, and Mrs. Witchit of St. Alban's Street, Weymouth.

Old Ammabel had been years and years in the employ of James

Loder and all her feudal loyalty was concentrated on the old gentleman with the gastric ulcers. Ruth, her actual mistress, she disliked.
She disliked her with one of those lodged, rooted, mysterious dislikes,
which are the secret tragedy of so many human dwellings. Ammabel
regarded Rodney as a dangerous atheist, partly because of various
conversations with Ruth which she had overheard, and partly because
in her tenderness and pity for the master of the house she felt instinctively that the young man lacked sympathy for his father. She was
talking about her master now to Mrs. Matzell.

"All I say is, when his time comes he'll be as sure murdered by
that boy and that mean, mimicking girl, as if they had done it by
pison."

"You speak no less than gospel, Ammabel," replied Mrs. Matzell,
whose ruddy countenance twitched, jerked, and one might almost say
exploded, with her desire to be the person revealing tragical truths
rather than the person receiving them, "but I can tell you that our
poor Captain be tormented worse nor Mr. Loder for all his ulcers.
'Tis worse to suffer in mind, and it's the mind with him. What's *your*
opinion, Mrs. Piddle, being in a Doctor's house as you are, about my
poor dear Captain? We'll let alone what drove him to be like he is.
But as I see it, Mrs. Cobbold stirs up his poor brain whenever she
comes anywhere a-nigh him."

"I thought he never saw Mrs. Cobbold these days," threw in Mrs.
Piddle. "At least that's what Doctor thinks. If thik evil woman,
Doctor thinks, came as nigh thy master as I be to thee now, he would
fall to raving. What Doctor thinks is *that summat* did happen twixt
the two on 'em, but 'twere all Mrs. Cobbold's fault for leading the
poor man on. Her led him on, Doctor thinks, so as to taunt his
conscience with her, all his livelong days! Doctor thinks 'twould do
no good to either party to send him to this here Brush—begging
your parding since he's a relation—for this here Brush is—"

But Mrs. Matzell interrupted.

" 'Twould be over my body, Sarah Piddle, and no ways else, that
the Captain would go to *that* man! I know what I'm talking about,
because I've seen what I've seen in our house, and I tell you the
Captain's a quiet, God-fearing, self-respecting gentleman to what
he'd be if they took him into that place."

All the women glanced furtively at Mrs. Chant. No one knew just how things stood between Mrs. Chant's master and the director of Hell's Museum. A silence ensued, during which they each called up the image of some member of their own family whose shaky wits might require aid from the ambiguous specialist.

The Servants' Hall at Peninsular Lodge was in some ways the least unpleasing room in the house. Its chief characteristic was its faded neutrality. The ancient wall-paper was almost indistinguishable, as the lamp on the big table shone upon its discoloured surface. The walls were hung, too, with portraits of bygone Cattistocks, so dirty and uncared-for, that, in sheer shame at their condition, the owner had removed them from his front room.

All the time the discomforting idea of Dr. Brush was weighing upon these wedding-less guests their faces reverted to that pathetic weariness of a life of woman's toil which the spice of scandal had temporarily removed. Mrs. Monkton's countenance grew more pinched, more bitter; Mrs. Witchit's more benevolently helpless; old Ammabel's gloomier; Sarah Piddle's more gross and earthy; Mrs. Wix's paler and more stricken with years; Mrs. Matzell's—she was a short, red-faced woman—more care-burdened and vulnerable. All of them, unlike men in a similar situation, reverted with fatal acquiescence to the burden and the weight of life's day-by-day assaults upon the soul.

It had only been by the use of her authority as his old nurse, and by threatening to spend her own money, that Mrs. Chant had got leave from her master to order the cold brawn, the cold tongue, the cold chicken that now tempted these guests, but thoughts of the Work-house, of their relations, of their masters, and above all of Dr. Brush, led them at this moment to drop their knives and forks and sink sadly into themselves.

"Open the window a trifle for me, me girl, will 'ee?" whispered Mrs. Chant to the deep-bosomed Mrs. Witchit, who was sitting next her at the end of the table.

The fish-monger's wife extricated her portly form and went to the window and did as she was bid. But instead of recovering them from their temporary gloom the damp mud-scented airs that had climbed the upland from the shallow backwater that separated Chesil from the main-land only increased it. Such sea-birds as chose to break the silence, in their voyaging from the West Bay to Weymouth Bay seemed to leave their discordant cries behind them as they flew, the drifting, disembodied voices, not so much of flight and disaster, as of a beating against insoluble mystery.

But of all the living denizens of the two boroughs, the ones who heard these things least, who thought of them least, were these elderly, hard-worked, domestic women. Over their houses in Weymouth— prisons that had drunk up their youth, their blood, their life, as they toiled in the service of men and the children of men—those land-marks of the Inanimate, the Spire, the Nothe, the Bridge, the White Horse, the old King's Statue, the noble bulk of Portland, with the crying of their seagulls by day and by night had brooded and yearned in vain. They heard them not, these victims of house-care, or if they heard them they heeded them not. In the steam of their kettles, in the smoke of their chimneys, half the natural responses to the life of the race they served had evaporated from their devoted veins.

Matters soon cheered up, however, in the Servants' Hall of Penin-sular Lodge when various neglected aspects of the day's great "Fee-asky" were brought forward for discussion.

Perhaps the lady, at this curious collation, who received the most dramatic respect from the others was Mrs. Wix, and this not because her daughter was engaged to Benny's tutor, but because her daughter, as well as the tutor, had left the church door in Mr. Ballard's car after the portentous announcement. Not a woman present had failed to gain some private word with Mrs. Wix to-night. After their hostess, who really knew less than anyone about what had happened at the church, as she had remained at home to prepare for the reception of the married couple, Mrs. Wix was the centre of the stage. Over and over again Mrs. Wix had to repeat her enlarged version of Curly's confused version of the clever Sippy's cautious and calculated per-version of what he had heard from his uncle.

Every human gathering, whether of elderly servants or of elderly members of parliament, falls inevitably into a natural rhythm of its own; a rhythm that gives it form and shape as a psychic entity. According to this spiritual rhythm in the Servants' Hall at Chickerel, whenever either Mrs. Chant or Mrs. Wix opened their mouths all the rest of the conversation ceased. The only chance Mrs. Matzell had of obtaining equal respect was to repeat for the tenth time that evening her account of the return of Daisy to Old Castle Road, Daisy, it seems, had returned without her mother, bringing the news that the disappointed bride had gone off with Mrs. Cobbold to spend a few days at High House.

"What did Mr. Ballard look like, Eliza," enquired Mrs. Witchit suddenly, "when he brought Mr. Muir to the front-door?"

One of those occult silences immediately occurred, by means of which a group of human beings indicate their recognition of the arrival of a point in the conversation where the devil is likely to break out. Into this silence, broken only by the hissing of the kettle in the adjoining kitchen, and the distant whining of Yellow, Benny's dog, who had been temporarily shut up, the voice of Lizzie Chant rose, projected itself, established itself, throwing out, as an airplane might scatter pamphlets, little separate mental pictures of what was in the wind.

"I never saw Mr. Ballard," she said. "He took Curly home when he'd dropped Mr. Muir, and 'twas my son who drove Mr. Muir and our Benny over to Brunswick."

The silence that fell when she ceased was exactly as if in the midst of a company of ordinary witches the Witch of Endor had spoken.

It was the old Spy Croft parlour-maid who broke up this awestruck pondering on the ways of fate. Ammabel was so used to hearing the groans of James Loder and seeing him thrust his knuckles into the pit of his stomach while an atheist son and "a mean, mimicking girl" gloated over his pain, that she was aware of a feeling of superiority over these others, none of whom knew what real tragedy meant.

"Old Poxwell," she had been thinking indignantly, "Old Poxwell worse than the master? And worse because *mind* be worse than *body?* Oh, the Lord-a-Lord, the Lord-a-Lord! If they'd seen my master twist on floor, like a waspy what a kitten have caught, they wouldn't talk about their Captain and his mind. The Captain may have done what the Lord forbids but he doesn't twist and groan and hug his poor stummick. These ignorant torpids have no idea what is seen and known in *some* houses in Weymouth. The Captain's mind! What would they say and do if they knew all I know, of what the dear Lord

allows us to suffer, when we are old? The Captain's mind! Them
as talks of folks' minds being the trouble, dunno what *I* know. 'Tis
our poor carcasses what be the plague! Master would exchange his
stummick for the Captain's mind any Sunday afternoon!"

With these thoughts in *her* mind old Ammabel turned to Mrs.
Monkton and asked that lady whether Mr. Ballard had come straight
back to Trigonia House after taking Curly home. Curly's mother felt
a little uncomfortable when she heard this question, for she was,
herself, only too well aware that Mr. Ballard had not brought her
daughter home till late in the evening, and then had brought her back
in such a disturbed state that the girl had gone straight to bed. Mrs.
Wix had a most agitating vision of that beautiful grey dress lying all
crumpled and creased across a chair.

"I were out, my own self," replied Mrs. Monkton, "so I can't tell
'ee for sure. And me darter were takin' her English lesson with Mr.
Gaul. She be mighty fond of her lessons, me darter be. She's a-going
to follow after her fayther, I shouldn't wonder, who in's time were a
grand scholard."

"What a day of days this has sure been!" exclaimed Mrs. Witchit in
a rich contemplative voice. "Witchit were near church-door when
the quality comed out, and he said 'twas a wonder to see 'em all so
crestfallen. He said Mrs. Lily were as white as paper, and if it hadn't
been for pride and shame would have sat down on ground and cried
pitiful. He said Daisy kept shutting her eyes when she stood holding
her mother's hand till Mrs. Cobbold took the poor woman away. He
said Daisy went off with the Loders then and Miss Ruth were left
to wheel the old gent in his bath-chair while Daisy walked in front
with Mr. Rodney. They didn't wait for the bath-chair, he said. They
passed quite close to him, he said, and were walking so fast and so
excited like that they didn't see him. He said their eyes were so
shining and they were talking so quick they never saw him. He said
how kind of Mr. Rodney to take such an interest in a school-girl like
that. But I knows Witchit, and what he *meant* was that he thought
Mr. Rodney were taking advantage, and instilling ideas of bridal
nights and such-like into that young girl's head."

"I wouldn't wonder," broke in old Ammabel, "that he weren't
right there, Mrs. Witchit. I've been watching Master Rodney quite

a lot lately and he's forever making excuses to meet Miss Daisy. I expect he is—as you say—putting thoughts he ought not—being an atheist—into that dear young soul's pure mind."

It was Mrs. Wix who was the occasion now of the creation of another of these sacrosanct deathly silences, while Lizzie Chant spoke. Mrs. Chant had, it seemed, like the purveyor of the Marriage-Feast in the Gospel, a trick of saving the best wine of scandal till the last, and it was for such nectar as this that Mrs. Wix, extracting her immemorial piece of crochet-work from a black satin bag, and pushing her chair from the table now tactfully prepared the way.

"I keep thinking, Eliza, how you must have felt when you come down this morning and found Mr. Cattistock gone and stove in kitchen lit and kettle on. I hope whatever's happened to the poor gentleman he had a good breakfast inside of he! That's what I always said to my husband when he went off to his work. 'Lay up a good foundation, Herbert', I said, 'for none of us knows what lies afore us when us leaves our threshold-stone'."

Mrs. Wix's last word—which was the syllable "stone"—seemed to be falling into a gulf of stillness so profound that echoes of its descent came to every ear as if from far away. Indeed the noise of "Yellow", scratching at the door of Benny's room where he had been shut up, became so loud, in this awe-inspiring hush, that Mrs. Witchit was heard murmuring to herself:

"That dog wants something."

Mrs. Witchit being a giver rather than a taker among men was always finding that someone wanted something, and it seemed probable now that she might get up from her seat and go upstairs to the dog, if this silence were prolonged, but at last their hostess *did* open her mouth, and pregnant with significance were her words:

"He had no milk to his tea. I don't know how I failed to keep back a little, but I don't take milk me wone self, and how could I know he would want breakfast afore dawn? How could I know it? Tell me that!"

"You *couldn't* know it, Eliza," responded Mrs. Witchit. "There's no one but the good God could know it."

But Lizzie Chant fell into deep sadness, her old wrinkled face puckered up in the lamentable pondering of vain wishes.

"If only, if only," she thought, "I'd left a drop of milk where he could have found it!"

It was at this point that Mrs. Monkton's vigilant and wary countenance jerked spasmodically with the itch of enquiry.

" 'Twas when you were having your own cup o' tea," she said, "just after calling Benny, that Jobber Skald came with that fish from Witchit's, weren't it?"

An electric quiver of resentment passed through Mrs. Chant's thin frame at the bluntness of this inquisition.

"That's done for *you*, Mam!" she said to herself. "I'll never ask *you*, with your pertinent questions, to my master's house again!"

"No," she replied with an air of the lightest and most casual consideration, "I think it was *before* I took Master Benny his hot water that the Jobber called with the fish. I think 'twas just after I'd come down. Yes, it must have been just about six that he came, but anyway, 'twere hours and hours after the master were gone."

A deep, protective instinct—almost below the level of her own consciousness—now stirred beneath the voluminous bosom of Mrs. Witchit.

"I mind well," she began, drawing everybody's startled attention to her by the intensity in her voice, "I mind well that I said to Jobber the last time he were in shop, 'I be invited to Eliza's at Chickerel, come Thursday night, but I'm sure Eliza won't have thought of what to order for her wone friends, seeing she'll have to cater for a new mistress and for new ways'."

The quavering high-pitched voice of Sarah Piddle now broke in.

"You said Jobber were mighty funny when 'a came, and that he brought his fish-basket into kitchen and asked in a graveyard voice for Mr. Cat'stock? What *I* do say is, 'tis a thousand pities the Doctor ain't here,"—a smile ran round the table, for Mrs. Piddle's infatuation with old Higginbottom was well-known to them all—"so that he could diagnose this case proper and say whether the Jobber were in his right wits or whether he were drunk. 'Tis likely enough he'd been up all night at some Public-House by Harbour and that the sailors down there—that's what *I'd* say, if I were Doctor—dared him to call at Chickerel."

"Well, as I looks at it, Eliza," said Mrs. Monkton in a hard, clipped, pecking tone, like a vicious raven summoning up the case against the murderer of Cock Robin, "your master had reasons of his own for giving his lady the go-by. He may have heard, of course, that Mr. Skald threatened to insult him on his wedding-day, and even offer him violence, for we've all heard such tales, but as I looks at it myself—" at this point the didactic tone of the woman became so unsympathetic to the easy-going Dorsetshire gossips around her, for the Trigonia House landlady came from Salisbury, that they began murmuring and whispering to each other, even while she laid down the law—"and feels it," she went on bitterly, "in me bones, 'twasn't nothing to do with his quarrel with Mr. Skald that made him run off like this. *'Twas because he had some other woman.* I've a-heard from a good reliable quarter that he used to meet one of those dancing women at the Regent's, and as I looks at it, Eliza, it was—"

But Mrs. Chant, who had made several vain attempts to interrupt this rasping voice, now rose to her feet in righteous indignation.

"When I asked you to Mr. Cattistock's house, Mrs. Monkton," she burst out, her whole, thin frame shaken with emotion, " 'twasn't to speak shame of him and evil of him afore us all. 'Tis my dear master's bread ye have eaten. 'Tis his wine ye have drunk. 'Tis his house ye are in. If you can't hold a civil tongue in your head, Mrs. Monkton, the best thing you can do—"

But Mrs. Monkton had already divined what was the best thing she could do, and having risen quickly from the table, glancing defiantly upon them all, she was already putting on her hat and cloak. No sooner had the outer door shut upon her than there was a general sigh of relief, and a warm wave of emotional sympathy rose from all sides and enveloped the trembling little woman at the head of the table.

"Don't 'ee mind, Lizzie dear," cried Mrs. Witchit. " 'Tis they Wiltshire ways, that's what it be! Mr. Witchit 'isself, though I'm not the one to say it, were born on Sarum Plain. 'Tis they east winds there, I reckon. 'Tis the terrible thin earth there that makes these harsh voices and these bitter tongues!"

To soothe her ruffled nerves and to win converts to her amiable and partial view of her master's flight, Mrs. Chant now produced and opened a second bottle of Cattistock's sherry wine.

"I never liked they Wiltshire foreigners," said Curly's mother. "There were one o' they peddlers that me sister Phem used to buy Bulls' Eyes from, for she's shop in Weymouth Road, but they never tasted proper-like to *my* notion. The pep'mint in 'em weren't what it should be. 'Twern't hot, as you might say. 'Tis a marvel what a many peddlers I've seen in my time from Salisbury, and nary a one of 'em sold real old-fashioned sugar-candy nor pure Bulls' Eyes."

These allusions of Curly's mother to their ancient interest in peddlers and sweets warmed the old gossips' hearts still further, as they sipped their vanished magnate's wine. Sarah Piddle was actually moved to lift up an appropriate ditty in her thin treble voice.

"A boat, a boat, to cross the ferry!
And let us all be blithe and merry!
And laugh and quaff and drink brown sherry!"

" 'Tis warm and cosy in here," she went on, "now that there Wiltshire witch be traipsed off. What us must do in this here world is to follow our fathers what were afore us. There've been Piddles in Darset, I reckon, ever since Preston Brook ran into the sea. And there'll be Piddles in 'un when Harbour Bridge be like Backwater Bridge!"

"Would your master, Lizzie," broke in old Ammabel, for her family came from Hampshire and there was therefore no way of boasting of a blood equal to that of the Piddles, "be as angry as Mr. Loder'd be if he found we'd a-drunk all this wine?"

Quite honestly—though doubtless she would have lied if need had been—Lizzie Chant explained that when she had first asked Mr. Cattistock about these invitations and had mentioned a little wine he had nodded and smiled.

"I don't deny," Mrs. Chant went on, "now that we're all friends here and that that Salisbury bitch be gone, I don't deny master be close-fisted; I don't deny that in some respects you might call him a— a hoarder. But I've never known Mr. Cattistock not to act like a gentleman when the moment came."

"I be so deaf," protested Ammabel addressing herself to Mrs. Wix, "that I couldn't catch whether you said Mr. Ballard had told Curly in what form he received his communication from Mr. Cattistock."

Mrs. Wix hesitated. There had been a struggle going on in her mind for some while as to how much it was lawful to reveal to these bosom cronies about what Sippy Ballard had said. Now—warmed by the sherry—she made her plunge.

"Mr. Ballard told my daughter," she began, and the silence that followed this announcement was of that awful and sacred kind to which allusion has already been made, "told my daughter that 'twas a telegram Mr. Cattistock sent. What it said, or why Mr. Cattistock sent it, or where he was when he sent it, Mr. Ballard didn't say. My daughter told me she had great difficulty in persuading Mr. Muir to accept a lift from Mr. Ballard."

Mrs. Witchit looked at Lizzie Chant, and Sarah Piddle looked at Mrs. Matzell, while Ammabel looked nervously at the door, as if the woman from Salisbury might be listening outside. But turning from the door the old Spy Croft servant now fixed her eyes upon the little black satin bag on Mrs. Wix's lap, upon which lay, untouched as usual, the piece of crochet-work.

"Mr. Muir has the same proud ways as his father before him, but I felt sorry for him when he were at our house yesterday. He hardly spoke to a soul. Does Mr. Muir know, Mrs. Wix, ... about ... your ... about Curly and Mr. Ballard?"

The hush, throughout the room, that fell like a palpable presence round these portentous syllables, was more profound than any that had yet fallen within these walls. No one but the aged Ammabel would have presumed to refer to so intimate a matter, and, as it was, her Hampshire audacity dumbfounded Mrs. Wix. All the women's eyes in the lamp-light turned towards that lady, and so thunderstruck was she that she actually took up her crochet-work and extracted from it her crochet-needle. With this between her finger and thumb she turned towards the Spy Croft servant and made sundry little prods into an untouched piece of bread that lay by her plate.

"A handsome girl, like my darter," she said, prodding the bread, while her old face puckered up with the momentousness of the occasion, "has many fine men to choose from, when and where she may be, and what she tells them or doesn't tell them is her own concern. She and Mr. Muir will soon be married, and that should stop all mouths, I should hope, though *some* mouths, and some tongues, too, be busier with their mischief than waspies round a jam-pot!"

"Be it the truth, or be it not the truth, Eliza," said the good Mrs. Witchit hurriedly, in her rich, motherly voice, "that Jobber Skald were seen yesterday on esplanade, walking, like he was keeping company, along-side of Mrs. Cobbold's companion?"

Back went the crochet-needle into its proper place, and Curly's mother, heaving a sigh of untold relief, hastened to take advantage of this timely aid.

"All I know about *that*, Mrs. Witchit," she remarked, "be what my darter mentioned, afore she went to bed tonight, feeling footsore and forspent. She said when she were waiting for Mr. Muir, this morning, while he were buying roses for she, her met Mr. Fogg from High House, and *he* told her there were fine doings last night at Cobbolds'. He said the Companion were out all night and hadn't sent no word. He said his Missus were all for calling up Police-Station, but Jerry Cobbold said 'No'. He guessed the young lady were with Jobber Skald's Pa and Ma, and that 'twould be disturbing a decent family to make a rumpus. Mr. Fogg said he laughed a lot at his Missus and made sport of the Companion's cleverness. 'They be old sweethearts,' he said, 'and 'tis for *that* she took this job at the start along with we'."

There was a pause in the conversation now and the women who had come out from Weymouth began murmuring to each other that 'twere time to think about catching the bus home.

"What be taunting thee mind now, Eliza?" said Mrs. Matzell to their hostess, whose preoccupation with her own thoughts had become apparent to them all.

"I were thinking of Master Benny," Mrs. Chant confessed quickly. " 'Twere in me mind how he were behaving at Miss Le Fleau's. He went to sleep, Mr. Muir said, on a sofy-bed along wi' he, but Miss Le Fleau's Martha be a particular kind of body, and I hopes to goodness Master Benny won't have none of his tantrums on this here sofy-bed!"

Everyone got up at this point, as if the particular Martha at Kimmeridge House had put them in mind of their duties. They were all in their out-door things and old Ammabel, nervous about missing the bus, had already gone, when to the general consternation there came from the front of the house, clear and unmistakable, the sound of the opening and shutting of doors and of heavy footsteps and of men's voices.

"The master brought back dead!" was Lizzie Chant's first wild thought . . . then "Mr. Muir with Benny!" . . . then "that terrible Jobber again!"

But as she stood listening, and all the women with their hats and their wraps on listened with her, there came the not-to-be-mistaken tones of Mr. Cattistock himself.

"He's back! He's safe!" her nurse's heart cried, and the same untold relief relaxed her nerves as it had done forty years ago when the little Dogberry returned alive from a boating accident.

Never have wedding guests vanished so completely at the appearance of a bridegroom as these poor ladies vanished, and Mrs. Chant, moving to the window to close it before she returned to the kitchen, looked out for a moment into the darkness. The window opened on a field at the back of the house, a field that rose to the summit of a low-lying ridge from which the West Bay was visible. It was to the summit of this incline, which was only a short distance away, that Benny's mother had been wont to stroll of an evening, in the days before her confinement, and it had become a morbid amusement of late with old Lizzie to pretend to herself that a certain lonely post, of unknown origin, locally known as "the Grey Woman" which stood upon this hill, was that young married woman's solitary figure, still staring out across West Fleet and across West Chesil, over the western sea. Lizzie had often thought of the woman's spirit as growing uneasy, wherever its abode was, at the arrival of another mistress at Peninsular Lodge, and to-night, as she glanced at that dark up-land whose outline was clearly visible in the moonlight, she was startled, but not overmuch surprised, to see a second post standing by the side of the first one. But she heard Cattistock's voice, calling her impatiently now, and leaving the window she hurried into the kitchen to meet him. It's a wonder she didn't cry out: "There are two posts!" for what she'd seen dominated her consciousness completely. Later on the fantastic notion visited her that Ammabel, who certainly was thin as a post, had, in her anxiety about catching the bus, hurried west instead of east, but during the whole of her meeting with Cattistock Lizzie's feeling was that she *had* been permitted to see the real dead woman standing beside the pretended one.

"Your friends have gone?" said her master, smiling grimly into her haggard face. "I've timed myself well then."

"Where . . . what . . . why?" gasped the old nurse. "Oh, Master Dogberry, how could you"—*there are two posts*—"act like this? How could you"—*there are two posts*—"let it happen like this?"

"The Doctor's with me, Lizzie," he said curtly, giving no other explanation, "but there's no reason"—he looked at the big warm fire and he surveyed the cold brawn, cold ham and cold chicken about half of which was untouched—"you should light a fire as late as this in my room. Doctor won't stay, only I thought I'd ask him in for just a bite because I knew the place was full of good food. What have you given them to drink? My best sherry? Well, well! I suppose you'll say a day like this doesn't come often. Only the point is—*it hasn't come today*! Lizz, old friend, I *couldn't* do it when it came to the point, and that's all there is! I found I'd sooner risk everything here, risk making the Poxwells, Cobbolds, Loders, and all the rest of them enemies for life, risk upsetting all the 'golden opinions' they've now got of me in Portland, risk giving 'Tensia a cruel, deadly hurt—but she'll be all right, really! I hear she's gone to High House for to-night. Lucinda called up the Doctor. I'm glad of that! The old man would have tormented her to death with his jubilations. She'll never forgive me, and I shan't blame her. I couldn't do it, Lizz, when it came to the point. And that's the long and short of it! I've been with the Doctor all day. Well—we mustn't keep him any longer. Just clear away all this mess and set the table again. Pull it near the fire. That place of the Doctor's is damned cold, Lizz. I wouldn't be surprised if I'd caught a chill watching him in his Lab. It's devilish queer what he does—I don't know what to think! You have to be a scientist, I suppose, to get the hang of it. There! I mustn't shout like that. I'll be waking Benny."

"Master Benny's not here, sir."

"Not here?"

"He's staying the night in Brunswick Terrace."

"With Muir?"

"Yes, sir."

"Was that fixed up, after or before?"

"After, sir."

"All right, but Chant must fetch him back tomorrow morning. You'll tell him that—eh?—if you see him before I do. Oh, yes, and let's have whatever's left of that sherry you had out. How many bottles did you open?"

"Three, sir. Three, Master Dogberry."

"*Three!* Three bottles of sherry and I don't know what for *these things?* Brawn is very expensive. They don't seem to have eaten much, though—for so many of 'em—Well, this brawn will last me a long time, and Benny likes brawn, too, doesn't he? Doesn't he like brawn?"

"Yes, sir, Master Benny be very fond of brawn, sir."

Mr. Cattistock lifted up the plate containing this popular edible and sniffed at it.

"I expect the brawn will be quite enough for the Doctor and me *now*," he remarked as he put it down.

"With the chicken, of course, sir."

"No, Lizz, no, you spendthrift. *Without* the chicken."

As he walked back to his study, where his brother-in-law was standing by the empty grate wrapt in deep thought, words such as these passed through his mind:

"Instead of the whitest body in the world—to eat brawn with Dan! That's the final upshot. Brawn with Dan in the Servants' Hall. Daniel Brush and brawn! The fat and the lean are so delicately balanced in brawn; and firmness and leanness in Daniel. Let me see! It costs three and six, when it's in glass jars. For three and six you can eat as much brawn as you like. But one of his dogs, he says, costs nearly a pound. That is, if it's in good fettle. Well, if I hadn't cried off this business, I should be sitting now by a good fire in my study, drinking whisky and watching the clock go round. Nine ... ten ... eleven ... till it was time to go up to her. There'd have been no need for me to eat brawn in the Servants' Hall then or to watch the Doctor in his Lab either. What is the power they've got? Well, whatever it is, a man has to pay for it."

"All well I hope in your domain?" was his brother-in-law's greeting.

"Yes, the old trots are all cleared off and she'll have supper ready in the Servants' Hall in a minute. Benny's sleeping with his tutor in Weymouth. So I needn't have worried about him at all. Sit 'ee down, Dan, sit 'ee down. There's no good standing, though it *is* so blasted chilly in here."

They sat down on opposite sides of the empty grate.

"Have one of mine?"

"No, thanks. I always smoke these."

"Can't get her out of my mind, Dan. I suppose she'll never speak to me again."

"Oh, I don't know! I wouldn't say that. She'll probably marry someone else and invite you to the wedding."

"What *did* you say to that reporter from the 'Circular', Dan? How clever of the chap to go to you!"

"I told him you had come to the conclusion that with your bachelor habits you couldn't make a beautiful woman happy; that you regretted causing all your friends so much inconvenience; that your lawyer and Hortensia's lawyer were discussing the financial aspects of the affair; and that you hoped there would be no permanent ill-feeling."

Cattistock pondered for a moment. Then he said:

"You did very well, Dan. But you're still sure, are you, that 'twas the moment to mention lawyers and settlements?"

The Doctor sat straight up on his chair and pulled up his coat-collar. He began heartily to wish he'd never left his own house. What a man Dogberry was! Of course this case of his was all perfectly simple! He was suffering from—and the Doctor spoke to himself in his own scientific language for several seconds—combined with—and he added a few more words of classical origin.

"My hope is to avoid lawyers altogether," repeated Cattistock.

"But you said the Loders would deal with the claims she'll bring?"

"It's 'Loder and Crouch' now," corrected Cattistock. "The old boy's out of it. He spends his whole time, now, they say, talking to his ulcers."

"Well, anyway, you said that if a settlement—"

Cattistock smiled.

"What I say and what I want the Circular to say, Dan, are two different things. The great thing is to distract the attention of the public. Your phrase about my feeling I was too set in my ways to make a brilliant woman happy was splendid. But I rather wish you hadn't said anything about lawyers and settlements."

The Doctor hunched his shoulders and thrust his hands deep into his pockets. He felt as if he was in a night train between Basle and Zurich. *Had* the man said there was a fire, somewhere in this accursed house, or had he imagined it?

"I can't do anything for him of course," he thought, "unless I can get him to talk freely. But it's all pathological. The great fool is simply riddled with neuroses. They stick out of him. He bristles with them. But he'll go down to his grave thinking he's a miser, a clever, maniacal miser, that everybody has taken for normal. Oh, the bitten and blistered fool he is! Oh, the congenital and convoluted fool he is! He thinks he is a formidable, irresistible, unscrupulous machiavellian man of blood and iron; whereas—God! how I'd love to have you mentally exposed to the limit! What juices of rich truth about the system of things could be sucked from analysing you, what treasures of neurotic strata unearthed!"

Hunched up and miserable in that cold leather chair—for Cattistock was as partial to leather chairs as the Jobber—Dr. Brush turned his pale, neutral, de-personalized, ticket-collector's face upon his friend's great chin, protruding eye-brows, and prominent ears. He had, during this day of comparative intimacy, come to regard the man much more as a desirable patient—that is to say as a desirable field for exploration —than as any sort of relative. And as he looked at him now smoking so sullenly cigarette after cigarette as if to warm himself by their minute glow-worm ashes, he thought:

"I don't know which is the most exciting: cutting truth out of dogs or coaxing it out of men. But this I know: that I would help every dog in the world to die howling and reduce every woman in the world to a cold sepulchral pulp, like Mrs. Cobbold, if I could add only a page to the great Folio of *verified and verifiable truth!* How lovely, how exquisite are this man's lies and self-deceptions! God! I could watch him and experiment on him for a hundred years! Oh, how I wish I could buy a cartload of healthy Dogberrys as easily as Murphy can buy healthy Dogs! And Murphy himself. How beautifully complicated his sadism is, with its delicate feelers and its subtle arts of self-protective concealment! Murphy was drawn to the vivisection-laboratory as inevitably as trappers to traps or in the Middle-Ages those holy torturers to their castle-prisons. How Brother Dogberry does smoke and think to-night! He's thinking of the soft limbs of Hortensia Lily that won't lie by him or on him or under him to-night. What a head he's got—what a head! But it isn't *to the head* that a man's thoughts are confined. They float round him in a vortex not yet fathomed; they retreat behind him into some magnetic causal dimension for which at present we have no name. Why doesn't he light another candle? Those are both going out. Well, let them go out! Brother Dogberry's skull is certainly an uncommon shape, and you can see—damn those candles!—you can see its shape from the way his hair is cropped, but—"

Mr. Cattistock got up in silence at that point, for the couple of candle-ends he'd lit on the chimney piece were indeed flickering down to annihilation, their small black wicks drowned in grease. He now struck a match, which, as its light flared up between them in that cold, fireless room, caused the countenance of Dr. Brush to manifest itself like a ghostly countenance at a séance—the cheeks visible at their extreme edges, the bridge of the nose visible, one side of the mouth visible, and one point on the ridge of the forehead visible. With the match Cattistock lit a candle-end that emerged from a flat candle-stick on the table and by slow degrees this dwarf luminary's feebly ignited wick emitted spasmodic darts of light.

That miraculous projection of human personality that we call by such names as countenance, visage, face, features, physiognomy, lineaments, was now, in the case of Dr. Brush, thickened out and solidified so it no longer resembled an apparition. It did not, however, become all at once itself, as Cattistock's face did. Something about the inbred character of Dr. Brush, something in his inmost soul that did really tend to correspond to a Faustian "Larva" or "Lemur", seemed to retard his physiognomy in the re-taking on of its human shape. Thus thickened out and solidified, as Cattistock's new candle-end spluttered, but not yet quite humanized, Dr. Brush's face arrived at resembling the faces of the most revolting epoch of human decomposition, when, if we saw our dead beneath their trim coffin-lids, we would be quickly converted to cremation.

"Damn you, Lizzie!" Cattistock rapped out now as he stopped telling himself a story of what it would have been like to have Mrs. Lily waiting for him up there, nervous, feverish and fond, in cool-lavendered linen sheets, and went to the door and opened it.

But not a sound emerged from either kitchen or Servants' Hall, and he returned grumbling, and sat down with a groan, rubbing his forehead with that portion of his hand that lies below the palm and is so momentously eloquent to the palmist.

Once more Dr. Brush fixed his eyes on the skull of his brother-in-law, now undergoing this gloomy massage as it bent forwards over its owner's knees.

"What he thinks in his skull," Dr. Brush said to himself, while his own neutral cranium resolved itself into its normal lineaments with the steadying of that little flame, "is that he dodged his wedding *because of his miserliness;* because, when it came to the ultimate point his insane love of money rose up like a demon, and struck down with one ferocious blow the whole fruition of his desire. Yes, you may rub your head. That is what's going on, in there, you old clod-poll! The populace who waited outside that Church, on the other hand, and who know of course all about Tissty Clive, will put his insult to Hortensia entirely down to her. 'He was off with his dancing-girl'. And all the while, I, who sit looking at this man's skull, know perfectly well that the real cause of his getting up before dawn this morning and walking all those miles over the downs to me, was something belonging to that fluctuating, immeasurable, immaterial mind-circumference, that extends, my good friend, far beyond the limits of that hard pate of yours. Rub on, rub on, brother Dogberry. By all the rubbing in the world you won't get the feel of those soft limbs out of your frontal-bone!"

As if aware of the not altogether sympathetic thoughts of his relative, Cattistock now rose to his feet, uttered another curse upon his old nurse, went to the door and opened it wide. Absolutely silent was the whole house! He made a movement to go off down the passage, but instead of doing so he called out:

"Hurry up, for God's sake, Lizz. The Doctor's hungry."

"She must be cooking something," he thought. "They never take a man's word. They can't believe that a person could be content with cold brawn."

He went back to the room and hunted about in several drawers till he found two more candle-ends. These he squeezed into the candle-sticks on the chimney piece and meticulously lit them. Sitting down again he fixed a sardonic stare upon his brother-in-law.

"Do you really get anything valuable from all this experimentation, Dan?" he asked.

The Doctor cast down his eyes.

"Anything," Cattistock went on, "to make all this bother and all the suffering you cause really worth it?"

"It is rather cold in here, Dogberry, isn't it?" Dr. Brush answered, rising from his chair. "Do you mind if I put on my over-coat while we're waiting?"

He went out to get the object he referred to, and he thought to himself as he put it on, looking down the dark passage leading to the kitchen,

"I don't like the smell of this house. I never have. It's not hygienic. Mrs. Lily's lucky to have escaped living here."

When he came back he found Cattistock with a bottle in his hand.

"Here, my boy," was the welcome he got. "This'll warm you up, better than that coat!"

But when Dr. Brush saw the two yellowish glasses—like the ones associated with the process of cleaning people's teeth—that were now lugged out, he firmly declined the offer.

"They haven't been rinsed out for weeks," he thought.

But the owner of Peninsular Lodge was in a mood to be extravagant with his drink to-night. Looking about for a modicum of water he set eyes on a tumbler that Mrs. Chant must have balanced on the edge of the book-shelf, containing some of Curly's roses that Mrs. Wix had brought for her. Snatching out the flowers and flinging them on the table, Cattistock diluted his drink with their water, and continued doing so, as he went on refilling his glass from the bottle.

The men were facing each other now in their seats by the empty grate. A faint fragrance, wafted from Curly's roses on the table, reached their nostrils, while the door, which, in getting his coat, the Doctor had left ajar, blew suddenly wide open. Neither of them bothered to get up to shut it, for the Doctor's mind was in his laboratory, and Cattistock's was once more pretending that Hortensia was waiting for him upstairs. Damp, floating airs, neither pleasant nor unpleasant, came drifting down the long passage and entered their room, but they brought no sound of life with them. Lizzie might just as well have gone off with the last of her wedding guests. The two men with their heads half-turned to the grate fell into their separate tracks of thought as completely as if they had been two strangers waiting side by side in a railway-station. Every now and then the open door gave a little creaking sound, as if it said "Shut me! Shut me!" while Curly's roses, which were not moss-roses, went on wafting forth their dim garden-fragrance from amid a litter of Circulars and scattered ashes and broken match ends.

And the Doctor thought:

"That gorilla-cranium over there is perfectly right! Experiments on dogs have *not* been of anything like the practical value my colleagues claim. I know *that*. And it's silly and tricky of them to pretend that the dogs don't suffer. They suffer horribly. Murphy would see to that in any case, for that is why he is here. And of course, since human beings are what they are, there are Murphys in every university, in every hospital, in every laboratory. About once a week it comes over me that I really must sack Murphy, but I never do, for he knows the ropes. He knows how to get hold of the dogs."

Here the Doctor ceased to think in logical phrases, though words, those animated eidolons that resemble the astral entities hovering over graves, still played a part in what went on in his consciousness. He recalled how he had heard the struggle between Murphy and Zinzin—he had no notion of the identity of the girl—and had made it clear that there were to be no more unprofessional "voyeurs" in his scientific Inquisition.

"But whether that'll stop it, is doubtful," he thought, while the indescribable image of what he had seen that day resolved itself into something his intelligence could handle. "When I hear my sweet hypocritical colleagues," he thought, "like so many clever politicians,

defending experimentation as a humane duty for the curing of disease,
I feel that the human race is so contemptible that the sooner some
totally different creation takes its place, the better for the universe!
Man is a loathsome animal, prodigious in his capacity for a particular
kind of disgusting cruelty, covered up with ideal excuses. If I were
allowed—as no doubt we *shall* be in half-a-century—to vivisect *men*,
I'd gladly let the dogs alone. Comical, comical! It's comical but it's
also a little ghastly! I wonder if our sentimental devotees comprehend
what we real scientists are like. Mad! That's what we're like. It's
a vice. *I know what it is.* And I know what I am. I am a madman
with a vice for which I'd vivisect Jesus Christ."

Dr. Brush sat up as straight as a scarecrow as he thus formulated in
his secret heart his views upon himself, staring into the dead cinders
of Cattistock's grate. The candle-light flickering down upon him
gave him—only Cattistock was too absorbed in his own thoughts to
notice anything—a curiously malignant and even phantasmal detachment. What he really looked like—with his white face balanced
above his new light-coloured over-coat, a garment that somehow
suggested stables and the race course—was the Hanged Man of
Gipsy May's Tarot cards. His body had the rigidity of a corpse just
then, owing to the intensity of his thought, and his features for the
same reason had lost all intelligent and even intelligible expression.

"It's all lies," his thoughts went on, "this chatter about the grandeur
of truth and the noble virtue of pursuing it. There's nothing grand
about truth. There's something frightful about truth! Really wise
people spend their lives in forgetting 'God's truth', which is the
horrible reality, and creating a truth for themselves. *That* is the wise
life! I'm a madman, whose vice it is to enjoy pursuing the horrible
truth created by God."

While these thoughts marched, one after another, through the
brain of Daniel Brush, as if they had been an unending procession of
Elsinore sentries, clanking their halberds to the grinding noises of the
ice-floes, Cattistock, a little dazed by the liquor he'd drunk, allowed
his inner mind even greater liberties. When Dr. Brush denied that the
thoughts in Cattistock's skull were circumscribed by their material
container he certainly approached nearer to what Cattistock felt than
to what he believed. As he thought of the satiny smoothness of

Hortensia's legs as he had hoped not only to feel them in bed but to see them exposed for his pleasure when she rose in the morning, he felt as if his thinking ego were not inside this cold room, with the open door and the fireless grate, but as if this cheerless room were one fleeting and phantasmagoric object, among others, inside his thinking ego. But clever psychologist as Brush was, Cattistock beat him altogether to-night, if to beat an analysing truth-hunter is to be something totally different from what he has diagnosed you to be! With his unshaven chin poked forward on the back of his knuckles, as he rested it on his clasped hands, with his thick eyebrows working up and down, as if they had been too long in one position and wanted to stretch, with his low, broad forehead wrinkling a little, as he gave the skin over his frontal skull-bone sundry automatic twitches, Cattistock became aware that the real cause of his fooling his lovely bride and half the Town, the real cause of his sitting here in this miserable room instead of stealing up, step by triumphant step, to where, breathing hard with excitement, and whiter than the sheets she lay between, his woman awaited him, was as obscure and inevitable a compulsion as that which had led him, on the night of the wreck on Chesil, to swim out to that floating cask. He actually felt now the same sort of integral impulse, in all his muscles and bones, as he had felt then, and again it was as if from his physical frame itself, from its mysterious diffused life, rose up the decision he had made and was even now confirming.

As he sat, therefore, bowed down there, with his great chin on his folded hands and the air from the long passage blowing in through the creaking door, he reviewed the whole course of his days upon earth. A blind, obstinate, unyielding purpose gathered within him that seemed to spring from something in his being that certainly was not limited to his skull, but on the other hand, seemed much more like an emanation from his vigorous muscles and his athletic bones, as he bent and crouched, than from any superincumbent spiritual entity. Released by the whiskey he had drunk, with its faint flavour of flower-stalks, from all doubt and misgiving, the underlying consciousness of his powerful physique, his body consciousness, that terrible will to mastery that had dominated him while he wrestled with the waves that night, seemed now to articulate itself and to reveal its purpose. And the purpose thus revealed, as he saw it now, blindly reached after, furtively fumbled after, through all the years of his life, was something quite definite, but something, too, free from the usual vulgarities of gross ambition. Struggling there now, as his bristly chin pressed itself into his knuckles, to articulate this something, it seemed to him that what it really was was *power-in-suspension*.

In other words it was revealed to him now, in this upheaval of self-recognition, that it was no *overt* assertion of power he wanted, no worldly exercise of power, but the feeling that he was detached from all other men by his secret possession of what others, if they had it, would flaunt and flourish, but that he would hold, to the bitter end in volcanic reserve. To hold the thunder without scattering the bolts; it was this that now articulated itself to him as his real passion.

His idea of himself emerged into awareness, at this crisis in his days, as if he were a solitary arsenal of explosive energy, that must never be allowed to explode. An obscure, demonic pride in him held the human race in such contempt that all explosion, all hurling of thunderbolts, all external domination, presented itself as a confession of vulgar weakness. The sudden rising up within him of the subconscious Being who had driven him, after a sleepless night over the hills and made him walk, sometimes even, as he now remembered, actually run, across those long miles of dark country side till he reached the Brush Home, was an incontrovertible piece of knowledge. This knowledge, that had clarified itself just in time, was that to bring Hortensia into his life would undermine, dissolve, corrupt, disintegrate the grand secret of his days.

"She would spend my money," he had kept repeating to himself all that sleepless night. "Spend my money, spend my money, spend, spend, spend, *spend* it!"

He knew he wasn't the traditional sort of ordinary miser. He had no particular mania for the touch of gold as gold. What he wanted was to have it there as a mystical power-in-suspension, to have *the real thing there*, while other men swaggered and flaunted and strutted with the mere show of it! And to have it in secret—that was the main thing! It was the *secrecy* of power, of power unused, concealed, unknown even, to the very end, that alone satisfied his pride. Vulgar, vulgar, his heart told his heart, was this desire to be recognized, to be hailed as the winner in the great subterranean competition. He would like to die without one living soul of this contemptible race knowing him for what he was, knowing that he had held them in the palm of his hand! As it was *now*, though these fools called him the richest man in Weymouth, not a soul of them knew that in reality he was one of the richest men in England. Yes, his secrecy, his secrecy was his life! Only by his secrecy could he satisfy his pride, only by their not knowing, by their *never* knowing!

But it was just this secrecy that a woman like Hortensia, once settled snug and quiet there at his bed and board, would—it had come over him with a final, deadly certainty—inevitably destroy. Even if he kept his money from her, she would know, she would know! She would worm herself into his life *in order* to know. The truth was, when you got down to the depths, so he told himself now, he wanted in his direct masculine way, what every woman wanted, a certain mysterious, unknown life-tract, that he could govern without completely understanding it, and without ever boasting of it! Women were stronger than men, he thought, in that they could enjoy this mysterious kingdom and rule over it, without having to keep their feelings secret, even indeed while in full intimacy with other person-alities about it! This they could do because they could always sink into Nature and draw new strength from Nature when their in-discretions and their social betrayings of themselves had apparently given everything away.

"But a man cannot do that; a man to preserve the power of his identity must keep to himself. A man who doesn't—even when living with a woman—*live alone* is only half a man. But women, though they admire a man's loneliness and in a sense prefer it, are driven on by an accursed fatality to undermine it and destroy it!"

Thus did Dog Cattistock articulate what he thought to be his inmost soul, while all the while that ghastly Lemur hanging there opposite him, that corpse-man, sweating the wise sweat of the cunning of corpses, was finding, as he sat up so erect in his new over-coat, just as if he had a rope under his expressionless face, that Dog Cattistock had not the smallest, faintest, remotest inkling of the real causes of his actions!

It is interesting to think of the telepathic waves of magnetism, whether recognized or not, that must have been passing to and fro just then between Peninsular Lodge, Chickerel, and High House, Weymouth. The two Poxwell sisters were certainly present in some kind of reality in that chilly room that night, where the air, blowing in from the long passage, was so full of the indescribable house-smells of half a century of Peninsular Lodge existence! Even at the very second when the man who crouched down there, chin against knuckles, was tearing himself free of Hortensia, the man who hung there, like a cadaver in a straight waistcoat, was analysing Lucinda as if he were embracing a vivisected, half-anaesthetized, snarling panther.

But however much the Poxwell temperament, inheriting from the demented Captain so much more than the Captain would have cared to concede, diffused itself through that shabby room, it was not less of a shock to both the men when there came a sudden violent ring of the front door bell. The ringing of a bell is always charged with the electricity of drama, and the first thought that passed through Cattistock's mind was: "It's 'Tensia!" and in spite of all his resolutions a flood of happiness rushed through him as he rose to his feet and listened.

Dr. Daniel Brush also rose to his feet and the brothers-in-law stared at each other. Brush, the man, thought: "I hope it's not Mrs. Cobbold sent as an ambassador," a thought which Brush, the pathologist, immediately translated as: "I hope it *is* Mrs. Cobbold sent as an ambassador!"

"Why doesn't Lizzie come to the door?" Cattistock remarked sharply, and going into the hall he turned towards the long passage and called: "Lizzie! Lizzie Chant! Lizzie! Come! I want you!"

But instead of waiting for Lizzie to come, his excitement was so intense that he rushed to the front door and pulled it open while Brush with a doctor's instinct to be ready for immediate action began hurriedly pulling off his over-coat and hanging it with delicate care upon a peg. A sick, labouring moon, ill-shaped and blurred by mist, threw its distorting light on the heads of three persons out there, those of a young girl and two men. Cattistock, with Brush behind him, saw at once who they were, and at once these two clever ones realized the meaning of this invasion.

It was Captain Poxwell himself! And the old man was accompanied by his grand-daughter Daisy and by his lawyer, Rodney Loder.

"We came," began Daisy at once in her clear rounded voice, raised a little, and trembling a little, but perfectly under control, "we came because grandfather wanted so much to speak to you. Grandfather thought that it must be *because of him* that you didn't come today. I told Mr. Loder how troubled grandfather was, and he said to get a taxi and let him do what he wanted. We told the man to wait, and the taxi's over there in the road now."

"Don't 'ee visit the sins of the fathers on the children, Dogberry Cattistock!" cried the old man himself, shaking off Daisy's hand. "I never liked 'ee, ye know—but that's not here nor there. That's a gentleman's privilege, *with us;* though 'tis true in certain foreign places you and me would have, long ere now, been knife-sticking. But whether I've liked this wedding or no, Dogberry Cattistock, I can't endure to think that you ... are leaving ... are jilting my daughter 'Tensie because of what everyone says of me—of me and— of me and my other daughter. It isn't, Dogberry Cattistock, the right time for thee and me, to settle our private account. We can do that another day and I haven't come for that. I've come to take you to 'Tensie out there at Lucinda's. So don't say ye can't listen, nor heed, nor come. I know the pride of a man's heart and I know the pride of a woman's heart; but if you'd come, in Rodney Loder's taxi, straight to High House, I'm sure to Almighty God that you and 'Tensie would fall into such favour and prettiness with each other that you couldn't help letting by-gones be by-gones. I know what I am, and I don't deny it. I know I shall be damned in the other world and I know I'm tormented in this. But ye musn't consider—"

Till this moment Rodney Loder had kept himself in the background, allowing the Captain his fling, but when the old man's remorseful volubility showed no sign of abating, but on the contrary every indication that he was prepared to make a speech as lengthy as that of the foster-father at the tent-door of Achilles, he felt it incumbent upon him to assert himself.

"Perhaps you wouldn't mind, Mr. Cattistock," he said quietly, coming forward towards the door, "if we came in for a minute or two? Our taxi's here. We won't bother you for long, but Captain Poxwell—"

"Come in, come in, of course, Loder," said the master of Peninsular Lodge hurriedly and kindly. "I'm sure we'll be able to satisfy the Captain. I'm glad you came, my dear," this was addressed to Daisy, upon whose shoulder he laid his hand. "You all know my brother-in-law, don't you? Help the Captain up the steps, Dan. That's the way! Come in here, all of you."

Once inside the house, with the door closed on the ticking of the taxi in the road, Cattistock managed with the assistance of the Doctor to get his guests into his desolate and chilly study. The old man let Daisy take his coat and stick from him and settle him in the leather chair lately occupied by Dr. Brush. Rodney sat down on the smaller arm-chair, where Cattistock had been brooding over the grate, and beside which the half-empty whiskey bottle still stood in the littered fender. As for the Doctor, he brought up to the table a high chair from the side of the room and sat there, quiet and erect, his hands clasped in front of him and a vacant, almost stupid expression on his face, like a weary ticket-collector who is waiting patiently for the *next* train to come in. Cattistock carried to the Captain's side the only other seat in the room, which was an old piano-stool covered with faded plush. Towards this object he waved his hand.

"Sit down, my dear," he said with a friendly grimace. "You're the only one I'd dare offer *this* to!"

But Daisy in an absent-minded way was collecting Curly's scattered roses. When she had got them together she stood by the side of the table, but at some distance from the Doctor, arranging them into a neat nosegay, not without a quick glance round the room for an opportunity to put them into water.

"Take those home with you, child," said Cattistock kindly. "I'm sure I don't know how they got here, but you're welcome to them, if you like them."

Daisy gave him a straight look with her grey eyes. She was puzzled at herself for not feeling more indignant with the man who had made her mother the laughing-stock of the town, but instead of feeling indignant she felt—now that he was not to be her step-father—more friendly to this self-possessed, harassed-looking person, with such smouldering excitement in his roving eyes, than she had ever felt before. Her chief concern, however, was with the Captain, and with the bunch of roses in her hands she now sat down by his side on the piano-stool and looked appealingly at Rodney.

Rodney, far more concerned with her than with her grandfather or anyone else, responded quickly to her appeal.

"We mustn't stay more than a minute, Mr. Cattistock," he remarked. "I'm afraid we can hardly persuade you to do what Captain Poxwell has in his mind."

"I've said to him what I came to say, Rodney," interrupted the Captain, speaking quite calmly and rationally, and then with a certain shiver. "It's chilly, to-night, you know."

Cattistock caught the old man's eye fixed on the bottle on the floor, and hurriedly looking round for a glass he picked up his own, poured some whiskey into it and handed it to him.

"Forgive the glass," he said, "but an old sailor like you, Captain, won't—"

Breaking off, as he realized the absence of water, he made a movement towards the door, but the Captain stopped him,

"Don't bother, Dogberry," he said. "This is all I want . . . just to warm my old bones."

Thus speaking he tilted back his head and poured the whiskey down his throat. The candle light from the chimney piece, as he did so, fell upon his long lean neck accentuating its corded muscles as they distended in the act of swallowing.

Rodney, from where he sat looking anxiously at Daisy, turned to watch the old man drinking, and thought to himself:

"He's exactly like a picture of a man drinking."

"I doubt," began the Doctor suddenly while Daisy, balancing herself on her stool, fixed him nervously with her grey eyes and then deliberately closed them, "whether it would be any use, just at present, for our friend here to see your daughter, Captain. If I know anything of women,"—he spoke in a low emphatic, authoritative voice, a voice that clearly impressed the old man, who had now sunk back again in his chair, holding the empty tumbler in his hand—"it's always better to wait till a propitious moment, a propitious . . . what shall I say? . . . mood, and then, and not till then, make our . . . whatever move we want to make."

But the Captain turned to Cattistock.

"You'll say it isn't me, Dogberry. But I know better." And the old man fetched, in the presence of them all, one of those calamitous sighs that spring from a broken spirit. "But I've done my best for her . . . haven't I, Daisy? I've . . . always . . . done my best . . . for . . . my daughters . . . haven't I, Daisy? For your mother, I mean, and for . . . for Lucinda, too."

The Doctor, still sitting straight up at the table, turned his expressionless, ticket-collector's face towards the Captain.

"One day," he said, speaking very low and very quiet, "I'll tell you, Sir, something about Mrs. Cobbold that will interest you. No, not *now*—" for a look had come into the Captain's eyes like that of a hooked fish, on the bench of a boat, who catches a glimpse of the waves—"*another time;* but neither you"—he put a tone into his voice that caused the old man's tremulous mouth to work convulsively, as if he were biting at something—"nor she," he went on very slowly, "are what you think you are."

There was a heavy silence in the room, during which Cattistock crossed over to the chimney piece and moved both the candles till they were behind the old man. He seemed to do this quite automatically, but Daisy followed the gesture with gratitude in her eyes, now wide-open again and full of some interior resolution, for the result of his action was to throw the Captain's face into such deep shadow that neither the Doctor, nor anyone else there, could see his mouth, as it made those disconcerting movements.

Out of the shadow, however, which now obscured the figure in the arm-chair, a voice rose that was disturbing to them all.

"I'll give you all my shell-boxes and all my cowries, Doctor, if you'll make her swear by her mother's womb to leave me alone! I've got more cowries than they know about, and I'll give them all to you . . . tell him I mean it, Daisy! . . . if you make her swear she'll never come . . . never, never,"—his voice began to thin itself out, till it was almost inarticulate . . . "come walking and beckoning and swaying her hips and pouting her lips, and smiling like she does, in front of my cabin-window!" He paused and then in quite a different voice, a voice restrained and rational, but which, for that very cause, was yet more disturbing: "Tell him what I call my cabin, Daisy. Tell him what it is and how I never answer, never open the window, when she comes, never look out once! I've blocked up the window, haven't I, Daisy?—Daisy knows I have!—blocked it up with shell-boxes. No, no, no, Doctor. I don't want her secrets. She was always one for secrets and I never meddled with 'em. It's to swear on her mother's womb to let me alone—that's all I want. For her to leave me alone!"

He leant forward eagerly, so that the front of his high Poxwell forehead was just beyond the shadow, giving the impression that what spoke now was some orifice in that fragment of grizzled skull, where his brains were most troubled, not his hidden mouth at all.

"Shall I tell you something, Doctor? Shall I tell you something, Dogberry, and you, too, Rodney Loder? It takes a man who's sailed the deep sea to know it." He lowered his voice to a whisper. "They've got a sting in them. That's their secret.—It's all right, Daisy . . . don't 'ee shut your dear eyes and frown . . . I'm telling 'em soft and careful; no maidie could mind how I'm telling 'em, only I *must* tell 'em;—It's this sting's poison that they always leave behind! When she sways her hips, and pouts her lips, outside my window she has to hum a little tune so I shan't notice her sting. And do you know what she hums? She hums "Take her off to Devonport . . . Take her off to Devonport . . . take her off to Devon-*port* . . . as you have done before!"

That exposed fragment of the old man's head, protruded into the candle-rays, which seemed to contain a medium of speech in more direct touch with the disturbance of the brain than the one that really functioned, appeared to be what now chanted the famous village-green burden.

All this was so distressing to Daisy that she let Curly's roses drop upon her lap, and raising her hands, pressed both her wrists hard against her closed eyeballs, while her fingers covered the throbbing of her temples and sank into her wavy hair. If the young girl suffered under the Captain's wild words, Rodney, who was watching every movement she made, was yet more troubled. He had never felt such a rush of protective tenderness for anyone in his life as he felt towards her then! Hardly realizing what he did he actually got up from his seat, hurried across to her and laid his hand, with as much solicitude as if she had been hit by a bullet, on one of her shoulders. The girl seemed conscious of his reassuring touch, but they had come to know each other so well that without a word breathed he understood that she wished him to leave her alone to deal with her nerves in her own way, and removing his hand he went back to his seat and sat down again with a strained smile.

But the old man went on in total obliviousness of the effect of his ravings.

"Oh, what a paradise it would be," he cried, in his high-pitched, querulous Poxwell voice, a voice that made Cattistock think most uncomfortably of Mrs. Lily, "if a person could get their sting out of his mind! They sting us, I tell 'ee, . . . that's what they do . . . and the sting itches and itches till anyone could scratch out his brains! You're wise not to come near' em, Rodney me boy. Cupper's Compass! But how they *can* sting! Hark 'ee, Dogberry, hark 'ee, me great grinning lad, if 'twas *because of her sting* you ran away from church-door, I can tell you—Don't 'ee mind so, Daisy, if I *do* speak out!—I'm not going to blame 'ee! Mum's the word with the Captain, Dogberry. I'm not the one to—"

As Daisy shifted uneasily on the piano-stool, her hands still hiding her face, a few of Curly's flower-stalks slipped down from her lap to the carpet, a carpet that had not felt Mrs. Chant's broom for days and days. Cattistock, who now that Rodney had gone back to his seat was standing near her, automatically, as any man might have done, went down on his knees, picked them up, and laid them on her lap with the rest. But just as he rose, they were all arrested by a prolonged and penetrating howl from Benny's room upstairs, expressing the desperation of the dog "Yellow" who had been shut up there.

"Damn that dog!" muttered Cattistock, and then he thought: "But what on earth has happened to Lizzie? I must go and see."

It was Rodney's destiny, therefore, who always gave his own neat garments a timely brush with his hand, even when he rose from kneeling at Holy Communion, to behold in astonishment his present host rush from the room with trousers dusty and rumpled and not so much as giving them a fillip with a finger. But the owner of Peninsular Lodge had been feeling obscurely uneasy about Lizzie for some time. Why on earth hadn't she appeared? Was she undergoing a sudden fit of shame-faced self-obliteration on this night of "il gran rifiuto"? Leaving the room without closing the door, Cattistock now hurried

down the passage. Entering the kitchen he found the big kettle
emitting clouds of indignant steam, its impatient lid leaping up and
down like the iron hat of a hidden Jack-in-the-box. But there was
no sign of Mrs. Chant.

"Lizz! Lizz! he called. "Lizz! Where the deuce are you?"

The door into the Servants' Hall was ajar and he could see the place
was lit up. Yes! When he entered it he found it to be not only lit up
but threatened with a conflagration. The small modern lamp which
stood in the centre of an old table by the fire, a table with places
suitably laid for two persons, was flaring abominably. Much lamp-soot
had fallen on this table and the cloth was blackened. The window
looking out on the moonlit upland, where that post stood, was wide
open and an in-rush of chilly air came blowing into his face.

Looking out of his window something made him call Lizzie's name
into the moonlight night and to his complete amazement he was
answered by a faint voice that apparently came from the direction of
that post up there that they called the Grey Woman. Thoroughly
disturbed and puzzled he left the window and hurried out at the back
of the house.

"Lizz! Lizz!" he kept calling as he hastened up the hill towards the
post.

No sooner had Cattistock left the room than his brother-in-law
rose from his chair by the table.

"Did you see my machine, Mr. Loder, when your taxi drove
up?"

Not Rodney, however, but the Captain himself was the one who,
it appeared, had noted the large Hell's Museum car standing at the
edge of the road.

"Your taxi will cost you a fortune, I'm afraid," said the Doctor
as he put on his great-coat.

Rodney smiled and shrugged his shoulders grimly in a typical
lawyer's fashion.

"Make her swear, Doctor," the old man called from the threshold
after that light-coloured great-coat as it passed through the front door
and disappeared down the steps, "Make her swear not to torment
me!"

When he turned back into the little "study", where Rodney and

Daisy had already exchanged an anxious word, he sat down chuckling and wagging his head.

"Did I handle him well, Daisy? Did I handle 'em *both* well, Daisy and Rodney? Hee! Hee! Hee! I fancy I did, my chickabiddies, I fancy I did! And Dog Cattistock—aye! what a pity our friend the Jobber wasn't here to see me do it! I laid it on and spared not. Didn't I, Rodney? Didn't I, Daisy? He won't run away from any girl of mine at the church-door again. Will he, Daisy and Rodney?"

After this rush of bravura, a physical reaction of old age came upon Captain Poxwell and he soon began to nod as he settled himself comfortably in his chair.

Rodney fell to conversing in whispers with Daisy. Daisy was dressed in a navy blue suit that made her figure look particularly soft and youthful, while the little faded black cloak she still wore round her shoulders threw into relief, even in the faint light of that poorly-lit room, the bloom of her cheeks and the rosiness of her lips under the shadow of her felt hat. As Rodney whispered some questions to her and she bit her lip and frowned almost crossly in her desire to give him a weighty, grown-up, well-considered answer and not a hurried childish one, he thought in his heart that the time would come soon when he would find it very hard not to bring their attraction to each other into the open.

"Is it 'virtue' that has kept me from kissing her, from making love to her, all these days?"

"No," he decided, as he watched the flickering above her head, of what might well have been, for all they'd seen of his ways, the last couple of candles their host possessed, "no, it's not virtue. It's just pure, simple intelligence! I *know* with a girl like Daisy to rush her, to bewilder her, to startle her would be a crazy way to act—that is, if you felt as I do. Of course, if you *didn't*—but I can't get any perspective, except a sort of indignant protectiveness, on a deliberate attempt to corrupt Daisy."

A pallid smile, which Daisy caught at once on his face, and which infinitely puzzled and rather worried her, followed the notion of some shameless seducer setting out to corrupt this sturdy mistress-mother of Quinquetta; but Rodney's pessimism had not left room for excessive, Quixotic gallantry, and he did not forbid himself the piquant pleasure

of imagining what it would be like when the time for making love to
her did arrive. Of this time he had begun to think now, as he listened
to her slow, hesitant, well-weighed words, when all of a sudden both
his thoughts and her words were interrupted by a distant cry in
Cattistock's voice.

"Dan! Dan! Dan!"

Rodney and Daisy rushed down the passage; not, however, till the
girl had given a quick glance at her grandfather asleep in the chair, nor
till she had carefully closed the door upon him. The back door to
Peninsular Lodge was half-way down a little passage-way between the
kitchen and the scullery. At the door of the kitchen they stopped to
listen. But the only sound they could hear was a faint whining
upstairs, where "Yellow" was now pathetically crouched inside the
closed door of Benny's playroom. Finding nothing in the kitchen
except that Jack-in-the-box of a kettle-lid, dancing now a positively
frantic dance, they went into the Servants' Hall. Here they found a
smouldering fire, a table laid for two with an extinguished lamp upon
it, and a round of brawn sprinkled with soot.

Another call from Cattistock, however, made them rush to the back
door through which as they approached it, they could feel the night
wind blowing. Just outside the house, in a cobble-stone yard, they
found Cattistock on his knees by Lizzie Chant's prostrate body,
trying to bring her back to consciousness. He was apparently using
the most primitive and violent methods, just as if she were a person
rescued from drowning, or a person who was drunk, or someone from
whom death by freezing had to be driven away.

Doctor "Dan" himself could have hardly been more authoritative
than Daisy became at this surprising juncture, and it was not very long
before, carried upstairs to her own bed by her master and Rodney, and
tended, in her bed, by this spirited young woman, old Lizzie Chant
began to show signs of returning from the sanity of Not-Being to the
insanity of Being.

"Lie down, sir! Lie down! Or I'll take you back!"

This remark was addressed by the master of the house to the dog
he had just released from Benny's room and who was jumping up
against the old woman's bed.

"Where did you find her?" whispered Rodney.

"She'd wandered out of the house for some unknown reason," Cattistock replied in equally low tones. "It was by a mere caprice I found her. I went up the slope at the back of the house, as far as a post there is there, that in old days we used to call 'the Grey Woman' and there she was! She must have felt nervous and in great want of fresh air after a lot of friends she's been regaling. I brought her back from up there and we walked down merry as crickets and talking of old days, when she went dead off, there where you found me. I was afraid she'd done for herself that time. She fell so quick I couldn't break her fall. That's why I shouted like that for Dan. But on my soul, Daisy my child, you're more useful than Dan could possibly have been; do you know that? Well, well, I know who does know it! Ha, Mr. Loder? But if I *had* turned up in that crowd today this conservative infant wouldn't have been living here! No, no! She'd have stuck to the Captain, just as the Captain himself would have stuck to any of his ships! Eh, Daisy, my dear? Isn't that true?"

But Daisy had the best of all possible excuses for disregarding this praise, praise that had come so nearly to being that of her step-father, for she had to interpret the faint whispers of her patient.

"Mrs. Chant is saying something to you, Sir," she said emphatically.

Mrs. Lily had been trying in vain for months to make Daisy call him something different from "Sir", but without effect. Cattistock himself rather liked it. He found it piquant and engaging.

"What is it, Lizz? What is it, Nannie?" he said to the old nurse.

Part of his roughness to-night to Mrs. Chant was due to a secret fancy he had, which happened to be totally unfair, that the old lady was drunk.

"She is saying someone's at their post I think," said Daisy.

"The Post?"

And Cattistock bent over the old woman and with an indescribable intimacy in his voice, an intimacy that proved them inseparably one, far more one than if they had been the most passionate of amorists or the most loyal of relations, he asked her what she was saying.

"Coom nigher, Master Dogberry," she whispered. " 'Tis for thee wone ear."

And when he had bent low down over her, and Daisy and Rodney had drawn back a little, he heard her faint, wispy voice, like the voice of the wind in the telegraph wires that go over the loneliest stretches of the Dorset hills where she was born:

"There were two on 'em to-night, Master Dogberry; there were thik Grey 'Ooman and Another along o' she, whom thee and me do mind."

13

PUNCH AND JUDY

It was August, a day or two after the August Bank-holiday, and Weymouth was crowded with visitors. Up and down the esplanade people moved in two parallel streams, broken here and there into eddies and criss-cross currents, as new-comers joined the throng from across the road, or clambered up the stone steps from the beach.

The calm faces of the Janus-like Jubilee Clock rose out of the unending procession as if it had been a light-house amid confluent tides, as if it had been the Shambles Light-ship itself, where the tides of the two bays meet. It was nearly opposite the Jubilee Clock, which itself was opposite the short crowded street to the railway station, that the real Weymouth sands began. On the Brunswick Terrace side of the Clock there was very little sand, under most conditions of the tides none at all, for the pebbles sloped steeply down to the water, and the water itself was deep. It was west of the Clock, to the right and to the left of the place where the road, near the old King's Statue, dis-embogued itself of donkeys and goat-carriages and toy-vendors and sweet-sellers and handcarts and bath-chairs and fruit-trucks and children's perambulators, that the Weymouth sands proper stretched out, so nobly, so generously, so hospitably, and so astonishingly far into the sea!

It is indeed hard to imagine any expanse of sand—sand the element "nighest bordering upon Heaven" to the hearts of children—more perfectly adapted by nature to the friendly purposes of a watering-place than the sands of Weymouth. So far do the sands extend that from the days of George the Third, the town's historic patron, to the days when Jerry Cobbold discovered the genius of Tissty and Tossty there could have been seen numbers of stalwart horses at this August season passing to and fro from one to another of the bathing-machines which it was their task to pull out far enough from the shore to allow for bathing, though the more adventurous swimmers were forced to leave even these outposts far behind if they wished to reach any water out of their depth. But for boys and girls content with paddling, this smooth semi-cirque of shining ripples was an arena of undisturbed bliss. Nervous mothers and responsible elder sisters could rest in peace with their books and their sewing, ensconced in sun-warmed security on the hot dry sand above, while over the expanse of *wet* sand, between them and the actual water, little excited groups of bare-legged children and infants could always be seen digging with their wooden spades miniature moats and castles and canals. Gulls would come gliding in over the heads of the swimmers, cutting the air obliquely, like flying torpedoes, in their daring approaches, and then with a reversed motion of their powerful wings whirling sea-ward again, uttering their harsh but reassuring cries.

The scene on this particular afternoon, largely because of the warm diffused sunlight which fell from a filmy, feathery sky, and because of the absence of any blustering wind, had an air that resembled the air of Watteau's "Embarkation to Cythera". There was the same ideal atmosphere, as if the whole crowd, both in and out of the shining water, had been removed several degrees from the pressure of daily reality, had been transported, just as they were, to the magic shore of some halcyon sea, where "birds of calm sat brooding on the charméd wave". Nor was the scene devoid of its own inherent aesthetic contrasts. That difference, for instance, between the *dry* sand and the *wet* sand, which had remained in the memory of Magnus as a condensation of the divergent experiences of his life, heightened the way everything looked from the esplanade till it attained the symbolism of drama. On the dry sand sat, in little groups, the older people, reading, sewing, sleeping, talking to one another, while on the wet sand the children, building their castles and digging their canals were far too absorbed and content to exchange more than spasmodic shouts to one another. The free play of so many radiant bare limbs against the sparkling foreground-water and the bluer water of the distance gave to the whole scene a marvellous heathen glamour, that seemed to take it out of Time altogether, and lift it into some ideal region of everlasting holiday, where the burden of human toil and the weight of human responsibility no more lay heavy upon the heart.

There, above, on the *dry* sand, there were forever limning and dis-limning themselves groups and conclaves of a rich, mellow, Rabelaisian mortality, eating, drinking, love-making, philosophizing, full of racy quips, scandalous jibes, and every sort of earthy, care-forgetting ribaldry. But as these mothers and these fathers, these uncles and these aunts from hundreds of Dorset villages—for there is still a noteworthy air of real West-Country exclusiveness about Weymouth Sands—formed and reformed their groups of Gargantuan joviality and exchanged remarks upon the world that were "thick and slab" with the rich mischiefs of a thousand years, while, I say, the *dry* sands of Weymouth received the imprint of these mature glosses upon the life that went crying and weeping by, gathering I know not what of less human commentary upon its devious ways from the King's Statue, the Church Spire, the turf-covered Nothe-Fort, the outlines of Portland and the White Nose, the *wet* sands of Weymouth were imprinted by the "printless" feet, light, immortal, bare, of what might easily have been the purer spirits of an eternal classical childhood, happy and free, in some divine limbo of unassailable play-time.

Between the donkey-stand, where the bathing machines hide the sea, where Magnus could remember in his childhood actually bathing from one machine that bore the Royal Arms, and the Jubilee Clock, the sands die away. Here the pebbles begin and the water offshore almost immediately grows deep. It was here that Marret's father, Mr. Jones, had set up this summer not only a permanent platform upon which to erect his Punch-and-Judy Show, but also a private and personal tent of his own in the interior of which—although, properly-speaking, he had no licence to provide Public Refreshments—he was wont sometimes to serve, or rather to make Zinzin and Marret and Tiny serve, tea and bread-and-butter.

At the moment, on this particular afternoon, when the hands of the Jubilee Clock, across all its faces, pointed to the hour of four, Magnus, strolling along the beach, stopped at the outskirts of a crowd of children gathered before the miniature stage.

"*Judy! Judy! Judy! Judy!*" screamed Marret's father from inside his coffin-shaped stage.

"*Judy! Judy! Judy! Judy!*"

There was something unique—like no other sound in the world—about this more than brazen challenge. It was brutal, it was heartless, it was shocking, and yet there was about it, some indefinable quality—possibly simply the revival of his childhood—that flicked at Magnus' navel. Mr. Jones' voice was a very powerful one and possessed the penetration, and something of the harshness, of those Babylonian sackbuts that proclaimed the worship of the Graven Image set up by Nebuchadnezzar. It was like a savage chorus of age-old mockery, as if all the Mimes and Mummers of Antiquity, without pity or sensitiveness or remorse, were jibing at our modern sympathies. And when the first curious emotion, that of the revival of the infant in him, passed away, Magnus did actually imagine a long procession of all the neurotic acquaintances he had, a procession including Captain Poxwell, and Perdita Wane, and Peg Frampton, and Sylvanus Cobbold, and the highly-strung little Benny, advancing over those grassy Downs towards Hell's Museum, where the Cobbolds' father had died, and where for all he knew Mr. Edward Loder was still confined. He seemed to hear this incorrigible beady-eyed little reprobate, this Panurge, grown corpulent, with the huge red nose and the nut-cracker chin who now was banging the stage so viciously, leaping up out of a rabbit-hole beside those despairing pilgrims and calling out in his ferocious Babylonian intonation:

"*Judy! Judy! Judy! Judy!*"

"Yes, there's something," Magnus thought, "profoundly unchristian, antichristian even, about Mr. Punch. And how this chap catches the character of the pot-bellied rogue—God! how he smells of sour brass and strident brutality, like the bawdy-house signs in those streets at Pompeii!"

Magnus found himself wondering whom he knew in Weymouth who most resembled this irrepressible and paunchy villain. There! He caught it under the man's own inspired intonation.

"There's something," he said to himself, "of Punch in me, in Gaul, in Jerry, in old Poxwell, in the Jobber! Punch must be the eternal embodiment of what Rabelais calls the 'Honest Cod', the essential

masculine element, in every living man. I know who *is* a
born Punch—though he hasn't a pot-belly—and that's Sippy
Ballard."

It is extraordinary what satisfaction Magnus derived, all the rest of
the performance—which he felt no inclination to leave—by identify-
ing the official with Punch. When the Ghost groaned and gibbered
at the wretch, Magnus felt exactly like the Ghost; he felt he *was* the
Ghost. And as for the moment when the Hangman came on the stage
he felt such a close identification of himself with this indispensable
official that his fingers twitched as Punch dodged the merited rope.
He was in a harassed, touchy, jumpy mood these days. All through the
spring and summer, in fact ever since the fiasco over Cattistock's
wedding, Curly had been putting off their marriage with first one
excuse and then another. Her last excuse was that she didn't like the
Corporal's wife, and Magnus as long ago as June had had to break
it to this experienced traveller that it was no use his retaining a room
for them.

He turned and looked about him, trying to visualize this familiar
spot as if he were seeing it for the first time. Was there any town in
the world by the English sea that equalled this old Georgian resort?
It was so integral with itself, and it seemed now, in that August
haze, as if it had risen in its complete totality—Spire and Statue and
Nothe and Breakwater and all its ivory-misted rows of houses—
straight out of the glittering bay. It seemed an immaterial, an insubstantial thing to him just then, a thing made of the stuff of thought!
It was as if in all its long nights and days an impalpable thought-image
of it had been wrought, that on such an afternoon as this substituted
itself for the solid reality.

The comedy was over now and the little group of spectators melted
away and went in search of new amusement. While this retreat was
in progress Magnus found himself confronted by both Marret and her
sister Tiny who with their little ornamental bags at the end of poles
were trying desperately to extract their due of pennies from their
escaping audience. Ashamed of an initial instinct to run away, the
nervous tutor soon went further in his propitiation than really was
necessary, and impulsively asked whether their father was supplying
tea in his tent that afternoon. The girls implored him to come in,

which he did at once to their surprise and pleasure. While they were at the tent-entrance they were joined by other persons anxious to have a cup of tea on easier terms than was possible in the ordinary shops.

To Marret's astonishment and to the awestruck delight of Tiny, the celebrated Tissty and Tossty turned up, escorting their rustic parents from Radipole, together with an extremely deaf old man, of equally humble station, who was the clerk at Radipole Church. Magnus was surprised at the affability and relaxed good-nature with which the dancers treated their relatives and was impressed, too, at the complete freedom from any snobbish embarrassment which characterized their attitude to Herbie Dandin, the Radipole Clerk. They were dressed exactly alike, in cream-coloured skirts and cream-coloured sweaters and hats. They both wore sandals and neither of them had stockings on.

Magnus had often met Miss Gloria Clive and Pansy Clive, for so the sisters called themselves, behind the stage at the Regent, and he was amazed to see them transformed into Glory and Pansy Rugg, the goodnatured daughters of old Gideon and Hepzibah Rugg.

It was indeed a unique event, this visit of the old people to Weymouth and the girls were devoting themselves to making it a memorable day in their lives. They had put them into seats in one of the front rows for the afternoon's performance at the Regent, and then with an infallible instinct for what they would like best and what Mr. Dandin would like best, they had brought them to the beach to have tea at the Punch-and-Judy Man's.

"Rugg, not Clive, today, Mr. Muir," Tossty was saying now, as he entered the tent with them.

Once inside, he left the Radipole party and carried a canvas chair to the back of the enclosure. Magnus had prolonged his Bank Holiday to escape from teaching, hoping to enjoy one or two long and perfect afternoons with Curly, but he had not obtained hitherto more than a few hours with her since August began. Her absence from the beach today was especially bitter because it was his birthday. Magnus was forty-seven today and he had promised himself to celebrate the occasion by taking his girl for a long solitary row. He had fixed upon Preston Brook—a little stream running out into the sea between the cliffs—as the objective of this excursion, and he had pictured himself pulling up their boat, with Curly's help, in that lonely spot and gathering sticks and driftwood to make a fire.

It was a very different scene from the one he had conjured up that he saw before him now in Mr. Jones' Refreshment Tent, and charming as these beautiful girls were, in their rôle of Glory and Pansy Rugg from Radipole, he gave himself up to angry and bitter thoughts.

Curly had said she would be busy all day at the Wishing Well and too tired to see him afterwards, but although he knew that this first week in August *was* a busy one for her, there were troublesome suspicions in his mind. His suspicions about Sippy Ballard had commenced on that ill-fated twelfth of February when they stood together in the crowd at the door of the Church, and when Ballard had whispered so eagerly to the girl, and between them they had forced him to enter that odious car.

As the various guests settled themselves down at last and began to accept cups of tea from Marret and Tiny, Magnus was impressed by the exquisite sea-scents and sea-sounds that came floating in. He could hardly listen to poor Hepzibah trying to reply to Herbie's banter, which, since Mr. Dandin was such a bold one as to his tongue and so impenetrably sealed up as to his ears, was no easy task, so poignantly did all the old sensations of hot summers on Weymouth beach hit him to the heart. All the lesser smells, such as the smell of tar, of fish, of shag-tobacco, of ancient seaweed, of human sweat, of stale cake, of girls' cosmetics, of children's wet clothes, of men's new clothes, were caught up, as it were, and included, in the larger smell of the hot sunshine itself pouring down upon sand and pebbles.

One little incident and one only broke the current of his feeling. He suddenly realized that Marret—hitherto in good spirits—was silently weeping. Catching her quietly by the arm he asked the girl in a whisper what the matter was, and after looking at him quickly she whispered back:

"The police got after me. They made me leave him and come back to Father."

This was all Magnus could get from her and she soon was serving the tea as before.

The dark proud face of Tossty, with her splendid eyes and her dramatic silences, the pale, passionate face of Tissty with her dazzling white skin and her excited, emotional gestures, created an arresting foreground as the two girls began now to deliberately drop their metropolitan superiorities and laugh and nod and exchange glances and twit Mr. Dandin and whisper things into the ears of their mother, and listen with respect to the laconic remarks—for he was a South Dorset shepherd more voluble with his dog than with the human race—made by old Gideon.

Magnus never afterwards forgot—no! not to the end of his days— all his subtle feelings and sensations in that tent! Watching the two dancers in their innocent cream-coloured frocks and with their extravagantly touched-up faces, he felt as if they represented all that mysterious evasiveness in women that he was suffering from with Curly. His recognition of this came to him while he was exchanging superficial remarks with Zinzin, who was a small, slippery, gliding, iridescent person, curiously suggestive of a fresh-caught mackerel, but from whose form, instead of the smell of a fish, there emanated a strong odour of Opopanax mixed with human perspiration.

Back again, always back to Curly, wandered his deeper conscious-ness. She had of late been more reckless about what he thought with regard to her relations with Ballard, and not only so but she had had several violent quarrels with Ballard himself. Steadily, all these summer months, as she read her "Pansy novelettes" in the little rustic shelter by the Wishing Well, she had grown more lovely to look at. And it was as if the consciousness of her increasing beauty had given her a certain independence of both her men. Indeed it was not only Magnus—though he had no suspicion of this—who found the girl's attitude to her marriage disturbing and mysterious. Her anxious and puzzled mother had of late taken to coming upon her suddenly, and with premeditated unexpectedness in her Wishing Well Retreat, for the truth was that Mrs. Wix had begun to wonder in her heart *who the new man was.*

Tissty and Tossty's mother went on patiently retorting to the heavy-handed jocularity of the Radipole clerk, while her father grew more and more taciturn. Magnus, as he stole repeated glances at the shepherd's face, finally came to the conclusion that, like certain animals, he possessed the power of sleeping without the usual indications of sleep!

"He is asleep at this moment," Magnus thought. "His eyes are glazed."

"How can 'ee utter such words, Herbie," protested the old woman, "in the presence of God and me tidy girls? They be beer-shop words and Gideon don't like to hear 'un spoke. Glory and Pansy have always been the well-behaved maidies they be now. They did always wash them's necks when they was little, and both on 'em were always clean and sweet and spry, with their fingy-nails all shell-shiny. None set eyes on 'em but they made mention of it."

Mr. Dandin screwed round, on the pivot of his thin neck, his scarecrow physiognomy, with its retreating chin and enormous knobly nose and stared at each of the company in turn. But the responses he received were torpid. The old clerk was so used to having that lacklustre, bored look fixed upon him that he had come to assume that this look was the natural look of the human race! It certainly was the look of the whole Radipole congregation when he repeated "And with thy spirit", in the Church responses. It had been the look of Shepherd Rugg all the way to Weymouth in the 'bus this morning. Herb had only to turn his face towards any living thing and the eyes of that thing grew as glazed as the eyes of old Gideon. When he went to his privy these autumn mornings and just glanced through the wet mist over the nettles and burdocks of Mr. Cole's hedge to catch the yellow eye of Mr. Cole's great sow, the creature, in plain pig-language, told him he was a nuisance.

And Herb Dandin *was* a nuisance. He was not a vicious man, nor was he a malevolent man, but he had only to wink at a pig for the animal to get that look. Thus when the Radipole Clerk heard Hepzibah tell the company that Tissty and Tossty washed their necks when they were little, he winked at everybody present, one after another, without moving hand or foot from the exact position he had assumed when he first sat down, a habit he had learnt from the thousand Sundays of his clerk-ship.

"Parson Hussey," he said, "have many times told I about our Tissty and Tossty being such scholards with them's dainty legs. Parson Hussey told I he've 'a seed 'un dance 'The Cowslip' many a warm

May night, on Squire Coot's lawn. Squire Coot be a friend, s'now, or cousin or summat, to wold Mr. Ludlow of White Nose, what found thik girt heathen stone, they called the Cuddlin' Stone, out to Portland."

Magnus, as he sat at the back of the tent listening vaguely to several conversations at the same time and exchanging perfunctory remarks with Zinzin as she presided over the tea-making, was struck by the way Tissty and Tossty treated Mr. Dandin.

"It is, of course," he thought, "because they know they won't have to see the old man again for a whole year. But they *are* nice. I never knew how nice they were."

And then as that fatally *double* sound of the sea went on, systole, diastole, centripetal, centrifugal, flow-in, ebb-out, the long planetary rise-fall, up-down, pendulum swing of this self-contradictory universe, it seemed as if some destiny-drenched lust-sobbing force within him was carrying him forward on such a foam-crest, that he felt he must and *would* possess her, possess that maddeningly sweet body of hers, even if he had to ravish it by force!

"No, it were Farmer Coot, *that* were, me Dearies," Magnus now overheard Mr. Dandin explaining to Tissty and Tossty and their mother. "Farmer Coot were no relation to Squire Coot, though both on 'em lived in village. Farmer Coot were a church-going man, a God-fearing man 'a were, and took round collection-plate afore Communion, but Squire Coot were a friend to Mr. Ludlow of White Nose, what holds Cuddlin' Stones, and such-like Pretties, of more valley than serving the Almighty!"

"I can imagine her bed," Magnus was thinking to himself now, "though I've never been up those attic-stairs. I've heard them talking about the window being just above it. How lovely her face must look, these moonlit nights, with that casement-window open above her and the clematis swaying in the wind!"

The mind of a teacher of Latin and a reader of Greek is a queer thing. No sooner had Magnus in his justifiable indignation at her teasing ways imagined himself ravishing Curly by force in her own maiden bed, than such a blind passion of pure love for her swept over him that the blood rushed to his head and he squeezed his bony hands together.

"Oh, Curly, my darling, my life!" he cried in his heart, "never, never could I hurt you!"

At this moment the proprietor of the place entered the tent himself, and after looking grimly around began beckoning to Zinzin to come out. Marret and Tiny Jones were at that moment standing by Magnus' side with a cup of fresh tea and some bread-and-butter, and the teacher asked Marret in a whisper what it was that her father wanted. But Zinzin heard this question; and turning from a protracted interchange of slang words and gesticulations with Mr. Jones, swung round.

"He wants to begin another turn." she remarked. "He says there's a bigger crowd on esplanade. He thinks we're giving too much attention to *this* business, when it's the show that pays."

"Does he do *all* the parts?" enquired Magnus.

Zinzin nodded.

"I help though, don't I, Marret? But Tiny's the clever one of the family, isn't she, Marret? You see it's so narrow, our show-stage, and Marret's too big to squeeze in, when he's there. Isn't she, Tiny? So the little one has to do it."

A totally different odour from any of the preceding ones, and one that resembled turpentine, hung at present about the person of Zinzin and hovered round Magnus. This must have been the ordinary working emanation of this "mackerel of the sea", for she now went off with Mr. Jones.

It was not turpentine or tar, or any hot summer smell, that thrilled just then the senses of Tossty Rugg, *alias* Clive, as she threw one of her beautiful legs across the arm of her wicker chair and contemplated its noble curves. What came back to her was a certain dewy field beyond Radipole Church in spring time and the indescribable smell of cowslips. The sea-shore murmurs floating in, the children's voices drifting by, the disputes among the boatmen, the raucous shouts of Mr. Jones, all of these stirred up memories in her that seemed to go back, so deep they lay, to the time when she used to come to Weymouth "under one hat", as they say, with Shepherd Rugg's bride. And her mind as she gazed languidly at the white flesh of the leg she was swinging, turned with an almost passionate self-congratulation on the way she had manipulated her long intrigue with Jerry, never

once letting that arch-disillusionist solve the real secret of her life.
With that impenetrably hidden secret she dallied luxuriously now,
as her dark-brooding eyes lingered upon her sister's beauty, upon that
soft white neck, with its delicate blue veins, and upon those superbly
modelled breasts. For the truth was that long ago, when they were
little girls together, and her own beauty was undeveloped, the fair-
skinned Tissty was the dark Tossty's one and single passion.

"Oh, little Tiss, little Tiss!" she said to herself now, "and you are
the only one in the world that knows it! It's loving you, like I do,"
the said to herself, "that's given me the power to handle Jerry. Jerry's
the kind of man," she said to herself, "and no one, not even Lucky,
knows it as well as I do, who *has to have what he can't understand*. But
I never could have got him, never kept him, if you hadn't been always
first, little Tiss, first, last, and everything else! How sweet you look
in that jersey, Tiss! It suits you to a T to wear jerseys! It never *did*
suit me. Has Cattistock seen you yet in your jersey? Exquisite little
fool! Anyone but you would have long ago landed that man. I told
you, I begged you, I warned you, little Tiss, not to let him know you
cared for him—and you *didn't* care for him till the wreck. Damn
him and blast him! You're in love with the brute, kid; I know it!
It's being in love that makes you so sweet to Mother and Dad today.
Goodness, kid, you've given yourself too often to that great hulking
stiff, with his damned chin! You've been with him, Tissy, too often.
I *know* it, you've got the look, and it's bad for your work, and Jerry
knows it, without being told! I watched him today, how carefully
he was looking at you. You've been sleeping with him too often,
Tiss, in spite of my—" and at this point the dark girl's thoughts
became so much a matter of visual images, that it would be hard to
translate them into words. They were shameless, too, these images,
and scandalously realistic. For the proud, reserved girl allowed
herself, as women will, actually to visualize the kind of encounter
between her sister and Cattistock that she complained of as too
frequent.

"The truth is," she concluded, "Tissy and Mrs. Lily are birds of a
feather. They're both born to it. It must go with their kind of soft
flesh and milk-white skin. I saw Jerry looking at Mrs. Lily in such
a funny way yesterday. He always laughs at her to me—but I don't

know! He's never looked at me like that. It's odd, rich man though Cattistock is, neither of his women love him for his money. I wonder if he knows that? Probably not."

Whatever may have been the cause of Tissty's relaxed sweetness, as she talked to her mother, her mood at least made it easy for Magnus, who was always afraid of both these girls, to go boldly up to her and beg to be introduced to her parents before he left the tent.

Shepherd Rugg's eye kindled just a little as he held his hand.

" 'Tis many a time, sir," he said, "that your father have passed me and 'they',"—"they" was the way he always referred to his flock—"as he came across White Horse valley. 'Twere one of Mr. Muir's favourite walks *that* were; and as ye knows, Mr. Muir were allus one for talking natural like the gentleman he were, with anyone who knew 'un to speak to. Many a time I've a seed Mr. Muir take out's watch to make sure 'a wouldn't keep nobody waiting for tea. He were one for them little flower-weeds, too, I do mind. Many a afternoon I've a-seed 'un with a nosegay of them things, as 'a came fast along, over Sour-Bit Drove, with his eye to the south, when it did look like rain to sea-ward!"

It sometimes happens that a contemplative person, whose head is full of contrary thought-currents, receives, in a quick, unexpected revelation, a view of the world as it exists when many separate, far-off moments of insight, that have caught our landscape under a large and reconciling light, melt and fuse themselves together. Such a view of things it was, that came over Magnus, when he heard Shepherd Rugg speak of those "flower-weeds" and that "rain to sea-ward". All the calm monotonous years of his father's life seemed to be gathered up in that one moment, as he saw him hurrying along, past the shepherd and his flock, with that little bunch in his hand and his eye on the rain over the sea.

That was always the best of the Weymouth Sands. The people who came to enjoy them were local people, as their own boatmen were. It was as if cowslips and cow-droppings mingled with sea-horses and cowry-shells.

Even when out of the tent and up on the esplanade Magnus was still followed by the brazen, goatish, rammish cry:

"*Judy! Judy! Judy! Judy!*"

He chose the esplanade to walk upon because it meant the quickest advance, and he had a queer desire to see Sylvanus Cobbold that afternoon though he could not have explained exactly why he wanted to see him. As he walked through the crowd his mind ran upon Mr. Gaul who nowadays was always to be seen with Peg Frampton.

"Will those two hit it off?" he wondered. "She looks like a vicious, perverted boy! I know the type in boys well, but I've never met it in a girl. I can . . . *not* . . . conceive . . . how . . . old Gaul . . . will . . . cope . . . with her."

Mr. Gaul was, as a matter of fact, at that very second of time, doing his best to "cope"—and that not ignobly either—with this difficult little person. All the world was on the sands today, and though it was a tradition among the ladies and gentlemen of the town to declare that they avoided the sea-front when the place "was full of excursionists", the only person who had ever really acted on this principle had now been dead some years! This was Magnus' Father, who, when he had to walk from Brunswick Terrace to the station, always went by little side-streets behind the Burdon Hotel. Mr. Gaul and Peg Frampton were snugly ensconced on the lower ridge of the pebble-beach near where the lads were bathing.

Peg had a passion for seeing boys bathing and Mr. Gaul—esteeming it the business of a philosopher to understand all, and of an admirer to pardon all—had willingly yielded to her idea of what was a retired spot. Peg was thinking, as with her mouth more open than usual and her crimson lower lip more drooping than usual she lay on her face watching the bathers, how strange it was that although she was no longer officially and formally "unhappy", as she was last winter, when Daisy and she used to hide their letters to each other in that Rodwell wall, she was not yet, no! not even now, what she herself secretly regarded as honestly and entirely happy. She felt affectionate towards Mr. Gaul and certainly very grateful. She had fits of quite fierce protective instinct with regard to him, especially as concerned the advantage taken of him by tradesmen, boatmen, bus-men, landladies, especially from Salisbury with cheeky daughters, but the flavour of his quaint character it is doubtful if she got.

Peg was what might be called a born "Passionist". To abandon herself—that was her idea of bliss, to abandon herself to the intense and furious slaking of some sort of body and soul thirst. Well, it was certain that she did not find in the Philosopher of Representation anything that in the remotest degree resembled the slaking of such thirst! Certainly this girl, with her high Mongolian cheek bones and deep-set hollow eyes, with her abandoned look, with her long, hot, erotic-desperado fingers and her consumptive chest, found nothing of the pleasure which some found, from just sitting still and looking at the sea. She still required the dangerous, maddening nerve-quiver of vice to render existence bearable.

As she watched these bathers now her whole nature shivered like a harp-string in response to the excited feelings that they aroused. When the two of them had approached that exciting spot, she had replied by a brief, uncivil, heedless "what?" repeated more than once as her companion spoke of the parts played in the history of mythology by the masculine and feminine principle.

Meanwhile, Mr. Gaul, not relucting to compare himself with an Emperor, did his best to bethink him of the indulgence of Marcus Aurelius towards his dissipated Faustina. There indeed *was* something just a little resembling the big round, prominent eye-stare of the Imperial Stoic in Mr. Gaul's look, especially when he could take off his spectacles without blinking at the sun. This he certainly could not do now, for it was still mid-afternoon, and for a person with weak eyes the pebbles had a blinding dazzlement, as they flung back the hot rays. So he had to be as tolerant as he could to his little Faustina's impassioned interest in these Weymouth gladiators, while he turned upon them spectacles bought in St. Mary's Street.

"I do like him," thought the poor lust-driven girl as her whole nature flowed and writhed like a passionate Sea-Undine round the glittering bodies of the naked lads, "but Oh, I must come here more often! I must come her every afternoon! What a fool I've been not to come here every afternoon! But I *do* like him."

After a few minutes she sat up, hugging her knees.

"Why can't you love just as you want to," she thought, "just as much, just as often, and just as many? It's supposed to be wicked. I wonder if it *is*. I don't care if it is! I'd sooner go to Hell and be let do it, than go to Heaven and never do it again!"

"Richard!"

"Yes, dear."

"What do you say in your book about being wicked as people would think I am, always wanting to look at boys and so on? Is it wrong, Richard?"

Mr. Gaul turned a perplexed, perspiring face towards the questioner, but he had his answer ready.

"It seems to me, Peggie," he said in a tone of measured decision, "what you represent at present is the third rung of the philosophic ladder to the Contemplative Ecstasy. When you have reached the ninth rung you will find—you will lose—I mean you will gain—"

But the girl interrupted him.

"Are we really going to the Regent tonight?"

And the sudden anticipating of happiness that this prospect gave her brought back so vividly her old lonely and miserable dangling round the doors of Cinemas with boys like young Witchit that to his blank astonishment she suddenly burst into passionate weeping.

"You don't know what it means to me, you don't know what it means!" she sobbed.

She was perfectly right. Whatever her feelings represented they did not represent any rung in any philosophic ladder. Mr. Gaul, with the best intentions, could not conceive or imagine what was the matter. Like other philosophers, however, he was growing more and more accustomed to putting up with insoluble mysteries.

There was such a crowd on the esplanade that Magnus decided he had better get down to the sea's edge. They had assured him in the tent that Sylvanus had been seen by the donkey-stand. He swung round, therefore, when he reached the Clock, grasping his stick tightly and pulling down his cap over his forehead.

"Once down by the water," he thought, "there'll be no chance of missing him."

He had not left the esplanade, however, when he was suddenly accosted by a familiar voice and there stood the Jobber before him!

"Mr. Muir!"

The man jerked this out with a hoarse gasp of recognition.

"I'm gladder than I can tell you, Mr. Muir, to see you, to catch you like this. Here, Mr. Muir, I want—" In his excitement he seized Magnus by the lappet of his coat—"to talk to you a minute, to ask you, to beg of you, but I can't talk here. Where could we—"

But at that very second, by some special dispensation of Providence, two sailor boys of His Majesty's Navy got up from a seat quite close to them. Precipitantly, the Jobber pulled Magnus down into the places left by these lads, which were at the end of a long bench.

"*Where is Miss Wane?*"

It would be impossible to compare the intensity of these words to any earthly vibration. Their accent resembled the accent of those terrible scoriac syllables wherewith Dante makes the souls of his sons of perdition ask their single blood-freezing questions; questions that almost turn asker and answerer alike to stone. Such, and not less than such, was the petrifying force of the Jobber's intensity, as he clutched at Magnus, gazing into his face.

"I don't—know!" the teacher replied, feeling an overpowering rush of amazed pity.

He was deeply shocked, not only at the tone of the Jobber's voice, which seemed to come from somewhere *below* the pit of his stomach, but by his appearance, which had changed since he last saw him to a devastation that was unbelievable. The man's large, saturnine countenance, dark with that monumental look of bronze sculpture that had always struck him as something Spanish rather than Norse, sagged and wilted. In some indescribable way it had grown *indistinct*. It looked like a landscape over whose lineaments a whole ice-age had passed. Magnus examined this tragic map of glacial destruction very closely as he listened to him, and he noted that it was not only the nose and nostrils and lips that were, so to say, confounded. The cheeks had become bloated and pendulous. Dummy Skald's face had grown in fact to resemble the face of a real dummy, at which, for the fun of the fair and out of pure sport, the gods had been aiming missiles. It moved about among men like an "Aunt Sally" of the immortals. All the capricious flickerings of normal emotion had deserted his face. All the lesser human interests—of which the man never had very many or very lively ones—had oozed out of it. It was like the face of some wandering Belisarius, blind to the world, who had lost his guide. Something was left, however. Something had spoken from out of this perambulatory Image of desolation.

"*Where is Miss Wane?*" it had said, and the words kept repeating themselves in Magnus' mind and along with them, his own foolish ineffectual answer.

"*Where is Miss Wane?*"

It was like some ultimate babbled, burbled, blubbered *sob*, uttered by the whole human race, after Science has killed God, tortured the last animal to death, suckled all babies with machines, eaves-dropped on the privacy of all souls, and made life to its last drop an itch of the blood and a weariness of the will. Magnus couldn't get the echo of it out of his mind. And he thought, as he watched the dense procession of holiday people, pushing, jostling, scolding, chattering, perspiring, their parasols and parcels, their skirts and trousers rustling so uncomfortably past the tragic face at his side, that perhaps it would be a good thing if human nature *were* completely changed, and Science did create a fresh race of Sippy-Cattistocks, to cry their "Judy! Judy!" in a new accent. Certainly that feeble reply of his: "I don't—know," had reducèd Dummy Skald to complete Non-Existence. It seemed to Magnus, as if he had already joined the ranks of those Homeric *Kamontes* he was always thinking about, those sad troops of the enfeebled Dead, who were sub-conscious, sub-sensitive, sub-normal, sub-substantial.

Magnus was aware of a smell proceeding from him that was like the smell of an extremely aged tramp. It was not indeed only the Jobber's countenance that was ravaged. His dress had completely changed its character since the tutor had last seen him. It was no longer the dress of a well-to-do seafaring man. It would be hard to say exactly what it did resemble. Perhaps it was like the attire of one of those hangers-on about the Weymouth docks who were not accredited longshoremen or stevedores, but just wharf-side loiterers, pickers-up of anything that came their way. He was a little too tragic and a little too desperate in appearance for Magnus even to imagine him as one of the shabbiest of those respectable elderly fishermen, or retired boatmen, who row people across the Nothe Ferry.

"I only know," added Magnus, "that Jerry has heard nothing of her. He thinks she is still in the town though. He said that to me only yesterday; whereas Mrs. Cobbold—"

"Eh? What's that? What does *she* say?"

"She says that Miss Wane has either gone home to Guernsey or that she's——"

The Jobber looked at him a moment and then gave vent to a low guttural chuckle.

"Or on the streets, eh? Yes, that's what she *would* say. Is her sister still with them, up there, or has she gone back? She told me a month ago that——"

"Mrs. Lily's still with them," the teacher replied, "but she tells me, every time I see her, that she's going back 'tomorrow'. Do you still see Captain Poxwell, Mr. Skald? I've seen nothing of Daisy all this summer."

The faintest flicker of human interest came into the Jobber's face.

"I saw her yesterday," he said. "She's with the Loders when she's not with the Captain. They tell me Mrs. Matzell, over there, is ill."

The Jobber was silent, while the ripple of human interest, excited by the mention of Daisy, died out of his eyes. For a long while he held his peace, and Magnus continued to curse himself for his lack of invention or inspiration about Miss Wane. The unhappy man by his side was now squeezing him unmercifully against a youth with a neat straw hat on, who was reading Hardy's "Well-Beloved".

As Magnus glanced down at this book he caught the word "oolite", and the word seemed to dance before him. A baby, somewhere on their crowded seat—somewhere beyond the boy with the straw hat— was holding by a string a rose-coloured toy balloon, an object which kept tapping the shoulders of the promenaders, and was indeed once tossed back by a spiteful old man with a vicious flick that sent it rebounding against its owner's head. It was upon this rosy toy that the word "oolite" now fixed itself, like a label on the surface of a red moon, and although the Jobber's stony island was hidden from their eyes at that spot by Weymouth Pier, the tutor had the sensation that the whole of Portland, with all its people and all their passions, was no more solid than this airy, floating ephemeral balloon.

"By Dum!" exclaimed the Jobber at last. "I never thought of *that!* She may have got Ellen up at the Head to hide her. There are lots of deserted stone sheds up there where a person, who wanted to, could hide forever! 'Twas the smugglers' head-quarters in old times. By Dum!"—and he struck his corrugated forehead—"I thought Ellen

talked funny to me about her, Mr. Muir. Yes, I did, at the time, and
then I went and forgot it, Mr. Muir. But at the time I did! And she
is a funny one, Mr. Muir. You don't know, her, I suppose—the
landlady at the Head? Some say she's her husband's half-sister, and
that her daughters are also her nieces, 'Melia, Celia and Sue; you
don't know *them*, either, I expect? Nowadays they're always on the
sands with Cobbold."

In his eagerness to get Magnus to agree to the notion, not indeed an
impossible one, that Perdita was hiding from him in the neighbourhood
of the Sea-Serpent's Head, where they had spent their first night,
Dummy Skald inclined his great ravaged face close to the tutor's, and
as he did so Magnus was aware of a villainous odour of what struck
him as being, not whiskey, but rum. Now it happened that Muir,
though not averse to whiskey or even gin, loathed the smell of rum! A
sailor on one of the old men-of-war, when he was a child, had taken
him on his knees and breathed upon him from what had seemed a
very Avernus of sickly-sweet brimstone. Thus the rum on the
Jobber's breath considerably alienated the tutor's sympathy.

He now hurriedly lit a cigarette, an action which, by the law of
imitation, set the reader of the "Well-Beloved" upon lighting one,
too. As for the Jobber, he put his empty pipe into his mouth and
began biting its mouthpiece savagely.

"By Dum! If that's the ticket why haven't I thought of it before?"
but as he hissed these words through his closed teeth, he sighed heavily,
as if in his heart he knew the fallacy of this hope. Then Magnus had
an impulse to say something very unwise.

"Jerry said," he remarked, "that he was *certain* she was somewhere
in Weymouth. He said it so strongly that I had a feeling that he *knew*
where she was."

The tormented stare in the Jobber's eye-sockets concentrated itself
and narrowed itself, but it did not soften.

"Yes, I know," he growled. "He's given me that feeling in a lot of
talks, but I don't believe it, Mr. Muir, I don't believe it! I don't
believe she's in Weymouth."

"Have you gone to the police?"

Magnus blurted this out as inevitably as the elder Muir would have
done, to whom Weymouth policemen were like a personal body-guard

for the protection of the teaching of mathematics. He was surprised
at the glance of contempt the Jobber gave him.

"Well," he said rising, for in his own mind he was obstinately bent
upon seeing Sylvanus that afternoon, "Well, one thing at least I'd do if
I were in your place, Skald, and that is, go the round of everyone you
know in Weymouth and make 'em swear if they see Miss Wane on
the—in the road anywhere—to follow her home and let you know at
once where she lives. If I were in your place, Skald," he repeated,
warming to his advice, as he saw the end of this uncomfortable
interview, "I'd make this little town ring and ting with your spies,
all watching, all waiting for her! It mayn't answer for a day or two,
or for a week or two, but sooner or later—if she's in Weymouth, and
my instinct agrees with Jerry's that she is—you mark my words,
you'll find her." He had his hand extended now—"But let me just
add one word, Skald, if you'll not think me impertinent. I'm a good
deal older than you ... ten years, I shouldn't wonder! ... Don't 'ee
go to the drink as a consolation. It's a bad comforter, the drink is.
Better say your prayers, Jobber Skald, and that's the truth. Better
say your prayers!"

He went off with his face a little flushed from the audacity of his
last words. As he pushed his way through the moving crowd he felt
a pang of shame. Who was he to talk to this man about prayer? What
impulse had led him to "drop", as Jerry Cobbold would have said,
such a "brick" as that? He turned and looked round. The Jobber
was still on the bench, his hands clasped on his lap, sitting bolt upright. As Magnus peered at him between the intervening forms their
eyes suddenly met, and one of those indescribable looks passed from
one to the other that make up so large a part of the mystery of human
contact.

"I wish I hadn't said that about prayer," he thought, as he moved
away, "though it's just what father would have said! I *was* father at
that moment."

He was now across the esplanade and had his back to its crowded
procession. Here he felt an almost uncontrollable desire to return to
that man on the bench. But he suppressed it.

"What's the use?" he said to himself. "If I only talk to him as
father used to talk to tramps I shan't do him any good."

He was standing now on the top of one of the flights of stone steps that descend from the esplanade to the dry sand. A row of little bare-legged children were sitting on the bottom step, while beside them, propped up against a miniature sandcastle, an enormously fat old grandmother was reading the Melcombe Regis Circular. Two infants, hardly more than babies, were sprinkling little spade-fuls of sand on the sides of this castle, while armed with a brilliantly coloured bucket, upon which was a picture of Brighton, another infant, a very solemn little boy, was, like the Israelites without straw, struggling to make mud-pies without water. Letting Sylvanus go for a further minute, Magnus sat down on the top step and fixing his eyes on a small wet place in the sand, near the melancholy mud-pie failures, where the little worker in dryness had produced water from his own body, he fell to conjuring up, in a vein of nervous craving that was unusual with him, such a voluptuous scene in that never-yet-visited attic room that it transformed sand and urine and newspaper and infants' bare legs and the folds of the old lady's black gown and biscuit crumbs and flies and a beautiful specimen of riband seaweed kept in its place by pebbles, into lips that smiled as they had never smiled before, into limbs that yielded as they had never yielded before, and into a passion-ate response such as he had only dared even to imagine once before, and then it was under the excitement of that wreck.

A shrill bark from a woolly dog, of a ridiculously diminutive size, that he now observed for the first time—for it had been hidden by the newspaper—on the old woman's lap, roused him from his trance and recalled him to his purpose. He ran down the steps, pushed past the children, apologized to the old woman, and set off rapidly towards the wet sand.

It was an animated spectacle at that hour, the whole crowded shore, and through it all now, following the fragile, friable margin-line of the tidal windrow, he hurriedly made his way. The sun poured down from a sky that was almost cloudless now, its blue intensity only modified by a delicate film of Chinese-white on the sea's horizon. *There he was!* Yes; it was not very difficult to make out that giant figure in the tweed suit, as he stood, with long, bare legs, his boots and socks held firmly by the boot laces, and a little soldier's cane flicking the air. Listening to his words with intense absorption were

two feminine figures, who, to the eyes of the tutor from Brunswick
Terrace, seemed a pair of the most uninteresting young women he
had ever seen.

Magnus had never been to the Sea-Serpent's Head, and if he *had*
it is likely enough he would have missed the quality of the Gadget
family, but to the soul of Sylvanus these short, stiff girls in pink frocks
and be-ribboned hats were of absorbing and enthralling interest. Vases
of precious odours they were, urns of celestial unguents, vessels of
paradisiac myrrh and cassia, whose receptive souls were reed-pipes
through which the Absolute played without a pause, played all night
and all day, on the beaches and on the sands, on the rocks and in the
quarries, played tunes that taught Sylvanus, even as the Spirit taught
Faust:

> "Alles vergangliche
> Ist nur ein gleichnis."
> "All appearance is but a symbol."

"I've got used to him now," thought Magnus, "without his
moustache; it makes his face look much weaker, but it makes it more
sensitive."

Sylvanus' discourse must have become too nebulous for his holiday
audience, whether on land or in the water, as he thus stood, like
inconstant manhood in the song, "with one foot in sea and one foot
on shore", for 'Melia and Celia were the only faithful ones left of the
crowd of young people he had had about him. Sue Gadget had never
been the ardent devotee of Sylvanus that her sisters had become. Sue
had a tenderness for men of action, and more than once, since his
loss of Perdita, she had had the audacity to condole with Jobber
Skald.

Nearby where Sylvanus was talking to 'Melia and Celia there was a
pleasure boat pulled up on the edge of the pebbles whose stern lay low
in the wet sand. The boatmen to whom it belonged were out in the
bay, and with the tide on the ebb they had left this boat to take care of
itself. Magnus, feeling a sudden access of tiredness, seated himself on
this sand-locked stern, not without noticing the boat's name, which
was Calypso. Like a magic touch, through all his worries and
obsessions, this classical word swept the mind of the teacher to the

far-off realms he loved, and in a flash between that glittering bay, flecked with darting gulls, airy yachts, gaily loaded rowing-boats, and the vaporous cloud feathers of that halcyon sky, the tall figure of Sylvanus struck him as the eternal recurrence of some undying "gleichnis".

Sylvanus evidently did not recognize this man seated on the stern of the Calypso, for he went on with his rich, deep, low-murmured monologue, addressing himself solely to the two young girls, who with bare feet, each holding her shoes in her hand, kept their dazed, spectacles eyes fixed upon him, while their innocent mouths remained open. Magnus took not the smallest notice of what the man was saying, but he felt peaceful and happy as he sat on the Calypso's stern. All the fussiness, all the fretting life-worry of his usual expression left his face. The lines of his mouth grew formidable, almost majestic, his nostrils quivered like those of a proud horse.

"Water and Sand," he thought, "are what I want. The inanimate, not flesh and blood. I am *really* happier at this minute, than I am with Curly!"

His mind raced on from image to image of the Homeric mythology.

"I'm not the only one in Weymouth who reads Homer," he said to himself as he moved his fingers along the curves of the Calypso which were so blistering hot from the sun that in some places they emitted minute bubbles of tar, "but I fancy I *am* the only one who accepts Homer's philosophy as my own and Homer's religion as my own."

And then an odd thing happened to him. He caught sight of a large, derelict piece of cork, the sort of piece of cork that fishermen use to keep their deep sea nets from sinking out of sight. This large piece of cork lay half-embedded in the sand. But no sooner had he caught sight of it than a rush of happiness, so intense, so overwhelming, took possession of him, that he was as one transported out of himself. That piece of cork lifted him up, wafted him away. That piece of cork became all the summer afternoons when he and the elder Muir had set out from Penn House to walk to Redcliff Bay. That piece of cork became the splash of waves into all the rock-pools from the Coast-Guards to Preston Brook.

He sighed heavily, rose from his seat and, moving straight up to Sylvanus, took off his cap to these two girls, who to him looked so incredibly uninteresting, but who to Sylvanus were the "still un-ravished brides" of an unutterable revelation. The tall man's coun-tenance resembled the map of a Terra Incognita that is about to be inscribed by its discoverer. But by degrees he came to himself, his hand in that of Magnus.

"You mustn't leave Sue too long, sweethearts," he said in a quiet and rather wistful voice. "Your mother would never forgive me if she came to grief, and she's different from us! She's an explorer."

'Melia and Celia did not even throw one glance at the intruder. They lowered their eyes; they gave their skirts a few twitches; and they went off sea-ward, evidently intending to follow the retreating tide, to where—some three hundred yards away—the bulk of the boys and girls were paddling.

The two men sat down where Magnus had been seated, and as the ghost-conveying boat on the livid marsh, under the vermilion bastions of Dis, sank down to its gunwhale under Dante's weight, so the Calypso sank in the sand, under the weight of Sylvanus.

"We haven't seen as much of each other as I would have liked," Magnus began, "but the Bill's a difficult place for me to reach, and I've really had very little time since I've been teaching Benny Cattistock."

Sylvanus disregarded this polite opening as completely as if Magnus had merely sneezed.

"Did you want to ask me anything?" he said.

"I know you have your own affairs to attend to," Magnus went on. "We all have that. And I know your chief interest is your own mystical system. But sometimes it seems to me as if we really ought—"

"Is it about Marret Jones?"

The realistic directness of the man's approach to bed-rock topics did not disturb Magnus. Polite circumlocutions were not really native to his spirit, although from nervousness he habitually used them. He smiled now and shook his head.

"Is it about your friend, Curly Wix?"

He laughed and again shook his head.

"Is it about the girl Dummy Skald has lost?"

"On my soul, Cobbold, you seem to think that nothing's important except what's happening to girls. What I wanted to ask you was

whether you think people about here realize that there is vivisection
going on at the Brush Home? Because I can assure you that it *is* going
on there."

Sylvanus raised his hand to his face where the familiar moustaches
used to hang.

"Listen, Mr. Muir," he said, and he turned his long neck round
upon him with that curious turtle-head movement that used to be so
disturbing to Gipsy May: "This is my last day at large. They . . .
are . . . going, . . ." He spoke with a soft but significant emphasis . . .
"*they are going to lock me up.* Jerry has done his best . . . but all he'll
be able to do will be to have me sent to Brush's place . . . where my
father was before he died, and where Edward Loder went. Whether
he is still alive I don't know! Lots of us Weymouth people end at
Brush's. Hardly an old family round here but has someone there. So
you see I shall have plenty of chances to find out about that vivisection business. Don't 'ee look like that, Muir. I'm not afraid.
Since her father made all that fuss and got Marret back I've been a
bit lonely up there at the Bill. I shan't be lonely at Brush's. They'll
let me have the run of the grounds, and no one will bother to stop
my talking *to the others!* That's the privilege of Bedlam. They let
you talk!"

As Magnus listened to the words, issuing thus calmly from the
shaven face at his side, a deadly sickness took possession of him. He
saw life from a new angle, as if all his days he had been swaddling
himself in cotton-wool and now he touched the spikes! It was not
exactly that he pitied this man. There was something in Sylvanus
that thrust pity a thousand leagues away, something that made it seem
misplaced, like pitying Maiden Castle or Hardy's Monument, but
it was the revelation of the cruelty of the world that turned his
stomach, its monstrous cruelty. Little had he guessed what he was
doing, what he was fooling with, when he came to Sylvanus that
afternoon. The man's tone was so final, and Magnus was so un-
worldly, that he felt no inclination to question his ghastly announcement or even to utter any protest. The aura that emanated from
Sylvanus' whole personality was so charged with the gravitation of
necessity that it seemed impertinence to disturb him by discordant
clamour. But he did murmur one faint interrogation.

"What makes you so sure of their arresting you tonight?" he said in a low voice.

"My good sir," replied Sylvanus. "Three times today I've started talking on the esplanade. It was about three, I think, for I noticed the Clock, when I tried it last, and that was the end. Their Police-Superintendent himself was up there. He gave me one last chance. I've only to step on the esplanade and begin a few words, Mr. Muir, and they'll take me up. They're watching us now. They know I'm going to do it . . . and so I am! We understand each other perfectly. They've made all their arrangements. The warrant's already out. I'm on a sort of parole *now*. They'll take me to the Police Station for tonight. Tomorrow some local Magistrate—probably that little skipping Ballard—will sign my conviction. They'll send for Jerry at once and for some fool of a doctor, and it'll be that County Asylum, or Brush's! Jerry will pay for Brush's, and there I shall be. One night in gaol, my friend, and then the Sanitarium at His Majesty's good pleasure!"

A long, silent look passed between the two men.

"Couldn't you," whispered Magnus—he felt as if the esplanade were bristling with an immense Battery of Artillery, that at that moment might open fire—"couldn't you follow your star, and do your job, *just as well*, without breaking their rules?"

"Impossible," the other breathed. "I've decided all this, months and months ago. You saw yourself how many people listen to me down here. Just those two girls! On the esplanade I always draw a crowd. Well, Muir, I must be off! If you have a chance of being nice to Marret, don't 'ee miss it . . . or to May, either, or to those kids from the Head. I'm not posing as any heroic, ironical Socrates. I'm taking it easy, because I've gone through the worst already. I'll sleep sound tonight, Muir, and sounder still tomorrow night! Why not? God isn't only on Weymouth Sands."

Magnus thought:

"It's incredible that they should put a man like this away only for gathering crowds on the esplanade. I wonder . . . I wonder if—"

What came into his head were all the wicked rumours going about Weymouth with regard to Sylvanus, his seduction of young girls, his abducting them to that lonely house near the Bill. Mrs. Cobbold had,

HH

for months, been whispering to him the most sinister things, and he had heard tales about him, too, in the town that were simply unbelievable. Even Miss Le Fleau had expressed a wish, and that quite recently, that the authorities would intervene.

"It brings our town into disrepute," the old lady had said, "and I'm sure the police ought to do something. The place won't be safe soon for young girls to go about alone in. I can't bear to think of it. It keeps me awake at night."

With these thoughts rushing through his brain Magnus took the bull by the horns.

"By the way, Cobbold," he burst out. "You're sure this police trouble *is* about your speaking? You don't think it has been worked up by that Punch-and-Judy man over his daughter? I saw her just now and she seemed—"

He was astonished at the spasm of anger that convulsed the tall man's face.

"They're my friends," he cried hoarsely. "Friends, I tell you. May, Marret, little Peg . . . They're my friends. They understand me and I them. It's God between us, man! Can't you see? Can't everybody see? It's through them I touch God!"

Magnus was silent. He felt anything but reassured. The man's allusion to Peg troubled him especially. Was he really a seducer of young girls?

"Do you . . . mean . . . Peg Frampton?" he blurted out.

Sylvanus caught his changed mood in a flash.

"I mean—my *friends!*" he cried angrily. "Who has any right in this town to interfere with my friends? Muir . . . Muir . . . you begin to talk as your father would have talked!"

Nothing could have been more calculated to alienate the teacher from him than these unlucky words. Magnus knew well the old-fashioned, conventional prestige that his father possessed in Weymouth. The other side of his father, that secret, elemental life he had inherited from him, what did any of these people know of *that?*

"All I can say is, Cobbold," he found himself saying, while he looked at him with an electric flush of indignation, "is that if you've been . . . 'making friends' . . . with the daughter of Cattistock's partner, you're in for trouble! I begin to see light on the whole thing now. This young Ballard has had a hint from Mr. Frampton, probably from Cattistock himself. You'd have been a lot wiser, Cobbold, to confine your ... 'friendships' ... to girls of the lower classes ... to girls like those two I saw with you just now."

The tall man made no reply. With one glance that indicated to his interlocutor that their conversation was at an end, he began shaking the sand out of his boots, preparatory to putting them on, and when this was done to his satisfaction he bent down, and without attempting to dry his feet, proceeded to struggle, for it was not an easy process, to pull on his stockings. From his bent form by the boat's side there rose an emanation of human sweat mingled with sun-blistered paint.

Magnus was conscious of a vivid pang of remorse. Who was he to take a conventional view of this strange being's doings?

"Well, Cobbold," he said. "I won't bother you any more. But I'll tell you what I'm going to do. I'm going straight to High House to see your brother."

The man wrestling with the stocking made no response.

"*And then* I'm going to talk to Rodney Loder, for what you must have, if these demons really do take you up, is a clever lawyer."

Not a sign, not an indication from the crouching figure that he even so much as heard what was said to him! The fellow's obstinacy annoyed Magnus, but he thought:

"I'd be in a funny mood, myself, I daresay, if I were in danger of landing in Hell's Museum. Well! I'm off to Jerry's, anyway! The sooner *he* knows, the better, whatever happens."

He gave one last glance at the preoccupied man.

"Goodbye, Cobbold!" he said and this time he fancied that he caught some kind of a response from above the obdurate stocking, but what he heard sounded to his classical ears like two Latin words rarely found in juxtaposition, like the words "Caput ... Anus".

"Eh? What's that?" he said.

But Sylvanus was silent.

Left alone on his crowded bench, from which the crimson toy-balloon still tapped the elbows of the passers-by, Jobber Skald remained motionless, like an image of desolation carved in a darker, rougher stone than his native oolite. At length he slowly and stiffly rose to his feet.

"I'll get a drink," he thought, and he stood hesitating for a second, pondering in his mind where was the nearest bar.

Suddenly the short, square figure of the devoted Bum presented itself to his sun-dazed eyes.

"Skipper!" said Bum Trot in an unnecessarily loud voice, as if he were shouting against the wind from prow to stern of the Cormorant.

"Well?" groaned Skald.

" 'Tis she what sent me to keep 'ee in me eye. She be fine worried about 'ee."

"I'm all right," muttered the Jobber.

"Oh, skipper, but ye bain't, ye bain't! Ye be far from all right. Ye be a walking corpsy, and they that knows 'ee best do know it."

The Jobber was clearly not untouched by his henchman's faithful concern. A sudden impulse rose in his heart and depicted itself upon his grief-ravaged face.

"Come," he muttered, "come, old friend. I want to talk to you."

They left the esplanade, crossed the road, went a step or two up King's Street, and turned into the first tavern they came to, over the entrance of which hung a sign-board with the words "The Flag-Ship". Here in an almost empty bar-room, over foaming tankards of beer—and for once the Jobber raised no question as to whose brewery it came from—the master of the Cormorant unburdened his breast.

"I found her where I left her, Bum, when I went back that day. She was glad to her heart's core that I hadn't found him, and to tell 'ee the truth, Bum, I were glad enough myself. 'Twasn't a pretty thing to do, nor an easy, to leave her that dark morn! Well! We stayed, as you and the missus know, all that day and all the next, scarce going a stone's throw away from the Head. She thought I'd given up my oath to do for the Dog, and I never said no single word to her anent it, neither for nor against. 'Twere better I had, old friend, 'twere better I had! For the hour came at last—a time and times and half a time, woe be to all!—when she found out that that Chesil-stone were still in my pocket, yes and in my heart, God damn and wither my soul! in my heart, too. 'Twere a bitter moment when she found that, Bum, the bitterest I've known, and I've known many, afore and since! There were words between us, terrible words, my boy, words that . . . words that . . ."

His feelings overmatched him at this point, and to Mr. Trot's consternation his head bent forward over his beer, and sobs that seemed to proceed—so deep they were—from the place where the navel string of mortal men is cut at birth, shook his whole powerful frame.

Bum Trot had only once before seen the "skipper" weep, and that was when "the Dog" made his first move in the process of getting the stone quarries into his hand. But those were different tears! These that were now mingling with the froth and the dregs of what actually was—for the Flag Ship was a tied house—ale from a barrel of Cattistock-and-Frampton, were tears of the most self-obliterating passion of tenderness that Bum had ever seen shed.

When the woe-stricken man finally recovered his self-control and tossed off the dregs of his beer thus diluted with another salt than that which comes from the sea, the agitated Mr. Trot found himself almost relieved, in spite of there being so much the less to reveal at Cove House, when he discovered that the Jobber had exhausted his confessional mood. The only remaining scrap of information for the distracted Mrs. Trot that he could come at was the fact—and this they had guessed already—that a day or two after he had lost her he had gone to Guernsey to see Perdita's aunt, and that, though this secretive and cautious old woman did her utmost to tell him nothing, it was fairly clear that she had been hearing regularly from her niece, and was in no way perturbed about her.

While Bum Trot was doing his utmost to coax his master to return home by the ferry rather than by the bridge, the doorbell of Sark House, in Ranelagh Road, was ringing with a furious and frantic importunity. It was none other than Ruth herself, Miss Le Fleau's secret choice for Magnus, if a thoughtful Providence should ever take Curly to Itself, who was thus driven to invade these ambiguous precincts. But Ruth, though she rang violently, and though she prayed earnestly that her father's pain might cease before he died, retained all the while a large portion of her consciousness entirely calm, occupied indeed with matters far removed from both James Loder's ulcers and this teasing delay at the doctor's door. What she was thinking about were certain greenish-coloured fish that she had seen that afternoon below Sandsfoot Castle as she took care of Captain Poxwell. They had dark fins, erect and very sharp. She wondered to herself if they were in that pool still or if they had gone out with the tide.

Miss Le Fleau would have been simply staggered had she realized the calm depths and placid gulfs of inhuman detachment, far beyond anything Magnus knew, that lay beneath the tender solicitudes of this girl's gentle and devoted life! Ruth Loder was agitated as she conveyed the doctor to Spy Croft in her taxi, over her Father being in danger of his life, but what really diffused itself through her mind in spite of many twinges of nerve-to-nerve sympathy was a mysterious, inscrutable sense of satisfaction that she lived where there *were* greenish-coloured fish and where greenish-coloured fish could *go out on the tide* . . . Even when old Ammabel let them into Spy Croft, a few minutes later, and informed them that the master was worse, this inhuman girl—whose whole life was outwardly a long, patient devotion—breathed in with infinite satisfaction, after the unpleasant aroma of Sark House that peculiar smell of not only dead, but dried and embalmed seaweed, mingled with the odour of ancient woodwork, scorched by the sun, and cracking and peeling, into whose faded varnish had sunk the sun-blistered sea-salt of half a century of gala summers.

It was not that Ruth's reserve, the under-life with which her nature was sub-charged, was a furtive or guilty thing as it was with Rodney. When, only a second or two after her thrill of pleasure at getting home and inhaling the familiar sea-side smell, she and Dr. Girodel entered James Loder's bedroom, she carried her private underworld of well-being—full of greenish-coloured fish, floating and drifting, full of sunlit waters, rocking and tossing—quite unashamedly to her father's bedroom.

But is was shocking to see the old man as he received them and glared at them on their entrance! He had long ago, in fits of pain, inured his daughter to seeing him naked. He was stark naked now. He was stretching himself out on the extreme edge of the bed, so that having no support for his head, or for his buttocks, he might balance himself upon the middle of his spine, as a plank, in the game of see-saw, is balanced on its wooden cross-beam. Mr. Loder, by long and bitter experience, had found out that, when you have ulcers, uncomfortable positions are better than comfortable ones. And, moreover,

it was still a comfort to this old man to harrow the feelings of those
who yet had feelings to be harrowed. His daughter knew well
enough that he had not stripped himself naked, nor had stretched
himself out like this, *until they began to ascend the stairs.* He could
torment and scare little Lettice, the under house-maid, without
having to proceed to such lengths as these, but with Ruth and with
Girodel, he was prepared to let himself go. Instead of ceasing these
pain antics as with smiling face and outstretched hand the little doctor
approached him, James Loder actually had the gall, in the midst of
his acute suffering, to make a gross reference to the trade of an
abortionist.

Ruth moved to the window, while Girodel by a mixture of per-
suasion and astute muscular pressure got his patron into his white
night shirt and into his bed, but when safe under the sheets the
General, for Girodel kept calling him by Sippy's nickname, made it
worse for them by launching out into so vivid, so revolting, so realistic,
and at the same time so emotional a description of his ulcers,
that Ruth, with a distressed and angry flush on her white cheeks
and even a faint spot on her smooth forehead, abruptly left the
room.

As soon as she was gone there followed in the front bedroom of Spy
Croft one of those contests that in her perverse belligerency Nature
loves to evoke. It was a contest between savage pain avenging itself
on what is free from pain, and heartless cynicism trying to jest while
flesh and blood suffers. And it was Pain that won. The old man
fixed his eye upon the doctor and remarked:

"There's a red circle of them in here!"

And it was as if out of the stomach of the recumbent figure—who
soon had the bed-clothes off again and his shirt pulled up—an actual
circle of red, pustular sores, livid, festering, pullulating, exhaling,
reeking with fetid odours like crimson tussocks in a blood-red swamp,
were projected towards the hypnotized abortionist through the space
between them. The General was a strong personality, Lucky an
extremely weak one. And thus it was brought about that Pain, with
Malice to help it out, was more than a match for Cynicism with
nothing to aid it except professional aplomb.

"There's a wicked old name for this 'ring of roses' inside me. They dance in a circle, you know," said James Loder with hideous distinct-ness. "It isn't Hans Carvel's ring this time young man! It's a more uncommon kind of a ring."

And then, to Girodel's confounding, the astonishing General sud-denly burst into the old nursery doggerel:

"Ring-a-Ring of Roses!
A pocket full of Poses!"
"Ashes!"

His utterance of the concluding word, "Ashes", was made in an accent of such crumbling, crashing, climaxing finality—as if these ulcers of his were in the throbbing midriff of the universe—that the abortionist, his bravura completely blasted by the metal-sick fumes of this projectile of Hell, simply turned tail and, fleeing incontinently from the room, slammed the door.

The indescribable satisfaction of having driven away both his doctor and his daughter brought at once a real surcease to the General's sufferings. He pulled down his night-shirt and he pulled up his bed-clothes; and with the same look on his face with which he was wont to caress his cat, he actually lit a cigarette from the medicine table at his side.

"I believe I shall live another year in spite of them all," he thought.

With his head reclining comfortably on his pillow the General now became acquainted with the inmost secret of the wisdom of Epicurus—namely that simply *not to be suffering* in this world is Paradise enow! He was disturbed by footsteps and whispers outside, and presently two gentle knocks, followed by two quick, sharp ones, assailed his door. The General smiled, and converting his lips into a small, round orifice, blew out several neat rings of tobacco smoke that slowly ascended to the ceiling. As he watched these rings, and sent others after them from his pursed-up lips, he permitted himself a sigh of satisfaction that at least he was in his own house and not in the Hospital.

"Come in!" he called out quite vigorously and the runaway Lucky, attended this time by the aged Ammabel, re-entered the room.

The sympathetic servant, whose wrinkled face was all tense and drawn with emotion, asked him with infinite concern how he felt now. And the General, acting as he always did with this old woman, made light of his sufferings.

"Not nearly as bad as your rheumatism, Belle," he averred. "Besides —what is a man here for, if not to learn to endure a few pin-pricks!"

Ammabel looked as if this was what her brave master naturally would say, but Girodel contemplated the man in amazement. He had never seen him with Ammabel before. It was a completely new aspect of the General's character. Deftly and quickly he examined the patient now, left some fresh powders on the table with the other sedatives, shook hands with him warmly, and withdrew.

As soon as he was gone the General took stock of the thin, pinched line of the woman's mouth and the clamped, bolted look of her stoical regard. Hurriedly he held out his hand to her.

"Don't 'ee worry, Belle, old girl! I'm good for another twelve-month."

Instead of shaking his hand the old woman raised it to her lips and kissed it, and then went on mumbling and fondling it.

"She's the only one of the whole lot who cares," he thought.

And he made up his mind that he would conceal from her how much he suffered even more carefully than before.

Meanwhile Ruth—still feeling a most evil taste in her mouth from her experience in that bedroom—changed her dress, her stockings, her shoes, put on a light, soft, straw hat, gave some orders to the wide-eyed Lettice and left the house. She walked quickly to where the nearest buses passed and took a bus for the King's Statue. Clambering down here with the rest of the passengers she hurried alone across the road and, skirting the donkeys and ponies and goat-carriages, made her way almost at a run, so faint for the elements she felt, to the sea's edge.

It was the hour of sunset. In fact the crimson, unclouded sun, sinking down into the waters of the West Bay, was already invisible from the esplanade. An interesting change had passed over the Weymouth sands. The "dry" sand was almost entirely deserted, while the "wet" sand and the water, now much deeper as the great evening tide began to flow in, were crowded with bare-limbed boys and girls. Most of these paddlers were young excursionists whose train for Yeovil, or Sherborne, or Dorchester, or even Salisbury, would leave ere long and who wanted to sate themselves, before they left, with sand and sea. These were augmented, too, now by the town's own youth, free from work in shop, workshop and office, and easily distinguished from the visitors by their more matter-of-fact air and the absence of holiday attire.

Itself invisible, the after-glow of the sunset gave the sands an incredible look of enchantment. Some of the pools and canals in the wet sand that the children had made gleamed as though, ere they were deserted, buckets of liquid gold had been poured into them. Local fishermen, their figures dusky and workman-like against that holiday expanse, were going about near the sea's edge digging giant holes to get sea-worms for bait, holes that were so much deeper than any that could be dug with wooden spades, while all over the wet sands, gleaming bright in those red-gold reflections, were little worm castles, where the worms had thrown up sandy reproductions of their own shapes. But by degrees the golden reflections died away and a curious chilliness, that gave to the dark blue water a cold, untouchable marbly look, and to the sands themselves something unfriendly and remote, established itself there, a chilliness that was the chilliness of a cemetery across which a gay procession of intruders has come and gone.

Ruth as she watched all this was aware that the hairy legs of the worm diggers and their great steel spades made her feel mysteriously sad. It was as if with the approaching darkness, and the chilly rising of the tide, and the near departure of the familiar seven o'clock train, the magic enchantment of those shores vanished away. Those dusky worm diggers were like remorseless grave diggers of another vanished day of pure delight. Questions of work and wages began to heave up their heads. The irresponsible Homeric hour had fled, and in place of it the sad, austere Hesiodic wisdom had begun to prevail. Sand in their shoes, slippery riband-seaweed in their hands, shell-boxes as glittering as old Poxwell's pressed against their breasts, tired, crying, scolding, quarelling, vomiting, urinating, with pathetically helpless star-fish and jelly-fish from the free sea perishing cruelly in their hot, human clutches, many of the holiday people were already moving slowly down King's Street towards the Station, preferring—or at least the children's mothers preferring—to sit for half-an-hour on a dusty bench rather than lose the chance of a choice of pleasant window seats, when the seven o'clock train to Dorchester was actually ready.

But Ruth was not one to allow a momentary sadness to spoil her evening, any more than she would allow the sight of a naked man playing at "Marjery-Daw" to do it, and she soon began following the windrow along those sands with her accustomed response. It is hard to suppose that any strip of planetary surface, even one over which the sea-tides advance and recede, can be so totally oblivious to the shifting impressions of our race's tragic comedy as to retain no trace, no memory, no memorial, of words that have once been spoken there. It is still harder, when we come to the works of man's hand to reconcile ourselves to this annihilating obliviousness. When for nearly a hundred years the thoughts of men and women have been eddying, drifting, revolving, round the Statue, the Spire, the Bridge, the Fort, it is difficult to think that the spiritual intensity of no human words, words roused by feelings of anguish, ectasy, treachery, heart-rending indignation, maniacal concealment, has the least effect upon them! That this *is* the state of the case, however, many among us, and not only scientists, feel quite confident. Such intelligences are equally alive to the fact that it is impossible to imagine any corpse more dead, more hopelessly and irredeemably unconscious, than the Spire, the Bridge, the Fort and the Statue!

The wind had dropped completely by this time, and with a full tide running high and showing signs of swallowing up every vestige of the wet sand, and even a little of the dry, there descended upon that whole shore the sort of atmospheric expectancy that makes human thought become most intense and evokes the feeling that Nature herself is waiting for some oracle. More often than not, Nature waits in vain. But on this day there *did* happen to be a sort of oracle delivered, though its utterer, in spite of being of an old Wessex family, was a complete stranger to the town.

At such a time as this, with a high tide running, with an invisible, cloudless sunset, with a cessation of every breath of wind, it was a memorable experience for old Higginbottom's new partner to be led by the old man and little Caddie along the beach. Very slowly they advanced along the pebbly slope, for the wily old gentleman knew how enchanting it was in this hushed hour, and he wanted, above everything else in the world to keep Dr. Mabon with him. He wanted him to live at the "Turret" with them. He wanted him to be Caddie's guardian.

When Magnus returned to Brunswick Terrace after accompanying Jerry to the Police Station he found himself going over again and again in his mind every detail of this event. He had waited outside the building seated on a bench in the glare of the setting sun till Jerry should re-appear. There had been a little boy there whose parents had been arrested and whose sister had gone into a neighbouring bar to get a drink. The child was crying piteously but he had a whip-top clutched in his hand and his tears had stopped when Magnus coaxed him into making his top spin on those sun-lit bricks.

It was of this the tutor thought now as he washed his hands in the bath-room, a room at the back of Miss Le Fleau's house. It was Windsor Soap he used, for he loved its healthy, disinfectant smell— Miss Le Fleau's own piece of private lavender-scented soap lying, pure and sacred, on its own separate china dish—and as he produced an abounding lather, almost worthy of the Jobber's method of dealing with soap, he gazed out, between the clean muslin curtains, at the Spire of St. John's.

"I'm doing," he thought, "what I made that kid at the Police Station do. I'm *washing my hands*. There are only two ultimate gestures of the human race. That of Jesus when He drove out those brutes from the Temple, and that of Pilate when he washed his hands."

He could tell from the sounds and silences in Kimmeridge House that tea had been cleared away and supper was still pretty far in the offing, so when he had dried his hands, still looking at the Spire and thinking of his Father, which he always did, for some reason, when he was using a towel at that back window, he hurried stealthily down stairs and out of the house.

Down at the sea's edge he thought of Homer's famous phrase "wine-dark".

"He *must* have been thinking of this colour," he said to himself for the hundredth time, "but it isn't reddish at all. It isn't even purple. It's dark blue, like Miss Le Fleau's sapphire ring. We're all astray about the Homeric colours. *Glaucous*, for instance I *know* is that peculiar blue-green of the leaves of sea-poppies!"

Whatever "colour", however, tha tfull-brimmed tide may have been as it heaved forward and sank back over the cold, brown pebbles, it pleased him to blend its deep, inflowing volume with the inside of Kimmeridge House, with that back window looking out on the Spire, and with the feeling of washing his hands. An expression came into his face that was neither his daily "worried" expression, nor his formidable look when he gave himself up to the elements. It was a placid, peaceful expression, such as he must have had many a time on that esplanade when he was in his cradle. He touched in his mind some new conclusion about life, in its ebbings and flowings, that he had never formulated before, and even now he couldn't quite catch it. But it had to do with what he had felt as, like Pilate, *he washed his hands*.

Three figures were now approaching him, walking along the edge of the sea. They came from the eastward direction, not the direction of the town. Magnus surveyed them with some interest and a faint surprise. They turned out to be old Higginbottom, little Caddie, and a middle-aged man who was a stranger to him. Every now and then they would stoop down and pick up something from the beach at their feet, and little Caddie would make hurried scrambled rushes over the wet stones, where the sea had drawn back, and return with some small treasure-trove in her hand, or with a scream of dismay as a wave overtook her. Old Higginbottom appeared pleased to encounter Magnus.

"Let me introduce you," he said. "to Dr. Mabon, my new partner. The doctor's going to take my place, Magnus, as time goes on. This is Mr. Muir, Dr. Mabon! I told you about him just now. I'm going to slip out lad, slip out, me boy, from now on!"

The Latin teacher shook hands with his old friend's new partner and scrutinized him carefully. Though the sun had gone down every visible object seemed to assert itself through that vapourless air with an interior illumination, as if it were independent both of darkness and light. Among these objects Dr. Mabon's countenance asserted itself, and also the small entities which he held with infinite scrupulousness in the palm of one of his hands.

It would have been very difficult for Magnus to define what he felt as he kept his eyes fixed on this new Weymouth physician. There was certainly an element of astonished security, confidence, re-assurance, in his impression, and with this a fantastic sensation of unreality as if this man were a specimen of a new type of personality in the world. But simultaneously with this impression there rose up in the background of his thoughts all the old landmarks together, the Spire, the Statue, the Nothe, the Bridge. And what had these to do with this singular conchologist? But no one he knew in Weymouth had a face that pleased him more, unless it were his old friend Miss Le Fleau, and something about the indescribable calm of that whole occasion, the look of the beach and the sea and the fronts of those peaceful houses, made it impossible for any one of them just then, with little Caddie among them, to utter a word that was not solemn and significant.

The old doctor was evidently in an unusually emotional vein. He was clearly feeling that he was leaving his stage forever, and intro-ducing his successor, while Magnus, for all his Pilate-like washing of his hands, was solemnized by the thought of the man he had left in the Police Station.

"Dr. Mabon's a great traveller," announced the old gentleman. "He's been all over the world."

The stranger took no notice of this remark. He kept turning over the shells in the palm of his left hand with the fingers of his right.

"He looks like a Harpooner," thought Magnus.

And indeed there was something about the man's silent, self-contained, suppressed concentration that made one think of some intent, long-sighted master of a whaling ship, with eyes forever fixed on a far-off horizon.

"*What* did you call this one?" said little Caddie, taking up a long queer-shaped shell from his hand.

"A Solen," replied Dr. Mabon gravely, and then his whole face wrinkled up in a most whimsical smile. "Its shape is made like that for moving through the sand. It moves perpendicularly."

And he made a faint movement himself with his whole tall frame, as if he would willingly have exchanged his present incarnation for the life of a Solen.

"Dr. Mabon is writing a work on Ethics," said the old gentleman proudly. "He thinks that there's Science in everything else, but that our ethics are barbarous."

"What's this?" persisted Caddie, holding up a faintly-curved beautifully-indented shell, of a yellowish-brown colour.

"That's an Ostrea," said Dr. Mabon. "You see how equal its valves are, Caddie, and how small one of its 'ears' is! And look at all its' rays'! It's got about thirty. I've often counted them . . . Ostrea varia . . . It's a very good specimen, this is . . . perfectly equivalvular!"

And the stranger, looking at Magnus, smiled such a sympathetic, tender, and yet profoundly humorous smile, that the tutor thought: "I'd like to know this chap's philosophy. He's in advance of all of us. He sees far. He's like the Pilot of the Argo. God! I hope he stays here!"

"Oh! and what's this?" cried Caddie. "This is my favourite of *all* shells! Oh! it's so hard to find one that's not broken. I shall collect *these*, Dr. Mabon!"

Here for the first time since she'd been old enough to walk Magnus saw little Caddie begin to jump about like an ordinary child, Dr. Mabon seemed to have a special look for everyone, with its own humorous commentary upon the world, but a *different* commentary for each separate person in any group. He became very grave, however, when he had examined this particular shell and looked at Caddie.

"It's a Pholas," he murmured, and his voice was as caressing and tender as if he had been the god who had just created this fragile entity. "Pholas candida, and as far as I know it's peculiar to our English coast. It ought to be put into our national heraldry, this Pholas. It's far prettier than the Pilgrims' cockle-shells . . . don't you think so, Mr. Muir?"

"Dr. Mabon's writing a book on Ethics," repeated the old man.

"*This* is one of our commonest and one of our nicest shells," said Dr. Mabon hurriedly, not, however, without acknowledging, with a smile, his friend's persistence.

Magnus approached the conchologist with something like eagerness and took up between his fingers and thumb the shell he was now showing them.

"Yes, I remember!" he cried excitedly—"Mactra, Mactra . . . that's what it is! It's a Mactra . . . isn't it, Dr. Mabon? My father used to collect shells."

And from the fragile convexity of the Mactra there poured through him, quivering up through his finger-tips, a strange feeling of some secret continuity in experience that was the only thing that mattered.

"Barbarous," remarked old Higginbottom. "That's what he thinks our ethics are. Barbarous. I can't get him to say what he thinks of Brush. But I know what he thinks of psychoanalysis. For when I told him *my* opinion of it he said he agreed with me entirely. Didn't you, Dr. Mabon?"

"He must meet my friend, Gaul," said Magnus.

"What does ethics mean?" asked Caddie.

The stranger's countenance grew as sombre and drooping and his whole nature seemed as metagrabolized, as if the child had referred to a murder.

"My book's purely *biological*," he muttered.

And then with an obvious effort he indicated how antediluvian our behaviour to one another still was, even in the most ordinary human relations.

Magnus, thinking of the way he had left the Jobber on that bench, just telling him "to pray instead of drink," began to have a guilty sense that this explorer-physician, who looked like the skipper of a whaler in the Arctic Sea, could teach even a reader of Homer something.

"Pardon my talking shop, Dr. Mabon," he said hurriedly, "but how do you go to work with your neurotic cases, now that you've dropped psychoanalysis?"

His worried schoolmaster's mind was running upon Benny.

Dr. Mabon fixed his Harpooner's gaze upon the horizon, and as Magnus awaited his reply he had a sort of visionary "second-sight", according to which this queer new-comer, with his mania for shells, was destined to bring a completely new set of values into Weymouth.

"How *do* you, Dr. Mabon?" he repeated, with an almost petulant reiteration.

"*How* do you, Dr. Mabon?" the little girl chimed in, while her grandfather, making some of those affectionate but inarticulate sounds that always indicated that people were in the presence of Caddie, that Caddie was feeling something strongly, that Caddie must be gratified at once, confirmed the general craving for something unusual and oracular, which indeed the whole stretch of that calm beach and whole expanse of that dark blue water seemed to feel.

"*How do you, Dr. Mabon?*"

But this new personality upon Weymouth Beach seemed in his goings to and fro over the face of the earth to have visited China. Dr. Mabon smiled vaguely, without—this time—looking at anyone in particular. Perhaps he was smiling at the whole tidal sea, in some deep conspiracy with its mysterious ways. But all he said was—and he might have been addressing the White Nose, or its famous resident, Mr. Ludlow—"I do nothing but listen . . . and . . . move . . . perhaps . . . a few things that have got in the way!"

Having been persecuted till he uttered this oracle, Dr. Mabon did not retire into sulky silence the moment he had spoken. It was evidently as contrary to his system of behaviour to show touchiness and pride as it was contrary to his temperament to express himself in anything but fleeting humour. He was occupied now in lighting a cigarette, which Magnus had offered him, when they were all startled by hearing a resonant voice—a voice that Magnus recognized at once—crying in agitated tones something about "water". Little Caddie, whose surname was "Water," turned a puzzled and frightened face to her grandfather, who in turn looked angrily at Magnus making his loudest "Caddie is here" sounds.

"It's Jerry," thought Magnus. "He must be drunk or something. I must go over there."

Meanwhile Dr. Mabon, discreetly and tactfully, examined the Mactra Stultorum in the palm of his hand.

"Yes, yes," he said to himself. "Subdiaphanous, smooth, . . . radiate . . . purplish . . . gibbous . . . cinereous."

It had been Lucinda Cobbold who had felt a necessity for getting out of the house and down to the sea. Just about the time when the two doctors encountered Magnus the Poxwell sisters, in elegant Regatta clothes, stood on the seaward side of the Esplanade, in front of the house which its garden-loving tenant had named Fernlands. Mrs. Lily, who still found it impossible to decide anything about her

future, had just run in to see the Corporal's front rooms, but, like
Curly, she found the excuse of a strong reaction against the old man's
third wife a splendid excuse for postponing any final conclusion. In
her heart she thought, as Lucinda's desire "to do something" led
them to descend the steps to the beach:

"I mustn't make that mistake twice, that I made with Dogberry.
It seems I don't give men the impression of a *free* woman! I give
them the impression of a woman bound up with sisters and daughters
and fathers. *That*, I'm sure, was what frightened Dogberry. But
what a pity that the richest man in the place should lead the wretched
life he does! Why, *together* if we'd taken a bigger house, and given
parties, and entertained people, he could have assumed the position
that a man like him ought to assume! Well! if I *did* take these rooms
I'd seem a different woman . . . a free woman . . . I'd be starting my
life all over again. But I don't suppose I will. I don't suppose I
really will!"

Jerry, who had rushed to the Police Station just as he was, in his
old grey trousers, baggy at the knees, and his faded Panama hat, had
a particularly weary air that evening. He displayed his usual exaggerated deference towards his wife, he was polite and almost nervously
distant towards his sister-in-law, but it was not concealed from either
of the two women that he had trouble on his mind. It had been no
pleasant experience that he had been through at the Police Station.
He had come away full of a sick loathing for the human race, and the
interview he had with Sylvanus left him hopeless about his brother's
future. It seemed even doubtful, when it turned out that there were
definite charges against him about so many young girls, whether it
would be possible to have him committed as mentally unsound to the
Brush Home. Beneath his exaggerated politeness to his wife—for
always as his contempt for humanity deepened his punctilious propping
up of the status quo became more pronounced—he realized that his
old interest in Lucinda's convoluted morbidity was dead. What he
kept thinking of now was a certain fish, with a horrible eye, that
he had caught sight of at Witchit's in St. Alban's Street, when he
went to see the boy there about a job for which the lad had applied.
That dead fish's eye had given him an idea, one of his most lurid
and sardonic ideas, and he had so bewildered the elder Witchit by a

casual reference to it, that the fish-monger had been betrayed, and it was the one time in his life he was so, into a revelation of his own ferocious misanthropy. Obscene beyond obscenity this idea had been, and as it returned upon him now, while he gave his arm to Mrs. Cobbold, to help her down to the water's edge, he wondered if at one of his nights at the Regent he would be tempted to burst out into a paroxysm so appalling that it would land him where his brother was! As they stood now in front of what had become a miracle of "wine-dark" water, the thought came to him:

"If in one mortal cry—the most horrible ever uttered by a human throat—I could cram all this loathing, loathing, *loathing* into a single word . . . a word like the eye of that fish . . . I'd willingly gulp out a great gobbet of blood and fall dead on my face!" And he thought, "If you found me out, my sweetheart," and he pressed his wife's arm tenderly, "would you have the wit to ruin me?"

And with a sort of precipitous, headlong gusto he set himself to imagine what his existence would be like if he were driven out of his profession!

Weymouth Sands under the rising of the evening tide, yes! and the Spire and the Statue and the Fort, too, must often have been reduced to a meaningless proscenium *by what goes on* in human skulls, but as Mrs. Cobbold beneath the high forehead inherited from the Captain, imagined herself—as it was her destiny to do now—left quite alone, without either husband or sister, in those rooms at High House, her thoughts were so deadly that the poor lover of Trivia, now at peace in the Police Station, might have learnt from them what it was that induced his evasive Absolute to start at all costs setting a cosmos in motion!

"Did you see the yacht-race *to-die*, Sir?" said a cockney voice behind them, and turning with a simultaneous start they all three beheld the landlord of "Fernlands", bare-headed, in clean white shirt and sky-blue braces, and holding his pip ecourteously in his hand.

The Corporal's lady had not been feeling very well that day, and her physical discomfort had endowed her tongue with the hiss of a score of vipers. But when she had rushed upstairs from their tea table in the basement, almost beside herself with temper and nerves, the Corporal had merely sighed, murmured the syllables "Singapore," and gone out into the smallest enclosed space that has ever been called a garden. Here the imperturbable old soldier who had watered his flower-pots from the Ganges to the Euphrates, squatted on his heels on the gravel path and loosened the earth round every single one of his sea-resisting plants. By his side was his watering-can. In the reflected sunset his white-washed stones became glimmering milestones along incredible sea highways, all ending in Singapore. The road dust soothed him, the sound of the waves soothed him, the vesper bells at St. John's soothed him, and there was wafted through his old, cropped, snow-white pate —the stupidest pate and the pate of the most obstinate bore between the Spire and the Statue—a mysterious breath of indescribable reconciliation, a flowing, floating breath, that was at once a sigh of contentment in all the white-washed stones and cockle-shells and flower-pots that have ever comforted the human heart, and a sigh of relief that there *are* welcoming graves—at least in Singapore—to which old men can escape.

"Did you see the yacht-race *to-die*, Sir?"

"Hullo, Corporal!"

Jerry's voice shook with irritation.

"No, no! I can't say I did. I forgot there was a Regatta today! But we all watched it yesterday from the water—Didn't we, Lucinda? Didn't we, Hortensia?—from the water, Sergeant, from the water, the water, the water, the water!"

A non-commissioned officer of His Majesty's Forces is not slow, even if he has an extremely simple mind, in catching the quiver of exasperation in a personage of importance. The Corporal explained to his wife later, who made him repeat the story several times and completely recovered her equanimity as she listened to it, that "them Comedy Hactors 'ud do better to tike to some 'obby, such as siving a bit of garden from drying up in the 'eat, or siling a' yacht, or breedin' a few nice dawgs. They heats their bloomin' 'earts out, with nothing to do but theaytering and staring at the bloody wives."

"What did Jerry Cobbold *say?*" demanded the appeased cross-patch. "Tell me exactly now, Stupid! As if you was on your Bible oath."

"He said, 'We watched the Regatta yesterday, Sergeant'."

"That wasn't it at all! Say it as you did before. And you needn't try and make *me* believe he called you Sergeant, because Jerry Cobbold would know better."

Certainly none knew better than the third wife where an old soldier's "funny-bone" lay. The Corporal didn't often get angry, but he did on this occasion, and his voice ascended from that Brunswick Terrace basement and rang across the road.

"We watched the Regatta from the water. Isn't that enough? From the water, Sergeant, from the water, the water, the water, *the water!*"

14

TUP'S FOLD

It was November, and one of the wettest, wildest Novembers that the Dorset coast had known for many a year.

Very early on the morning of the twenty-first of the month—the day devoted in the calendar to the presentation of the Virgin—Sylvanus lay awake in his small cubicle, partitioned off by bare wooden boards, which, however, did not reach to the ceiling, from the other cubicles in that particular corridor of Hell's Museum. It was pitch-dark, but he could hear the rain beating against his barred window and the long-drawn howl of the wind as it swept round the whole isolated building. There was no Gipsy May between him and the wall to be rendered nervous by his characteristic movements, no Marret to cuddle up against him full of tender indulgence for the weird antics of her tall human Puppet, and when he propped himself up in those early hours and thrust his long neck forward after his fashion it was as if he were lifting up his cranium from the bottom of a deep, dark sea and swallowing, like the Sea-Serpent itself, great gulfs of liquid night.

The man derived a half-sensual, half-mystical pleasure from the mysterious pressure of this circumambient darkness. He embraced it with all his soul and rejoiced to feel it embracing him. It smelt faintly of the rain-sodden earth, but it had also an under-scent that was less reassuring, an obscure, sickly and complicated smell, as of chloroform, grown mephitic with long diffusion, mingled with the odour of soap and wash-buckets, and an acrid savour of bed-clothes, wooden-planks, sour food, human sweat, and the disinfectants used in lavatories.

Sylvanus was worried in his mind, not bitterly worried, but per-

ceptibly and teasingly worried. In his dealings with the Director of
Hell's Museum he had won many surprising psychological victories,
but he had been unsuccessful as yet in persuading Dr. Brush to close his
experimental laboratory, where the dogs were tortured, or to dismiss the
sadistic Murphy. He had made up his mind that something drastic,
something even startling and spectacular must be done.

"Human beings," thought Sylvanus, "are so constituted that no
revolution can be effected by words alone. 'In the beginning was *the
Act.*' "

Thus he pondered, straining forth his long, fantastic, close-cropped
cranium at the end of his turtle-neck, while the palpable darkness
pressed in upon it and about it, like a black, liquid mould taking the
print of a death-mask. And the pressure of the darkness became an
image to him now of the Absolute he worshipped, but at this hour, as
he lay in his cubicle, thinking and thinking, he was aware that the
ecstasy of his wonted abandonment to his God knew some diminishing, some hitch, some flaw, some abatement.

"I'm not in love with the child," he kept saying to himself. "I'm
not in love with her; I'm not in love with anyone."

But he couldn't get Marret out of his mind. She kept obstinately
mingling with his worry about the dogs and with his failure to make
Brush stop his cruel experimenting.

"I'm *not* in love with her. It *isn't* love. I've long since got beyond
all that!"

What kept coming back to him, do what he could to thrust it away,
was the pathetic passivity and docility of the girl.

"She's so tall," he kept thinking. "She's so tall and still."

Once this very night he had thought of her as a mermaid. That was
because she was so tall and so very still.

"It's funny," he said to himself. "She's helped me to get hold of
God; and yet there's a sweetness in her that I can't mix with God."

He tried in vain to analyse what he felt, but it was as if his great
Being, whose Centre was everywhere and his Circumference nowhere,
had an infinitesimal fragment of his rounded completeness *chipped off,*
leaving a tiny gap, a gap of too-sweet, too-dear Time in the bosom of
the Eternal!

"Well," he thought, "I shall see her soon, if Jerry posted my letter and if the Phoenix keeps his promise. It'll be a shame, though, if I get the Phoenix into a row. How unfair life is! Why should I be favoured as I am above the poor Phoenix?"

As the image of this fellow-inmate of Hell's Museum presented itself Sylvanus' old ultimate difficulty about his Absolute rose up against him. Why, if God was all, was there this *difference in luck* between one organism and another?

"Heigh-ho! this wicked difference in luck—in pure luck—was what you had to deal with at the roots of life. And how does it work in with the Absolute? How does it work in with God?"

Sylvanus had been in Hell's Museum now for over three months and the diagnosing of his "case" had proved the most interesting piece of analysis that Daniel Brush, in all his long experience as a psychiatrist, had ever undertaken. For one thing Sylvanus turned out to be a well-nigh perfect patient. He became so interested in Dr. Brush's de-personalized personality that he was ready to humour it to the utmost. And since the essence of this man's identity was to eliminate his identity and to become a pure, unblurred mirror in which reality could reflect itself, what Sylvanus constantly aimed at was to furnish the doctor with an increasing series of new layers, new levels, new strata of his precious objective truth. As a result of this, Daniel Brush had never known such persistent, unalloyed mental excitement as he experienced during these autumn months. The more he analysed Sylvanus the more he found to analyse. And what was so extremely satisfactory about it, from Brush's point of view, was that *the question of cure* never emerged at all. The Doctor could in fact drop the "doctor" and give himself up to experiment with Sylvanus as he had never dared to experiment with anyone, no, not even with Mrs. Cobbold!

That Sylvanus had been committed to him by the authorities as a man who, as Paley says of Socrates was "more than suspected of the foulest impurities", that he had been convicted of having lured away both Miss Frampton and Miss Jones from their lawful parents, lured them away to that lonely house of sinister repute near the Beale, and there corrupted them, meant nothing to the Doctor except as a piece of good luck in keeping this bottomless cask of psychological interest from escaping his inquisition.

The situation from the Doctor's point of view was flawless, but it had one extremely unexpected result. His contact with this surprising patient began to give him new scientific ideas. Sylvanus had the whip-hand over Daniel Brush in the simple fact that by holding his tongue he could deprive the man of these sacred theory-shattering pathological facts. The Doctor couldn't read the life-history of Sylvanus by telepathy. Sylvanus had to describe it to him. And he did this in such suggestive, punctual, exact detail that the result was that there slowly dawned upon Daniel Brush a totally new perspective in scientific psychology. Indeed compared with the illumination thrown upon the deepest secrets of life by these new ideas his old psychoanalytical theories appeared like fantastical fairy-tales! As free from the human desire for notoriety as he was free from all impulses of philanthropy Doctor Brush made no attempt to rush into publicity with these new and fascinating clues. He decided to develop them at leisure for there seemed no immediate likelihood of Sylvanus being set free, and he hoped to have time to formulate, on the basis of what he learnt from him, a completely new set of pathological hypotheses.

As has been hinted, Daniel Brush had in a sense to pay a price for these startling and original ideas. But since what he had to sacrifice were processes of thought involving purely materialistic concepts, this loss was less serious than it would have been had not his new "aperçu" lain at the extreme opposite pole from everything materialistic.

The grand difference between his old system and his new one lay in the hypotheses they respectively assumed with regard to the *locality* of all those dark, disturbing impulses, manias, shock-bruises, neuroses, complexes that he regarded as both the causes and the symptoms of human derangement. In his old system these volcanic neuroses were resident in an entirely subliminal region, a permanent underworld of the human ego from which they broke forth to cause unhappiness and anguish. This region was out of reach, and possessed locked, adamantine gates, as far as our ordinary processes of mental introspection went. To isolate and analyse these peculiarities *as aberrations* it was necessary to assume some kind of well-balanced norm, some measure of well-constituted functioning, from which all such "complexes" could be regarded as lapses.

But the essential point of Dr. Brush's old view of things was that you could only deal with the deep-sea fishes of the Unconscious indirectly, and by a kind of poetical symbolism. It was impossible simply to use your will and move about freely, spontaneously, rationally, and like a natural-born native, at the bottom of this interior sea! Thus, as in the early religious systems, only certain initiated adepts, who had the ritual-patter at their finger-tips, could interpret the mysteries of this arbitrarily-invented region, this *other-world*, debarred to all who could not utter the correct "open-sesame."

Daniel Brush's new theory, on the other hand, abolished this distinction between conscious, and sub-conscious as arbitrary and dogmatic, and, in place of this hard-and-fast division, regarded the whole ocean of human experience, with all its maddest and most unspeakable delusions, as *always open* to flashes of intelligent exploitation by minds that cared to dive into that deep sea.

Dr. Brush after analysing Sylvanus night by night till a very late hour, and in the process, without a breath of controversy, suffering an insurrection in his own ideas, used to lie awake till three or four in the morning, not listening to the winds and rains of those wild nights but lost in concentrated thought. Had people come into his room and *seen* him there thus thinking after his fashion they would have seen a face more totally devoid of human expression than any they had ever seen. The appearance of Doctor Brush in the process of thinking, between three and four in the morning, was in truth rather a disturbing phenomenon. It was a Husk with a human head, out of which all identity had evaporated, like smoke out of a bottle.

One of these clue-thoughts that came to the Doctor after analysing Sylvanus was that not only from the surface of that sea within us *but from all levels and depths of it* we have the power of coming into contact with one another. It is then, Brush thought, that our personalities emit luminous rays, like certain electric fish. He came to the conclusion that no generalizations can possibly cover the ghostly, twisted, tangential tricks with which the mind deals with its own submarine devils, its sub-tides down there, its sub-reefs, its sea-serpents. It was the unequalled objectivity of Daniel Brush's mind that was the cause of this mental "volte-face".

Had he been an old-fashioned, orthodox psychoanalyst, his obstinate theories would have been squeezed and bent and hammered till they found room, willy-nilly, for the theory-breaking Sylvanus. But Brush was a fanatic of objectivity. It was the pursuit of what he called "truth," not any particular set of theories about it, that was his absorbing passion. Thus when Sylvanus came into Hell's Museum, like a wandering Teiresias into the purlieus of Dis, the Doctor lacked all protection against the towering invader. To bed and board he had to welcome him! Impervious to the waving of the Plutonian sceptre Sylvanus simply came on and on and on, and in the end it was the practitioner who was practised on!

Matters at the Brush Home suddenly began to change in many serious respects. The truth was that Dr. Brush had never been a very practical Director. He was a man whose reputation had always depended rather on his intellectual achievements than on his conduct of his Institution. And now as he sailed recklessly forward—"stemming nightly to the pole" in his insatiable mental skiff—over the untraversed sea of Sylvanus' perversities, he began to lose touch with the affairs of Hell's Museum and to leave them more and more in the hands of subordinates. Daniel Brush went about these days like someone in a trance. Nothing except his precious interviews with his insidious patient had the least interest for him. His assistants came to him for advice, for orders, for help, and he had nothing to say to them! He put them off. He lost his temper with them. The breaking up of that mysterious "equator-line" between Conscious and Unconscious and the merging of these two worlds into one equally fantastical continent began to lead to the spasmodic introduction of new methods in the psychiatry of Hell's Museum, methods that originated directly from Sylvanus' experiences at "Last House," methods such as had certainly never been used before in this Wessex Sanitarium.

Sylvanus himself had assuredly never met a listener in any degree approaching Daniel Brush. What he was always suffering from in his girls—who otherwise were so receptive—those unaccountable fits of irrational jealousy, those wild, hysterical outbursts, those moods that were, so to say, the actual crying aloud of the "Yang" itself, were quite absent in this intellectual fanatic. It was a little, it is true, like talking to yourself in a mirror—so perfect was the Doctor's de-personaliza-tion—but *that* didn't bother the man from Portland Bill. If the

Doctor, by a lifetime of scientific "yoga", had made himself into an Inanimate, to talk to an Inanimate exactly suited Sylvanus. It was like talking to the rope in his cliff shanty. He came more and more to confess himself as freely to the Doctor as if the fellow had really been his good, strong, patient, quiet rope, his rope that did nothing but dangle down, however Trivia might dance.

On this particular twenty-first of November, which was an anniversary never forgotten by Sylvanus, for it was the date of his first sleeping in Last House, it must have been about four o'clock when he first woke up. Not only was it all pitch-dark, but the same wild, tumultuous wind that had been blowing off and on all the month tossed the thin, small, West-Country rain in splashing, intermittent volleys against his window, volleys that swept the pane with the impact of weeping faces whirling by in the impenetrable night. About five o'clock the rain showed signs of abating and the wind lessened. He turned on the electric light and flooded his cubicle with a distressing bluish-tinted glare.

"Oh, for the candles of Last House!" he sighed in discomfort.

Hurriedly he put on his clothes.

"She'll be there by six," he said to himself, "if Jerry posted my letter."

When he was dressed he opened his cubicle door and stood outside in the pitch-black corridor listening intently. It was a small corridor containing three more cubicles identical with his own, but only one of these was at this time occupied. He was holding his boots in his hand, and he had been so excited at the thought of what lay before him that he had only half pulled on his socks, which protruded from his toes as he walked, and trailed, wrinkled and ruffled, along the bare boards.

Arrived at the inhabited cubicle he very gently turned the handle and whispered into the deeper darkness of its recess:

"Time to get up, you Bird of God!"

A crop-headed, middle aged man jumped up at once into a sitting posture.

"I'm with you, sir!" he jerked out. "I wasn't asleep. I was watching for you."

His intonation was neither what is usually called "educated" nor

what is called "uneducated." It was the tone of a substantial burgess
in a small town.

"Is your great-coat there?" whispered Sylvanus. "It's still raining."

"It's here," said the man. "Go back to your room, sir. Don't stand
waiting. I'll come in a jiffy."

On returning to his room Sylvanus turned out the light and sat
down in the darkness on his low couch-bed. The patient he had just
roused, although by no means "cured," had been promoted for his
impeccable good behaviour to some temporary official post, a post that
gave him the privilege of a pass-key. It was Sylvanus' knowledge that
he could always count on this fellow's assistance that had given him
the assurance to write to Marret and even to appoint a definite hour
and a definite meeting-place.

How slowly the seconds passed!

"He's got his braces on now. Now he's doing them up. Now he's
putting on his collar."

Constantly Sylvanus pictured and counted out every stage in the
progress of the man's dressing. Listening intently as he could, though,
he couldn't hear him make the least sound. Not a creak, not a rustle,
broke the silence of that little corridor. And yet in other portions of
Hell's Museum there were all manner of curious, disturbing little
half-sounds as if a number of demented rats were engaged in the task
of pursuing hundreds of female mice in order to disembowel them.
Sylvanus put on his over-coat now, for he began to feel deadly cold.

"It's a terrible morning for her to be out in," he thought. "She's
got no fear of wind and rain, but she may feel lonely on those hills."

Again he listened; and it seemed to him as if from all the people
under that roof, as they tossed about, or as they lay stone-still, little
ghastly whispers kept mounting up and floating through his door and
out of his window, whispers that left behind, as birds might leave
behind their droppings, images of obscenity and evil. The darkness
was so thick around him, as he listened, that by its very density it
seemed to destroy and swallow up the intervening barriers of the
place, all the walls, all the doors! The darkness made the whole
dwelling one huge vault, a vault that was full of brain-tortured
unresting ghosts who could neither realize their dolorous identities
nor forget them, but were forever stumbling and fumbling and

groping in pitiful bewilderment under the pressure of the grey, cold, invisible rain—worse than the visible one—of the implacable malediction of heaven. And like Teiresias in Hades it seemed to be the destiny of Sylvanus to find rational articulation, if nothing else, for the blind gibberings of these poor ghosts.

The unusual privilege accorded to his present companion of possessing a pass-key was only one instance among several others of the effect he had worked upon the Director by distracting, confusing, and subtilizing his intelligence. After passing several gratings and iron doors, and descending several flights of stairs, Sylvanus was unable to keep his nerves as calm as he had expected when he actually saw his friend beginning, with stealthy caution, to unbolt the great folding doors of the main entrance! As he watched his figure there in the phantasmal light of the entrance-hall, for to get the bolts moved in silence took quite a long time, he could not help thinking of this worthy man's obstinate illusion that he was a Phoenix.

These old classical, biblical, mediaeval appellations, how they hung about the world! They were an endless armoury of masks always available for purposes of auto-hallucination. How curious it was—when anyone thought seriously about it—the particular famous names that mad people assume! Like ghostly simulacra they were, these ancient syllables, doomed to drift about on the tradewinds of Time, like empty snake-skins or newt-skins, all silvery hollow masks, till they were seized upon, like these magic syllables Phoenix, to cover up the tragic nakedness of a new generation of witless anonymity.

Another thing had struck Sylvanus as curiously heart-piercing in this House of Ghosts, and that was the way Sex itself, the great life-urge of the world, fell away and dwindled and receded. It sank, this thing, from occupying the first place in human life to occupying the ninth or the tenth. Its results were here only too clearly; but its living manifestations seemed minimized, sterilized, paralyzed. Anyone who has been in Bedlam will bear witness how forlornly correct Sylvanus' observation was. As a matter of fact it is curious how the illusion should ever have got about that mad people are often happy and cheerful, and merry and gay! As a matter of fact upon an insane asylum lies exactly the same kind of sick, inert, bewildered, unearthly sorrowfulness that Homer depicts as the prevailing condition of those faint spirits, who in the realm of Hades "no longer behold the sweet sun". Yes, the sadness, the dispiritedness, the inert hopelessness that is the dominant atmosphere of such a place is almost identical with that twilight kingdom where only the drinking of blood enables a mother to know her own son! And it would seem that just as with the loss of their bodies "the noble nations of the dead" feel no longer the urge of amorous desire, so in the atmosphere of Hell's Museum considerations of excrement played a larger part than those of the heart. That terrible and startling indifference to *personal appearance*, to the state of one's dress for instance, that is such a noticeable characteristic of these societies of the damned, is a fearful and significant hint as to how the implacable Goddess of Desire, when by her ravages she has reduced her victims to this condition, leaves them in contempt, and glides away, to impoison and drive to madness other, fairer, fresher, younger, less plague-spotted souls!

"Is it raining still, George Pounce?"

His use of his friend's name betrayed how excited Sylvanus was. He generally called this excellent man not by the name with which his godfathers and godmother had baptized him, but by the wind-blown snake-skin into which he wantonly had slipped! This was indeed a curious and strange metempsychosis; for Mr. George Pounce, late of High Street, Dorchester, had contracted the illusion that he was a Phoenix.

A quiet bachelor tradesman, George William Pounce had become a passionate ornithologist. From the study of living birds he had pressed forward till he became a skilled amateur taxidermist. Then he had fallen sick of a villainous influenza, an attack that made him delirious for weeks, and even after his bodily recovery left him with wits fatally impaired.

"I could stuff a Phoenix for you!" he had remarked once to Mr. Ludlow, the Antiquary, and it was in the mythic feathers of the only rare bird he had never stuffed that he came to Hell's Museum.

In these cases of insane transformation it is pathetic to note the accommodating malleability and flexibility of the mind's diseased logic. This man, for instance, was not utterly and entirely a Phoenix. He remained George Pounce. But he was a George Pounce who, under certain particular conditions, would flap his thin, short arms up and

down, while under others he would run screaming through the halls
and corridors, with the notion that he was on fire. It was the rarity
of these burning fits—for the flapping of his arms would occur without
any trouble to himself or to others—that made Pounce one of the
most harmless of the Doctor's inmates and was the cause—coincident
with the general loosening of discipline to which reference has been
made—of his being trusted with the key.

He was flapping his arms now as he stood in that windy doorway
contemplating the impenetrable darkness.

"That will do, Bird of God," said Sylvanus quietly. "We'd better
get away while we can!"

He crossed the threshold as he spoke, and Mr. Pounce, his arms
suddenly quiet again—as they generally seemed to be, when matters
pertaining to practical human life compelled his attention—closed the
unwieldy doors behind them, and they set forth.

It was not raining any more now, and the wind had dropped.
George Pounce, from his long ornithological pursuit, could have led
the way blindfolded to Tup's Fold, which was the spot Sylvanus had
mentioned in his letter. It was only a couple of miles away, but it
stood on much higher ground than the Brush Institution. What
Tup's Fold really was, was an old excavated tumulus or barrow, that
had been surrounded in more recent times by rough stone walls, and
was still half-covered by an unfinished piece of straw thatching. It
stood on a high commanding ridge of the chalk hills and from it—in
daylight—could be seen the whole curving expanse of Weymouth
Bay, from Portland to St. Alban's Head.

The taxidermist was silent for nearly a mile of the way, though he
walked with a firm step. Perhaps he felt shame for having waved his
arms, or perhaps the re-assumption of normal mortality could only be
achieved in silence. Sylvanus himself was silent, too, and for a very
definite cause.

In the agitation of rousing Mr. Pounce and setting off in time he
had omitted saying his prayers. And now, the more emotion he had at
seeing Marret again the more necessary he felt it to be, to propitiate
his elemental gods. Eccentric as Sylvanus' litany was, he had repeated
it so often that he had a tendency to gabble it at a crisis, mumbling the
words like a weary priest muttering a familiar office.

"O earth!" Sylvanus mumbled in a very low voice, but quite audibly, while the dense darkness seemed to be swallowing up both the wind and the rain. "O divine ether! O sun, that beholdest all things and hearest all things! O Sea, that hath comforted me and sustained me from my youth up! And you O Wordless and Nameless, that dwellest equally in all wisdom and in all folly, guard Olwen and Lily and Lottie and Nelly and Polly and May and Peg, and especially guard Marret."

Here in still more emphatic earnestness—if such distinctions can be made in the matter of scarce-audible prayer—Sylvanus went on, in the most homely and realistic manner, to inform the earth, and the sun, and the divine ether, and even the sea who knew her so well, that Marret was the daughter of Mr. Jones, and lived not far from the Harbour Bridge in Weymouth proper. The fact that it was impossible just then to catch the faintest glimpse of any of these great Powers except the earth, and hardly even of her, meant nothing to Sylvanus. If he had been walled up in the heart of the Great Pyramid he would have periodically given vent to this gabble of cave-man supplication. He always preferred to kneel down, if it were possible, on these occasions, so it was a comfort to find he had no difficulty in lagging behing his swift-footed guide.

There was not the faintest visible trace of dawn as yet, and yet it would have been impossible for Sylvanus, had he been roused from the deepest sleep, not to feel it was near to a new day. The darkness itself seemed of a different texture from the darkness of midnight. As it pressed down upon eyelids and nostrils and lips and hands, it seemed penetrated by a faint magnetic chilliness, like the touch of a resurrected god's breath!

It was close to a mole-hill that he knelt and it was an ecstasy to him thus to feel the dawn's presence in the mould before he could see a streak of it in the sky. Plunging his hands into the rain-soaked soil, thus thrown up above the surface of the chalk he tried, as he always did, to de-humanize himself. And as he squeezed the wet earth of the molehill, the whole vast expectancy of that rolling Down-land, waiting like an enormous beast for the Dawn's coming, seemed to reach his consciousness and flow through his veins with a touch of something that was *live*-cold, like the shivering nipples of a She-

Leviathan. And as Sylvanus buried his forehead in that rain-drenched mole-hill he felt the night receding out of the body of the earth like the water of an ebbing sea-wave receding out of the crannies of a pebble-bank, and as he felt the night receding, he felt the dawn—the wet fungus-breath of the invisible horses of the dawn—stealing into the very substance of this dark chalkridge.

Rising straight up on his knees now and snuffing the darkness he suddenly became transported with the feeling that he was more and also less than a man. His thighs seemed to become the thighs of a colossus, as they sank into the slope of that hill! His neck as he stretched it upwards and backwards, felt like the neck of an ante-diluvian tortoise. Through his trousers, for the ground was soaking-wet, he felt the impact of the great round-bellied one with the rock-bound heart. She was waiting for dawn, the million-breasted, sleep-chilled, rain-soaked Mother of Beasts and Men, and such feelings as he had then may very well have created the dawn-mad Orion. Like Orion Sylvanus was now snuffing the far-off dawn-smell, while his knees were buried in the wet earth and his head was turned towards the cold tides of the fish-bearing sea. Like Orion he still strove towards his God through the loves of the daughters of God. Like Orion he lived an ambiguous double-life, between the *Kamontes*, the "worn-out underground ones", and the eternal children of the ether.

A shout from Mr. Pounce, a ringing cry, in a clear young-girl's voice, from Marret, and Sylvanus rushed forward. There was Marret, waiting for him! And with her was young Larry Zed from Lodmoor. She had not been scared or worried at all—as Gipsy May in her suspicions and reservations would certainly have been—by the approach of Mr. Pounce. She knew "the Old Man of the Beale", as they called him in Easton, too well to have expected anything else. She had brought with her a regular feast in a large basket, and before Sylvanus had time to consider the weight of these viands, Larry Zed presented himself before his eyes as the pack-horse who had carried them.

All four of them stood close together for a while, at the entrance to the thatched portion of Tup's Fold. They were drawn by a power outside their control towards the eastern quarter of the sky, and

Marret instinctively put off the opening of the basket. Meanwhile young Zed pointed out to them the bright spot of light on Lodmoor which he knew so well.

"May has lit she's lamp!" he said.

George Pounce, who was no stranger to the green-eyed lad, argued with him then quite hotly as to whether another spot of light they could make out, far to the left of the Lodmoor one, was or was not a light at the White Nose. Young Zed maintained that the White Nose "never had no lights" but the taxidermist, who knew the place well, declared that you could see for miles away the lamp in the window where Mr. Ludlow, the antiquary, lived.

The dawn they were waiting for still delayed its appearance, and after some whispered conversation between Marret and Larry, the boy, who had learnt the art from Gipsy May, set himself with the air of one at home on rain-soaked hills to the task, in spite of the dampness of all available kindling, of lighting a fire, and it was then that Marret, hurriedly placing her basket at the complete disposal of George Pounce, took Sylvanus aside.

"We can go off now," she said. "It may be harder, later on! You never can tell what'll happen. No, no, you *must* come. Us haven't got so long together this blessed morn!"

She accordingly led him off along the ridge of the high Down, while Mr. Pounce, fraternizing very happily with Larry, and coughing and choking in the smoke of the new-lit fire, explored what the girl's great basket contained.

But Sylvanus and Marret walked away alone along the crest of the hill. Two tall figures they were, as they walked off side by side, and as through the smoke of his fire young Zed watched them, a deep and solemn feeling surged up in his heart.

"Her do love thik man," he thought, "same as I do love she. Me Nothing-girl be nought to I, same as I be nought to she. Us be both cast-off. Wold May don't mindy about such things as me and me Nothing-girl do. Wold May be like she's girt cat. 'Tis by reason of being Gipsy-born, I reckon. Gone now. They be gone now. He be *in there* where I were afore. And the poor man ain't got a moustache left. He've a-moulted hisself like a wold owl! But 'tis him she do love and none other. Him and not Lal. And so it must even be."

Thus, as with eyes smarting from the smoke he had raised, he bent over his fire, young Zed adjusted his nature, disturbed to its very depths, to that renunciation that is as ancient as our troubled race.

"And so it must even be," he repeated, as he applied himself to yet new Promethean tricks learnt from that friend whose own erratic affections seemed like those of "she's wold cat".

On and on Sylvanus led his girl, and on and on she led him, for no one—not even the psychological Doctor—could have separated and divided the impulse that held them, that drove them. Suddenly he stopped, held himself erect, raised his bare head high and snuffed at the air.

"It's coming," he whispered in a low vibrant voice.

And he was right. Like the first flicker in the eyelids of a dead man restored to life, a wan indescribable lifting of darkness took place in the far-off horizon, over the southeastern waters, close to St. Alban's Head. He tightened his arm round her waist. Well knew he that stillness, that quietness in her, that mute, untrembling trance, that made her always seem to his touch even taller than she was.

Minutes and minutes flowed over them, and the link between them became like another dawn, whiter, ghostlier, more inscrutable still, mounting up through a yet deeper dark. Then came a time when the whole wide stretch of waters threw open its tremulous dawn-porches to their intense gaze. Grey, and yet not grey, metal-livid rather, like the dumb glimmer of ten thousand sword-blades, the sea unrolled its leagues of shivering expanse. It grew whiter and ever whiter, and its whiteness was not the whiteness of death, nor yet the whiteness of light or of life. It was the whiteness of the spirit. It was the whiteness of that mysterious act of creation that came even before the word. Nor did this whiteness last for long. It lasted long enough to add something of its own immortal nature to the mortal weakness of their human feeling. But then, soon, too soon, it began to fade, and its place to be taken by something else. And what now took its place was the natural, the secular diffusion of ordinary daylight, of the accustomed, the familiar, the common day, one more day, just one more, among all the other days that had spread themselves out over two human lives.

The girl turned her face towards him, when this change came, but instead of raising it up to his own, she pressed it against his chest, against his heart, and there she remained, with her long bare arms, protruded from her black cloak, clinging tightly about him. She was too nearly one with him—only one tall pillar of darkness in darkness they formed now—for her to note the difference between the sickly-sweet Hell's Museum smell of the garments they had put on him and his old clean-scented tweed clothes. Knowing all, knowing how near the end of their time it was, knowing how hard it would be ever to snatch a meeting like this again, she yet felt happier than she had ever felt in all the days she could remember.

And Sylvanus was talking to her now, old Sylvanus, still talking, always talking, and his words became to her as the air-cleaving gulls, that she had so often seen without seeing, darting, dipping, swaying, hovering, along the Weymouth Sands. Proud and strange, proud and even blasphemous, his words were, and they were cold and remote, too, but not more cold, not more remote than the dawn she had just seen.

"Whenever you hold in your hand," he was saying, "a wet pebble by the sea's edge, you must believe you are holding me. Whenever you snatch up a handful of wet sand, by the sea's edge, you must believe I am holding you. I can *never let you go*, even if I wanted to! You're more real to me than anyone in the world, even than Jerry! Shall I tell you a queer thing, girlie? Last night when I was—"

They were interrupted by the voice of young Zed out of the darkness. The lad was running towards them.

"Coom quick, Mister!" he cried. "Coom quick, Marret! There be trouble with the loony. He'll be doing summat, lookso, if ye don't make haste!"

What had happened was indeed simple enough under the circumstances. That phantasmal whiteness upon the horizon had been almost as exciting to Mr. Pounce as to Sylvanus and Marret. He had left Larry's side and scrambling out of the hollow tumulus had brushed against the lad's fire which had begun to grow a little out of control. Here he had scorched one of his coat-sleeves. This was enough, combined with the magnetic influence of the dawn to start a psychic conflagration, or what Dr. Brush would have styled "an elation-response to unusual stimulus". George Pounce was in fact, when they reached the spot, whirling round and round on his own axis, like a frantic dervish, his stumpy arms and his poor spatulate fingers— the fingers of a born taxidermist—sticking out like the spokes of a wheel that has been stripped of its circumference. It was an extra-ordinary sight, this fire in the grey dawn, this smoke, this revolving man!

They approached in wonder this whirling figure who might indeed have been engaged, at the edge of this ancient barrow, in some pre-historic fire-dance. Strange was it to see him appear and vanish again in the smoke! To recover the burning Phoenix from his self-induced flames presented itself indeed as a harder task than Sylvanus had ex-pected. The truth was that the presence of young Zed, whose own wits were never far *on this side* of the Pass Perilous, aggravated the man's disorder, and prevented these self-ignited blazes from dying down as quickly as usual. It was pitiful, and at the same time grotesque, to see this sturdy human form, spinning round on the edge of the old chieftain's rifled grave, his figure appearing and disappearing in that pallid dawn-light, as cloud after cloud of smoke from Zed's real fire kept rolling over his head! Heart-rending, too, were the curious sounds the poor man kept muttering, sounds that some unconscious imagination in his demented brain—the brain of an ornithologist— caused to approximate to the anguished croakings of some great bird in mortal distress. At last his galvanic movements ceased and he stood trembling and choking in the drifting smoke.

It was then that Marret approached Sylvanus.

"Good-bye," she said, making no attempt to take his hand.

The tall man and the tall girl stared at each other in tense silence. By some kind-unkind chance a great cloud of smoke rolled between them, and the girl accepted the sign. Clutching Larry by the arm, who had already possessed himself of the basket, she hurried down the hill; nor did she once look back. Up went Sylvanus' hand to his face, for it was always at a crisis like this that he was wont to tug at his great moustache. But he laid his arm instead on the shoulder of Mr. Pounce. As he watched their retreating figures, Zed swinging the basket and Marret with her small head, in its boy's cap, hanging down a little on one side, he was aware of a sensation in the pit of his stomach as if there were an umbrella inside him that was blowing inside out.

But he kept his eyes fixed steadily upon them till their forms vanished behind a curve of the hill. Then his hand dropped from the shoulder of the resuscitated Phoenix and his whole figure drooped and wilted in the grey dawn. It was one of those moments in a human being's life when the will to live drains away, like water from a dam that has been lifted.

"I beg your pardon, sir?" gasped Mr. Pounce hoarsely, fancying that Sylvanus had commented upon his recent fire-dance.

But the tall man's commentary had been of the sort that the Doctor would—at least three months ago—have termed a response to auto-stimulus.

"Caput . . . Anus," he repeated several times, while he stared at the spot upon which Marret had stood before the smoke intervened.

On their return to the Home, Mr. Pounce, a little anxious for his reputation as an inmate on parole, hurried into the main building, leaving Sylvanus to follow his own devices.

In every man's life there are moments when a desolation takes possession of him which resembles the terrible look which a dead planet might turn upon a lonely voyager travelling through space. At such a moment the heart feels as if an abyss of hopelessness had suddenly been revealed to it through some ghastly crack or crevasse in the buoyant etheric expanse. And it seems to him then as if, at some grim signal, what he had really known all the time had been relentlessly shown him, the ancient cosmogonic jest, the old un-redeemed treachery. Like an infinitely forlorn face, stripped of all comfort, this ghastly vision of things limns itself against the sur-rounding nothingness. Nature has piled up all her resources to hide the yawning void through which this frozen look bids us despair. Viaduct after rainbow-viaduct have our own hearts thrown across this fissure in the familiar landscape, but perhaps it will only be when the Original Jester himself repents Him of His Joke and ceases to cry "Judy! Judy! Judy!" across our shining sands that that look out of the void will melt away. Or perhaps—

But the tall man—whose influence upon young women was regarded as so much more dangerous than that of Mr. Jones or Mr. Frampton—felt, as that cold grey day established its normal supremacy over the scattered buildings of Hell's Museum, that any prolongation of the desolation he experienced just then would end by making him the kind of inmate who—like poor Edward Loder—cared no more *whether he came out or not.*

Sylvanus stood on the gravel-path that led to the Doctor's private residence and contemplated a garden-fork that someone had left stuck deep into a heap of manure. Had this tool been a hoe he would have passed it by. Had it been a rake he would have disregarded it. Had it been a pick he would scarce have noticed it. But he had so often used a fork, just like this, for various purposes at Last House, that the mere sight of it stirred up his old fighting-spirit.

"What was it that the poor old Jobber was always muttering?" he thought. " 'A time and times and half a time'. Well . . . if I *am* destined to die in this place . . . and if I'm *not* destined ever to see Marret again . . . at least I'll *fight!* That's the whole thing. Suffer . . . be miserable . . . feel like a worm cut in half . . . but one thing a person *can* do, till he's stone-dead, and that's fight . . . even though his fighting is all done in the circle of his own mind!"

He felt so grateful to the fork that he actually stepped on the dung heap and, bending down, kissed its handle. To kiss the handle of a garden fork would not have arrested any particular attention *where he was,* but it would have fatally lent itself to Perdita's impression of him, as one who, even when alone, was forever acting and showing off. Perdita's view of his character, and indeed the Jobber's view, too, would have been accentuated had they witnessed the sequel.

After walking briskly forward with a happier step, now he had seen the fork in the dung, for both these objects seemed to belong to everything that was outside the Brush Home, it occurred to his superstitious mind that the dung heap might feel neglected. Back therefore he went, and pulling out the fork with a jerk, while with the emergence of the tool came forth a heavy warm scent of long-buried cow droppings, he raised the prongs to his face and kissed *them.* Then he replaced the tool where he had found it and hurried off again.

Entering the Doctor's house, without summoning his servant, and going straight to his study, he found little Benny Cattistock alone there, waiting for his uncle.

"Do you think I might sit down?" he asked the child, who was lying on the floor reading a newspaper. "This boy," Sylvanus thought, "oughtn't to be always feeding his manias from the papers. Why hasn't that fool Muir swung him off this sort of thing?"

Benny's eyes were dilated with fascinated and horror-struck curiosity.

"I'm reading about it!" he cried. "It's in that paper ... what I knew they were doing ... what they got Yellow for ... only they'd never tell me anything! I tried to peep through the key-hole once, but Murphy found me ... It tells of how they get 'Hypo-Toxin'."

"How *do* they get it?" enquired Sylvanus. "I do not even know what it is."

Benny struggled to make it clear to him. It was not altogether clear,—probably it was not *that* even to the men who did it—but it was clear enough to contract Sylvanus' forehead with lowering attention.

"Wait a minute, Benny! Isn't that word *Hypno-Toxin*, not Hypo-Toxin?"

Benny's face, which had begun to cloud with irritation at this correction, lit up when he saw how interested Sylvanus was.

"Yes! Yes!" he cried. "That's it! I got it wrong. They've got a dog they're keeping awake, keeping it always awake—and they do it ... you see it tells everything ... to get something from it. When you've wanted to sleep for days and days, and can't sleep, your spine— I think it's your spine—begins to cry. And that's what they're looking for. It's only a drop. It's only the tiniest little drop. And they take it out of the dog and put it in a little glass bottle ... Oh, so careful! ... so as not to spill it. It's someone's business ... like Murphy ... to keep the dog awake ... and do you know how he does it, Mr. Cobbold?"

The child's face became convulsed with a babyish frenzy, and stamping on the newspaper and with the tears streaming from a reddened face, began kicking and scuffing the trampled pages about the room in the kind of tantrum that Magnus by this time knew only too well.

"That'll do, Benny. Quiet, my lad!" said Sylvanus.

The boy turned to him with clenched fists, and Sylvanus thought to himself:

"God! how like his chin is to his father's! I never realized how like they were."

But the boy recovered himself now and went on.

"They don't tell the truth, Mr. Muir says, when they say they give them Anna's Ethics. They say they always put dogs to sleep with that stuff. So they're just liars, Mr. Cobbold, aren't they, when they *keep* them awake till they get that drop?"

Sylvanus saw clearly enough that unless young Benny had pretty soon some tremendous reassurance his whole nervous system would be affected.

"Does that double-dyed fool, Muir," he thought, "encourage him in all this? But the boy's right; and what can a person do? We can't tell him that they don't torture dogs."

"I should say he is!" he now replied to the boy, in hearty confirmation of his opinion of the head of Hell's Museum. "But there are lots of them far worse than your uncle Dan, sonny, and that's the truth. You'll go after them and bring them to book when you're grown up! But now you must make *me* your man-at-arms. I'll deal with your uncle now. I've got a good yew-tree shaft to my bow. Have no fear. But you run off now quick, before uncle Dan comes. You wait and see what happens. We're fellow conspirators, that's what we are."

When the boy had gone Sylvanus put his hand into his pocket where there was a parcel of sandwiches given to him by Marret. These he proceeded to swallow, one after another, with incredible speed.

"From the brain, under the not-sleeping torture," he thought, "into the cerebro-spinal column. Caput . . . Anus! Caput . . . Anus! What a race we are!"

He had finished the sandwiches and was lying back in the Doctor's biggest chair feeling a craving for sleep when Daniel Brush entered.

"Hullo!" he said. "I've been hearing fine stories about you. You're a nice parole-patient, you are, and so's your friend Pounce!"

Sylvanus remained where he was and surveyed the man quizzically. He thought to himself.

"You wait, my lad. You wait a bit!"

Dr. Brush took off his coat and fidgeted uneasily about the room. He felt something was in the air; but he attributed it to this excursion to Tup's Fold, the details of which, in many exaggerated versions, had already been circulating freely. At last he sat down opposite his patient and an extraordinary duel began which was fought at one and the same time on the rational, the imaginative and the occult level. It was also fought—strange as it may sound—on the sexual plane.

"Doctor," said Sylvanus, opening the struggle with a terrific lunge of his sword-arm, "I'm not going to utter one word more, I'm going to keep as silent as Hardy's Monument, until—"

"I know perfectly what you're going to say, Cobbold! Until I've closed my little experimental laboratory? Have you heard anything, or seen anything lately, Cobbold, that's set you off?"

Sylvanus shook his head. As a matter of fact he had heard nothing of vivisection for several weeks.

"It's all for so little, Doctor!" he cried, suddenly sitting bolt upright and clenching his fists on his knees. "It isn't for an Elixir that would make us Immortal. You don't get *that* from pinching and prodding and torturing animals. I can't understand it! A man like you, who bleed if you're pricked, who laugh if you're tickled, how you can torment these dogs to such wretched purpose, for such a poor, paltry result? If you were going to make us Immortal by it, or reveal to us the nature of God by it, I'd *still* say it was wrong. But, as it is, it's monstrous! Your dogs suffer beyond what even you like to think about—and what are the results? Nothing really stupendous or world-shaking. If you ask my opinion, Doctor, I tell you this whole crime of vivisection will be horribly paid for in human suffering. That's the way the gods always work. This vivisection of yours is the worst sin of our age—of the age of *The Star Wormwood* as that Russian says—and it will be horribly avenged! The worst of it is, Doctor, that in these avengings the innocent suffer equally with the guilty."

Daniel Brush's countenance was not so much, as the poet says, "a book wherein could be read strange matters" as he listened to his prisoner-patient, as it was a title-page whereby what lay within was carefully concealed in an indecipherable cryptogram.

"You touch on a large question, my friend," he said quietly, pulling up one of his cuffs—for he was now in his shirt-sleeves—and examining some little abrasion on his wrist. "A large question," he repeated, looking, not at Sylvanus' excited face, but at the man's gaunt knees on which his fists rested as he leaned forward.

The Doctor's "sang froid" proved more like oil on a smouldering flame than on a rising wave, and Sylvanus' voice gathered resonance.

"I know what you're thinking," he cried. "You're thinking I'm 'elated'—in other words, mad like the rest. No, I'm *not* mad, Doctor, but if I were—! No, I tell 'ee. If your unrighteous Science, defying all God's decency and pity, calls itself the test of sanity, then give me the insane! Abominable cruelty remains abominable cruelty, whether it's performed on dogs by scientists or on his enemies by Tiberius! Come on! I take your challenge, Doctor. The insane *versus* the sane! God turns to Bedlam for His worshippers. The lost soul of pity finds lodgement where the demons dwelt till now!"

The resonant voice—that voice which had seduced Olwen and Lily and Lottie and Nelly and Gipsy May and Peg Frampton and Marret Jones, apart from anything he *said*—became inaudible now for a minute while Sylvanus fixed his eyes on the man opposite him. He seemed to be labouring under the illusion that he was still uttering words, and that his words were such that none could hear without a change of heart, for as he straightened his body and thrust forward his turtle-neck, till his whole El Greco skull seemed about to hurl itself like a cannon ball at his hearer, there was a gleam of unearthly triumph in his eyes. Then his voice rang forth with the ring of an antiphonal chant of which the opening strophe has been inaudible.

"His babes and sucklings have deserted him! They have become wise and cruel like the rest. And God, even the Absolute, has found Himself and known Himself and returned to Himself in . . . in . . . in . . ."

His voice died down, but this time it sank in a different manner than before. It sank as if his words had been some kind of foaming liquor, pouring forth from a bottomless cask, whose flow had been suddenly stopped. His "in . . . in . . . in . . ." was like the final drops, dripping down from the bung-hole when the spigot had been turned. If it could be said that this torrent of wild words had any effect on the Doctor at all, what it apparently did was to induce him to lie back at full length in his chair and give himself up to a luxury of relaxation.

"I'd like to get a crowd of your patients, Doctor," he went on, and there was a fretful peevishness and human irritation in his tone that was a new note, "and make 'em smash every vivisection-apparatus you've got! All those straps, that some reputable firm manufactures for you, all the fragile little glasses for bottling *Hypno-Toxin* that's been produced in cerebro-spinal columns by agonies of sleeplessness, all your machines for peering into living brains and entrails and hearts! I'd like to see that laboratory of yours combed out, raked out, scoured out, sucked out, vacuum-cleaned, stomach-pumped, disinfected, clystered, *gutted!* Don't you see that the mere fact of your *being allowed* to do this—for your chatter about giving 'em anaesthetics is all my eye—it's those nicely-manufactured straps that hold 'em so still—proves that we've given up trying to touch the secret of life by being just and righteous and pitiful. Good God! Given up the whole direction we've been making toward, from the beginning! How did it ever get into the world at all, this idea of *not* being cruel? But once in the world, *it has done it*. It's the only thing that has changed anything—changed Nature herself! If God's been vivisecting us, it may be the one single 'drop' He's got out of the whole ghastly experiment! And this is what you're prepared to throw away, as your cleaning-man might throw away your precious phial of *Hypno-Toxin!* As long as we can put off death for a few wretched years, in our cowardice we give you 'carte blanche' to make the dogs scream. Save us from death and you can squeeze all the agony you like out of our dogs!"

"One moment, Cobbold—" Doctor Brush did not change his position. He still lay back with an almost voluptuous air in his big chair, but he now pulled up his cuff again, and bent his head forward, peering down at that spot on his arm that so persistently tickled. "If it's any comfort to you, my friend, I may as well tell you that I gave up my experimental laboratory here more than a month ago. Mr. Cattistock is going for a trip—perhaps you didn't know that either— and has had to cut down his subscription. As to your bête-noir Murphy, you'll be glad to hear I refused him a recommendation for any other place. He indicated that he intended to go in for raising water-cress. I commended this decision."

Sylvanus' whole frame underwent a process of sagging and wilting. He felt like a man who had struck out with a broadsword and beheaded a popinjay. The fact that vivisection was no longer practised in Hell's Museum and that Murphy had gone was a deep comfort to him, but at the moment it was like the discovery that the tyrant he had disciplined himself by vigil and fasting to overthrow in the power of the Lord had perished of a jungle-fever. He felt a complicated humiliation, too, and an anger against Brush, which itself increased his shame. The fellow had let him talk, just wanting to hear what he would say, and knowing that, any minute, by a single word he could put an end to his harangue. He contemplated the relaxed and restful posture in which the Doctor was awaiting his reply to this little surprise.

At certain crises in life Nature Herself comes to our rescue by a peculiar power of her own—a power that is blinder, swifter, more formidable, than even instinct, and without knowing what we are doing, or why we are doing it, we fling ourselves pell-mell, hugger-mugger, helter-skelter, *into the breach*. There are some who call this power impulse, but what it feels like is an organic leap of our whole vital force, something that can *only* leap—like a ponderous beast—when it is in its last ditch.

Sylvanus, as he sat there, felt that he really was in the last ditch. He was beginning to recognize the grim and crushing fact that the Doctor did really regard him as demented, as demented as poor George Pounce, only with no hope that they would give *him* a pass-key. But great, creative nature, the mother and accomplice of miracles, came to his rescue by flinging him upon one of those subtle hand-to-hand psychic struggles with this man which always threw the problem of madness into the background.

"Doctor," he said suddenly, making no comment of any sort at all upon what he had just heard of the closing of the laboratory.

"Yes, Cobbold?"

"Is it your view that the world comes into being from purely mechanical causes?"

Doctor Brush sank even lower than before in his chair.

"Not from those alone, Cobbold," he replied. "But they played their part then as they do now."

"Do you believe in God, then?"

"Perhaps."

"In Immortality?"

"I wouldn't deny it off hand."

"In prayer?"

"As a subject for experiment."

"Have you any tendency, yourself, Doctor—"

Sylvanus having been given his cue by Nature was now interfering with her by trying to be too clever.

"—any tendency to mental aberration?" "I am glad I asked him that," he thought. "It may make him think a bit."

The man certainly assumed a very odd expression when Sylvanus put to him this direct, this simple interrogation.

"Sometimes, my good Cobbold," he said slowly, "I think I am the unhappiest person in this whole establishment. Do you realize that at this moment there is nothing that would give me greater pleasure than if you were to pick up that poker and knock my brains out?"

Sylvanus once more shuffled himself forward to the edge of his chair and sat at attention. Once more he held his long, lean thighs apart, once more his clenched fists were resting on them while he leaned forward. He was thus in the precise position that rowers assume, at the beginning of a race, when they are waiting the signal. The Doctor, on the contrary, was lying back now at full length in his low chair, his chin sunk into his neck, his arms drooping, his legs straight out and side by side, while of his feet, nothing of them but the heels touched the carpet. As Sylvanus gazed at the Doctor and pondered upon this startling remark, there came over him a very curious sensation. He suddenly found himself seized with a queer feeling, as if the Doctor, stretched out there before him, was really a *woman!* Do what he could to concentrate his thought on the problem of the Doctor's unhappiness, he could not resist a weird, irresistible vibration, that reached him as he looked at the man stretched out in that chair, that he was dealing with a personality that was feminine. Sylvanus, although, as Magnus had correctly divined, he had nothing of the character of Punch in him, had an exaggeratedly male identity. Entirely free from the least flicker of erotic perversity, a freedom very rare among prophets, philosophers and priests, Sylvanus was, at this particular second, as he clenched his strong fists on his lean thighs, seized with a mysterious spasm of turbulent erotic emotion.

"Caput—Anus!" he cried in his heart, "What in the devil's name is happening to me? Am I going mad? Is it with *this* that it begins? Are you really 'flapping' over there in that chair, you little fool? Are you really wanting me to 'tart' you? *If not*, why do I feel—"

Thus, in place of any modern jargon, Sylvanus in his simplicity used his old Public School expressions. But it now began seriously to enter his stirred-up wits, as a startling but quite real possibility, that he had at last stumbled on the secret of the Doctor's partiality to him and his passion for conversing with him. This would explain, too— for the unscientific mind of Sylvanus began to seethe with wild hypotheses—the man's power of self-negation and the almost humiliating way he had of imbibing another person's ideas.

"You poor devil!" thought Sylvanus. "What I feel now as I look at you is quite reason enough for your being unhappy. We need an opposite sex, just as plants need water."

Thus while a mysterious contact of his eyes with those of Dr. Brush—full of the interchange of magnetic currents that troubled his senses and perplexed his mind—increased the queer sensation he was experiencing, he remarked gravely: "I can't understand, Doctor, how anyone like you can be unhappy when you have only to walk to a place like—" he was going to say Tup's Fold but he could not utter those syllables—"a place like the White Horse to get the sense of . . . the sense of . . ."

He paused, feeling confused, puzzled, how to convey to this man, lolling there in his shirt-sleeves, inspirations that came from Something so "deeply interfused" as was the spiritual Presence he referred to. He found himself talking to the man, too, exactly in the tone he always used when he talked to women, and he had an odd feeling that his relaxed and reclining interlocutor was amused, just as a woman would have been at the notion that the Director of Hell's Museum had only to walk—to the White Horse, in order to recover the resources of his spirit. He stammered on awkwardly, trying to indicate his own methods of emotional recuperation, but something about the Doctor's quizzically lifted eyebrow and the almost Mona-Lisa-like equivocation of his flickering smile gave him the feeling that there were dimensions of sophisticated mentality in the world to which these simple spiritual secrets of his own life were totally inapplicable. And what was Daniel Brush thinking all this while?

He was thinking in terms, if you could put such a complicated procession of mental adjustments into a rational order, in terms of a vein of philosophical reverie that had nothing whatever to do with the differences of the sexes. But it was true, all the same, that the peculiar *trend* of his thoughts had been drawn directly from former conversations with the singular person now addressing him.

"Here we two sit," thought Dr. Brush, "in this square room in the midst of these chalk hills, so many miles as the crow flies, from the salt sea, so many miles, as the plummet sinks, from the mathematical centre of the earth. And between our two personalities, that now touch through the rays of our optic 'neurones', there is of necessity attraction and repulsion, and he is trying to work psychic magic on me, and I am trying to work psychic magic on him."

Three months ago Dr. Brush would never have allowed his thoughts to take this particular line. Indeed he would never have *had* thoughts of this semi-mystical nature. But at least the man was true to his maniacal pursuit of what he called "Truth". If Truth began to look different to him, well! it must be followed all the same!

"Two men," he thought, "never meet, save on those special occasions when they are attracted by love, without thinking at every point: 'I am subtler, deeper, wiser, more dangerous, more complicated, than you are!' But, Nom de Dieu! what a load of self-satisfied balderdash I've brought down on my head! I must break this up. And there's always only one way to do it—one infallible way of asserting one's superiority and that's to be ironic, mocking, supercilious. When you're that, you dodge it all; spread your wings; off and away! But—damn the chap!—it's the trick of *the inferior intelligence!* But—perhaps—there *is* an irony ... well, at any rate, I can't stand any more of *this!*"

And the Doctor, a very Proteus in mental somersaults, called up—using the actual introspective device he had learnt from his patient—an electric current of ferocious mockery. He sat straight up in his chair, as he resorted to this trick, and he even rose and lit a cigarette.

"But I was only joking, my good Cobbold," he said. "You

needn't sermonize me! I was parodying the sort of dramatic 'narcissism' and sentimental tom-foolery that you get among the half-educated. Don't we Doctors know it in our profession? You get your own back from the universe by your voluptuous self-pity, by being such an interesting Sensitive. 'The most unhappy man in the Brush Home is Brush!' Hasn't that got the true ring of the hypocrisy of self-pity? Bah! my dear boy, I am an exceptionally happy person."

The foolish face of innocent bewilderment, mingled with tokens of a really deep outrage, with which Sylvanus received this information seemed to satisfy the Doctor. He actually came over to the tall man, walking gingerly across his flowered carpet, as we are told Agag walked when he saw Death to the windward, and snapped his fingers.

"I don't give *this*," he cried, "for anyone's pity! I'm a singularly happy man."

Then he smiled at Sylvanus, as he stood there by his side, a smile that resembled that appalling smile described by William Blake, which can only be smiled once in a person's life-time, and as Sylvanus saw him smiling this smile he began to receive once more that extraordinary impression, and—what was worse—to feel again that curious feeling which put him to shame. A wave of uncontrollable anger with the man followed this feeling, an anger that was accentuated by the fact that he was being forced to experience erotic emotions *without any accompanying pleasure*. He, too, rose to his feet and the pair looked at each other for a second without a word.

Then it chanced that the Doctor's great clock over the mantelpiece began to strike, and it struck with the intonation of a certain Portland clock near the bowling-green at Easton. This sound was to the exile from Last House like the crowing of the cock to Peter. He felt that the Doctor *had* fooled him. He felt bitterly alone. He felt without friends, without future, without hope. In the expressive popular phrase, *he felt the draught;* and this superficial "draught", composed of the bleak corridors of Hell's Museum, suddenly made him feel as though his very Absolute had forsaken him. It was only of his mental humiliation that he consciously thought, as he stood in this spiritual "draught", but his poor, battered, lank, grotesque body felt a bewildered distress of its own that seemed to go down to the bottom of its being.

"It is *I*," said the lean, lank, turtle-necked body of Sylvanus in Hell's Museum, the body that had been stripped of its friendly tweed and swaddled in the prison-garb of the Home, "It is *I* who know where the compass is pointing now; and what *I* say, to the Spirit that has landed me here, is—'Lama Sabachthani?'"

With the dying away of the last reverberations of that clock a thirst for Marret came over Sylvanus that made him howl like a famished wolf. He did actually give vent to a cry that seemed hardly human.

"Good God, man! What have I said? What have I done?" cried Daniel Brush, taking to himself, and to his clever devices, the credit for this beast-howl issuing from the body of his patient.

But Sylvanus seemed to have caught "the prevailing tone", as one might say, of the place he was in. Casting aside every vestige and shred of self-respect, and humiliating himself before this man to the uttermost, yes! even to the extent of mentioning Marret's name, he rushed weeping from the Doctor's study. As he went, as he held the door open to go, he found himself uttering, quite without any intention of doing such a thing, one of those childish jingles of his which it seemed a fatality of his nature to be always stringing together. This persistent tendency of the man—he would probably die uttering some gibberish that rhymed with "anus"—was a pathological illustration of Wordsworth's subtle hint that rhyme drugs and stupifies the poignancy of feelings that otherwise could not be borne.

> "I'm an ass, I'm an ass, I'm an ass, my God!
> An ass that's tasted carrot—
> You fill me full with the grass of the sod—
> But you take away my Marret!"

As he uttered the final line of this doggerel of despair, he turned his great, white, parsnip-shaped face, with the tears streaming down it, full upon the Doctor.

"Damn your soul!" he cried savagely. "You are not a man!"

When he was gone, the first thing that Dr. Brush did was to pull up his shirt-cuff and survey with concentrated concern the little spot on his wrist which refused to stop tickling.

"Shall I never do it? Never do it?" he said to himself.

And what he meant by "do it" was to grow as impersonal in his relations with Sylvanus as he had compelled himself to be over the end of his experiments on dogs. There are things that happen in the world that have an effect out of proportion to their apparent importance. It is as if there were always blowing a faint, supernatural wind through the world, holding a secret of assuagement for troubled hearts, that is only perceptible when it can find a straw, a feather, a gossamer-seed, a leaf, in the débris of circumstance light enough for it to stir.

As Sylvanus that night went down the corridor to his cubicle he was saluted through the other's half-open door by the demented ornithologist.

"Good-night, sir!" whispered George Pounce, in a tone full of respectful consideration.

"How nicely he said that!" Sylvanus thought. "He'd have said it just like that if the world were coming to an end tomorrow."

Sylvanus was right, and he might have concluded furthermore that an Absolute that could roll away the stone of its sepulchre, through so simple a salutation from the mouth of a Loony, even if he *had* been trusted with the key to Hell's Museum, was an Absolute not devoid of one power at least attributed to the most fabulous of birds. Such an Absolute had the power of renewing itself from its own ashes.

"Good-night, George!" replied Sylvanus in his normal voice.

15

LOST AND FOUND

ON the second morning after Marret's visit to Tup's Fold, Magnus Muir, still a bachelor-lodger with his friend Miss Le Fleau, sat talking with that lady in the drawing-room at Kimmeridge House, amid the furniture that he had known from childhood. As he listened to Miss Le Fleau, upon whose black satin lap lay a touching evidence of her devotion to him, namely a white, woollen bed-jacket for Curly, he contemplated a rose-wood chiffonier on which, in a little book-case, stood all his old prize editions from Weymouth College.

"I was miserable in those days," he thought, "much more miserable than I've been this autumn, for all poor Curly's moods! Well! I suppose everyone lands themselves in some wretched pass by following their temperament! After all it's my chief happiness to see her . . . if only once a week! How sweet she was to me yesterday!"

His mind wandered from Miss Le Fleau's words to that Upwey Attic and to the unusually voluptuous intimacies that the girl had allowed him to enjoy there last night. *What did this mean?* Did it mean that she was losing her "nervousness" about being made love to? Could it mean that what he still so obstinately, so patiently awaited, was really, at last, on the verge of materializing?

His eyes left his friend's calm neutral face, the face of a morning-after-morning sitter and knitter in a room full of old furniture, of Penn House furniture, in a room where between a green leather edition of Ruskin and an inlaid table covered with Meissen tea-cups, stood a maiden-hair fern on an old gilded stand, and wandered off to a large, oblong Chesil-Beach pebble—also from Penn House—upon which had been painted by his mother, nearly half a century ago, a picture of the Great Eastern, the ship that had laid the Atlantic cable.

Curly had been so incredibly sweet to him last night! It was just as if she had *planned* to have her mother go off to spend the evening with Aunt Phem over the shop!

"Yes," he now remarked, "I hate to see him. I hate to meet him. He's just drinking himself to death! I *can't* believe any girl would be so cruel as to deliberately go on hiding herself away while a decent chap like this goes to the devil. My own feeling is she's dead. I didn't think so at first. Jerry was so sure about her still being in Weymouth that I thought he knew where she was. In fact I hinted to *him* that I thought Jerry knew. He never believed it! I think he must have had an instinct how it was, some curious sixth sense about it. And that's why he is in such despair. He's almost sure she's dead, but not *quite* sure—and that's the worst state a person could be in. He . . . was . . . very . . . *fond of her*, Miss Le Fleau!"

"Does he still go on talking in that wild way about doing some hurt to Mr. Cattistock?"

"No, no—at least I don't think so! In fact I can't imagine it, looking the way he does. But unless by some miracle that girl turns up, I tell you the chap's done for. He *can't* go on. It's humanly impossible. I met that man of his the other day, on the esplanade— I daresay you don't know him, his name's Trot—and he said it was all they could do to make him eat anything these days. He said he always went with him now to that 'Pub' down by the Harbour and had struck up an understanding about him with the bar-maid. You don't know, I daresay, Miss Le Fleau, what comfort and support those bar-maids are, to men who are unhappy. They keep 'em from suicide very often. Yes, they do."

"I've no doubt they do," said Miss Le Fleau smiling resignedly. But what she thought was: "Oh, the darling fools that men are! We torment them, we humour them, we look after them, we drive them to perdition, and all the while they are so blind, so stupid, that it's hard to bear it!"

"Did Martha hear any news, Miss Le Fleau, as to how old Loder is when she took your note to Ruth?"

The old lady bent her head and knitted in silence. It always hurt her in some obscure, sidelong manner when Magnus referred in this careless casual way to Miss Loder. Long ago in her secret heart the wise old woman had decided that if, by any Providential intervention such as the Black Death invading Upwey, or the girl being drowned in the Wishing Well, Magnus became free again, it was Ruth who was best qualified to make him happy. Miss Le Fleau's judgment was infallible, but what she had not yet fully grasped was that the passion of love is like the Sword-Bridge to the Castle of Carbonek. It will as lief lead to death as lead to life! She therefore gave him time to intensify his enquiry a little while she let fall a remark without raising her head about the way Rodney and little Daisy Lily had been so much together all this summer.

"It's all right, of course. We all know what a trustworthy young man *he* is, and what a good, sweet child *she* is . . . but still . . . considering what sensitive things young girls' hearts are it does seem strange to me that her mother—"

"Her mother never goes near her!" interrupted Magnus. "Since Jerry left Lucinda and took rooms with that woman Tossty at Dr. Girodel's, Hortensia hardly goes out at all. *She's* Mrs. Cobbold's companion now."

Miss Le Fleau looked grave. Recognizing her failure suitably to steer the conversation, she lifted her eyes from her lap and remarked that Ammabel had told Martha that Mr. Loder was dying.

"I fear it's a rather distressing end, too, from what Martha tells me," and she fell to giving lurid details, though still in the gentlest tone, about the old man's complaint. At one point she interrupted herself, as old ladies will, to pick up a copy of the Melcombe Regis Circular which lay by her side. "Did you see this about Dr. Brush having to give up his Experimental Laboratory, whatever that means, for lack of funds?"

Magnus looked at her sharply.

"Does it mention Mr. Cobbold?" he asked.

"Oh, no! It's only a couple of lines," she replied, and once more, waving the Brush Home away, she came back to the Loders.

But Magnus, looking at the carefully watered maiden-hair fern in its delicate china pot, allowed his attention to wander from James Loder's death-struggle with his ulcers. He instinctively avoided, too, any further thought about the Brush Home. The furniture helped him in this. Not one single piece of this dignified Penn House furniture but had some sweet, youthful, tremulous, forbidden imagination projected into its grain, into its texture, into its colour, into its pattern. And he set himself to recall, voluptuously, passionately, just as if they had been the Homeric flowers he was always reading about, "violet, amaracus and asphodel, lotus and lily", as indeed they were, for her loveliness had steadily increased since the spring, all the swan's-down softness, all the marbly whiteness of Curly's limbs.

What *did* it mean that she had let him come up into the Attic? What *did* it mean that she had let him caress her upon her bed? Magnus was so unused to girls that he had no notion how lightly, how absent-mindedly, and with how little in it but a vague good-heartedness and a wish to give where 'tis safe to give, they will bestow their lesser favours, favours that bind not a jot either themselves or the recipient.

But Curly was, as a matter of fact, an unusually cold and chaste girl. She was temperamentally proud, shy, reserved, and especially so in regard to her body. Such a girl is more than monogamous. She has an Artemis-like dislike, an angry, nervous, irritable dislike, of being so much as touched when she is not in love. Magnus, in his old-fashioned manner, frankly attributed this reserve in his girl to purity, modesty, chastity, maidenliness. *And he was right.* Dr. Brush's latest theories would have heartily corroborated this simple view. But although to be made love to, when she was not in love, was an irritation and an annoyance to Curly, it affected her deeper nature so little that it was something she *could* easily put up with for any important purpose of her own. Indeed it is likely enough that many professional prostitutes are as chaste as she was!

The tutor was therefore completely justified in being roused to new hope as he stared at the diaphanous filaments of that maiden-hair fern, hanging so airily and lightly above the old gilt-bound school-prizes and above the pebble carrying on its surface the Great Eastern. He had not possessed her in the final sense, but she made no real resistance until quite near that consummation. Certainly he had enjoyed her in a way he had never been allowed to enjoy her before, and he kept asking himself:

"What did it mean? What did it mean?"

"With any other young girl," Miss Le Fleau was remarking, and as Magnus looked at those aged fingers, that soft white wool, that black satin, a curious peace began to insinuate itself among his worries.

All women, since they carry within them a portion of that primordial womb of darkness wherein creation once slept undisturbed, convey something of "this peace that passeth understanding". Every woman's lap, as she rests, nursing, sewing, pondering, chattering, is a cradle of eternal nirvana, capable of soothing the most troubled brain. And touching him now with a faint scent of Eau de Cologne, this smooth black satin, those aged fingers, brought back endless hours when weary of his restless boy's hunt for half-understood sensuality, he had come to this woman's side. He thought of it always on grey, still autumn mornings, mornings when the scent of Eau de Cologne was not easily blown way! How this white wool and black satin flowed in with the whole character of Weymouth, its spire, its clock, its two royal statues!

This old woman's limbs covered with her smooth dress brought peace, while Curly's, as he had seen them exposed last night, roused up the impulse that set the cosmos whirling! Suddenly something came over him that he had quite forgotten, thinking so exclusively about the liberties she had allowed him, something that happened at the last. She had wanted him to go before Mrs. Wix came back, and as they stood in the cottage doorway she had suddenly moved forward and thrown her arms round his neck, that gesture that *never once* she had spontaneously made before, that gesture about which he had told himself so many stories, that gesture which he had imagined when he had longed for her so desperately on Chesil on the night of the storm! With her arms round his neck she had pressed her face to his and kissed him passionately. She did this awkwardly, for she was not used to giving him kisses. He remembered how foolish he had felt when her dear lips in the darkness collided clumsily with his aquiline nose. And then, as he went off, she acted as if she had really at last given him a piece of herself. She acted as if she did not wish to add anything to her kiss.

"With any other young girl," the old lady was saying, still edging cautiously in the general direction of Spy Croft, "we should all be worried at her being left with that old man, and Mrs. Matzell ill, too, and only a maid about! But she's an exceptional child. You can feel as if she were well over twenty, instead of being—hardly seventeen! I don't wonder that dear Ruth, who has such wisdom in these things, is glad for her brother to—"

It was Martha, her lace cap covered with purple ribbons, who interrupted at this point, knocking at the door and turning its handle simultaneously.

" 'Tis only to tell 'ee Master Magnus," she said, "that Mr. Gaul be outside squinnying up at windy."

Magnus gave a hurried, unceremonious nod to Miss Le Fleau.

"Thanks awfully, Martha," he cried as he rushed downstairs.

He found his friend waiting on the pavement with a very dejected air.

"Do you mind coming to my room for a minute, Muir?" he said gravely. "I have something I want to ask your advice about."

It was so very rare for Mr. Gaul to ask advice of *him* that Magnus went with him with alacrity, being urged on by that rather ambiguous curiosity with which we learn of the agitations of our friends.

"It's a beautiful morning," Magnus said as they walked along, "after all this rain."

Mr. Gaul did not even trouble to give him a look, far less to comment on this platitude.

Then the Corporal met them, returning from his weekly visit to old Higginbottom about his lumbago.

"If he refers," thought Magnus, "to that damned second wife of his, I'll tell him what Curly says about his third one."

But what the old world-sentinel referred to lacked every vestige of interest for the two egoists. He told them that Caddie Water had trouble with her throat and he went on to say that the old doctor must think well of his new partner as he was letting him prescribe for his case. Then he wandered off to changes at Dr. Girodel's.

"He's coming on, *that young man be*."

"Pardon me, Corporal, but we've got an engagement that won't wait," and Magnus looked at him exactly as the elder Muir used to look at the garrulous School Porter.

"I suppose this Corporal," he said to Gaul when they reached Trigonia House, "knows every faintest smell, whether of dust or snow, or rain, or tar, or gull's droppings, or bilge-water, or bad fish, or bathchair polish, between 'The Turret' and 'Fernlands'?"

But Mr. Gaul cut short this assuaging enquiry.

"Do you mind not speaking in the passage," he whispered. "*He's* in there!" and he made a jab with his thumb in the direction of Mr. Ballard's room.

It was then that Magnus realized for the first time that the car, covered with mud and dust, and looking as if it had not been cleaned for days, that was standing at the curb, was none other than the "Tirra-lirra" car!

No lowered voices, however, no tip-toe movements, could conceal from the Wiltshire landlady this morning visit. She turned to her daughter who was helping her to wash up.

"There's summat on, my charmer," she said, using an expression of endearment that she had picked up in a Canon's family in Salisbury Close, "there's summat on that's as serious as King's Evidence ... Mr. Ballard going and coming since eight o'clock this morning, and now these two, glaring and staring, and nudging in whispers, like a couple of executioners! And don't let's forget to bear in mind how you saw that Gipsy from Lodmoor pass the door so early this morning, muttering funny-like to herself and dragging a heavy load, nor how that picture of your blessed Dad fell from its nail. The Lord be up to summat, my charmer; he be up to summat. But ' 'tis His Doing and So Be Still', as Canon's wife used to say to Maria the cook when he killed a mole on his lawn."

Once having seated his friend safely in his own room Richard Gaul explained the circumstances that made him come to him that morning.

"You know," he said gravely, "that Miss Frampton and I have been seeing a good deal of one another this autumn?"

Magnus nodded, with equal gravity. The fact referred to was indeed well known in every lodging-house between the Harbour and the Spire.

"Nothing had been Decided," Mr. Gaul went on. "Nothing *may* be Decided. My book remains of course the first and the last consideration. And what ... effect ..." He spoke as an astrologer might speak of the approach to each other of Jupiter and Mars, "what ... effect ... intercourse with Miss Frampton ... may ... have ... on ... my book it is hard to say."

Magnus' curiosity began to ebb and his attention to wander.

"If Gaul has only called me here to talk about the effect of Peggie on his Philosophy, or of his Philosophy on Peggie, he's wasting my time;" and the catch came drifting into his head: "Thus did Bacchus conquer India, thus Philosophy Melinda."

But the sight of Ballard's car had sent his own mind off on his own affairs in a whirling gyration of agitated panic. These two girls had invaded the peace of Brunswick Terrace with a vengeance!

"Was she so sweet with me," Magnus thought, "because she is intending to marry Ballard instead?"

"She has asked me," continued Gaul, "well! not exactly *asked* me, but arranged the subject before my intelligence so that I thought of it myself—to risk spending a night with her at Swan Villa ... you know? ... where the Backwater used to be ... while Frampton's away on some business affair. Do you think, Muir, that it would be safe for me to do this?"

"Oh, perfectly safe, very, very safe," replied Magnus absent-mindedly.

"You *really* ... think so?"

His voice was so astonished and so intense that Magnus woke up.

"What's that Gaul? I'm so sorry! I don't think I quite caught just what you said."

Mr. Gaul rose to his feet, took off his spectacles and rubbed them against the tassels of a bracket bearing a photograph of the late Canon's garden in Salisbury.

"I asked you whether," he said with a forced laugh—and never had a more hollow sound paid homage to the Laughter-Loving One— "whether it would be safe for me to stay the night with Miss Framp-ton, when Mr. Frampton is away."

An irrational irritation with his philosophic friend seized upon Magnus. Compared with the ghastly possibility that his own Love had run off with this skipping pond-fly of a Sippy, what did it matter whether Metaphysics and Desperation lay together at Swan Villa or at Preston Brook?

"I wish you'd call her 'Peg', Gaul," he said crossly. "When

everyone knows her as Peg it's absurd to call her Miss Frampton."

"But *do* you, Muir?" the young sage repeated, while Magnus became aware that some disturbance in Gaul's absence had strewn the floor with at least three sheets of manuscript, an accident that had passed entirely unobserved by the writer of them.

"Do I *what?*"

"Do you think it would be safe?"

"You mean he might come home unexpectedly and give you a hiding?"

Mr. Gaul's spectacles had been rendered considerably more obscure by the dust of those tassels. He removed them spasmodically again and, still on his feet, rubbed them so violently against the seat of his trousers that one of their lenses slipped from its horn-rim and fell to the floor.

"Blast the things!" cried Mr. Gaul, and when he had groped on the floor for the lost glass and placed it on the table he thrust his one-glass spectacles upon his nose and glared through them angrily.

"If you can't see what I mean," he cried, "without having to be told in realistic medical language, all I can say is, Muir, that you are—"

Magnus beheld in his mind the deep-sunken eyes with their dark dissipated look and the red under-lip with its pathetic droop.

"That poor little girl!" he thought, feeling a spasm of shame, "and we great hulkers discussing her! Her life's in her soul, after all, just as ours is!"

He gave his friend a not altogether sympathetic glance.

"You mean," he remarked, "you might get the pox?" He rapped out these gross words lowering his thick eyebrows and screwing up his eyes. "Get it on the ground of her having gone about such a lot, among—"

He was interrupted by the mocking, impish sound of that accurst Tirra-Lirra! He shrugged his shoulders, glanced at the window, and spoke more gently to Mr. Gaul who was engaged in making vain attempts to insert the escaped disc into its empty frame. As Magnus watched his repeated failures to do this, that arrogant horn outside was blown again.

Mr. Gaul looked up.

"I believe he is making signals," he remarked. "Yes," he went on, "I really believe he is doing that *for us*."

Magnus stared at him and turned angrily towards the window from which nothing could be seen.

"For *us*? God! they may have told him I was with you here, and it's me he wants."

A wild, unreasoning, animal fear now seized upon him. He thought:

"*She is dead;* and Ballard's come to break it to me!"

Then his saner reason prevailed again and he said to himself:

"He isn't calling us at all."

Mr. Gaul had seated himself at the table and was fumbling with his broken spectacles. He suddenly looked up so pathetically and with such a confused, lost look on his bland countenance, that Magnus felt heartily ashamed of himself.

"Of course, my dear chap," he said in his kindest tone, "we can't be too careful. But wouldn't Peg be frank with you? And if she *has* taken risks and has suffered for it, wouldn't she tell you? I'd ask her with absolute freedom, Gaul. It's wonderful what cowardice we can carry off, if we are open about it, and laugh at ourselves! But, Gaul don't you think I'd better run down and see if Ballard really does want either of us?"

The author of "the Philosophy of Representation" glanced sadly at the floor, where it was too evident several of his pages had drifted.

"I must remember to get some more cockle-shells," he thought. "Yes, I think you'd better go down," he murmured. "I shall have to go down, too, because of these spectacles. I shall have to go to that place in St. Mary's Street. Yes, we had both of us better go down."

He uttered this so lugubriously that Magnus would have smiled if his growing uneasiness about Curly had not put an end to his smiling.

"Go down, go down, go down," Gaul repeated in a gloomy chant. "Yes, we had both of us better go down."

When they reached the pavement, there, seated in his car, was Sippy Ballard. He was sounding his horn in a mechanical way at intervals but his face looked white and he kept biting his lower lip and making an odd circular movement with his chin over his collar—a movement that Magnus had noticed before in him, but never in so pronounced a way. For half a second as he observed him making this queer automatic movement he saw the good-looking youth as if he were Mr. Punch on the gallows with the rope round his neck. The voice of Jones sounded in his ears: "*Judy! Judy! Judy!*"

Meanwhile Gaul, holding his spectacles in one hand and the unattached disc in the other and blinking helplessly in the presence of this new phenomenon tried to arrest his attention. Anxious to be off to the town and yet unfortified by any authoritative oracle from his friend, he gently poked him in the ribs.

"Then you'd advise me to go ahead?" he murmured. "I mean about Swan Villa."

Magnus gave him a confused glance.

"Certainly," he said, "certainly."

Then he proceeded to address the young man who was moving his chin so oddly.

"Do you want me?" he said, and stepping forward he laid his hands on the edge of the familiar car.

All the answer he got was yet another mechanical pressure of that frivolous horn. Tirra-Lirra! it sounded between the houses and the sea.

"Do you want me, Ballard?" he repeated. "What on earth's wrong? Is it from Curly you've come? Is it well with Curly?"

Then at last the handsome young man recovered his wits and looked down at him.

"Get in," he murmured laconically. "Get in here, for God's sake. I'll tell you as we go!"

Magnus turned to his friend.

"Don't worry about that little matter, Gaul. Be perfectly frank. Cover up your—your nervousness by jesting about it. Be open and shameless. It's always best to be shameless with them. Good-bye, Gaul!"

If S. P. Ballard had blown his horn when there was no need, it seemed to his passenger, jammed in so close to him by the wheel, that he didn't remember to sound it half enough as they drove past the Station and over the new viaduct dam by Radipole Lake.

In dead silence the young man drove, while one wild thought after another coursed through his companion's brain.

"Has he killed her to keep her from me?" he thought. "Is he taking me to see her body?" And then he thought: "No, no! He isn't like that at all! It's something quite different. *He's given her up.* They've quarrelled, and he's given her up. Oh, little Curly, Oh, my precious darling! Is this really the end, the end of all our trouble? Have you turned to me, at last, my only true Love?" And he concluded in his heart: "Yes that's it, that's evidently it. That's what she meant by what she said last night."

How clearly he could see her face as it was when they came down from the Attic, as it was when they stood, together in the kitchen, before she hurried him off! What was it she had said to him then?

"You have always been so kind to me, Magnus."

He hadn't paid much attention then. His senses were in such a whirl.

"So kind to me"—yes! that's what she said. *Kind?* Was that all he'd been? "Oh, Curly, my one of all, Oh, my little, little Curly!"

They were clear of the traffic now. But where was he going? This wasn't the way to Upwey! Why had he come *this* way? This led to Chickerel, not to Upwey! Then Ballard spoke. Clearly, without mincing words, he told him all. *Curly had gone off with Cattistock.* Magnus never afterwards forgot the look of that long white hill-road going up to Chickerel, its low hedges, its open, treeless uplands, the wind that suddenly came up, from across the West Fleet, over Chesil.

He accepted the worst in his deepest soul, while his brain, the surface of his mind, went on vainly, idiotically thinking, calling up one false hope after another. But Ballard's news had sunk, like that pebble painted by his mother, like that other one that people said the Jobber kept in his pocket, sunk sure and straight, down into his deepest soul! He had lost her. Gone, gone. It was all over. The surface of his nature, his reasonable mind, found itself astonished at his calm. He felt a little sick in his stomach. But what was that? A little dizzy and faint, too, so that he had to lean sideways, away from Ballard clutching the car's edge. But what was that? It occurred to him as if it were an

event in the remote past, in someone else's life, that in his agitation
that morning he had gone down to Miss Le Fleau's room without
touching his breakfast. What was it this tiresome boy was saying
now? He tried to attend to what he was saying, tried to fix his attention
on each word, as a man does who wants to prove he isn't drunk. But
underneath everything his deepest soul was washing, like an under-
tide, up and down, up and down, over that sunken stone, over the
boy's word that she'd gone off with Cattistock. Something at last did
sharply arrest his attention.

"*When* was that? *When* did she say that?"

And·Ballard went over it all again, wearily and patiently.

"It was yesterday afternoon. I was with her *all* yesterday afternoon, and I could see she was upset, had something on her mind she
was keeping back, and then she said: 'I'm sorry, Sippy, if ever'—"

"Yesterday afternoon!" thought Magnus with that silly, fussy,
intrusive top of his mind that still took an absurd interest in unessential
details, that still persisted in conjuring up impossible hopes against all
evidence. "Yesterday afternoon," he echoed dully, thinking to
himself: "She must have come straight from him to me! She must
have wanted to see us both at the very last. Had she said to *him*,
'You've been very kind to me, Sippy?'"

No doubt that's what she said! That was evidently her formula
with her men. Kind? Yes, he had been "kind", and Ballard had been
"kind". But kindness with girls is clearly not enough. They want
more than that! They want the money of a Cattistock. They want
to see the world. That indeed was apparently just what she *was*
seeing.

"My uncle telephoned to me at the Guildhall," Sippy was saying
now; "He says they're off this morning. He says he's taking her to
Italy."

Magnus was silent, gripping the side of the car with his fingers as a
man might grip the boards of a gibbet upon which his best friend is
being executed. He did not recognize it himself till long afterwards,
but something happened to him during that drive to Chickerel. After
this there was a solid level of stone, deep in his heart, of stone in whose
petrifaction was a single fossil—not an ammonite, but twisted like an
ammonite—a fossil that would remain there untouched, till it dropped

with a thud, into the bottom of his coffin, as the flesh left his bones.

"Do you think he'll marry her?" he said suddenly, as they approached Peninsular Lodge.

"How can *I* tell?" replied the other. "I don't suppose so. But you never know! If it goes on he may."

The outer surface of Magnus' mind was working firmly, calmly, normally now. That fossil, like petrifaction produced by seismic pressure, had already taken its permanent, imperishable form. And with his clearly working mind it struck him as curious that young Ballard should be treating him so considerately. But then how could you tell what Cattistock had said to him? He certainly did not miss the ironic queerness of their visit together to Peninsular Lodge. Who could have predicted among all the changes and chances that could possibly happen that the hour would ever arrive when he would be sitting in Lizzie Chant's kitchen, by Ballard's side, listening to the oracular discourse of Mrs. Wix.

Both the old women were seated, and it was clear that Mrs. Wix was upon very intimate and friendly terms with the aged housekeeper. It soon indeed became clear that the Upwey house was to be shut up for several months, perhaps forever, while Curly's mother made her domicile with her ancient gossip.

"What a dispensation of Nature," Magnus thought, "that a blow like this stuns you so completely that you're too numbed to feel the hurt!"

He did not realize that what he thought was numbness was really the turning into stone of a *woman-shell*, of a certain lovely tortuous conch of circles, a certain Ammonite with divine curves!

"Well," said Ballard, addressing both the old ladies, as he sipped a glass of brown sherry, "I suppose they're on the boat for Havre by now! Uncle telephoned to me, you know, from Southampton."

There was a long pause, during which Magnus found himself looking quietly about—now that the fossilized Curly lay so peaceful down there—to see where Mrs. Wix had put her crochet, for to his surprise that symbol of treachery was not on her lap. His astonishment was great—a sort of Alice in Wonderland astonishment—when he realized that Mrs. Chant was working hard, her aged fingers fluttering like wind-shaken straws in a barn-crack, at that identical bit of work!

"I suppose my Uncle has already been pretty liberal to your daughter, Mrs. Wix?" remarked the impertinent young man, beginning to feel what he would have called a bit squiffy.

The old women gave each other a sly glance, as much as to say,

"What gentlemen *will* say when you're alone with them!"

Magnus finished *his* glass of the absent magnate's admirable wine and addressed himself to Lizzie.

"I don't suppose the real relation between these two will ever be known," he said, speaking as gravely as if he had been talking to his friend in Trigonia House. "Women's characters change very quickly, don't they, Mrs. Wix?"

Curly's mother looked at Mrs. Chant from over her spectacles, a proceeding which made her eyes resemble those of a very wise, very crafty old frog.

"I don't think Curly's will," she retorted. "Am I telling these gentlemen the truth," she added, addressing Lizzie, "or aren't I telling 'em the truth?"

Mrs. Chant glanced furtively at the open door that led into the Servants' Hall through which she could see the window looking out upon "the Grey Woman". She was not by any means sure in her old mind what her life-long friend, *the first Mrs. Cattistock*, would feel towards such revelations! But she plunged in.

" 'Tis like of this, Master Simon," and she looked at Sippy. "This is how't be sir," and she turned to Magnus. "Master were always one to be shy of women-folk, 'cept where courtin' ways and haycock ways be concerned. Master could not endure—and I know what I be telling ye, for me and him have a-talked of it, many and many a night, when us has sat up when Master Benny were sick. He never could abide, I say, any sort of a 'ooman, whether she were old or young, meddling with his private life. It were for fear of her meddling with 'un in lovingness that 'a jilted Mrs. Lily. 'A always drop 'un, same as they were hot coals, soon as they clawed at's privy counsels, as you might say. 'Tweren't altogether the money, I'm telling ye, though 'twere that, *too*, on course. 'Twere that the Master do yearn to keep his wone soul in his wone belly! 'Tis for this cause 'a be more frighted of woon what loves and clings than of woon what keeps she's self *to* she's self, and respects pride and ensues it!"

The eyes of the diplomatic Mrs. Wix—whose ambassadorial credentials, in the form of the crochet-work, were thus found to be in the hands of a kindred spirit—literally shone at the conclusion of this noble defence of minding your own business. Her lips trembled with a desire to present to the company certain significant details from the life of Curly's father which bore on this principle. She confined herself to remarking that her daughter "were *the woon of all o' 'em* to keep she's self to she's self."

And it was then that Mr. Simon Pym Ballard, to Magnus' sardonic amusement—it was the first time he'd been in a position to *be* sardonic in this quarter—corroborated the trend of the conversation.

"I don't know whether you good people realize," he remarked in the oratorical voice that awed the rate-payers at the Guildhall, for his uncle's sherry was going more and more to his head, "but it was not only Hortensia Lily, née Poxwell, that was sacrificed at the altar of Mr. Cattistock's *Privacy*, as you, Eliza, have so admirably described it. He has more recently sacrificed—since we're all friends here!—a lovely Being we all know, a Being we have all admired, for her Person, a Person which has been generously displayed at a well-known local theatre, a Being who—"

But though he had become more cynical in the last couple of hours than he ever supposed any mortal man *could* be, Magnus found it impossible to endure the thought of Curly's proud body lying in a place still warm from the nakedness of Tissty.

"That'll do, Ballard! That's quite enough. Well? Do you want to take me over to Chesil before you go back to the Guildhall? I've a notion to find out what the old sea-bank looks like, on a calm autumn morning."

He rose quietly to his feet and put down his empty glass. He let his eye wander round Mrs. Chant's kitchen.

"Benny enjoying his holiday?" he enquired of the housekeeper.

"He've agone, with thik 'yaller' of his'n, to see old Mr. Cobbold at Brush's. Me nephy drove 'un in big car. Master took his wone little car when he and Miss Wix started for 'Truria'."

Etruria? Magnus sighed at the mention of the sacred word. What secret conultatisons at the Wishing Well, perhaps as long ago as August had conveyed such magic syllables from Dog Cattistock to Curly, till they came to Lizzie.

"And so that's what you're enjoying now! Well, good luck to you! I could never have afforded to take you in the storms in November, to 'the brooks in Vallombrosa, where the Etrurian shades'—"

No! these old women were perfectly right. Curly was, in some queer way—and he could admit it now, with that Ammonite lying so quiet down there—really more suited to this secretive, formidable, rich man than she had ever been to him. And what Ballard said about her being different from both Mrs. Lily and Tissty was perfectly true. Either of *them* would have wound her arms day and night round the man's neck, and when he got angry, and beat them, they would enjoy those blows. He'd have been driven to run away. But he never would need to run away from Curly. Yes! she was indeed in a profound sense, *born* to be the paramour, even the wife, of a great man of action . . .

"You're—not—by—any—chance—thinking of—"

Sippy had thrown out these words with some genuine concern when he finally left him on Chesil Beach.

"Good God, man!" he had replied. "Do I look like that?"

No! he cannot have looked in the least like that, though no doubt he looked different from the way he usually did in Miss Le Fleau's drawing room. He pulled out his father's heavy watch which he wore exactly as *he* had worn it, with it massive, well-worn gold chain. He had often felt a certain half-humorous uneasiness when he brought out this ancient time-piece in that Upwey Cottage. The elder Muir's watch regarded him now, on the crest of Chesil Beach, with unqualified approval.

"Tick! Tick!" it said. "Time ends all human folly."

And then it informed him with quiet emphasis that it was one o'clock. For the second time that day he remembered the fact that he had not broken his fast. This time he recognized that it was himself, Magnus Muir, the methodical Latin teacher, who was thus forgetful of the exigencies of the belly. But with a fossiled life in his heart, that was more recent than any to be found in Portland, he once more put the thought of food aside and turned a cold scrutinizing gaze, eastward and then westward, upon the curves of the enormous Beach on which he stood.

There is a spontaneous awakening of awe in the human soul when a person stands in the presence of any natural formation of the earth's surface that has no parallel in the whole circumference of the globe. The wind had shifted since his unforgettable drive up Chickerel hill and came now from the north. Thus it was prevented by the gigantic terraqueous bank itself from rousing to any further height the waves of the West Bay. But although divested of their usual grandeur by this accident, it could not be said that these waves slept in absolute tranquillity! Though no longer stirred up to terrific wrath, they did not cease from their rolling, tumbling, curving, cresting, restless activity, that immemorial sea-trouble, which, when it does cease, evokes the feeling that the waters have really been made a path for the feet of the Eternal. The sky itself had become clearer, and an army of ragged white clouds from the high plateaus of Mid-Dorset offered an aerial correspondence, as if they had been crossing some vast cosmogonic mirror, to the racing, tossing white horses that even yet, for all the change of wind, foamed and champed and careered towards the motionless beach.

That there should be a rim to this vast sea-cauldron, whether the waves towered high, or ran, as now, a monotonous, inverted race with the opposing wind, that there should be a rampart like this between the waters of the South Coast and what was practically the Atlantic had a monumental congruity that satisfied while it astonished the mind. But had an imaginative traveller, travelling South-West, who had never seen the sea, come bolt upon this Cyclopean Embankment, without a glimpse of Weymouth Bay to mitigate the spectacle, he certainly would have felt that the rooted earth and the unresting waters were divided here in a way worthy of the demiurgic artist. The presence of the narrow strip of backwater, known as the Fleet, on the land side of Chesil, enabled Magnus, as he gazed at all this, and saw it as perhaps—for he was at one and the same time benumbed and sensitized—he would never see it again, to isolate this vast ramparted curve of pebbles till its stupendous entity seemed to detach itself from all contact with the normal phenomena of the world. This phantasmal detachment, endowing the colossal Beach with nothing less than an astronomical remoteness—as if it had been a parallel formation with the far-seen configurations on the surface of the Moon—seemed to mark it out, this bastion of the elements, this multiform Conglomerate, made up of individual pebbles surpassing the very stars of the Milky Way in multitude, as the actual rim of all the land and all the water on earth, as the true shore of that great Homeric Oceanus, from whose bank the slope descends that leads to the dwelling place of the insubstantial dead.

Feeling all this as he stood here now, it seemed to Magnus as if it were he, and not his Love, who had passed down into that gulf, leaving the sweet light of the sun, passed down, not exactly to death, for as he had lightly indicated to Sippy Ballard, he had not the least impulse to destroy himself, but a world from which something—though its loss might leave other consolations—had been taken away, that could never—no! not even by a miracle—be given back.

But what was that? The long-drawn, unmistakable emphatic siren-call of an incoming passenger steamer suddenly struck his ear. The Channel Island Boat! So they hadn't stopped yet, coming in in the middle of the day! In the winter they docked in the evening. Oh, but how clearly he could remember one particular night, only a year ago it was, come January, when Mrs. Cobbold dispatched him to meet her companion, and he transferred the job to the Jobber.

Turning southward now, he moved hurriedly along the crest of the pebbled ridge till he reached the chaotic confusion of tumbled, jagged, slippery sea-rocks that lie along the base of the westerly cliffs of Portland. He climbed over a few of these until, feeling exhausted, he sank down on a rough limestone slab, overgrown with sharp indented rock-shells and gazed down into a rock-pool. Here living seaweeds, their lovely, light-floating filaments expanding in the swaying tide, revealed, as they stirred, all manner of rich, strange shells lying at the pool's bottom. Most of these as he gazed down, he could name, for the elder Muir had "collected" such sea-treasures and it always brought the old man's figure as he used to see it bending over such when he came upon them in his shore-walks.

Here, in this enchanted fissure, he could see purple and amber-coloured sea-anemones, their living, waving antennae-like tendrils swaying gently, as the tide swell took them. And tiny, greenish fish with sharply extended dorsal fins darted to and fro across the waving petals of those plants that were more than plants! But it was at the motionless shells at the bottom that he now gazed with his strongest sense of the past. Cowries he could see in plenty, and small gamboge yellow shells, and little pyramidal shells with alternate mother-of-pearl bands and black-green bands, and he could see one involved mother-of-pearl shell, with a tiny seaweed actually growing from its surface, the faint roots of which, against the pearl, took on, in those wavering, shifting, broken lights, an indescribable greenish tinge.

Suddenly he forgot his father's interest in these things, for against his will the shell-like radiance of his lost girl's flesh and blood, that incredible transparency her face used sometimes to assume, shot through his senses like an arrow, an arrow of sea-pearl!

Up he sprang and fleeing desperately from those rocks, as a lost soul might fly from an oasis in its perdition where the memories cut its feet, he made his way across Chesil, across the road, across the railway, till he came to the shallow mud-flats of the Fleet Backwater. Here he had never been with Curly, and as far as his troubled memory served him, only once, long ago, with his father. Had Ballard seen his face then he would have doubted the sincerity and questioned the weight of that lightly flung attestation that had induced him to leave him.

The singular Backwater across whose brackish mud margins he now hurried in his blind desperation had a character quite peculiar to itself. The saltish nature of these *stranded* waters, subject to risings and fallings in regard to their level, but never roused to any tumult comparable to the outer sea, gives to their sandy reaches, when they are traversed or even skirted by an observant wayfarer, a quality that is unique. The spot has a strange metallic look, a livid forlornness, as if the brackish element in its mud had not only killed any ordinary plant-growth in its salt-bitten bosom, but had rendered its own amphibious, marine mosses sea-pale, sea-chilly and sea-blighted.

Magnus soon found his way barred by wide stretches of treacherous-looking water, that seemed neither to belong to the sea nor to any recognizable portion of the earth. Cursing the place, and conscious still of that terrible mother-of-pearl arrow head in his vitals, he swung round now, and came pounding and splashing back, to the higher level that stretches towards what is called the Fleet Bridge. In this region he stumbled on nothing more consolatory than a few whitish-grey walls of Portland stone falling into slow decrepitude, and one or two ruined stone sheds, buttressed and plastered with weather-stained stucco. These edifices had grown so "native and endued" to that queer No Man's Land, that, like the great, overturned, black-tarred boats upon the slope of the Beach above them, they seemed to take the shape of ancient geological formations rather than of structures put together by the hand of man.

Thus if Magnus, as he lurched so miserably forward, really faint now from lack of food, saw around him a domination of the artificial by the natural, it was the dominance of a "natural" that in itself seemed a fragment of a derelict and deserted world. Across this Waste-Land drifted the stricken man, while at his feet, as they sank into that brackish mud, curious little, purplish-stalked marine plants stared up at the travelling clouds, their abortive leaves clammy and cold, and thick, too, with a self-projected sap, wherewith they protected themselves from the invading brine.

Standing still, when about fifty yards from the Bridge, he watched his own feet as they slowly sank into the mud, causing bubbles to rise that looked as if the mud-worms were blowing tiny balloons of their salt spittle. He took out his watch. It was nearly three . . . two hours since Ballard had left him! He turned his eyes on the grey arches of the Bridge above him, which now seemed the one remaining goal of his exhausted desire. Suddenly a solitary taxi-cab, coming down the hill from the village of Wyke, moved slowly across the bridge. Even as it crossed the bridge it hesitated and almost stopped, as if the sight of his own presence, down here among these mud-pools, had arrested its occupant's attention. And no sooner had it crossed over, than it did stop; and after a pause a woman's figure descended from it and stood in the road, making unmistakable signals to him.

A wild, impossible hope flooded his whole being and the depths of his heart were stirred. *It is Curly.* But no! This girl was thinner, taller, more fragile looking. Her whole air was different. With a quick step, all the same, and a much lighter one, he made his way towards this figure, while the figure itself, seeing she had his attention,

spoke a word to the driver of the taxi, and deliberately advanced to
meet him.

Yes, two hours had passed since the elder Muir's triumphantly
ticking watch had told Magnus it was one o'clock. But it was not
for him alone that clocks and watches ticked. Time the obliterater,
the restorer, the healer, the smoother out of our troubled footprints
from more than Weymouth Sands brought it about that at the exact
second when Magnus felt his heart so madly leap up at the impression
that he beheld Curly, the news that had sent him hugger-mugger to
this rim of the world reached Mrs. Lily and Tissty Clive, Cattistock's
two most interested ladies, and reached them simultaneously. Yes,
it was now just three by the Jubilee Clock—that Clock whose Janus-
faces had been watched by so many and with such multitudinously
different emotions, since in the great Queen's honour and in the
interests of Weymouth Sands it was set up—three o'clock in the
afternoon of the twenty-third of November, and the first act of
Jerry's fantastical fooling at the Regent's was at an end.

The world-famous clown had deserted High House now for quite
a long time, and had apparently been happier than he had been for
many a year, as he shared one of those ambiguous "upper rooms", at
his devoted Lucky's, with his mysterious Tossty, and gave himself
up to enjoying his particular form of pessimism to its last opal-tinted
drop. Most people assumed that it was the presence of his sister-in-
law at High House that afforded this punctilious observer of forms and
ceremonies his excuse for escape. Certainly no diplomatist could have
conducted a delicate transaction more exquisitely than Jerry did his
final flight from the courtly threshold of his lady's room to this
tatterdemalion ménage with the daughter of the Radipole shepherd.
He hàd managed it all so smoothly that there was no break at all, no
quarrel with Lucinda, no public scandal. He went often to dine with
the two ladies. He made as much use of the services of the competent
Mr. Fogg as he had ever done. But this was the first time since he
had changed the locality of his bed and board that the Poxwell sisters
had come to the Theatre and been actually present at a scene where
he played vis-à-vis with Tossty. When the curtain came down on this
first scene, which though such a short one, was followed by a long
interval of nearly a quarter-of-an-hour, Mrs. Cobbold talked rapidly

to her sister. She was persuading her to give up all thought of returning to Half-Way House. When she paused to take breath an observer would have been startled by her expression, which was sinister beyond anything that an ordinary onlooker could possibly analyse. Dr. Brush himself had begun in recent months to wonder whether in delving into this woman's secret life and humouring her morbidities, he was not practising vivisection upon her rather than psychiatry.

Mrs. Cobbold was really unusual in the sublety of her art of playing a She-Iago. She did it by self-deception. She never confessed even to herself, what she was doing. Her intellect was forever being tricked, most elaborately tricked, by the complicated perversions of her motives. She was forever telling herself morbidly sadistic stories, which, as she grew older and more jaded, became almost mad, but her grand engine for poisoning life, for undermining life, for bringing life down and crumbling it to pieces, was *the art of indirection*. She was the most indirectly malicious talker ever known in Weymouth, where talk, as in other fashionable places, was not always guileless. And she followed it up. She persecuted. She tormented. She ran people to earth. The only thing that at all excused her present wickedness in regard to her sister was that Hortensia did not really, not in her *deepest* nerves, dislike the situation! If she couldn't be trampled upon by Cattistock, she could at least be trodden upon by Mrs. Cobbold.

But grossly crude would it be to maintain—as in her breathing-spaces from her present masterpiece of indirection, over her husband's acting and Tossty's looks, she held up her proud, high forehead and gazed upon "Le Néant" like a blood-satisfied Medusa, that Mrs. Cobbold was entirely evil. Some mysterious life-impulse, bursting up from some crack in the marbly floor of her Mephistophelean beautitude, was always emitting flashes of a superb and defiant courage. Had the whole human race, in the circles of some immense Colosseum gathered together to see Mrs. Cobbold executed it is certain that she would never have blinked an eyelid, or lapsed one hair's breadth from her fortitude.

The subterranean struggle between herself and Jerry was of a very peculiar nature. She had inherited from old Poxwell a terrible vitality, a life-zest which, though it took an evil form, was never undermined by any feeling of futility. Jerry on the contrary was a pessimist to the bottom. Life to him was one long wearisome farce and he had only married her because to play with morbid humanity kept him alive.

As she sat now, gazing into that curtain before her and *through* it, gazing at the shops in St. Thomas' Street and *through* them, gazing at the old King's Statue, at the Jubilee Clock, at St. John's Spire, at the far-away White Horse and *through* them all, the beautiful sister by her side, as she stole glance after wandering glance at her profile, was struck, for all her familiarity, just as Perdita had been, by the woman's almost mystical air of dedication. The truth perhaps might have been, though such an interpretation had never occurred to Dr. Brush, that when with all her falsity she felt she was "dedicated," it was because she *was* dedicated! That all her morbid sadism and her malicious persecutions were the horrible scum and loathsome surface-froth of a crashing Power, that was destined one day to emerge and astonish all was not an impossible hypothesis . . .

The Theatre-attendants at the Regent that autumn were all of them lads, and it was no other than young Witchit who now, in his neat uniform, presented himself to the attention of Mrs. Cobbold and Mrs. Lily.

"What is it?" enquired Lucinda, who sat next the aisle, as the boy offered her a folded piece of paper.

"I don't know, lady," said young Witchit. "Mr. Cobbold gave it to me for you."

She took it in her hands—those plump, exquisitely-shaped hands with such short fingers—and opened it hurriedly, while young Witchit stole sidelong glances at the alluring Correggio-like sweetness, so extremely provocative to boys of his type, of her lovely sister.

"Thank you, sonny," she said. "There's no answer." Then she turned to Hortensia. "Let's go out into the foyer, 'Tensia, and have a cigarette. They're not nearly ready yet. Jerry's always so slow. And with that stupid, animal woman—"

They went out together, and it was at the end of the corridor, where they could sit down, that she told her the news.

"Dogberry has gone abroad with that pretty Wishing Well girl— you know?—who had an affair with Ballard and was engaged to Magnus. He's taken her to Italy."

It was then that Mrs. Cobbold discovered that she had not understood her pleasure-loving, easy-going, undomestic sister as completely as she fancied. She had prepared herself for one of those scenes that had recurred again and again between them since their childhood— false sympathy on *her* part and exaggerated abandonment on Hortensia's. Such, however, was not the manner in which things turned out today. What Hortensia did was to burst into a merry laugh.

"Poor old Magnus!" she cried. "What a face he will go about with, for weeks and weeks!" Her cheeks grew flushed with her merriment. "But it's Sippy who'll look the biggest fool! Why it's a regular Comedy of Errors; that kid fooling Magnus, and now fooled himself by Dogberry! Well done, old man! Well done!"

And her clear, rippling, silvery laughter rang in lovely peals down the corridor. Such can be the nature of a sympathetic sister that it must now be confessed that Mrs. Cobbold began a little to recover her good spirits. There seemed to be a chance that this laughter was a prelude to a fit of hysterics. But not the faintest sign of anything of the sort showed itself! Mrs. Lily's amusement at Sippy's discomfiture seemed to completely outweigh any personal emotion. The pretty woman kept chuckling over it. She seemed to rule out her own relations with Cattistock altogether. When she wasn't thinking of Sippy she was apparently thinking of Magnus. Just for one second, however, Mrs. Cobbold did look at her closely while a sudden most startling thought, like a flying wing, just dipped into the current of her consciousness.

"Has *any other man*," she said to herself, "taken the place of Cattistock?"

But the Second Act of the performance had now begun and the sisters rose from their seat, threw away their cigarettes, and re-entered the darkened house. That dipping wing touched Mrs. Cobbold's mind just once more and then departed.

"If there is another man," this fleeting thought whispered, "*Who is he?*"

The contrast between the reception of the news of Cattistock's elopement by the lady who was to have been his wife and the girl who *had* been his paramour was certainly striking. Neither Jerry nor Tissty and Tossty had anything to do in the last act of the programme, and Jerry was himself rather amused to see that his wife and sister-in-law intended to sit it out to the end. It is even possible he was a little piqued, for in his opinion the conclusion of any performance without himself and the Radipole girls was less than nothing. At any rate, before he had any idea how upset Tissty would be, he had in his general desire to propitiate the sisters, sent young Witchit again with a request that they come round to his private office. This was a most pleasant room with several large book-shelves that were much mellower and more scholarly in appearance than any in the rooms at High House, and here it was his invariable custom to take a cup of tea, after the play, with both Tissty and Tossty.

But Tissty seemed broken-hearted. The fair, passionate, peasant dancer had come of late to love this rich descendant of peasants. Of all the men she had ever known Cattistock alone seemed able to satisfy her insatiable sensual desires. Sensuality had of late transformed itself into an authentic passion, and the flight of the man without a word simply prostrated her. They had to get a substitute for her principal act, though she did dress and come on the stage. It was on the sofa in Jerry's office, a more comfortable couch than any in the girls' dressing-room, that Tissty lay now when the others came in, white and death-like and with her eyes tight shut. The other two still had on their stage-attire, but the girl on the couch had changed into her ordinary clothes.

"Don't 'ee mind too much, little Tiss! Don't 'ee, don't 'ee mind too much, my precious darling!"

Thus, on her knees beside her, in her gorgeous Gentian-blue tights and her belt of black ostrich feathers, the agitated Tossty gave vent to emotions that astonished even Jerry, though he was so well cognizant of the close link between the two. The girls had long ago been careful to unlearn their old Dorset dialect, and it sounded queer to Jerry to catch this "don't 'ee! don't 'ee!" in his Regent's office.

Tea was produced for the benefit of Tissty, without waiting for the appearance of the Poxwell sisters, but when the ladies did finally come in, it was this unfortunate collapse of the younger Radipole girl, that precipitated the crisis. The crisis, Mrs. Cobbold prayed, was for the nonce confined to her own consciousness, but it was of such a nature, resulting from so startling a revelation of her husband's duplicity, that it remained a serious question with her whether she had or had not the wit to conceal the effect it had upon her. It was Jerry's concern over Tossty's agitation, as the dark-skinned dancer in her fantastical costume kept flinging herself down by her sister's side that betrayed the shameless intimacy which existed between himself and Mrs. Lily. A glance and a touch between them—and the cat was out of the bag! Situations not a whit more explosive can go on, *have* gone on, without any of the parties involved being a penny the worse or a scrap the wiser. And so no doubt would this situation have gone on, in beautifully directed equilibrium, under the head of a master manipulator, if it had not been for the unpredictable vagaries of authentic passion— Tissty's for Cattistock and Tossty's for Tissty—breaking the rules of this school of artful gallantry.

Jerry must have felt that the Fates had turned against him, against all these meticulous proppings up of the Status Quo that resembled "a shining Pleasure-Dome with caves of ice" for he sank back in his mediaeval episcopal chair—smuggled in from that "Etruria" to which Curly was now whirling in an express-train—folded his hands over his knee and ransacked the utmost armoury of his spirit. He was dressed in a strange harlequin garb, of his own invention, that answered Tossty's blue tights with shimmering silver and pale rose, and the play of his mobile features, as he gathered himself together for the one exposure of his life that he really dreaded, had tragic-humorous reversions from high confidence to abysmal desperation, such as he had never equalled in any of his most brilliant stage performances! With one part of his subtle intelligence he was still searching for ways of escape, but with another, much deeper down, he was struggling to tap some ultimate acceptance of worldly exposure, some spring, some out-jetting of non-human defiance, that would enable him to re-create his life-illusion when all his elaborate "caves of ice" came crashing down, or melting, rather, about his head!

It is queer what odd little things come to a man's aid at such a toppling over of the spiritual towers of personality. What Jerry thought of now, with the part of his swift-moving intelligence that already accepted defeat, was that pebble in the pocket of the Jobber of which rumours had been filling the Weymouth taverns throughout this eventful year.

"Men and women are all the same," he thought. "They all want to live on the other side of the Moon, while they get glory for sweating in the Sun. It's the salt of our Sun-Sweat that turns our stomachs! If she finds me out, I'll change into the Jobber's pebble; and let her hate and let the other love, and let the waves roll over me as they will! No living person has caught me yet. Down pebble! Down soul of Jerry! Down to the bottom of the world! I'll smile . . . and smile . . . and smile—and be a pebble!"

The clown in the harlequin's dress was justified in his worst prediction. Mrs. Cobbold's fingers soon after she took her seat in her husband's office began dallying ominously with the gardenias in her bosom. Her eyes, having once seen in one single moment of emotional revelation during that agitation over the girl on the couch, *who it was* who had taken Cattistock's place, looked through them all, through the booklined walls of that pleasant room, through the shops of St. Thomas' Street, through the old King's Statue, through the Spire of St. John's, and out, away, through the White Horse too, into Le Néant!

"How clever he's been!" she thought. "So there's nothing between him and the dark girl; probably there never was. It's to meet 'Tensia he's taken those rooms in Sark House! And it's for him, all for him, not for the game with me, she's remained with us. Oh, Father, oh, Father, did you suckle us both then, when Mother died, with that bulging vein in your neck?"

On moved the hands of the Jubilee Clock. St. John's Spire murmured to its movement:

"Piety and Respectability will never perish from Weymouth Sands while I point upwards!"

The old King's Statue murmured to its movement:

"Honour your Father and your Mother that your days may be long by Weymouth Sands!"

The Harbour Bridge murmured to its movement:

"The tide rises, the tide falls;" while the clock itself, as its bowels rumbled with its effort at articulation, ticked out the words:

"Wet Sand . . . Dry Sand . . . Wet Sand . . . Dry Sand."

Perdita did not take very long in explaining to Magnus over their cup of tea in the Refreshment Room of Portland Station, how it was that she had made no sign of life all these long months. As he looked at her there, sitting by his side, this Companion of Mrs. Cobbold's that he had *not* met that winter day when she first arrived, he saw clearly enough without her telling him, why she had made no sign of life! She was indeed, he thought, even now, like a departed Cimmerian spirit, come back from among those "powerless heads of the dead".

"Yes," she told him, in her low, husky scrannel-pipe voice, "I had a bad illness after I got back. I didn't cross at once when I left him. I waited to see. But they all said he hadn't changed; they all said he still kept—you know about that I expect, Mr. Muir?—*that stone* in his pocket, and so I went back. It was after he had been to see my Aunt. But I couldn't . . . bear it. It was . . . too much . . . after . . . being with him . . . so I got ill. And I've only just—got well!" she added with a weak attempt at a lively smile.

She had left her bag at the pier, it transpired, and crossing the ferry had gone straight to Cove House. Mrs. Trot was alone, but from her she had learned that " the Master," as the woman called him, had got a mania for staying whole days and nights, of late, up at the Gadgets', at the place they call the Head.

"And that's where *you* are heading for now, I take it?" he murmured, glancing at her wasted figure and death-pale cheeks.

She nodded, pushed away the uneaten Bath bun on her plate, and finished her cup of tea. Magnus surveyed the few crumbs that were left on his own plate.

"She wins," he thought, "I lose. But I am the one who can swallow Bath buns."

She looked so weak and ill that he insisted on their taking a taxi.

"But send me off," he muttered, "if you'd rather go alone."

But she had not been using her instinct all this while without detecting a heart that had a fossil in it, a hidden petrifaction, of nine hours' eternity, a very ancient stone, shaped like an Ammonite, and yet it could shoot forth now and again, from where it lay, arrows of hurting that were tipped with mother-of-pearl! And she could not find it in *her* heart, for all its wild beating, to send this unhappy-eyed man away.

They had nearly reached the little town of Easton when Perdita suddenly cried out to the driver to stop. There before them, toiling up

the steep road with a heavy, covered basket in her hand, went the
unmistakable figure of Gipsy May. Magnus got out and saluted her.
As usual her rambling speech debouched down every possible vista of
information, except the one that would explain her presence there.
He persuaded her at length, however, to enter their taxi for she
admitted that her basket was heavy:

"Rowena's in it," she explained.

And, sure enough, a low "meow" from the confined animal
witnessed to the truth of this explanation at least. She indicated
presently that she had thought she might as well "look round S. C.'s
old place, while she was up here," and she seemed well-satisfied when
Perdita, as if too weak to struggle against any jolt to her purpose,
feebly requested the driver to take them to Last House. To herself
Perdita thought:

"The Powers have kept us alive. I am on my way to him. I *can't*
be unkind to a living soul today."

They stopped before that forbidding front-entrance to Last House.
She and Magnus both stared at the forlorn chain with its closed
padlock. The chain seemed to say to them: "Go away! Go away!"
and there were bits of paper and shrivelled dead leaves, evidently
blown in there from the road, that were also voluble.

"Gone," they said: "Gone, gone, gone—never to come back!"

But Gipsy May resolutely got out and placed the basket with
Rowena in it carefully on the ground.

"You may come with me for a minute if you want to!" she
remarked proudly, with the air of a princess in sight of her ancestral
drawbridge.

Telling the driver to wait in her feeble straw-like voice, Perdita
gave Magnus a pitiful little smile. They both followed the
Gipsy, Magnus offering, but without success, to take the basket from
her.

"She'll think she's left!" the woman said, clutching the handle and
giving him a fierce look.

When they stood, all three, the basket resting on the flagstones, in
front of the kitchen-door, Magnus and Perdita caught the woman's
cadaverous face, with its roving black eyes, turned away from them
towards Weymouth. Not the absent tenant of Last House himself

could have addressed some unseen object of superstition more automatically than Gipsy May did now.

"Enjoy theeself with her, then, Fisherman! Enjoy theeself,
Fisherman!" they heard her mutter, but the November winds in the
dead raspberry-canes of that forlorn garden carried her words west
instead of east.

But she now produced a big iron key from somewhere about her
person, and as if the fact that she was to be alone with her cat in a
moment had given her volubility she turned to them both.

"Those lawyers are no good," she announced confidentially and
even gaily. "Me cards were right! The Man with Three Staves
was right."

Had it been, as perhaps for all *they* knew it was, her own death that
had been predicted, she still would have been pleased that the ancient
Tarot wisdom was justified.

"That wicked young man came," she said, "with a policeman, and
turned us out of house."

"Wasn't Loder and Crouch managing things for you?" interjected
Magnus. "That's what Caddie Water told me," he added, looking at
Perdita.

At the name of Caddie, the Gipsy made a curious grimace, that
was neither derisive not pitiful.

"*Her* coffin'll be a little one," she said quietly, "*and* a pretty one.
Me cards have seen 'un where 'un lies."

"But Ballard had no right—"

Gipsy May gave him a look as old as all the sorrowful wisdom of
her tribe. She didn't deign to answer. That anyone should talk of
"right" in a world ruled by chance and the devil, in a world understood
only by "me cards," struck her mind as the height of simplicity.

"And Lal Zed be gone to work for Jones," she threw out, as if
this event followed naturally from her previous allusion to Caddie's
coffin.

"Are you going to live here, then?" enquired Perdita faintly,
looking nervously round for an available seat, for she felt as if her
legs had suddenly become floating clouds.

Meow? came sharply from the basket, and Gipsy May picked up
this covered receptacle of her only faithful friend.

"She wants Lal Zed to help with she's Toby," mocked the Gipsy, in a voice as high-pitched as the wind in the very key-hole into which she now prepared to thrust her big key.

"*You* shan't have no Toby chasin' you, shall you, Rowena?"

They watched her in silence as she went in. When she was well inside and had put the cat down she gazed at them through the door-chink, making that aperture too narrow for anything human to enter. Through this crack they could see her bright eyes above her hollow cheeks gleaming with satisfaction. She was like a triumphant elf, peering out of Child Rowland's Tower.

"Her lips look red as blood," thought Perdita, wondering whether she herself was going to faint.

"I can't wait here any longer," she suddenly said aloud, though she imagined she was only thinking this thought. "He may have gone when we get there."

The idea that, after all, they might reach the Gadgets' too late was so unbearable that with every drop of her life-force driven by sheer willpower into her tottering legs she started walking round the house. The world was just beginning to turn into a rocking, heaving, universal blackness when she found the driver was pouring some fiery drink from a little flask down her throat. This treatment brought her quickly round and her heart did the rest . . .

"Yes. He be in bedroom, in thik same wold room thee remembers mighty well, belike."

It was Ellen herself who thus greeted them as they passed in, under the indecipherable lineaments of the ancient sign-board.

"He ain't bed-rid nor nothing," she went on. "This be 'Melia and this be Celia and this be Sue—good girls, all on 'em, though Sue do take after her Dad, poor bustling maid!"

The "good girls" gathered round Magnus in the bar—Mr. Gadget having gone to Weymouth—while Ellen led, supported, and indeed almost carried the visitor upstairs.

"Will it . . . *hurt* . . . my going straight in?"

"Not a God's splinter, dearie! Aren't you his life-blood? Aren't you the marrow of his bones? In with 'ee, for Christ's love! We'll take care of your friend."

The romantic woman almost ran downstairs so that the lovers

might meet in peace. This whole event was to Ellen the greatest that
had happened in that house since she lay in the pains over her firstborn.
She caught Sue listening—just as her father would have listened—
at the foot of the stairs, and she indignantly dragged the child into
the bar-room calling to 'Melia to keep her there, while she herself
went into the kitchen.

"*Perdita!*"

He leapt up from the bed. He had only his vest and his drawers on.
His other clothes lay tossed about the room, and the room itself—for
they were all afraid of him in that house—was like a place that
ship-wrecked people had slept in after escaping from the waves. There
was not one single second of awkwardness, of embarrassment, not
even one of heart-beating tension, or of fixed, staring, awestruck relief,
or of frozen, spiritual ecstasy between them.

"Skald!" and the breath of her weak voice went wailing between
her teeth, as if her whole frame had become a thin bag-pipe against
his ribs.

"*By Dum?*" and as they pressed their bodies and their faces together
they were beyond any definite kisses, just as they were beyond astonishment, surprise, thankfulness, happiness even. He could taste the salt
of her tears, pouring, pouring, from what seemed like the whole
surface of her face, and she could feel herself rising and falling, up and
down, on the crests and troughs of his immense, slow, shaking sobs.
It was as if they were not just human lovers, not just sweethearts
finding each other again. It was as if they were animals, old, weak,
long-hunted animals, whose love was literally the love of bone for
bone, skeleton for skeleton, not any mere spiritual affinity, not any
mere sexual passion.

Skeletons, literally, they both were! His face was positively ghastly
in its disfigurement, in its tattered raggedness, and hers, though, her
features being less pronounced, it showed less emphatically, was the
face of the dead come to life.

"*By Dum?*" ... He lifted her up at last, clean off the floor. This he
did while his sobs were still heaving against her body and his mouth
was still contorted with crying. With an infinite, crooning, snarling,
growling tenderness, like a lioness with her first whelp, he lifted her up,
till her hair, loosened by their embrace, fell in wisps and swathes, and

then finally shook itself free, as he swung her about, till it hung straight down.

"Put . . . me . . . down . . . Skald!" she gasped at last. "I'm too heavy . . . you'll hurt yourself doing this!"

It is true he *was* gasping for breath when he obeyed her and laid her down on the bed. Here he sank on his knees on the floor, by the bedside, one heavy hand covering her entire face and the other holding her feet, while he pressed his forehead against her navel. He remained like this for such a long time, while into her nostrils stole the smell of his hand—which, unlike the mad King's did not so much "smell of mortality" as of the smoke of driftwood and the bitter stalks of fennel —that she fancied at last that in the reaction from his storm of feeling he had fallen asleep.

Magnus was not such a daring tippler of the elder girl's Meliodka as Sylvanus had been, but he amused them by the wry faces he made as he sipped the famous drink. Celia, too, he delighted by being ready to read aloud to them all from out of her ballad-book. All would have gone well in this, as in the case of the drink, had not some restless demon of misadventure put it into the head of little Sue to ask to be the one to choose what he should read. Had Magnus been as well versed in old ballads as he was in Latin and Greek, he would have sheered off at the opening words, for he would have known what he was in for, but on he went, and his voice rose and fell feelingly enough with that sorrowful lilt till he came to the last line.

> "Whan cockle shells turn siller bells,
> And mussels grow on every tree,
> When frost and snaw sall warm us aw'
> Then sall my love prove true to me."

At the last line the unfortunate man's voice broke in spite of all he could do; but it was the restless Sue, the one who had been responsible for putting him to such a test, who paid the heaviest price. Sue Gadget suddenly felt as if all the waves of the sea did not contain water enough to wash out the pity and trouble and pain and weariness of being alive in this world. Like many another practical young woman, living anywhere between Brunswick Terrace and Old Castle Road, little Sue found out her womanhood when she least expected it.

Magnus' voice trembled, thinking of Curly, but when Sue rushed out of the house and turned her face to the Sea-Serpent on the Sign, crying out to it as to the Ancient of Days, "Oh, why was I born, why was I ever born?" she was thinking of no particular man, or boy either, who had turned from her. She was thinking of nothing *in particular*. But thinking of nothing, or thinking of something, she became at this moment the mouthpiece of that motiveless, causeless, non-human grief in the world, that comes on the wind, that rises and sinks on the sea, and that seems older and more tragic than all our human agitations. Even while poor little Sue was still out there, consoling herself in thinking that she had never seen the Sea-Serpent's eyes so alive, Perdita came downstairs.

"Have you got a fairly large pocket, Mr. Muir?" she said.

Magnus stared at her, and very seriously began removing various objects from his left-hand pocket to his right.

"Pretty large," he replied. "Is it a present for Mrs. Cobbold?"

Then, while 'Melia and Celia looked on in astonishment, she handed him the stone which had been in the Jobber's pocket so long.

"No," she said and the words seemed to come to her by some sudden inspiration. "It's for my old friend, Mr. Gaul. It will keep the Philosophy of Representation from blowing away!"

THE END

155 J

39M